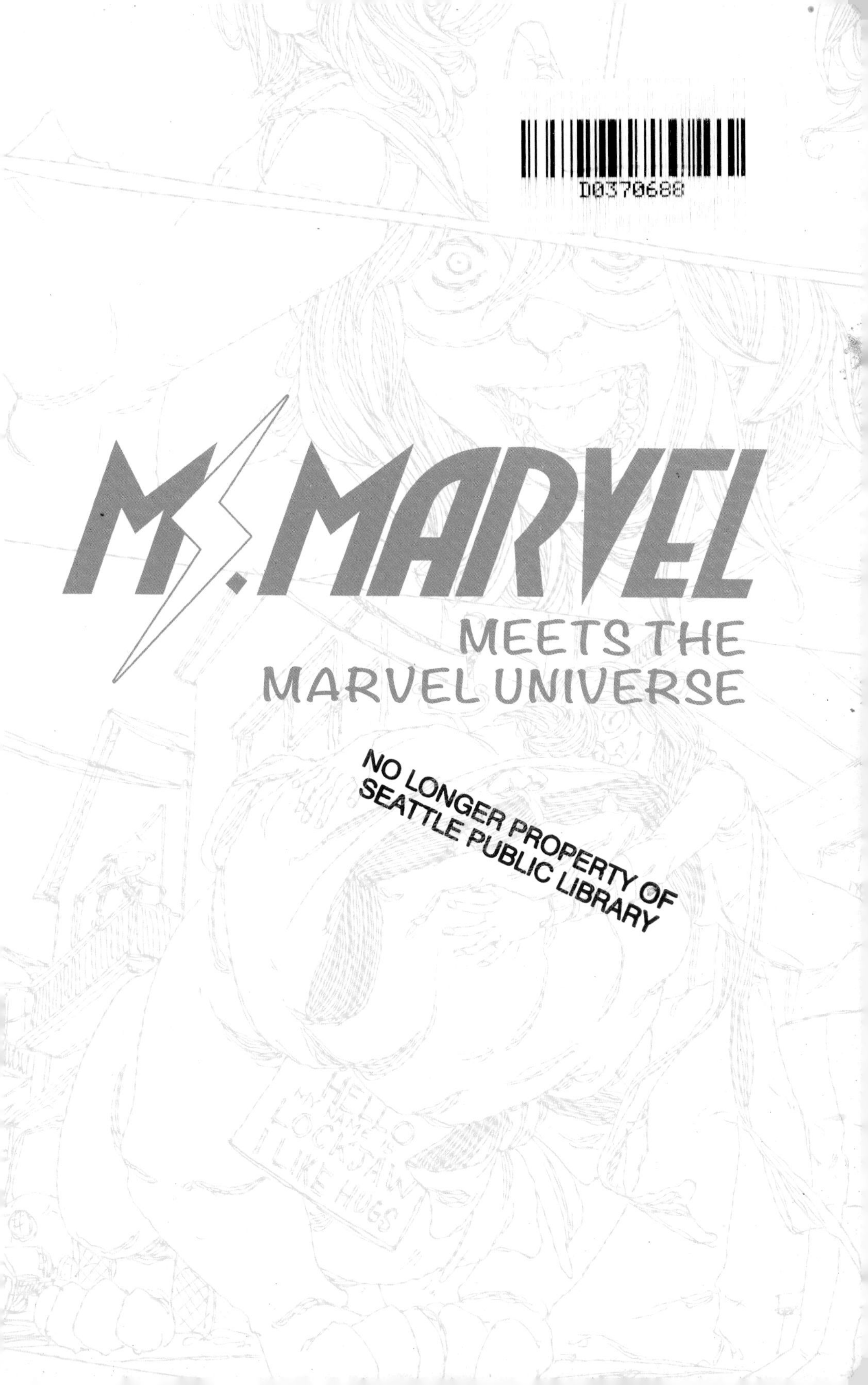

MS. MARVEL

MEETS THE MARVEL UNIVERSE

Contents

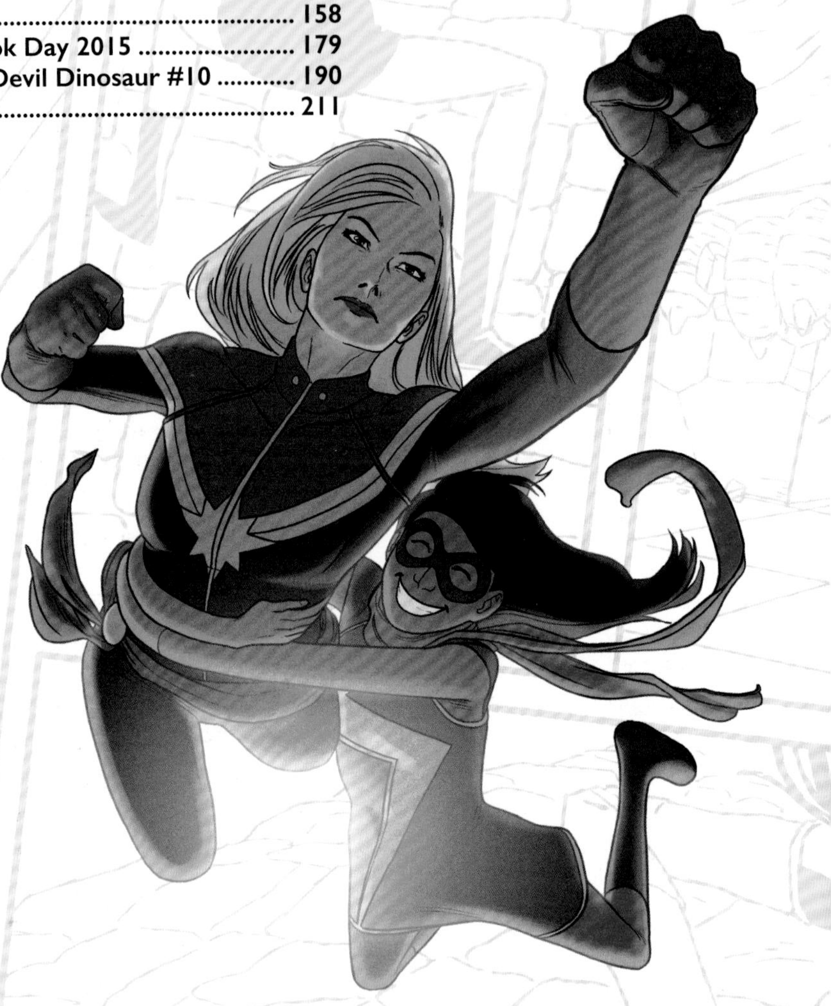

MS. MARVEL MEETS THE MARVEL UNIVERSE. Contains material originally published in magazine form as MS. MARVEL (2014) #6-9 and #17-18, S.H.I.E.L.D. (2014) #2, MOON GIRL AND DEVIL DINOSAUR (2015) #10, CHAMPIONS (2016) #1, AMAZING SPIDER-MAN (2014) #7-8, and FREE COMIC BOOK DAY #2015 (AVENGERS) #1. First printing 2020. ISBN 978-1-302-92362-4. Published by MARVEL WORLDWIDE, INC., a subsidiary of MARVEL ENTERTAINMENT, LLC. OFFICE OF PUBLICATION: 1290 Avenue of the Americas, New York, NY 10104. © 2020 MARVEL No similarity between any of the names, characters, persons, and/or institutions in this magazine with those of any living or dead person or institution is intended, and any such similarity which may exist is purely coincidental. **Printed in Canada.** KEVIN FEIGE, Chief Creative Officer; DAN BUCKLEY, President, Marvel Entertainment; JOHN NEE, Publisher; JOE QUESADA, EVP & Creative Director; TOM BREVOORT, SVP of Publishing; DAVID BOGART, Associate Publisher & SVP of Talent Affairs; Publishing & Partnership; DAVID GABRIEL, VP of Print & Digital Publishing; JEFF YOUNGQUIST, VP of Production & Special Projects; DAN CARR, Executive Director of Publishing Technology; ALEX MORALES, Director of Publishing Operations; DAN EDINGTON, Managing Editor; SUSAN CRESPI, Production Manager; STAN LEE, Chairman Emeritus. For information regarding advertising in Marvel Comics or on Marvel.com, please contact Vit DeBellis, Custom Solutions & Integrated Advertising Manager, at vdebellis@marvel.com. For Marvel subscription inquiries, please call 888-511-5480. **Manufactured between 3/13/2020 and 4/14/2020 by SOLISCO PRINTERS, SCOTT, QC, CANADA.**

10 9 8 7 6 5 4 3 2 1

collection editor JENNIFER GRÜNWALD
assistant managing editor MAIA LOY
assistant managing editor LISA MONTALBANO
editor, special projects MARK D. BEAZLEY
vp production & special projects JEFF YOUNGQUIST
research JESS HAROLD
svp print, sales & marketing DAVID GABRIEL
director, licensed publishing SVEN LARSEN
editor in chief C.B. CEBULSKI

MS. MARVEL
MEETS THE MARVEL UNIVERSE

MS. MARVEL #6-9
writer G. WILLOW WILSON
artists JACOB WYATT (#6-7)
& ADRIAN ALPHONA (#8-9)
color artist IAN HERRING
letterer VC'S JOE CARAMAGNA
cover art JAMIE McKELVIE & MATTHEW WILSON
assistant editor DEVIN LEWIS
editor SANA AMANAT
senior editor NICK LOWE
special thanks to David Namisato & Irma Kniivila

AMAZING SPIDER-MAN #7-8
"Ms. Marvel Team-Up"
& "Adventures in Babysitting"
plot DAN SLOTT
script CHRISTOS GAGE
penciler GIUSEPPE CAMUNCOLI
inker CAM SMITH
colorist ANTONIO FABELA
letterer CHRIS ELIOPOULOS
cover art GIUSEPPE CAMUNCOLI,
CAM SMITH & ANTONIO FABELA
assistant editor ELLIE PYLE
editor NICK LOWE

S.H.I.E.L.D. #2
writer MARK WAID
penciler HUMBERTO RAMOS
inker VICTOR OLAZABA
colorist EDGAR DELGADO
letterer VC'S JOE CARAMAGNA
cover art JULIAN TOTINO TEDESCO
assistant editor JON MOISAN
editors TOM BREVOORT
with ELLIE PYLE

MS. MARVEL #17-18
writer G. WILLOW WILSON
artist ADRIAN ALPHONA
color artist IAN HERRING
letterer VC'S JOE CARAMAGNA
cover art KRIS ANKA
assistant editor CHARLES BEACHAM
editor SANA AMANAT

FREE COMIC BOOK DAY 2015
writer MARK WAID
artist MAHMUD ASRAR
color artist FRANK MARTIN
letterer VC'S JOE SABINO
cover art JEROME OPEÑA
& FRANK MARTIN
assistant editor JON MOISAN
editors TOM BREVOORT
with WIL MOSS

MOON GIRL AND DEVIL DINOSAUR #10
writers BRANDON MONTCLARE & AMY REEDER
artist NATACHA BUSTOS
color artist TAMRA BONVILLAIN
letterer VC'S TRAVIS LANHAM
cover art AMY REEDER
assistant editor CHRIS ROBINSON
editor MARK PANICCIA

CHAMPIONS #1
writer MARK WAID
penciler HUMBERTO RAMOS
inker VICTOR OLAZABA
color artist EDGAR DELGADO
letterer VC'S CLAYTON COWLES
cover art HUMBERTO RAMOS & EDGAR DELGADO
assistant editor ALANNA SMITH
editor TOM BREVOORT

MS. MARVEL #6

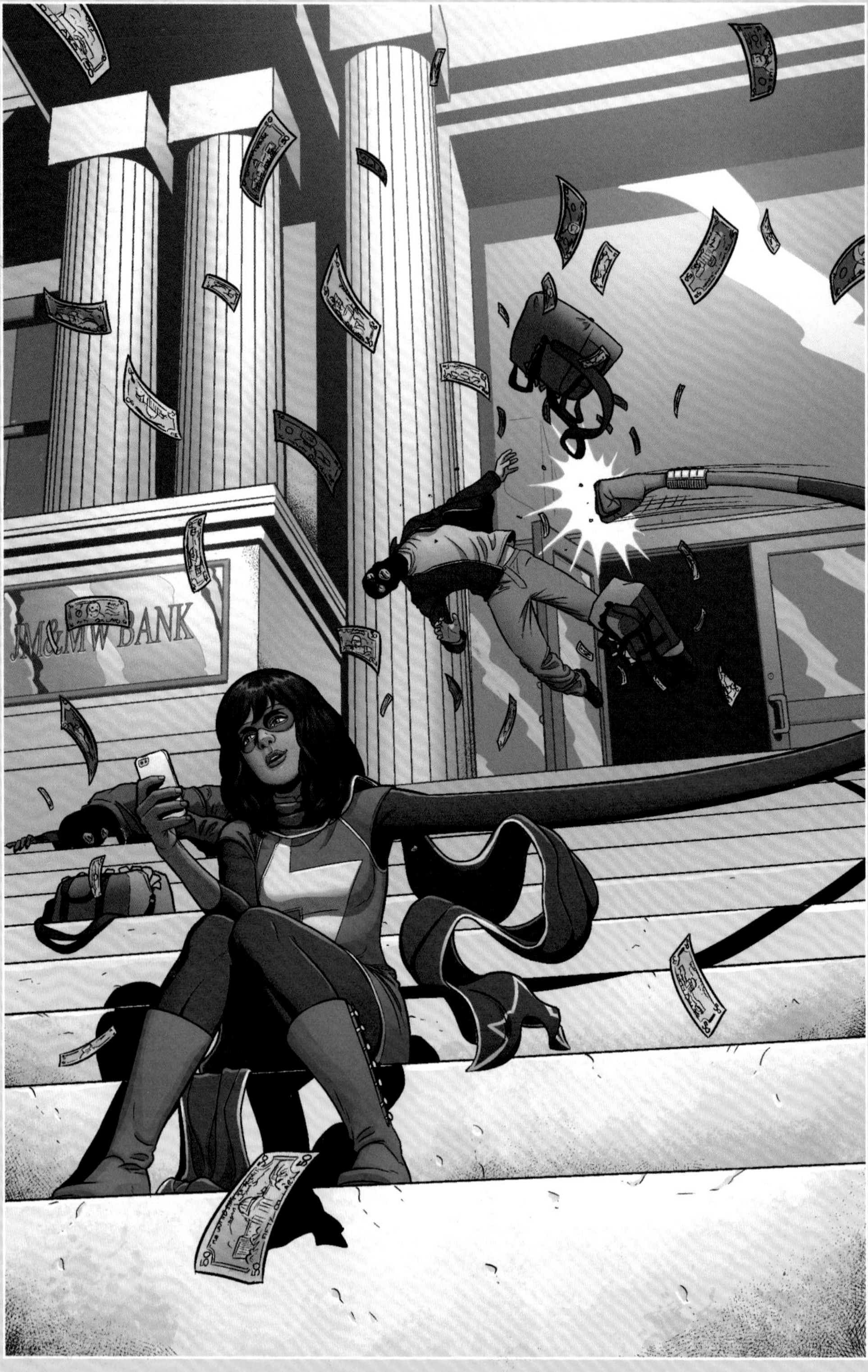
JM&MW BANK

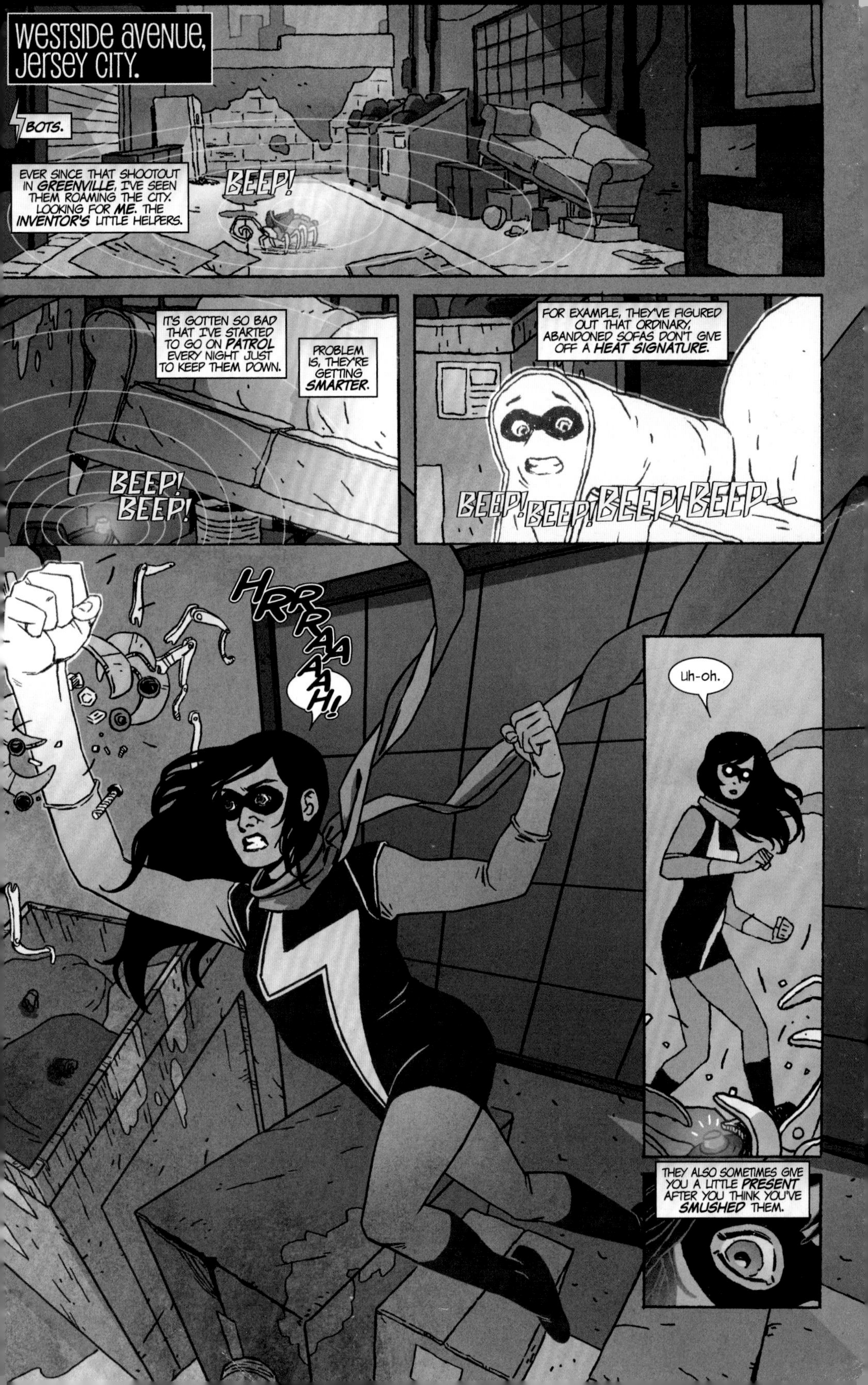
WESTSIDE AVENUE, JERSEY CITY.
BOTS.
EVER SINCE THAT SHOOTOUT IN GREENVILLE, I'VE SEEN THEM ROAMING THE CITY. LOOKING FOR ME. THE INVENTOR'S LITTLE HELPERS.
BEEP!
IT'S GOTTEN SO BAD THAT I'VE STARTED TO GO ON PATROL EVERY NIGHT JUST TO KEEP THEM DOWN.
PROBLEM IS, THEY'RE GETTING SMARTER.
BEEP! BEEP!
FOR EXAMPLE, THEY'VE FIGURED OUT THAT ORDINARY, ABANDONED SOFAS DON'T GIVE OFF A HEAT SIGNATURE.
BEEP! BEEP! BEEP! BEEP--
HRRRAAAAAH!
Uh-oh.
THEY ALSO SOMETIMES GIVE YOU A LITTLE PRESENT AFTER YOU THINK YOU'VE SMUSHED THEM.

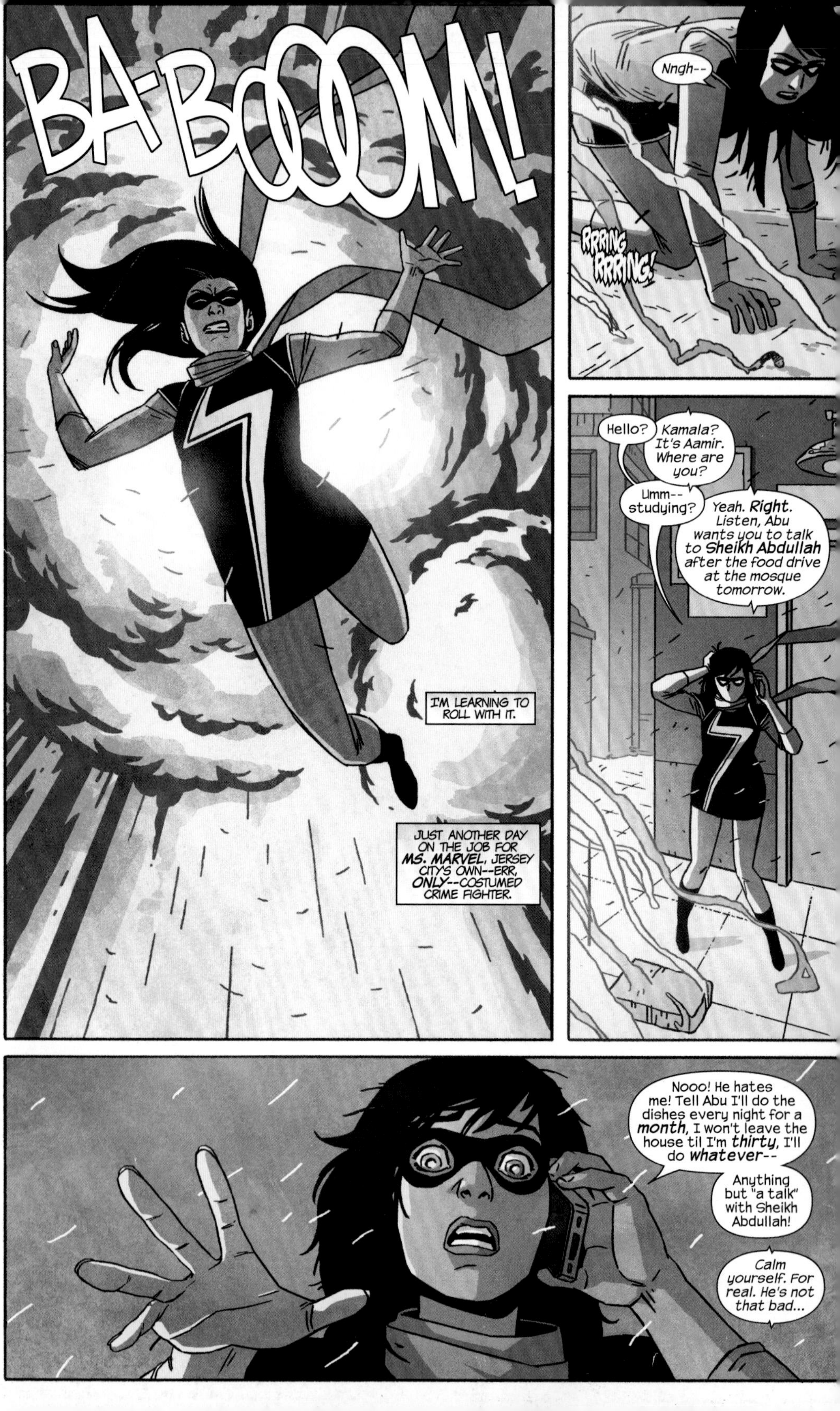
BA-BOOOOM!
I'M LEARNING TO ROLL WITH IT.
JUST ANOTHER DAY ON THE JOB FOR MS. MARVEL, JERSEY CITY'S OWN--ERR, ONLY--COSTUMED CRIME FIGHTER.
Nngh--
RRRING RRRING!
Hello?
Kamala? It's Aamir. Where are you?
Umm-- studying?
Yeah. Right. Listen, Abu wants you to talk to Sheikh Abdullah after the food drive at the mosque tomorrow.
Nooo! He hates me! Tell Abu I'll do the dishes every night for a month, I won't leave the house til I'm thirty, I'll do whatever--
Anything but "a talk" with Sheikh Abdullah!
Calm yourself. For real. He's not that bad...

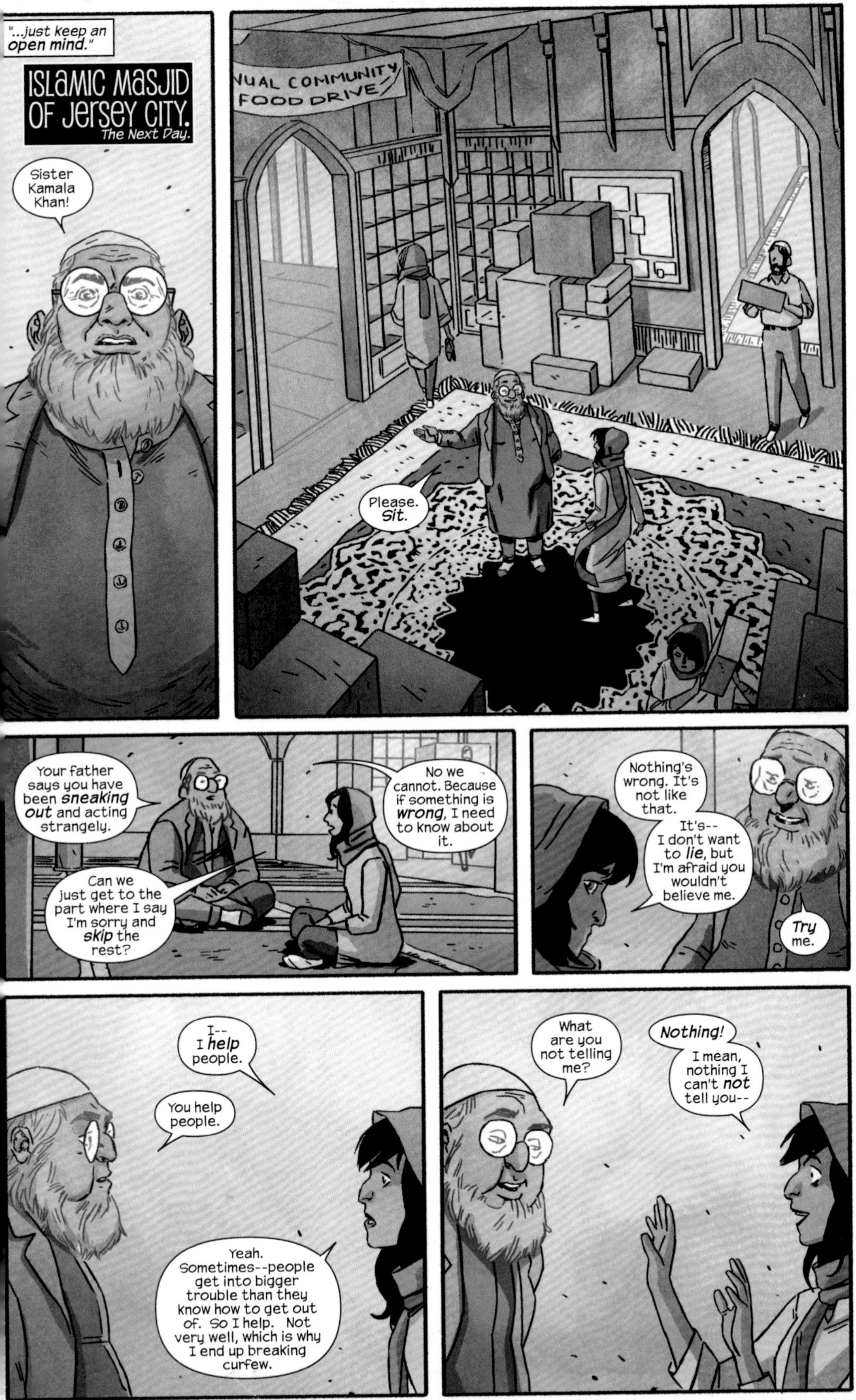
"...just keep an open mind."
ISLAMIC MASJID OF JERSEY CITY. The Next Day.
Sister Kamala Khan!
NUAL COMMUNITY FOOD DRIVE
Please. Sit.
Your father says you have been sneaking out and acting strangely.
Can we just get to the part where I say I'm sorry and skip the rest?
No we cannot. Because if something is wrong, I need to know about it.
Nothing's wrong. It's not like that.
It's-- I don't want to lie, but I'm afraid you wouldn't believe me.
Try me.
I-- I help people.
You help people.
Yeah. Sometimes--people get into bigger trouble than they know how to get out of. So I help. Not very well, which is why I end up breaking curfew.
What are you not telling me?
Nothing! I mean, nothing I can't not tell you--

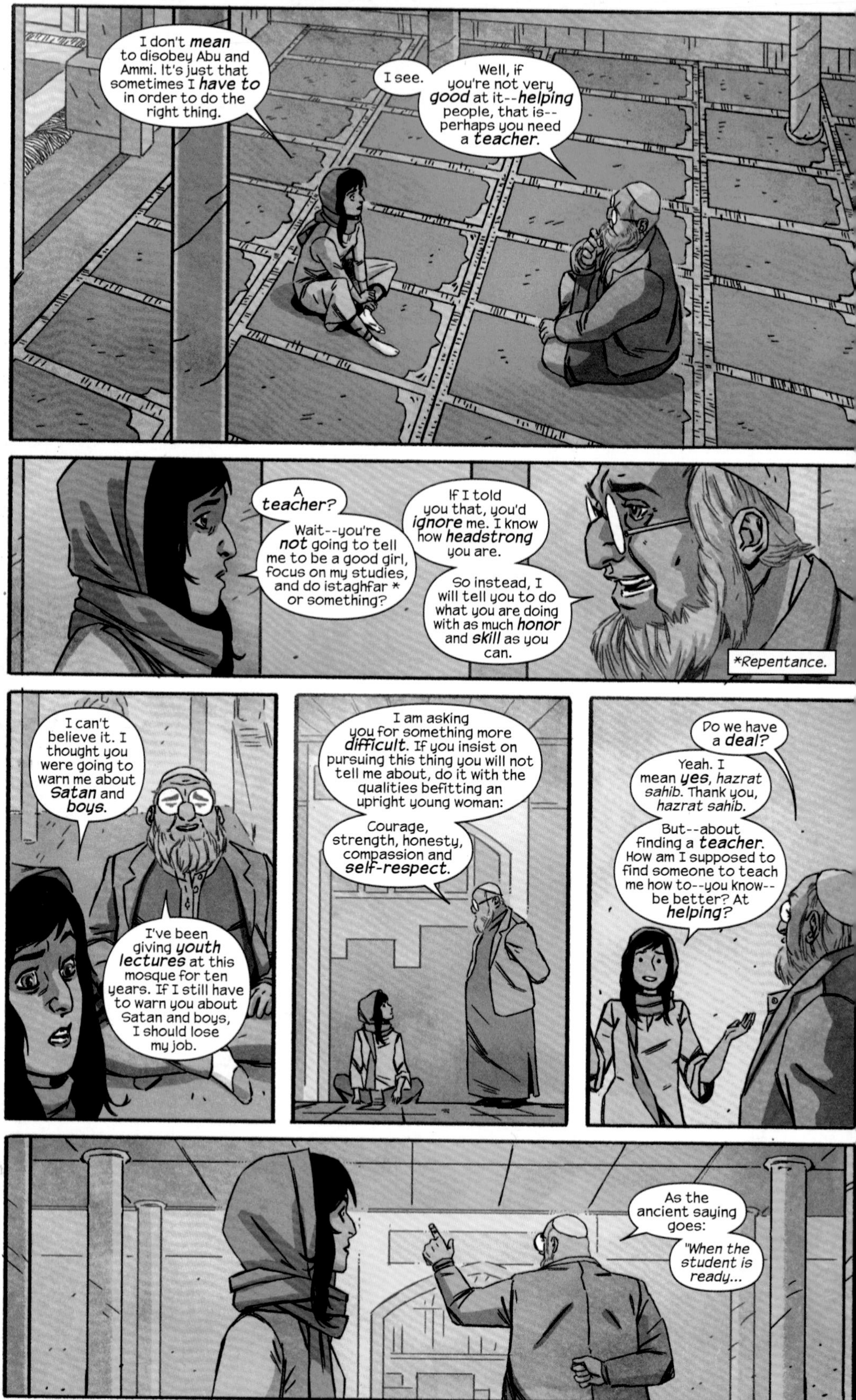
I don't mean to disobey Abu and Ammi. It's just that sometimes I have to in order to do the right thing.
I see.
Well, if you're not very good at it--helping people, that is--perhaps you need a teacher.
A teacher?
Wait--you're not going to tell me to be a good girl, focus on my studies, and do istaghfar * or something?
If I told you that, you'd ignore me. I know how headstrong you are.
So instead, I will tell you to do what you are doing with as much honor and skill as you can.
*Repentance.
I can't believe it. I thought you were going to warn me about Satan and boys.
I've been giving youth lectures at this mosque for ten years. If I still have to warn you about Satan and boys, I should lose my job.
I am asking you for something more difficult. If you insist on pursuing this thing you will not tell me about, do it with the qualities befitting an upright young woman:
Courage, strength, honesty, compassion and self-respect.
Do we have a deal?
Yeah. I mean yes, hazrat sahib. Thank you, hazrat sahib.
But--about finding a teacher. How am I supposed to find someone to teach me how to--you know--be better? At helping?
As the ancient saying goes:
"When the student is ready...

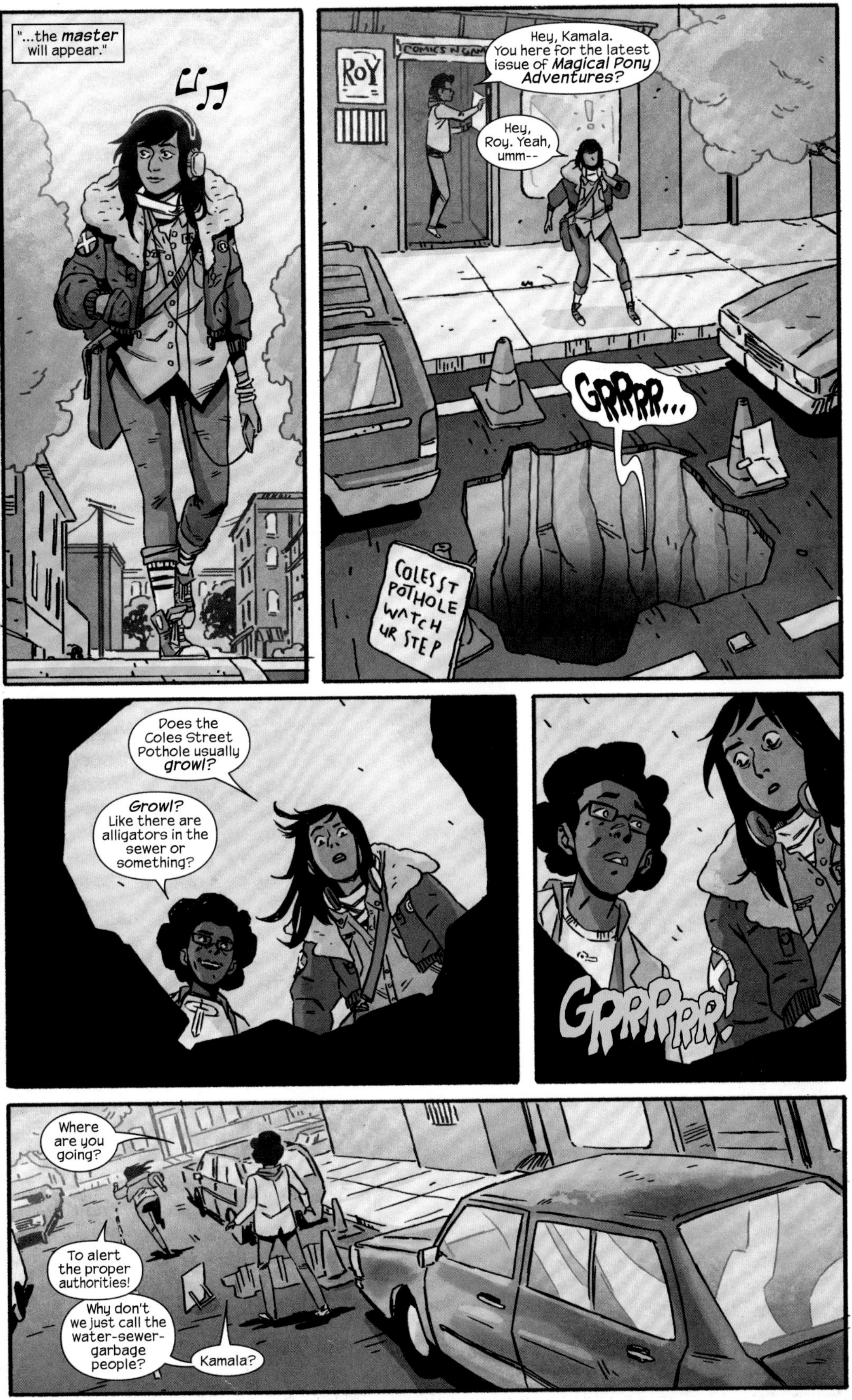
"...the *master* will appear."
Hey, Kamala. You here for the latest issue of *Magical Pony Adventures*?
ROY
Hey, Roy. Yeah, umm--
GRRRR...
COLES ST POTHOLE WATCH UR STEP
Does the Coles Street Pothole usually *growl*?
Growl? Like there are alligators in the sewer or something?
GRRRRR!
Where are you going?
To alert the proper authorities!
Why don't we just call the water-sewer-garbage people?
Kamala?

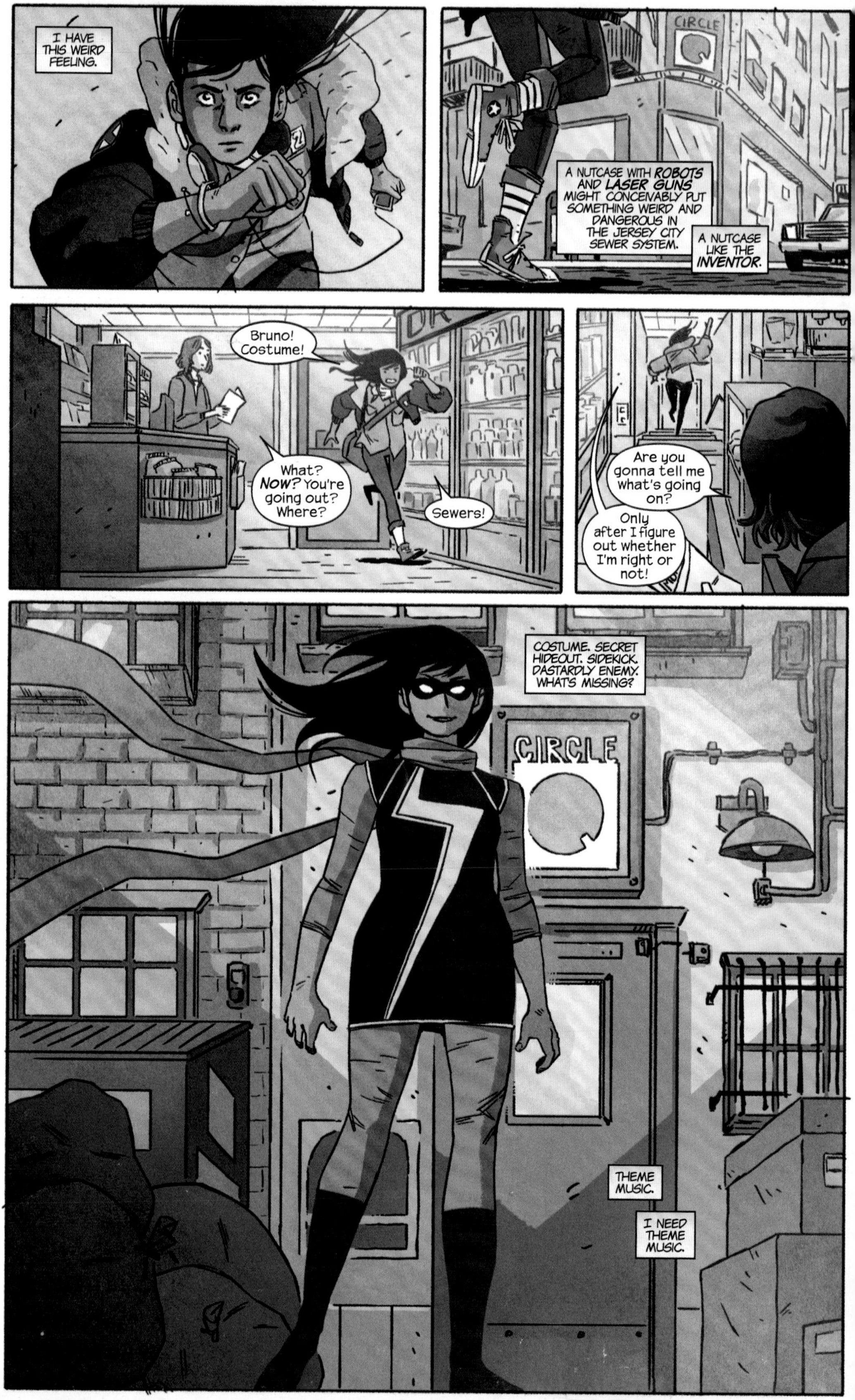
I HAVE THIS WEIRD FEELING.
A NUTCASE WITH ROBOTS AND LASER GUNS MIGHT CONCEIVABLY PUT SOMETHING WEIRD AND DANGEROUS IN THE JERSEY CITY SEWER SYSTEM.
A NUTCASE LIKE THE INVENTOR.
CIRCLE
Bruno! Costume!
What? NOW? You're going out? Where?
Sewers!
Are you gonna tell me what's going on?
Only after I figure out whether I'm right or not!
COSTUME. SECRET HIDEOUT. SIDEKICK. DASTARDLY ENEMY. WHAT'S MISSING?
CIRCLE
THEME MUSIC.
I NEED THEME MUSIC.

IT'S DARK. IT'S HUMID. AND THERE'S A STRANGE SMELL--LIKE STUFF *DECOMPOSING* AND OTHER STUFF *LIVING* IN THE DECOMPOSING STUFF.

BUT NO ALLIGATORS.

I'M STARTING TO FEEL A LITTLE BIT SILLY.

Ungh!

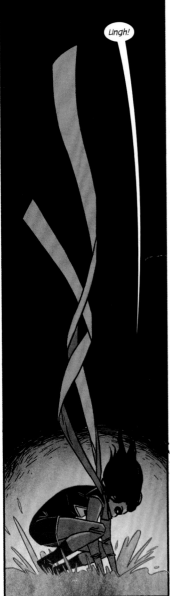

THE INVENTOR SEEMS PRETTY CRAZY, BUT HE CAN'T BE *THAT*--

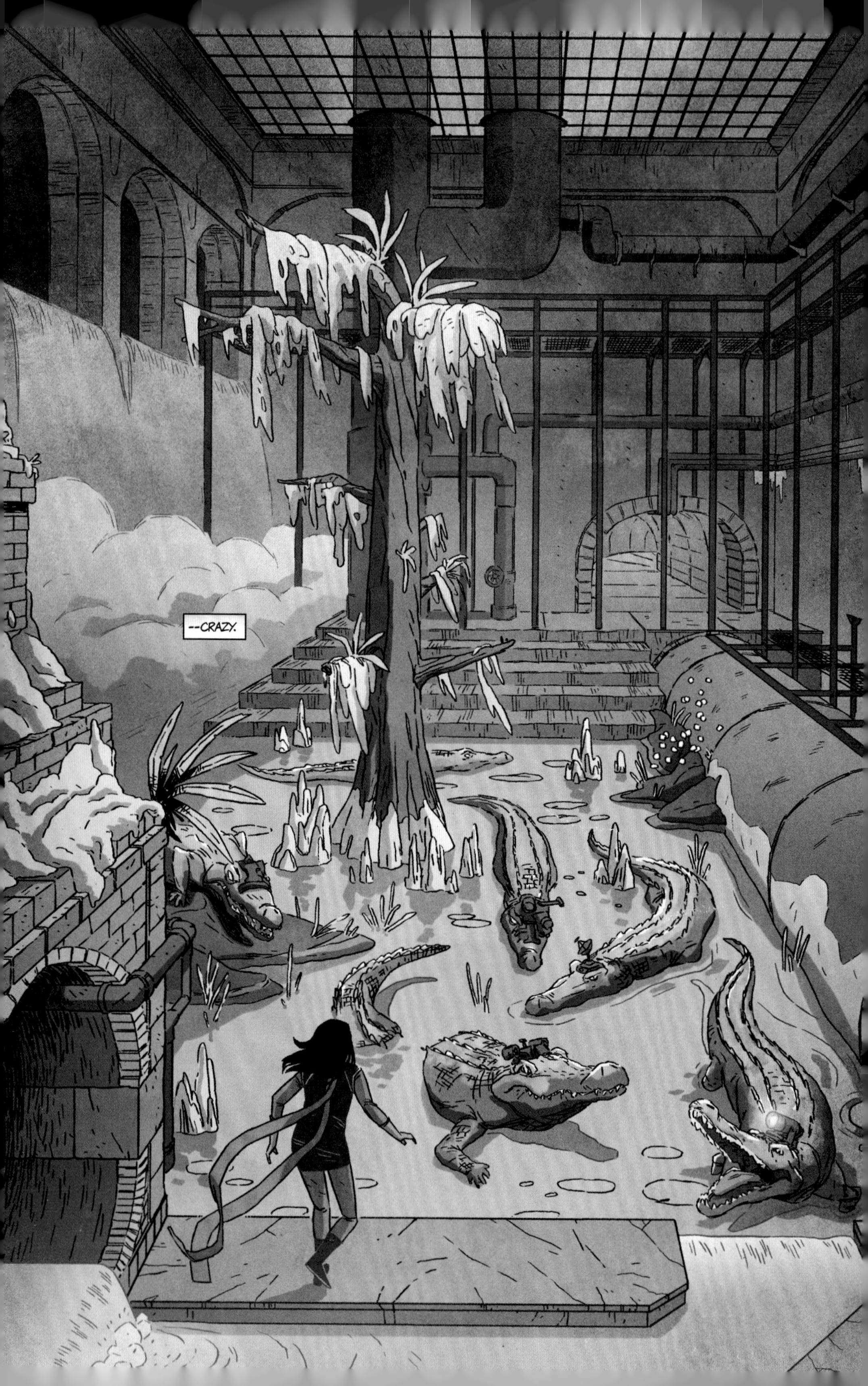
--CRAZY.

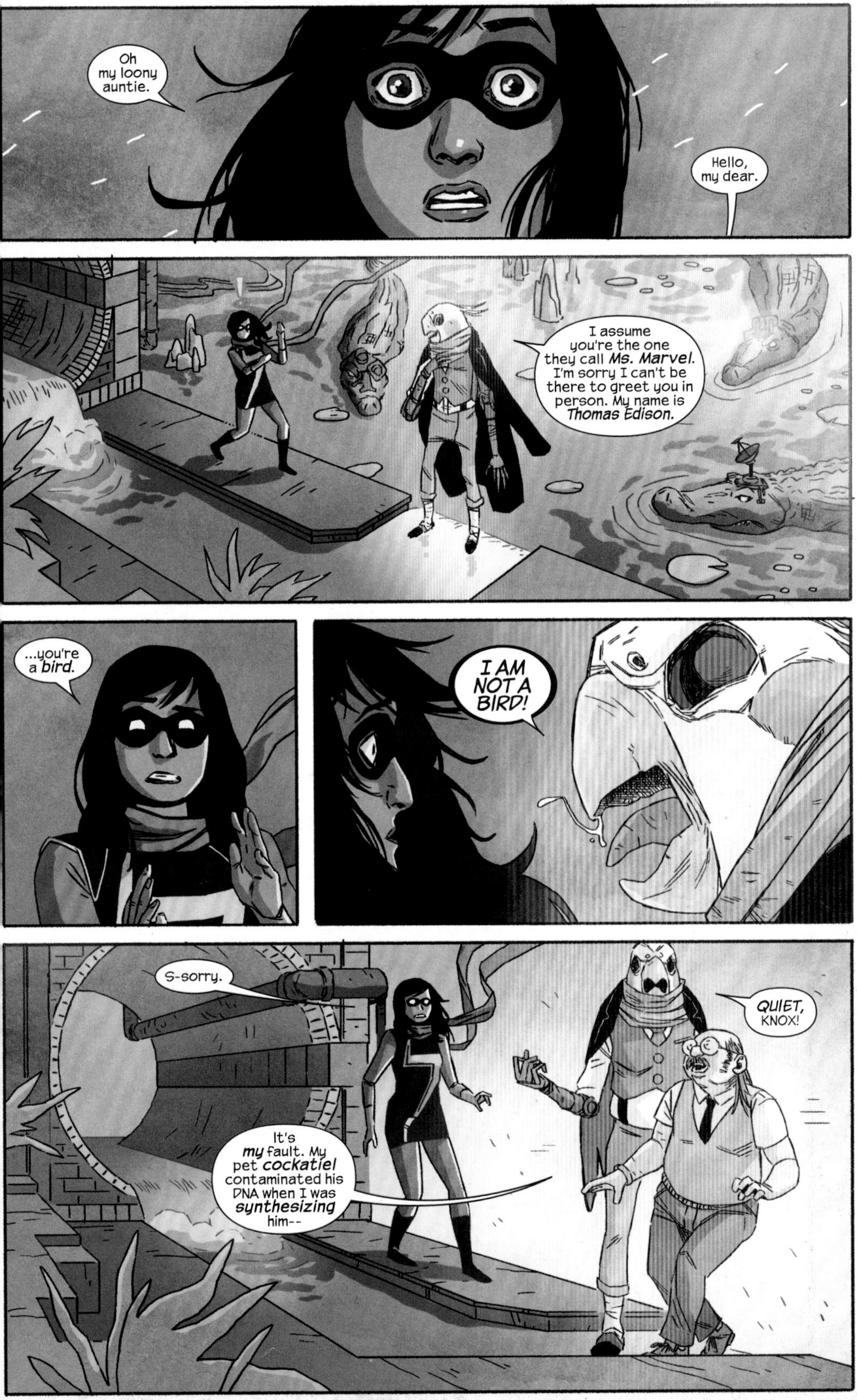
Oh my loony auntie.
Hello, my dear.
!
I assume you're the one they call Ms. Marvel. I'm sorry I can't be there to greet you in person. My name is Thomas Edison.
...you're a bird.
I AM NOT A BIRD!
S-sorry.
QUIET, KNOX!
It's my fault. My pet cockatiel contaminated his DNA when I was synthesizing him--

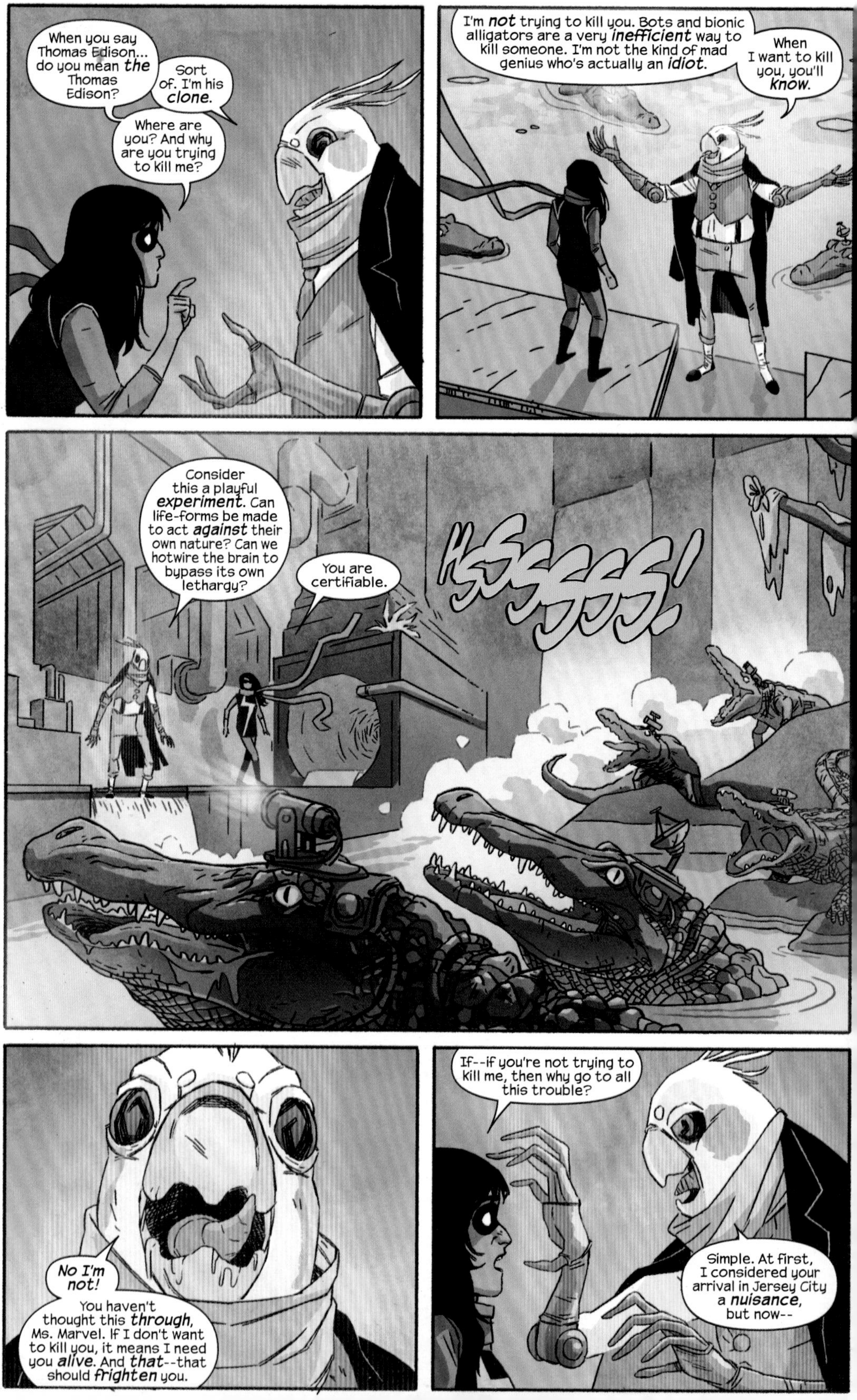
When you say Thomas Edison... do you mean the Thomas Edison?
Sort of. I'm his clone.
Where are you? And why are you trying to kill me?
I'm not trying to kill you. Bots and bionic alligators are a very inefficient way to kill someone. I'm not the kind of mad genius who's actually an idiot.
When I want to kill you, you'll know.
Consider this a playful experiment. Can life-forms be made to act against their own nature? Can we hotwire the brain to bypass its own lethargy?
You are certifiable.
HSSSSS!
No I'm not!
You haven't thought this through, Ms. Marvel. If I don't want to kill you, it means I need you alive. And that--that should frighten you.
If--if you're not trying to kill me, then why go to all this trouble?
Simple. At first, I considered your arrival in Jersey City a nuisance, but now--

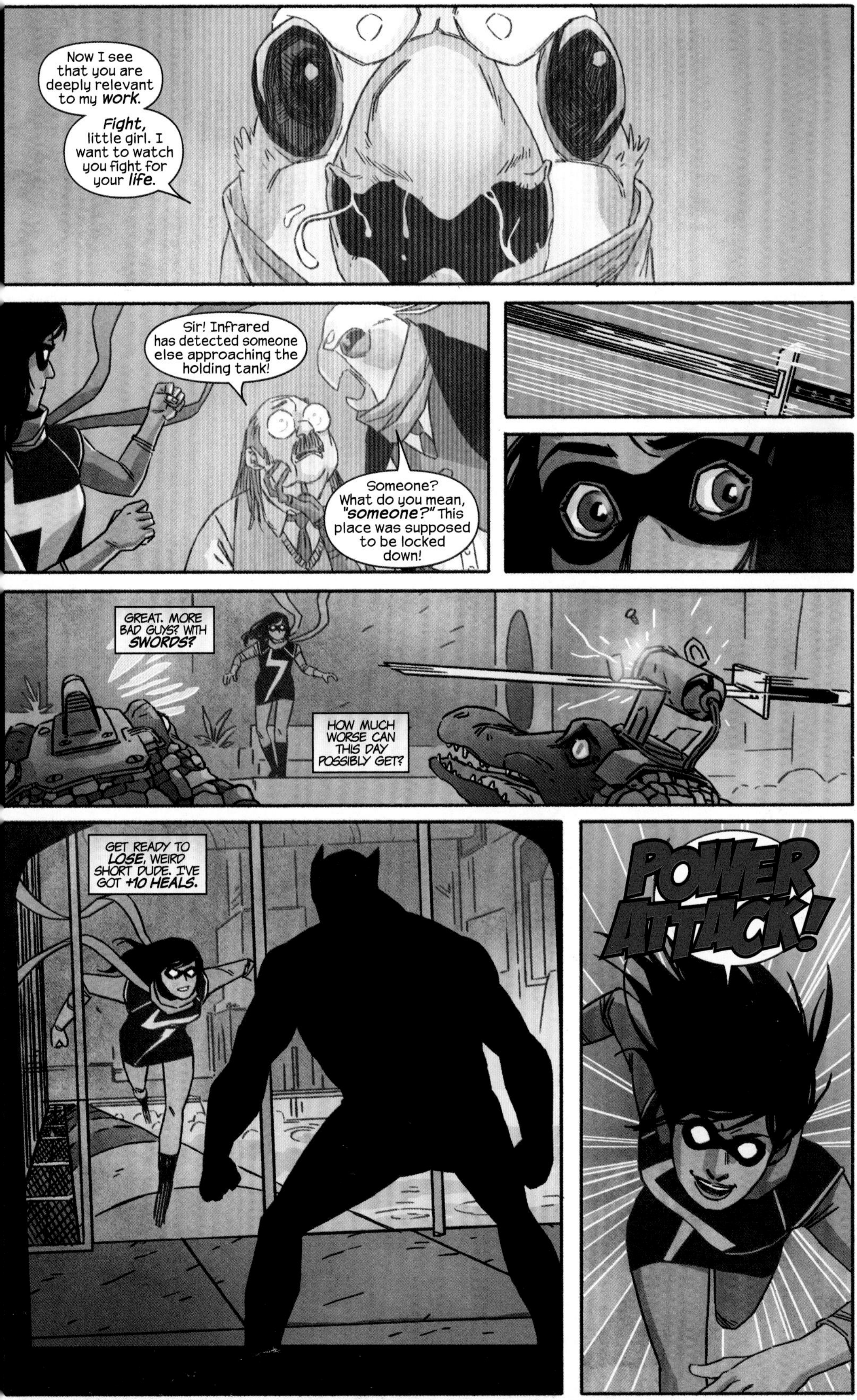

Now I see that you are deeply relevant to my work.
Fight, little girl. I want to watch you fight for your life.
Sir! Infrared has detected someone else approaching the holding tank!
Someone? What do you mean, "someone?" This place was supposed to be locked down!
GREAT. MORE BAD GUYS? WITH SWORDS?
HOW MUCH WORSE CAN THIS DAY POSSIBLY GET?
GET READY TO LOSE, WEIRD SHORT DUDE. I'VE GOT +10 HEALS.
POWER ATTACK!

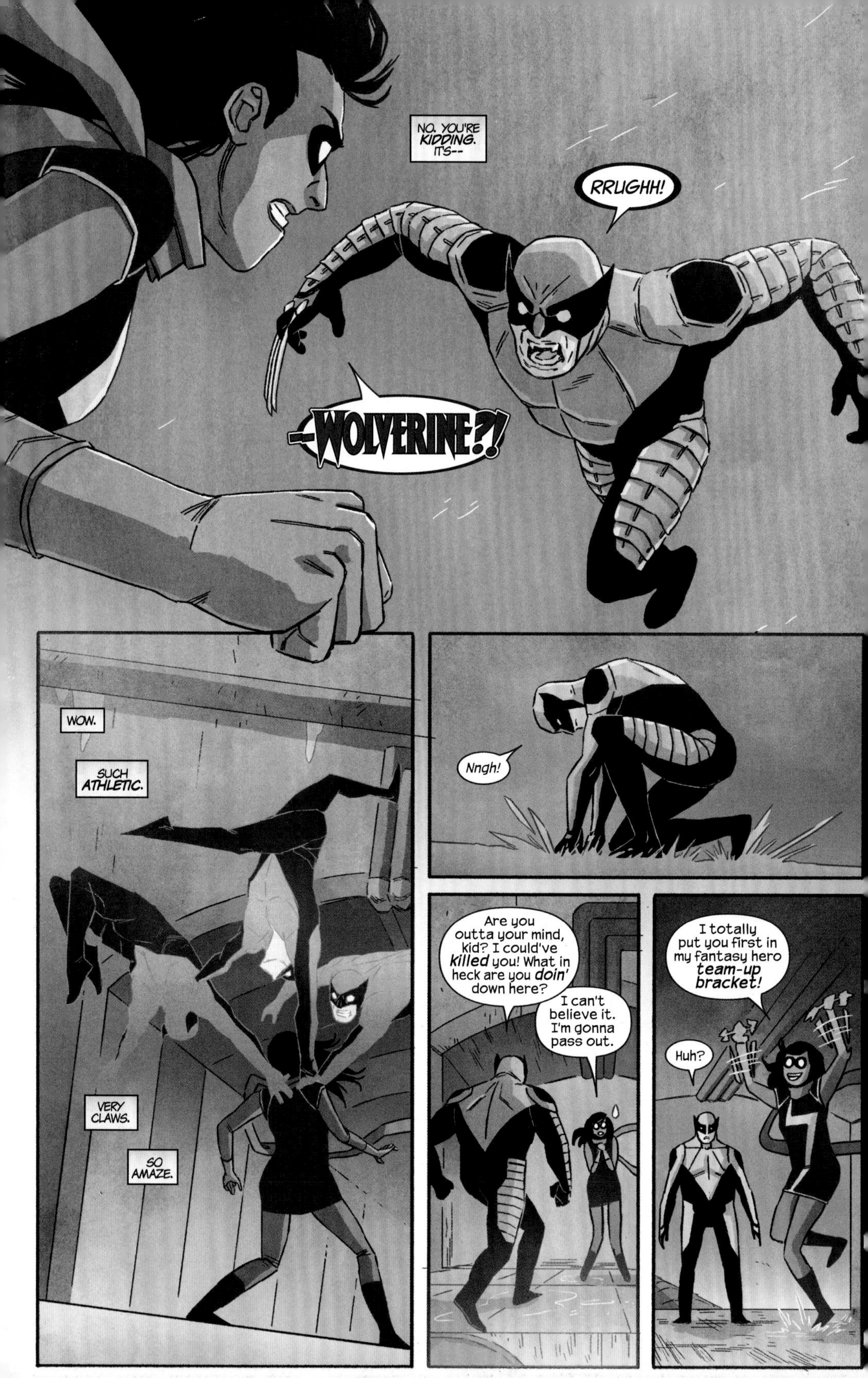
NO. YOU'RE KIDDING. IT'S--
RRUGHH!
-WOLVERINE?!
WOW.
SUCH ATHLETIC.
VERY CLAWS.
SO AMAZE.
Nngh!
Are you outta your mind, kid? I could've killed you! What in heck are you doin' down here?
I can't believe it. I'm gonna pass out.
I totally put you first in my fantasy hero team-up bracket!
Huh?

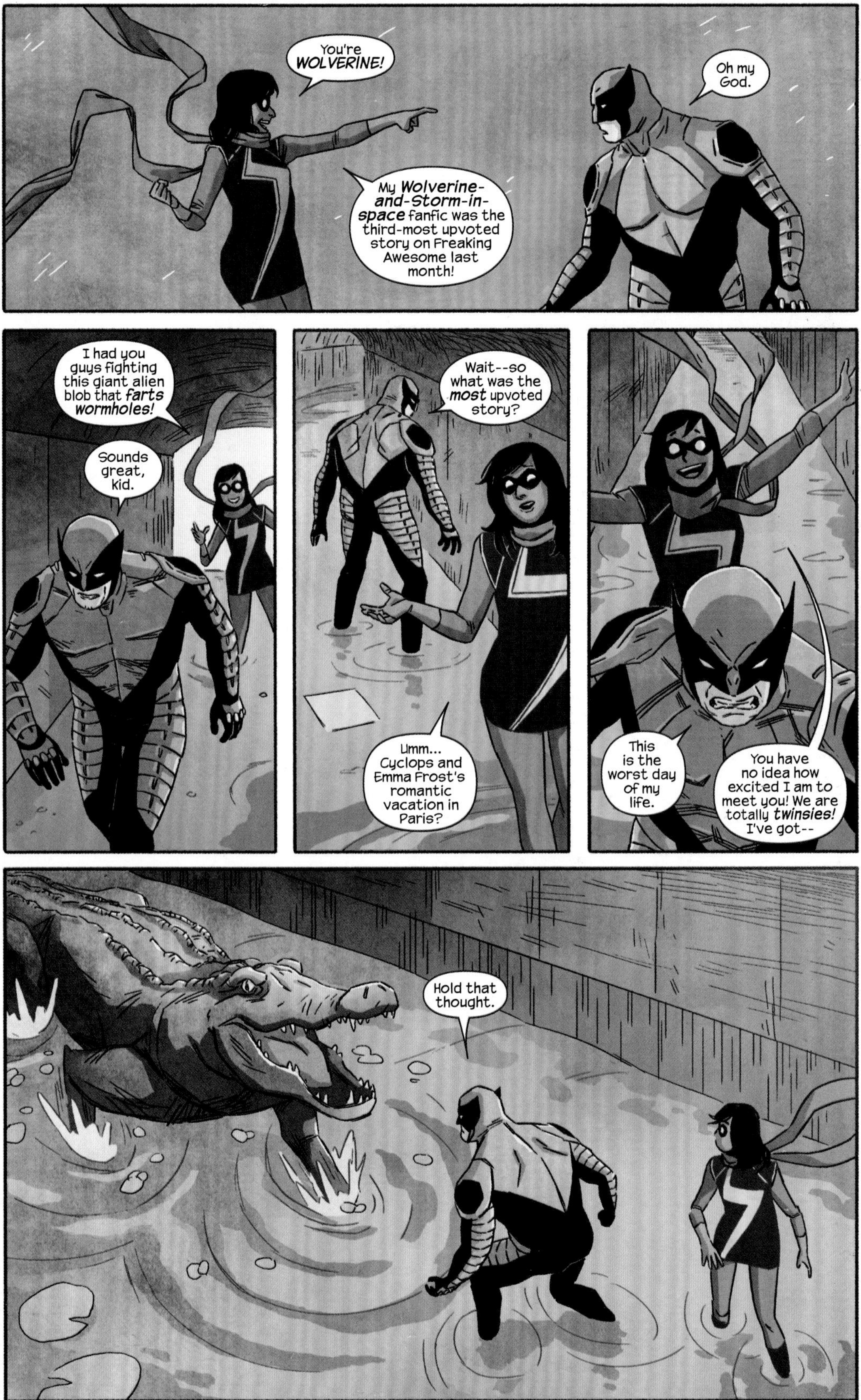
You're WOLVERINE!
Oh my God.
My Wolverine-and-Storm-in-space fanfic was the third-most upvoted story on Freaking Awesome last month!
I had you guys fighting this giant alien blob that farts wormholes!
Sounds great, kid.
Wait--so what was the most upvoted story?
Umm... Cyclops and Emma Frost's romantic vacation in Paris?
You have no idea how excited I am to meet you! We are totally twinsies! I've got--
This is the worst day of my life.
Hold that thought.

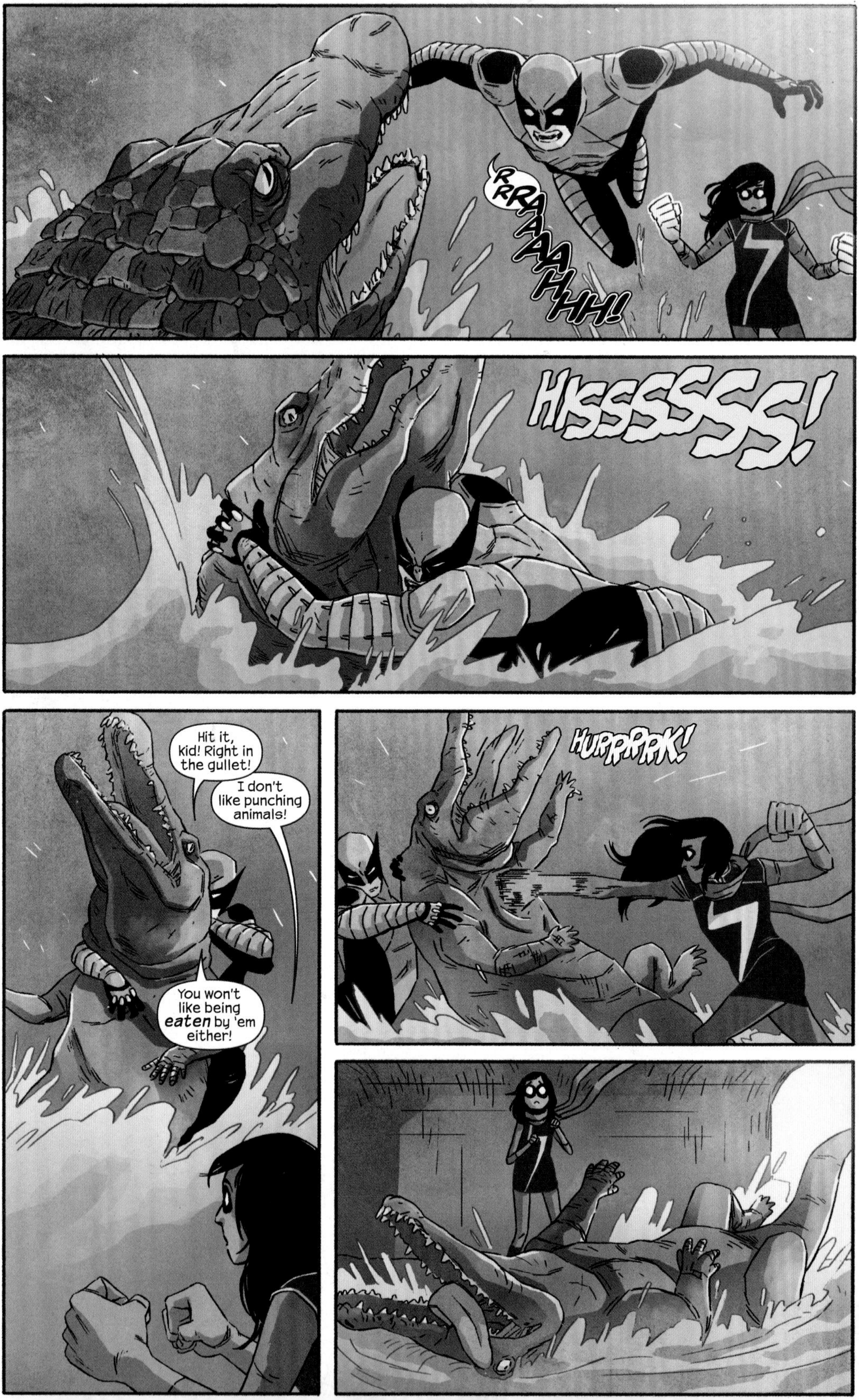
RRRAAAAHHH!
HISSSSSSS!
Hit it, kid! Right in the gullet!
I don't like punching animals!
You won't like being eaten by 'em either!
HURRRRK!

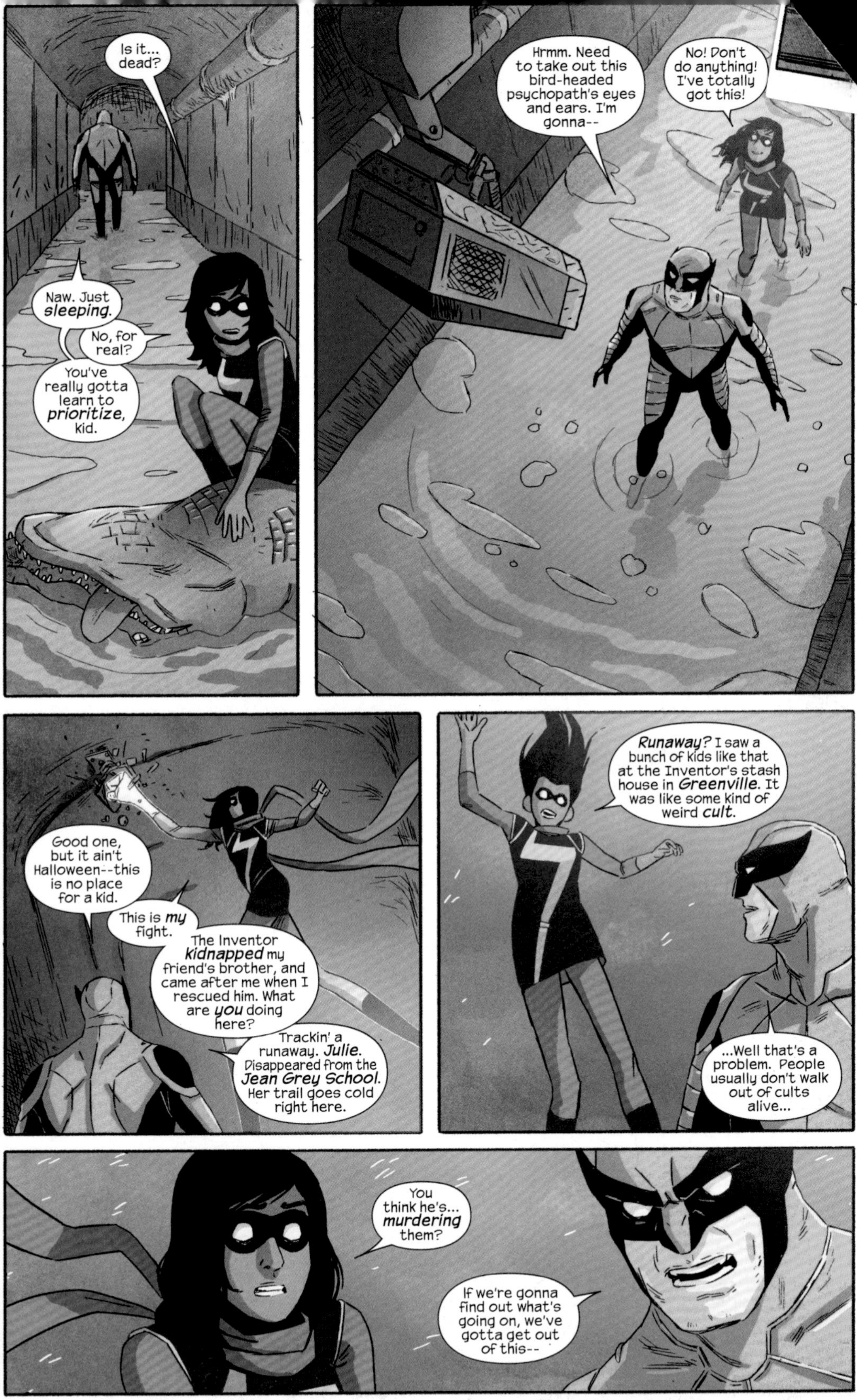

Is it... dead?
Naw. Just *sleeping*.
No, for real?
You've really gotta learn to *prioritize*, kid.
Hrmm. Need to take out this bird-headed psychopath's eyes and ears. I'm gonna--
No! Don't do anything! I've totally got this!
Good one, but it ain't Halloween--this is no place for a kid.
This is *my* fight.
The Inventor *kidnapped* my friend's brother, and came after me when I rescued him. What are *you* doing here?
Trackin' a runaway. *Julie*. Disappeared from the *Jean Grey School*. Her trail goes cold right here.
Runaway? I saw a bunch of kids like that at the Inventor's stash house in *Greenville*. It was like some kind of weird *cult*.
...Well that's a problem. People usually don't walk out of cults alive...
You think he's... *murdering* them?
If we're gonna find out what's going on, we've gotta get out of this--

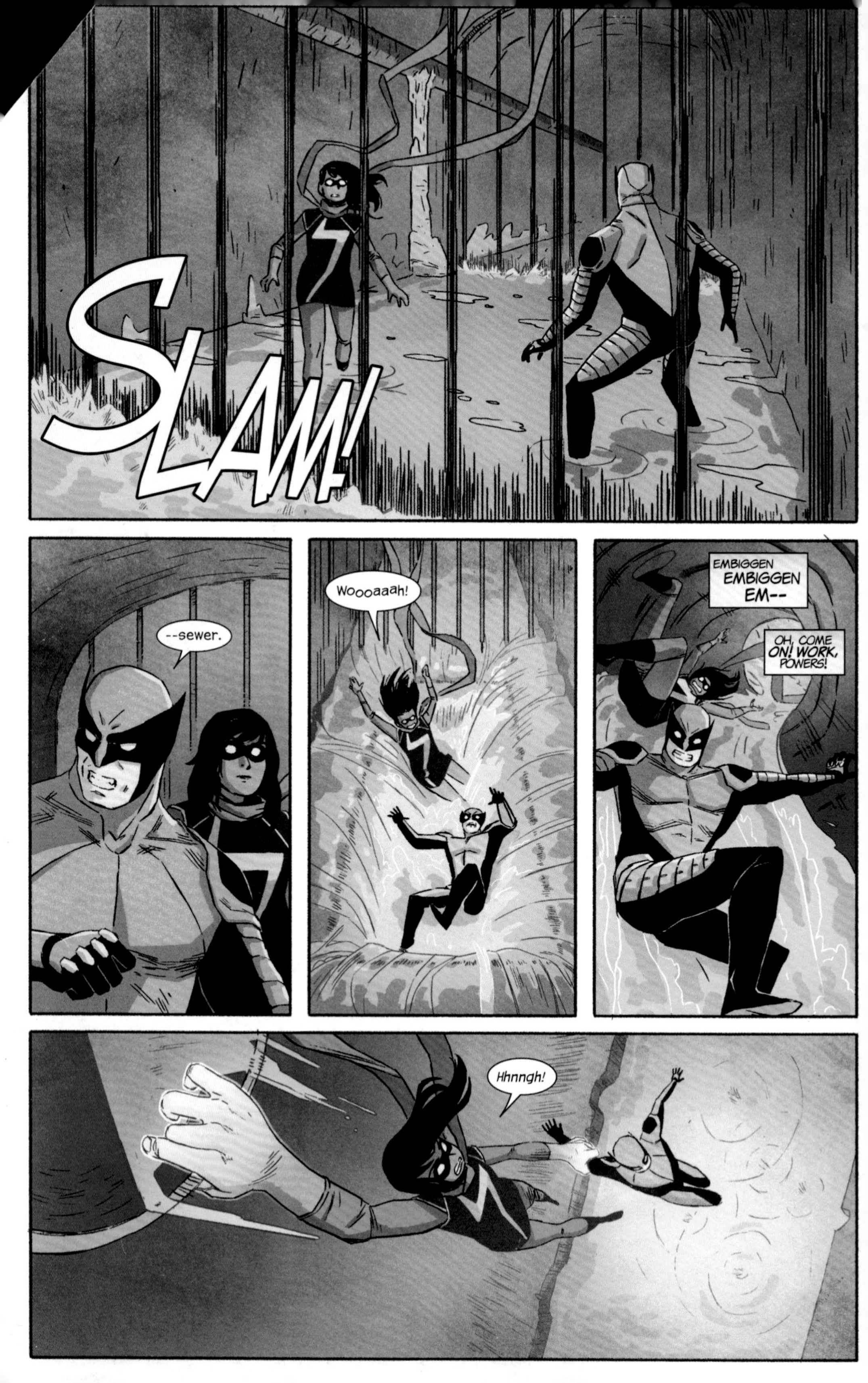
SLAM!
--sewer.
Woooaaah!
EMBIGGEN EMBIGGEN EM--
OH, COME ON! WORK, POWERS!
Hhnngh!

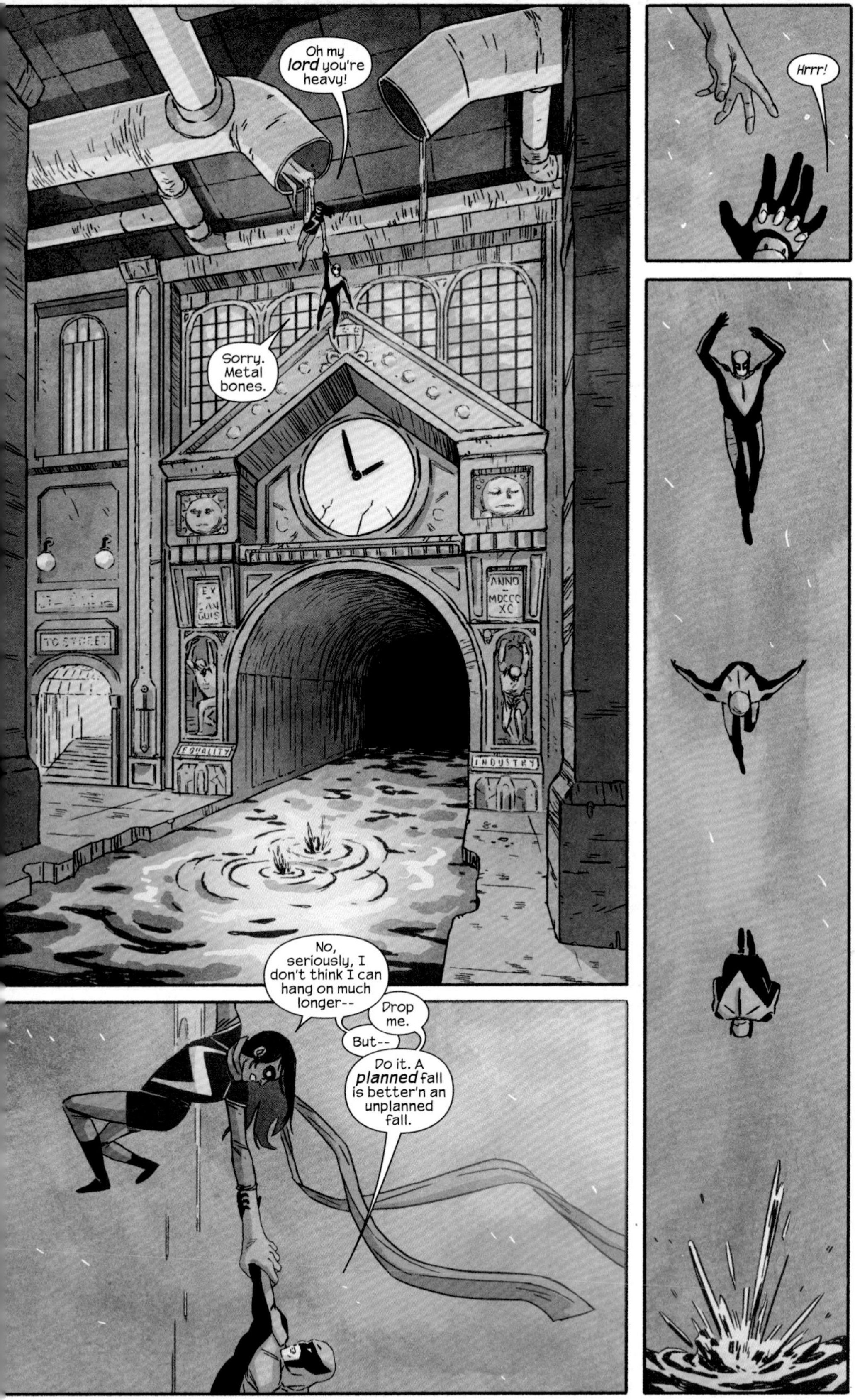
Oh my *lord* you're heavy!
Sorry. Metal bones.
TO STREET
EX SAN GUIS
ANNO MDCCCXC
EQUALITY
INDUSTRY
Hrrr!
No, seriously, I don't think I can hang on much longer--
Drop me.
But--
Do it. A *planned* fall is better'n an unplanned fall.

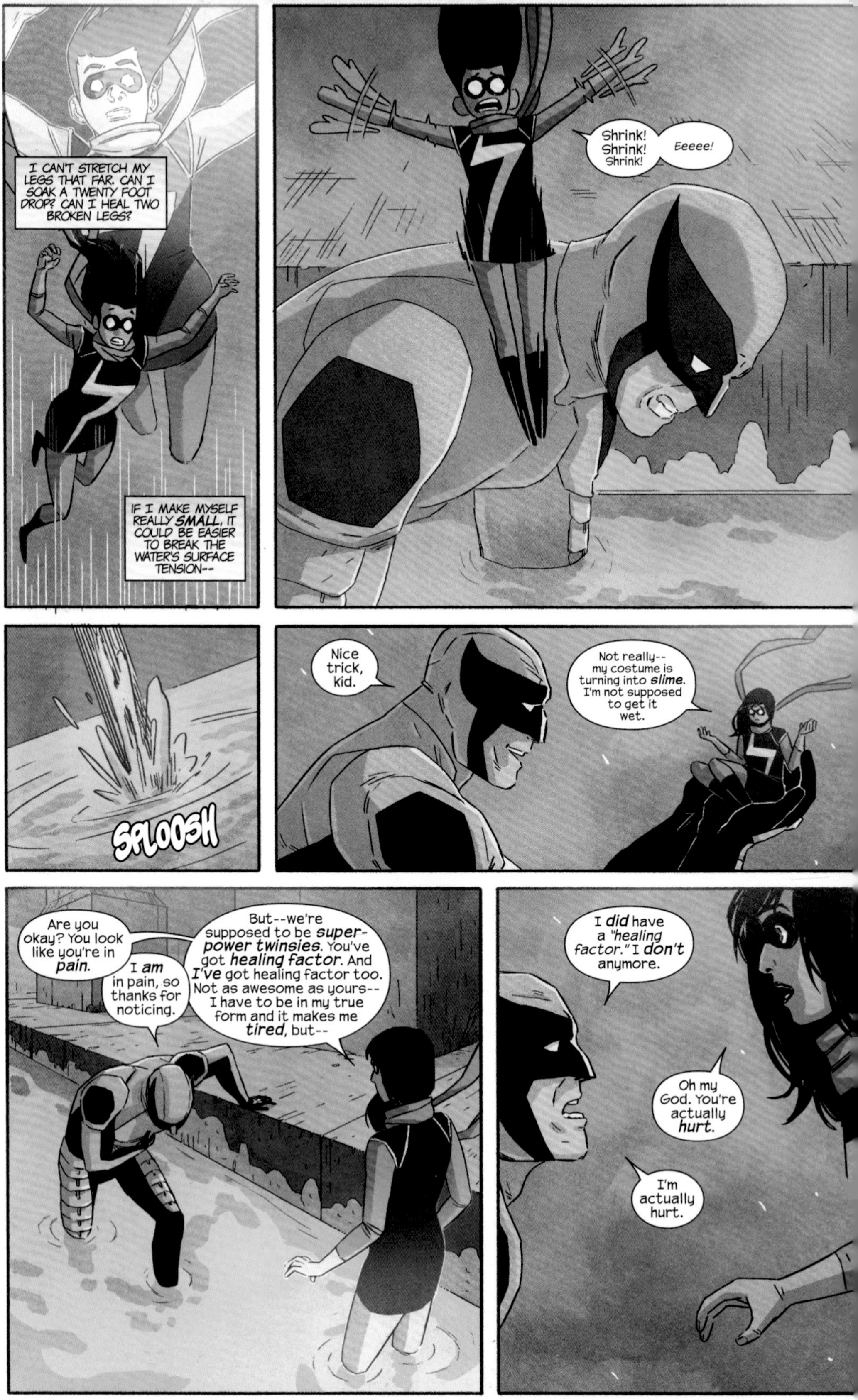
I CAN'T STRETCH MY LEGS THAT FAR. CAN I SOAK A TWENTY FOOT DROP? CAN I HEAL TWO BROKEN LEGS?
IF I MAKE MYSELF REALLY SMALL, IT COULD BE EASIER TO BREAK THE WATER'S SURFACE TENSION--
Shrink! Shrink! Shrink!
Eeeee!
SPLOOSH
Nice trick, kid.
Not really-- my costume is turning into slime. I'm not supposed to get it wet.
Are you okay? You look like you're in pain.
I am in pain, so thanks for noticing.
But--we're supposed to be super-power twinsies. You've got healing factor. And I've got healing factor too. Not as awesome as yours-- I have to be in my true form and it makes me tired, but--
I did have a "healing factor." I don't anymore.
Oh my God. You're actually hurt.
I'm actually hurt.

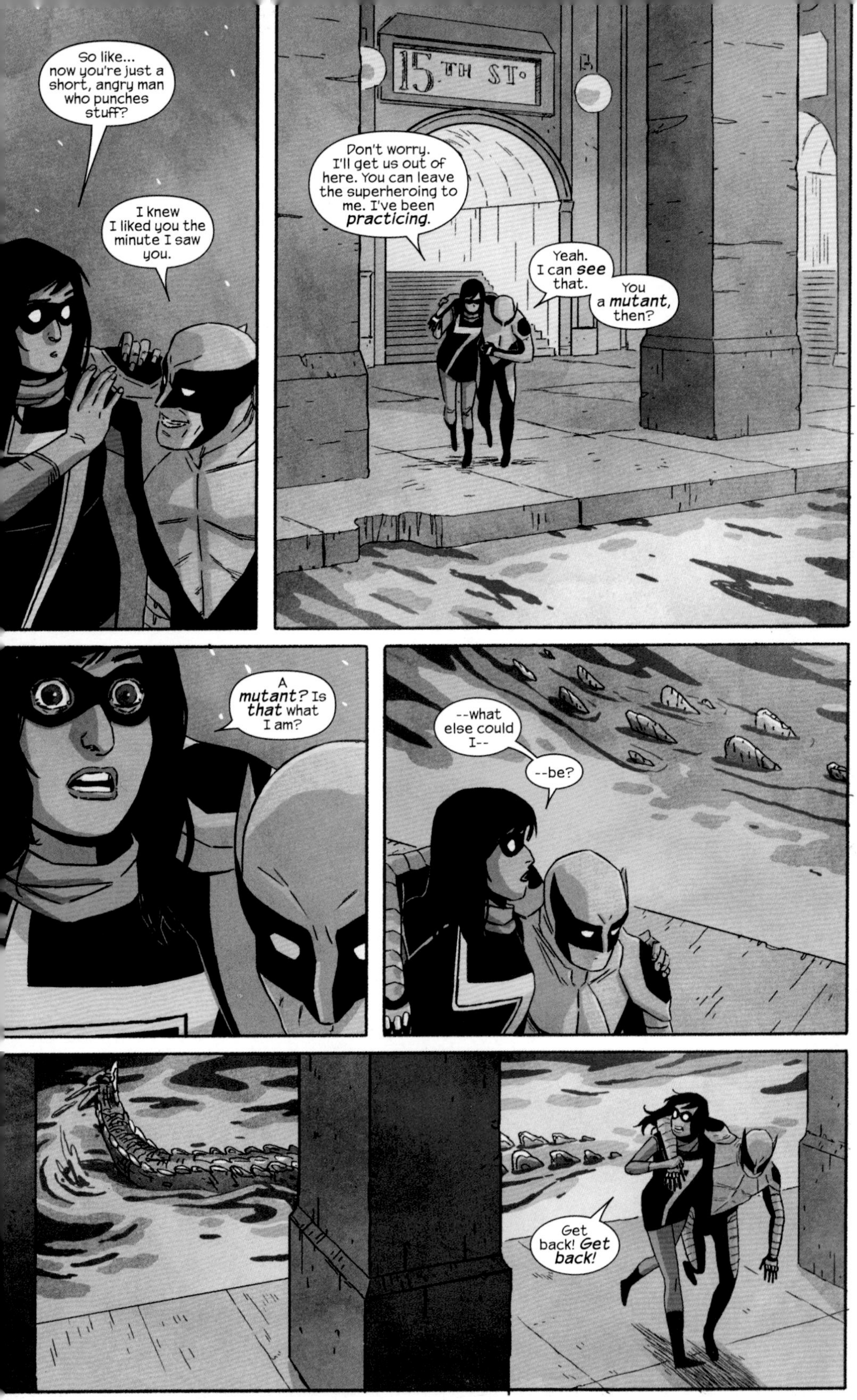
So like... now you're just a short, angry man who punches stuff?
I knew I liked you the minute I saw you.
15TH ST.
Don't worry. I'll get us out of here. You can leave the superheroing to me. I've been *practicing*.
Yeah. I can *see* that.
You a *mutant*, then?
A *mutant?* Is *that* what I am?
--what else could I--
--be?
Get back! *Get back!*

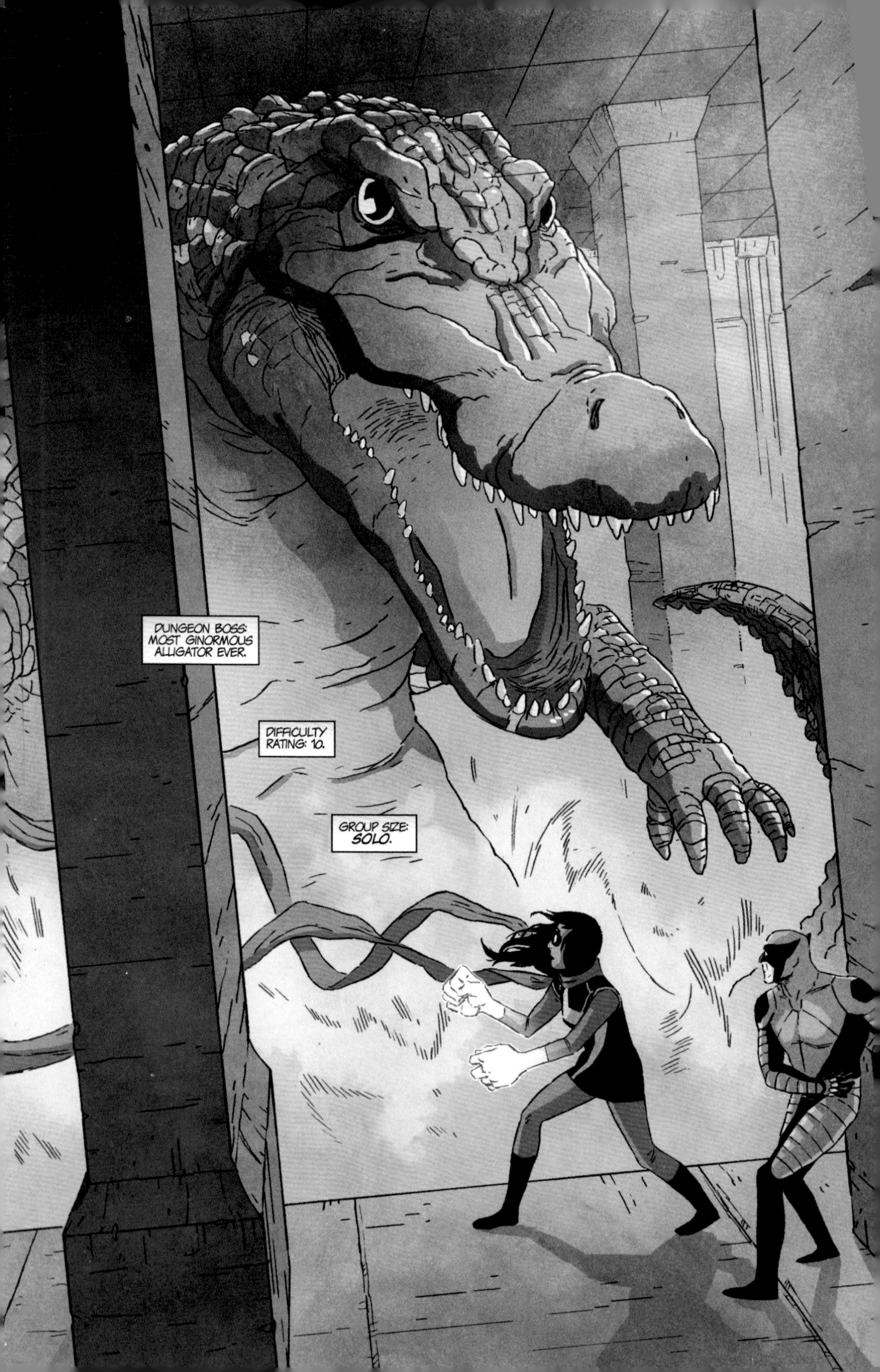
DUNGEON BOSS: MOST GINORMOUS ALLIGATOR EVER.
DIFFICULTY RATING: 10.
GROUP SIZE: SOLO.

MS. MARVEL #7

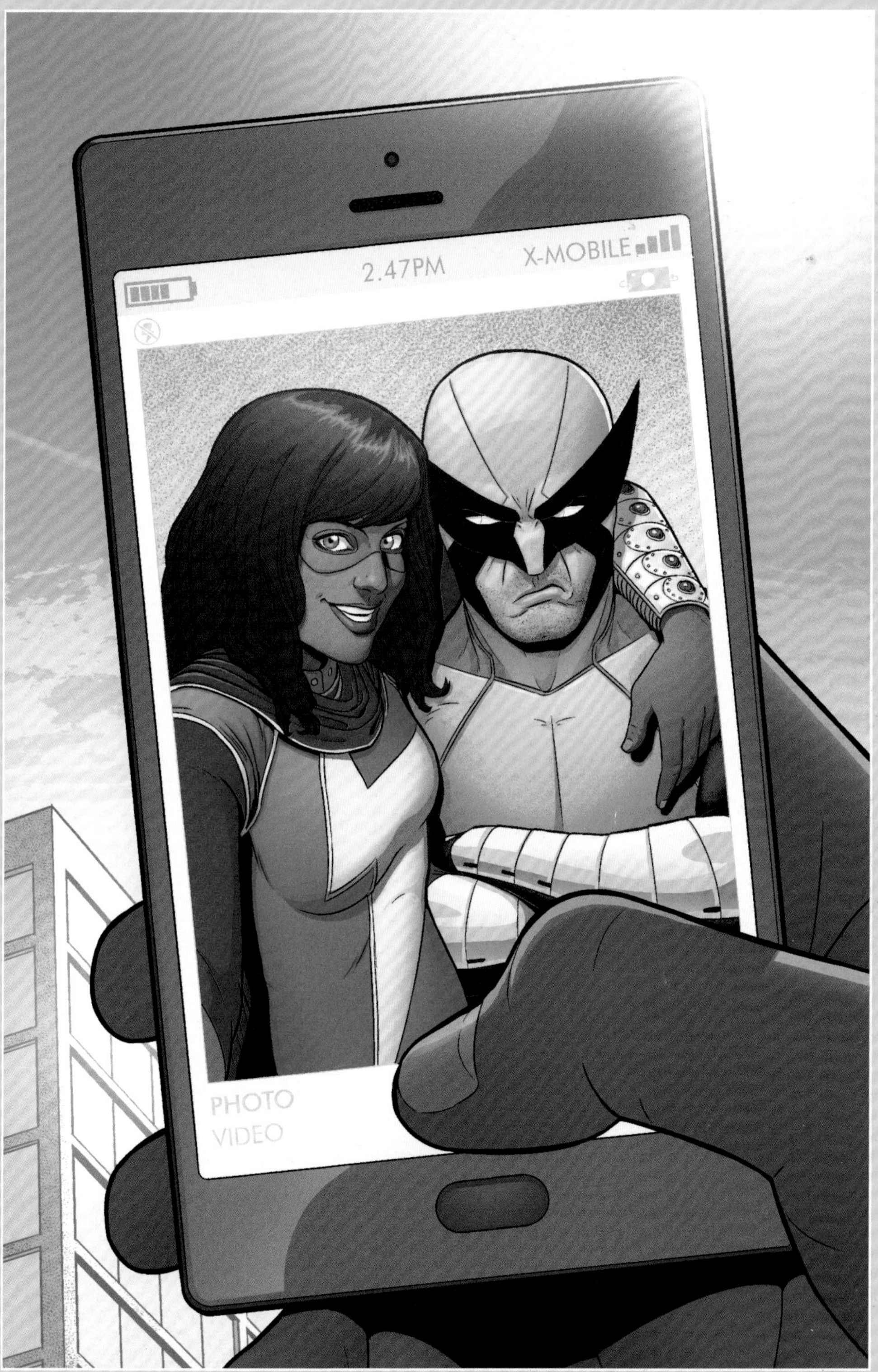
2.47PM
X-MOBILE
PHOTO
VIDEO

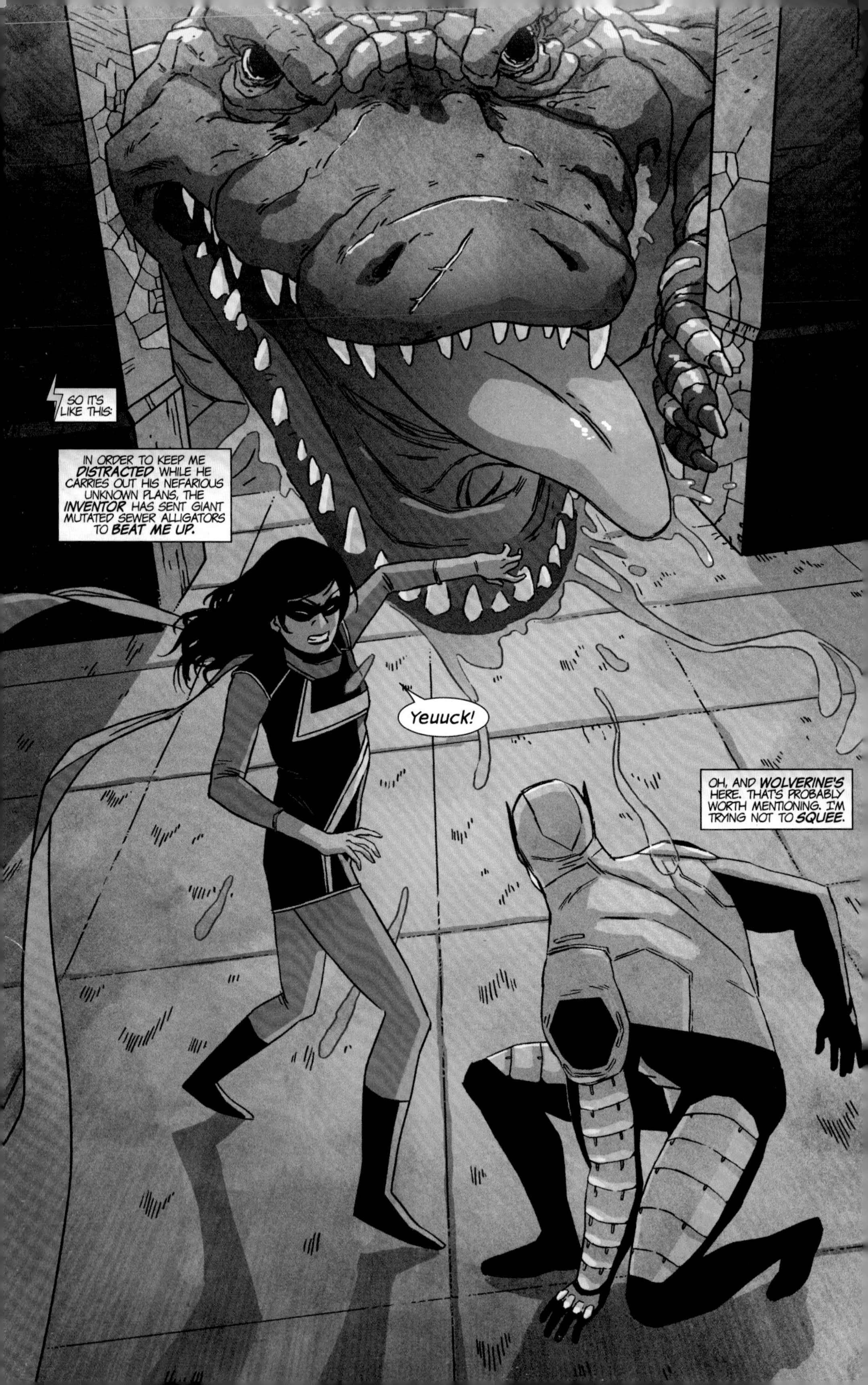
SO IT'S LIKE THIS:
IN ORDER TO KEEP ME DISTRACTED WHILE HE CARRIES OUT HIS NEFARIOUS UNKNOWN PLANS, THE INVENTOR HAS SENT GIANT MUTATED SEWER ALLIGATORS TO BEAT ME UP.
Yeuuck!
OH, AND WOLVERINE'S HERE. THAT'S PROBABLY WORTH MENTIONING. I'M TRYING NOT TO SQUEE.

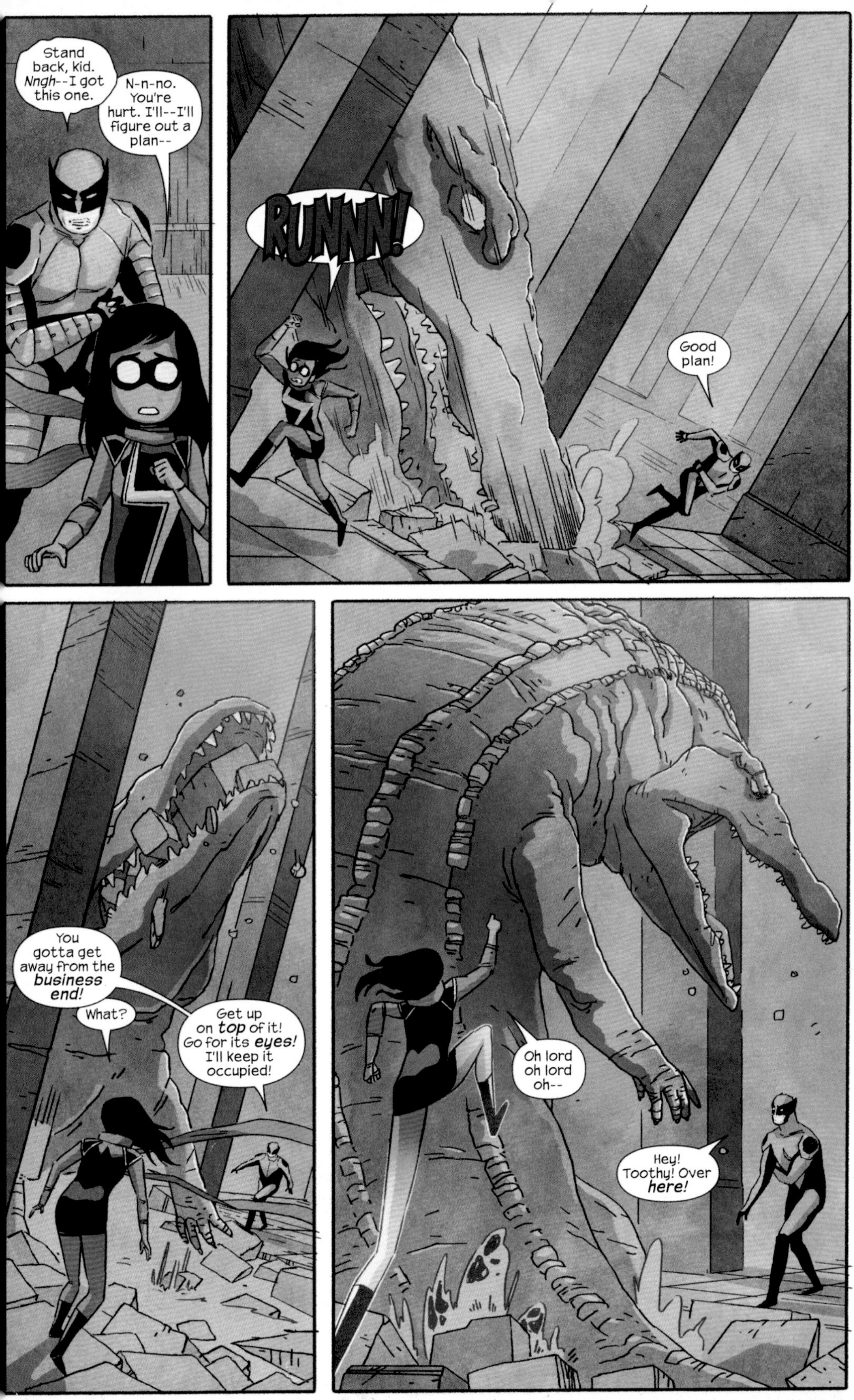
Stand back, kid. Nngh--I got this one.
N-n-no. You're hurt. I'll--I'll figure out a plan--
RUNNN!
Good plan!
You gotta get away from the business end!
What?
Get up on top of it! Go for its eyes! I'll keep it occupied!
Oh lord oh lord oh--
Hey! Toothy! Over here!

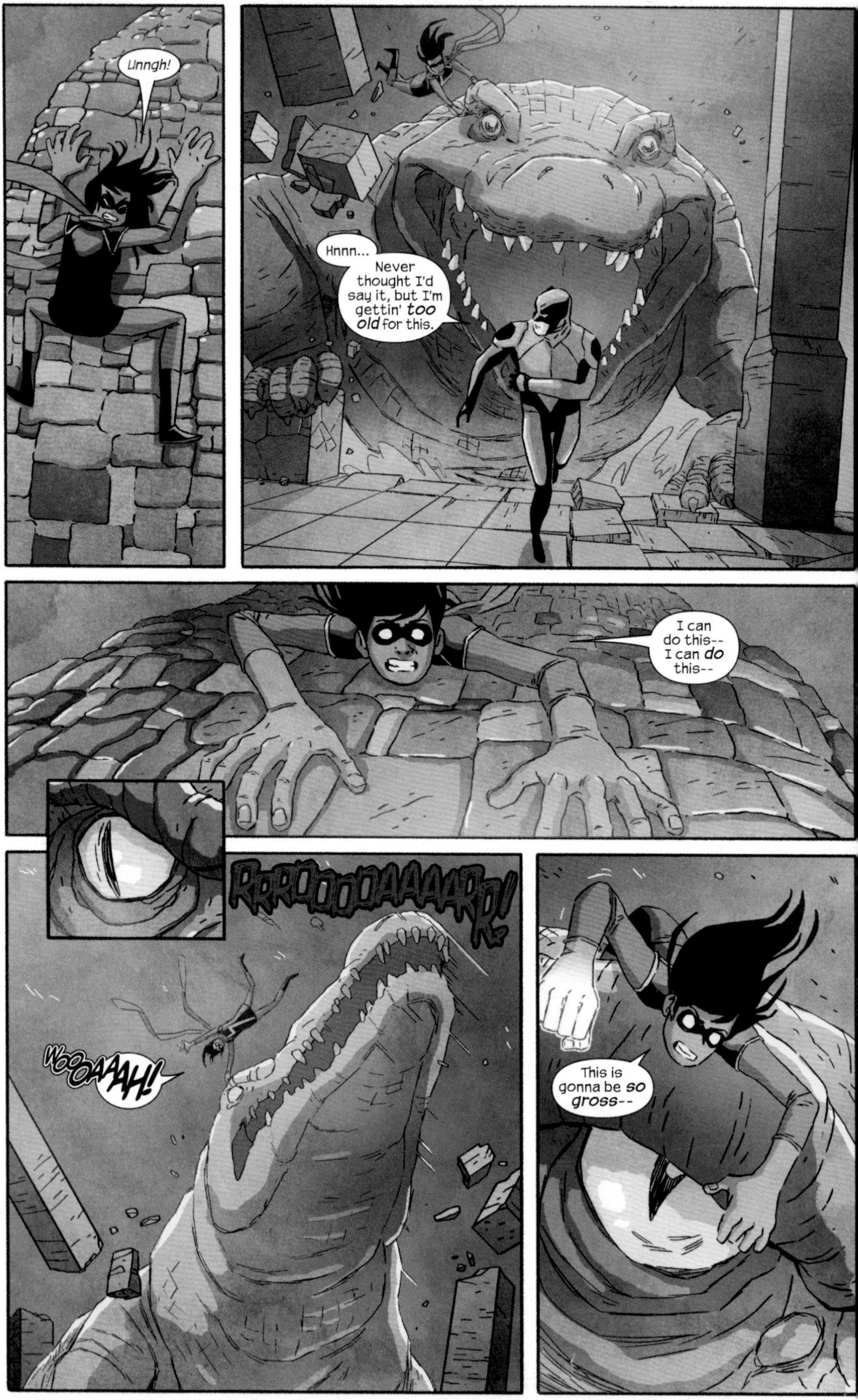
Unnngh!
Hnnn...
Never thought I'd say it, but I'm gettin' *too old* for this.
I can do this-- I can *do* this--
RRRROOOOAAAARR!
WOOOAAAH!
This is gonna be *so gross*--

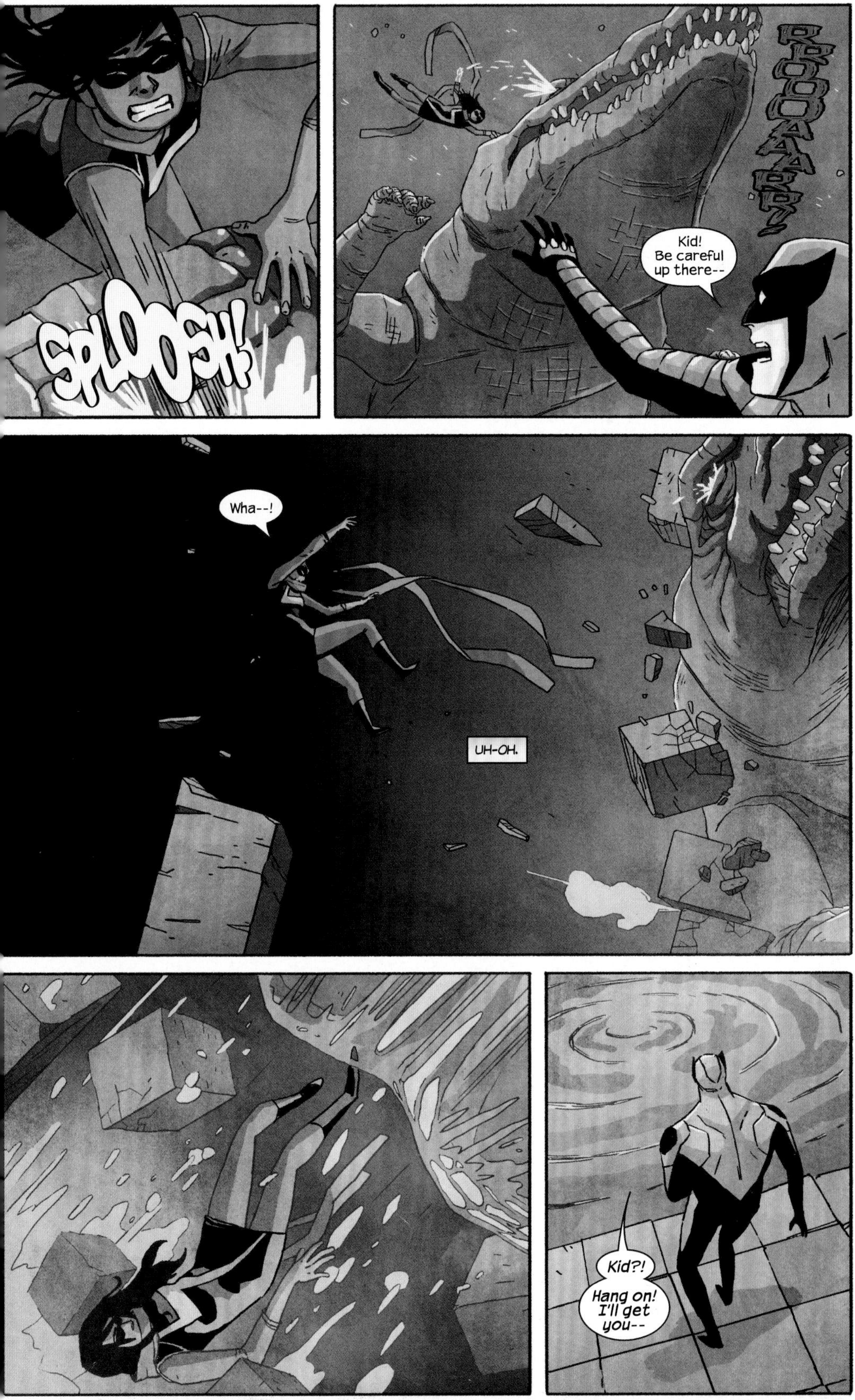
SPLOOSH!
RROOOAAARR?!
Kid! Be careful up there--
Wha--!
UH-OH.
Kid?!
Hang on! I'll get you--

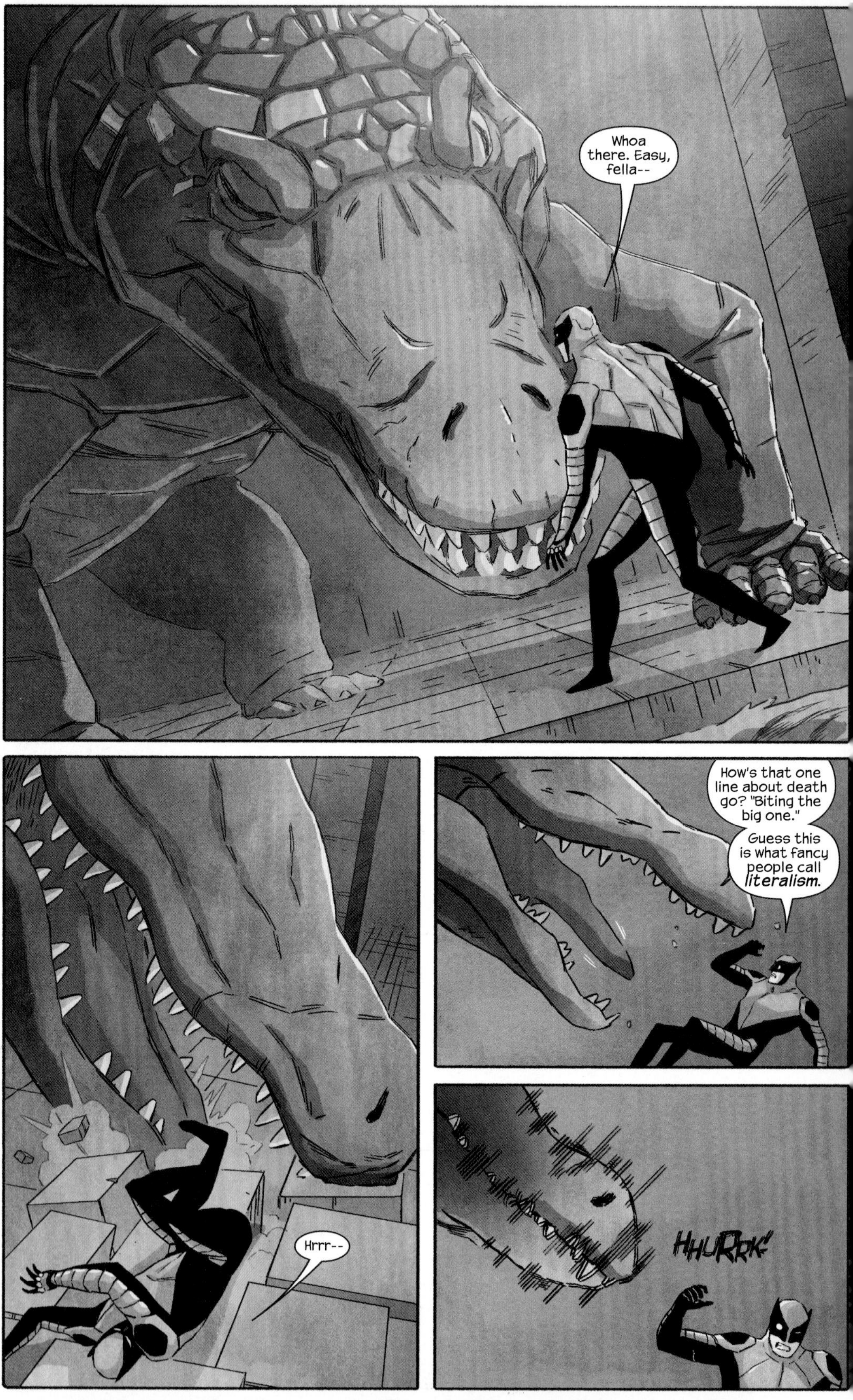
Whoa there. Easy, fella--
Hrrr--
How's that one line about death go? "Biting the big one."
Guess this is what fancy people call *literalism*.
HHURRK!

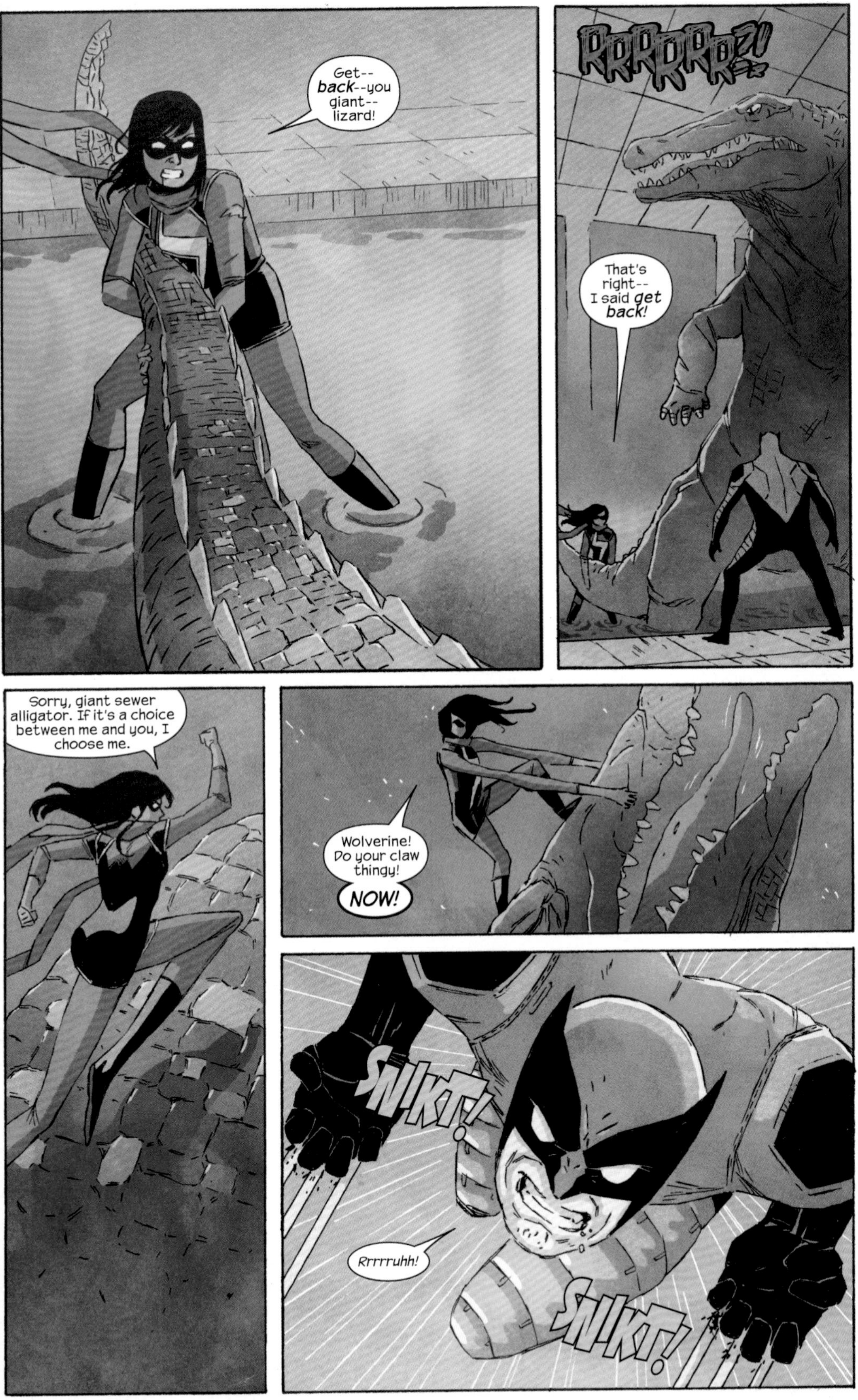
Get--
back--you giant--lizard!
RRRRRRRZ!!
That's right--
I said get back!
Sorry, giant sewer alligator. If it's a choice between me and you, I choose me.
Wolverine! Do your claw thingy!
NOW!
SNIKT!
Rrrrruhh!
SNIKT!

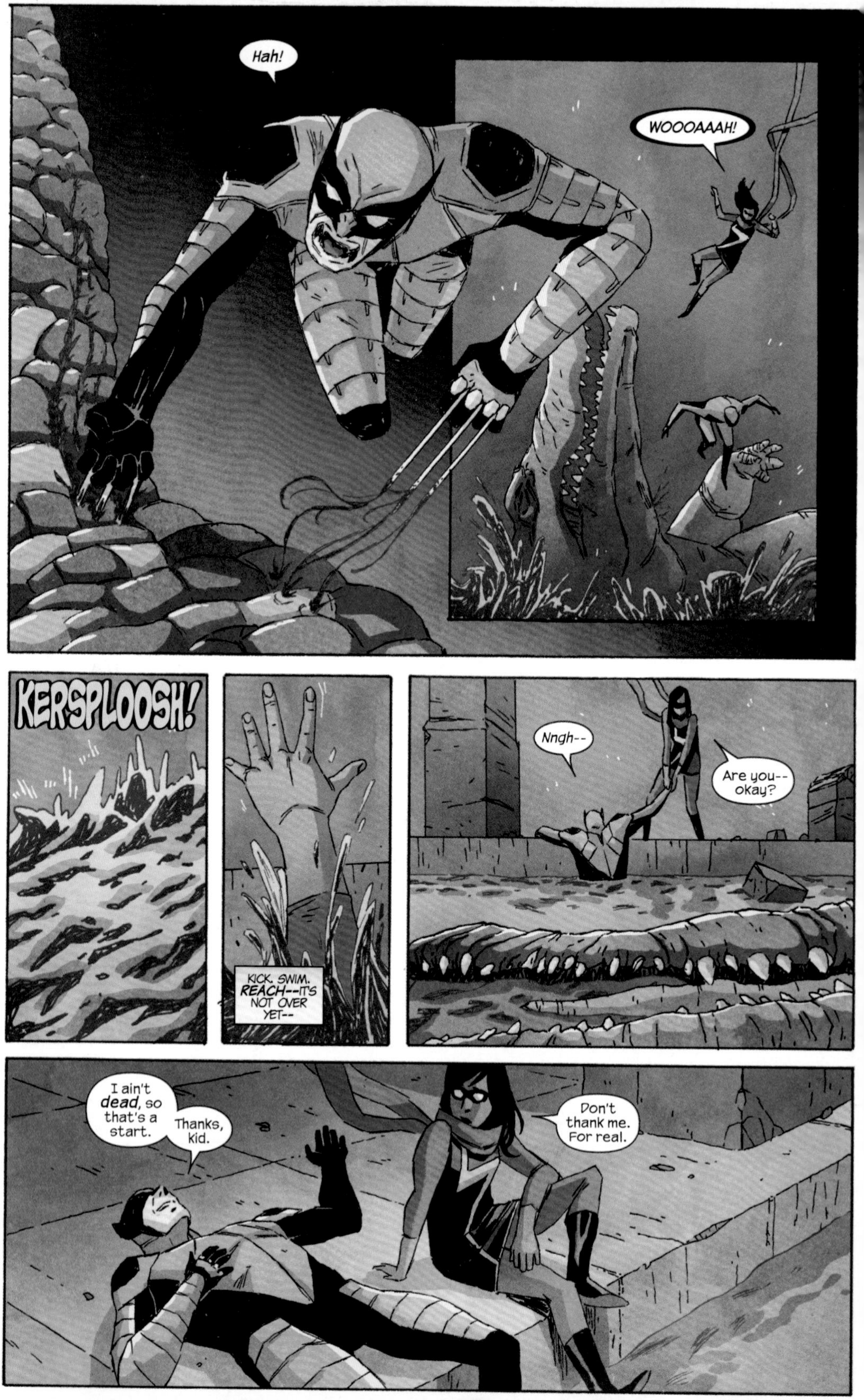
Hah!
WOOOAAAH!
KERSPLOOSH!
KICK. SWIM. REACH--IT'S NOT OVER YET--
Nngh--
Are you--okay?
I ain't dead, so that's a start.
Thanks, kid.
Don't thank me. For real.

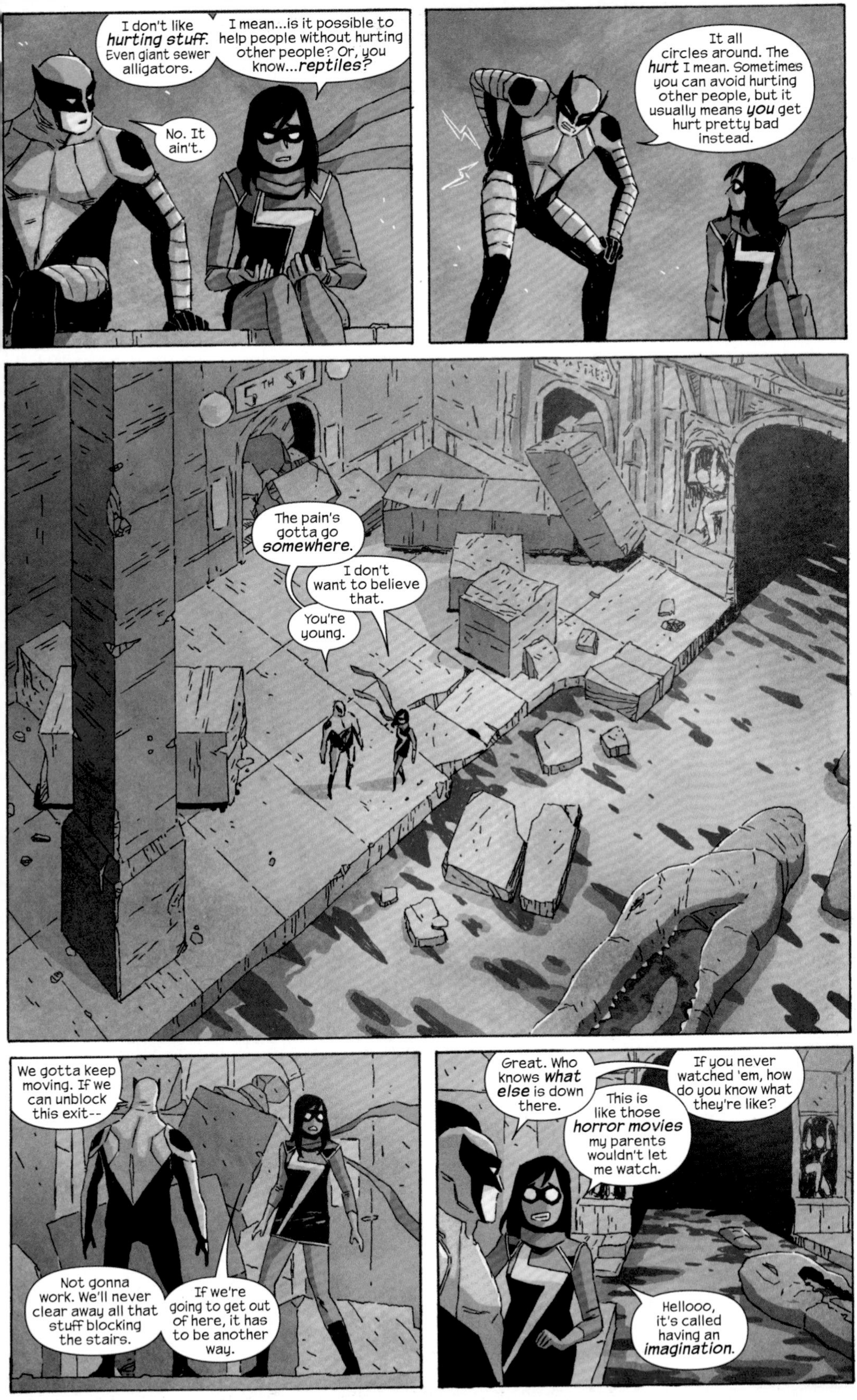
I don't like hurting stuff. Even giant sewer alligators.
I mean...is it possible to help people without hurting other people? Or, you know...reptiles?
No. It ain't.
It all circles around. The hurt I mean. Sometimes you can avoid hurting other people, but it usually means you get hurt pretty bad instead.
5TH ST
The pain's gotta go somewhere.
I don't want to believe that.
You're young.
We gotta keep moving. If we can unblock this exit--
Not gonna work. We'll never clear away all that stuff blocking the stairs.
If we're going to get out of here, it has to be another way.
Great. Who knows what else is down there.
This is like those horror movies my parents wouldn't let me watch.
If you never watched 'em, how do you know what they're like?
Hellooo, it's called having an imagination.

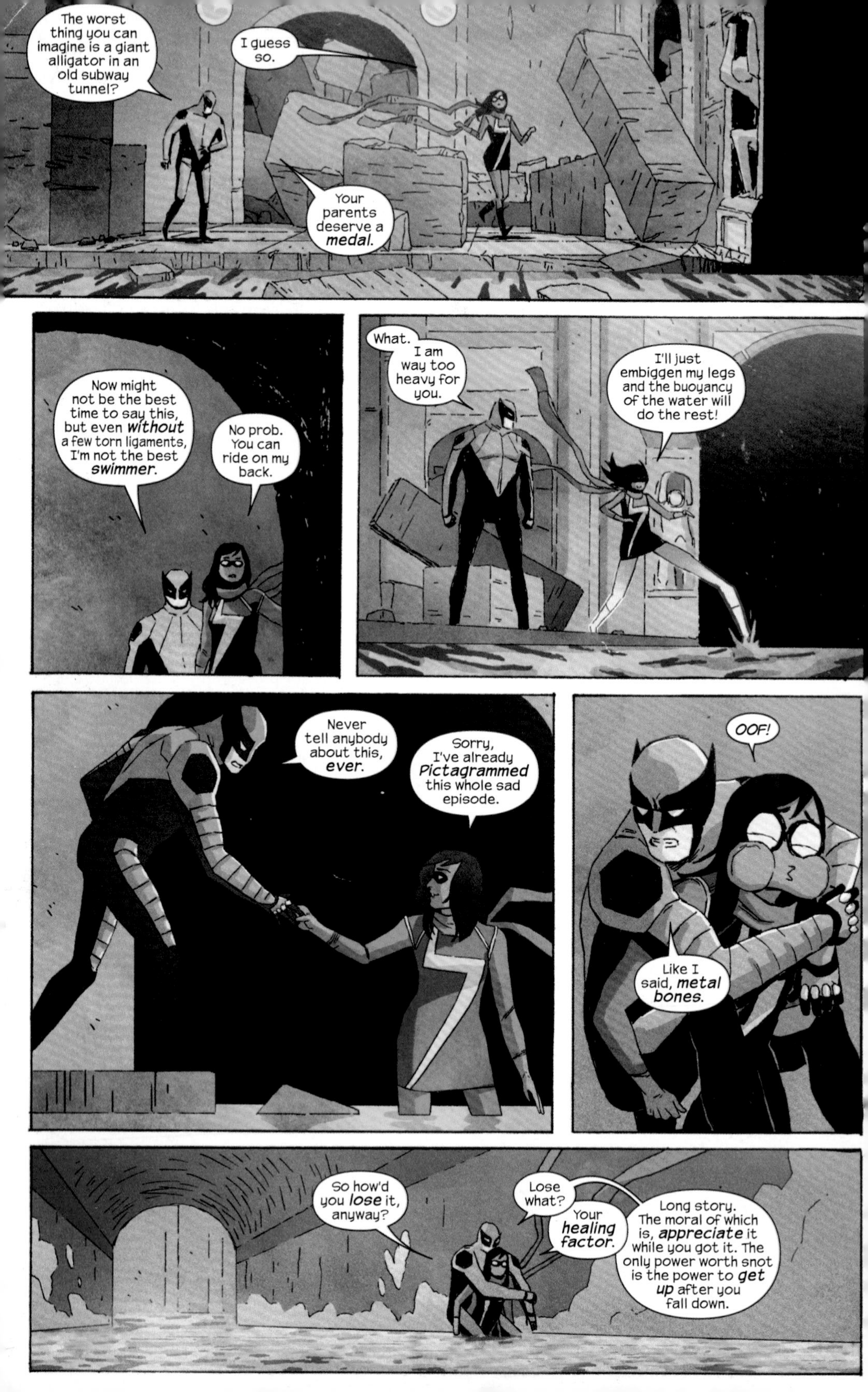
The worst thing you can imagine is a giant alligator in an old subway tunnel?
I guess so.
Your parents deserve a *medal*.
Now might not be the best time to say this, but even *without* a few torn ligaments, I'm not the best *swimmer*.
No prob. You can ride on my back.
What. I am way too heavy for you.
I'll just embiggen my legs and the buoyancy of the water will do the rest!
Never tell anybody about this, *ever*.
Sorry, I've already *Pictagrammed* this whole sad episode.
OOF!
Like I said, *metal bones*.
So how'd you *lose* it, anyway?
Lose what?
Your *healing factor*.
Long story. The moral of which is, *appreciate* it while you got it. The only power worth snot is the power to *get up* after you fall down.

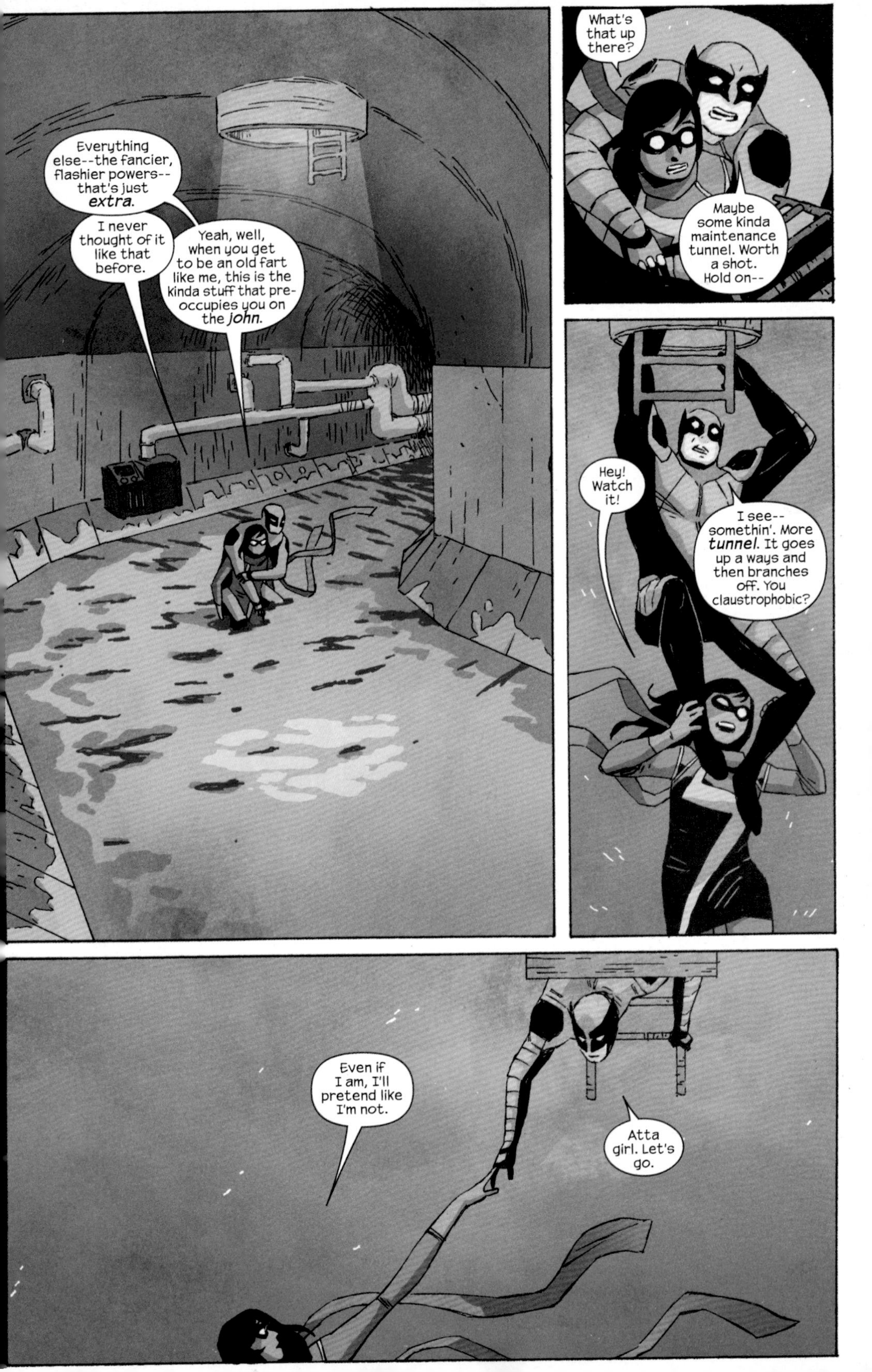
Everything else--the fancier, flashier powers--that's just *extra*.
I never thought of it like that before.
Yeah, well, when you get to be an old fart like me, this is the kinda stuff that pre-occupies you on the *john*.
What's that up there?
Maybe some kinda maintenance tunnel. Worth a shot. Hold on--
Hey! Watch it!
I see--somethin'. More *tunnel*. It goes up a ways and then branches off. You claustrophobic?
Even if I am, I'll pretend like I'm not.
Atta girl. Let's go.

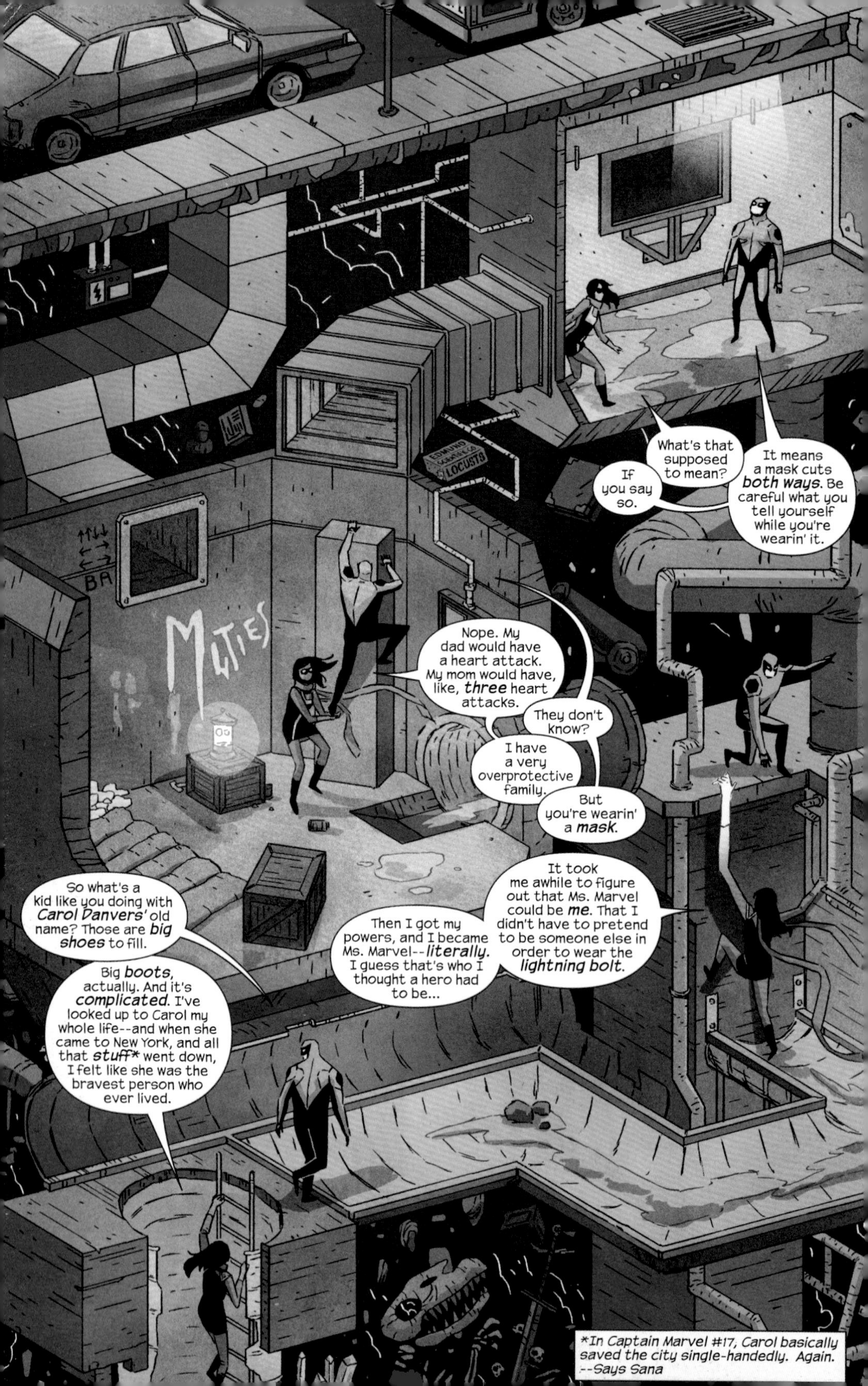
What's that supposed to mean?
It means a mask cuts **both ways**. Be careful what you tell yourself while you're wearin' it.
If you say so.
Nope. My dad would have a heart attack. My mom would have, like, ***three*** heart attacks.
They don't know?
I have a very overprotective family.
But you're wearin' a ***mask***.
So what's a kid like you doing with *Carol Danvers'* old name? Those are ***big shoes*** to fill.
Big ***boots***, actually. And it's ***complicated***. I've looked up to Carol my whole life--and when she came to New York, and all that ***stuff**** went down, I felt like she was the bravest person who ever lived.
Then I got my powers, and I became Ms. Marvel--***literally***. I guess that's who I thought a hero had to be...
It took me awhile to figure out that Ms. Marvel could be ***me***. That I didn't have to pretend to be someone else in order to wear the ***lightning bolt***.
**In Captain Marvel #17, Carol basically saved the city single-handedly. Again. --Says Sana*

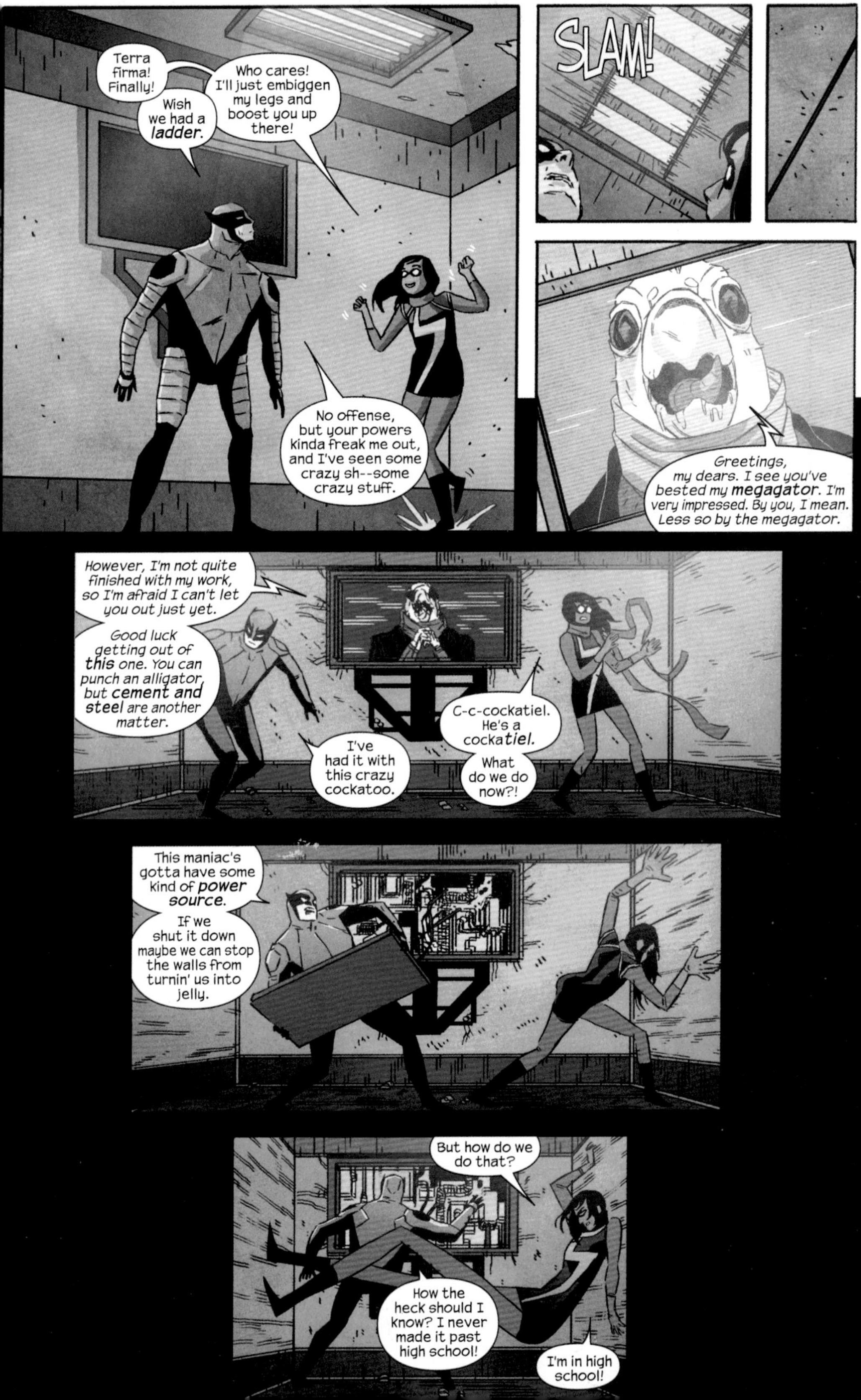
Terra firma! Finally!
Wish we had a ladder.
Who cares! I'll just embiggen my legs and boost you up there!
No offense, but your powers kinda freak me out, and I've seen some crazy sh--some crazy stuff.
SLAM!
Greetings, my dears. I see you've bested my megagator. I'm very impressed. By you, I mean. Less so by the megagator.
However, I'm not quite finished with my work, so I'm afraid I can't let you out just yet.
Good luck getting out of this one. You can punch an alligator, but cement and steel are another matter.
I've had it with this crazy cockatoo.
C-c-cockatiel. He's a cockatiel.
What do we do now?!
This maniac's gotta have some kind of power source.
If we shut it down maybe we can stop the walls from turnin' us into jelly.
But how do we do that?
How the heck should I know? I never made it past high school!
I'm in high school!

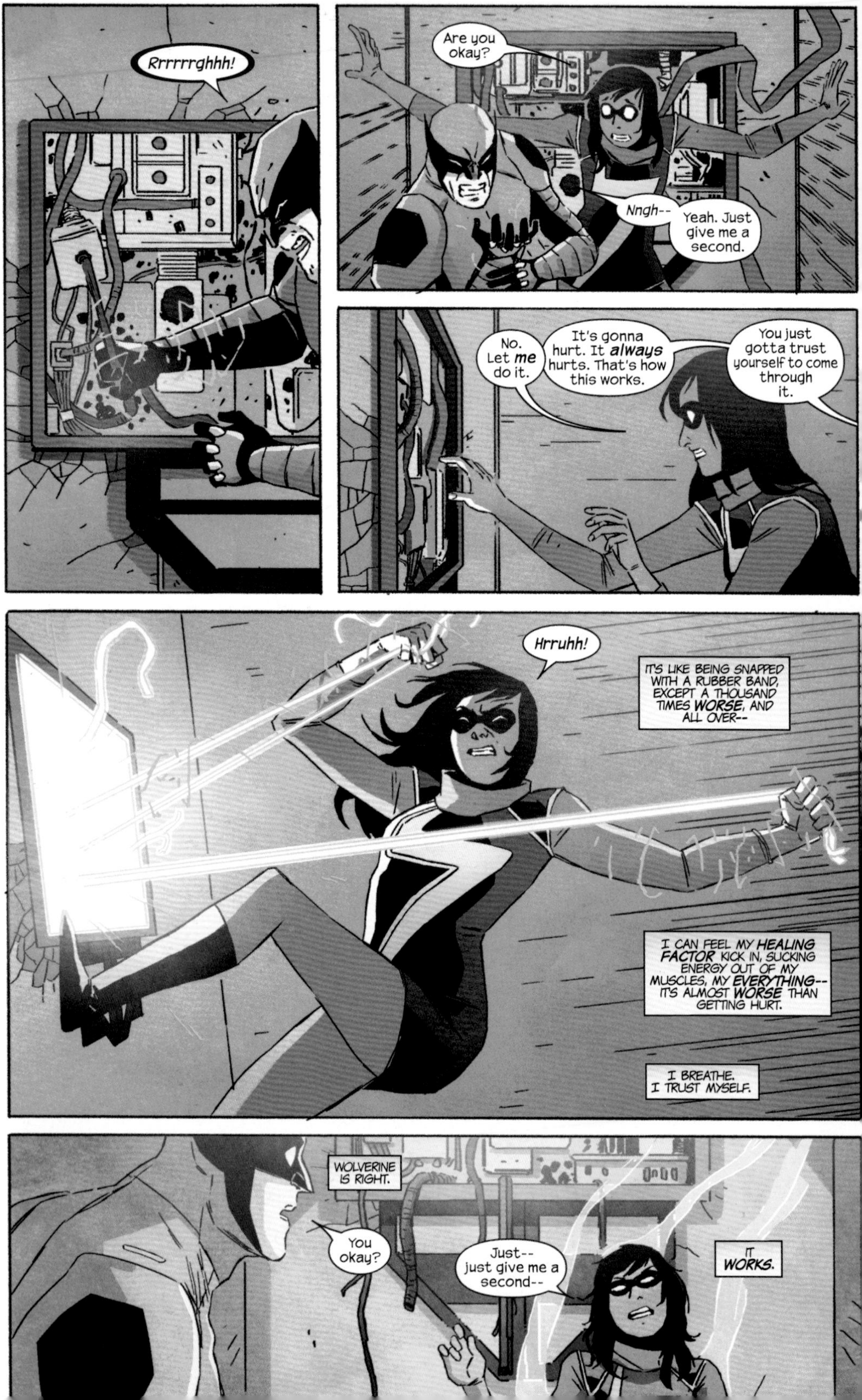
Rrrrrrghhh!
Are you okay?
Nngh--
Yeah. Just give me a second.
No. Let me do it.
It's gonna hurt. It always hurts. That's how this works.
You just gotta trust yourself to come through it.
Hrruhh!
IT'S LIKE BEING SNAPPED WITH A RUBBER BAND, EXCEPT A THOUSAND TIMES WORSE, AND ALL OVER--
I CAN FEEL MY HEALING FACTOR KICK IN, SUCKING ENERGY OUT OF MY MUSCLES, MY EVERYTHING-- IT'S ALMOST WORSE THAN GETTING HURT.
I BREATHE. I TRUST MYSELF.
WOLVERINE IS RIGHT.
You okay?
Just-- just give me a second--
IT WORKS.

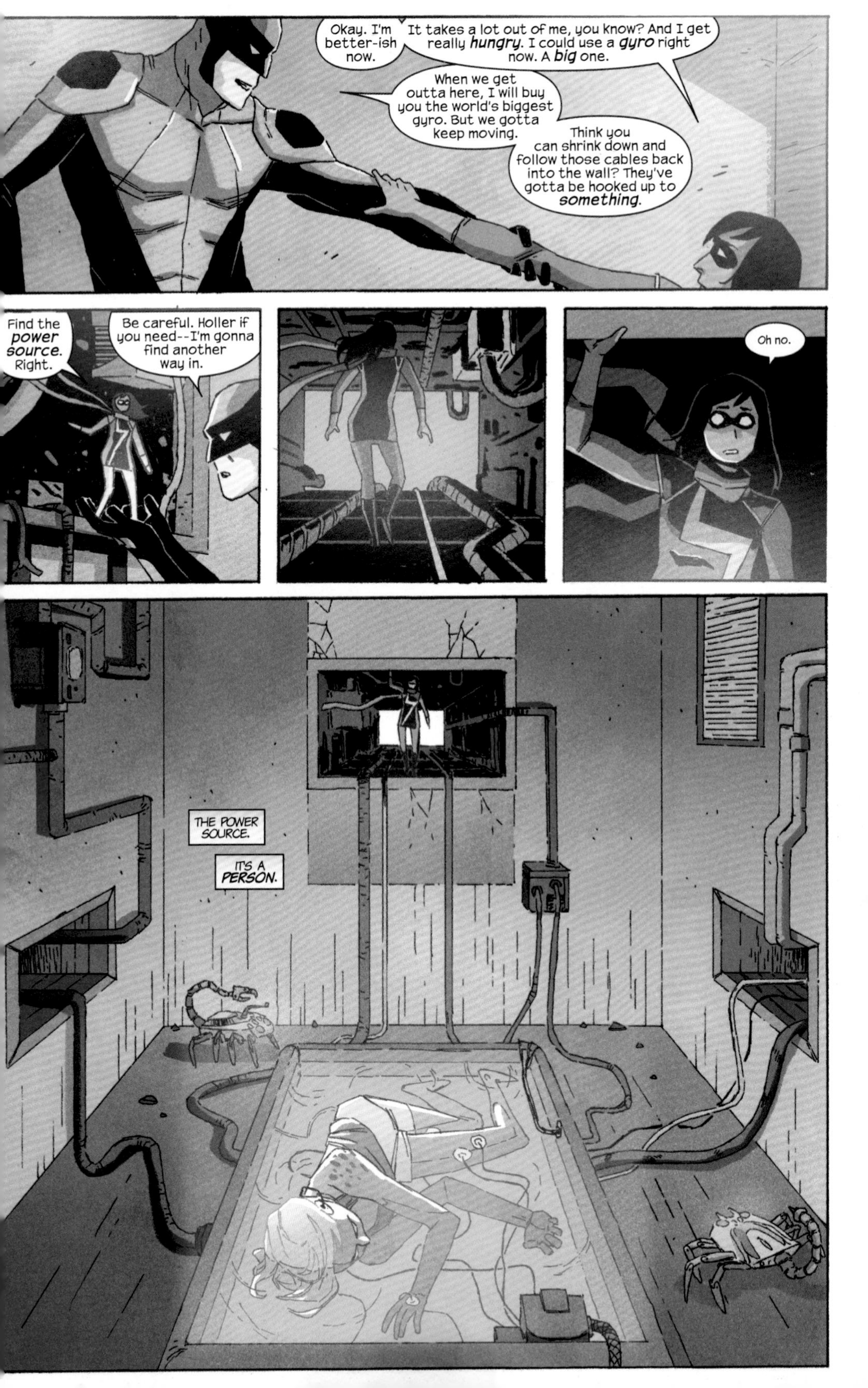

Okay. I'm better-ish now.
It takes a lot out of me, you know? And I get really *hungry*. I could use a *gyro* right now. A *big* one.
When we get outta here, I will buy you the world's biggest gyro. But we gotta keep moving.
Think you can shrink down and follow those cables back into the wall? They've gotta be hooked up to *something*.
Find the *power source*. Right.
Be careful. Holler if you need--I'm gonna find another way in.
Oh no.
THE POWER SOURCE.
IT'S A *PERSON*.

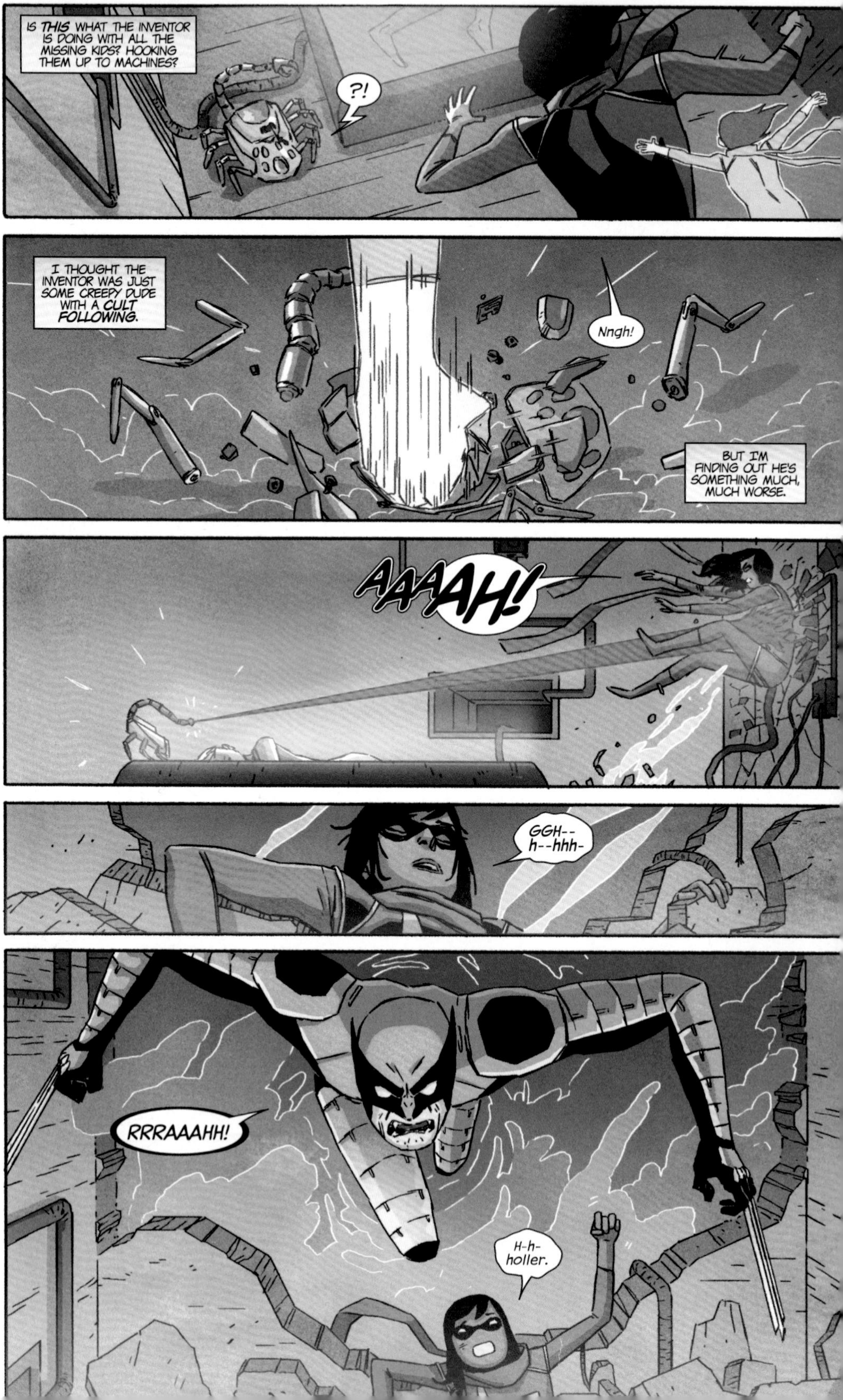
IS THIS WHAT THE INVENTOR IS DOING WITH ALL THE MISSING KIDS? HOOKING THEM UP TO MACHINES?
?!
I THOUGHT THE INVENTOR WAS JUST SOME CREEPY DUDE WITH A CULT FOLLOWING.
Nngh!
BUT I'M FINDING OUT HE'S SOMETHING MUCH, MUCH WORSE.
AAAAH!
GGH-- h--hhh-
RRRAAAHH!
H-h-holler.

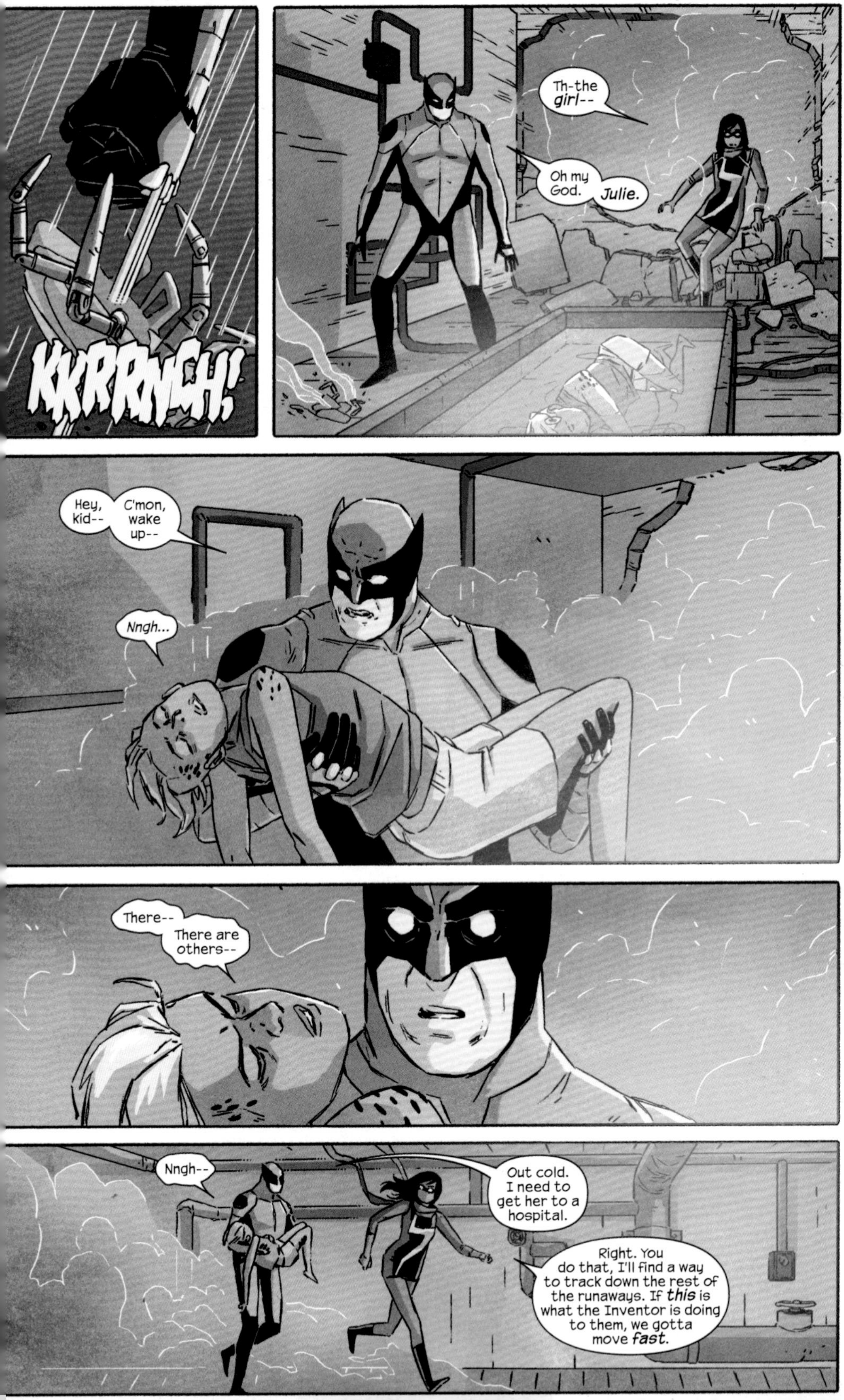
KKRRNCH!
Th-the girl--
Oh my God.
Julie.
Hey, kid--
C'mon, wake up--
Nngh...
There--
There are others--
Nngh--
Out cold. I need to get her to a hospital.
Right. You do that, I'll find a way to track down the rest of the runaways. If this is what the Inventor is doing to them, we gotta move fast.

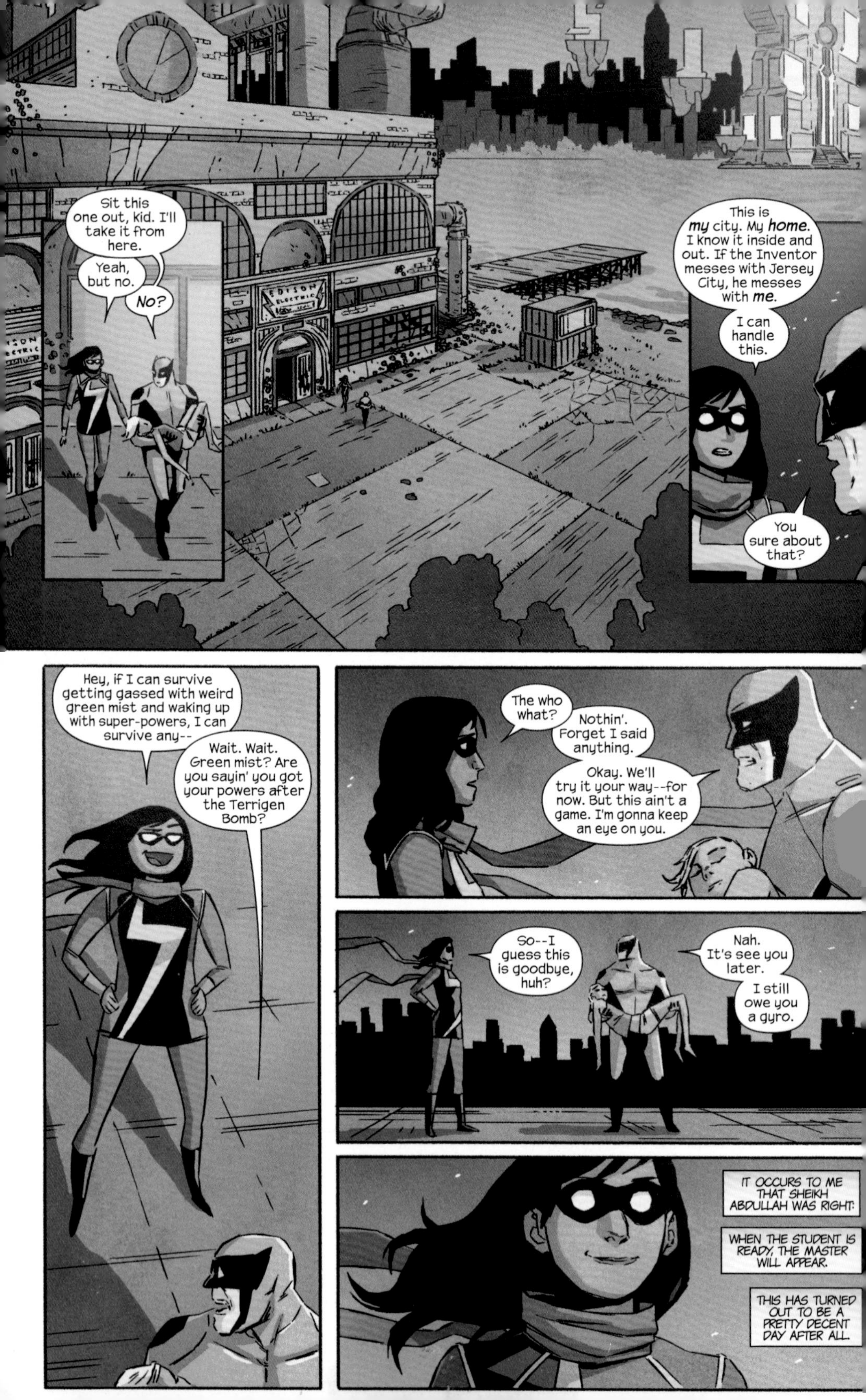
Sit this one out, kid. I'll take it from here.
Yeah, but no.
No?
This is *my* city. My **home**. I know it inside and out. If the Inventor messes with Jersey City, he messes with *me*.
I can handle this.
You sure about that?
EDISON ELECTRIC
Hey, if I can survive getting gassed with weird green mist and waking up with super-powers, I can survive any--
Wait. Wait. Green mist? Are you sayin' you got your powers after the Terrigen Bomb?
The who what?
Nothin'. Forget I said anything.
Okay. We'll try it your way--for now. But this ain't a game. I'm gonna keep an eye on you.
So--I guess this is goodbye, huh?
Nah. It's see you later.
I still owe you a gyro.
IT OCCURS TO ME THAT SHEIKH ABDULLAH WAS RIGHT:
WHEN THE STUDENT IS READY, THE MASTER WILL APPEAR.
THIS HAS TURNED OUT TO BE A PRETTY DECENT DAY AFTER ALL.

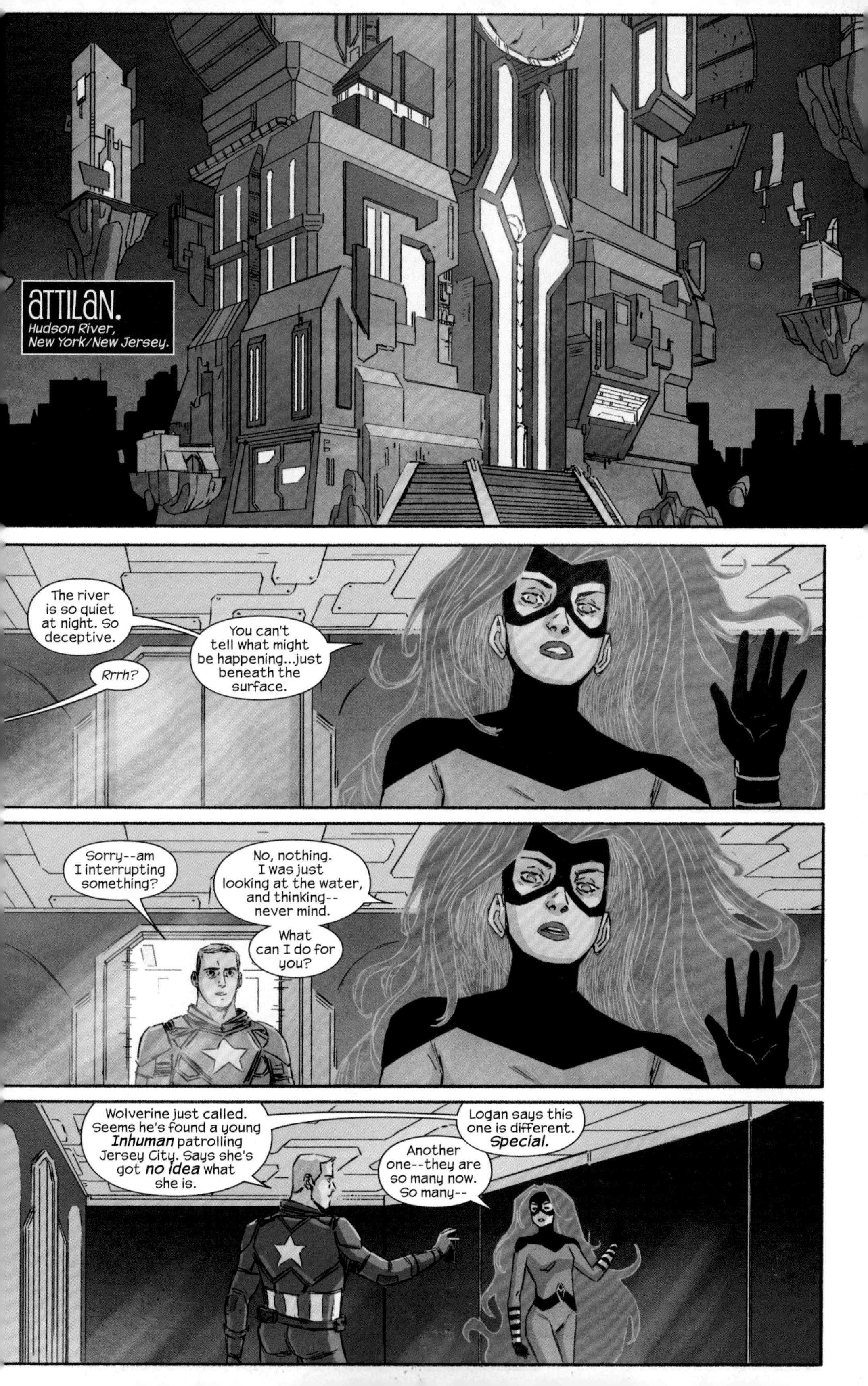
ATTILAN.
Hudson River, New York/New Jersey.
The river is so quiet at night. So deceptive.
You can't tell what might be happening...just beneath the surface.
Rrrh?
Sorry--am I interrupting something?
No, nothing. I was just looking at the water, and thinking-- never mind.
What can I do for you?
Wolverine just called. Seems he's found a young Inhuman patrolling Jersey City. Says she's got no idea what she is.
Logan says this one is different. Special.
Another one--they are so many now. So many--

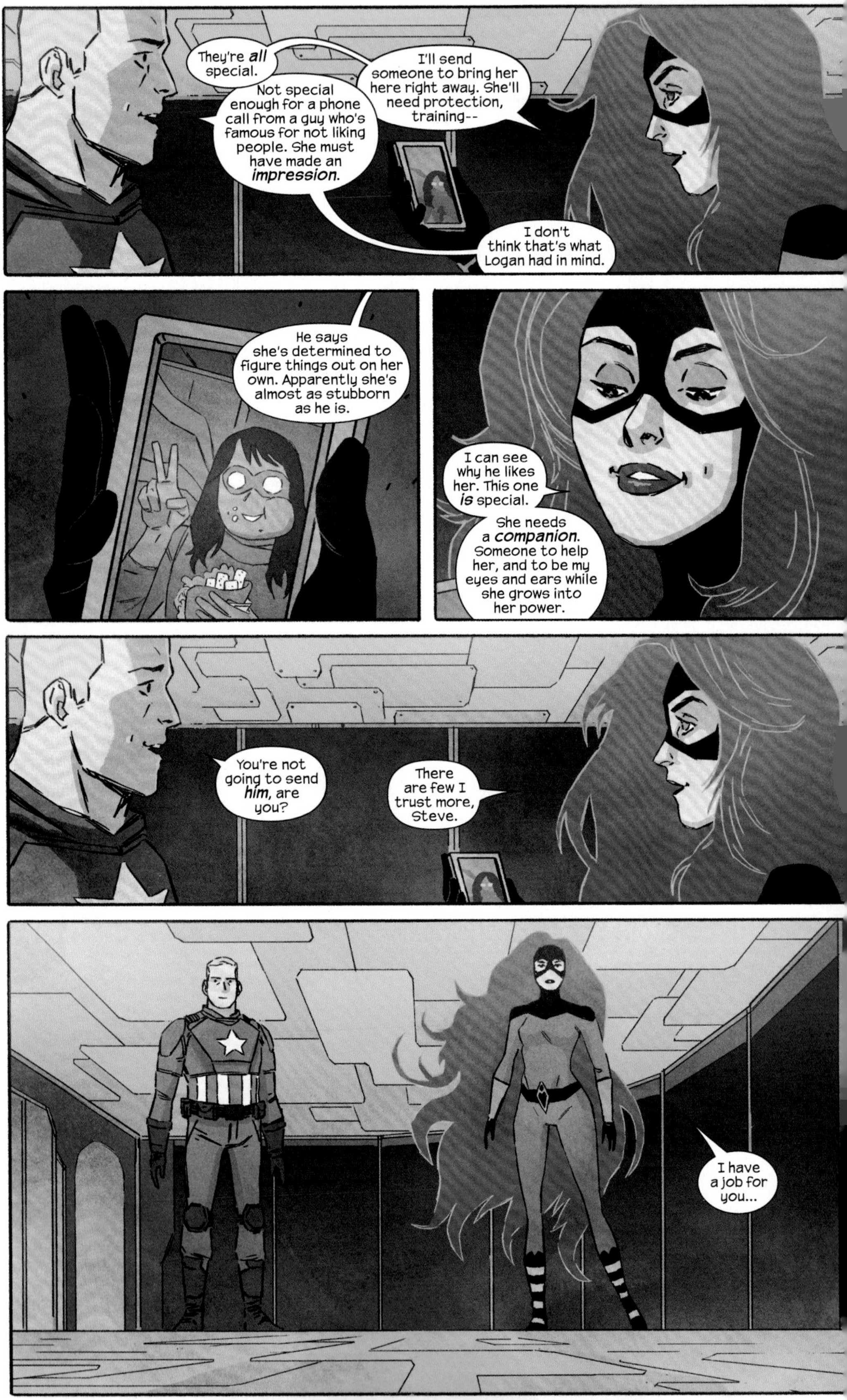

I'll send someone to bring her here right away. She'll need protection, training--
They're *all* special.
Not special enough for a phone call from a guy who's famous for not liking people. She must have made an ***impression***.
I don't think that's what Logan had in mind.
He says she's determined to figure things out on her own. Apparently she's almost as stubborn as he is.
I can see why he likes her. This one *is* special.
She needs a ***companion***. Someone to help her, and to be my eyes and ears while she grows into her power.
You're not going to send *him*, are you?
There are few I trust more, Steve.
I have a job for you...

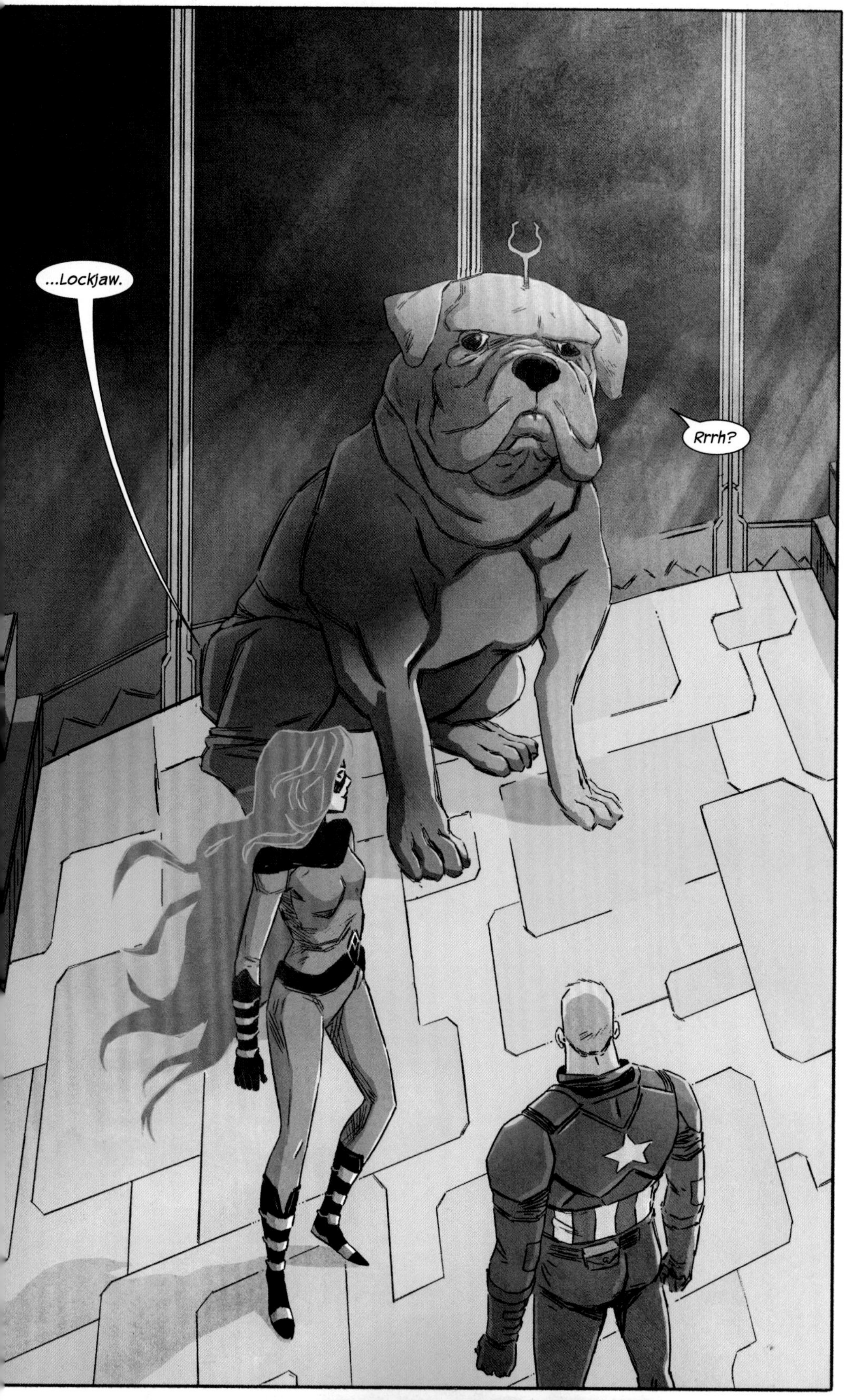
...Lockjaw.
Rrrh?

MS. MARVEL #8

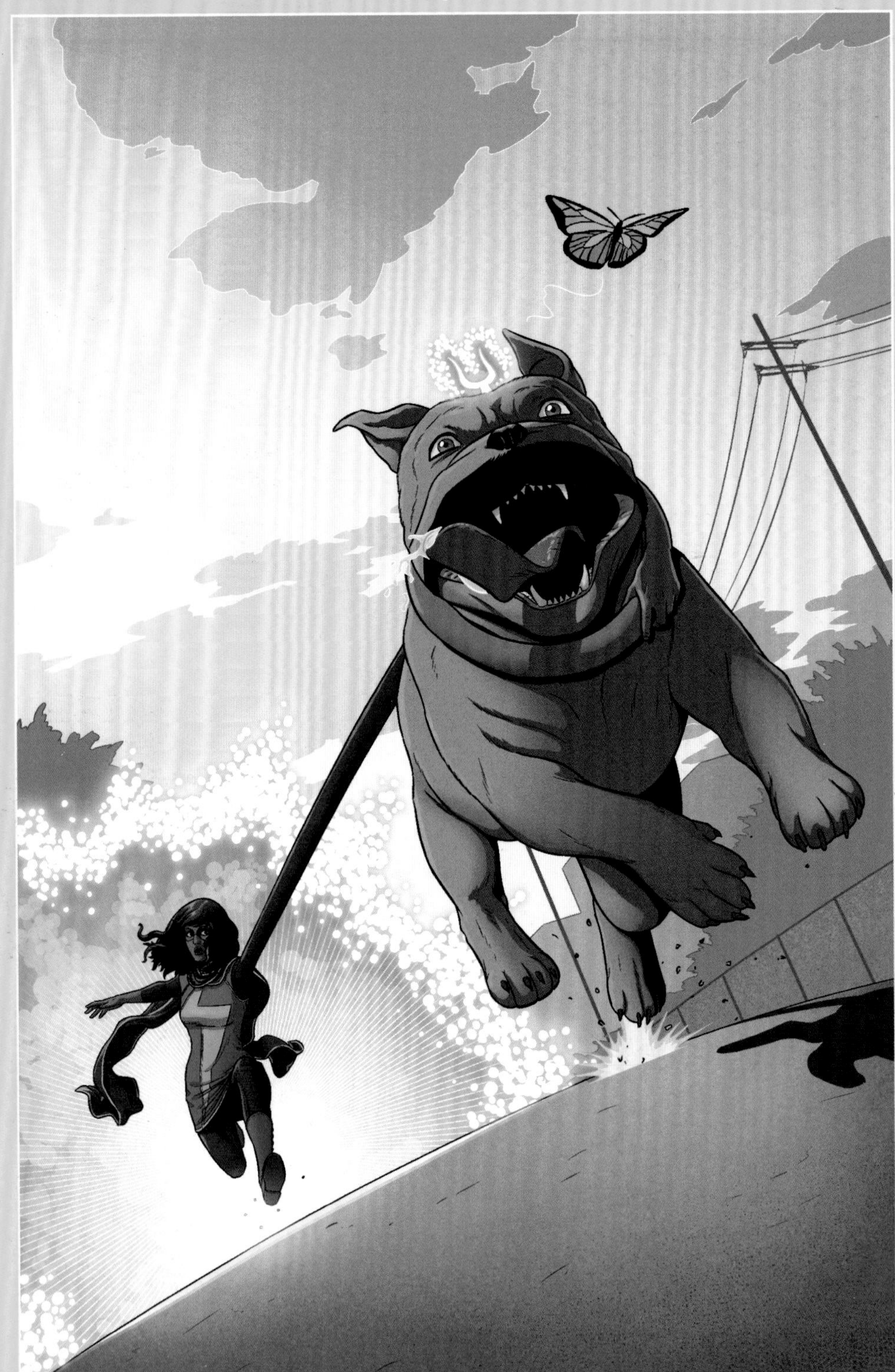

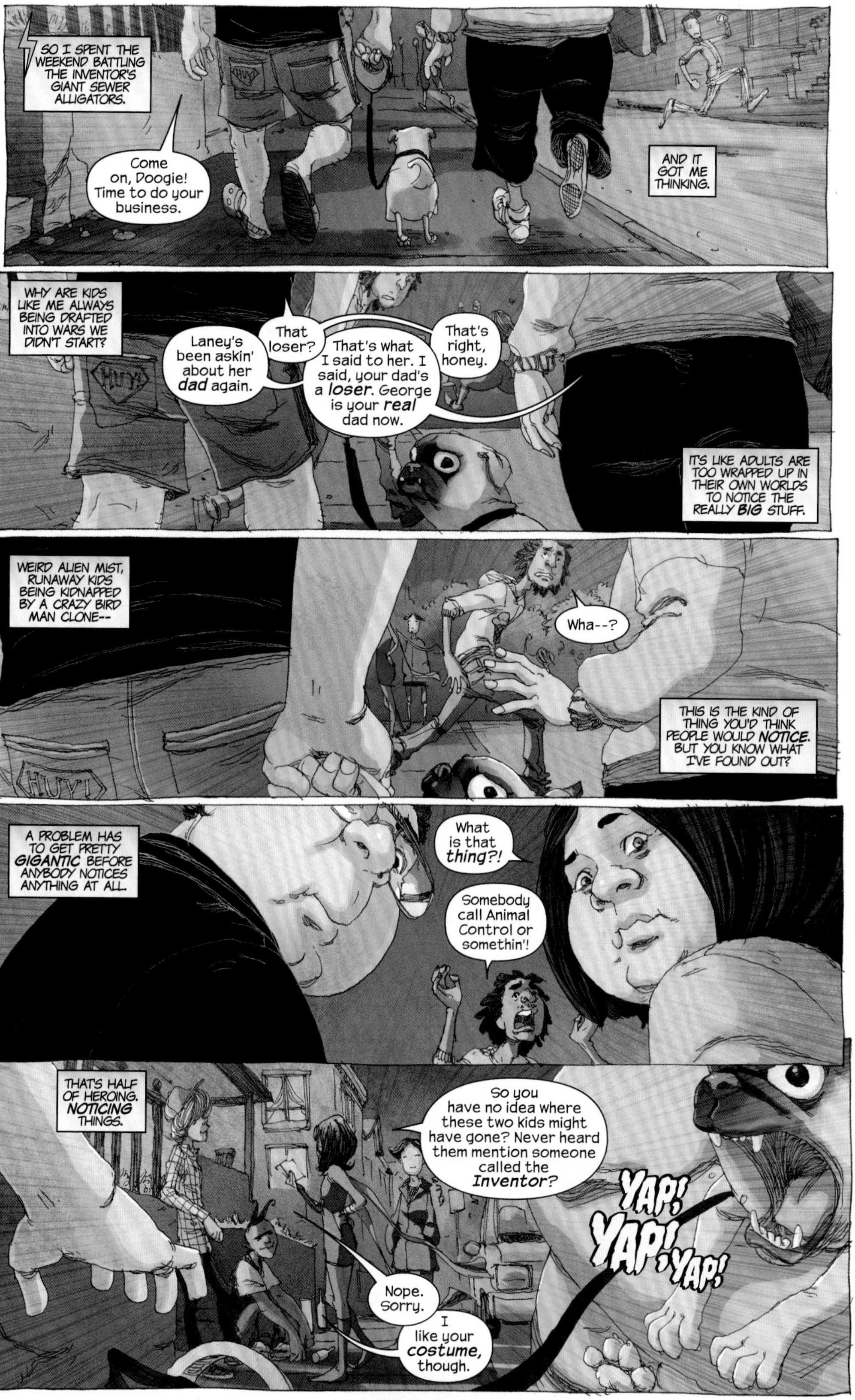
SO I SPENT THE WEEKEND BATTLING THE INVENTOR'S GIANT SEWER ALLIGATORS.
Come on, Doogie! Time to do your business.
AND IT GOT ME THINKING.
WHY ARE KIDS LIKE ME ALWAYS BEING DRAFTED INTO WARS WE DIDN'T START?
Laney's been askin' about her dad again.
That loser?
That's what I said to her. I said, your dad's a loser. George is your real dad now.
That's right, honey.
IT'S LIKE ADULTS ARE TOO WRAPPED UP IN THEIR OWN WORLDS TO NOTICE THE REALLY BIG STUFF.
WEIRD ALIEN MIST, RUNAWAY KIDS BEING KIDNAPPED BY A CRAZY BIRD MAN CLONE--
Wha--?
THIS IS THE KIND OF THING YOU'D THINK PEOPLE WOULD NOTICE. BUT YOU KNOW WHAT I'VE FOUND OUT?
A PROBLEM HAS TO GET PRETTY GIGANTIC BEFORE ANYBODY NOTICES ANYTHING AT ALL.
What is that thing?!
Somebody call Animal Control or somethin'!
THAT'S HALF OF HEROING. NOTICING THINGS.
So you have no idea where these two kids might have gone? Never heard them mention someone called the Inventor?
YAP! YAP! YAP!
Nope. Sorry.
I like your costume, though.

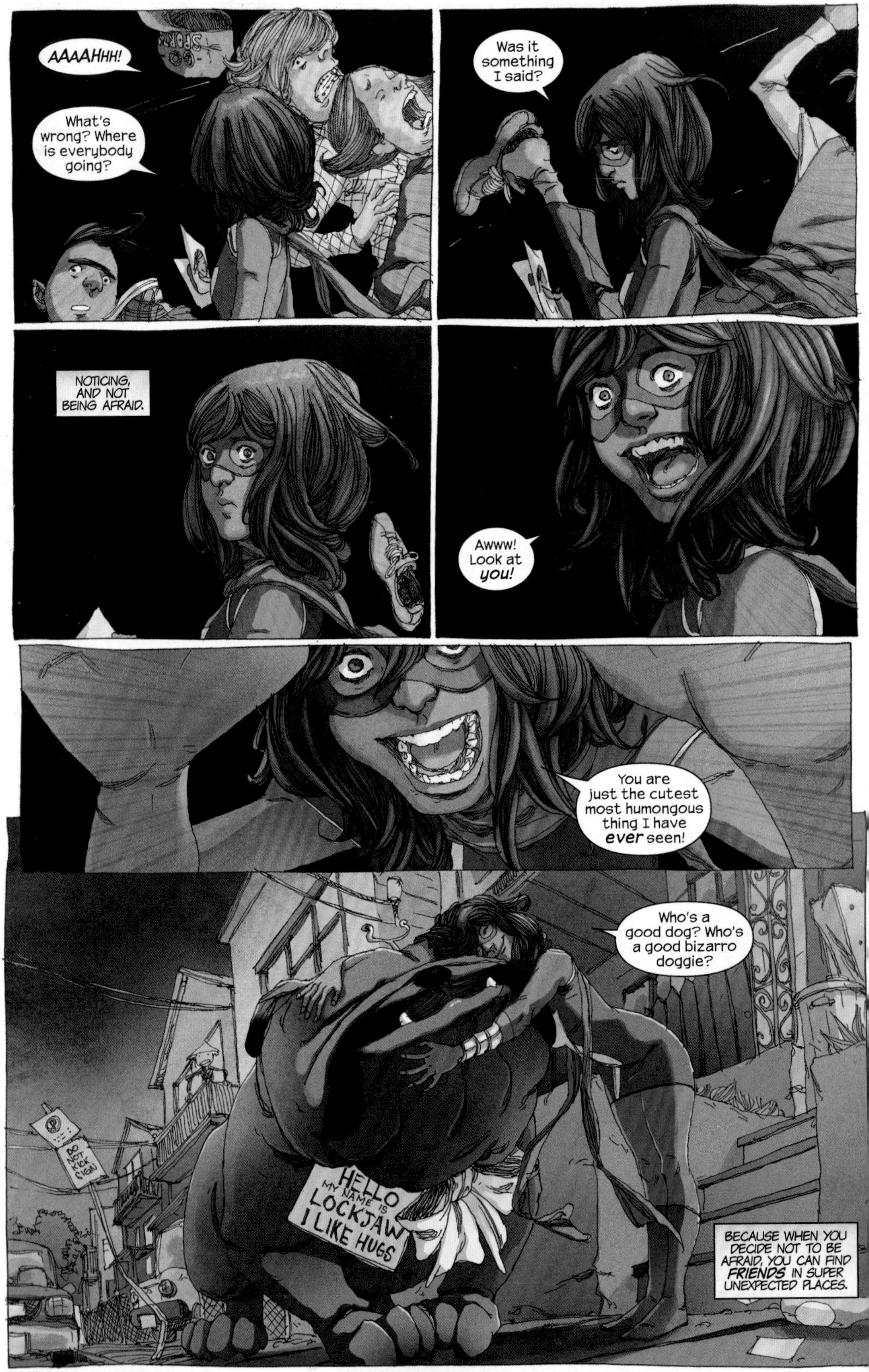
AAAAHHH!
What's wrong? Where is everybody going?
SPORK
Was it something I said?
NOTICING, AND NOT BEING AFRAID.
Awww! Look at *you!*
You are just the cutest most humongous thing I have *ever* seen!
Who's a good dog? Who's a good bizarro doggie?
DO NOT KICK SIGN
HELLO MY NAME IS LOCKJAW I LIKE HUGS
BECAUSE WHEN YOU DECIDE NOT TO BE AFRAID, YOU CAN FIND *FRIENDS* IN SUPER UNEXPECTED PLACES.

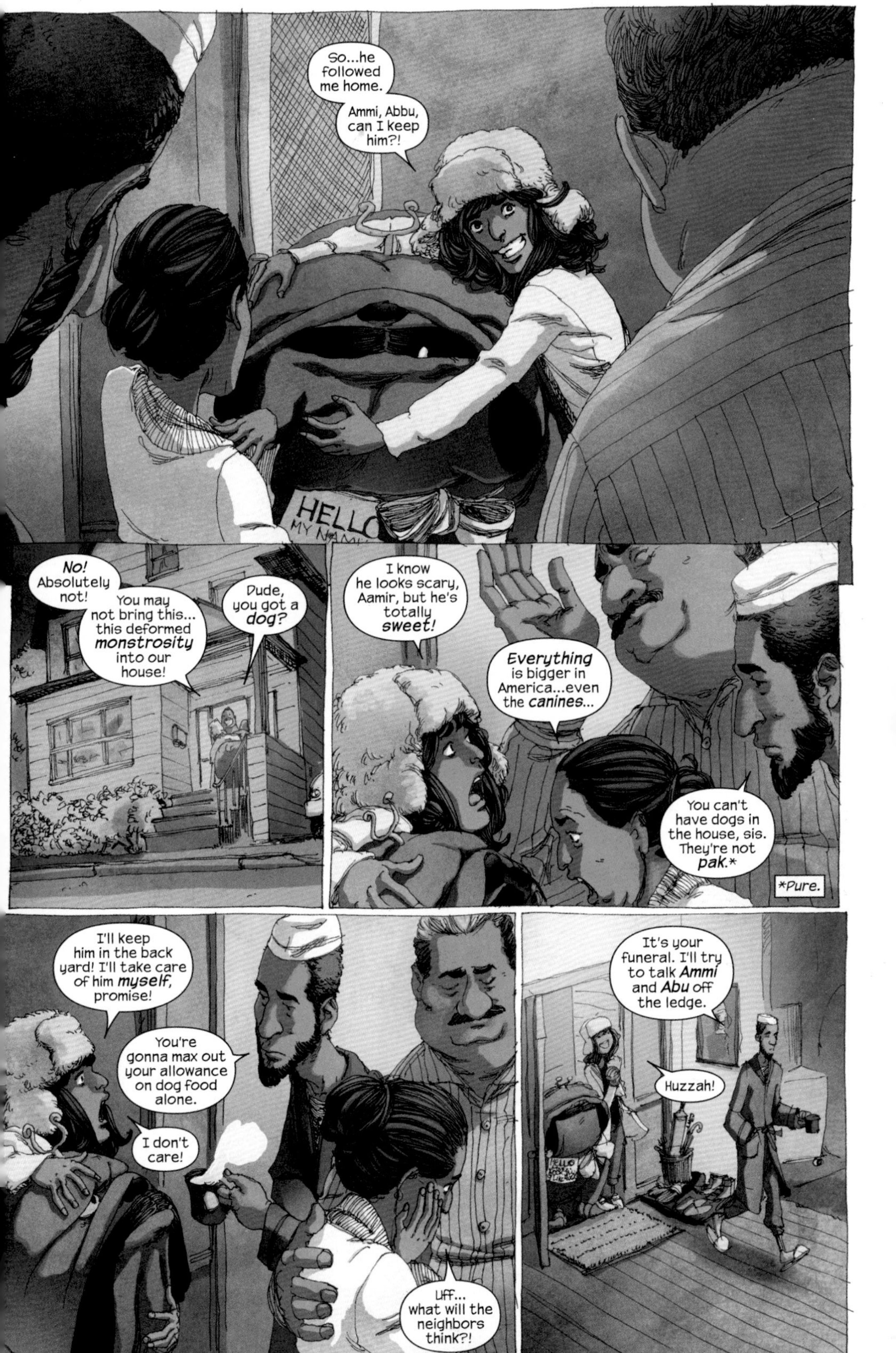
So...he followed me home.
Ammi, Abbu, can I keep him?!
HELLO MY NAME
No! Absolutely not!
You may not bring this... this deformed *monstrosity* into our house!
Dude, you got a *dog?*
I know he looks scary, Aamir, but he's totally *sweet!*
Everything is bigger in America...even the *canines*...
You can't have dogs in the house, sis. They're not *pak*.*
*Pure.
I'll keep him in the back yard! I'll take care of him *myself*, promise!
You're gonna max out your allowance on dog food alone.
I don't care!
Uff... what will the neighbors think?!
It's your funeral. I'll try to talk *Ammi* and *Abu* off the ledge.
Huzzah!

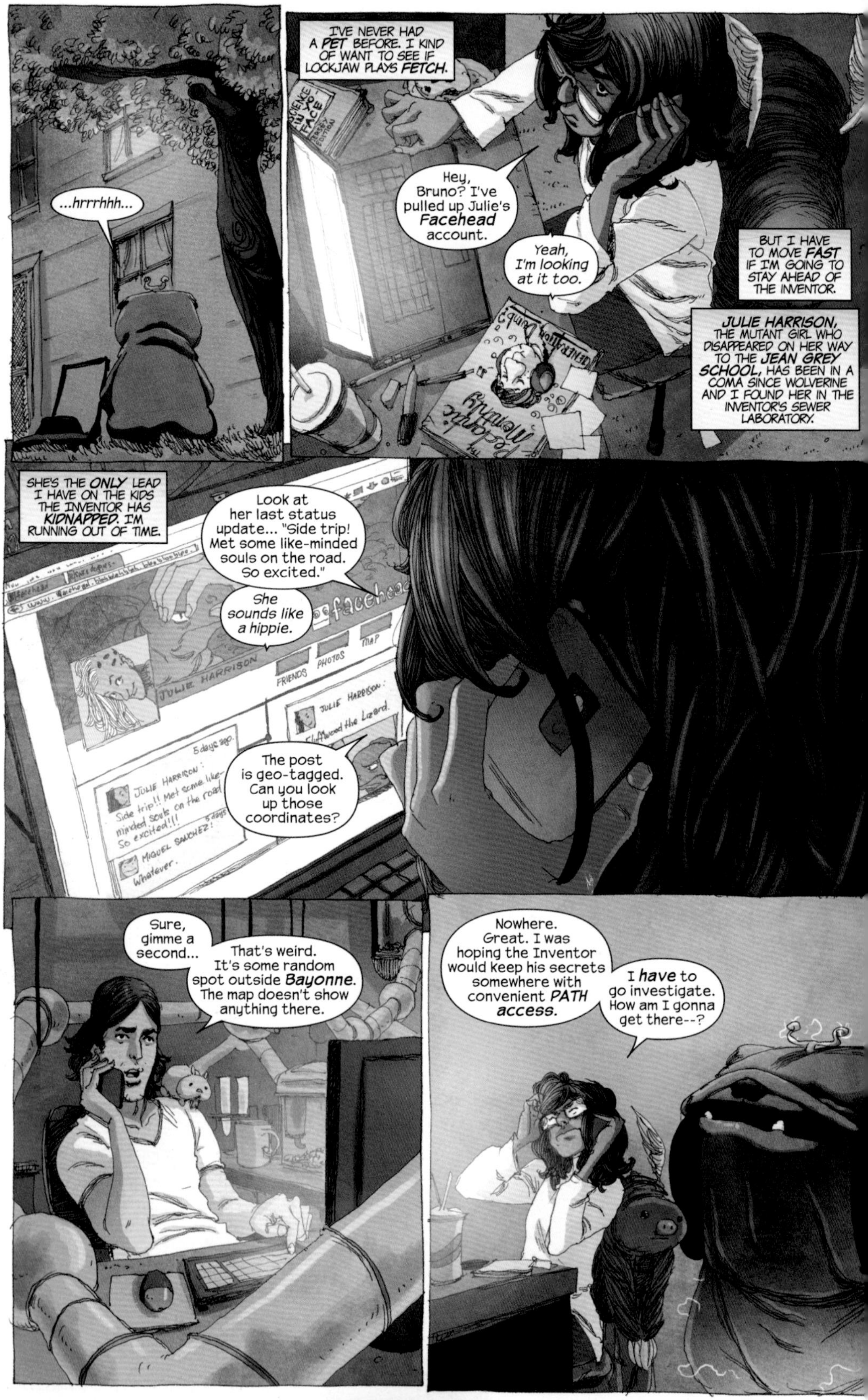
...hrrrhhh...
I'VE NEVER HAD A PET BEFORE. I KIND OF WANT TO SEE IF LOCKJAW PLAYS FETCH.
Hey, Bruno? I've pulled up Julie's Facehead account.
Yeah, I'm looking at it too.
BUT I HAVE TO MOVE FAST IF I'M GOING TO STAY AHEAD OF THE INVENTOR.
JULIE HARRISON, THE MUTANT GIRL WHO DISAPPEARED ON HER WAY TO THE JEAN GREY SCHOOL, HAS BEEN IN A COMA SINCE WOLVERINE AND I FOUND HER IN THE INVENTOR'S SEWER LABORATORY.
SHE'S THE ONLY LEAD I HAVE ON THE KIDS THE INVENTOR HAS KIDNAPPED. I'M RUNNING OUT OF TIME.
Look at her last status update... "Side trip! Met some like-minded souls on the road. So excited."
She sounds like a hippie.
The post is geo-tagged. Can you look up those coordinates?
Sure, gimme a second...
That's weird. It's some random spot outside Bayonne. The map doesn't show anything there.
Nowhere. Great. I was hoping the Inventor would keep his secrets somewhere with convenient PATH access.
I have to go investigate. How am I gonna get there--?

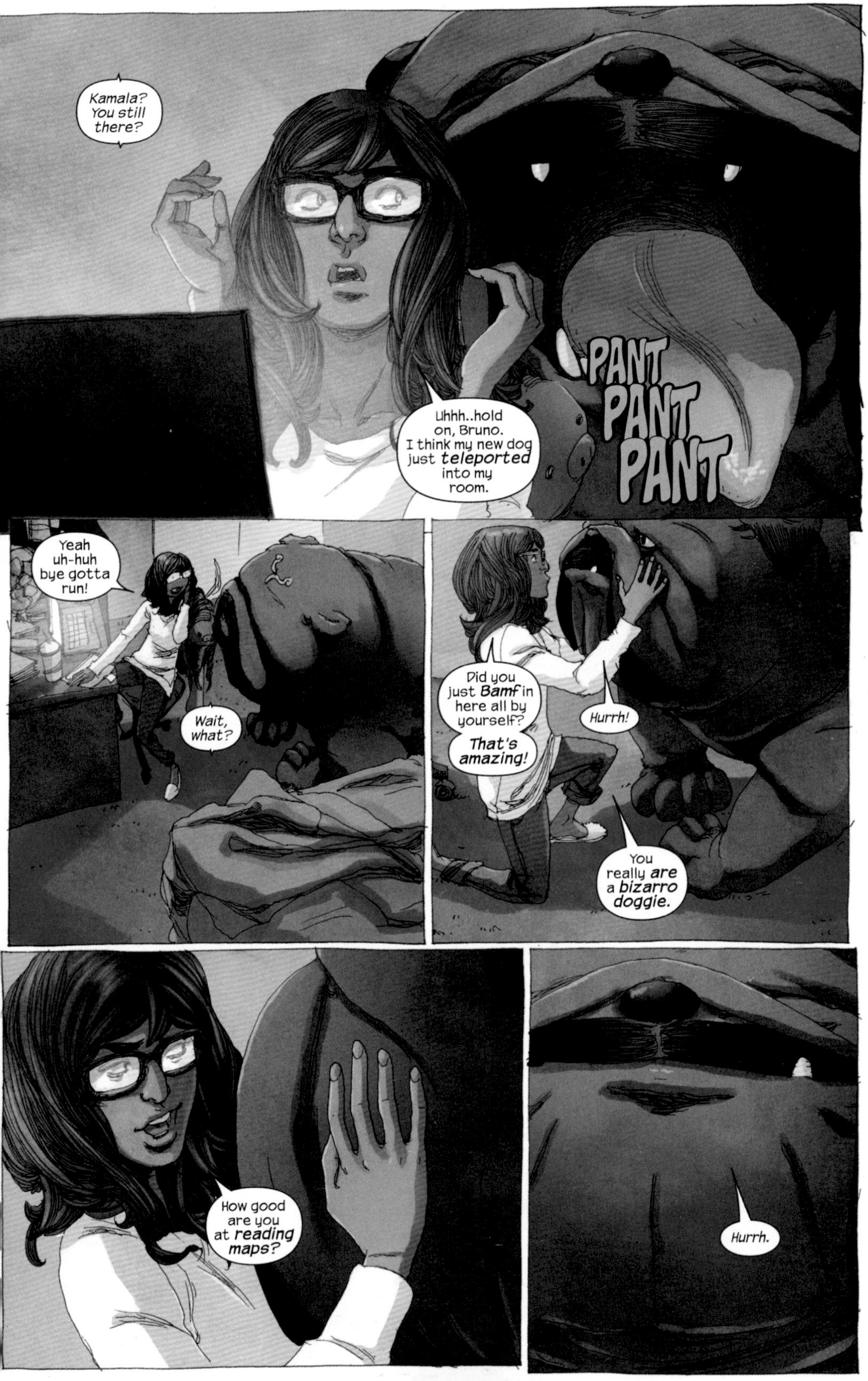
Kamala? You still there?
Uhhh..hold on, Bruno. I think my new dog just *teleported* into my room.
PANT PANT PANT
Yeah uh-huh bye gotta run!
Wait, what?
Did you just *Bamf* in here all by yourself?
That's amazing!
Hurrh!
You really *are* a *bizarro doggie.*
How good are you at *reading maps?*
Hurrh.

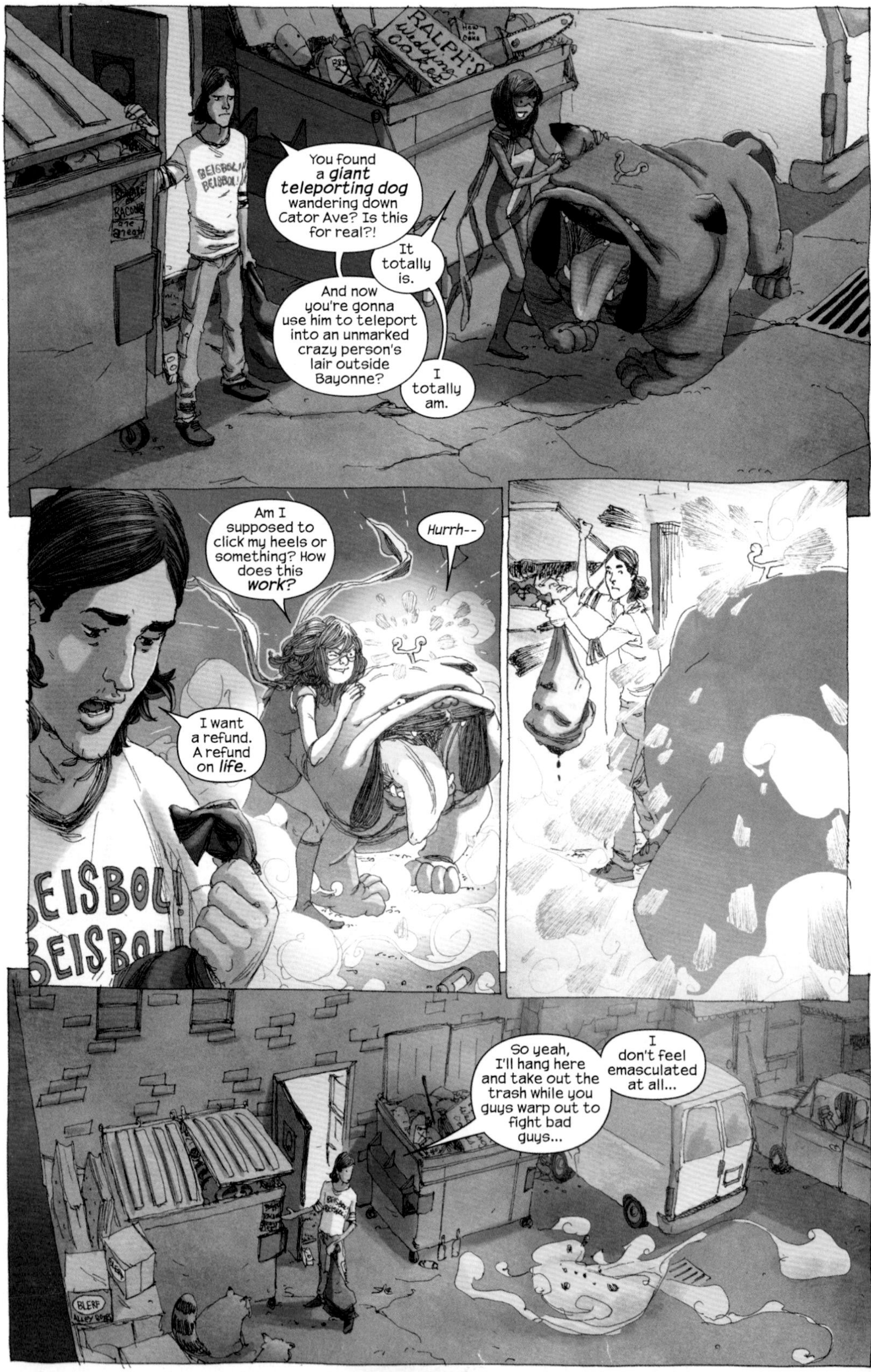
You found a giant teleporting dog wandering down Cator Ave? Is this for real?!
It totally is.
And now you're gonna use him to teleport into an unmarked crazy person's lair outside Bayonne?
I totally am.
RALPH'S Wedding Cakes
Am I supposed to click my heels or something? How does this work?
Hurrh--
I want a refund. A refund on life.
So yeah, I'll hang here and take out the trash while you guys warp out to fight bad guys...
I don't feel emasculated at all...

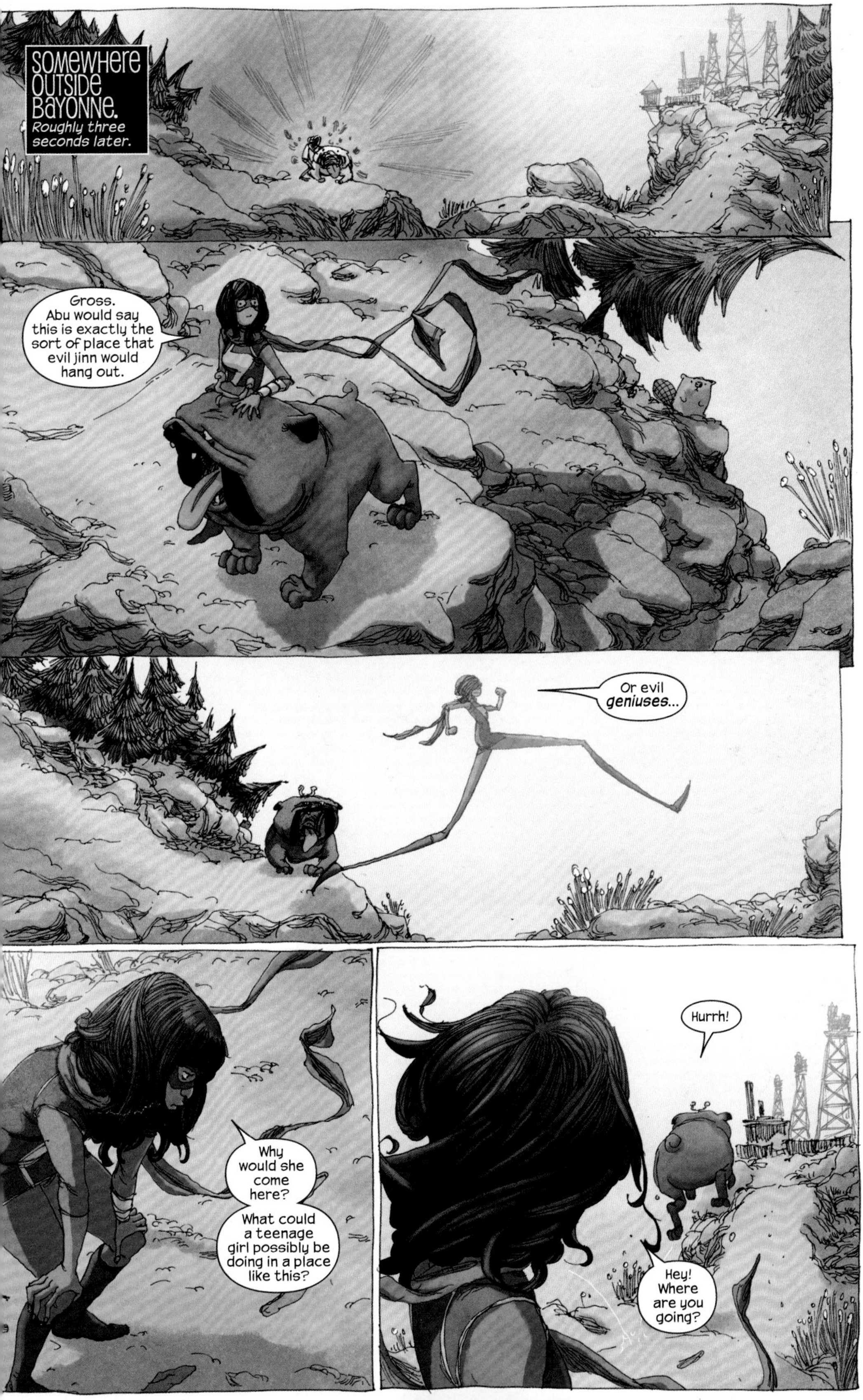
SOMEWHERE OUTSIDE BAYONNE.
Roughly three seconds later.
Gross. Abu would say this is exactly the sort of place that evil jinn would hang out.
Or evil *geniuses*...
Why would she come here?
What could a teenage girl possibly be doing in a place like this?
Hurrh!
Hey! Where are you going?

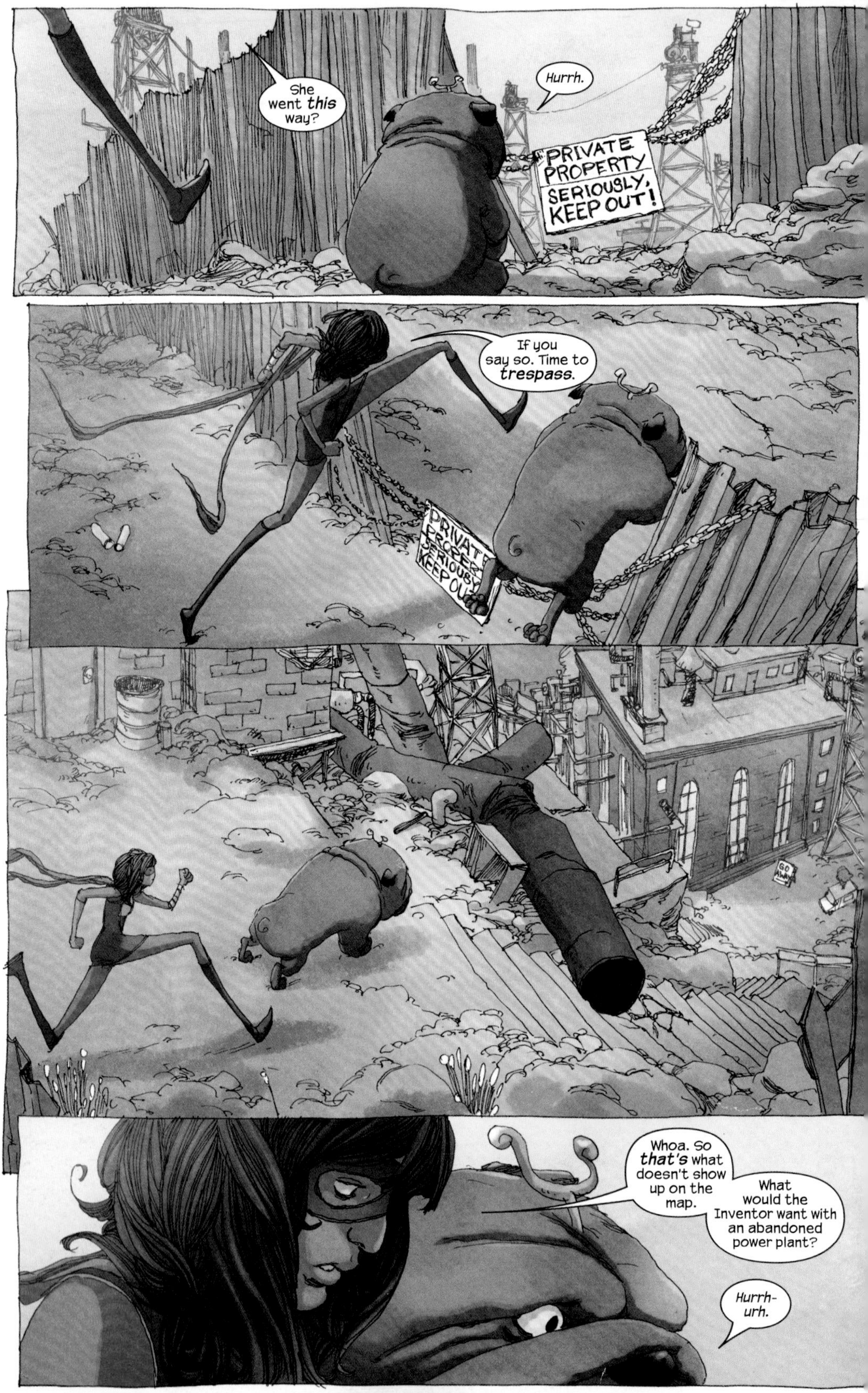
She went *this* way?
Hurrh.
PRIVATE PROPERTY
SERIOUSLY, KEEP OUT!
If you say so. Time to *trespass*.
Whoa. So *that's* what doesn't show up on the map.
What would the Inventor want with an abandoned power plant?
Hurrh-urh.

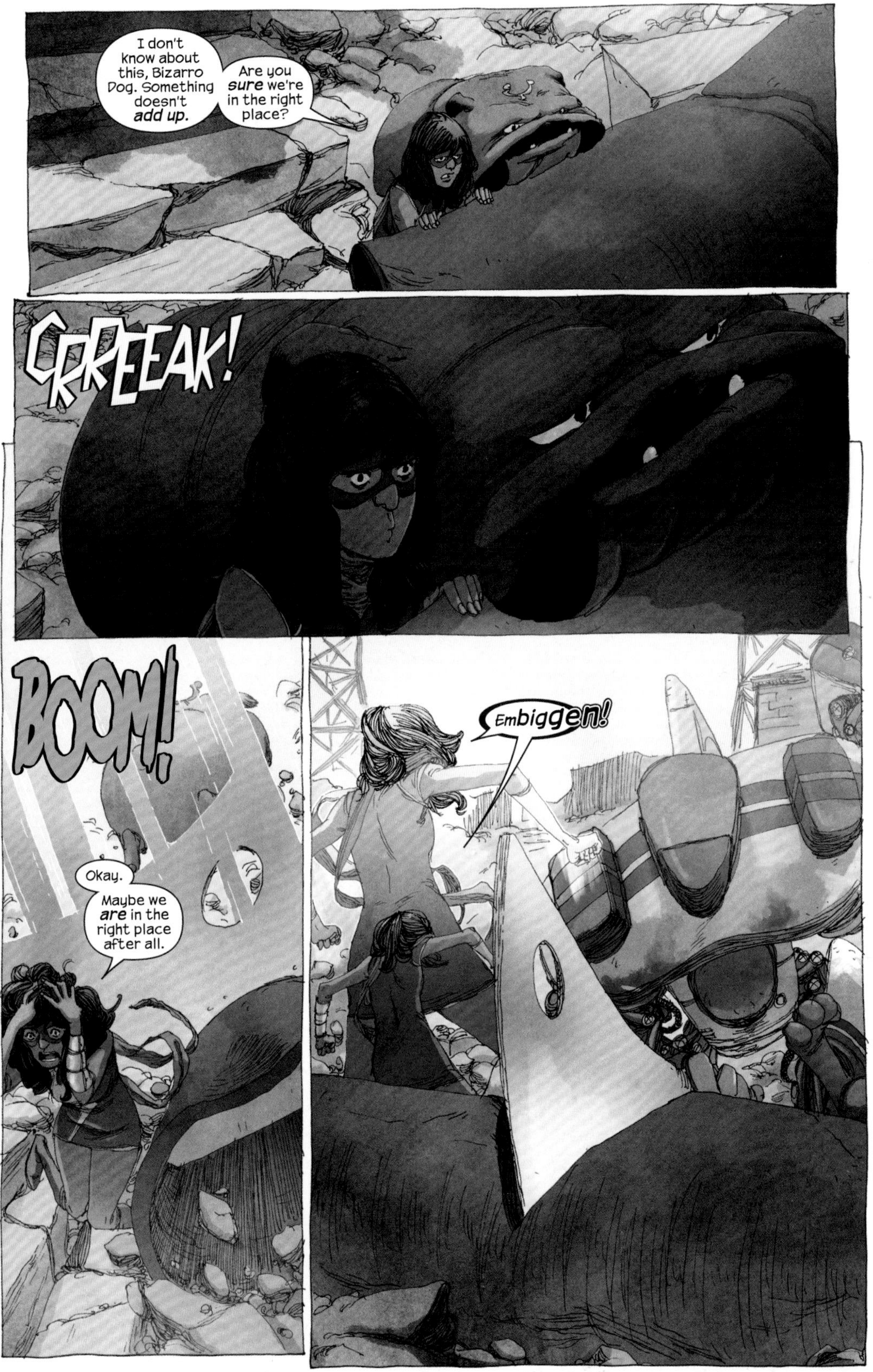
I don't know about this, Bizarro Dog. Something doesn't **add up.**
Are you **sure** we're in the right place?
CRREEAK!
BOOM!
Okay.
Maybe we **are** in the right place after all.
Embiggen!

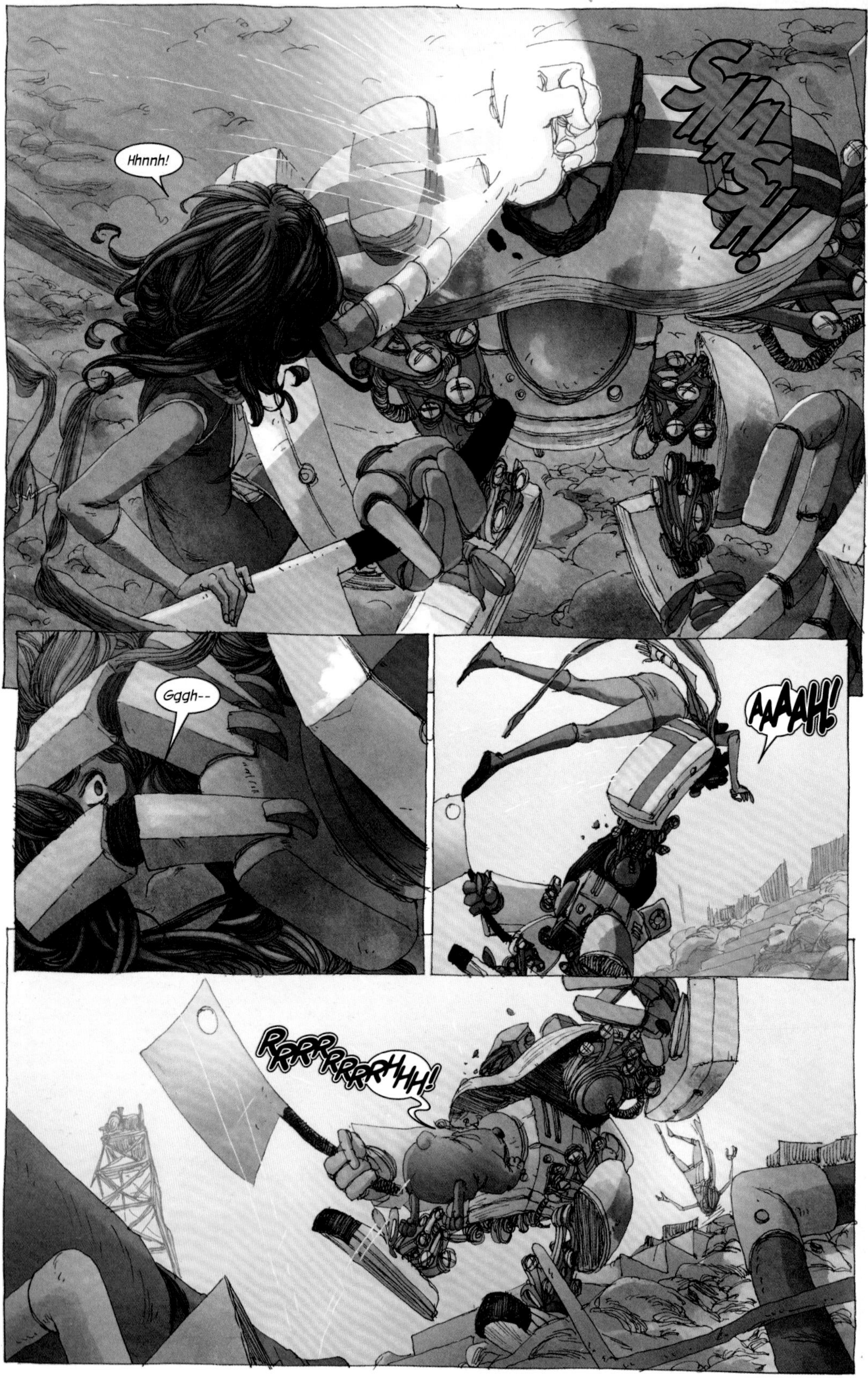

Hhnnh!
SMASH!
Gggh--
AAAAH!
RRRRRRRRHHH!

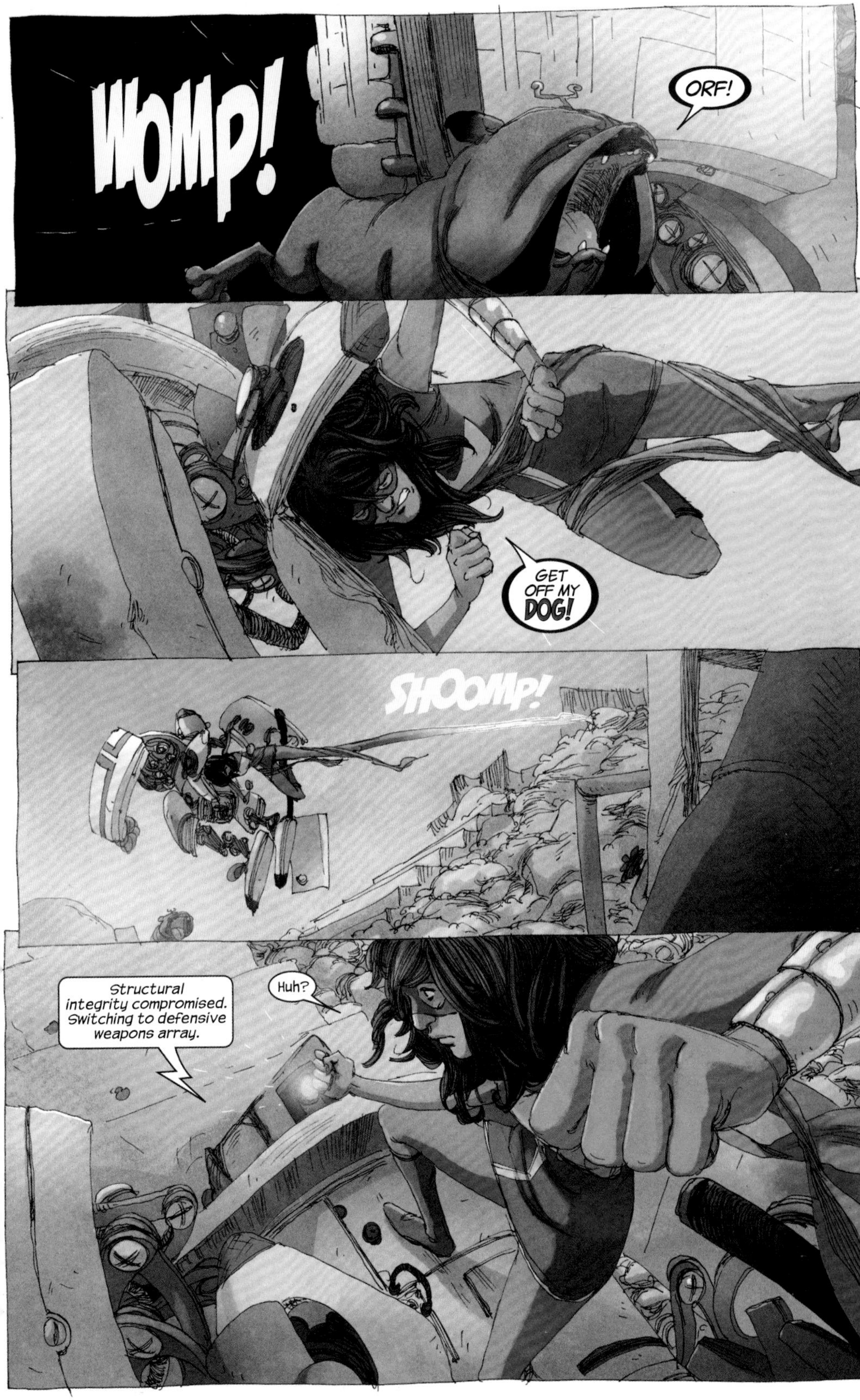
WOMP!
ORF!
GET OFF MY DOG!
SHOOMP!
Structural integrity compromised. Switching to defensive weapons array.
Huh?

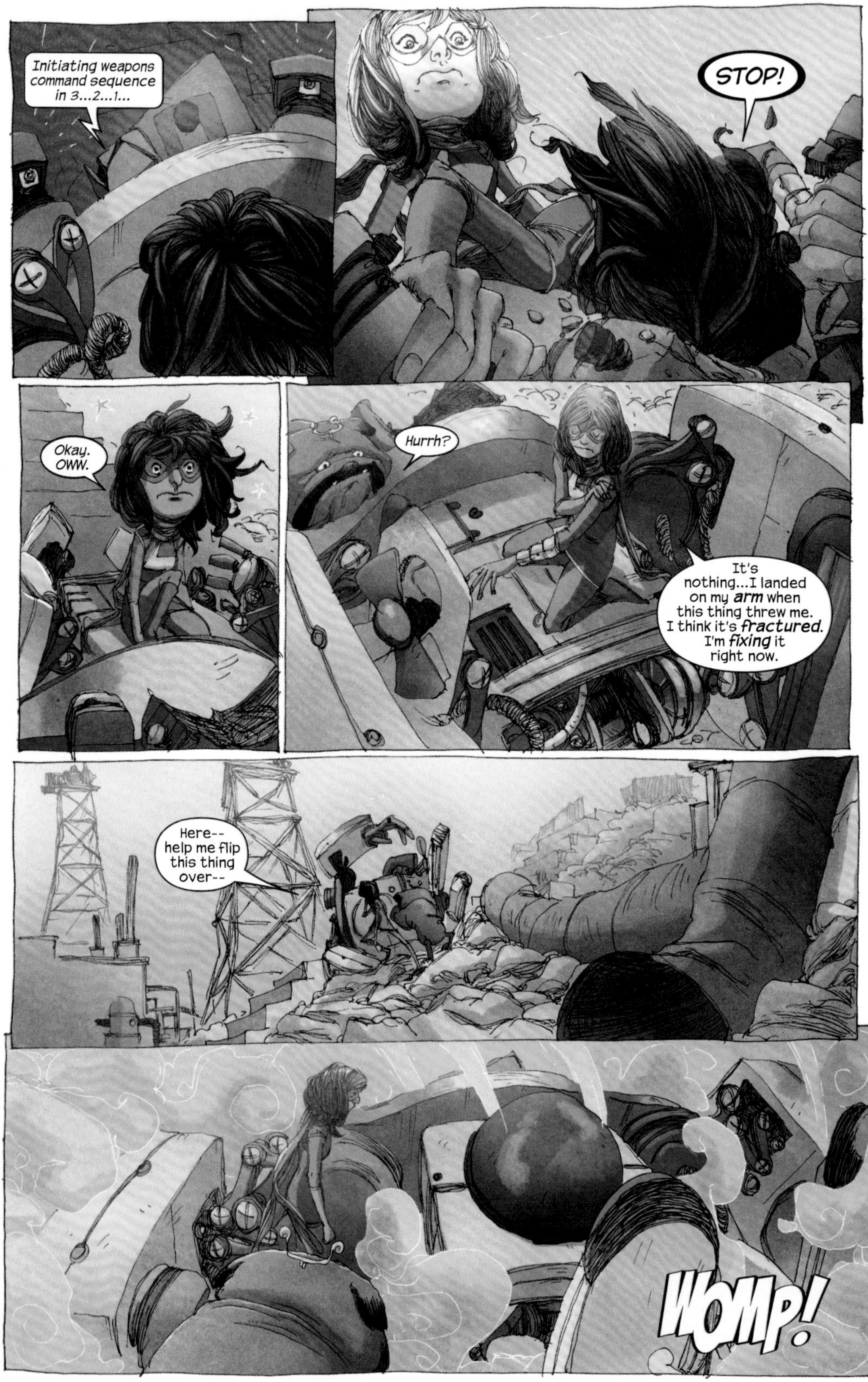
Initiating weapons command sequence in 3...2...1...
STOP!
Okay. OWW.
Hurrh?
It's nothing...I landed on my arm when this thing threw me. I think it's fractured. I'm fixing it right now.
Here-- help me flip this thing over--
WOMP!

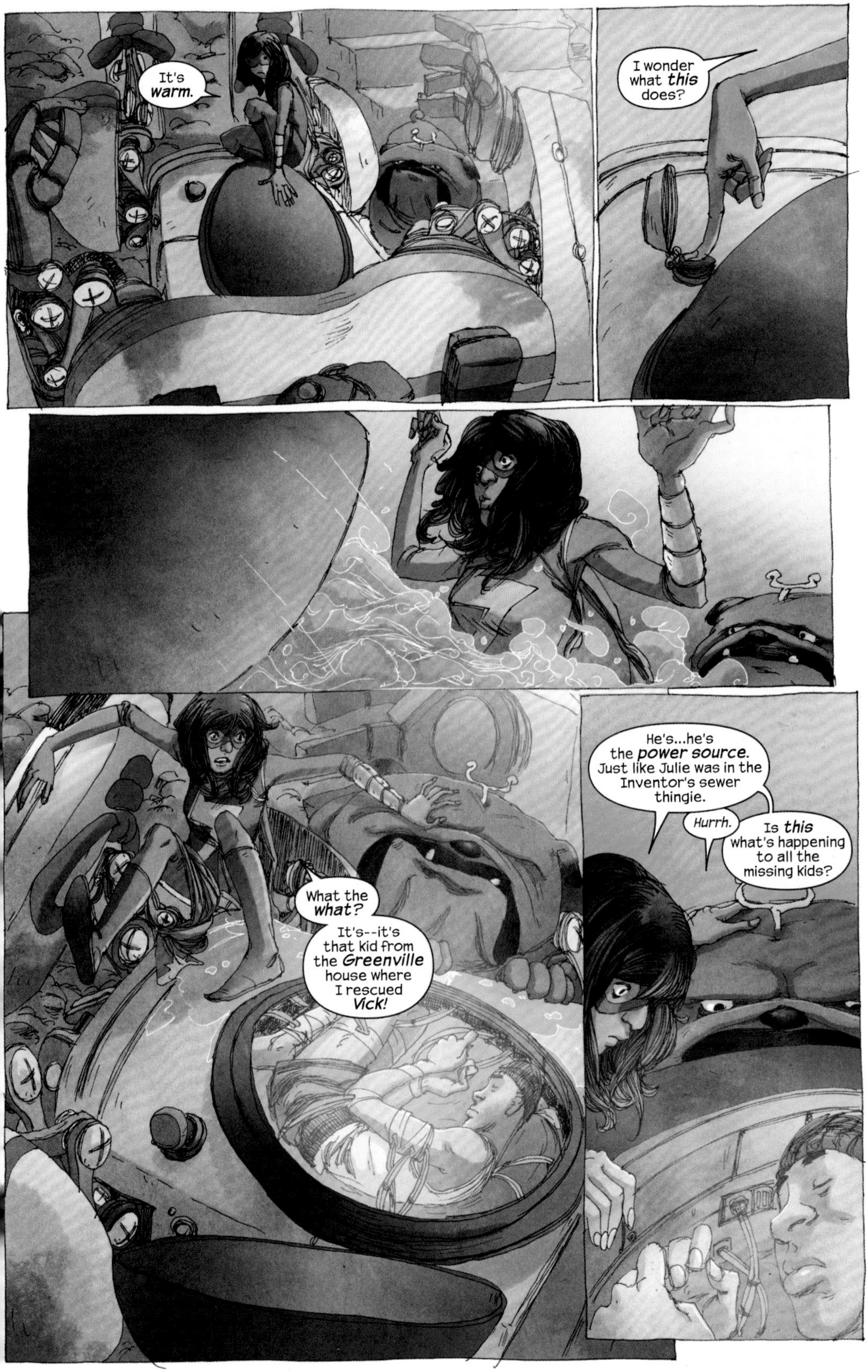
It's *warm.*
I wonder what *this* does?
What the *what?*
It's--it's that kid from the *Greenville* house where I rescued *Vick!*
He's...he's the *power source.* Just like Julie was in the Inventor's sewer thingie.
Hurrh.
Is *this* what's happening to all the missing kids?

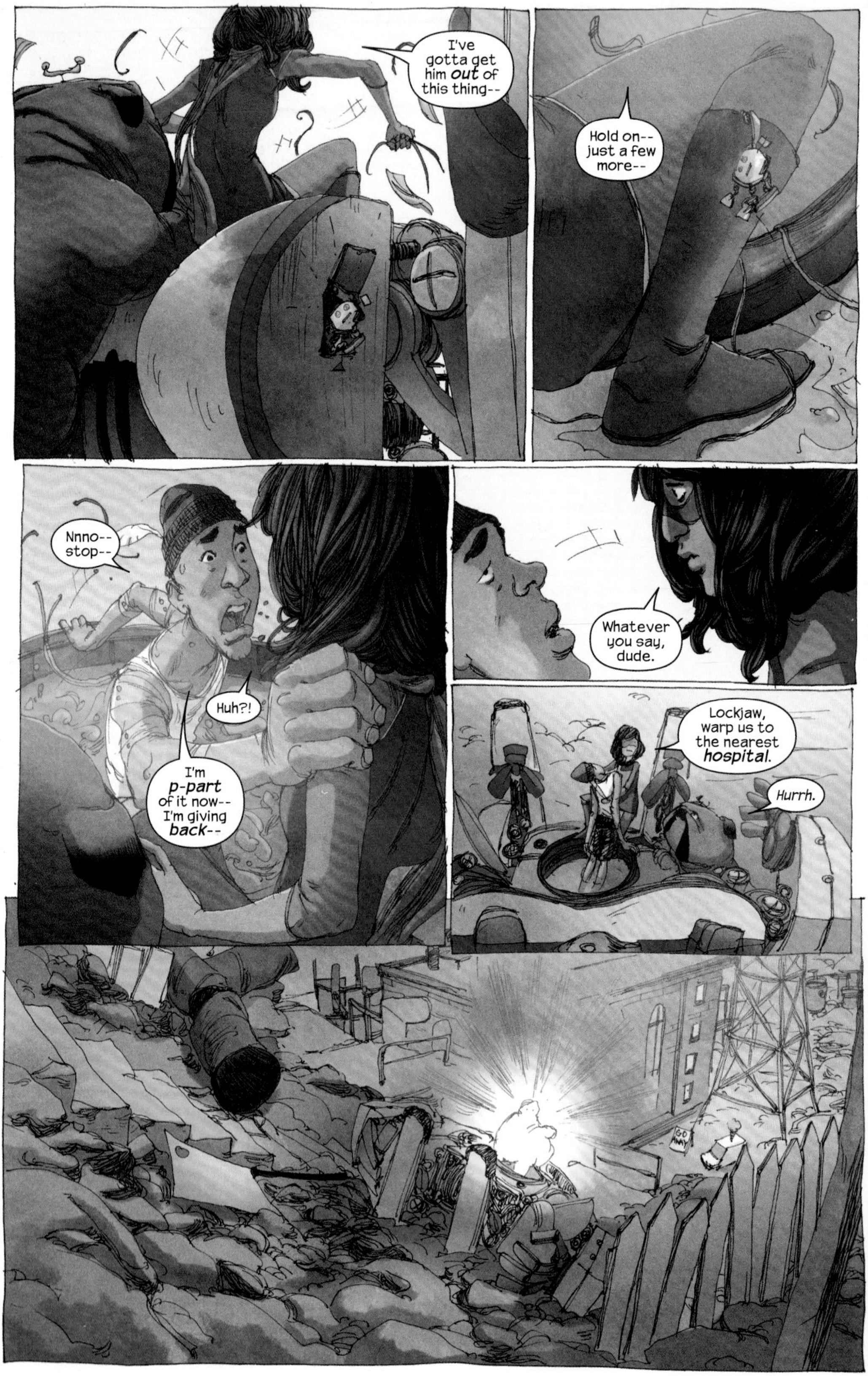
I've gotta get him *out* of this thing--
Hold on-- just a few more--
Nnno-- stop--
Huh?!
I'm *p-part* of it now-- I'm giving *back*--
Whatever you say, dude.
Lockjaw, warp us to the nearest *hospital*.
Hurrh.
GO AWAY

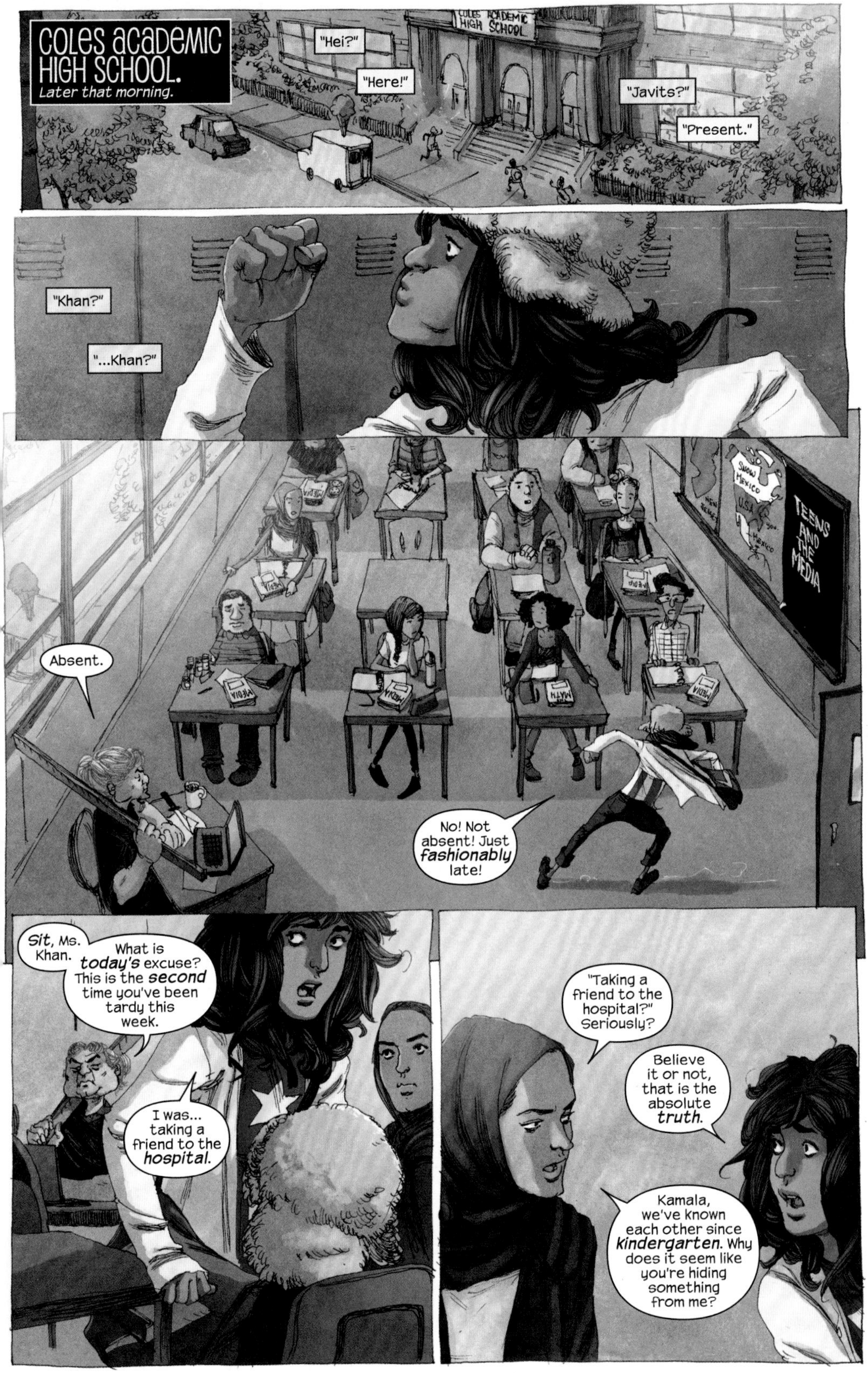
COLES ACADEMIC HIGH SCHOOL.
Later that morning.
COLES ACADEMIC HIGH SCHOOL
"Hei?"
"Here!"
"Javits?"
"Present."
"Khan?"
"...Khan?"
Absent.
TEENS AND THE MEDIA
No! Not absent! Just *fashionably* late!
Sit, Ms. Khan.
What is *today's* excuse? This is the *second* time you've been tardy this week.
I was... taking a friend to the *hospital*.
"Taking a friend to the hospital?" Seriously?
Believe it or not, that is the absolute *truth*.
Kamala, we've known each other since *kindergarten*. Why does it seem like you're hiding something from me?

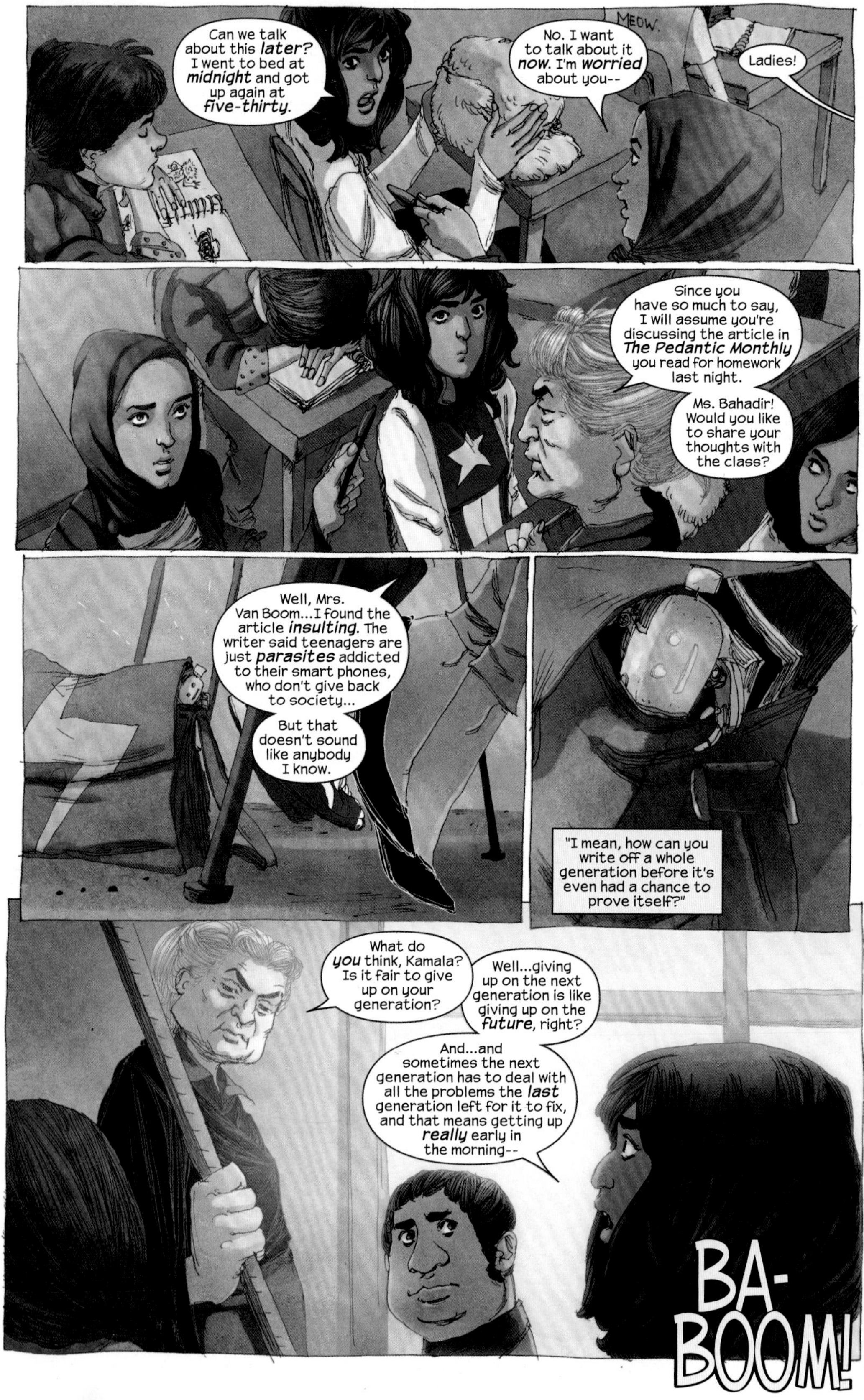
MEOW.
Can we talk about this later? I went to bed at midnight and got up again at five-thirty.
No. I want to talk about it now. I'm worried about you--
Ladies!
Since you have so much to say, I will assume you're discussing the article in The Pedantic Monthly you read for homework last night.
Ms. Bahadir! Would you like to share your thoughts with the class?
Well, Mrs. Van Boom...I found the article insulting. The writer said teenagers are just parasites addicted to their smart phones, who don't give back to society...
But that doesn't sound like anybody I know.
"I mean, how can you write off a whole generation before it's even had a chance to prove itself?"
What do you think, Kamala? Is it fair to give up on your generation?
Well...giving up on the next generation is like giving up on the future, right?
And...and sometimes the next generation has to deal with all the problems the last generation left for it to fix, and that means getting up really early in the morning--
BA-BOOM!

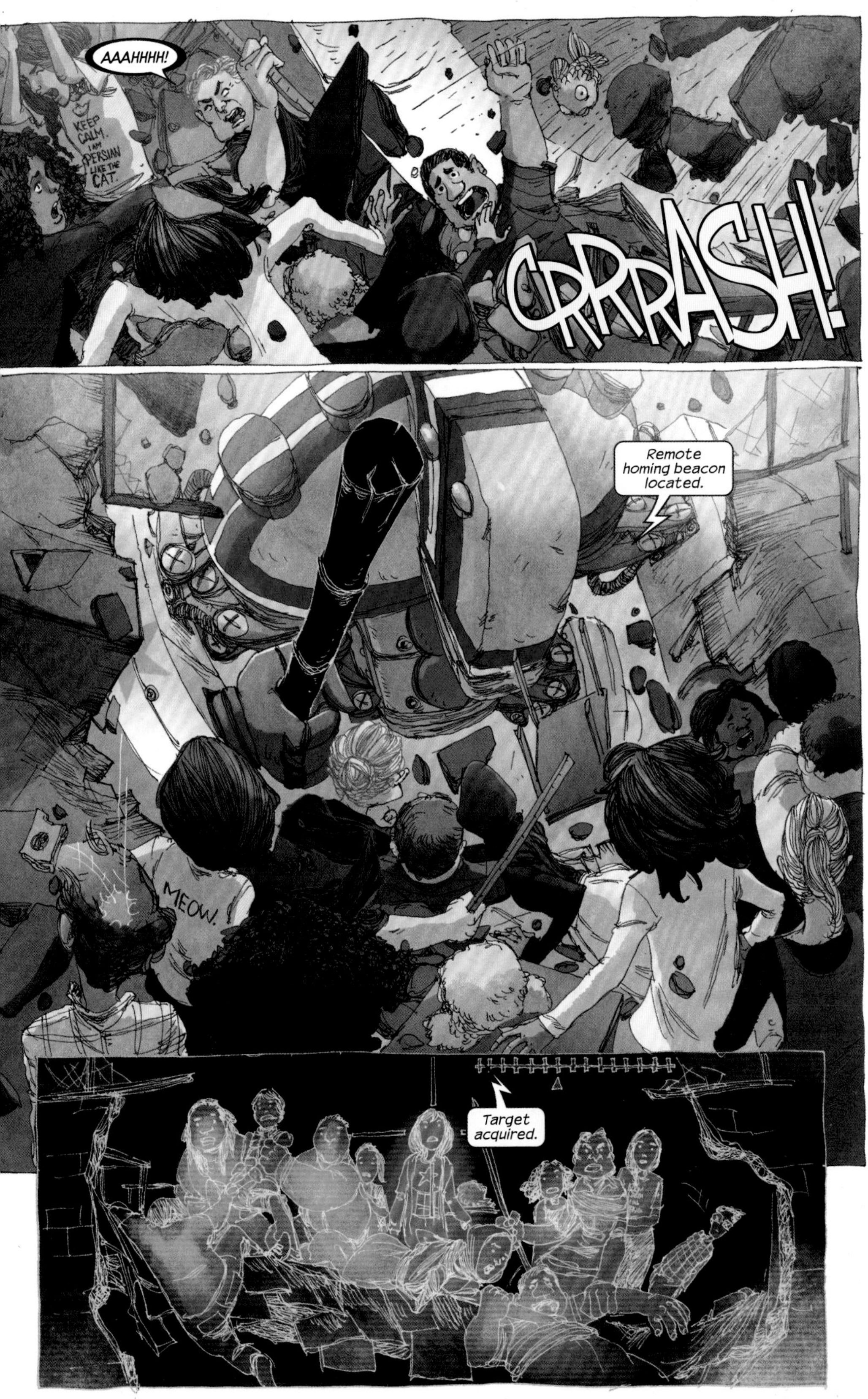
AAAHHHH!
KEEP CALM. I AM PERSIAN LIKE THE CAT.
CRRRASH!
Remote homing beacon located.
MEOW.
Target acquired.

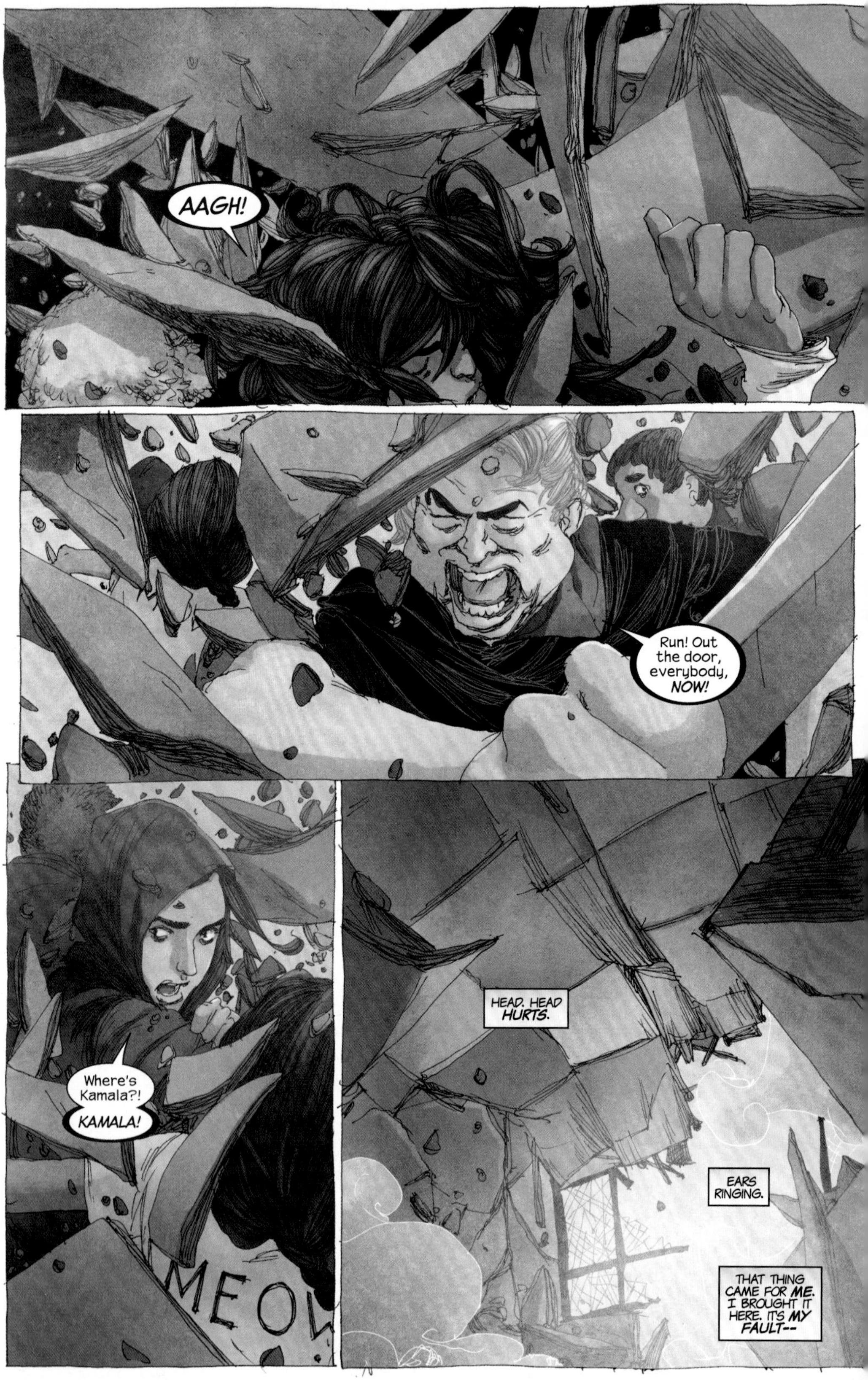
AAGH!
Run! Out the door, everybody, NOW!
Where's Kamala?!
KAMALA!
MEO
HEAD. HEAD HURTS.
EARS RINGING.
THAT THING CAME FOR ME. I BROUGHT IT HERE. IT'S MY FAULT--

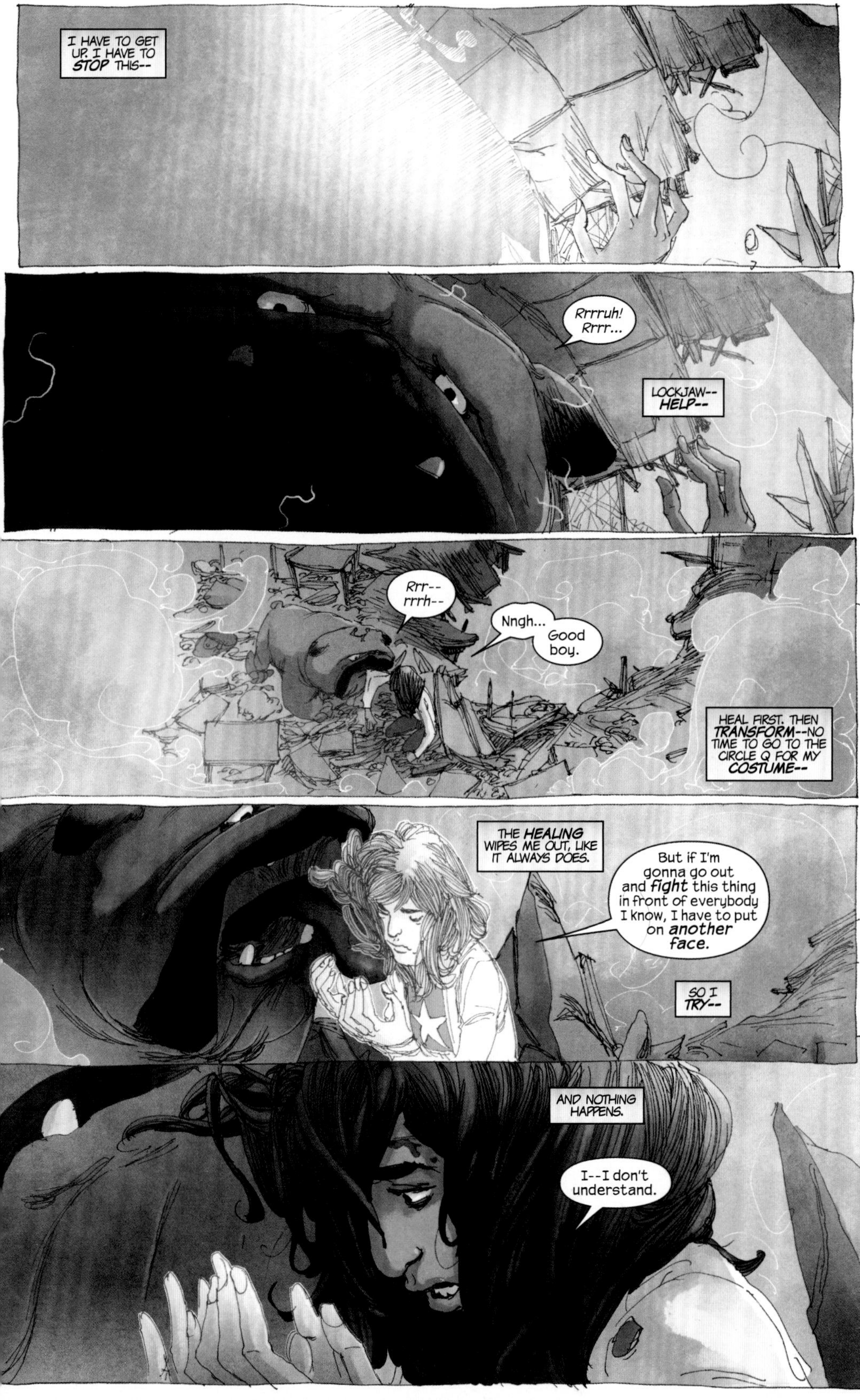
I HAVE TO GET UP. I HAVE TO STOP THIS--
Rrrruh! Rrrr...
LOCKJAW-- HELP--
Rrr-- rrrh--
Nngh... Good boy.
HEAL FIRST. THEN TRANSFORM--NO TIME TO GO TO THE CIRCLE Q FOR MY COSTUME--
THE HEALING WIPES ME OUT, LIKE IT ALWAYS DOES.
But if I'm gonna go out and fight this thing in front of everybody I know, I have to put on another face.
SO I TRY--
AND NOTHING HAPPENS.
I--I don't understand.

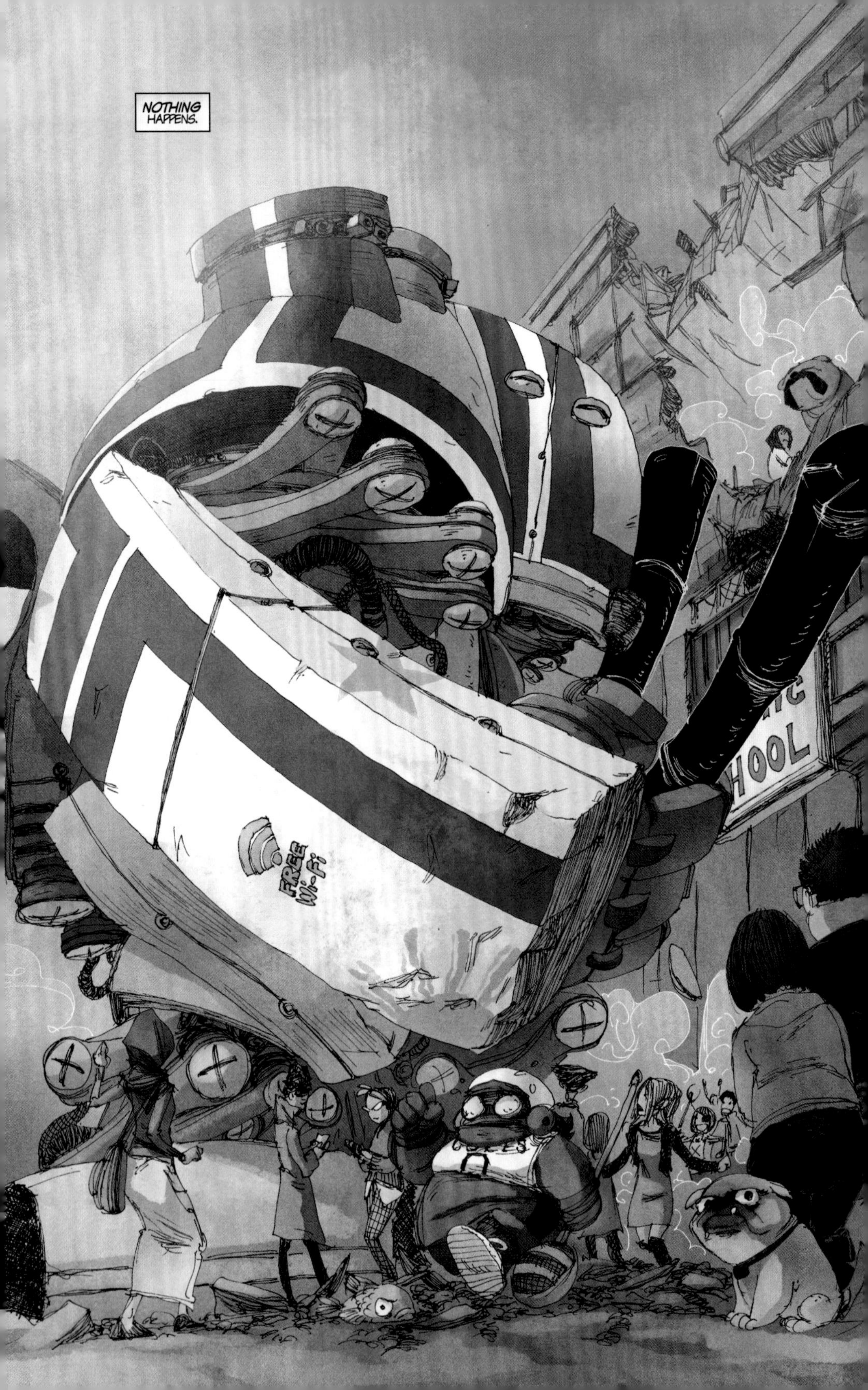
NOTHING HAPPENS.
FREE Wi-Fi
HOOL

MS. MARVEL #9

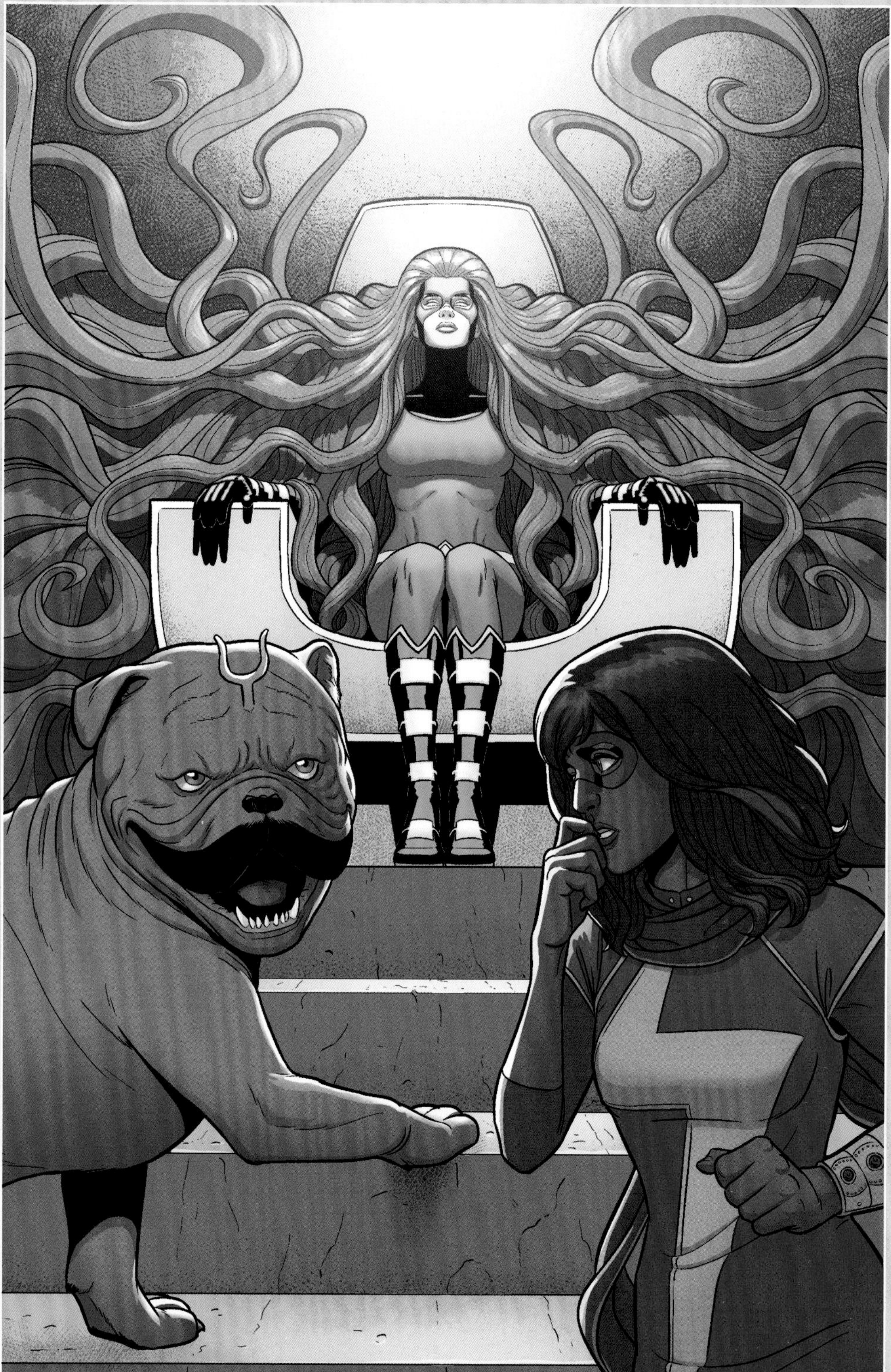

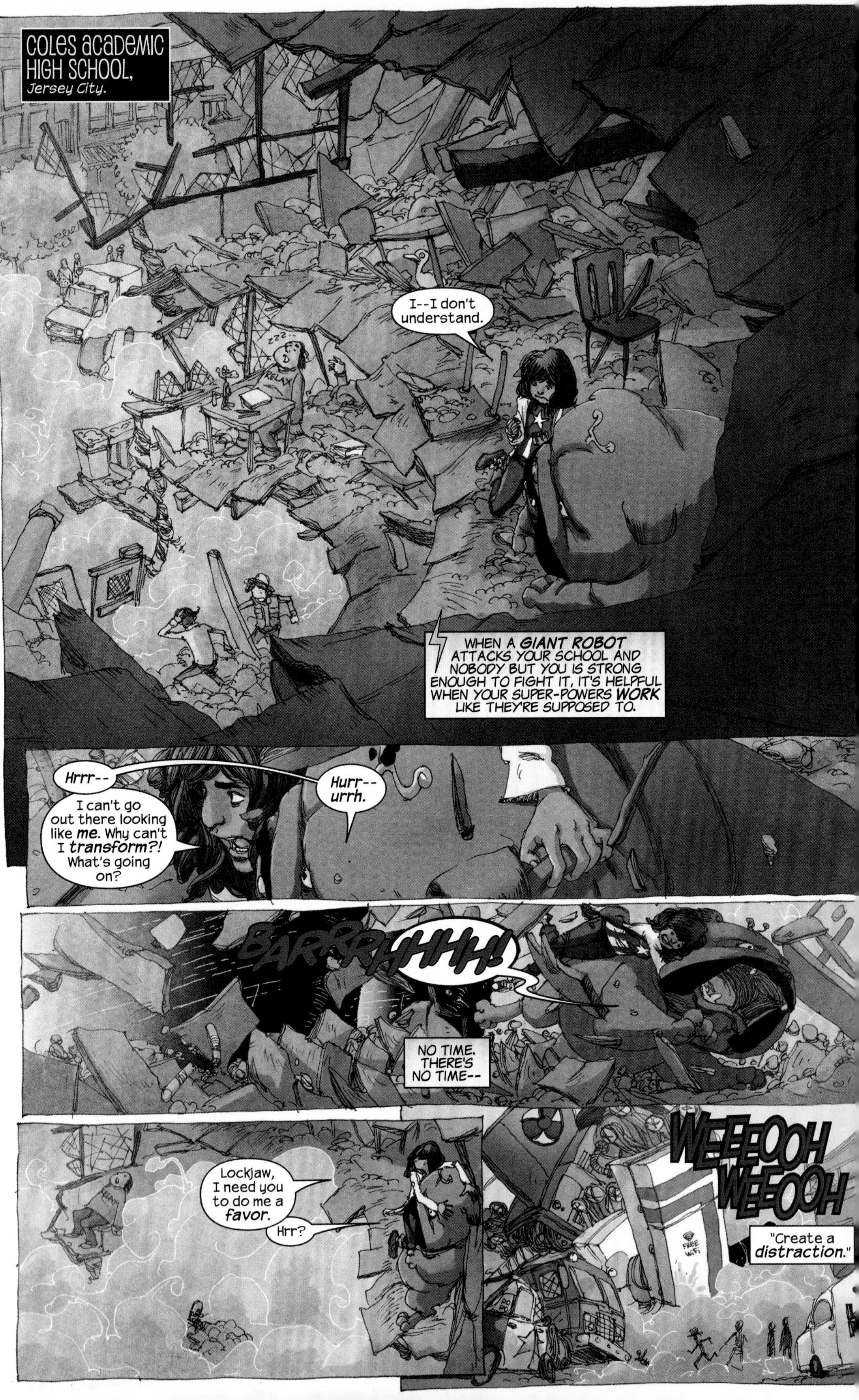
COLES ACADEMIC HIGH SCHOOL,
Jersey City.
I--I don't understand.
WHEN A GIANT ROBOT ATTACKS YOUR SCHOOL AND NOBODY BUT YOU IS STRONG ENOUGH TO FIGHT IT, IT'S HELPFUL WHEN YOUR SUPER-POWERS WORK LIKE THEY'RE SUPPOSED TO.
Hrrr--
I can't go out there looking like me. Why can't I transform?! What's going on?
Hurr-- urrh.
BARRRHHHH!
NO TIME. THERE'S NO TIME--
Lockjaw, I need you to do me a favor.
Hrr?
WEEEOOH WEEOOH
"Create a distraction."

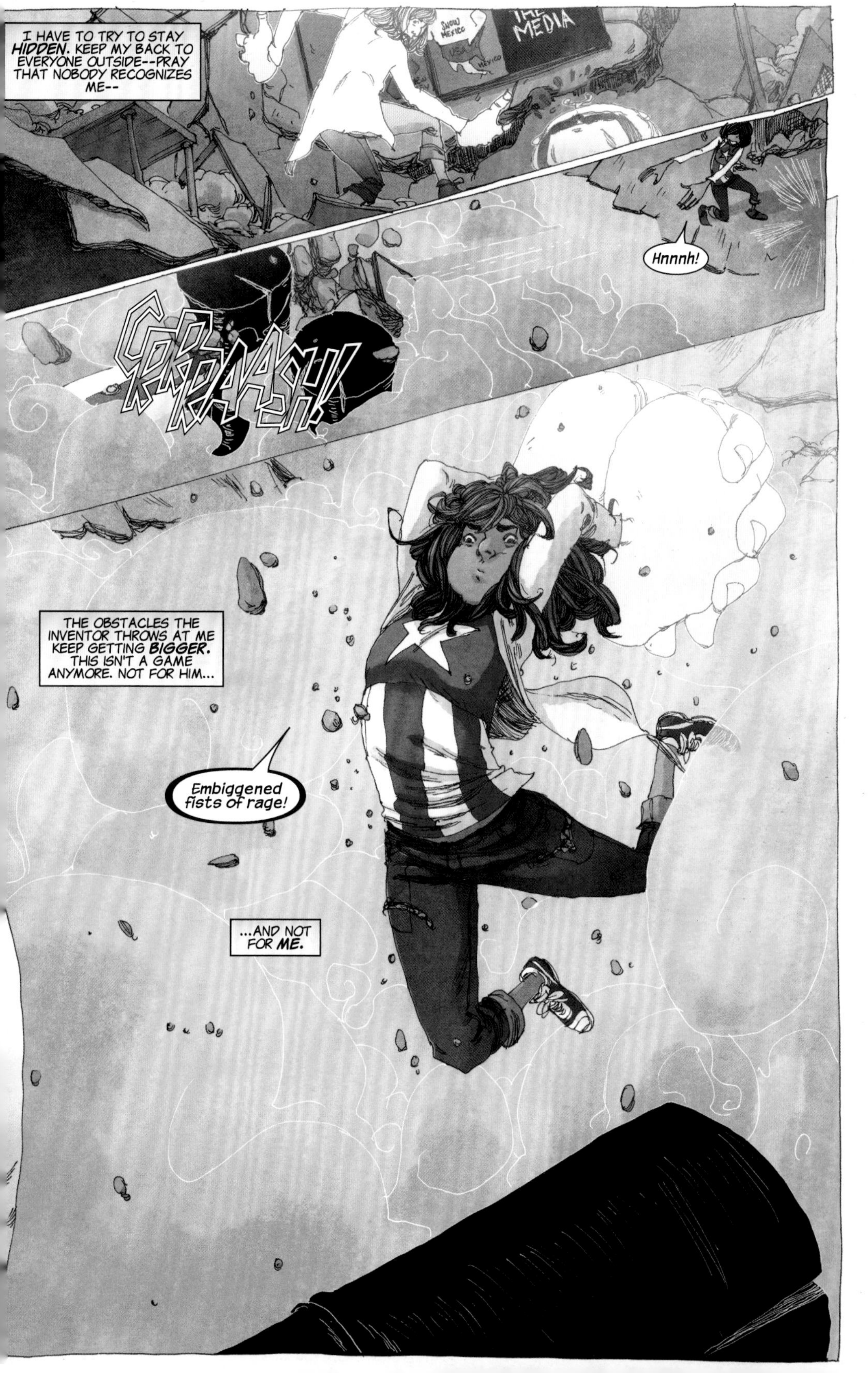
I HAVE TO TRY TO STAY HIDDEN. KEEP MY BACK TO EVERYONE OUTSIDE--PRAY THAT NOBODY RECOGNIZES ME--
THE MEDIA
Hnnnh!
KRRBBAASH!
THE OBSTACLES THE INVENTOR THROWS AT ME KEEP GETTING BIGGER. THIS ISN'T A GAME ANYMORE. NOT FOR HIM...
Embiggened fists of rage!
...AND NOT FOR ME.

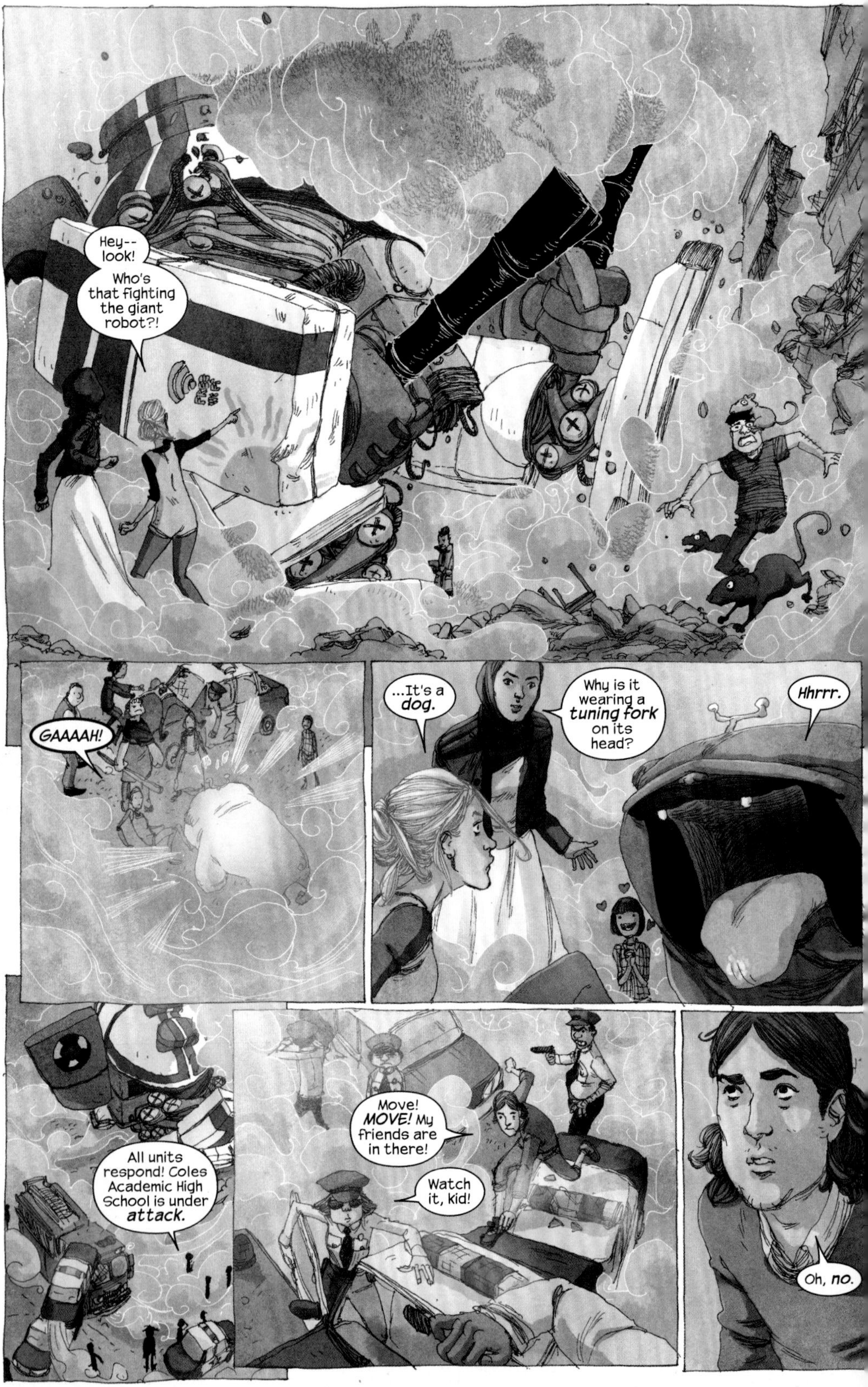
Hey-- look!
Who's that fighting the giant robot?!
GAAAAH!
...It's a dog.
Why is it wearing a tuning fork on its head?
Hhrrr.
All units respond! Coles Academic High School is under attack.
Move! MOVE! My friends are in there!
Watch it, kid!
Oh, no.

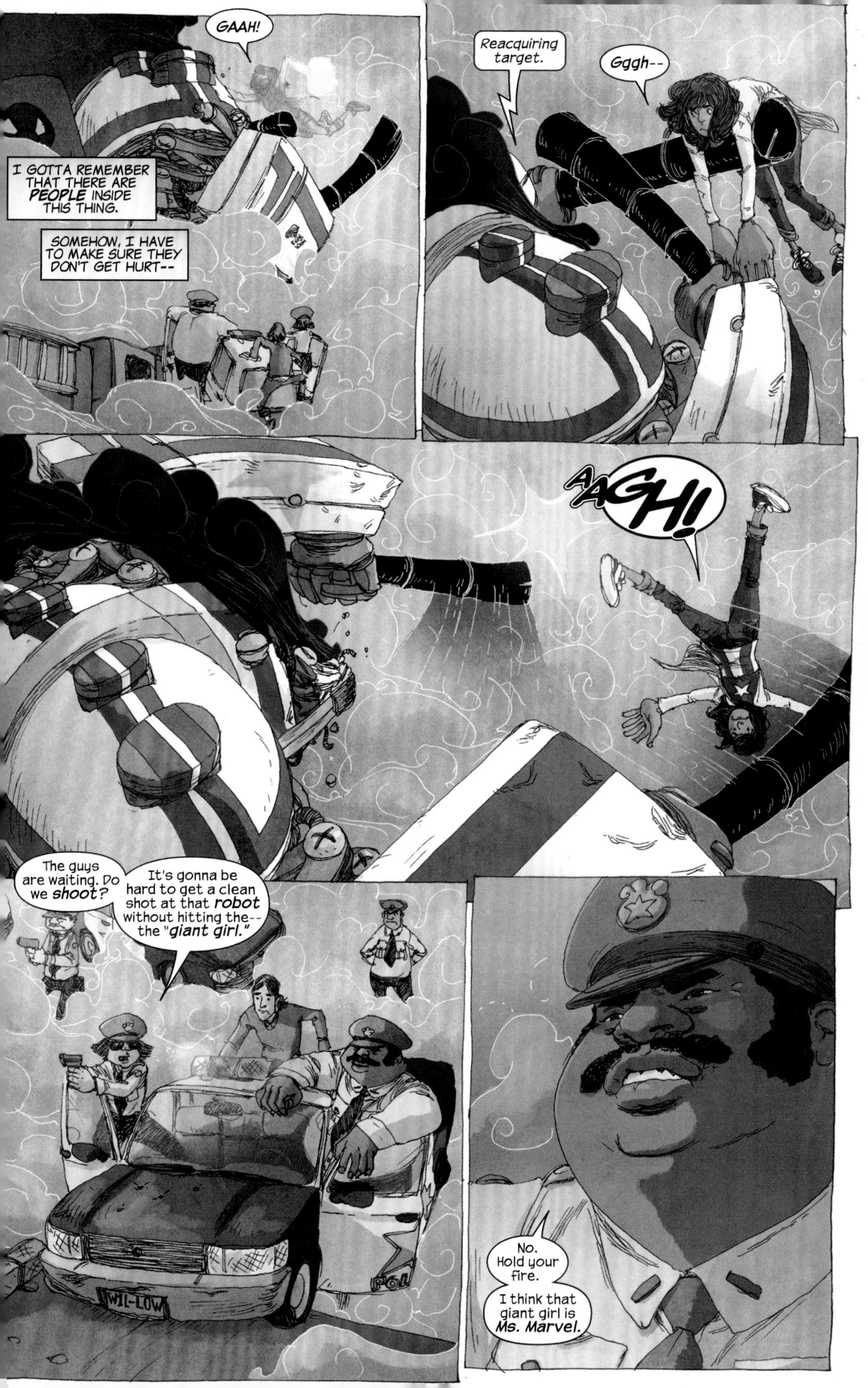
GAAH!
I GOTTA REMEMBER THAT THERE ARE PEOPLE INSIDE THIS THING.
SOMEHOW, I HAVE TO MAKE SURE THEY DON'T GET HURT--
Reacquiring target.
Gggh--
AAGH!
The guys are waiting. Do we shoot?
It's gonna be hard to get a clean shot at that robot without hitting the-- the "giant girl."
WIL-LOW
No. Hold your fire.
I think that giant girl is Ms. Marvel.

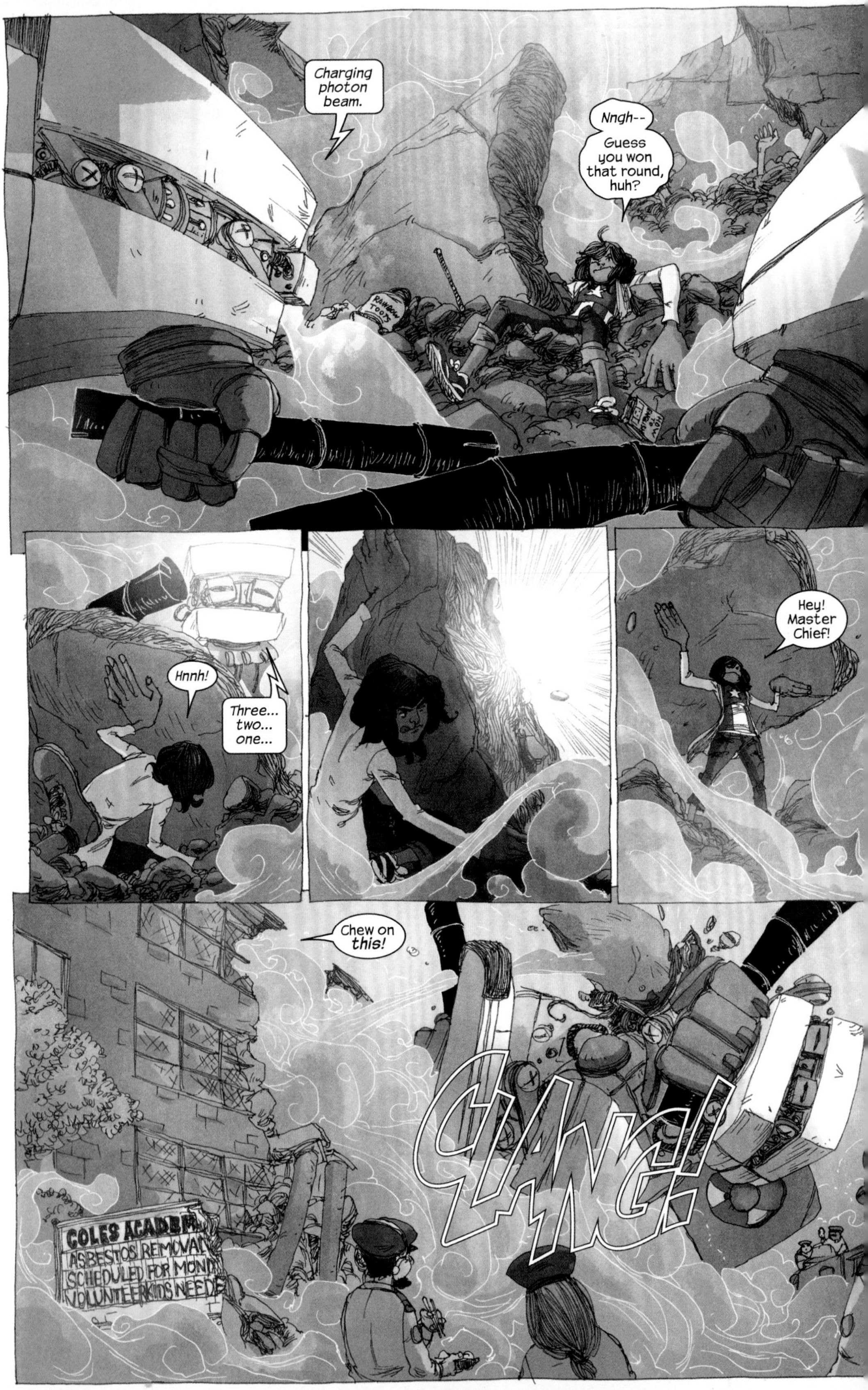

Charging photon beam.
Nngh--
Guess you won that round, huh?
RAINBOW TOOTS
Hnnh!
Three... two... one...
Hey! Master Chief!
Chew on this!
CLANG!
COLES ACADEM
ASBESTOS REMOVA
SCHEDULED FOR MOND
VOLUNTEER KIDS NEEDE

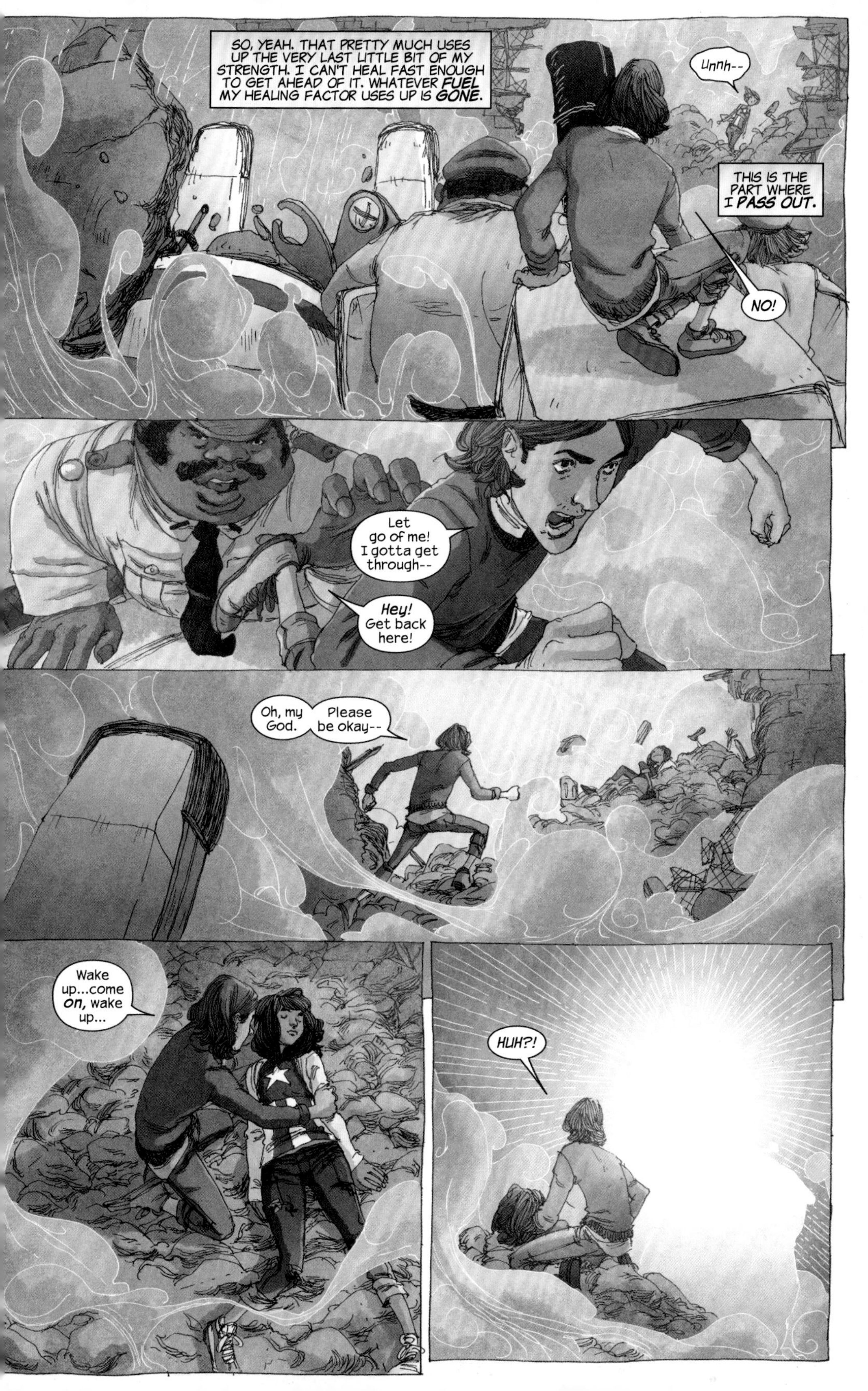

SO, YEAH. THAT PRETTY MUCH USES UP THE VERY LAST LITTLE BIT OF MY STRENGTH. I CAN'T HEAL FAST ENOUGH TO GET AHEAD OF IT. WHATEVER FUEL MY HEALING FACTOR USES UP IS GONE.
Unnh--
THIS IS THE PART WHERE I PASS OUT.
NO!
Let go of me! I gotta get through--
Hey! Get back here!
Oh, my God.
Please be okay--
Wake up...come on, wake up...
HUH?!

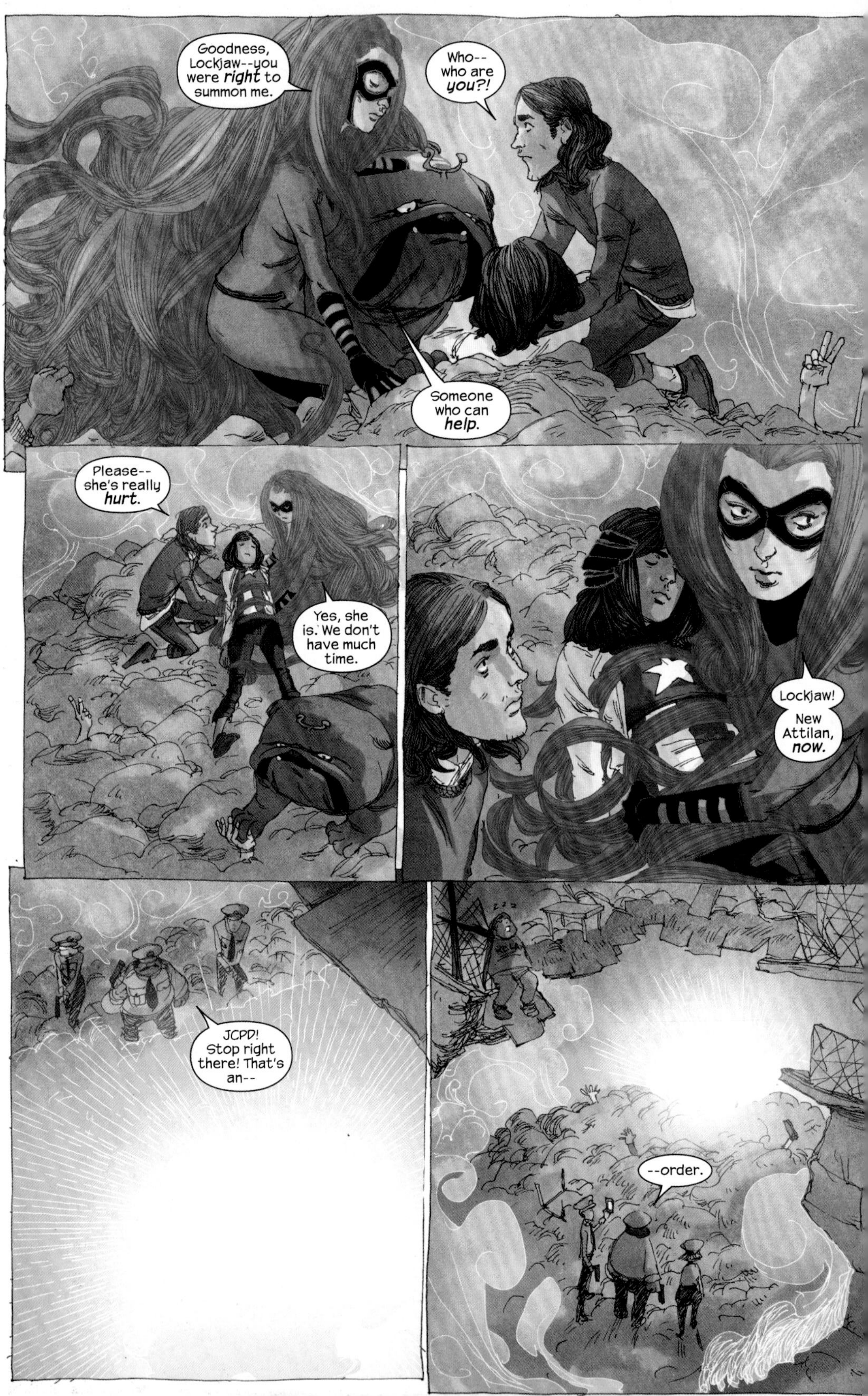
Goodness, Lockjaw--you were *right* to summon me.
Who-- who are *you*?!
Someone who can *help*.
Please-- she's really *hurt*.
Yes, she is. We don't have much time.
Lockjaw! New Attilan, *now*.
JCPD! Stop right there! That's an--
--order.

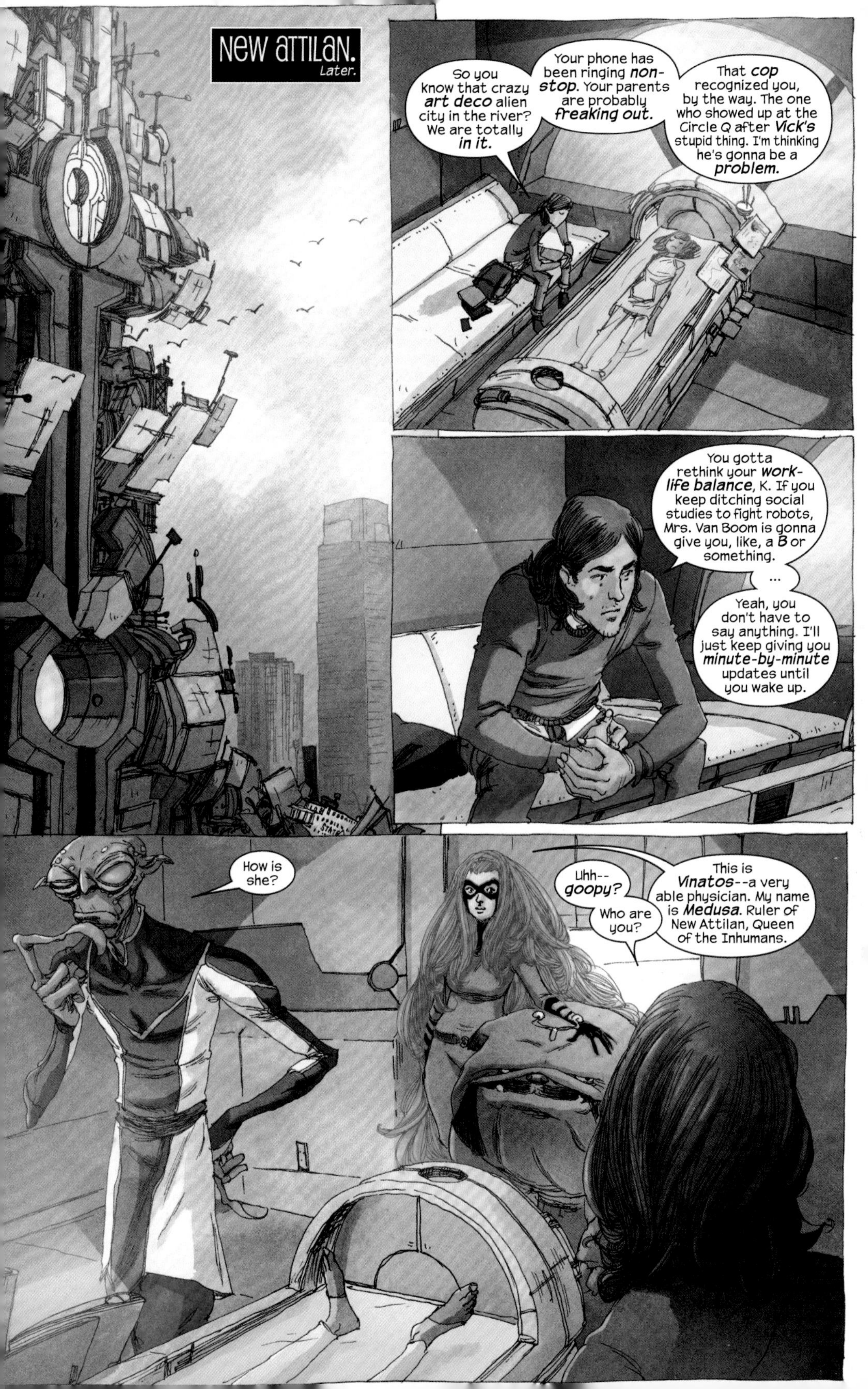
NEW ATTILAN.
Later.
So you know that crazy art deco alien city in the river? We are totally in it.
Your phone has been ringing non-stop. Your parents are probably freaking out.
That cop recognized you, by the way. The one who showed up at the Circle Q after Vick's stupid thing. I'm thinking he's gonna be a problem.
You gotta rethink your work-life balance, K. If you keep ditching social studies to fight robots, Mrs. Van Boom is gonna give you, like, a B or something.
...
Yeah, you don't have to say anything. I'll just keep giving you minute-by-minute updates until you wake up.
How is she?
Uhh-- goopy?
Who are you?
This is Vinatos--a very able physician. My name is Medusa. Ruler of New Attilan, Queen of the Inhumans.

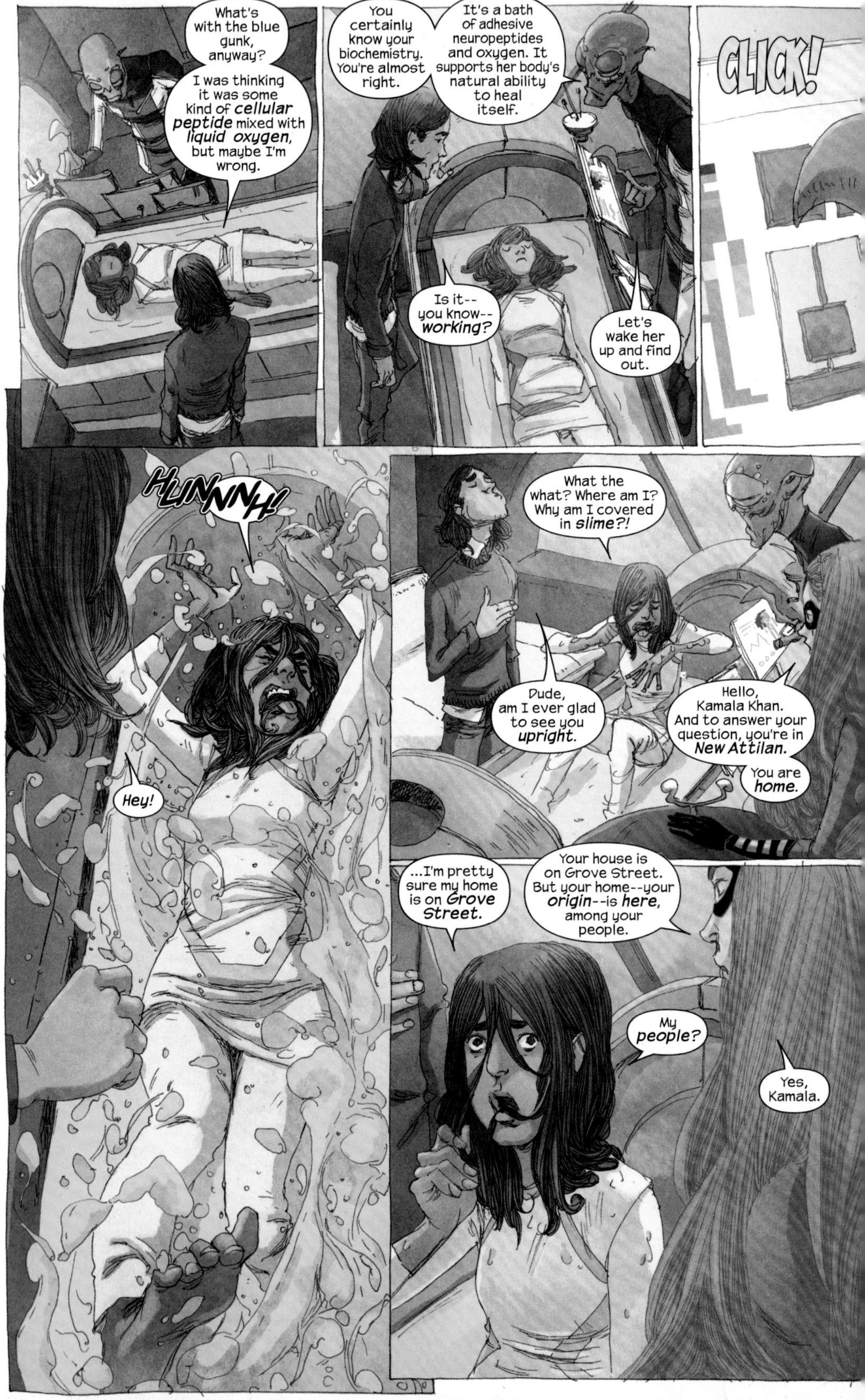
What's with the blue gunk, anyway?
I was thinking it was some kind of cellular peptide mixed with liquid oxygen, but maybe I'm wrong.
You certainly know your biochemistry. You're almost right.
It's a bath of adhesive neuropeptides and oxygen. It supports her body's natural ability to heal itself.
Is it-- you know-- working?
Let's wake her up and find out.
CLICK!
HUNNNH!
Hey!
What the what? Where am I? Why am I covered in slime?!
Dude, am I ever glad to see you upright.
Hello, Kamala Khan. And to answer your question, you're in New Attilan.
You are home.
...I'm pretty sure my home is on Grove Street.
Your house is on Grove Street. But your home--your origin--is here, among your people.
My people?
Yes, Kamala.

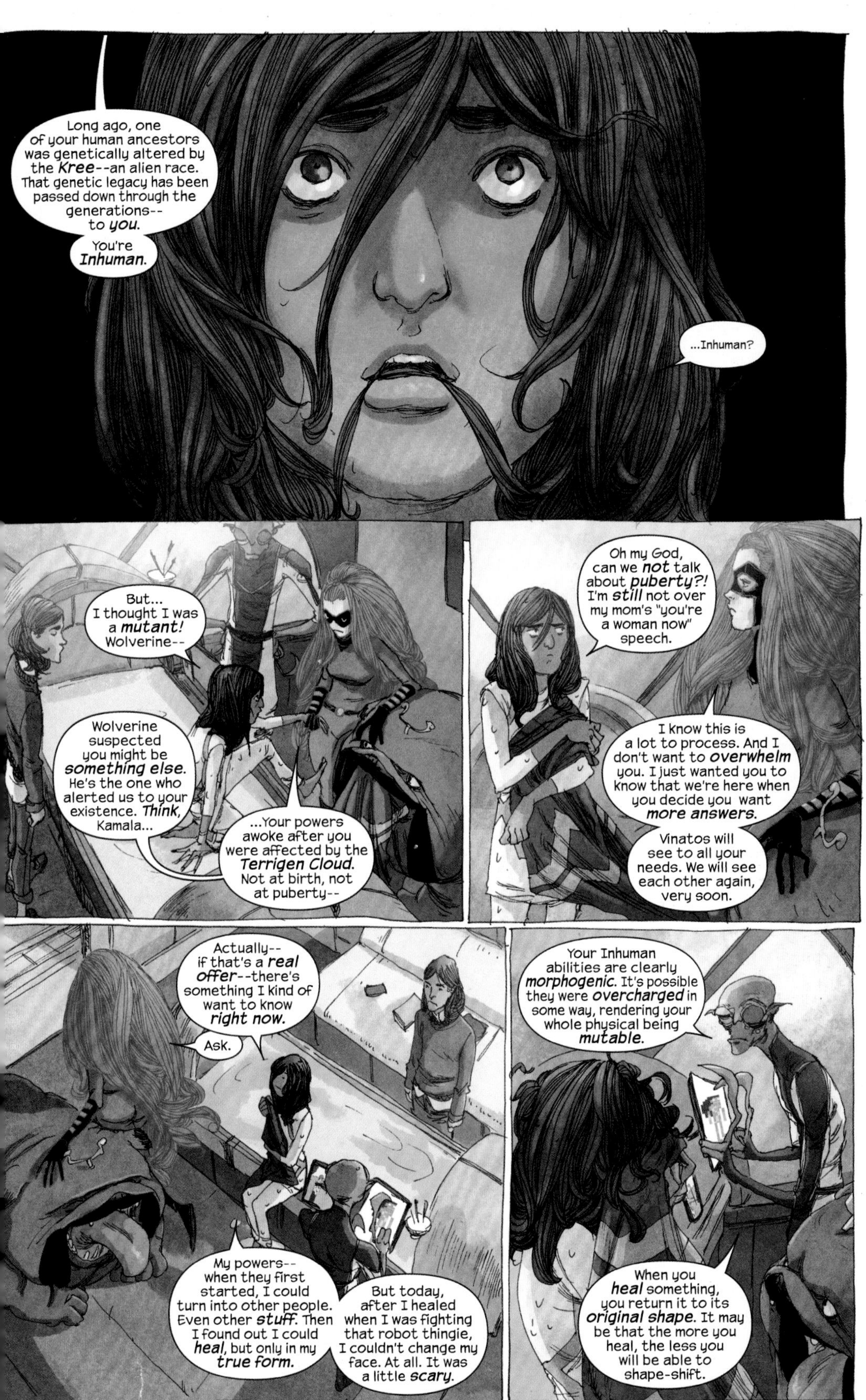
Long ago, one of your human ancestors was genetically altered by the Kree--an alien race. That genetic legacy has been passed down through the generations-- to you.
You're Inhuman.
...Inhuman?
But... I thought I was a mutant! Wolverine--
Wolverine suspected you might be something else. He's the one who alerted us to your existence. Think, Kamala...
...Your powers awoke after you were affected by the Terrigen Cloud. Not at birth, not at puberty--
Oh my God, can we not talk about puberty?! I'm still not over my mom's "you're a woman now" speech.
I know this is a lot to process. And I don't want to overwhelm you. I just wanted you to know that we're here when you decide you want more answers.
Vinatos will see to all your needs. We will see each other again, very soon.
Actually-- if that's a real offer--there's something I kind of want to know right now.
Ask.
My powers-- when they first started, I could turn into other people. Even other stuff. Then I found out I could heal, but only in my true form.
But today, after I healed when I was fighting that robot thingie, I couldn't change my face. At all. It was a little scary.
Your Inhuman abilities are clearly morphogenic. It's possible they were overcharged in some way, rendering your whole physical being mutable.
When you heal something, you return it to its original shape. It may be that the more you heal, the less you will be able to shape-shift.

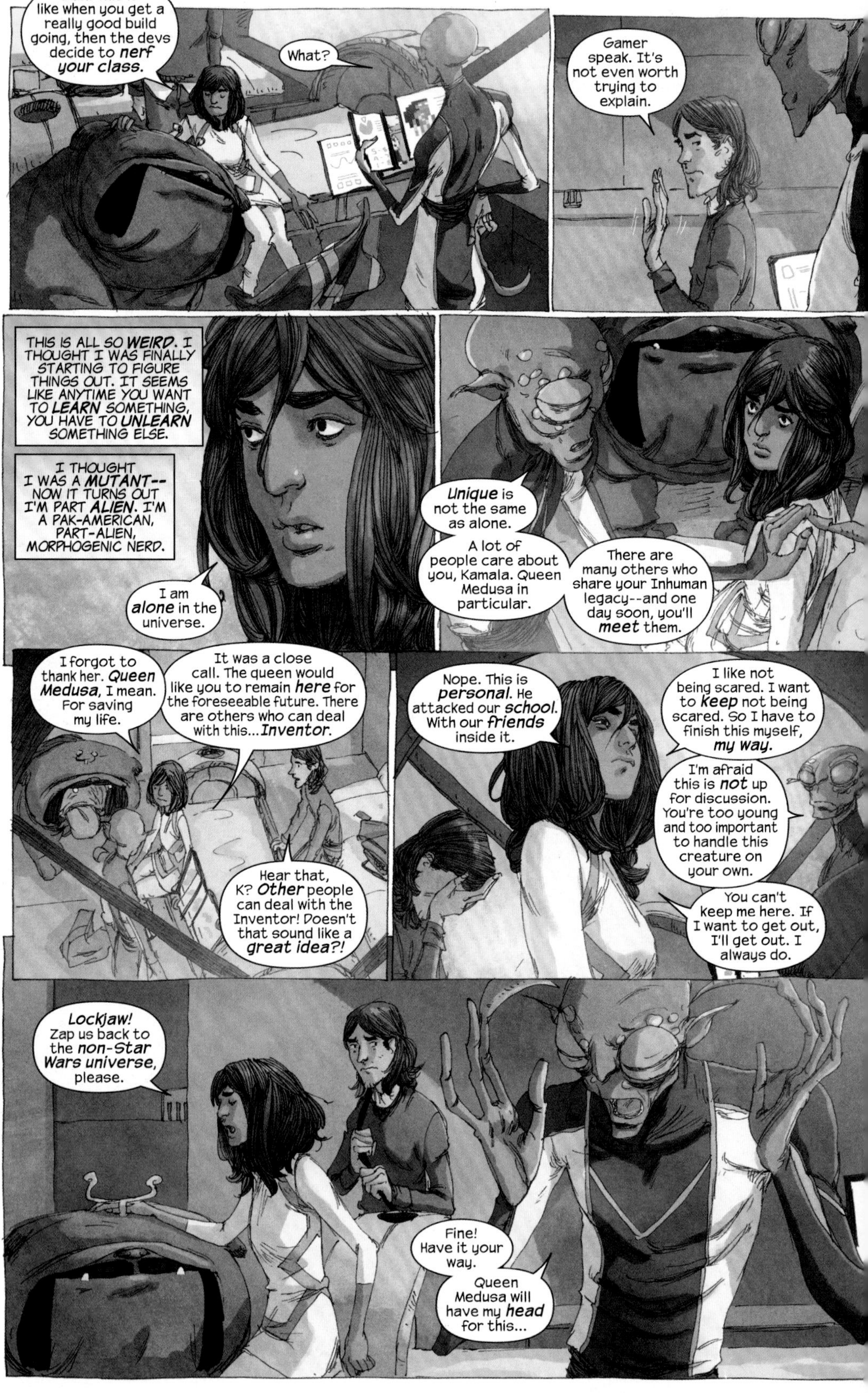

Man. This is like when you get a really good build going, then the devs decide to nerf your class.
What?
Gamer speak. It's not even worth trying to explain.
THIS IS ALL SO WEIRD. I THOUGHT I WAS FINALLY STARTING TO FIGURE THINGS OUT. IT SEEMS LIKE ANYTIME YOU WANT TO LEARN SOMETHING, YOU HAVE TO UNLEARN SOMETHING ELSE.
I THOUGHT I WAS A MUTANT-- NOW IT TURNS OUT I'M PART ALIEN. I'M A PAK-AMERICAN, PART-ALIEN, MORPHOGENIC NERD.
I am alone in the universe.
Unique is not the same as alone.
A lot of people care about you, Kamala. Queen Medusa in particular.
There are many others who share your Inhuman legacy--and one day soon, you'll meet them.
I forgot to thank her. Queen Medusa, I mean. For saving my life.
It was a close call. The queen would like you to remain here for the foreseeable future. There are others who can deal with this...Inventor.
Hear that, K? Other people can deal with the Inventor! Doesn't that sound like a great idea?!
Nope. This is personal. He attacked our school. With our friends inside it.
I like not being scared. I want to keep not being scared. So I have to finish this myself, my way.
I'm afraid this is not up for discussion. You're too young and too important to handle this creature on your own.
You can't keep me here. If I want to get out, I'll get out. I always do.
Lockjaw! Zap us back to the non-Star Wars universe, please.
Fine! Have it your way.
Queen Medusa will have my head for this...

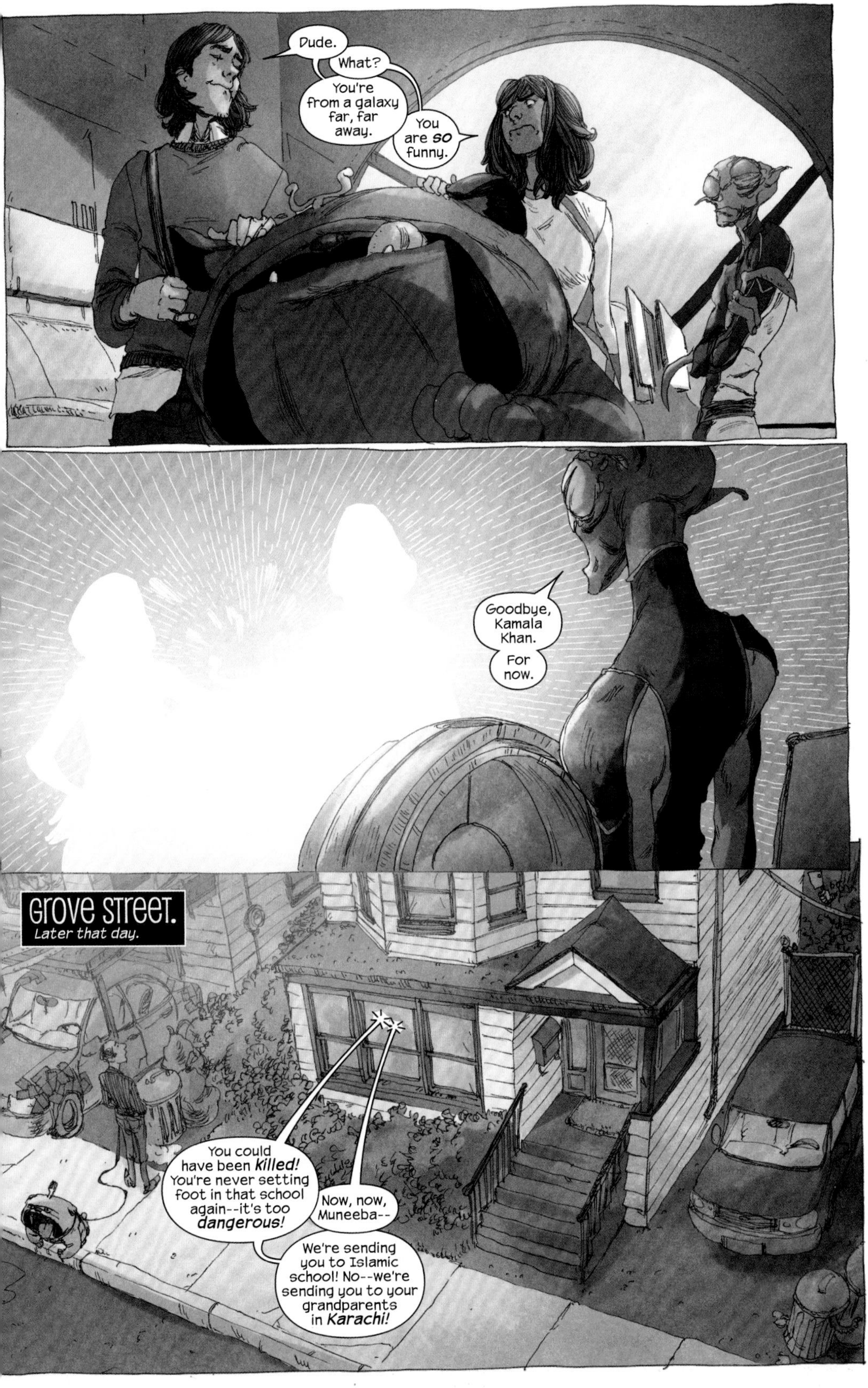
Dude.
What?
You're from a galaxy far, far away.
You are SO funny.
Goodbye, Kamala Khan.
For now.
GROVE STREET.
Later that day.
You could have been killed! You're never setting foot in that school again--it's too dangerous!
Now, now, Muneeba--
We're sending you to Islamic school! No--we're sending you to your grandparents in Karachi!

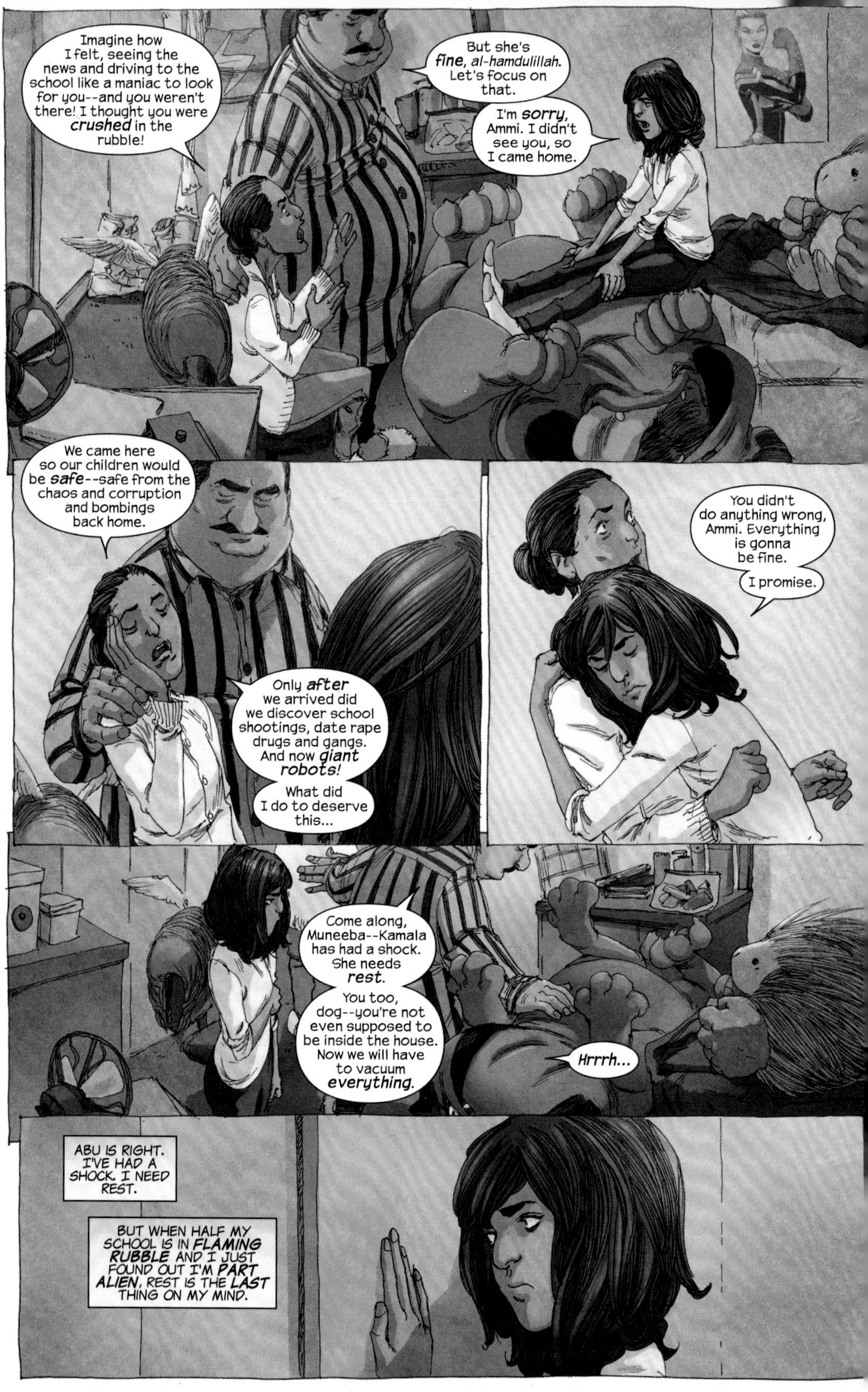
Imagine how I felt, seeing the news and driving to the school like a maniac to look for you--and you weren't there! I thought you were crushed in the rubble!
But she's fine, al-hamdulillah. Let's focus on that.
I'm sorry, Ammi. I didn't see you, so I came home.
We came here so our children would be safe--safe from the chaos and corruption and bombings back home.
Only after we arrived did we discover school shootings, date rape drugs and gangs. And now giant robots!
What did I do to deserve this...
You didn't do anything wrong, Ammi. Everything is gonna be fine.
I promise.
Come along, Muneeba--Kamala has had a shock. She needs rest.
You too, dog--you're not even supposed to be inside the house. Now we will have to vacuum everything.
Hrrrh...
ABU IS RIGHT. I'VE HAD A SHOCK. I NEED REST.
BUT WHEN HALF MY SCHOOL IS IN FLAMING RUBBLE AND I JUST FOUND OUT I'M PART ALIEN, REST IS THE LAST THING ON MY MIND.

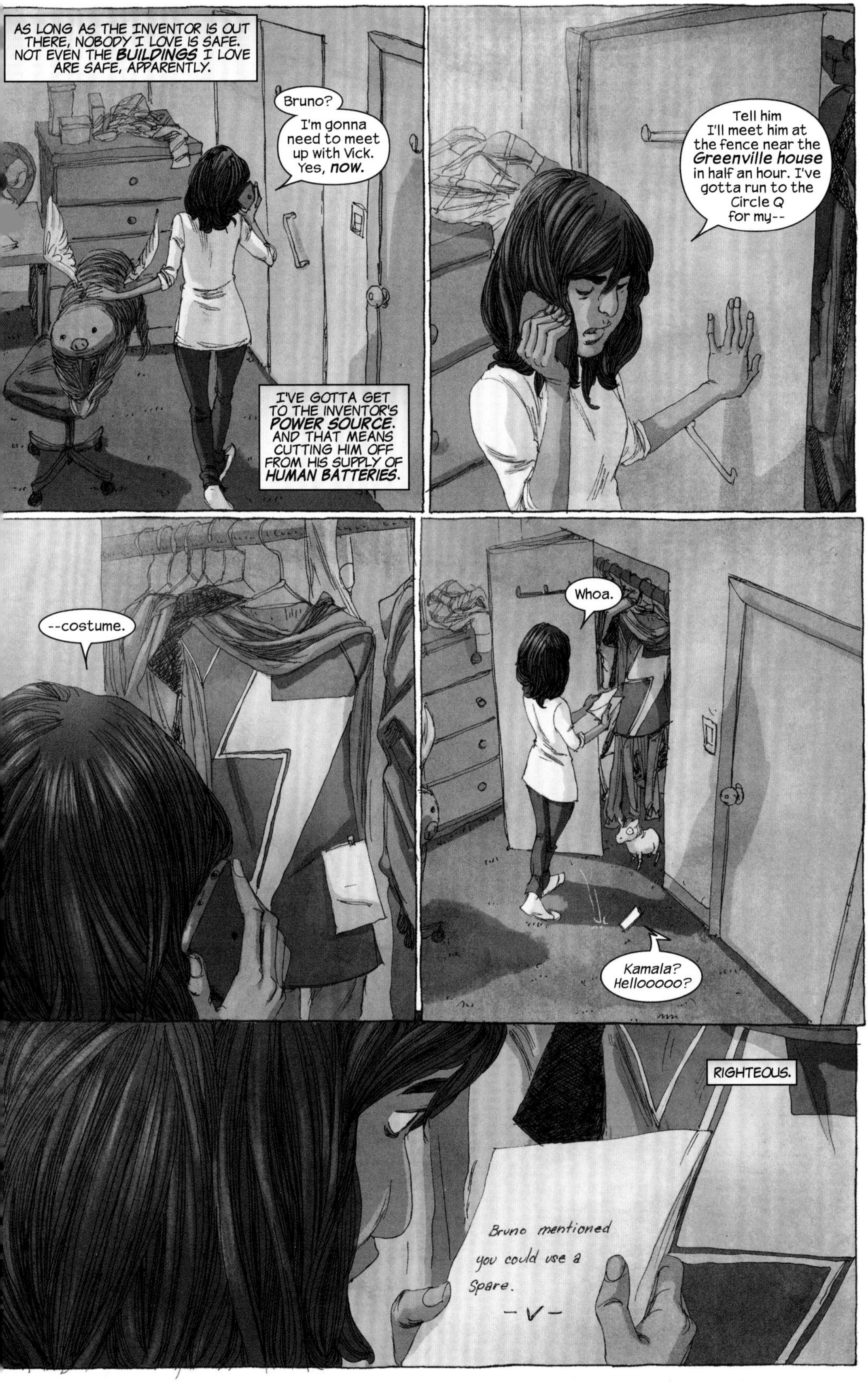

AS LONG AS THE INVENTOR IS OUT THERE, NOBODY I LOVE IS SAFE. NOT EVEN THE BUILDINGS I LOVE ARE SAFE, APPARENTLY.
Bruno?
I'm gonna need to meet up with Vick. Yes, now.
I'VE GOTTA GET TO THE INVENTOR'S POWER SOURCE. AND THAT MEANS CUTTING HIM OFF FROM HIS SUPPLY OF HUMAN BATTERIES.
Tell him I'll meet him at the fence near the Greenville house in half an hour. I've gotta run to the Circle Q for my--
--costume.
Whoa.
Kamala? Hellooooo?
RIGHTEOUS.
Bruno mentioned you could use a spare.
-V-

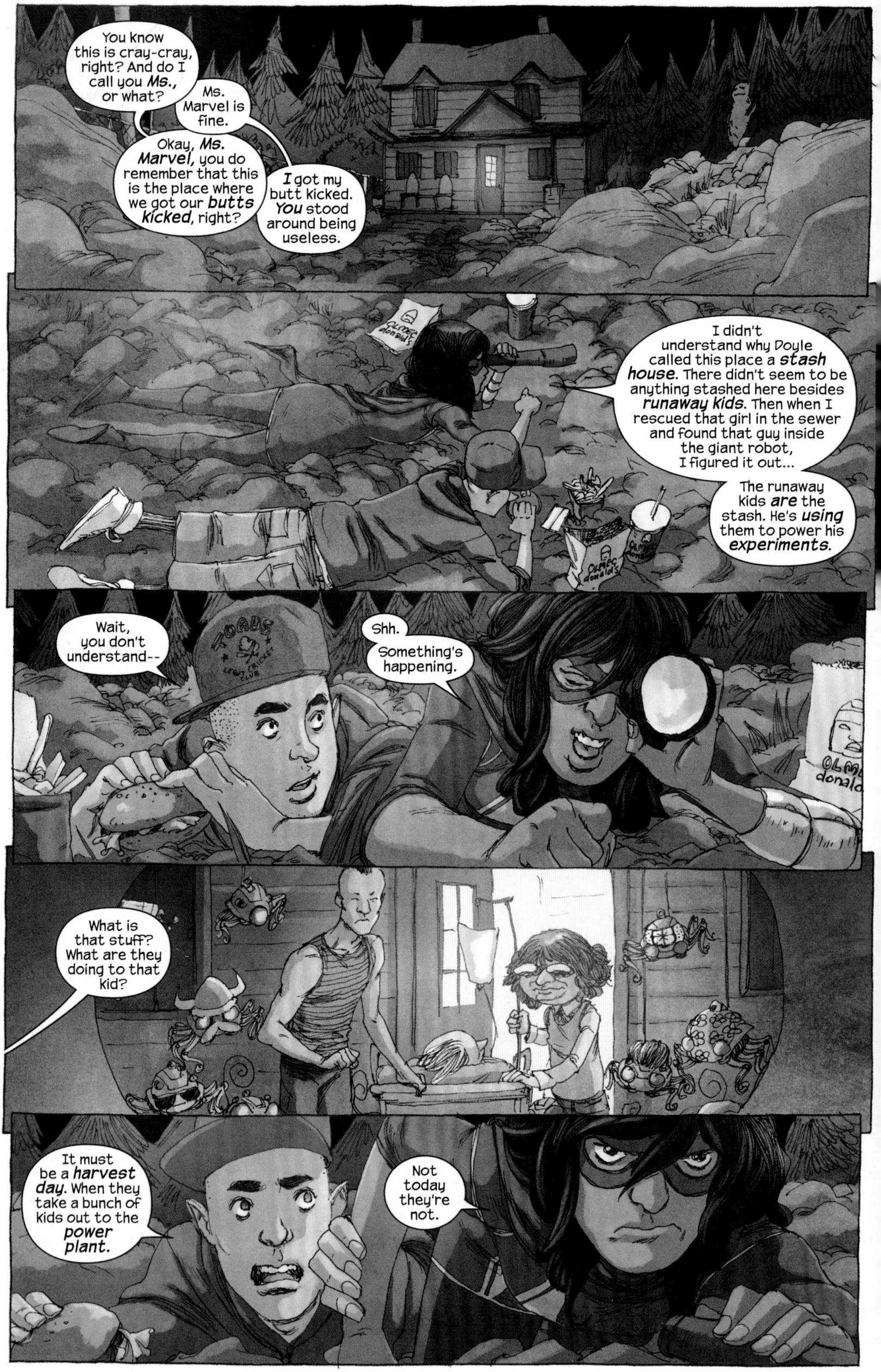
You know this is cray-cray, right? And do I call you *Ms.*, or what?
Ms. Marvel is fine.
Okay, *Ms. Marvel,* you do remember that this is the place where we got our ***butts kicked***, right?
I got my butt kicked. *You* stood around being useless.
I didn't understand why Doyle called this place a ***stash house***. There didn't seem to be anything stashed here besides ***runaway kids***. Then when I rescued that girl in the sewer and found that guy inside the giant robot, I figured it out...
The runaway kids ***are*** the stash. He's ***using*** them to power his ***experiments***.
Wait, you don't understand--
Shh.
Something's happening.
What is that stuff? What are they doing to that kid?
It must be a ***harvest day***. When they take a bunch of kids out to the ***power plant***.
Not today they're not.

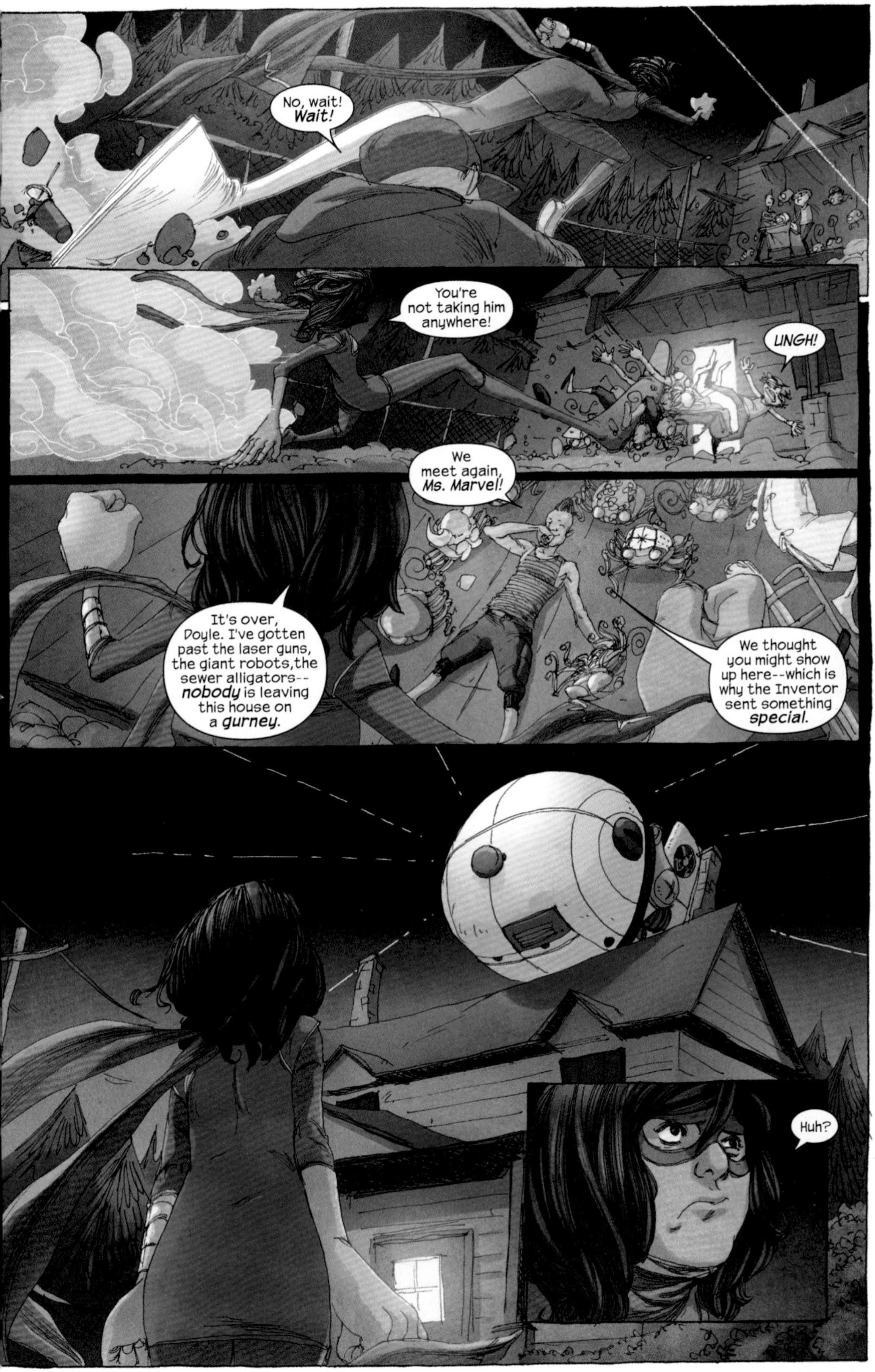
No, wait! Wait!
You're not taking him anywhere!
UNGH!
We meet again, Ms. Marvel!
It's over, Doyle. I've gotten past the laser guns, the giant robots, the sewer alligators--nobody is leaving this house on a gurney.
We thought you might show up here--which is why the Inventor sent something special.
Huh?

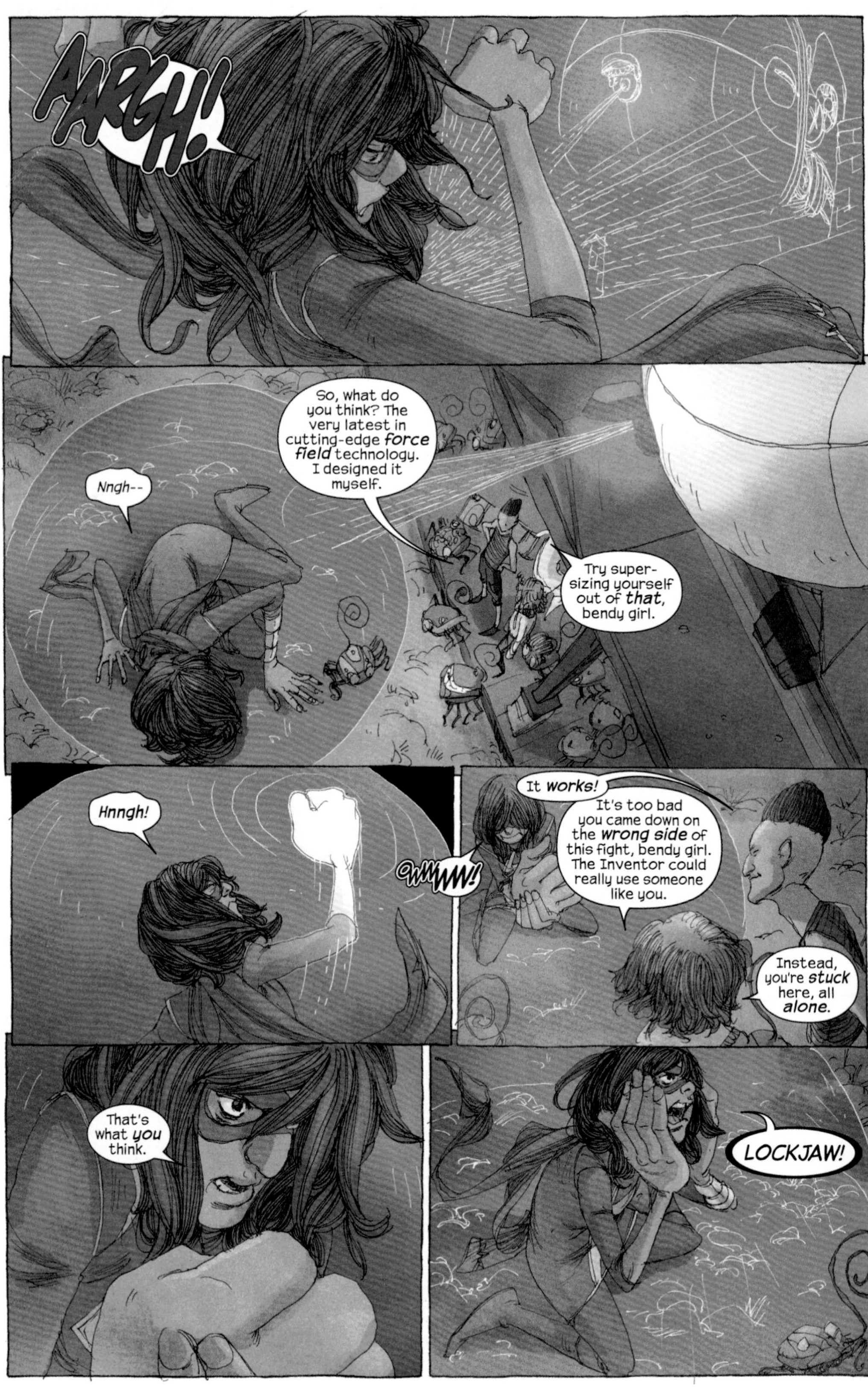
AARGH!
So, what do you think? The very latest in cutting-edge force field technology. I designed it myself.
Nngh--
Try super-sizing yourself out of that, bendy girl.
Hnngh!
OWWWW!
It works!
It's too bad you came down on the wrong side of this fight, bendy girl. The Inventor could really use someone like you.
Instead, you're stuck here, all alone.
That's what you think.
LOCKJAW!

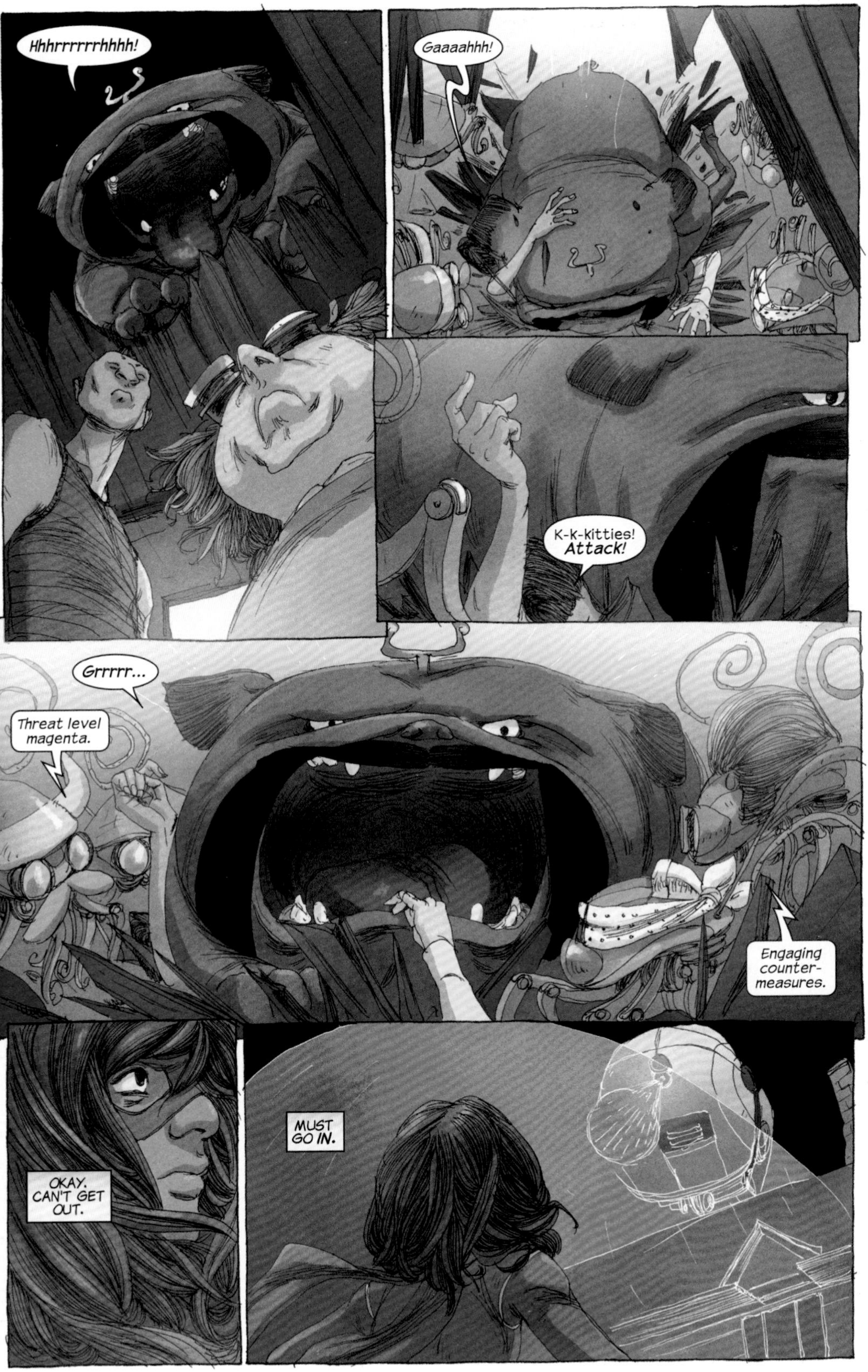
Hhhrrrrrrhhhh!
Gaaaahhh!
K-k-kitties! Attack!
Grrrrr...
Threat level magenta.
Engaging counter-measures.
OKAY. CAN'T GET OUT.
MUST GO IN.

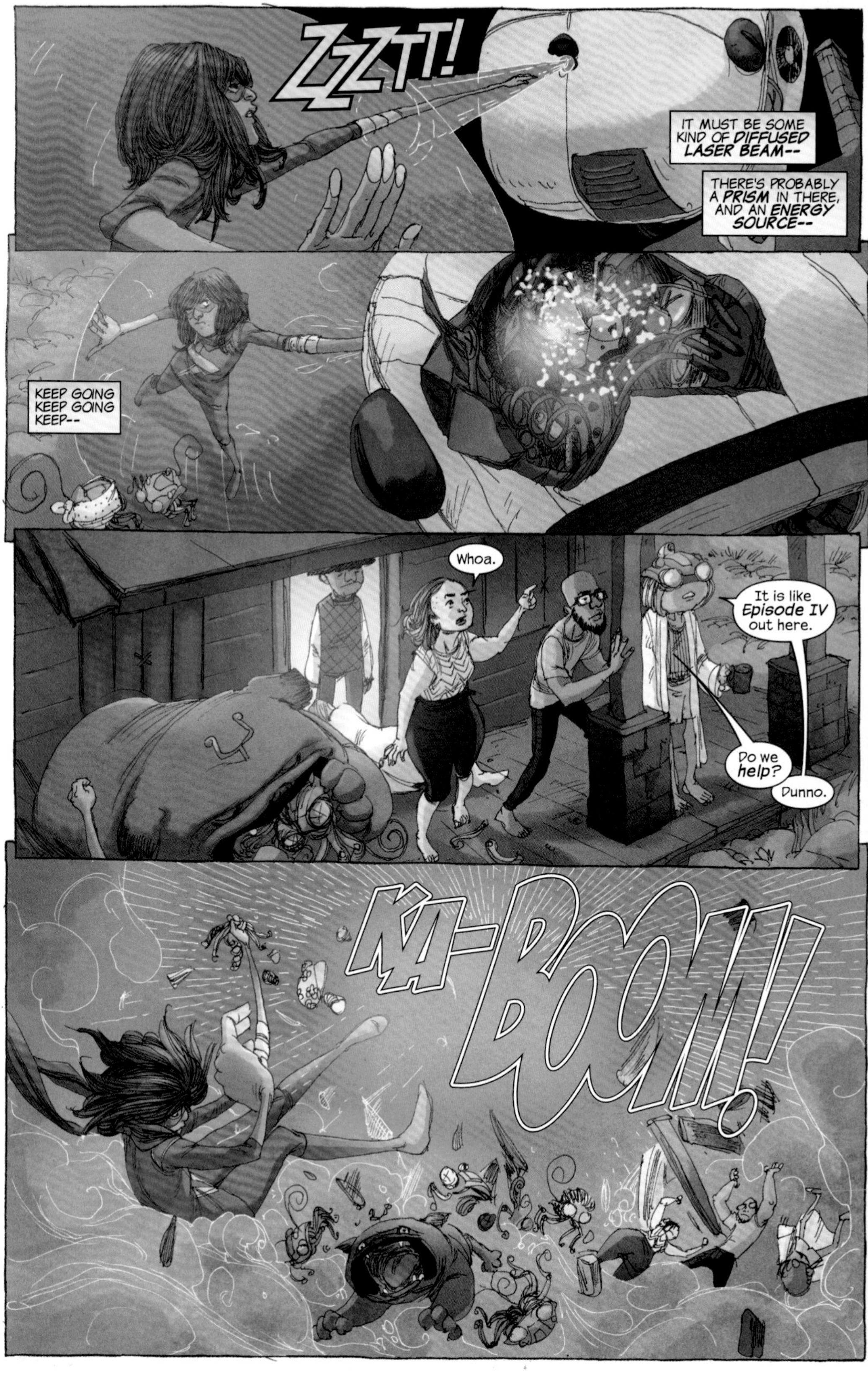
ZZZTT!
IT MUST BE SOME KIND OF DIFFUSED LASER BEAM--
THERE'S PROBABLY A PRISM IN THERE, AND AN ENERGY SOURCE--
KEEP GOING KEEP GOING KEEP--
Whoa.
It is like Episode IV out here.
Do we help?
Dunno.
KA-BOOM!

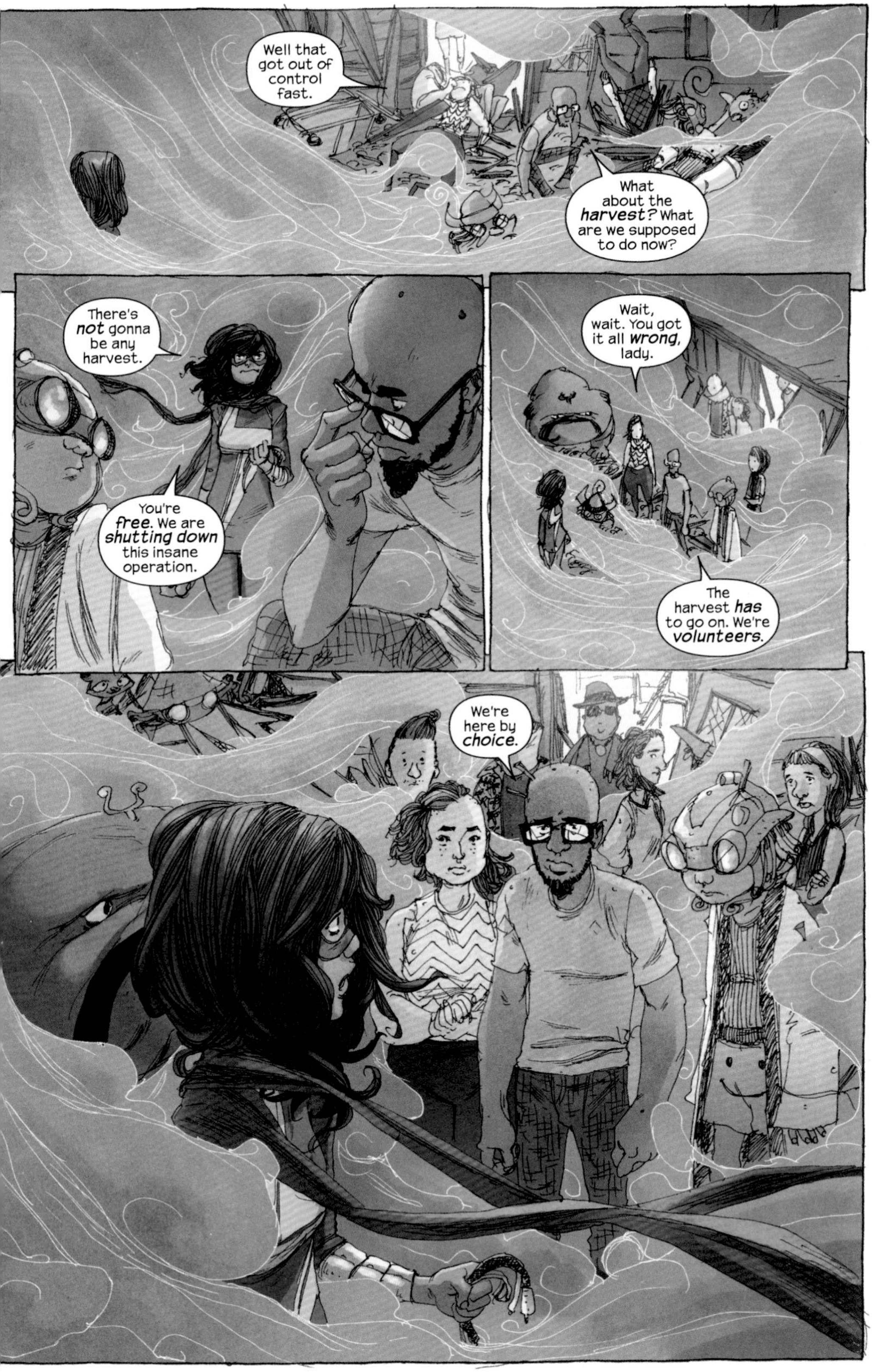
Well that got out of control fast.
What about the harvest? What are we supposed to do now?
There's not gonna be any harvest.
You're free. We are shutting down this insane operation.
Wait, wait. You got it all wrong, lady.
The harvest has to go on. We're volunteers.
We're here by choice.

AMAZING SPIDER-MAN #7

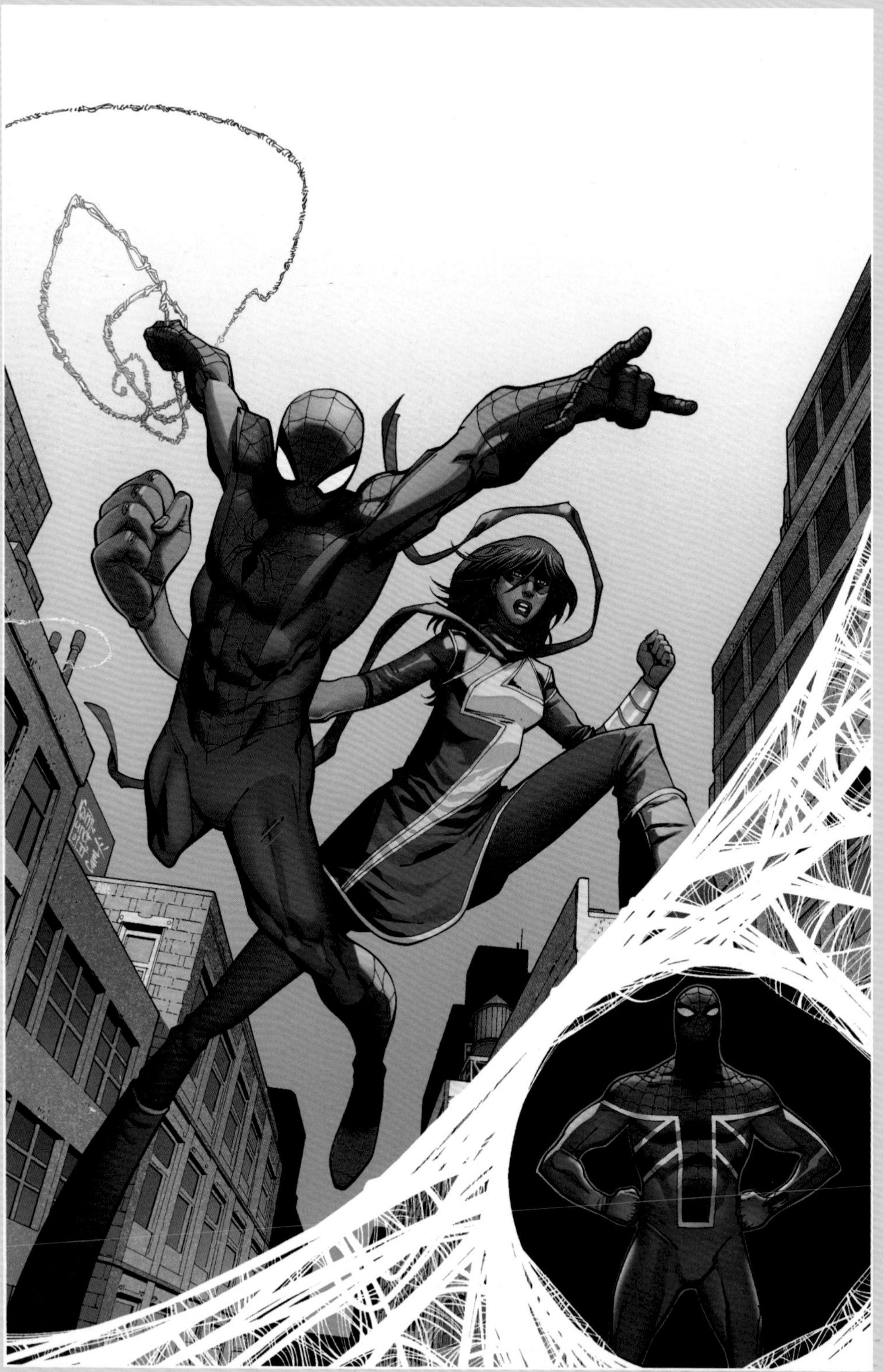

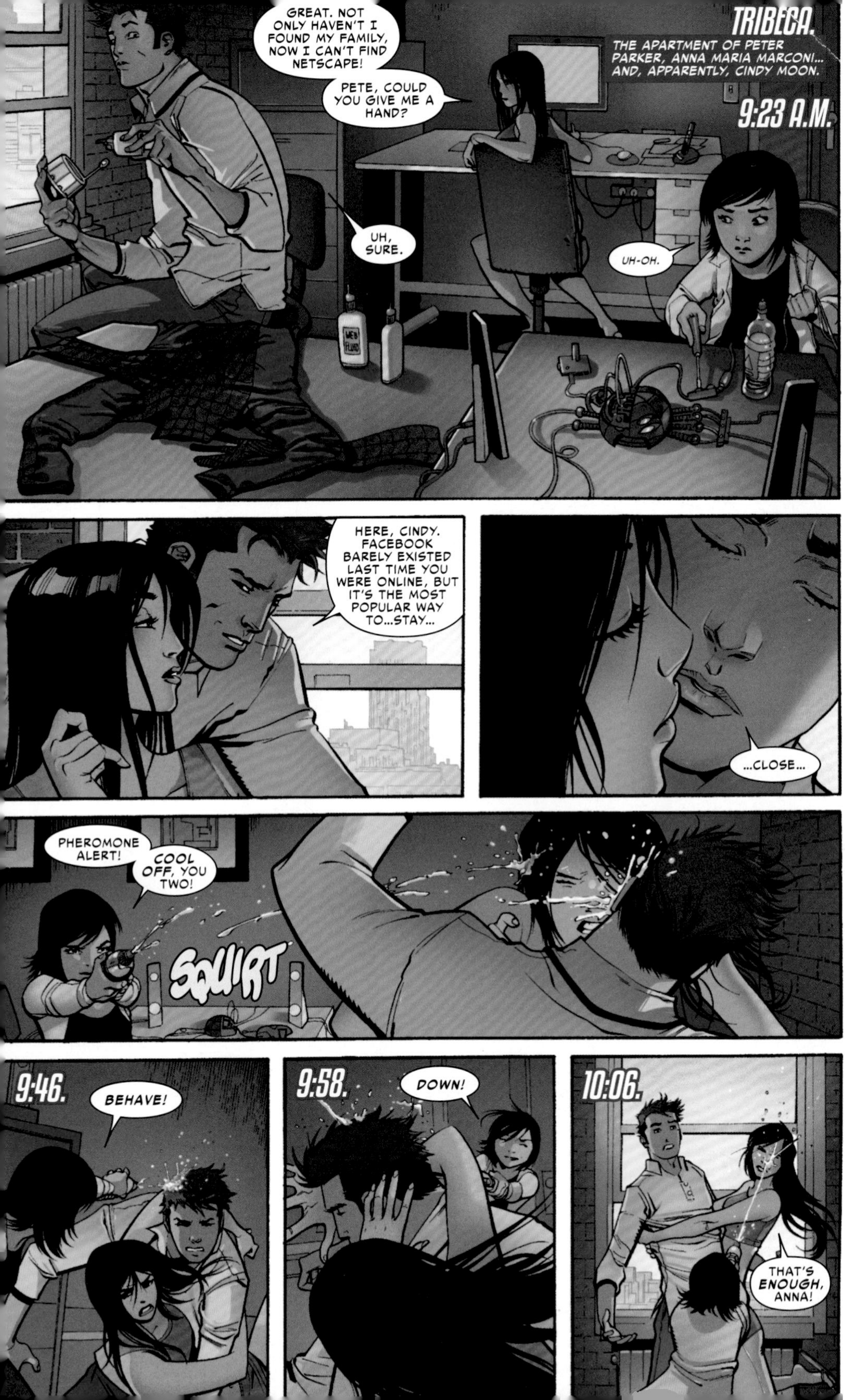
TRIBECA.
THE APARTMENT OF PETER PARKER, ANNA MARIA MARCONI... AND, APPARENTLY, CINDY MOON.
9:23 A.M.
GREAT. NOT ONLY HAVEN'T I FOUND MY FAMILY, NOW I CAN'T FIND NETSCAPE!
PETE, COULD YOU GIVE ME A HAND?
UH, SURE.
UH-OH.
WEB FLUID
HERE, CINDY. FACEBOOK BARELY EXISTED LAST TIME YOU WERE ONLINE, BUT IT'S THE MOST POPULAR WAY TO...STAY...
...CLOSE...
PHEROMONE ALERT!
COOL OFF, YOU TWO!
SQUIRT
9:46.
BEHAVE!
9:58.
DOWN!
10:06.
THAT'S ENOUGH, ANNA!

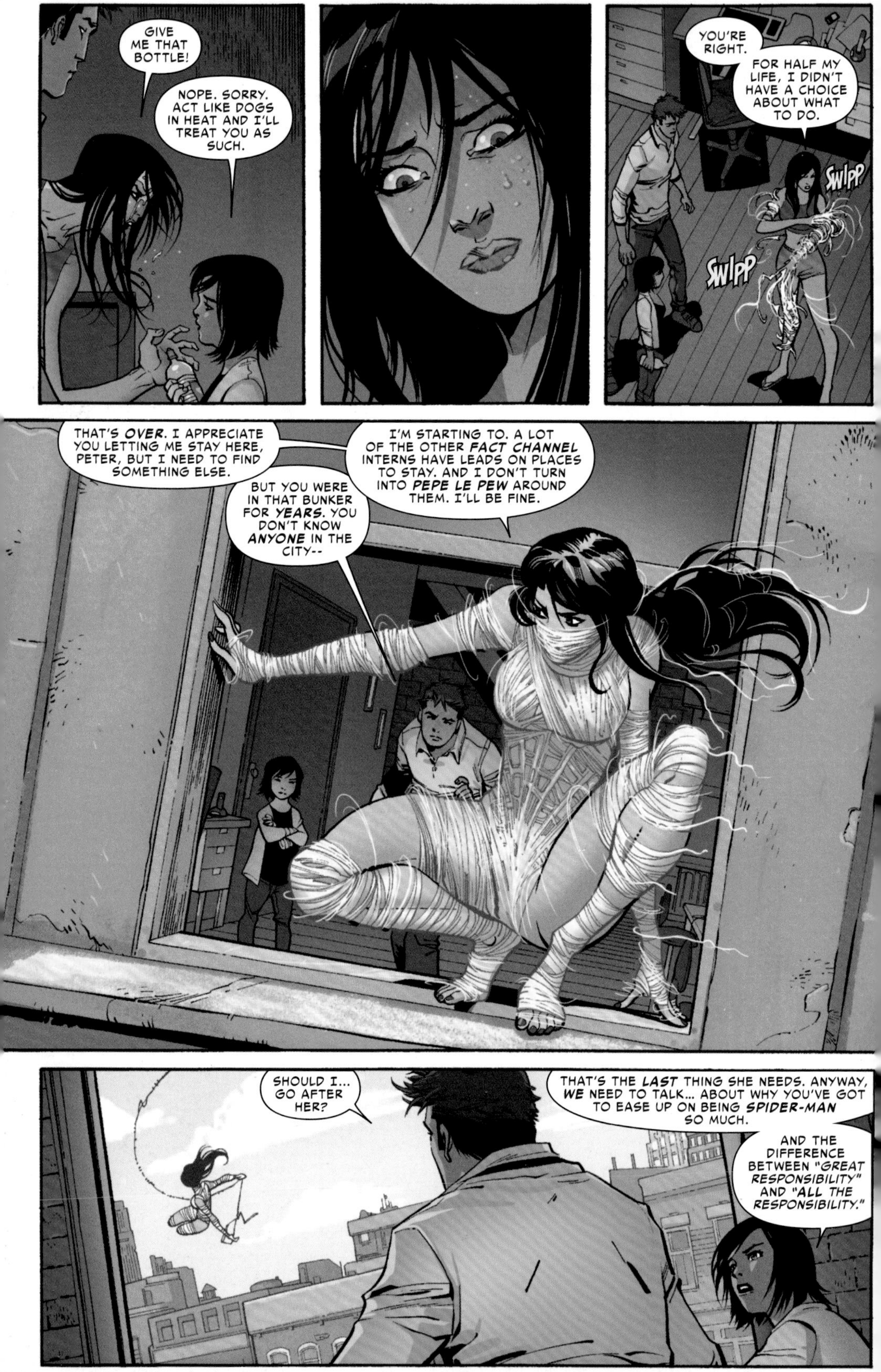

GIVE ME THAT BOTTLE!
NOPE. SORRY. ACT LIKE DOGS IN HEAT AND I'LL TREAT YOU AS SUCH.
YOU'RE RIGHT.
FOR HALF MY LIFE, I DIDN'T HAVE A CHOICE ABOUT WHAT TO DO.
SWIPP
SWIPP
THAT'S OVER. I APPRECIATE YOU LETTING ME STAY HERE, PETER, BUT I NEED TO FIND SOMETHING ELSE.
BUT YOU WERE IN THAT BUNKER FOR YEARS. YOU DON'T KNOW ANYONE IN THE CITY--
I'M STARTING TO. A LOT OF THE OTHER FACT CHANNEL INTERNS HAVE LEADS ON PLACES TO STAY. AND I DON'T TURN INTO PEPE LE PEW AROUND THEM. I'LL BE FINE.
SHOULD I... GO AFTER HER?
THAT'S THE LAST THING SHE NEEDS. ANYWAY, WE NEED TO TALK... ABOUT WHY YOU'VE GOT TO EASE UP ON BEING SPIDER-MAN SO MUCH.
AND THE DIFFERENCE BETWEEN "GREAT RESPONSIBILITY" AND "ALL THE RESPONSIBILITY."

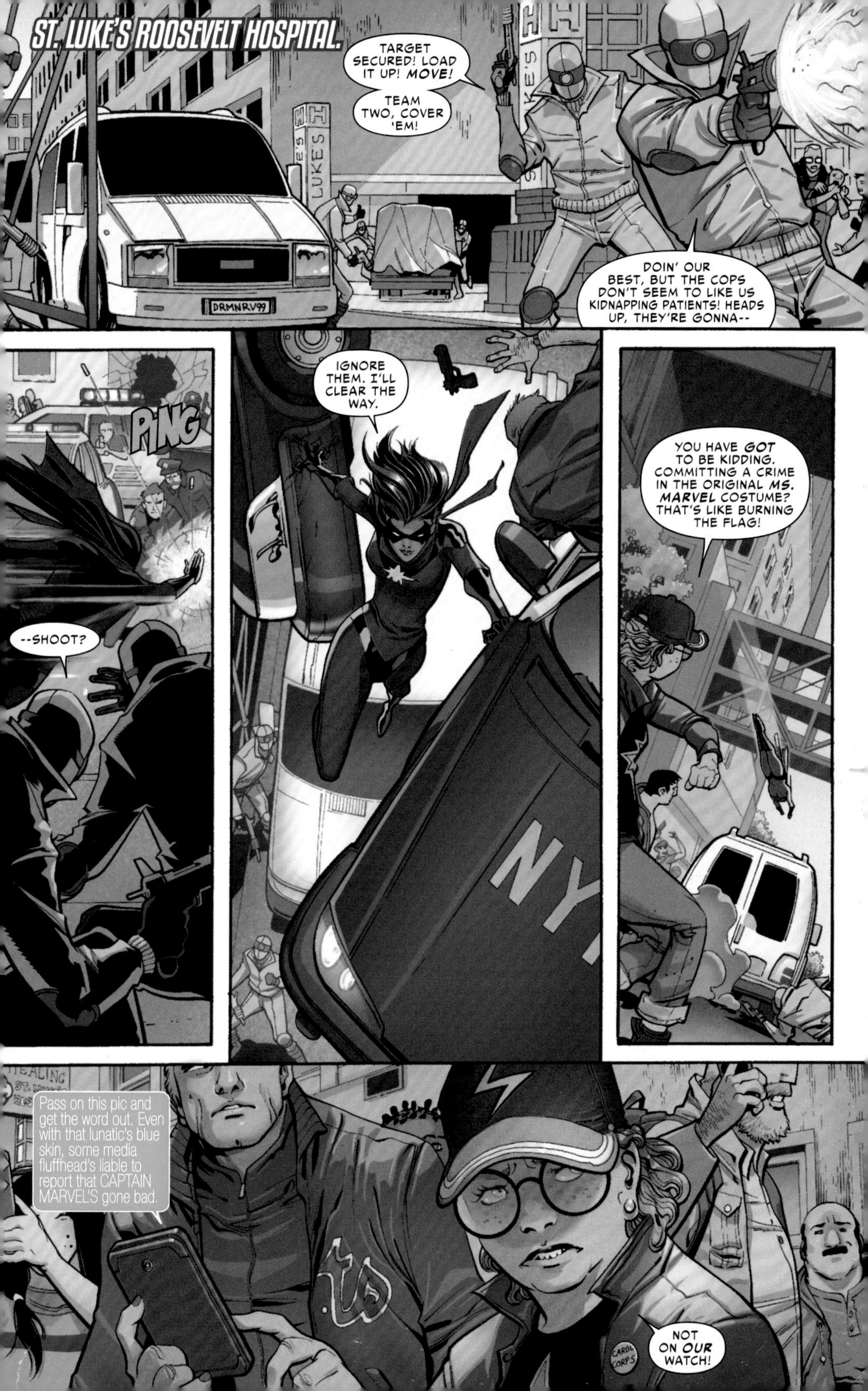
ST. LUKE'S ROOSEVELT HOSPITAL.
TARGET SECURED! LOAD IT UP! MOVE!
TEAM TWO, COVER 'EM!
DOIN' OUR BEST, BUT THE COPS DON'T SEEM TO LIKE US KIDNAPPING PATIENTS! HEADS UP, THEY'RE GONNA--
PING
--SHOOT?
IGNORE THEM. I'LL CLEAR THE WAY.
YOU HAVE GOT TO BE KIDDING. COMMITTING A CRIME IN THE ORIGINAL MS. MARVEL COSTUME? THAT'S LIKE BURNING THE FLAG!
Pass on this pic and get the word out. Even with that lunatic's blue skin, some media fluffhead's liable to report that CAPTAIN MARVEL'S gone bad.
NOT ON OUR WATCH!

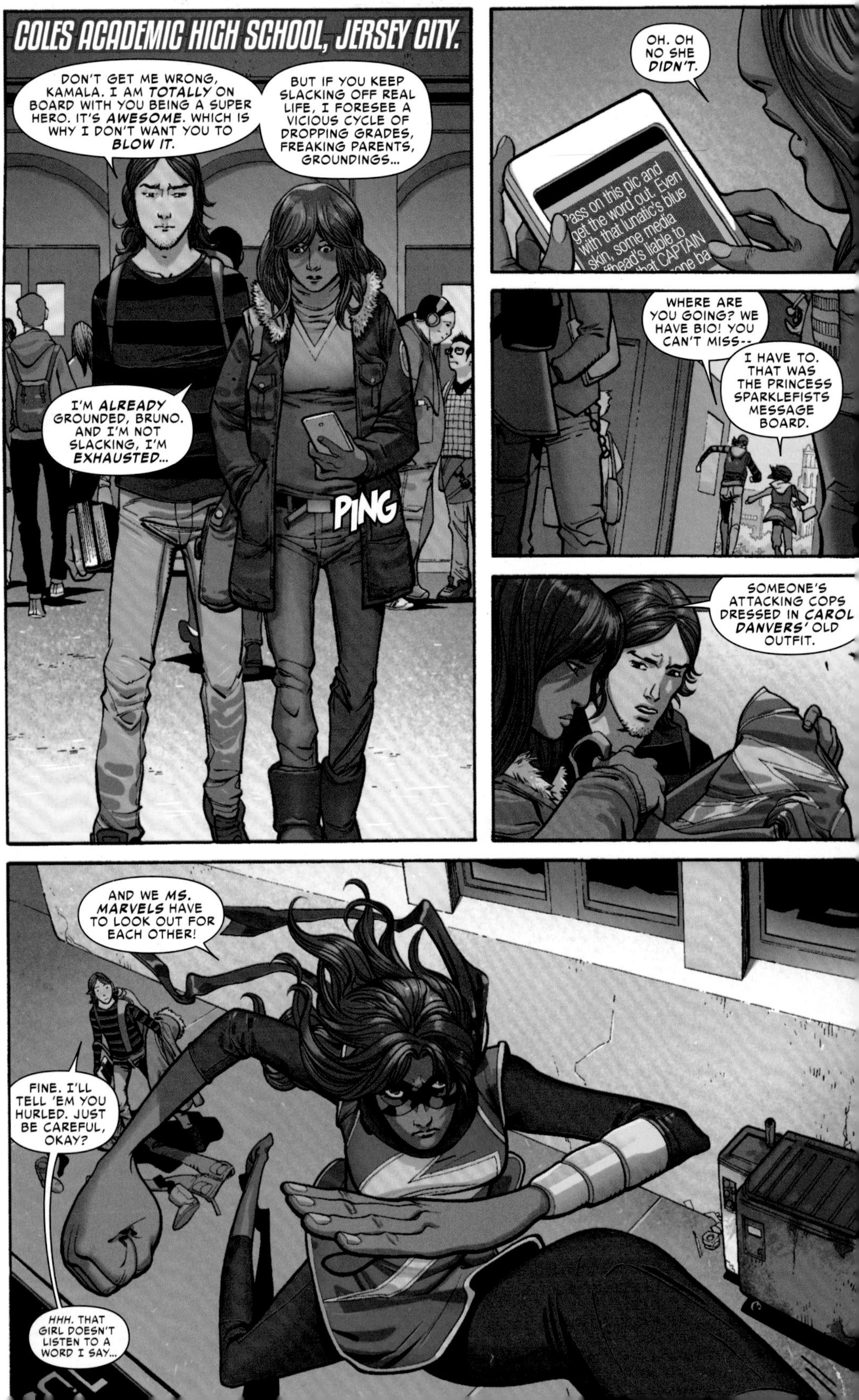
COLES ACADEMIC HIGH SCHOOL, JERSEY CITY.
DON'T GET ME WRONG, KAMALA. I AM *TOTALLY* ON BOARD WITH YOU BEING A SUPER HERO. IT'S *AWESOME*. WHICH IS WHY I DON'T WANT YOU TO *BLOW IT*.
BUT IF YOU KEEP SLACKING OFF REAL LIFE, I FORESEE A VICIOUS CYCLE OF DROPPING GRADES, FREAKING PARENTS, GROUNDINGS...
I'M *ALREADY* GROUNDED, BRUNO. AND I'M NOT SLACKING, I'M *EXHAUSTED*...
PING
OH. OH NO SHE *DIDN'T*.
Pass on this pic and get the word out. Even with that lunatic's blue skin, some media
WHERE ARE YOU GOING? WE HAVE BIO! YOU CAN'T MISS--
I HAVE TO. THAT WAS THE PRINCESS SPARKLEFISTS MESSAGE BOARD.
SOMEONE'S ATTACKING COPS DRESSED IN *CAROL DANVERS'* OLD OUTFIT.
AND WE *MS. MARVELS* HAVE TO LOOK OUT FOR EACH OTHER!
FINE. I'LL TELL 'EM YOU HURLED. JUST BE CAREFUL, OKAY?
HHH. THAT GIRL DOESN'T LISTEN TO A WORD I SAY...

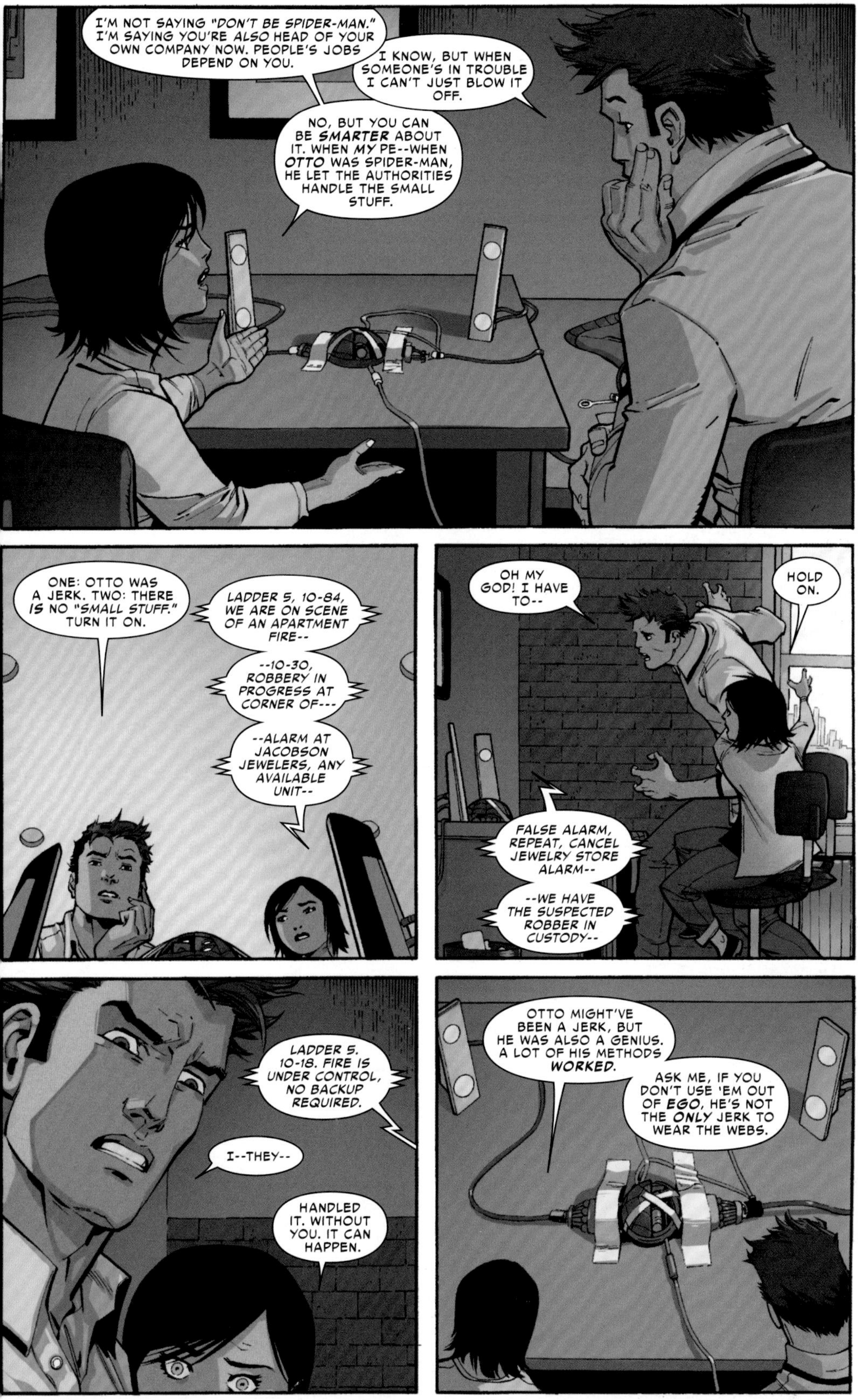

I'M NOT SAYING "DON'T BE SPIDER-MAN." I'M SAYING YOU'RE ALSO HEAD OF YOUR OWN COMPANY NOW. PEOPLE'S JOBS DEPEND ON YOU.
I KNOW, BUT WHEN SOMEONE'S IN TROUBLE I CAN'T JUST BLOW IT OFF.
NO, BUT YOU CAN BE SMARTER ABOUT IT. WHEN MY PE--WHEN OTTO WAS SPIDER-MAN, HE LET THE AUTHORITIES HANDLE THE SMALL STUFF.
ONE: OTTO WAS A JERK. TWO: THERE IS NO "SMALL STUFF." TURN IT ON.
LADDER 5, 10-84, WE ARE ON SCENE OF AN APARTMENT FIRE--
--10-30, ROBBERY IN PROGRESS AT CORNER OF---
--ALARM AT JACOBSON JEWELERS, ANY AVAILABLE UNIT--
OH MY GOD! I HAVE TO--
HOLD ON.
FALSE ALARM, REPEAT, CANCEL JEWELRY STORE ALARM--
--WE HAVE THE SUSPECTED ROBBER IN CUSTODY--
LADDER 5. 10-18. FIRE IS UNDER CONTROL, NO BACKUP REQUIRED.
I--THEY--
HANDLED IT. WITHOUT YOU. IT CAN HAPPEN.
OTTO MIGHT'VE BEEN A JERK, BUT HE WAS ALSO A GENIUS. A LOT OF HIS METHODS WORKED.
ASK ME, IF YOU DON'T USE 'EM OUT OF EGO, HE'S NOT THE ONLY JERK TO WEAR THE WEBS.

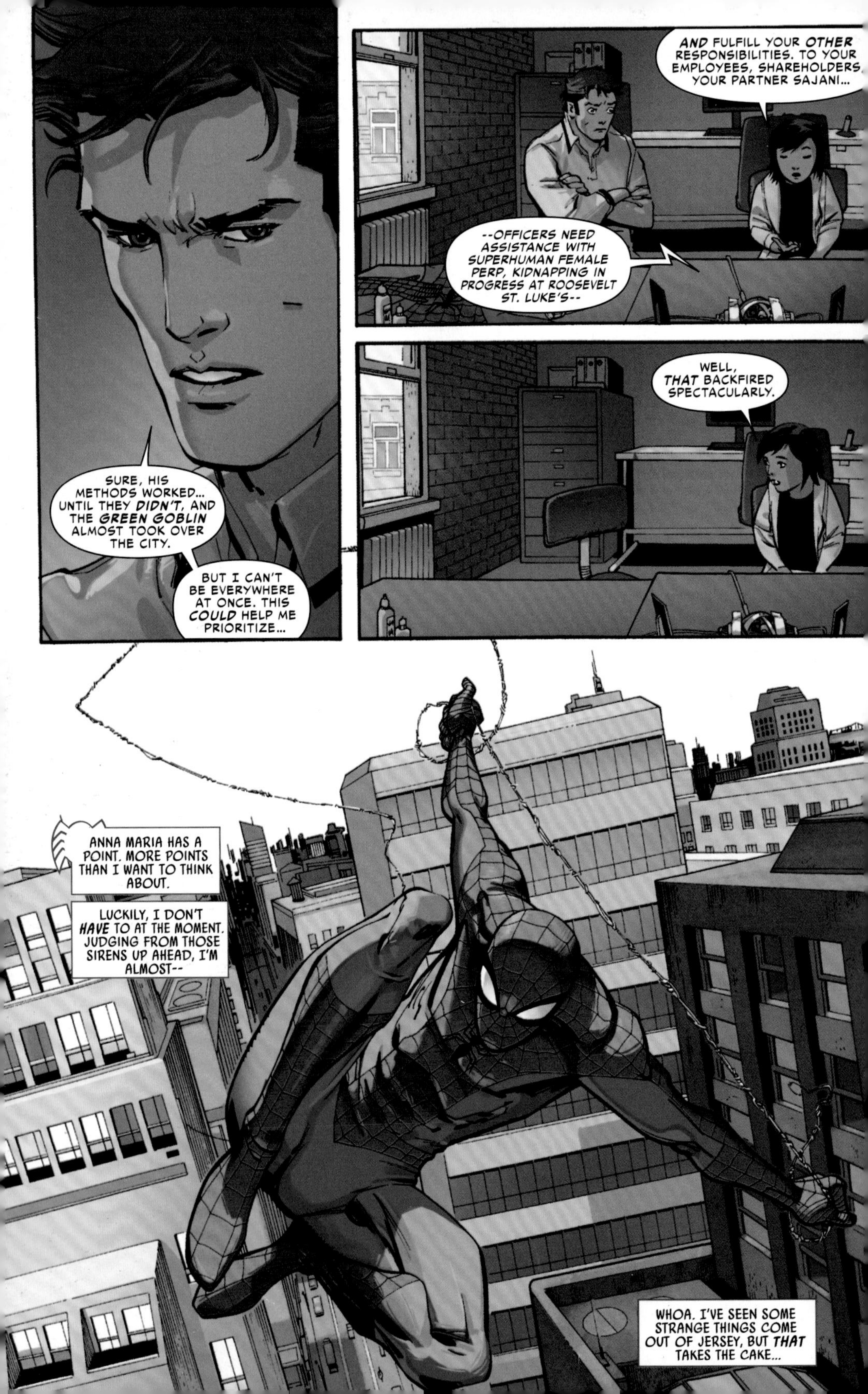
AND FULFILL YOUR OTHER RESPONSIBILITIES. TO YOUR EMPLOYEES, SHAREHOLDERS, YOUR PARTNER SAJANI...
--OFFICERS NEED ASSISTANCE WITH SUPERHUMAN FEMALE PERP, KIDNAPPING IN PROGRESS AT ROOSEVELT ST. LUKE'S--
SURE, HIS METHODS WORKED... UNTIL THEY DIDN'T, AND THE GREEN GOBLIN ALMOST TOOK OVER THE CITY.
BUT I CAN'T BE EVERYWHERE AT ONCE. THIS COULD HELP ME PRIORITIZE...
WELL, THAT BACKFIRED SPECTACULARLY.
ANNA MARIA HAS A POINT. MORE POINTS THAN I WANT TO THINK ABOUT.
LUCKILY, I DON'T HAVE TO AT THE MOMENT. JUDGING FROM THOSE SIRENS UP AHEAD, I'M ALMOST--
WHOA. I'VE SEEN SOME STRANGE THINGS COME OUT OF JERSEY, BUT THAT TAKES THE CAKE...

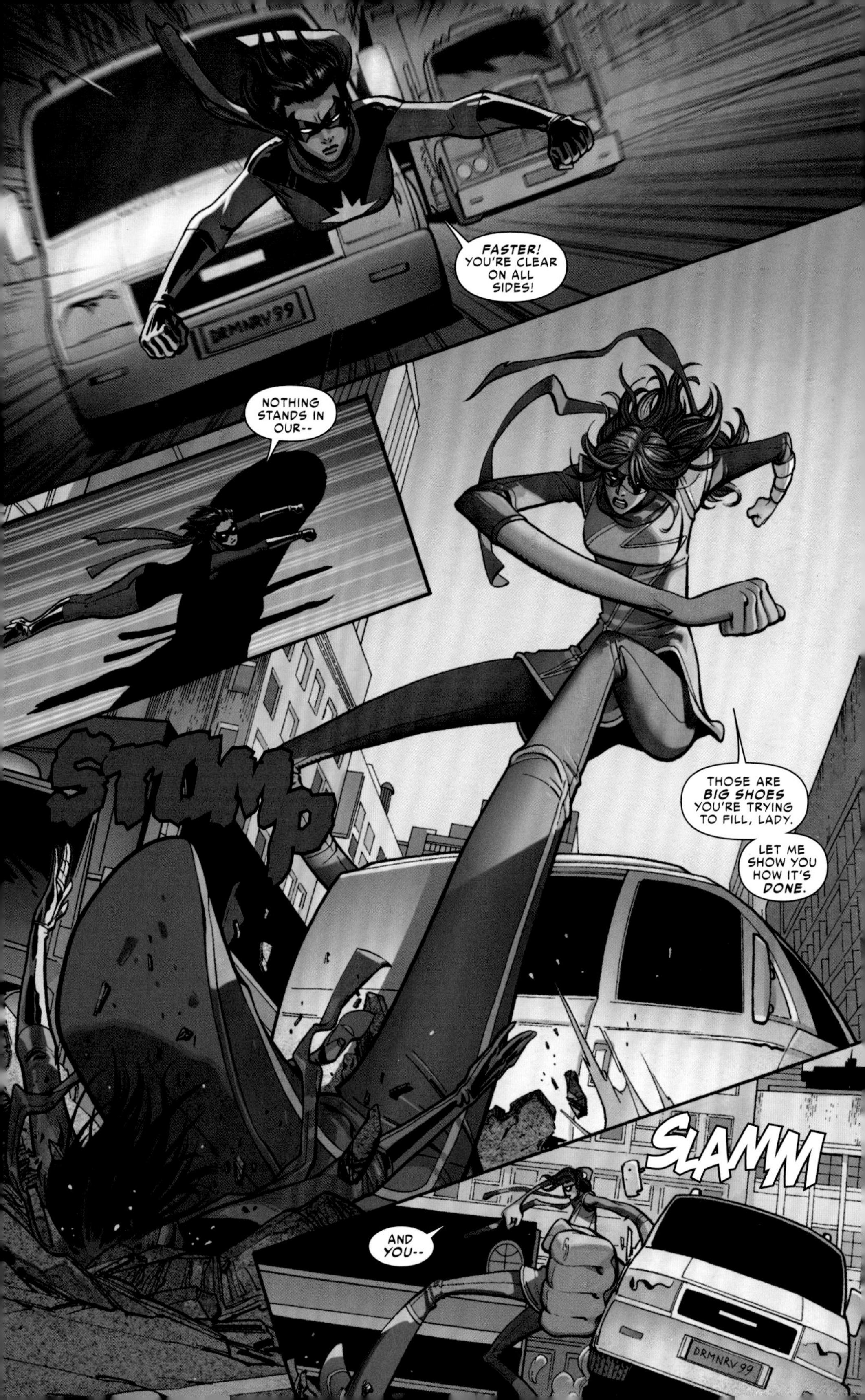
FASTER! YOU'RE CLEAR ON ALL SIDES!
DRMNRV 99
NOTHING STANDS IN OUR--
STOMP
THOSE ARE BIG SHOES YOU'RE TRYING TO FILL, LADY.
LET ME SHOW YOU HOW IT'S DONE.
SLAMM
AND YOU--
DRMNRV 99

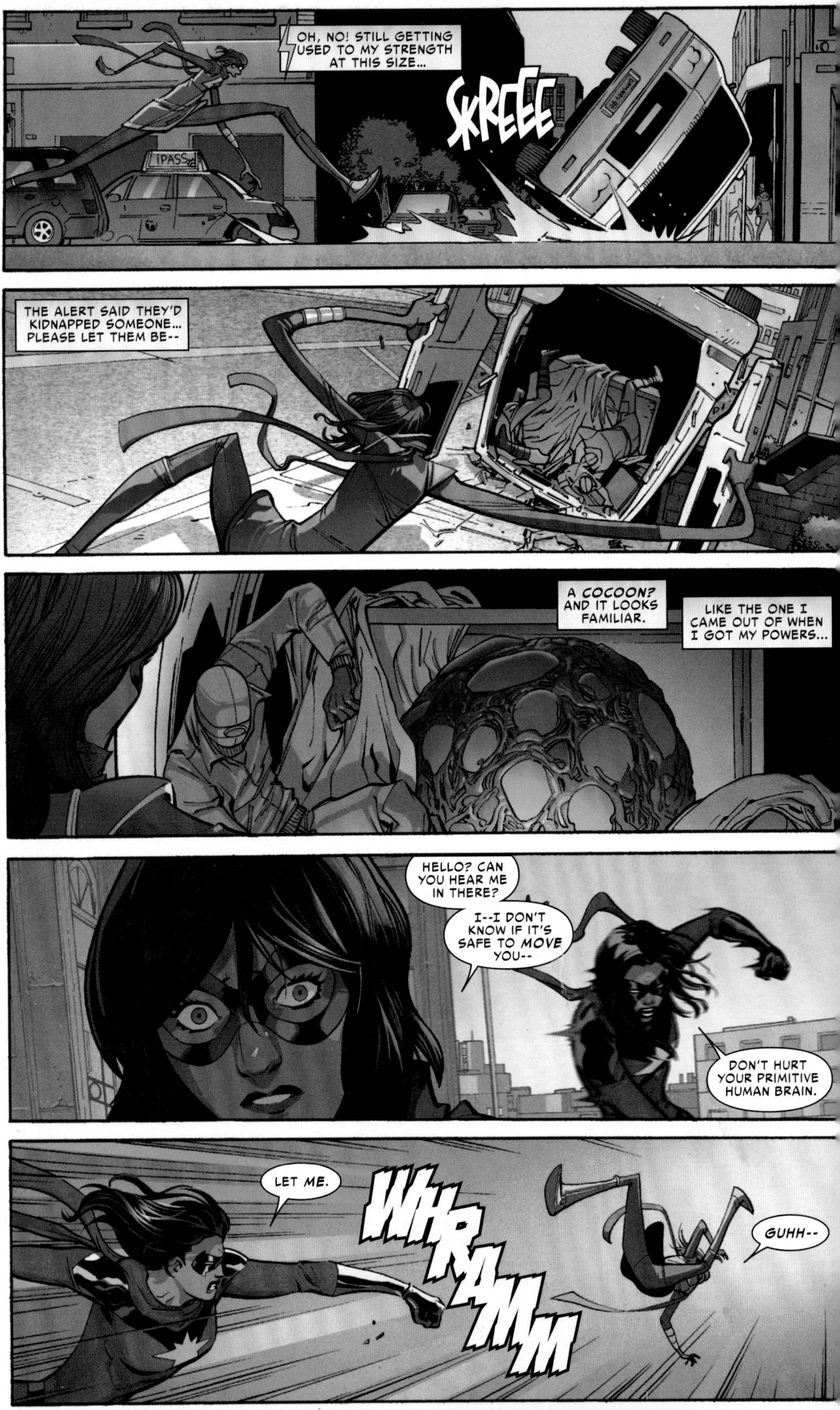
OH, NO! STILL GETTING USED TO MY STRENGTH AT THIS SIZE...
SKREEEE
THE ALERT SAID THEY'D KIDNAPPED SOMEONE... PLEASE LET THEM BE--
A COCOON? AND IT LOOKS FAMILIAR.
LIKE THE ONE I CAME OUT OF WHEN I GOT MY POWERS...
HELLO? CAN YOU HEAR ME IN THERE?
I--I DON'T KNOW IF IT'S SAFE TO MOVE YOU--
DON'T HURT YOUR PRIMITIVE HUMAN BRAIN.
LET ME.
WHRAMM
GUHH--

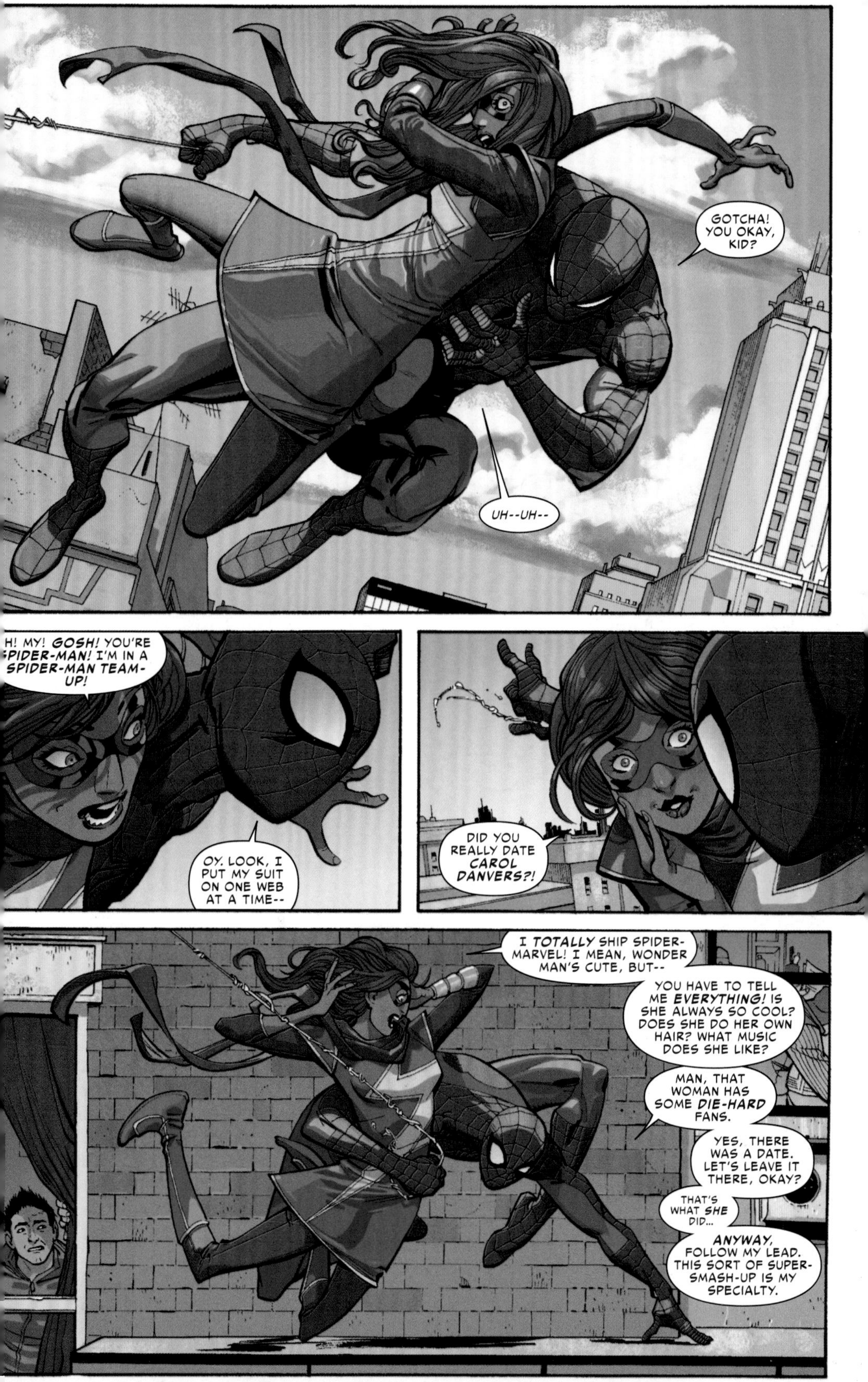
GOTCHA! YOU OKAY, KID?
UH--UH--
H! MY! GOSH! YOU'RE SPIDER-MAN! I'M IN A SPIDER-MAN TEAM-UP!
OY. LOOK, I PUT MY SUIT ON ONE WEB AT A TIME--
DID YOU REALLY DATE CAROL DANVERS?!
I TOTALLY SHIP SPIDER-MARVEL! I MEAN, WONDER MAN'S CUTE, BUT--
YOU HAVE TO TELL ME EVERYTHING! IS SHE ALWAYS SO COOL? DOES SHE DO HER OWN HAIR? WHAT MUSIC DOES SHE LIKE?
MAN, THAT WOMAN HAS SOME DIE-HARD FANS.
YES, THERE WAS A DATE. LET'S LEAVE IT THERE, OKAY?
THAT'S WHAT SHE DID...
ANYWAY, FOLLOW MY LEAD. THIS SORT OF SUPER-SMASH-UP IS MY SPECIALTY.

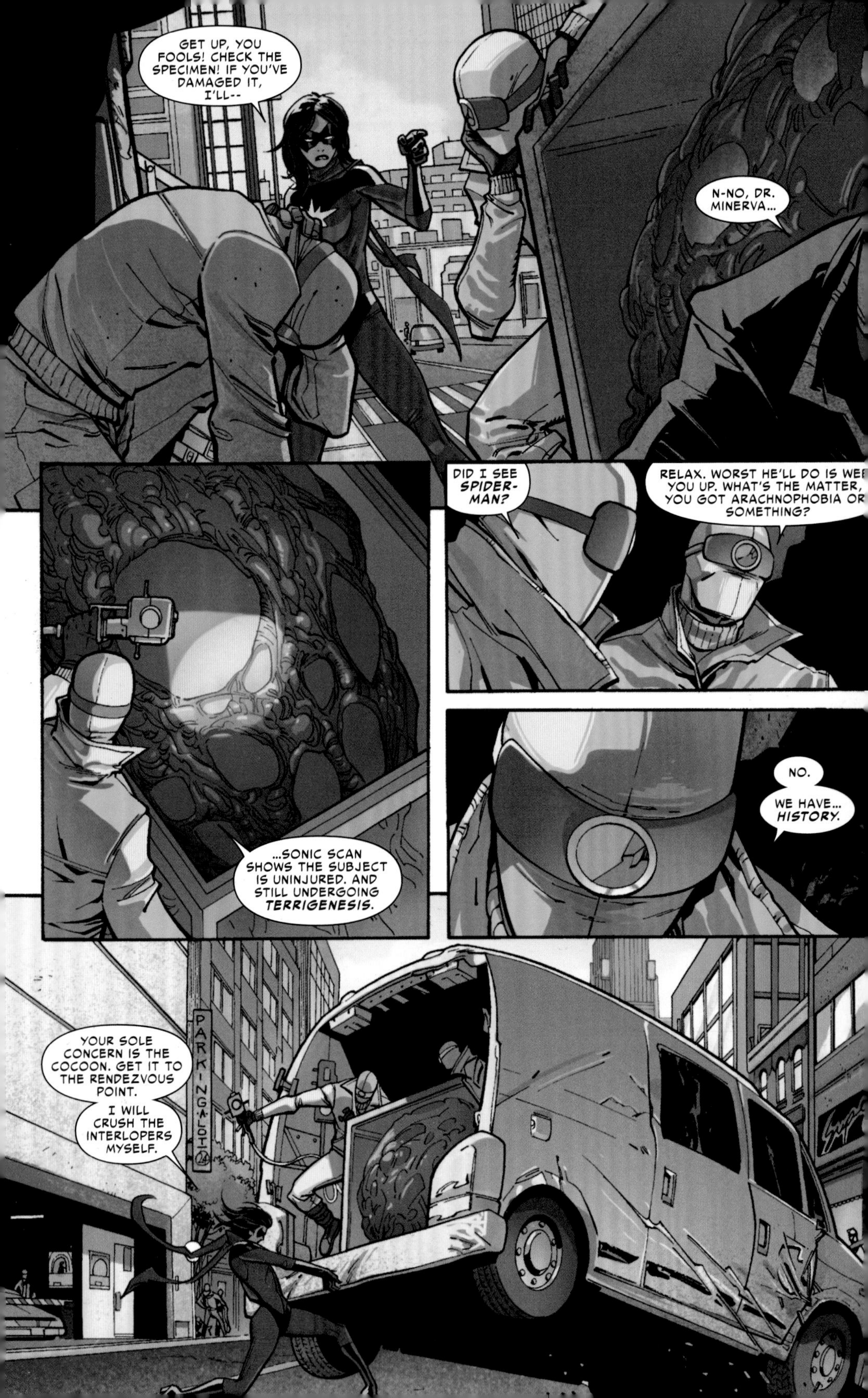
GET UP, YOU FOOLS! CHECK THE SPECIMEN! IF YOU'VE DAMAGED IT, I'LL--
N-NO, DR. MINERVA...
...SONIC SCAN SHOWS THE SUBJECT IS UNINJURED. AND STILL UNDERGOING TERRIGENESIS.
DID I SEE SPIDER-MAN?
RELAX. WORST HE'LL DO IS WEB YOU UP. WHAT'S THE MATTER, YOU GOT ARACHNOPHOBIA OR SOMETHING?
NO.
WE HAVE... HISTORY.
PARKING LOT
YOUR SOLE CONCERN IS THE COCOON. GET IT TO THE RENDEZVOUS POINT.
I WILL CRUSH THE INTERLOPERS MYSELF.

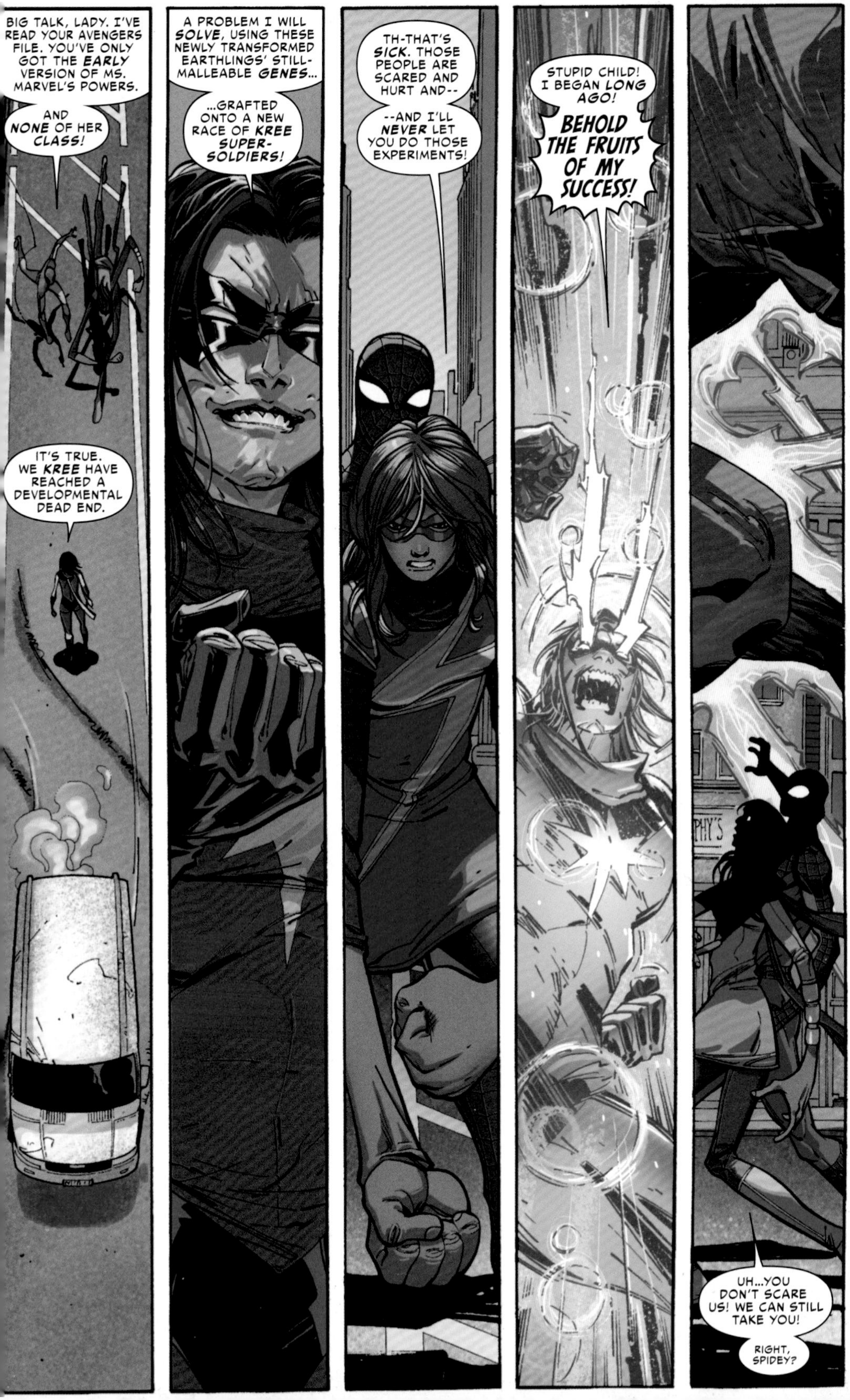
BIG TALK, LADY. I'VE READ YOUR AVENGERS FILE. YOU'VE ONLY GOT THE EARLY VERSION OF MS. MARVEL'S POWERS.
AND NONE OF HER CLASS!
IT'S TRUE. WE KREE HAVE REACHED A DEVELOPMENTAL DEAD END.
A PROBLEM I WILL SOLVE, USING THESE NEWLY TRANSFORMED EARTHLINGS' STILL-MALLEABLE GENES...
...GRAFTED ONTO A NEW RACE OF KREE SUPER-SOLDIERS!
TH-THAT'S SICK. THOSE PEOPLE ARE SCARED AND HURT AND--
--AND I'LL NEVER LET YOU DO THOSE EXPERIMENTS!
STUPID CHILD! I BEGAN LONG AGO!
BEHOLD THE FRUITS OF MY SUCCESS!
UH...YOU DON'T SCARE US! WE CAN STILL TAKE YOU!
RIGHT, SPIDEY?

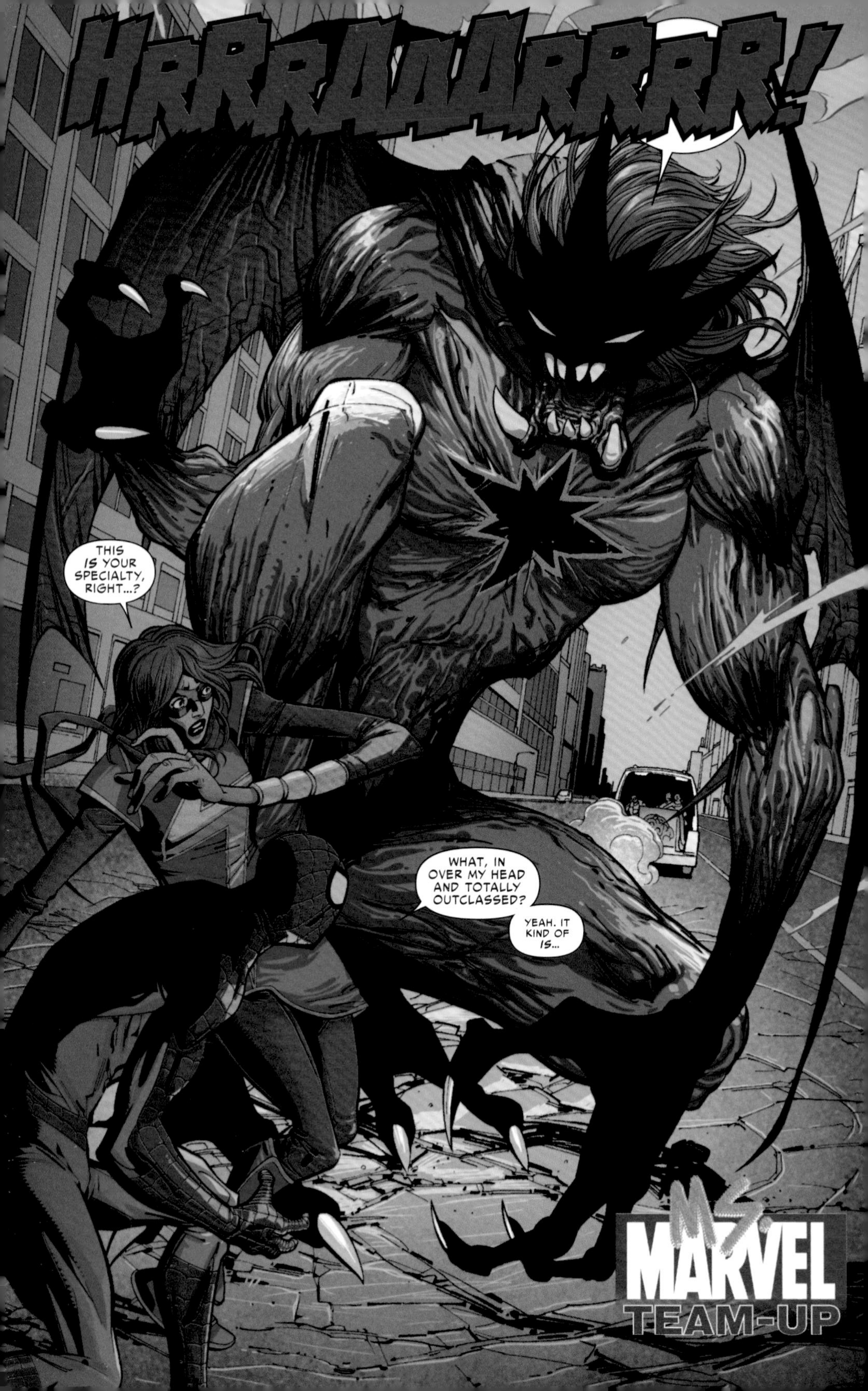
HRRRAWRRRR!
THIS IS YOUR SPECIALTY, RIGHT...?
WHAT, IN OVER MY HEAD AND TOTALLY OUTCLASSED?
YEAH. IT KIND OF IS...
MS. MARVEL TEAM-UP

AMAZING SPIDER-MAN #8

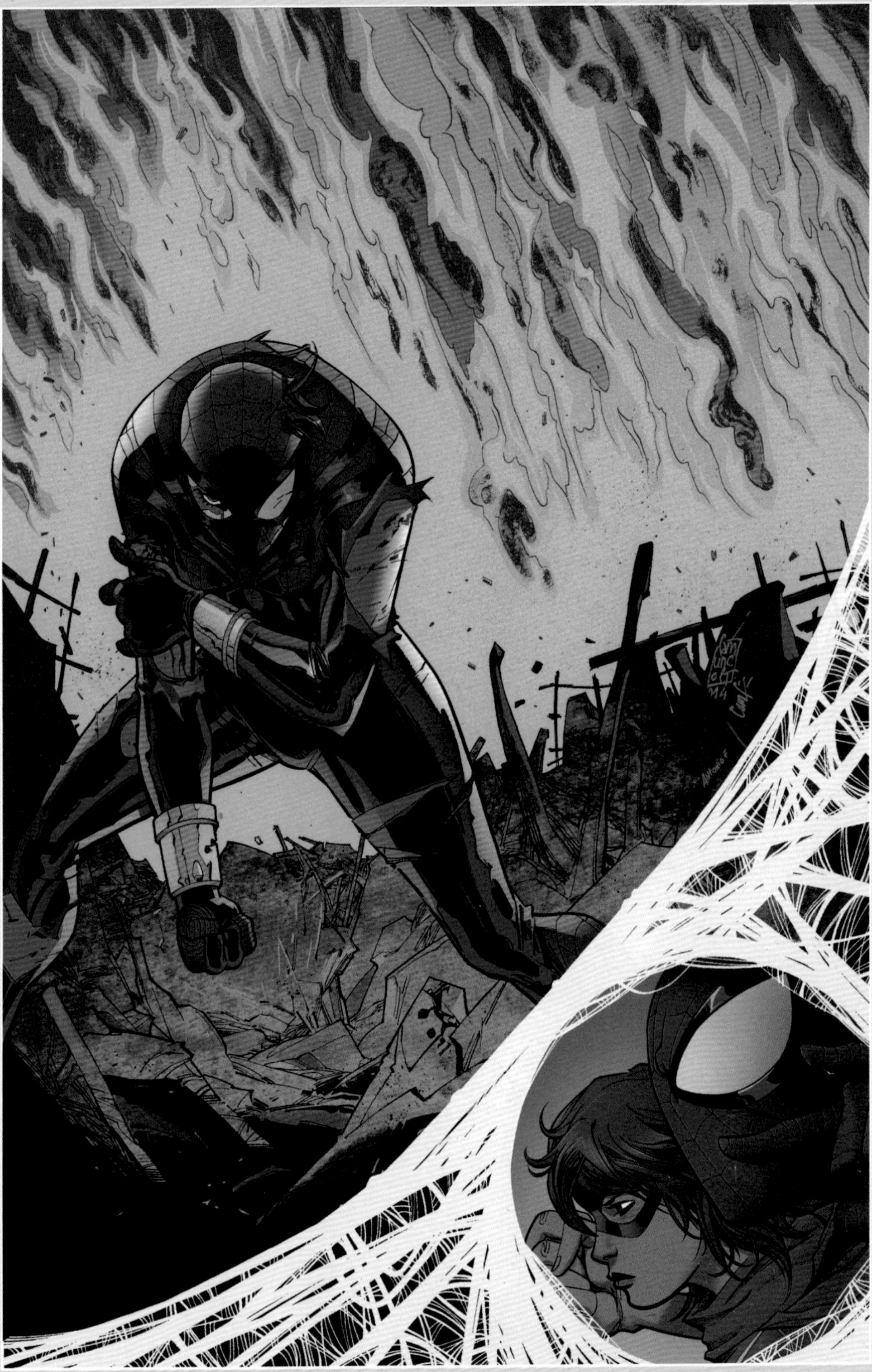

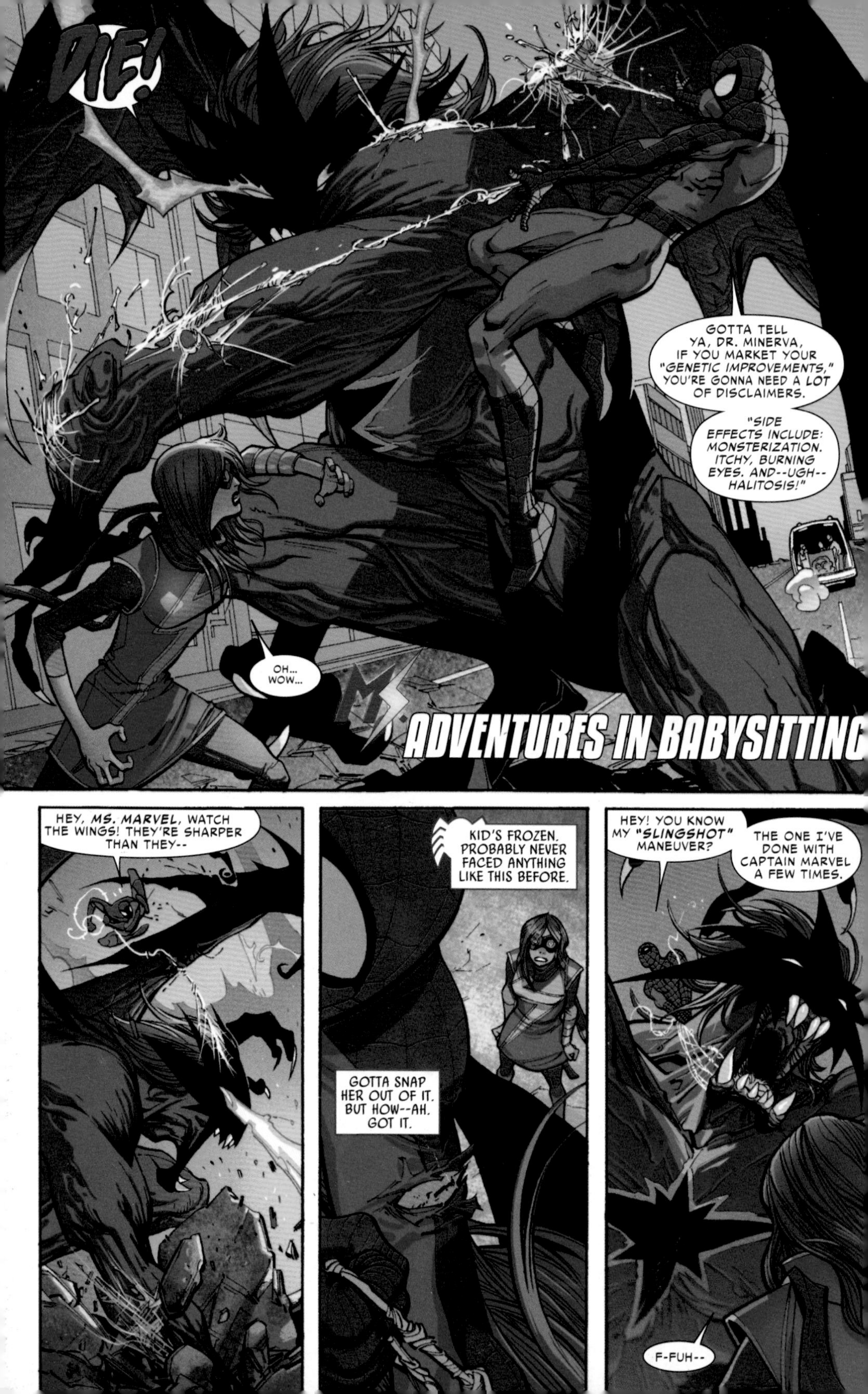
DIE!
GOTTA TELL YA, DR. MINERVA, IF YOU MARKET YOUR "GENETIC IMPROVEMENTS," YOU'RE GONNA NEED A LOT OF DISCLAIMERS.
"SIDE EFFECTS INCLUDE: MONSTERIZATION. ITCHY, BURNING EYES. AND--UGH--HALITOSIS!"
OH... WOW...
MS. ADVENTURES IN BABYSITTING
HEY, MS. MARVEL, WATCH THE WINGS! THEY'RE SHARPER THAN THEY--
KID'S FROZEN. PROBABLY NEVER FACED ANYTHING LIKE THIS BEFORE.
GOTTA SNAP HER OUT OF IT. BUT HOW--AH. GOT IT.
HEY! YOU KNOW MY "SLINGSHOT" MANEUVER?
THE ONE I'VE DONE WITH CAPTAIN MARVEL A FEW TIMES.
F-FUH--

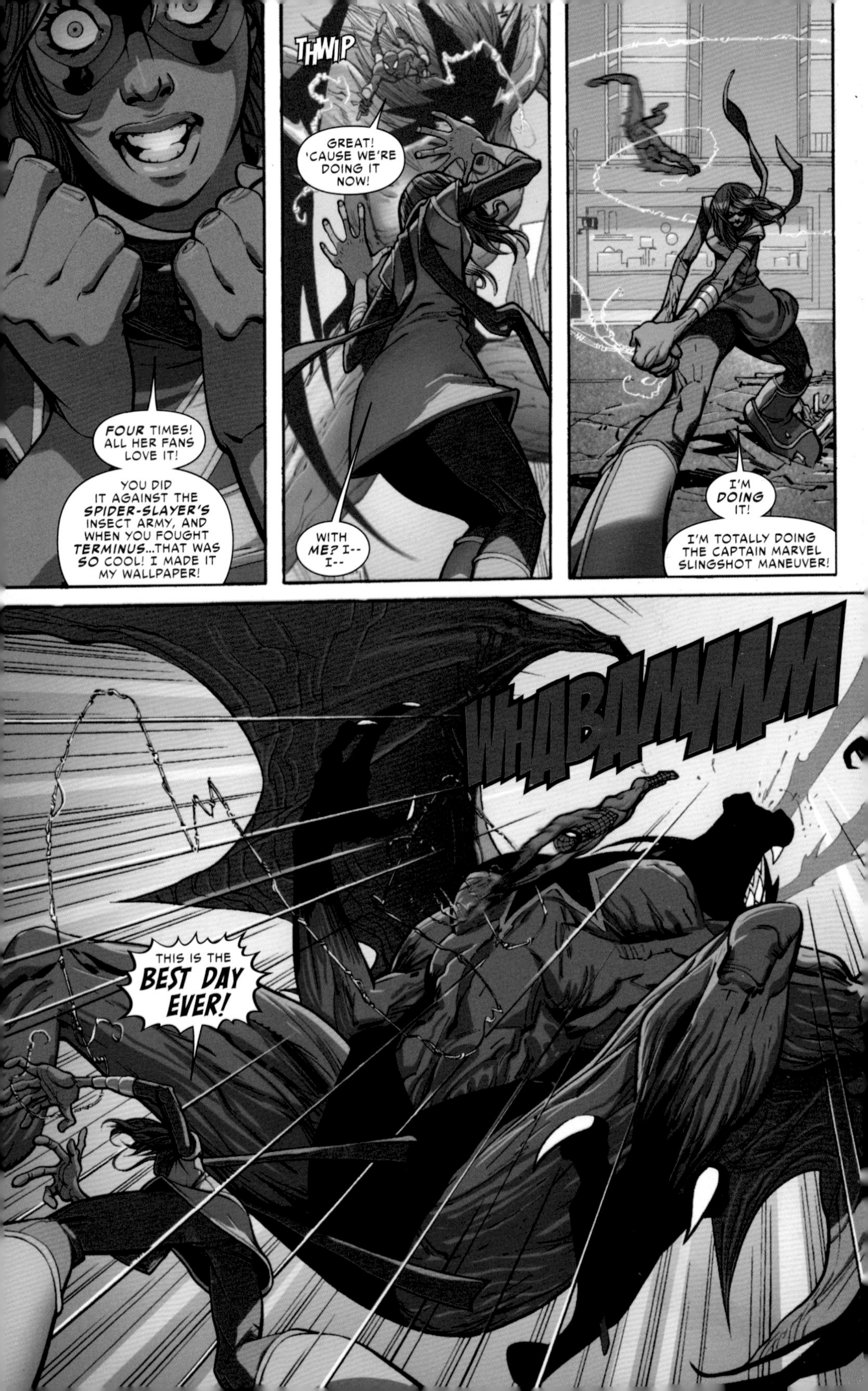
FOUR TIMES! ALL HER FANS LOVE IT!
YOU DID IT AGAINST THE SPIDER-SLAYER'S INSECT ARMY, AND WHEN YOU FOUGHT TERMINUS...THAT WAS SO COOL! I MADE IT MY WALLPAPER!
THWIP
GREAT! 'CAUSE WE'RE DOING IT NOW!
WITH ME? I-- I--
I'M DOING IT!
I'M TOTALLY DOING THE CAPTAIN MARVEL SLINGSHOT MANEUVER!
WHABAMMMM
THIS IS THE BEST DAY EVER!

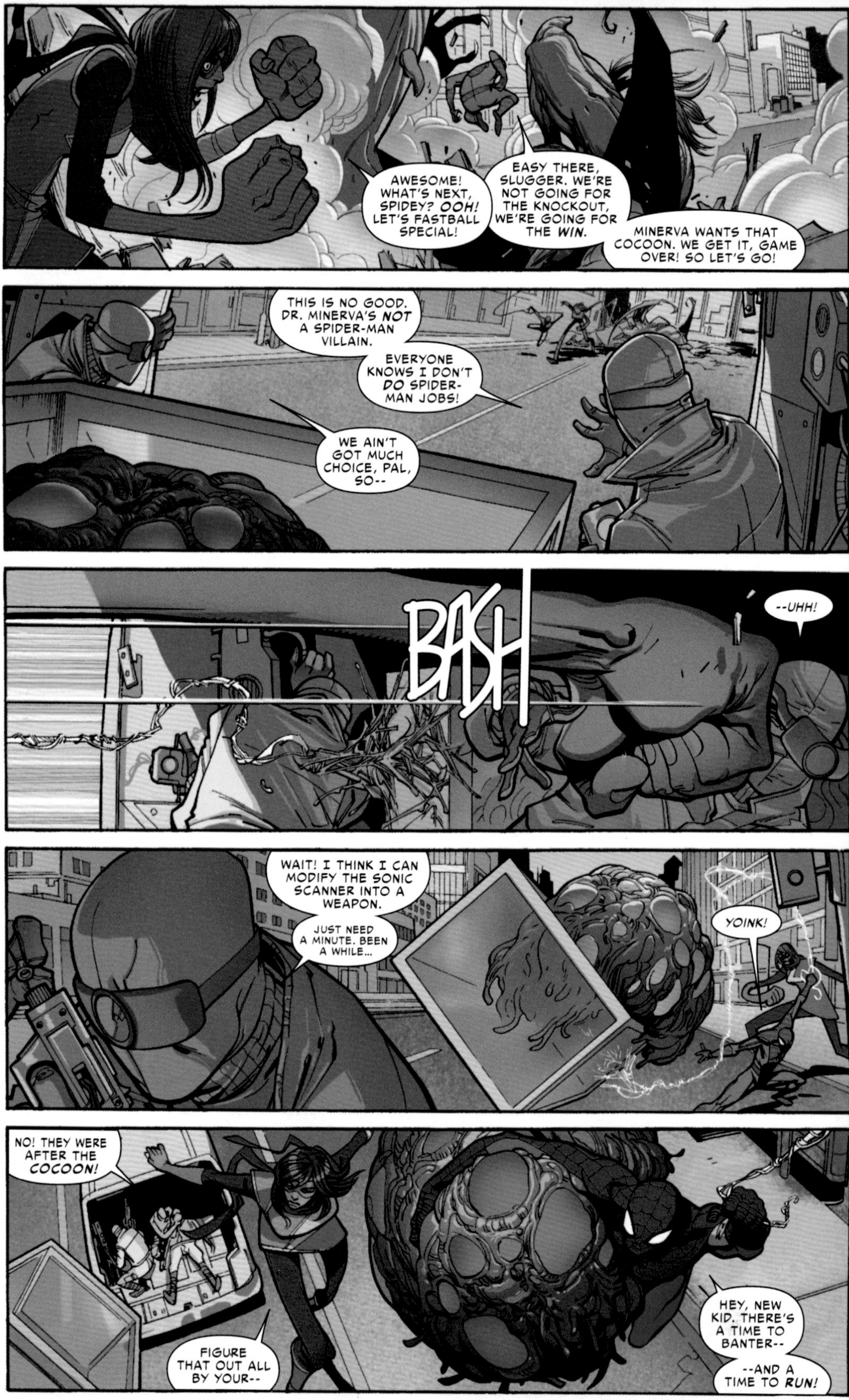

AWESOME! WHAT'S NEXT, SPIDEY? OOH! LET'S FASTBALL SPECIAL!
EASY THERE, SLUGGER. WE'RE NOT GOING FOR THE KNOCKOUT, WE'RE GOING FOR THE WIN.
MINERVA WANTS THAT COCOON. WE GET IT, GAME OVER! SO LET'S GO!
THIS IS NO GOOD. DR. MINERVA'S NOT A SPIDER-MAN VILLAIN.
EVERYONE KNOWS I DON'T DO SPIDER-MAN JOBS!
WE AIN'T GOT MUCH CHOICE, PAL, SO--
BASH
--UHH!
WAIT! I THINK I CAN MODIFY THE SONIC SCANNER INTO A WEAPON.
JUST NEED A MINUTE. BEEN A WHILE...
YOINK!
NO! THEY WERE AFTER THE COCOON!
FIGURE THAT OUT ALL BY YOUR--
HEY, NEW KID. THERE'S A TIME TO BANTER--
--AND A TIME TO RUN!

GIVE IT BACK!

BOGEY ON OUR TAIL. YOU GOT SUPER STRENGTH? CAN YOU CARRY THE COCOON WHILE I COVER YOU?

I--I...

LIKE *THIS*, I CAN--

PROVIDE A *LARGER* TARGET!

WHRAK

GAHH!

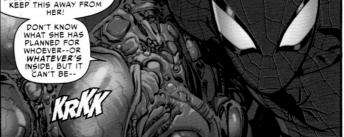

SHE'S RIGHT! WE NEED SPEED, NOT SIZE! GOTTA KEEP THIS AWAY FROM HER!

DON'T KNOW WHAT SHE HAS PLANNED FOR WHOEVER--OR *WHATEVER'S* INSIDE, BUT IT CAN'T BE--

KRKK

--IT'S HATCHING!

KRIK

SPROK

WOW! THIS IS CRAZY...

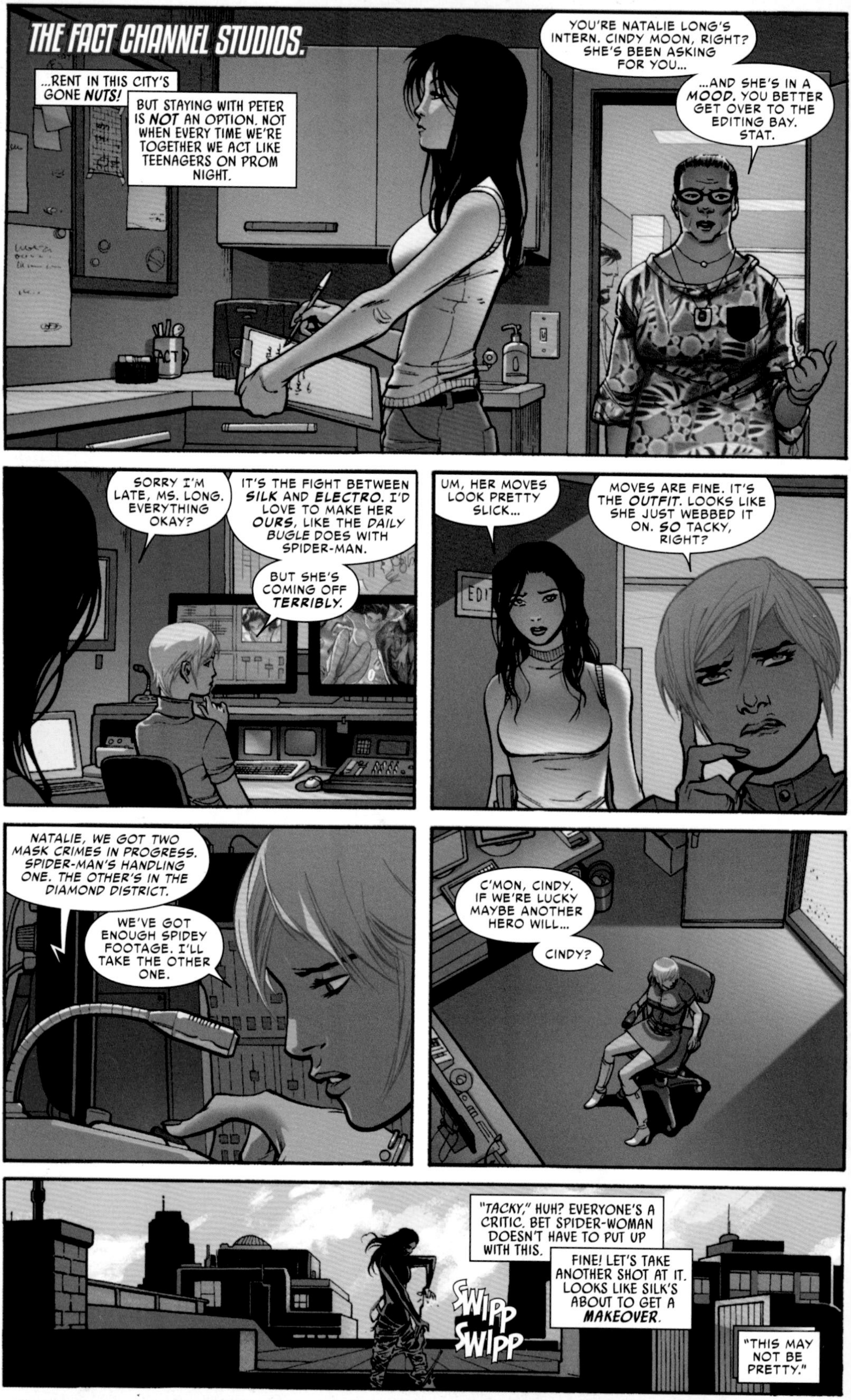
THE FACT CHANNEL STUDIOS.
...RENT IN THIS CITY'S GONE NUTS!
BUT STAYING WITH PETER IS NOT AN OPTION. NOT WHEN EVERY TIME WE'RE TOGETHER WE ACT LIKE TEENAGERS ON PROM NIGHT.
YOU'RE NATALIE LONG'S INTERN. CINDY MOON, RIGHT? SHE'S BEEN ASKING FOR YOU...
...AND SHE'S IN A MOOD. YOU BETTER GET OVER TO THE EDITING BAY. STAT.
SORRY I'M LATE, MS. LONG. EVERYTHING OKAY?
IT'S THE FIGHT BETWEEN SILK AND ELECTRO. I'D LOVE TO MAKE HER OURS, LIKE THE DAILY BUGLE DOES WITH SPIDER-MAN.
BUT SHE'S COMING OFF TERRIBLY.
UM, HER MOVES LOOK PRETTY SLICK...
MOVES ARE FINE. IT'S THE OUTFIT. LOOKS LIKE SHE JUST WEBBED IT ON. SO TACKY, RIGHT?
NATALIE, WE GOT TWO MASK CRIMES IN PROGRESS. SPIDER-MAN'S HANDLING ONE. THE OTHER'S IN THE DIAMOND DISTRICT.
WE'VE GOT ENOUGH SPIDEY FOOTAGE. I'LL TAKE THE OTHER ONE.
C'MON, CINDY. IF WE'RE LUCKY MAYBE ANOTHER HERO WILL...
CINDY?
"TACKY," HUH? EVERYONE'S A CRITIC. BET SPIDER-WOMAN DOESN'T HAVE TO PUT UP WITH THIS.
SWIPP SWIPP
FINE! LET'S TAKE ANOTHER SHOT AT IT. LOOKS LIKE SILK'S ABOUT TO GET A MAKEOVER.
"THIS MAY NOT BE PRETTY."

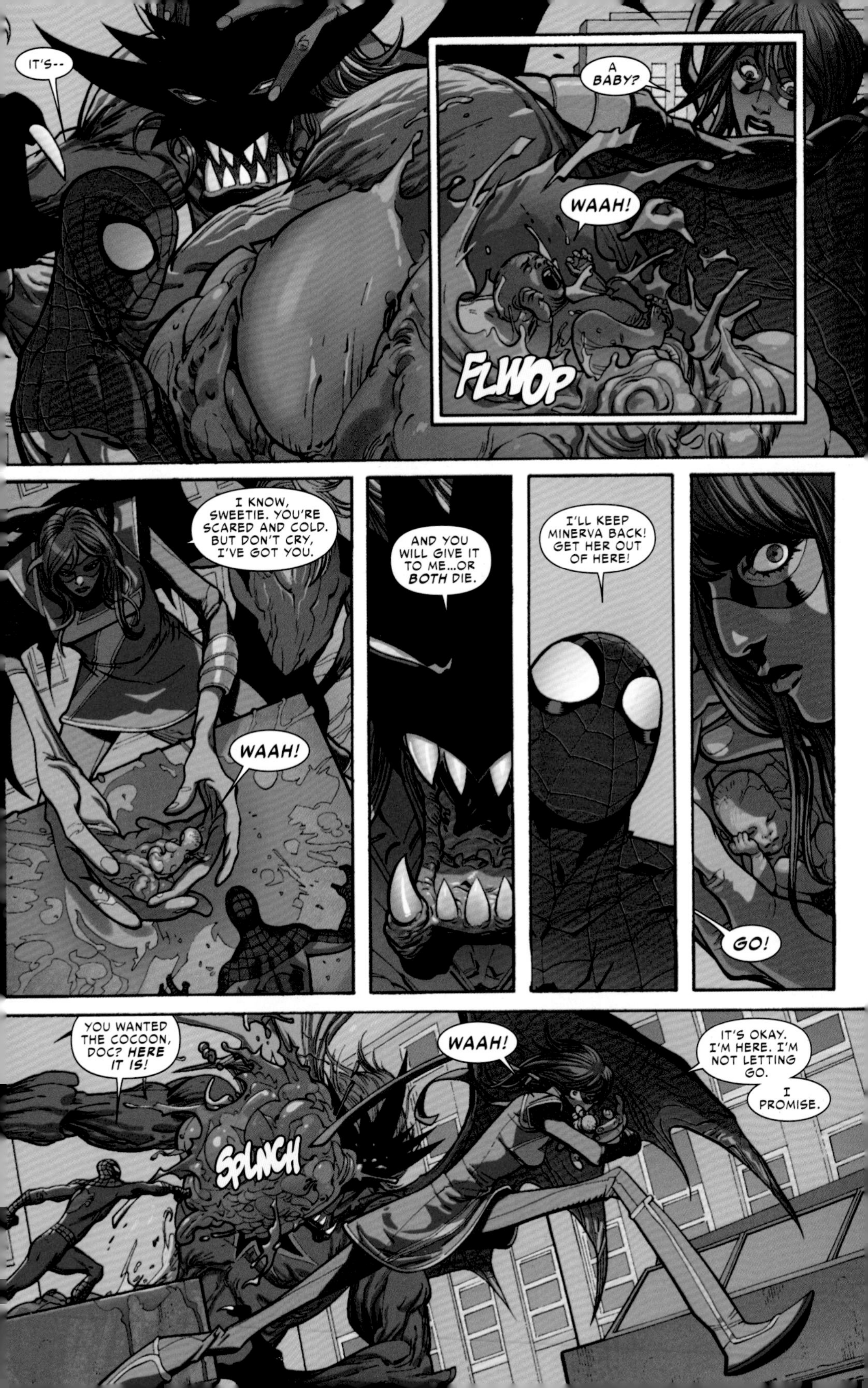
IT'S--
A BABY?
WAAH!
FLWOP
I KNOW, SWEETIE. YOU'RE SCARED AND COLD. BUT DON'T CRY, I'VE GOT YOU.
WAAH!
AND YOU WILL GIVE IT TO ME...OR BOTH DIE.
I'LL KEEP MINERVA BACK! GET HER OUT OF HERE!
GO!
YOU WANTED THE COCOON, DOC? HERE IT IS!
SPLNCH
WAAH!
IT'S OKAY. I'M HERE. I'M NOT LETTING GO.
I PROMISE.

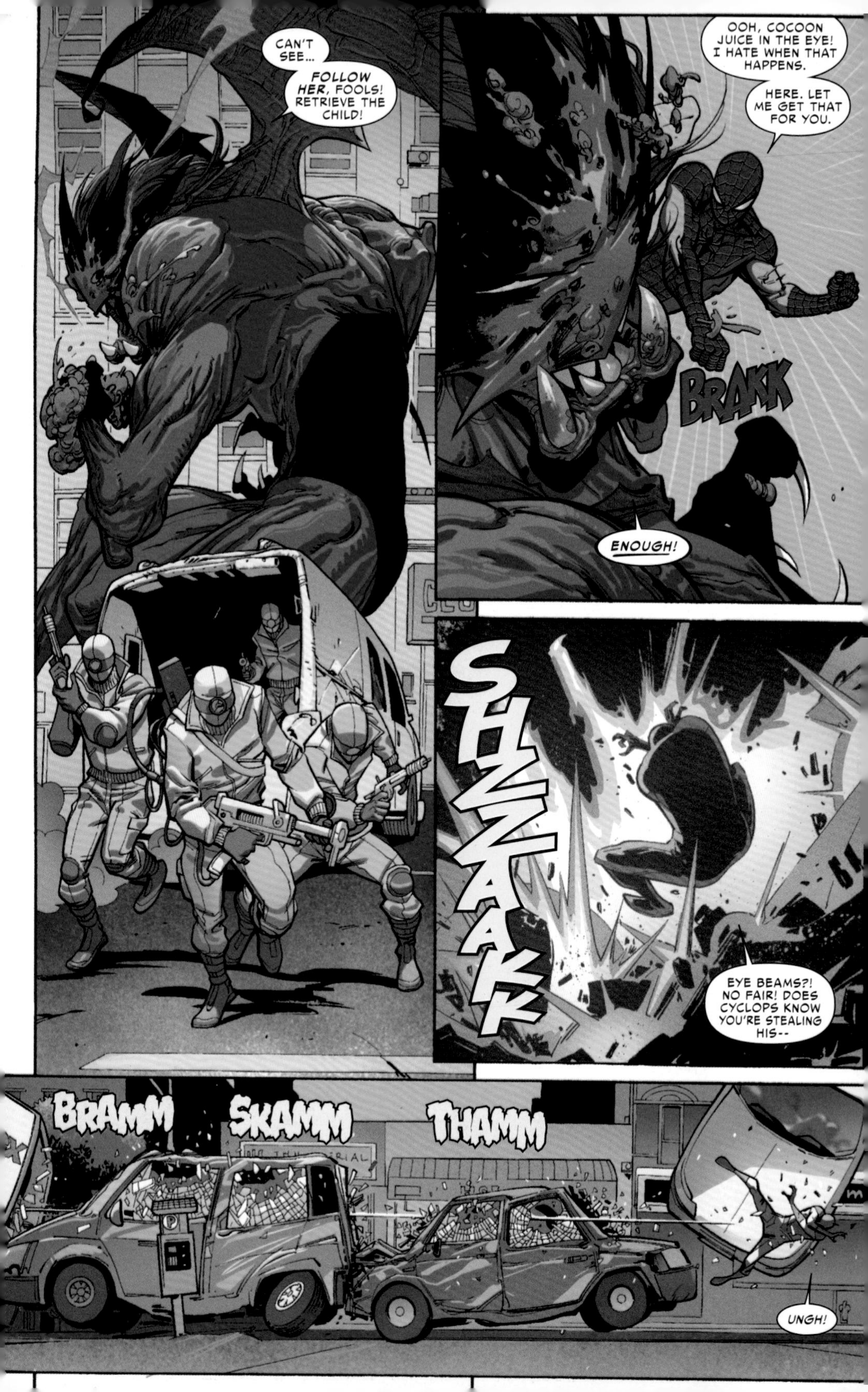
CAN'T SEE...
FOLLOW HER, FOOLS! RETRIEVE THE CHILD!
OOH, COCOON JUICE IN THE EYE! I HATE WHEN THAT HAPPENS.
HERE. LET ME GET THAT FOR YOU.
BRAKK
ENOUGH!
SHZZAAKK
EYE BEAMS?! NO FAIR! DOES CYCLOPS KNOW YOU'RE STEALING HIS--
BRAMM
SKAMM
THAMM
UNGH!

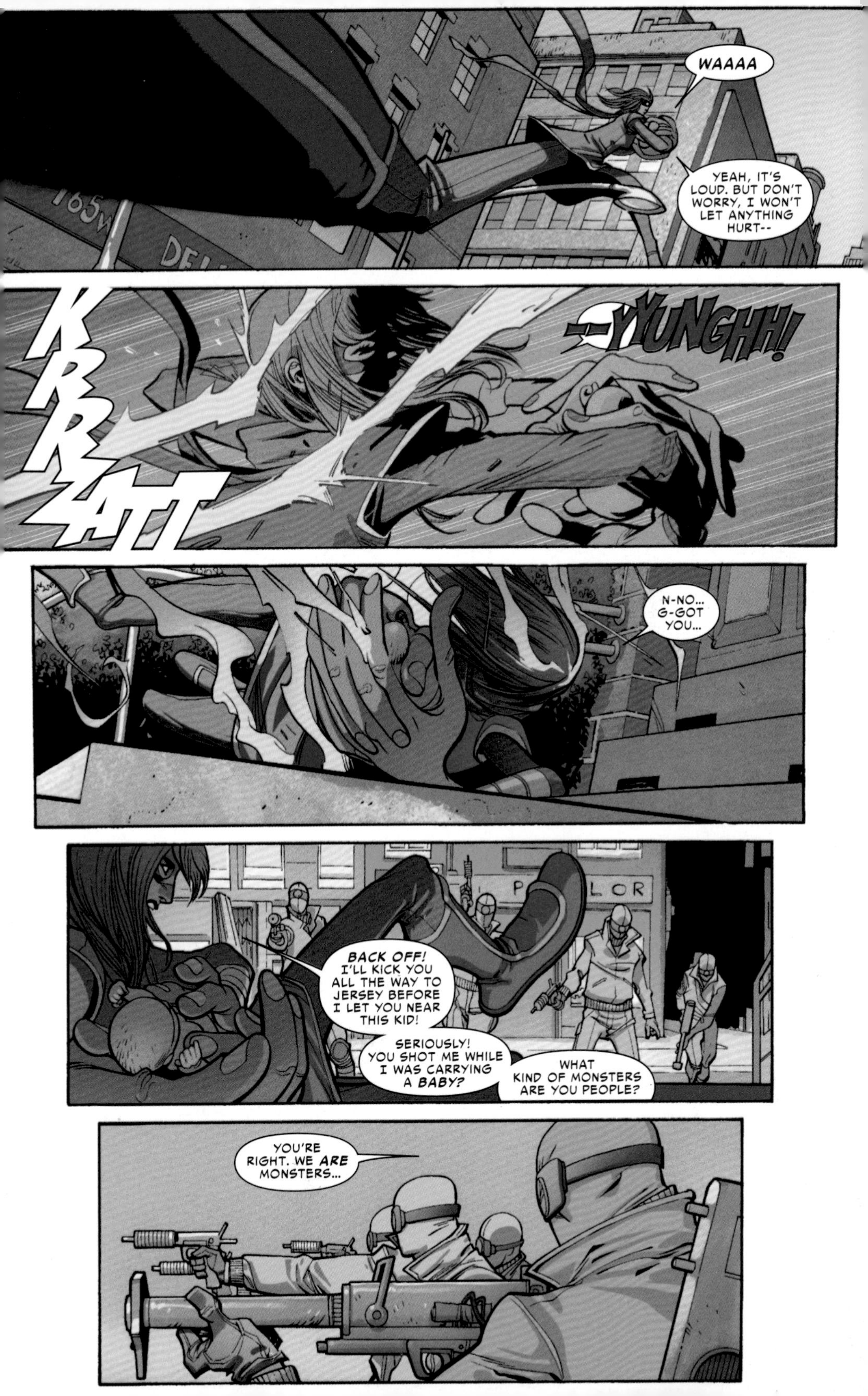
WAAAA
YEAH, IT'S LOUD. BUT DON'T WORRY, I WON'T LET ANYTHING HURT--
KRRZATT
--YYUNGHH!
N-NO... G-GOT YOU...
BACK OFF! I'LL KICK YOU ALL THE WAY TO JERSEY BEFORE I LET YOU NEAR THIS KID!
SERIOUSLY! YOU SHOT ME WHILE I WAS CARRYING A BABY?
WHAT KIND OF MONSTERS ARE YOU PEOPLE?
YOU'RE RIGHT. WE ARE MONSTERS...

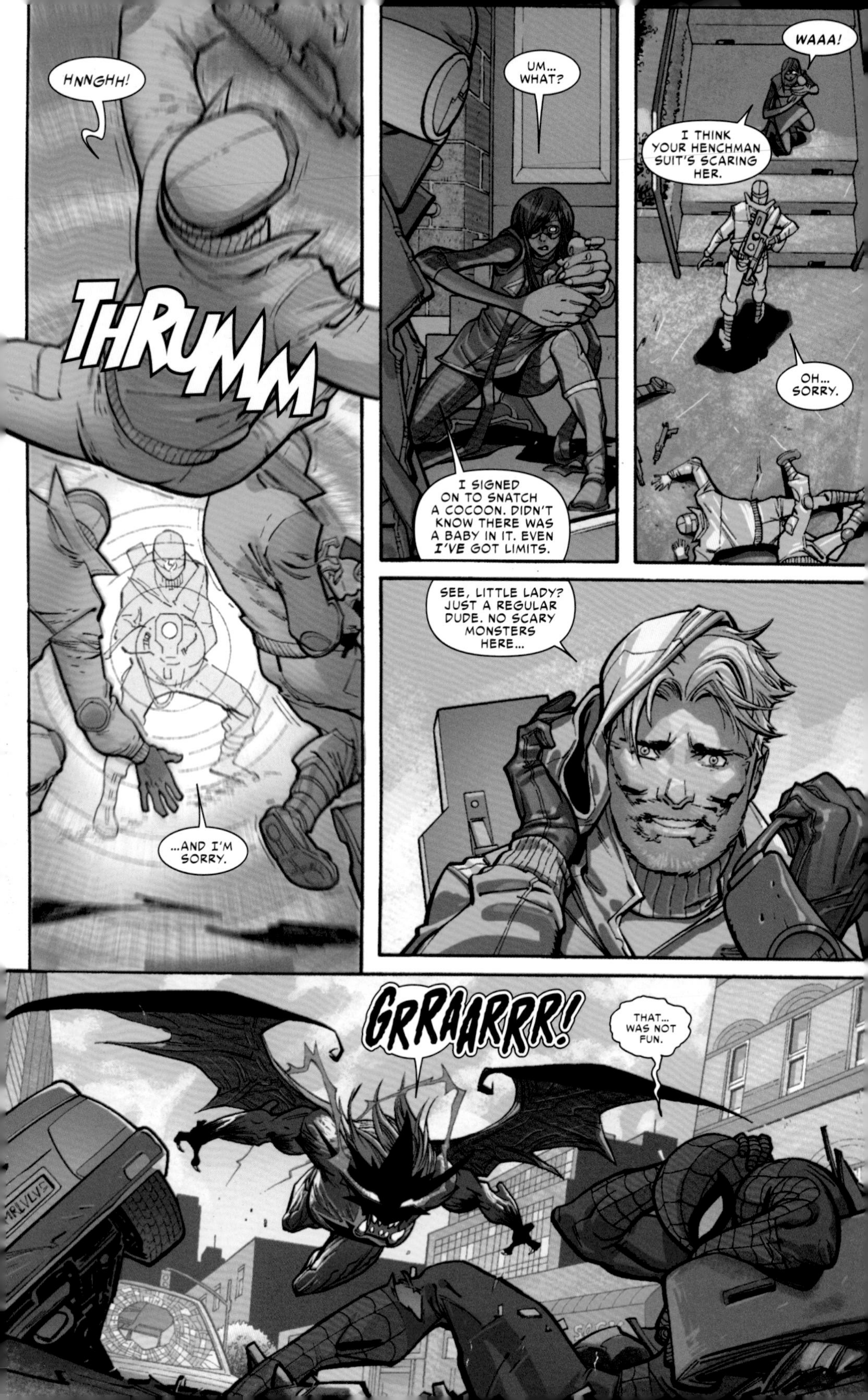
HNNGHH!
THRUMMM
...AND I'M SORRY.
UM... WHAT?
I SIGNED ON TO SNATCH A COCOON. DIDN'T KNOW THERE WAS A BABY IN IT. EVEN I'VE GOT LIMITS.
WAAA!
I THINK YOUR HENCHMAN SUIT'S SCARING HER.
OH... SORRY.
SEE, LITTLE LADY? JUST A REGULAR DUDE. NO SCARY MONSTERS HERE...
GRRAARRR!
THAT... WAS NOT FUN.
MRLVLVS

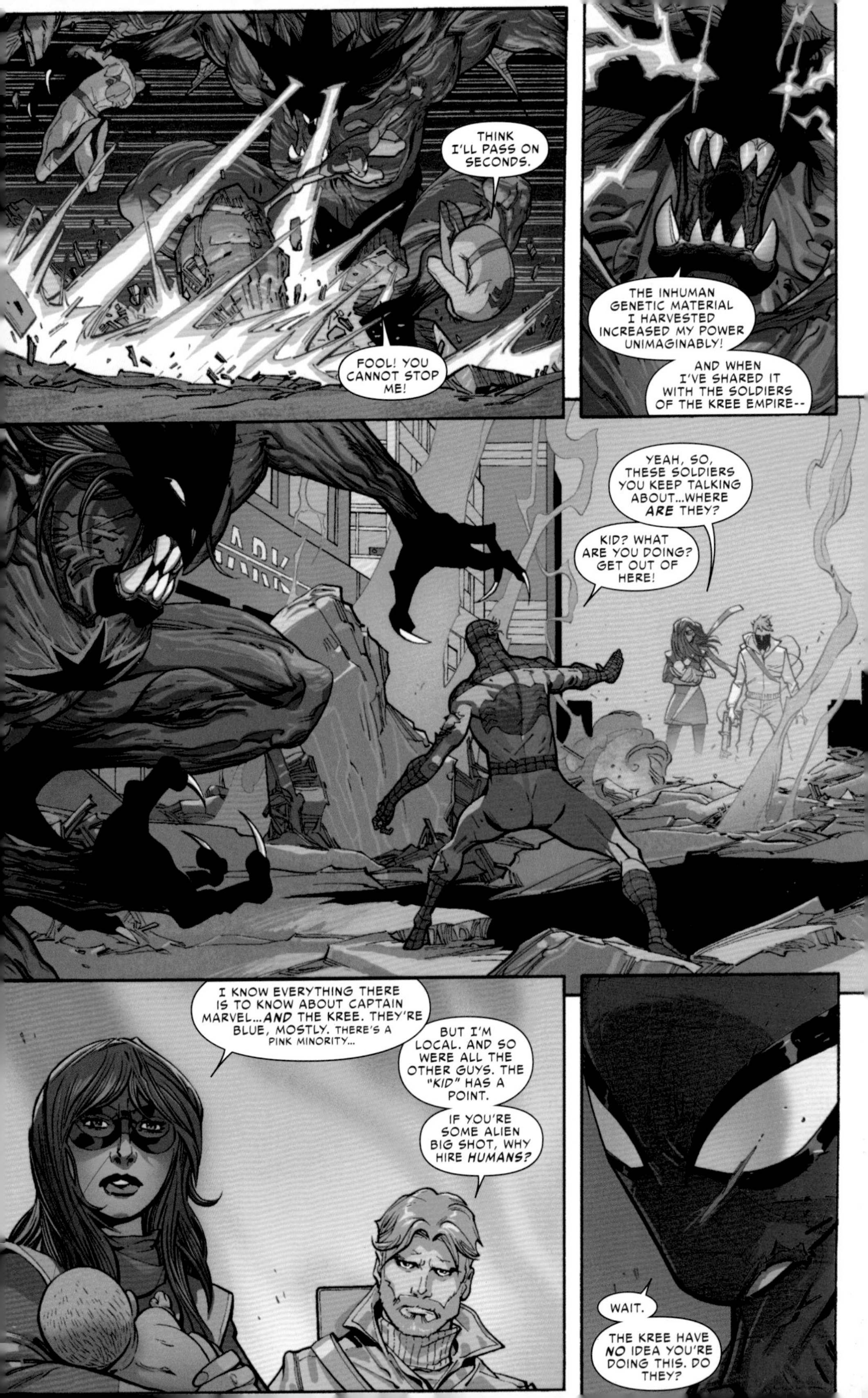
THINK I'LL PASS ON SECONDS.
FOOL! YOU CANNOT STOP ME!
THE INHUMAN GENETIC MATERIAL I HARVESTED INCREASED MY POWER UNIMAGINABLY!
AND WHEN I'VE SHARED IT WITH THE SOLDIERS OF THE KREE EMPIRE--
YEAH, SO, THESE SOLDIERS YOU KEEP TALKING ABOUT...WHERE *ARE* THEY?
KID? WHAT ARE YOU DOING? GET OUT OF HERE!
I KNOW EVERYTHING THERE IS TO KNOW ABOUT CAPTAIN MARVEL...*AND* THE KREE. THEY'RE BLUE, MOSTLY. THERE'S A PINK MINORITY...
BUT I'M LOCAL. AND SO WERE ALL THE OTHER GUYS. THE "*KID*" HAS A POINT.
IF YOU'RE SOME ALIEN BIG SHOT, WHY HIRE *HUMANS?*
WAIT.
THE KREE HAVE *NO* IDEA YOU'RE DOING THIS. DO THEY?

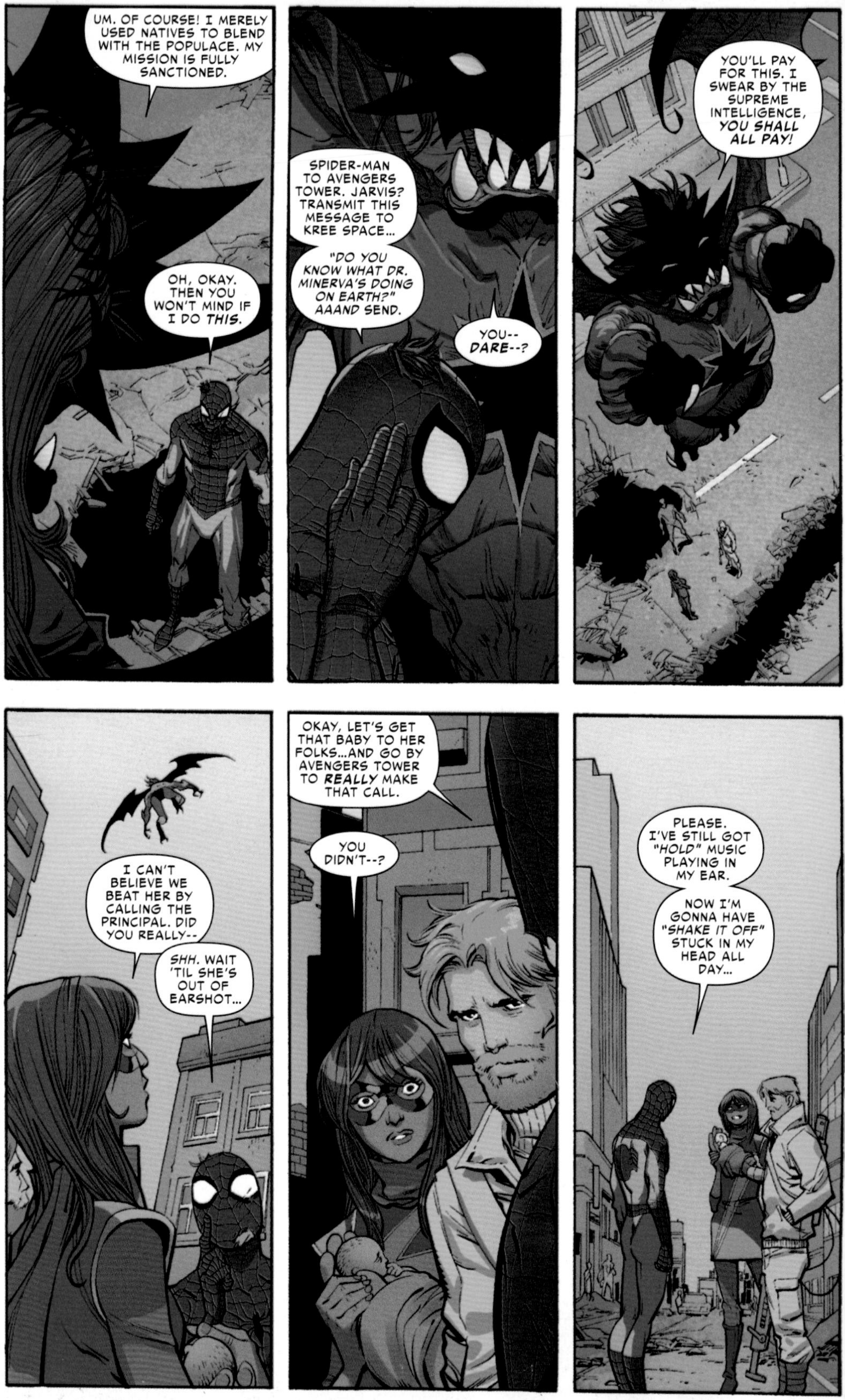
UM. OF COURSE! I MERELY USED NATIVES TO BLEND WITH THE POPULACE. MY MISSION IS FULLY SANCTIONED.
OH, OKAY. THEN YOU WON'T MIND IF I DO *THIS.*
SPIDER-MAN TO AVENGERS TOWER. JARVIS? TRANSMIT THIS MESSAGE TO KREE SPACE...
"DO YOU KNOW WHAT DR. MINERVA'S DOING ON EARTH?" AAAND SEND.
YOU-- *DARE*--?
YOU'LL PAY FOR THIS. I SWEAR BY THE SUPREME INTELLIGENCE, *YOU SHALL ALL PAY!*
I CAN'T BELIEVE WE BEAT HER BY CALLING THE PRINCIPAL. DID YOU REALLY--
SHH. WAIT 'TIL SHE'S OUT OF EARSHOT...
OKAY, LET'S GET THAT BABY TO HER FOLKS...AND GO BY AVENGERS TOWER TO *REALLY* MAKE THAT CALL.
YOU DIDN'T--?
PLEASE. I'VE STILL GOT *"HOLD"* MUSIC PLAYING IN MY EAR.
NOW I'M GONNA HAVE *"SHAKE IT OFF"* STUCK IN MY HEAD ALL DAY...

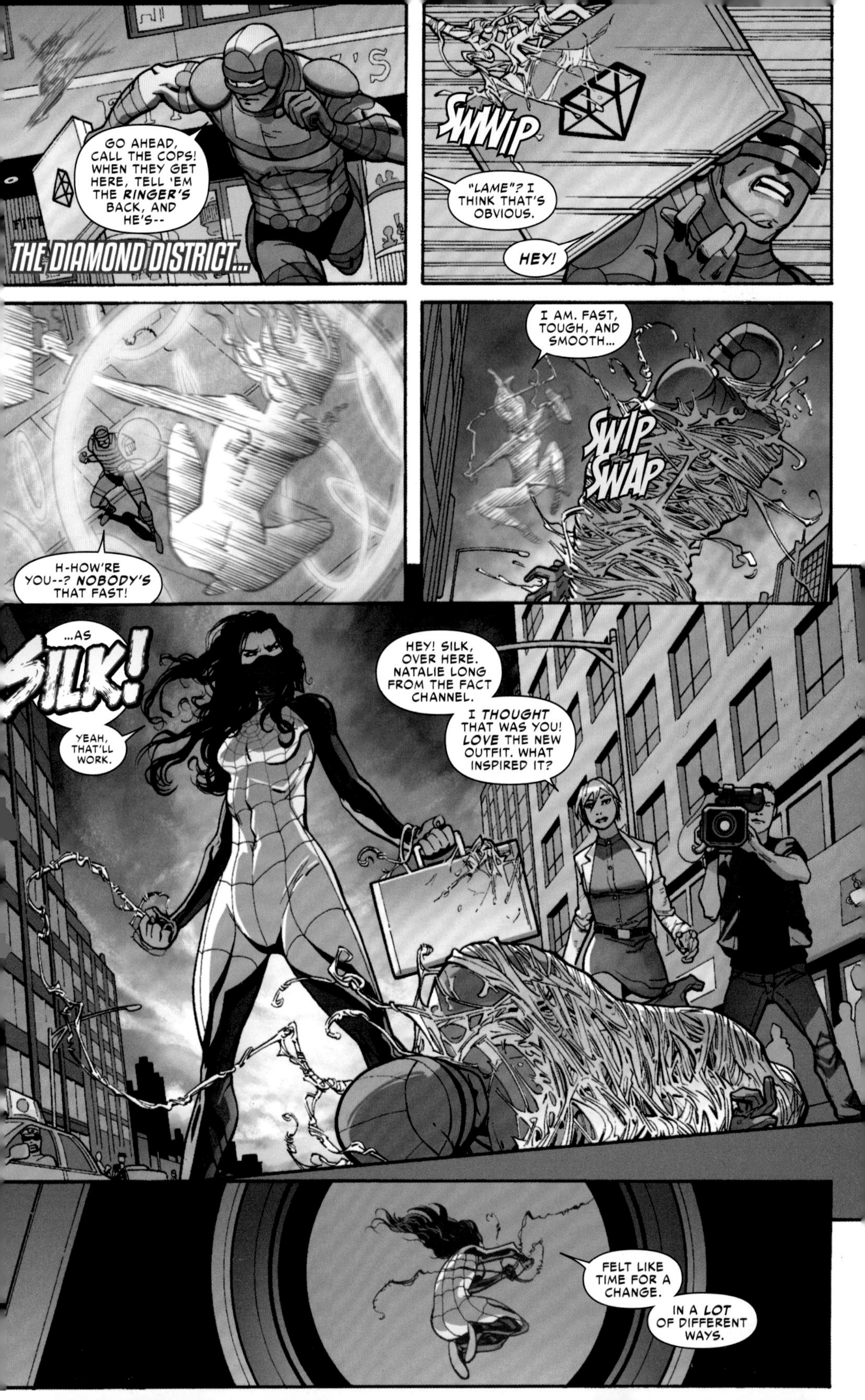

THE DIAMOND DISTRICT...
GO AHEAD, CALL THE COPS! WHEN THEY GET HERE, TELL 'EM THE RINGER'S BACK, AND HE'S--
SWWIP
"LAME"? I THINK THAT'S OBVIOUS.
HEY!
H-HOW'RE YOU--? NOBODY'S THAT FAST!
I AM. FAST, TOUGH, AND SMOOTH...
SWIP SWAP
...AS SILK!
YEAH, THAT'LL WORK.
HEY! SILK, OVER HERE. NATALIE LONG FROM THE FACT CHANNEL.
I THOUGHT THAT WAS YOU! LOVE THE NEW OUTFIT. WHAT INSPIRED IT?
FELT LIKE TIME FOR A CHANGE.
IN A LOT OF DIFFERENT WAYS.

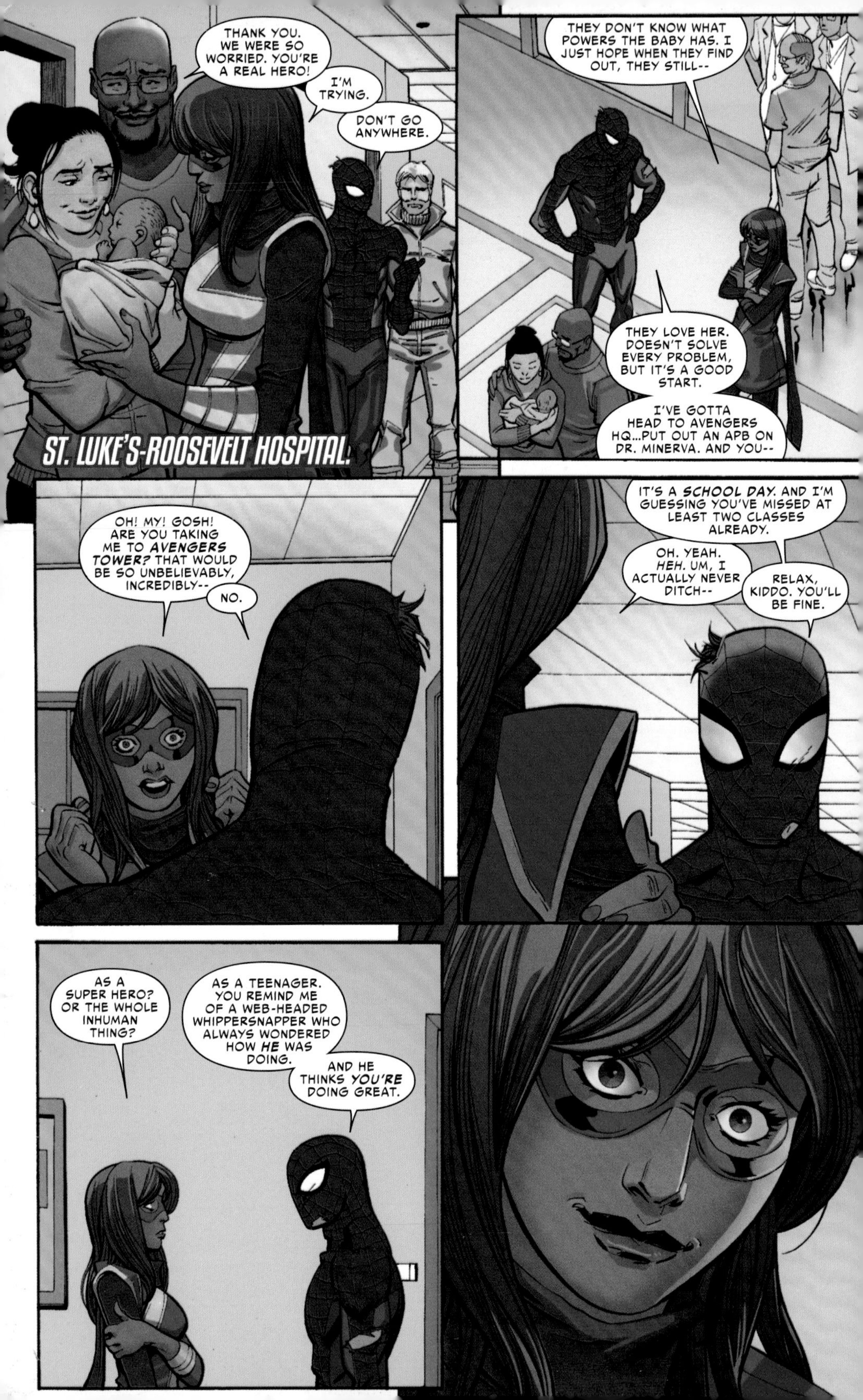
THANK YOU. WE WERE SO WORRIED. YOU'RE A REAL HERO!
I'M TRYING.
DON'T GO ANYWHERE.
ST. LUKE'S-ROOSEVELT HOSPITAL.
THEY DON'T KNOW WHAT POWERS THE BABY HAS. I JUST HOPE WHEN THEY FIND OUT, THEY STILL--
THEY LOVE HER. DOESN'T SOLVE EVERY PROBLEM, BUT IT'S A GOOD START.
I'VE GOTTA HEAD TO AVENGERS HQ...PUT OUT AN APB ON DR. MINERVA. AND YOU--
OH! MY! GOSH! ARE YOU TAKING ME TO *AVENGERS TOWER?* THAT WOULD BE SO UNBELIEVABLY, INCREDIBLY--
NO.
IT'S A *SCHOOL DAY.* AND I'M GUESSING YOU'VE MISSED AT LEAST TWO CLASSES ALREADY.
OH. YEAH. *HEH.* UM, I ACTUALLY NEVER DITCH--
RELAX, KIDDO. YOU'LL BE FINE.
AS A SUPER HERO? OR THE WHOLE INHUMAN THING?
AS A TEENAGER. YOU REMIND ME OF A WEB-HEADED WHIPPERSNAPPER WHO ALWAYS WONDERED HOW *HE* WAS DOING.
AND HE THINKS *YOU'RE* DOING GREAT.

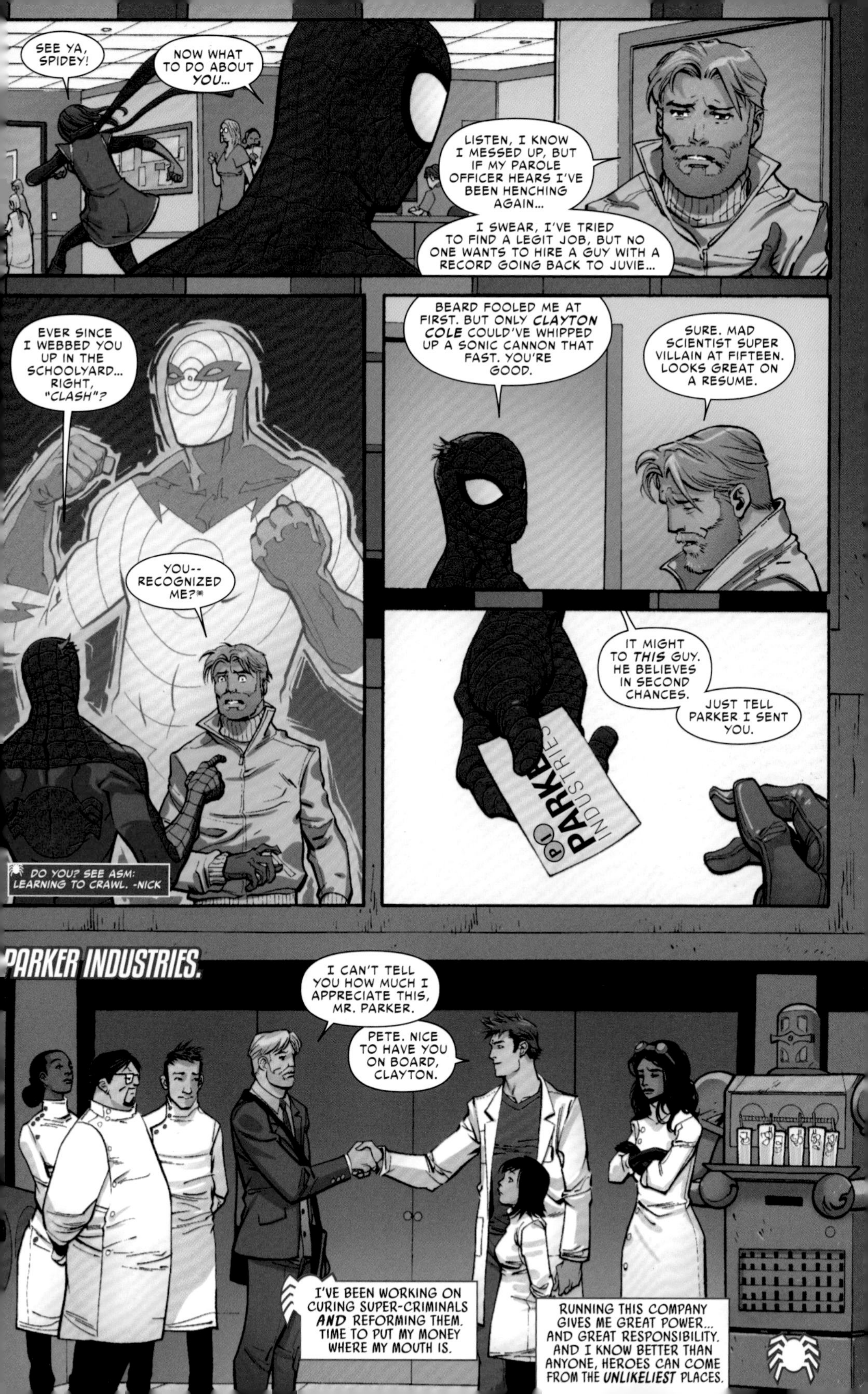
SEE YA, SPIDEY!
NOW WHAT TO DO ABOUT YOU...
LISTEN, I KNOW I MESSED UP, BUT IF MY PAROLE OFFICER HEARS I'VE BEEN HENCHING AGAIN...
I SWEAR, I'VE TRIED TO FIND A LEGIT JOB, BUT NO ONE WANTS TO HIRE A GUY WITH A RECORD GOING BACK TO JUVIE...
EVER SINCE I WEBBED YOU UP IN THE SCHOOLYARD... RIGHT, "CLASH"?
YOU-- RECOGNIZED ME?*
*DO YOU? SEE ASM: LEARNING TO CRAWL. -NICK
BEARD FOOLED ME AT FIRST. BUT ONLY CLAYTON COLE COULD'VE WHIPPED UP A SONIC CANNON THAT FAST. YOU'RE GOOD.
SURE. MAD SCIENTIST SUPER VILLAIN AT FIFTEEN. LOOKS GREAT ON A RESUME.
IT MIGHT TO THIS GUY. HE BELIEVES IN SECOND CHANCES.
JUST TELL PARKER I SENT YOU.
PI PARKER INDUSTRIES
PARKER INDUSTRIES.
I CAN'T TELL YOU HOW MUCH I APPRECIATE THIS, MR. PARKER.
PETE. NICE TO HAVE YOU ON BOARD, CLAYTON.
I'VE BEEN WORKING ON CURING SUPER-CRIMINALS AND REFORMING THEM. TIME TO PUT MY MONEY WHERE MY MOUTH IS.
RUNNING THIS COMPANY GIVES ME GREAT POWER... AND GREAT RESPONSIBILITY. AND I KNOW BETTER THAN ANYONE, HEROES CAN COME FROM THE UNLIKELIEST PLACES.

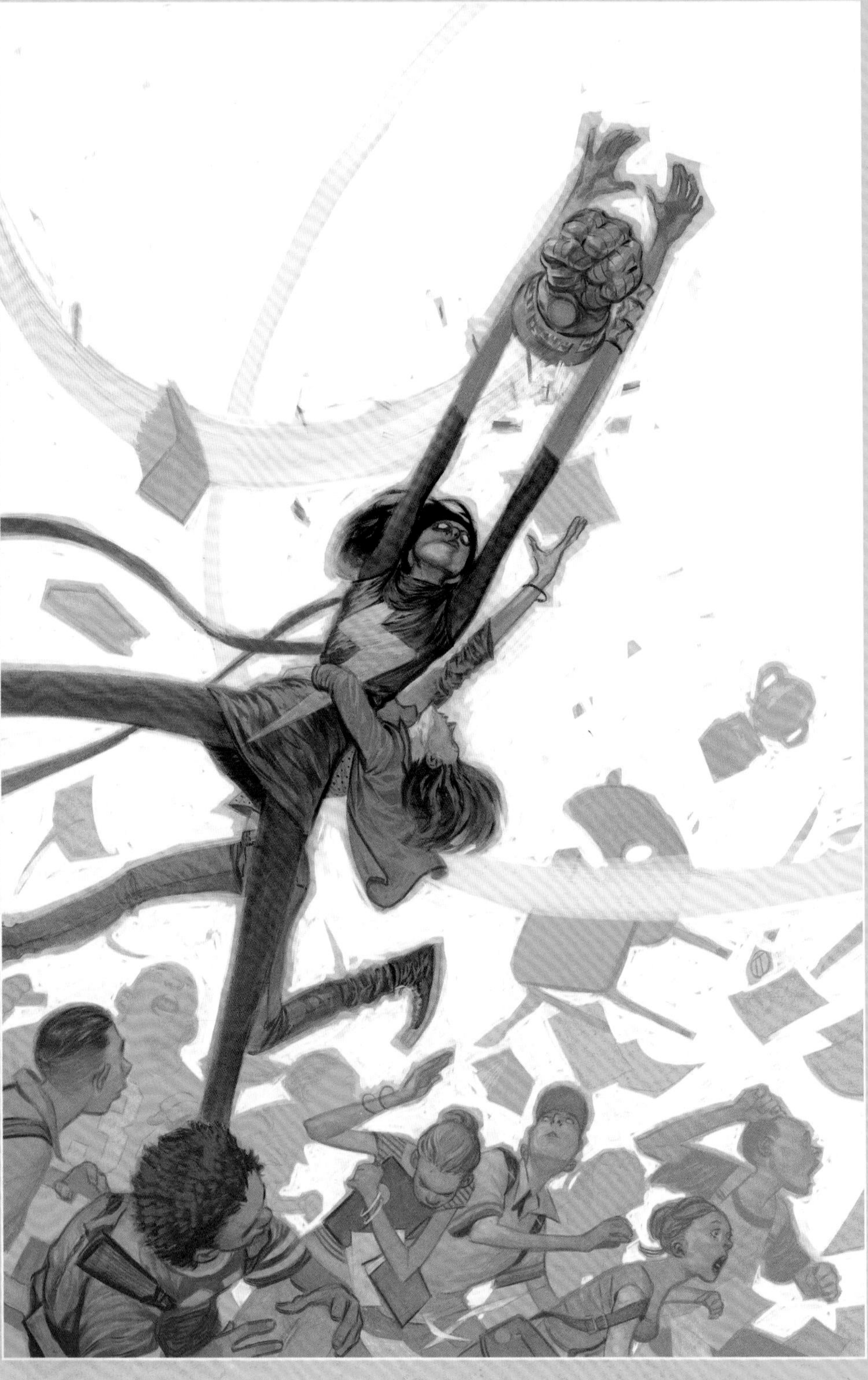

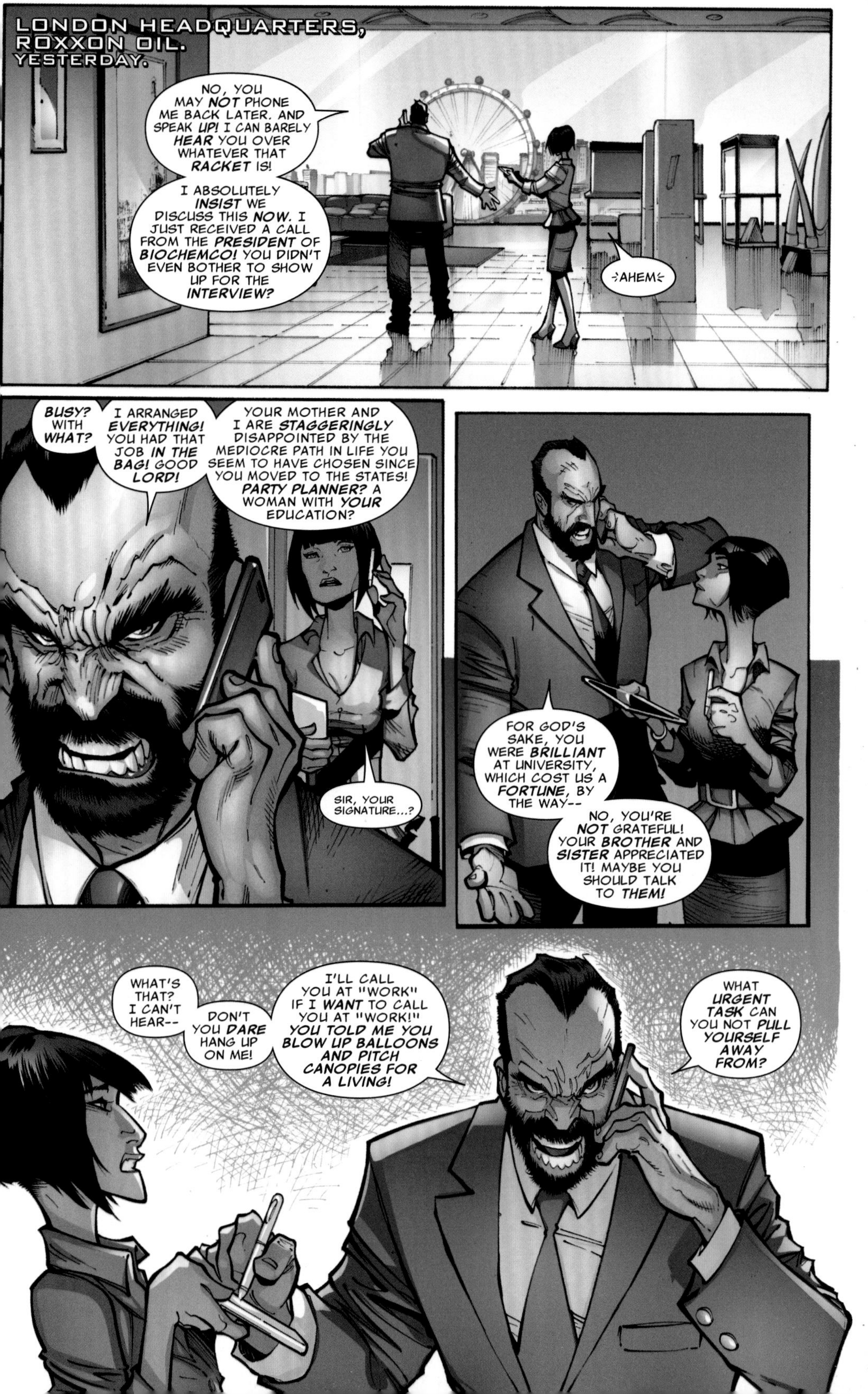
LONDON HEADQUARTERS, ROXXON OIL. YESTERDAY.
NO, YOU MAY NOT PHONE ME BACK LATER. AND SPEAK UP! I CAN BARELY HEAR YOU OVER WHATEVER THAT RACKET IS!
I ABSOLUTELY INSIST WE DISCUSS THIS NOW. I JUST RECEIVED A CALL FROM THE PRESIDENT OF BIOCHEMCO! YOU DIDN'T EVEN BOTHER TO SHOW UP FOR THE INTERVIEW?
AHEM
BUSY? WITH WHAT?
I ARRANGED EVERYTHING! YOU HAD THAT JOB IN THE BAG! GOOD LORD!
YOUR MOTHER AND I ARE STAGGERINGLY DISAPPOINTED BY THE MEDIOCRE PATH IN LIFE YOU SEEM TO HAVE CHOSEN SINCE YOU MOVED TO THE STATES! PARTY PLANNER? A WOMAN WITH YOUR EDUCATION?
SIR, YOUR SIGNATURE...?
FOR GOD'S SAKE, YOU WERE BRILLIANT AT UNIVERSITY, WHICH COST US A FORTUNE, BY THE WAY--
NO, YOU'RE NOT GRATEFUL! YOUR BROTHER AND SISTER APPRECIATED IT! MAYBE YOU SHOULD TALK TO THEM!
WHAT'S THAT? I CAN'T HEAR--
DON'T YOU DARE HANG UP ON ME!
I'LL CALL YOU AT "WORK" IF I WANT TO CALL YOU AT "WORK!" YOU TOLD ME YOU BLOW UP BALLOONS AND PITCH CANOPIES FOR A LIVING!
WHAT URGENT TASK CAN YOU NOT PULL YOURSELF AWAY FROM?

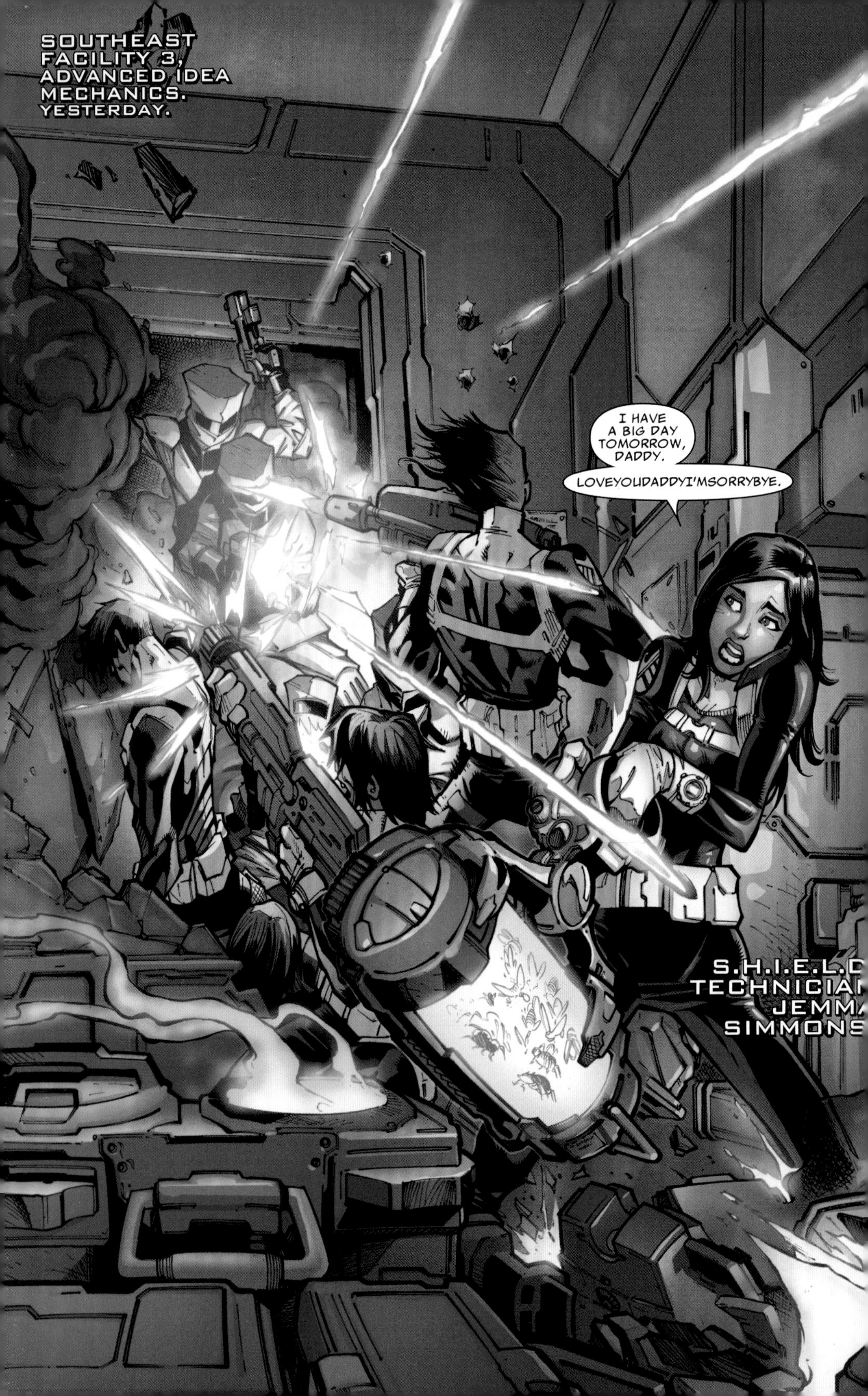
SOUTHEAST FACILITY 3, ADVANCED IDEA MECHANICS. YESTERDAY.
I HAVE A BIG DAY TOMORROW, DADDY.
LOVEYOUDADDYI'MSORRYBYE.
S.H.I.E.L.D. TECHNICIAN JEMMA SIMMONS

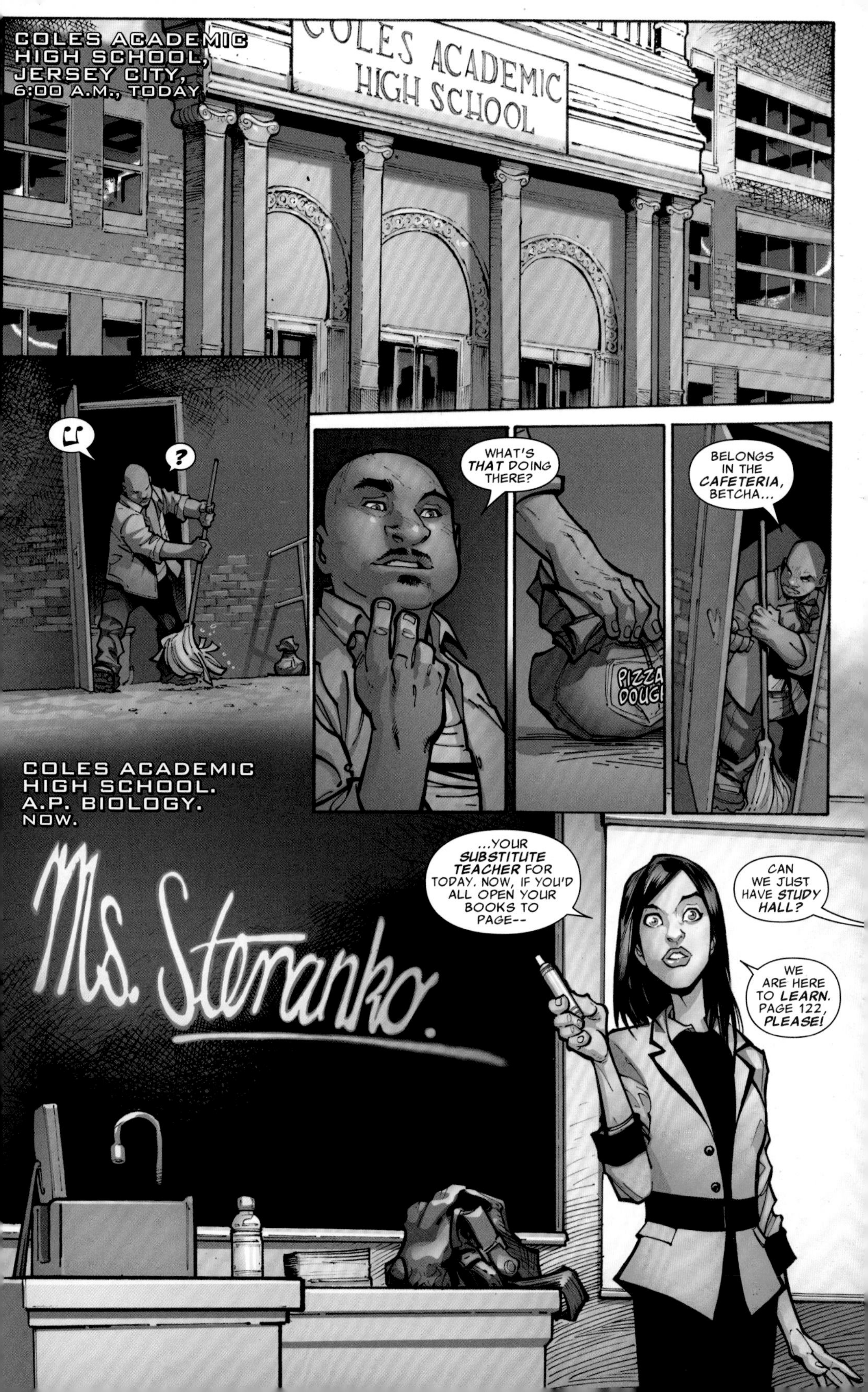
COLES ACADEMIC HIGH SCHOOL, JERSEY CITY, 6:00 A.M., TODAY
COLES ACADEMIC HIGH SCHOOL
?
WHAT'S THAT DOING THERE?
PIZZA DOUGH
BELONGS IN THE CAFETERIA, BETCHA...
COLES ACADEMIC HIGH SCHOOL. A.P. BIOLOGY. NOW.
Ms. Steranko.
...YOUR SUBSTITUTE TEACHER FOR TODAY. NOW, IF YOU'D ALL OPEN YOUR BOOKS TO PAGE--
CAN WE JUST HAVE STUDY HALL?
WE ARE HERE TO LEARN. PAGE 122, PLEASE!

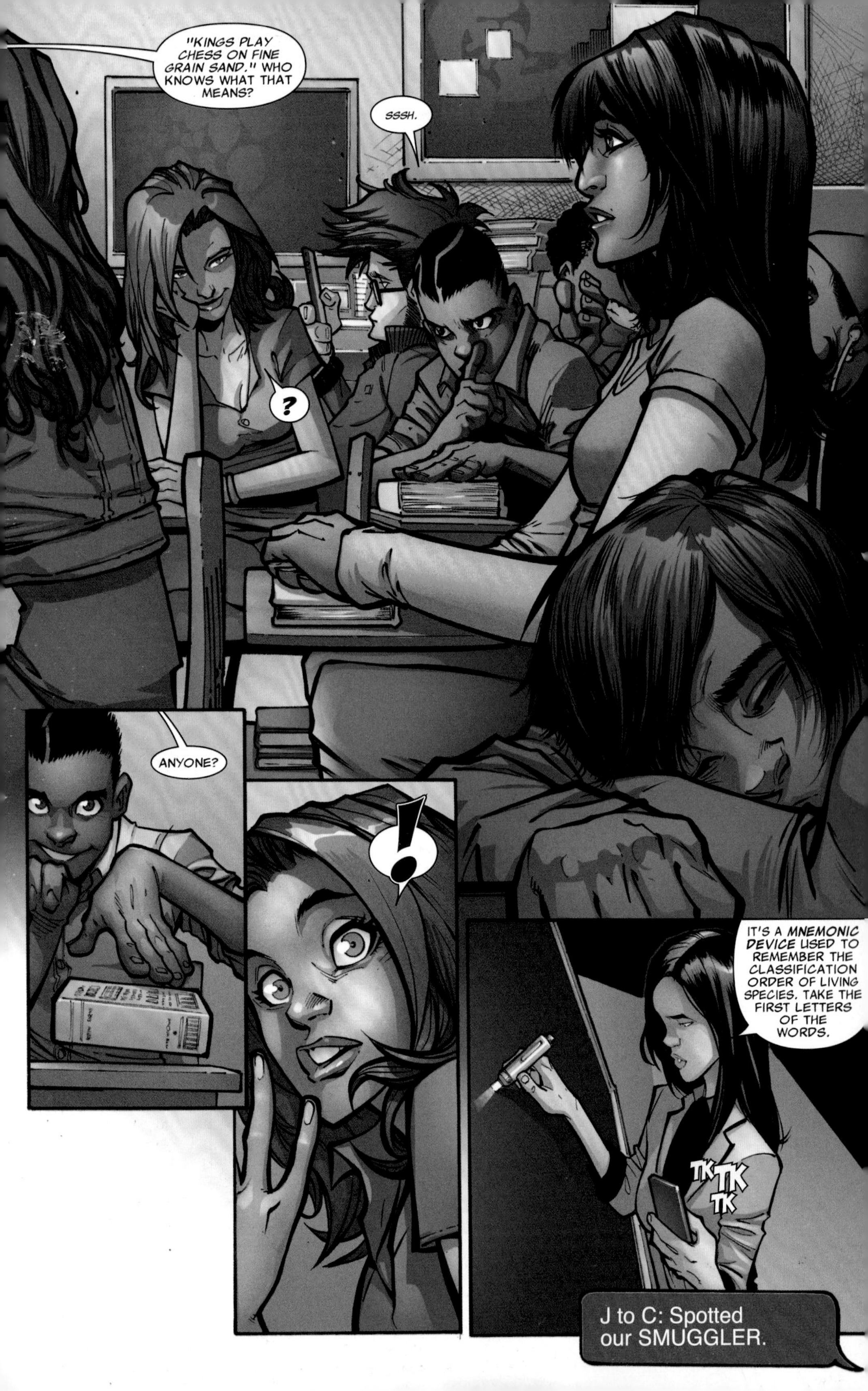
"KINGS PLAY CHESS ON FINE GRAIN SAND." WHO KNOWS WHAT THAT MEANS?
SSSH.
?
ANYONE?
!
IT'S A *MNEMONIC DEVICE* USED TO REMEMBER THE CLASSIFICATION ORDER OF LIVING SPECIES. TAKE THE FIRST LETTERS OF THE WORDS.
TK TK TK
J to C: Spotted our SMUGGLER.

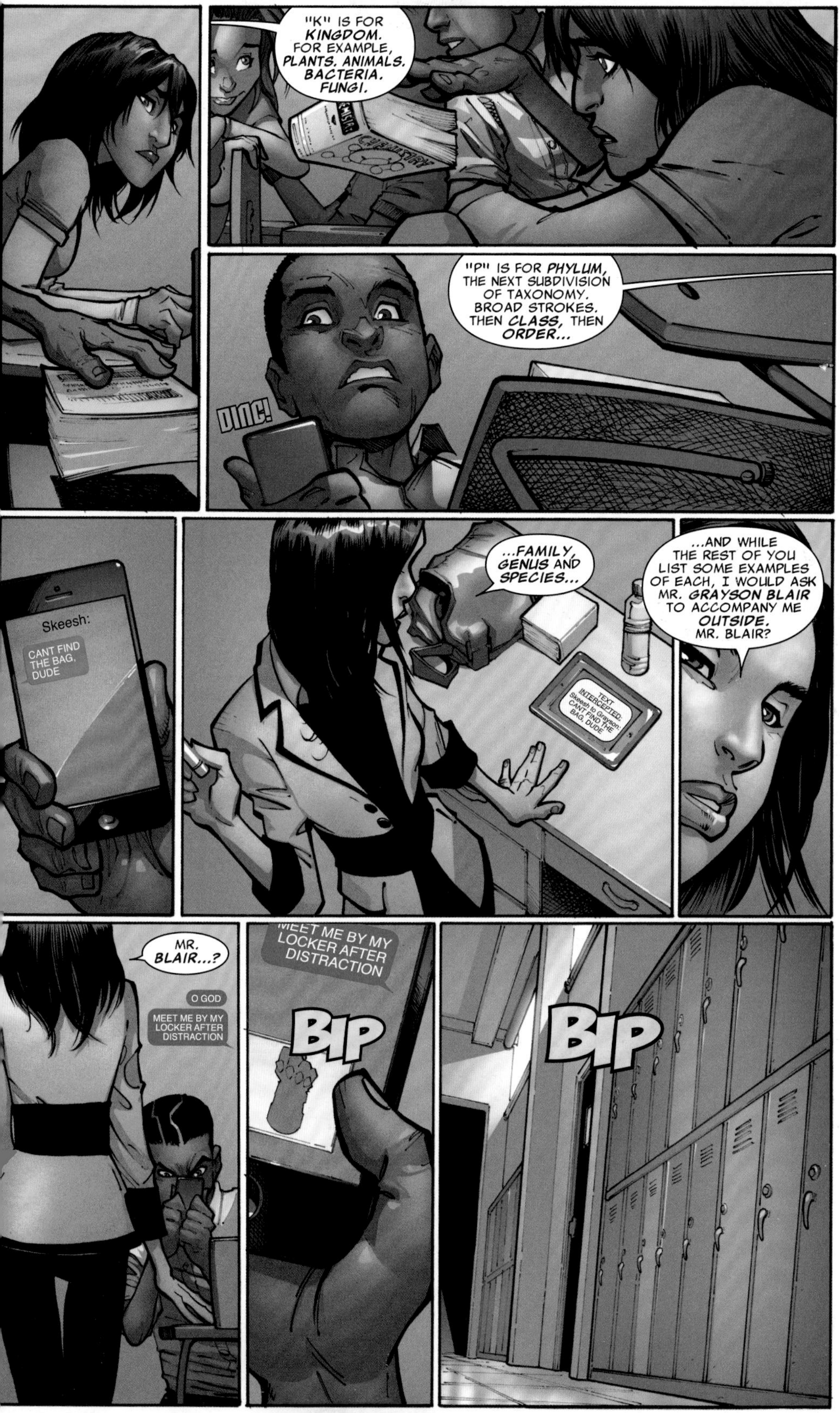
"K" IS FOR KINGDOM. FOR EXAMPLE, PLANTS. ANIMALS. BACTERIA. FUNGI.
"P" IS FOR PHYLUM, THE NEXT SUBDIVISION OF TAXONOMY. BROAD STROKES. THEN CLASS, THEN ORDER...
DING!
Skeesh:
CANT FIND THE BAG, DUDE
...FAMILY, GENUS AND SPECIES...
TEXT INTERCEPTED: Skeesh to Grayson: CANT FIND THE BAG, DUDE
...AND WHILE THE REST OF YOU LIST SOME EXAMPLES OF EACH, I WOULD ASK MR. GRAYSON BLAIR TO ACCOMPANY ME OUTSIDE. MR. BLAIR?
MR. BLAIR...?
O GOD
MEET ME BY MY LOCKER AFTER DISTRACTION
MEET ME BY MY LOCKER AFTER DISTRACTION
BIP
BIP

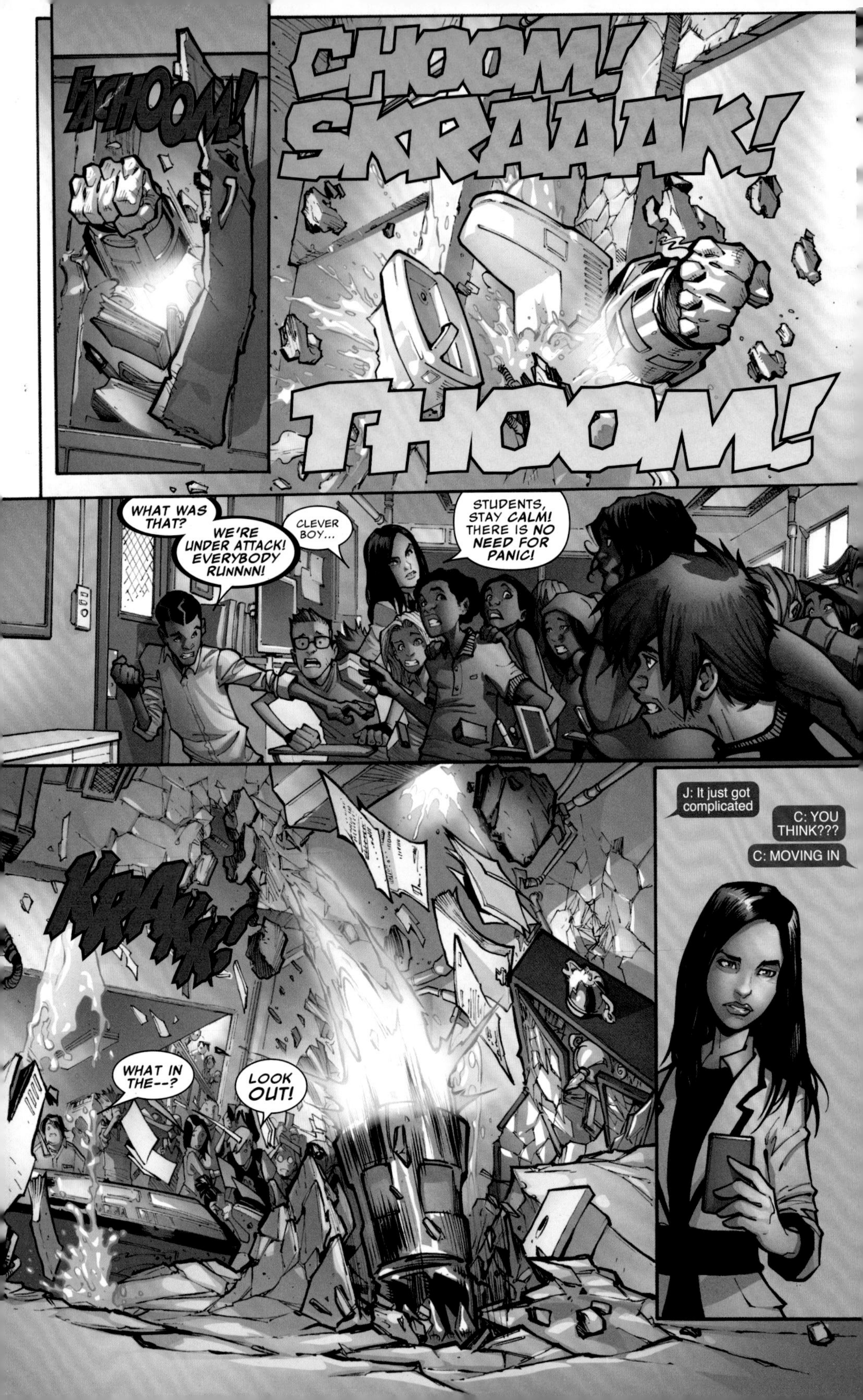

F-CHOOM!
CHOOM!
SKRAAAK!
THOOM!
WHAT WAS THAT?
WE'RE UNDER ATTACK! EVERYBODY RUNNNNN!
CLEVER BOY...
STUDENTS, STAY CALM! THERE IS NO NEED FOR PANIC!
KRAKK!
WHAT IN THE--?
LOOK OUT!
J: It just got complicated
C: YOU THINK???
C: MOVING IN

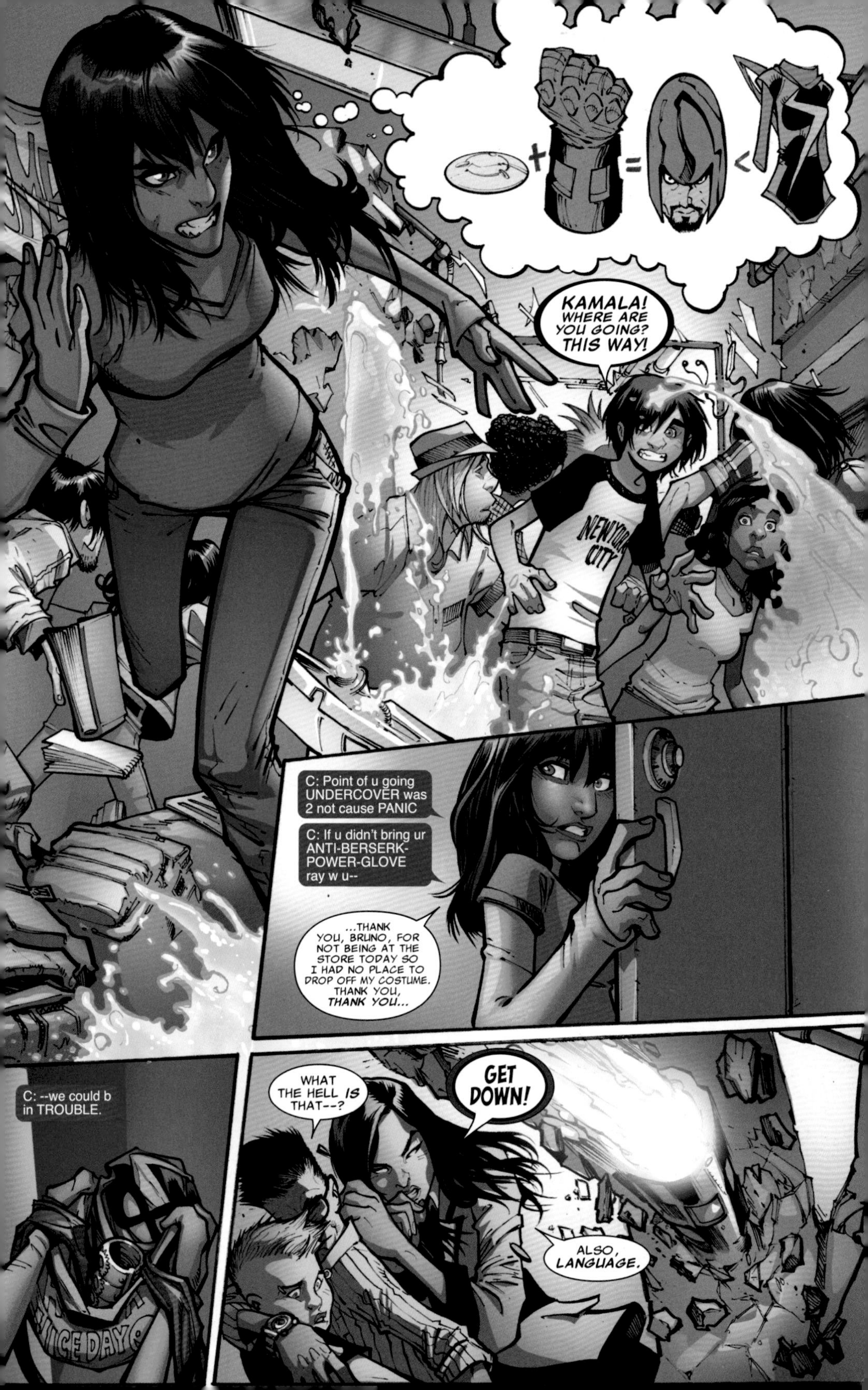
KAMALA! WHERE ARE YOU GOING? THIS WAY!
C: Point of u going UNDERCOVER was 2 not cause PANIC
C: If u didn't bring ur ANTI-BERSERK-POWER-GLOVE ray w u--
...THANK YOU, BRUNO, FOR NOT BEING AT THE STORE TODAY SO I HAD NO PLACE TO DROP OFF MY COSTUME. THANK YOU, THANK YOU...
C: --we could b in TROUBLE.
WHAT THE HELL IS THAT--?
GET DOWN!
ALSO, LANGUAGE.
NEW YORK CITY
ICE DAY

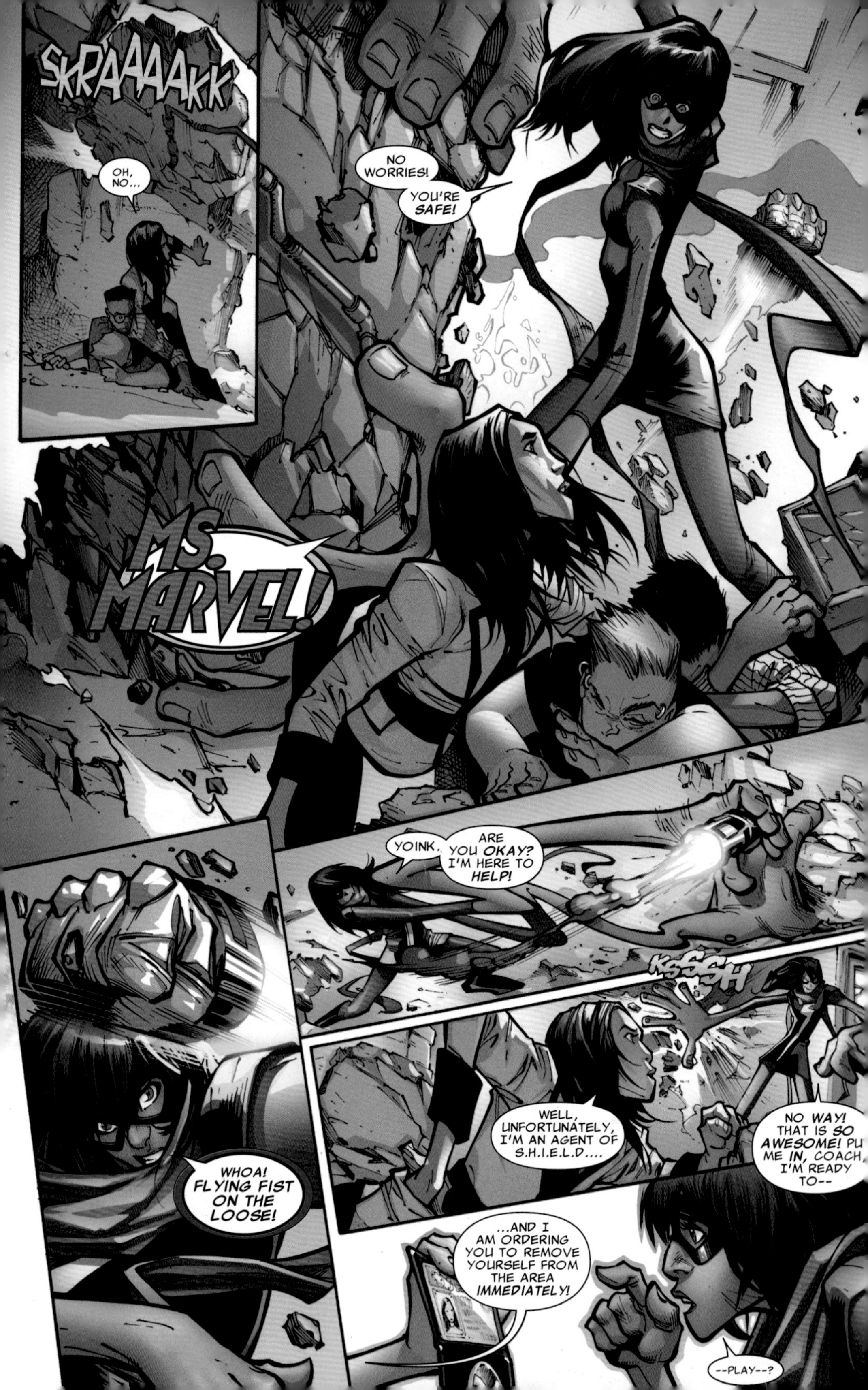
SKRAAAAKK
OH, NO...
NO WORRIES!
YOU'RE SAFE!
MS. MARVEL!
YOINK.
ARE YOU OKAY? I'M HERE TO HELP!
KSSSH
WHOA! FLYING FIST ON THE LOOSE!
WELL, UNFORTUNATELY, I'M AN AGENT OF S.H.I.E.L.D....
NO WAY! THAT IS SO AWESOME! PU ME IN, COACH, I'M READY TO--
...AND I AM ORDERING YOU TO REMOVE YOURSELF FROM THE AREA IMMEDIATELY!
--PLAY--?

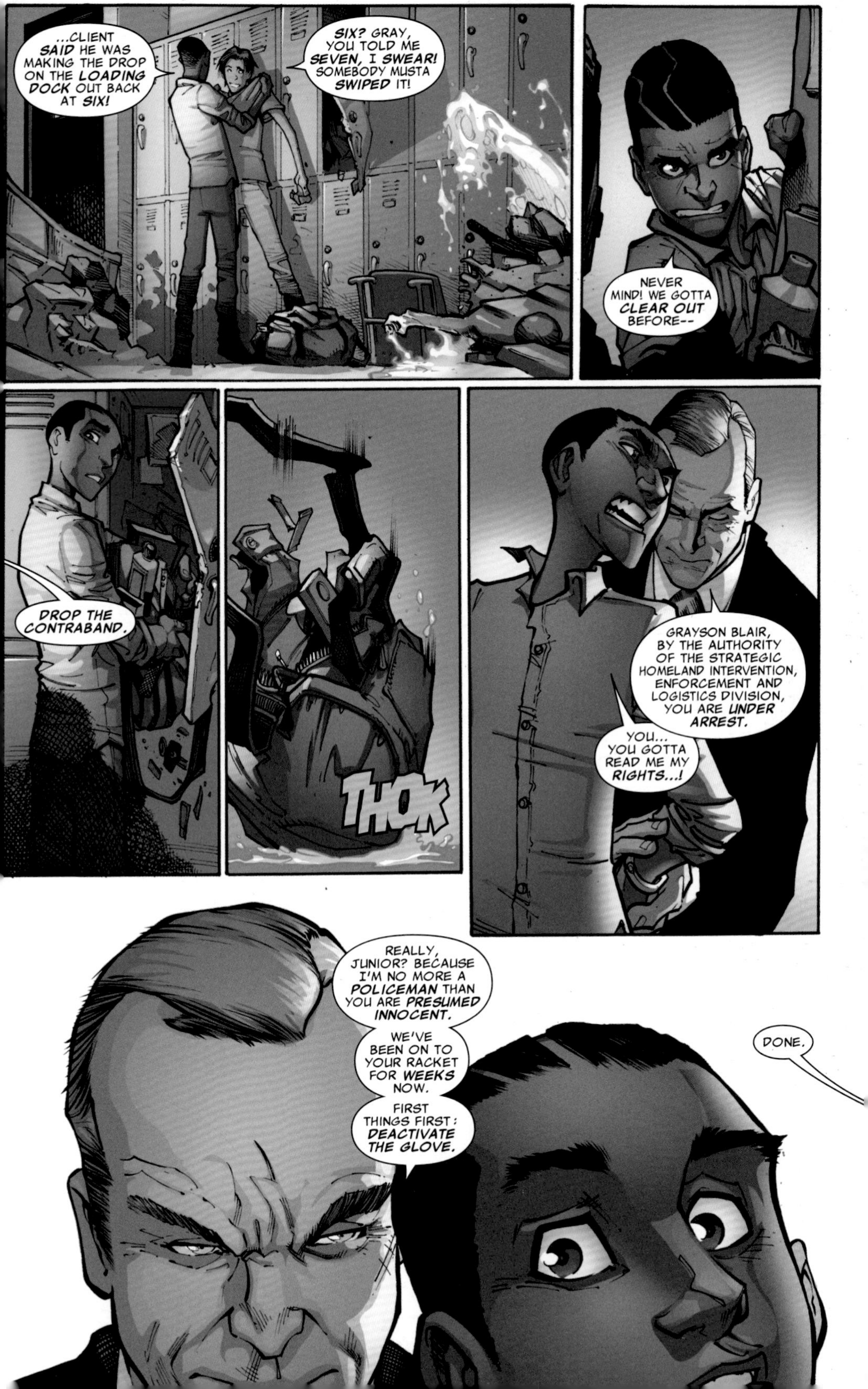
...CLIENT SAID HE WAS MAKING THE DROP ON THE LOADING DOCK OUT BACK AT SIX!
SIX? GRAY, YOU TOLD ME SEVEN, I SWEAR! SOMEBODY MUSTA SWIPED IT!
NEVER MIND! WE GOTTA CLEAR OUT BEFORE--
DROP THE CONTRABAND.
THOK
GRAYSON BLAIR, BY THE AUTHORITY OF THE STRATEGIC HOMELAND INTERVENTION, ENFORCEMENT AND LOGISTICS DIVISION, YOU ARE UNDER ARREST.
YOU... YOU GOTTA READ ME MY RIGHTS...!
REALLY, JUNIOR? BECAUSE I'M NO MORE A POLICEMAN THAN YOU ARE PRESUMED INNOCENT.
WE'VE BEEN ON TO YOUR RACKET FOR WEEKS NOW.
FIRST THINGS FIRST: DEACTIVATE THE GLOVE.
DONE.

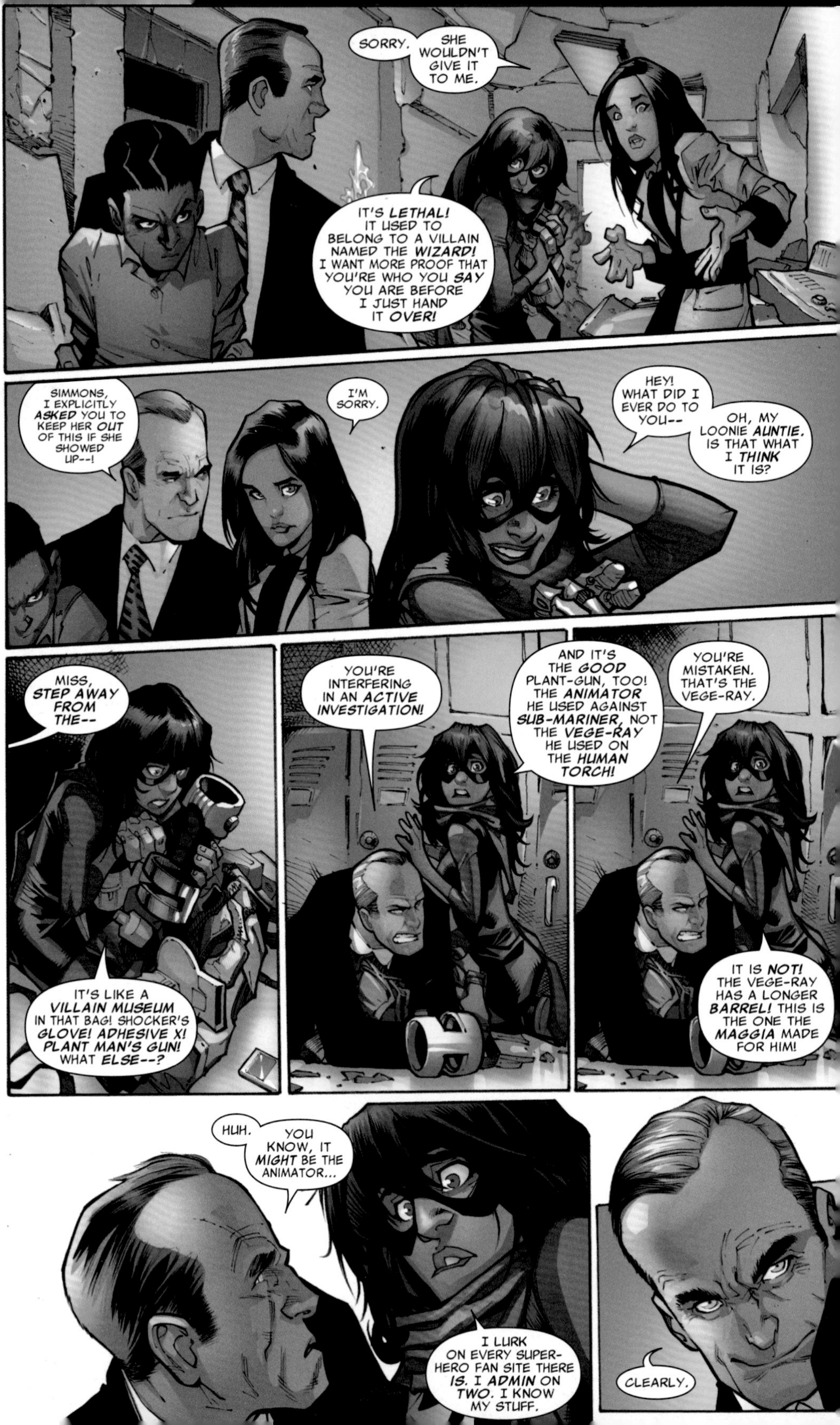
SORRY.
SHE WOULDN'T GIVE IT TO ME.
IT'S LETHAL! IT USED TO BELONG TO A VILLAIN NAMED THE WIZARD! I WANT MORE PROOF THAT YOU'RE WHO YOU SAY YOU ARE BEFORE I JUST HAND IT OVER!
SIMMONS, I EXPLICITLY ASKED YOU TO KEEP HER OUT OF THIS IF SHE SHOWED UP--!
I'M SORRY.
HEY! WHAT DID I EVER DO TO YOU--
OH, MY LOONIE AUNTIE. IS THAT WHAT I THINK IT IS?
MISS, STEP AWAY FROM THE--
IT'S LIKE A VILLAIN MUSEUM IN THAT BAG! SHOCKER'S GLOVE! ADHESIVE X! PLANT MAN'S GUN! WHAT ELSE--?
YOU'RE INTERFERING IN AN ACTIVE INVESTIGATION!
AND IT'S THE GOOD PLANT-GUN, TOO! THE ANIMATOR HE USED AGAINST SUB-MARINER, NOT THE VEGE-RAY HE USED ON THE HUMAN TORCH!
YOU'RE MISTAKEN. THAT'S THE VEGE-RAY.
IT IS NOT! THE VEGE-RAY HAS A LONGER BARREL! THIS IS THE ONE THE MAGGIA MADE FOR HIM!
HUH.
YOU KNOW, IT MIGHT BE THE ANIMATOR...
I LURK ON EVERY SUPER-HERO FAN SITE THERE IS. I ADMIN ON TWO. I KNOW MY STUFF.
CLEARLY.

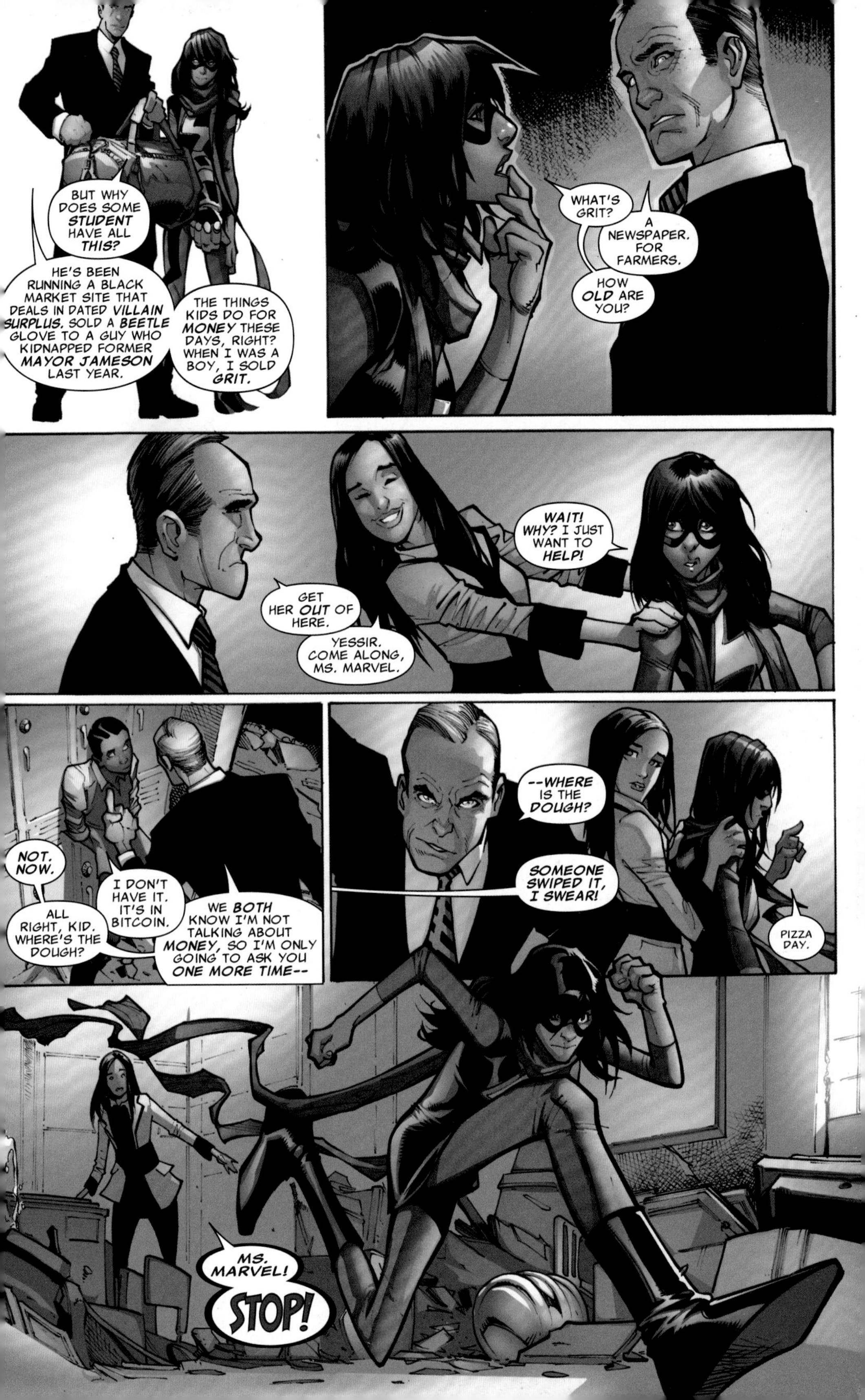
BUT WHY DOES SOME STUDENT HAVE ALL THIS?
HE'S BEEN RUNNING A BLACK MARKET SITE THAT DEALS IN DATED VILLAIN SURPLUS. SOLD A BEETLE GLOVE TO A GUY WHO KIDNAPPED FORMER MAYOR JAMESON LAST YEAR.
THE THINGS KIDS DO FOR MONEY THESE DAYS, RIGHT? WHEN I WAS A BOY, I SOLD GRIT.
WHAT'S GRIT?
A NEWSPAPER. FOR FARMERS.
HOW OLD ARE YOU?
WAIT! WHY? I JUST WANT TO HELP!
GET HER OUT OF HERE.
YESSIR. COME ALONG, MS. MARVEL.
NOT. NOW.
ALL RIGHT, KID. WHERE'S THE DOUGH?
I DON'T HAVE IT. IT'S IN BITCOIN.
WE BOTH KNOW I'M NOT TALKING ABOUT MONEY, SO I'M ONLY GOING TO ASK YOU ONE MORE TIME--
--WHERE IS THE DOUGH?
SOMEONE SWIPED IT, I SWEAR!
PIZZA DAY.
MS. MARVEL!
STOP!

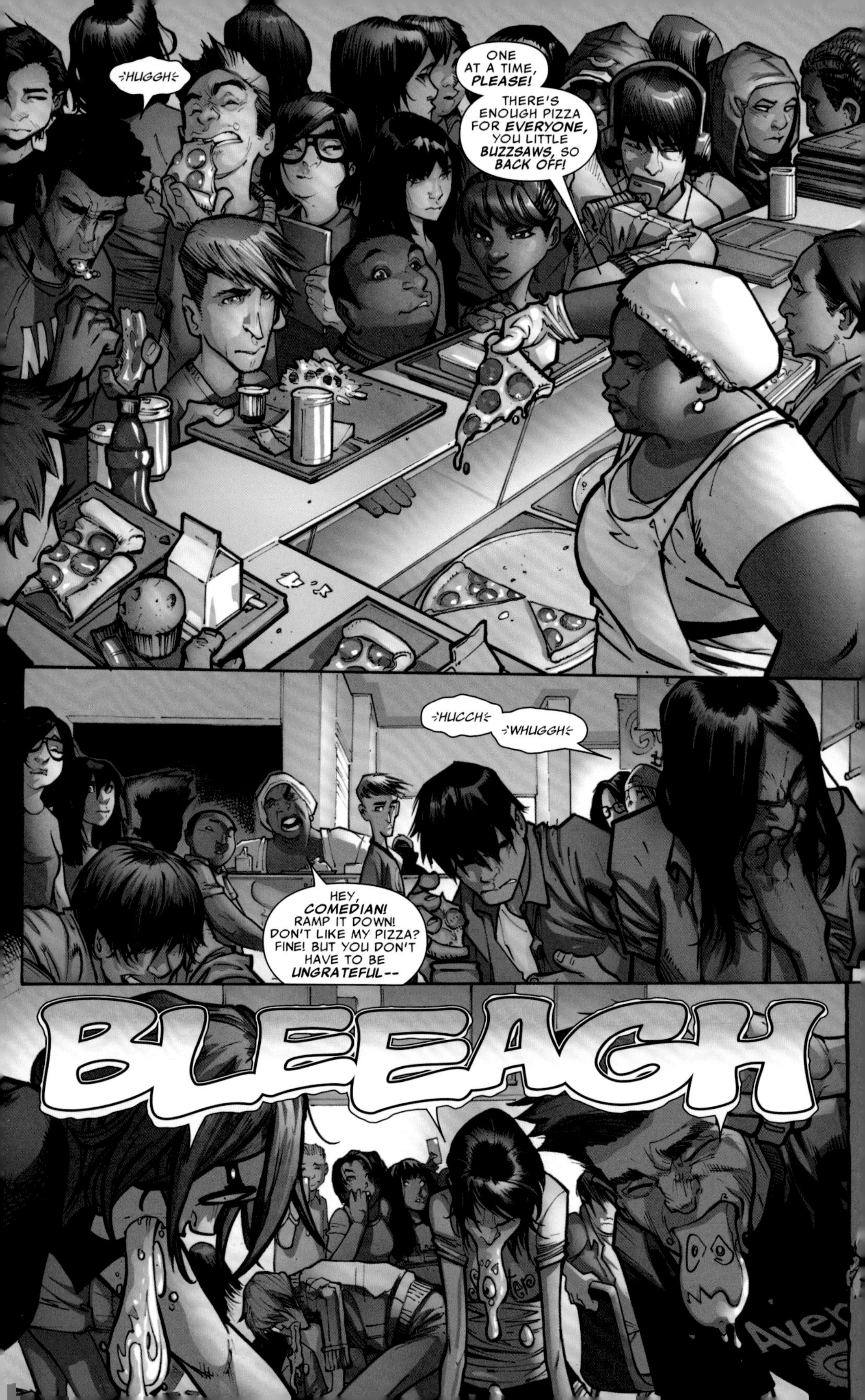
HUGGH
ONE AT A TIME, PLEASE!
THERE'S ENOUGH PIZZA FOR EVERYONE, YOU LITTLE BUZZSAWS, SO BACK OFF!
HUCCH
WHUGGH
HEY, COMEDIAN! RAMP IT DOWN! DON'T LIKE MY PIZZA? FINE! BUT YOU DON'T HAVE TO BE UNGRATEFUL--
BLEEACH

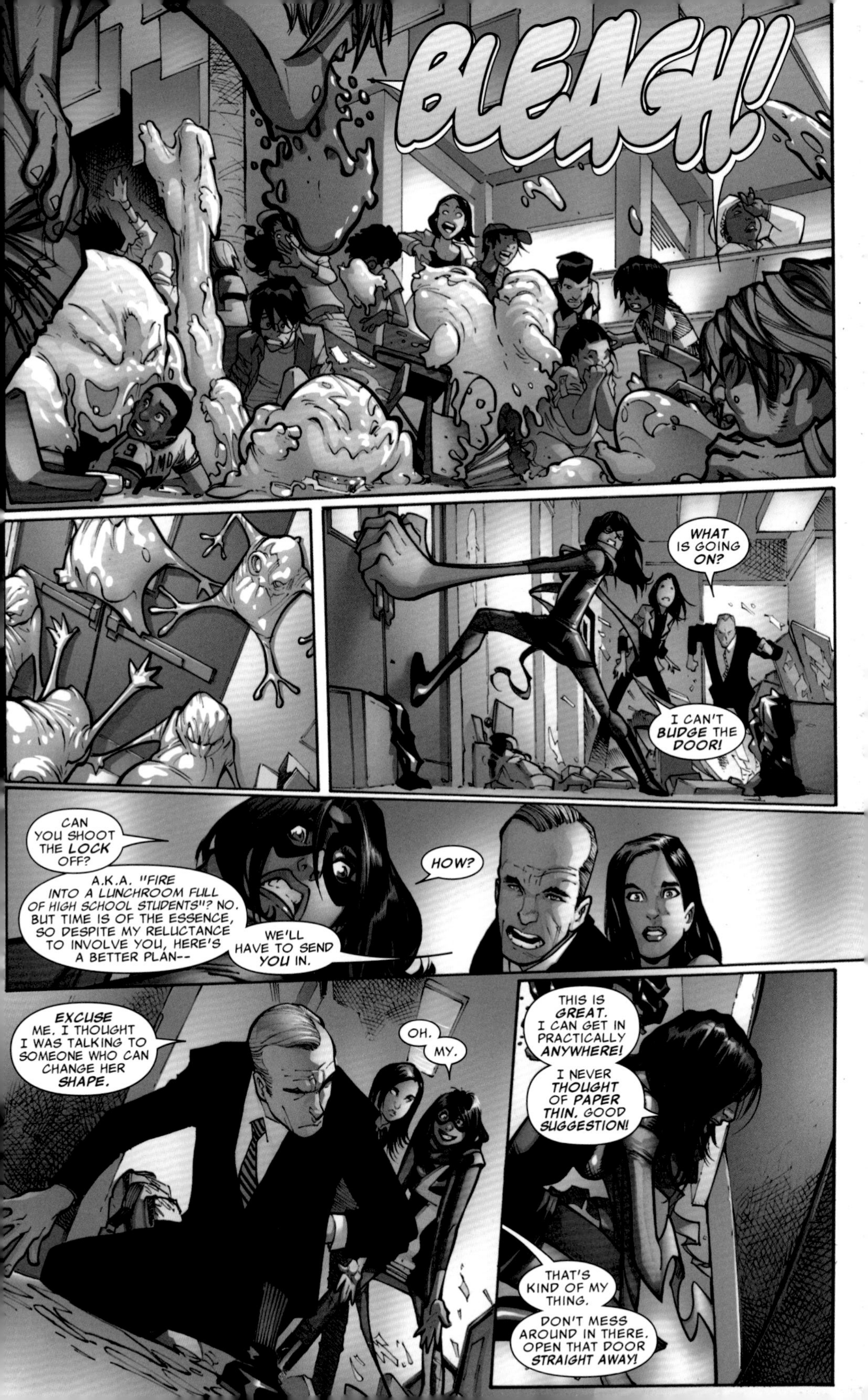
BLEACH!
WHAT IS GOING ON?
I CAN'T BUDGE THE DOOR!
CAN YOU SHOOT THE LOCK OFF?
A.K.A. "FIRE INTO A LUNCHROOM FULL OF HIGH SCHOOL STUDENTS"? NO. BUT TIME IS OF THE ESSENCE, SO DESPITE MY RELUCTANCE TO INVOLVE YOU, HERE'S A BETTER PLAN--
HOW?
WE'LL HAVE TO SEND YOU IN.
EXCUSE ME. I THOUGHT I WAS TALKING TO SOMEONE WHO CAN CHANGE HER SHAPE.
OH.
MY.
THIS IS GREAT. I CAN GET IN PRACTICALLY ANYWHERE!
I NEVER THOUGHT OF PAPER THIN. GOOD SUGGESTION!
THAT'S KIND OF MY THING.
DON'T MESS AROUND IN THERE. OPEN THAT DOOR STRAIGHT AWAY!

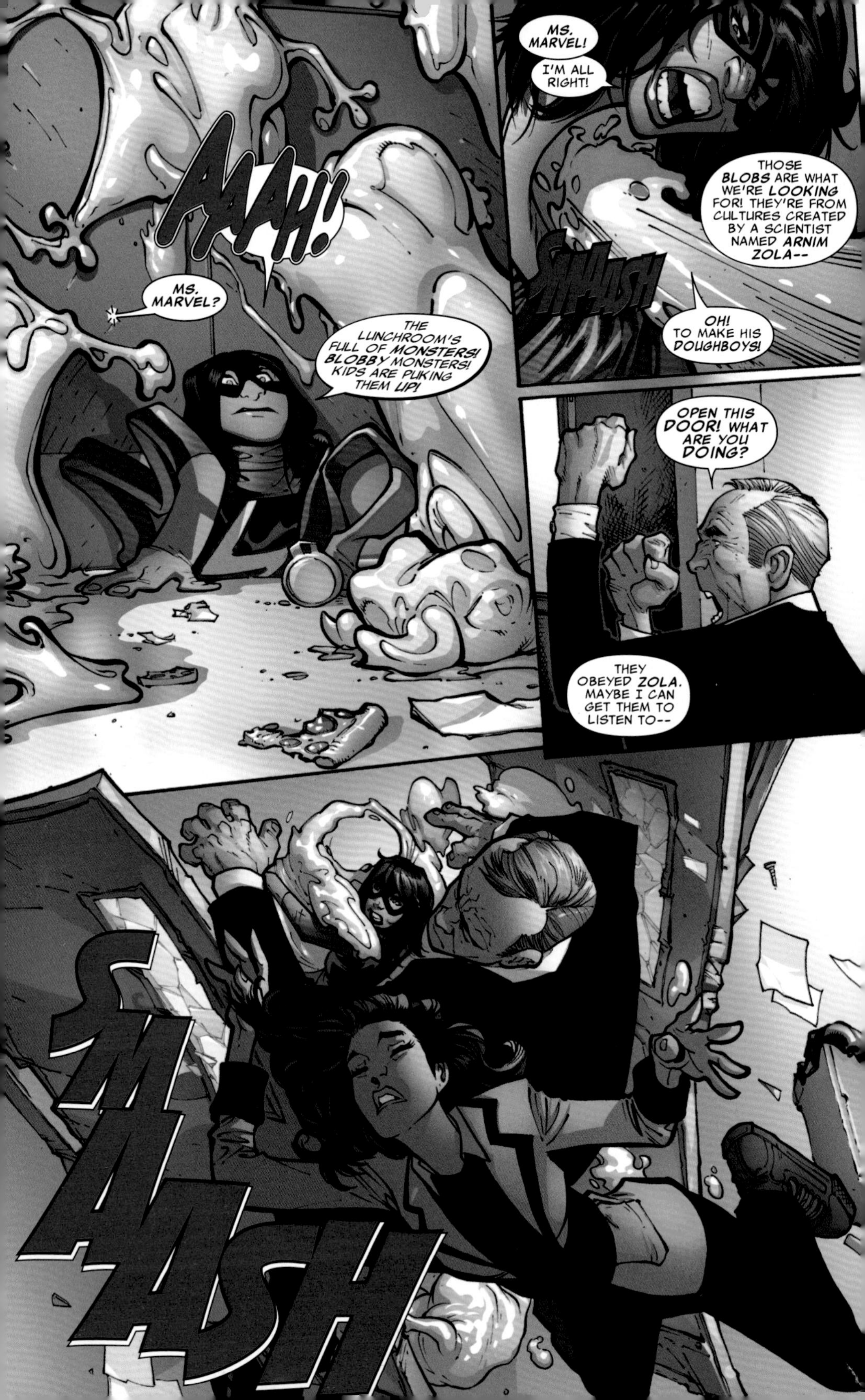
AAAAH!
MS. MARVEL?
THE LUNCHROOM'S FULL OF MONSTERS! BLOBBY MONSTERS! KIDS ARE PUKING THEM UP!
MS. MARVEL!
I'M ALL RIGHT!
SMAASH
THOSE BLOBS ARE WHAT WE'RE LOOKING FOR! THEY'RE FROM CULTURES CREATED BY A SCIENTIST NAMED ARNIM ZOLA--
OH! TO MAKE HIS DOUGHBOYS!
OPEN THIS DOOR! WHAT ARE YOU DOING?
THEY OBEYED ZOLA. MAYBE I CAN GET THEM TO LISTEN TO--
SMAASH

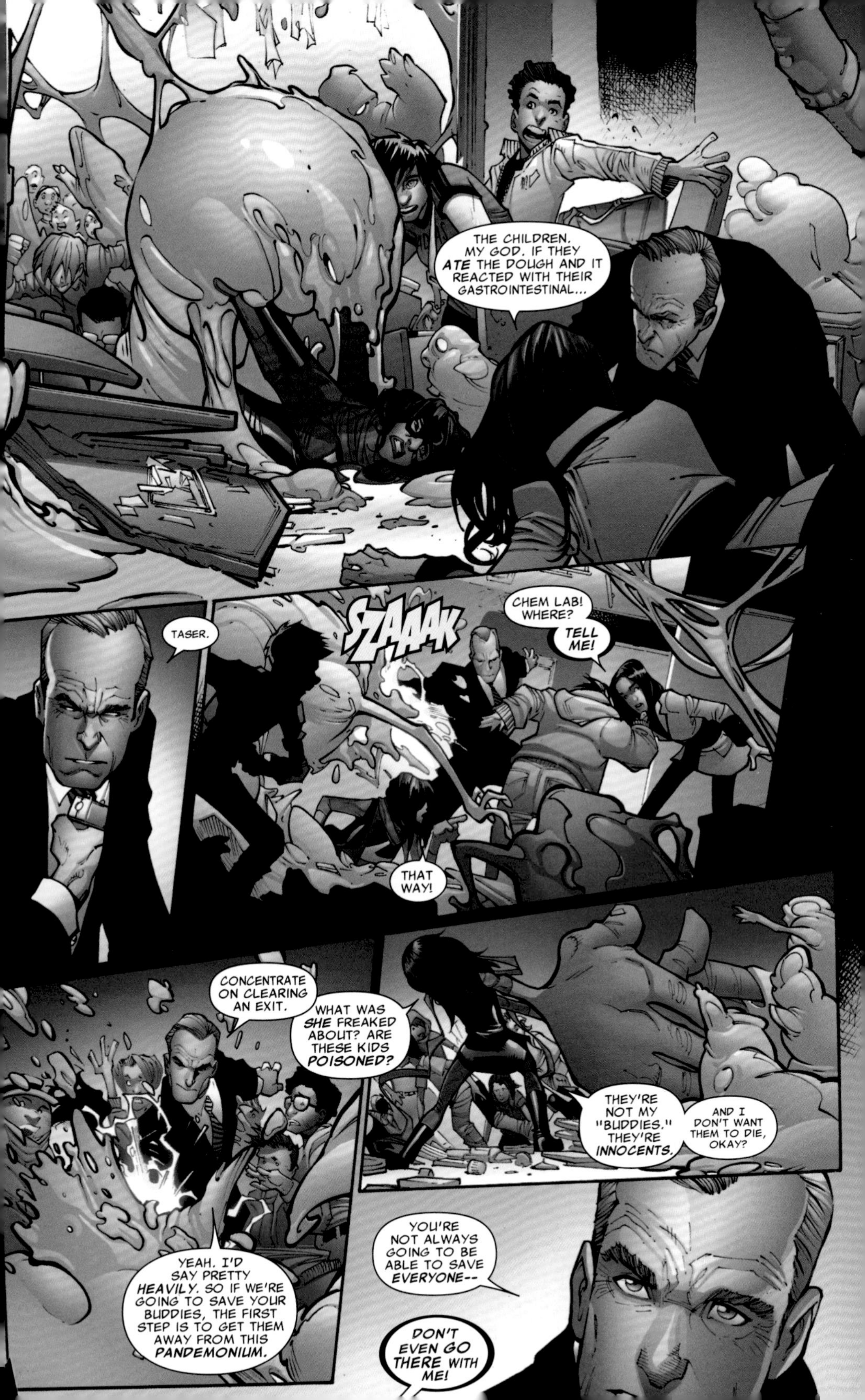

THE CHILDREN. MY GOD. IF THEY ATE THE DOUGH AND IT REACTED WITH THEIR GASTROINTESTINAL...
TASER.
SZAAAK
CHEM LAB! WHERE? TELL ME!
THAT WAY!
CONCENTRATE ON CLEARING AN EXIT.
WHAT WAS SHE FREAKED ABOUT? ARE THESE KIDS POISONED?
YEAH. I'D SAY PRETTY HEAVILY. SO IF WE'RE GOING TO SAVE YOUR BUDDIES, THE FIRST STEP IS TO GET THEM AWAY FROM THIS PANDEMONIUM.
THEY'RE NOT MY "BUDDIES." THEY'RE INNOCENTS.
AND I DON'T WANT THEM TO DIE, OKAY?
YOU'RE NOT ALWAYS GOING TO BE ABLE TO SAVE EVERYONE--
DON'T EVEN GO THERE WITH ME!

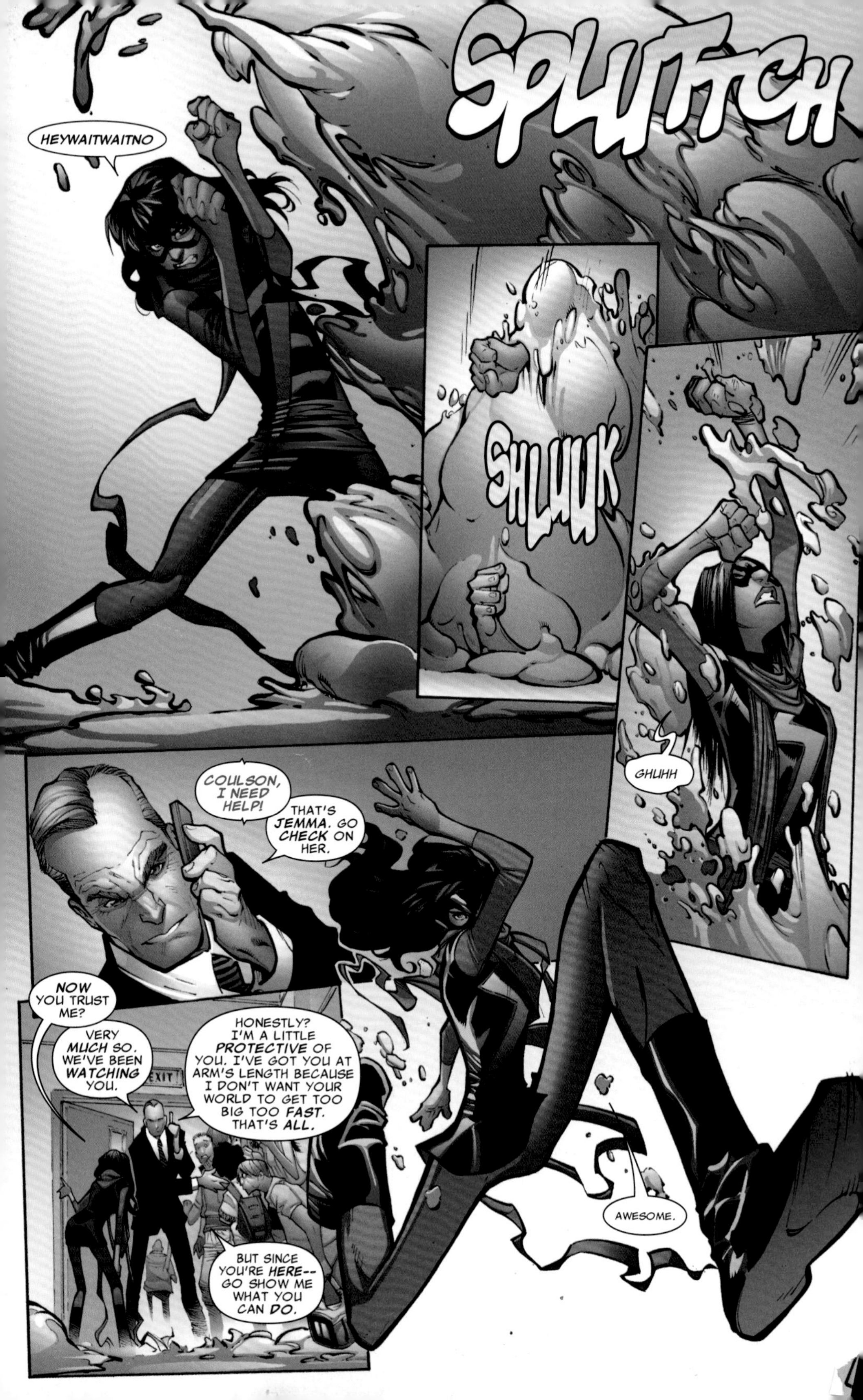
SPLUTTCH
HEYWAITWAITNO
SHLUUK
GHUHH
COULSON, I NEED HELP!
THAT'S JEMMA. GO CHECK ON HER.
NOW YOU TRUST ME?
VERY MUCH SO. WE'VE BEEN WATCHING YOU.
HONESTLY? I'M A LITTLE PROTECTIVE OF YOU. I'VE GOT YOU AT ARM'S LENGTH BECAUSE I DON'T WANT YOUR WORLD TO GET TOO BIG TOO FAST. THAT'S ALL.
BUT SINCE YOU'RE HERE-- GO SHOW ME WHAT YOU CAN DO.
AWESOME.
EXIT

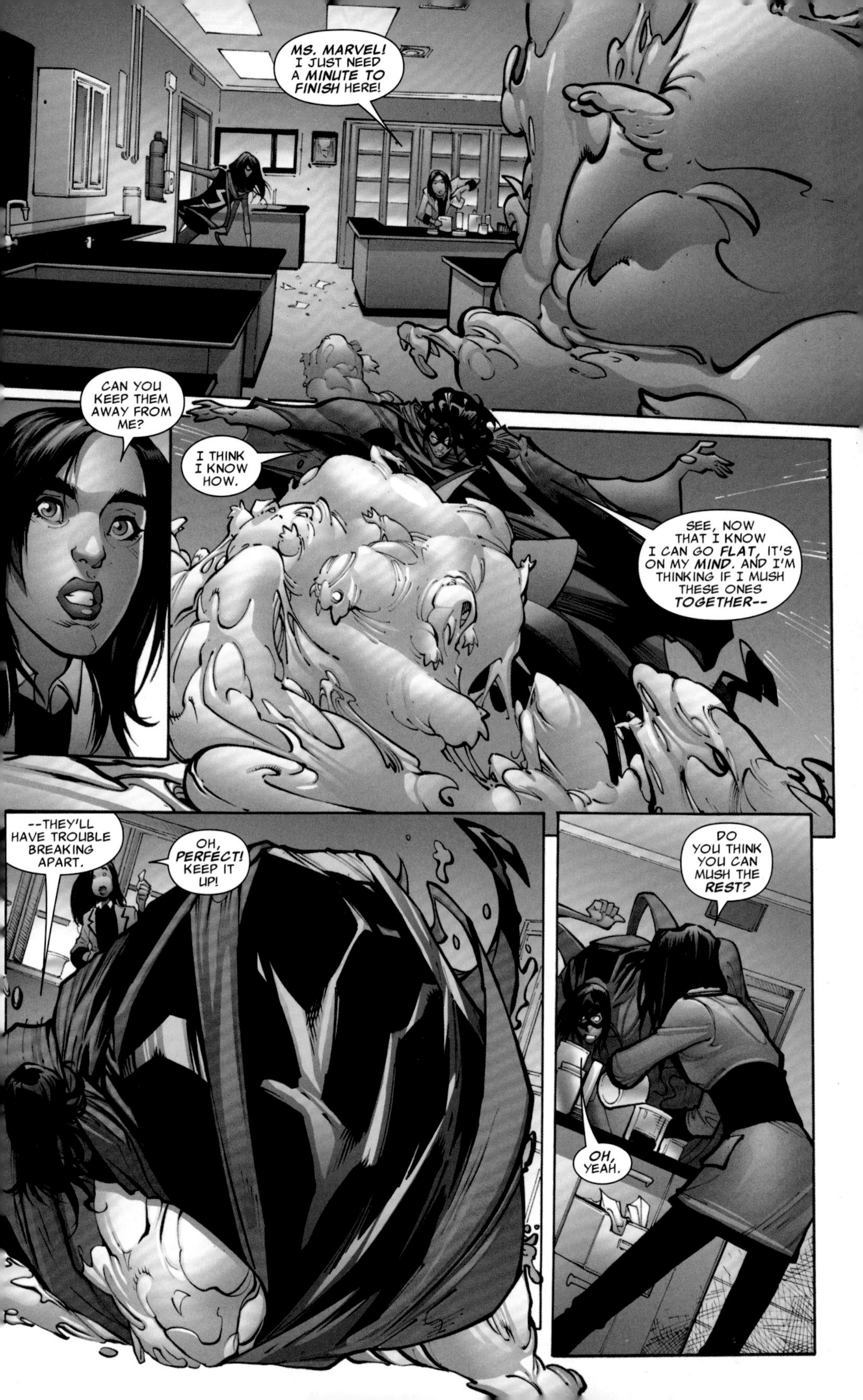
MS. MARVEL! I JUST NEED A MINUTE TO FINISH HERE!
CAN YOU KEEP THEM AWAY FROM ME?
I THINK I KNOW HOW.
SEE, NOW THAT I KNOW I CAN GO FLAT, IT'S ON MY MIND. AND I'M THINKING IF I MUSH THESE ONES TOGETHER--
--THEY'LL HAVE TROUBLE BREAKING APART.
OH, PERFECT! KEEP IT UP!
DO YOU THINK YOU CAN MUSH THE REST?
OH, YEAH.

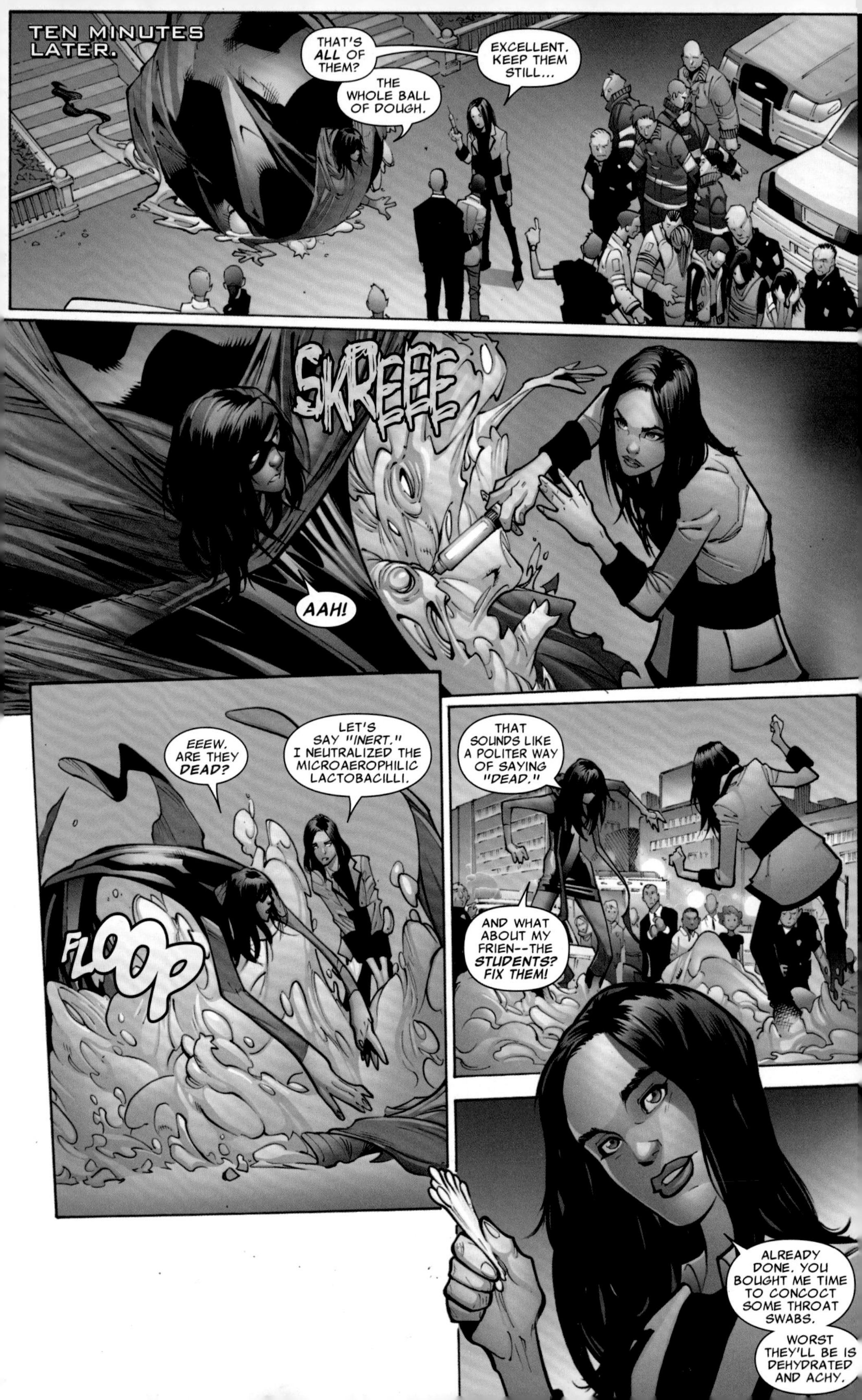
TEN MINUTES LATER.
THAT'S ALL OF THEM?
THE WHOLE BALL OF DOUGH.
EXCELLENT. KEEP THEM STILL...
SKREEE
AAH!
EEEW. ARE THEY DEAD?
LET'S SAY "INERT." I NEUTRALIZED THE MICROAEROPHILIC LACTOBACILLI.
FLOOP
THAT SOUNDS LIKE A POLITER WAY OF SAYING "DEAD."
AND WHAT ABOUT MY FRIEN--THE STUDENTS? FIX THEM!
ALREADY DONE. YOU BOUGHT ME TIME TO CONCOCT SOME THROAT SWABS.
WORST THEY'LL BE IS DEHYDRATED AND ACHY.

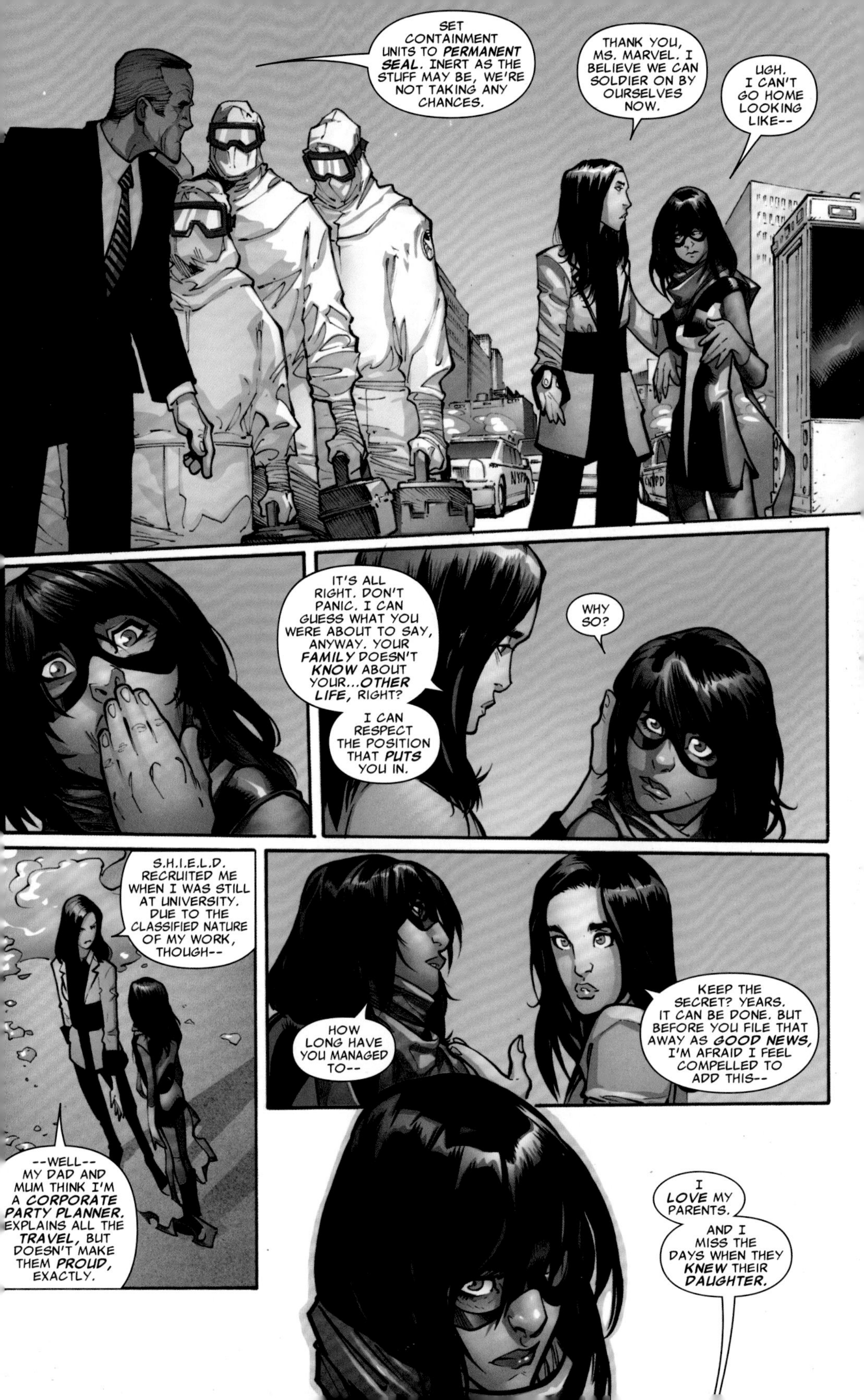
SET CONTAINMENT UNITS TO PERMANENT SEAL. INERT AS THE STUFF MAY BE, WE'RE NOT TAKING ANY CHANCES.
THANK YOU, MS. MARVEL. I BELIEVE WE CAN SOLDIER ON BY OURSELVES NOW.
UGH. I CAN'T GO HOME LOOKING LIKE--
IT'S ALL RIGHT. DON'T PANIC. I CAN GUESS WHAT YOU WERE ABOUT TO SAY, ANYWAY. YOUR FAMILY DOESN'T KNOW ABOUT YOUR...OTHER LIFE, RIGHT?
I CAN RESPECT THE POSITION THAT PUTS YOU IN.
WHY SO?
S.H.I.E.L.D. RECRUITED ME WHEN I WAS STILL AT UNIVERSITY. DUE TO THE CLASSIFIED NATURE OF MY WORK, THOUGH--
--WELL-- MY DAD AND MUM THINK I'M A CORPORATE PARTY PLANNER. EXPLAINS ALL THE TRAVEL, BUT DOESN'T MAKE THEM PROUD, EXACTLY.
HOW LONG HAVE YOU MANAGED TO--
KEEP THE SECRET? YEARS. IT CAN BE DONE. BUT BEFORE YOU FILE THAT AWAY AS GOOD NEWS, I'M AFRAID I FEEL COMPELLED TO ADD THIS--
I LOVE MY PARENTS.
AND I MISS THE DAYS WHEN THEY KNEW THEIR DAUGHTER.

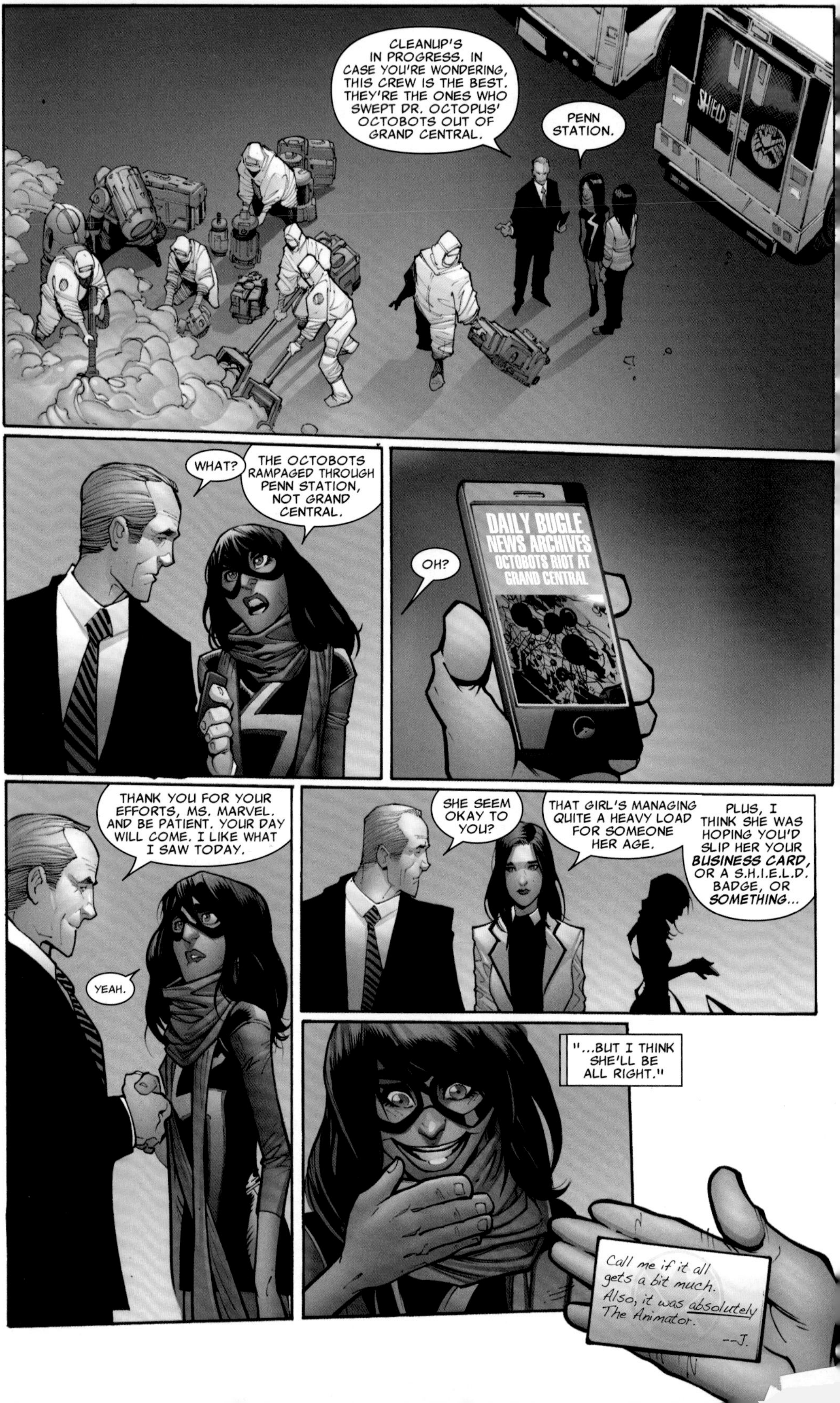
CLEANUP'S IN PROGRESS. IN CASE YOU'RE WONDERING, THIS CREW IS THE BEST. THEY'RE THE ONES WHO SWEPT DR. OCTOPUS' OCTOBOTS OUT OF GRAND CENTRAL.
PENN STATION.
SHIELD
WHAT?
THE OCTOBOTS RAMPAGED THROUGH PENN STATION, NOT GRAND CENTRAL.
OH?
DAILY BUGLE NEWS ARCHIVES
OCTOBOTS RIOT AT GRAND CENTRAL
THANK YOU FOR YOUR EFFORTS, MS. MARVEL. AND BE PATIENT. YOUR DAY WILL COME. I LIKE WHAT I SAW TODAY.
YEAH.
SHE SEEM OKAY TO YOU?
THAT GIRL'S MANAGING QUITE A HEAVY LOAD FOR SOMEONE HER AGE.
PLUS, I THINK SHE WAS HOPING YOU'D SLIP HER YOUR BUSINESS CARD, OR A S.H.I.E.L.D. BADGE, OR SOMETHING...
"...BUT I THINK SHE'LL BE ALL RIGHT."
Call me if it all gets a bit much. Also, it was absolutely The Animator. --J.

MS. MARVEL #17

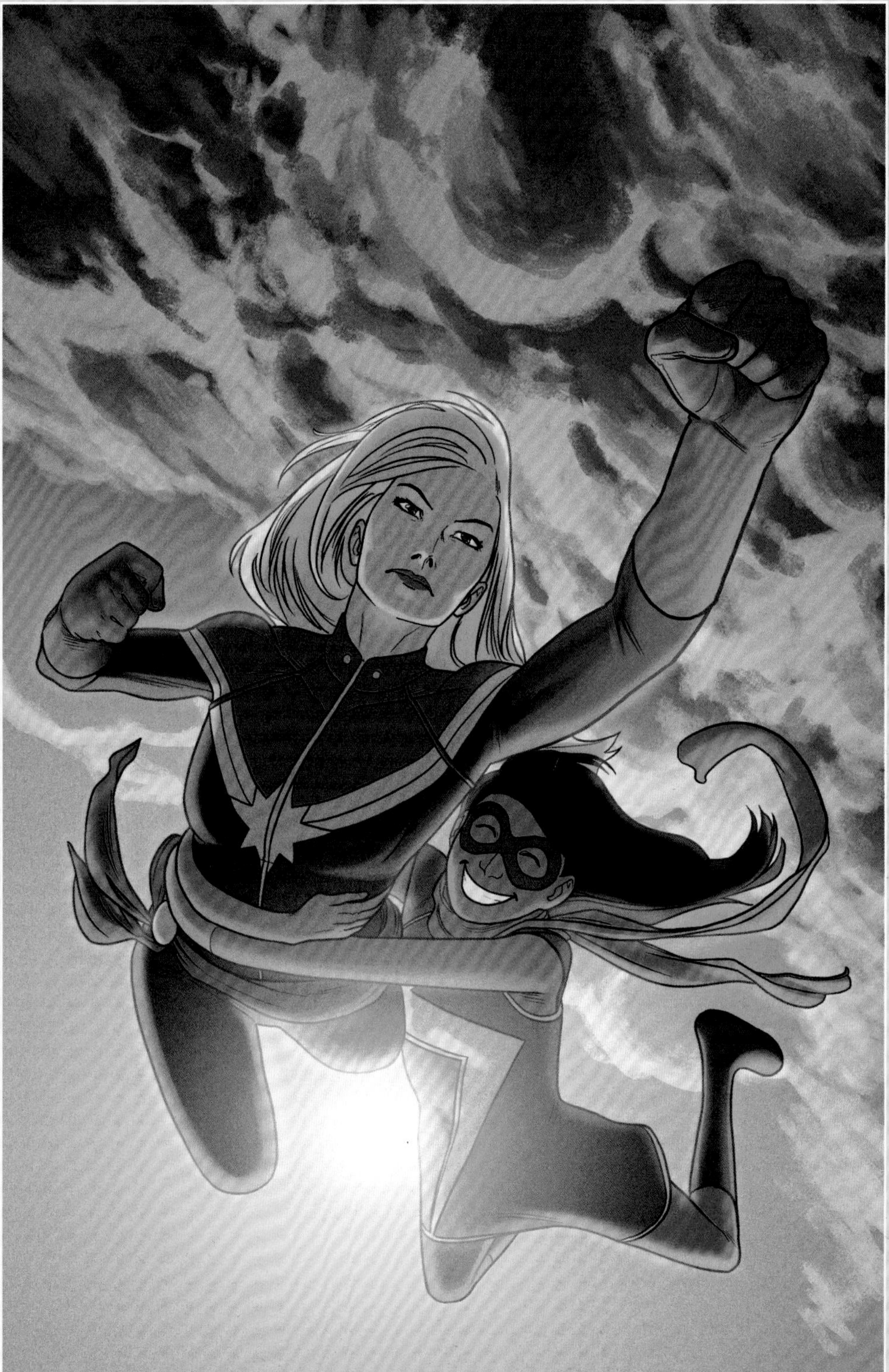

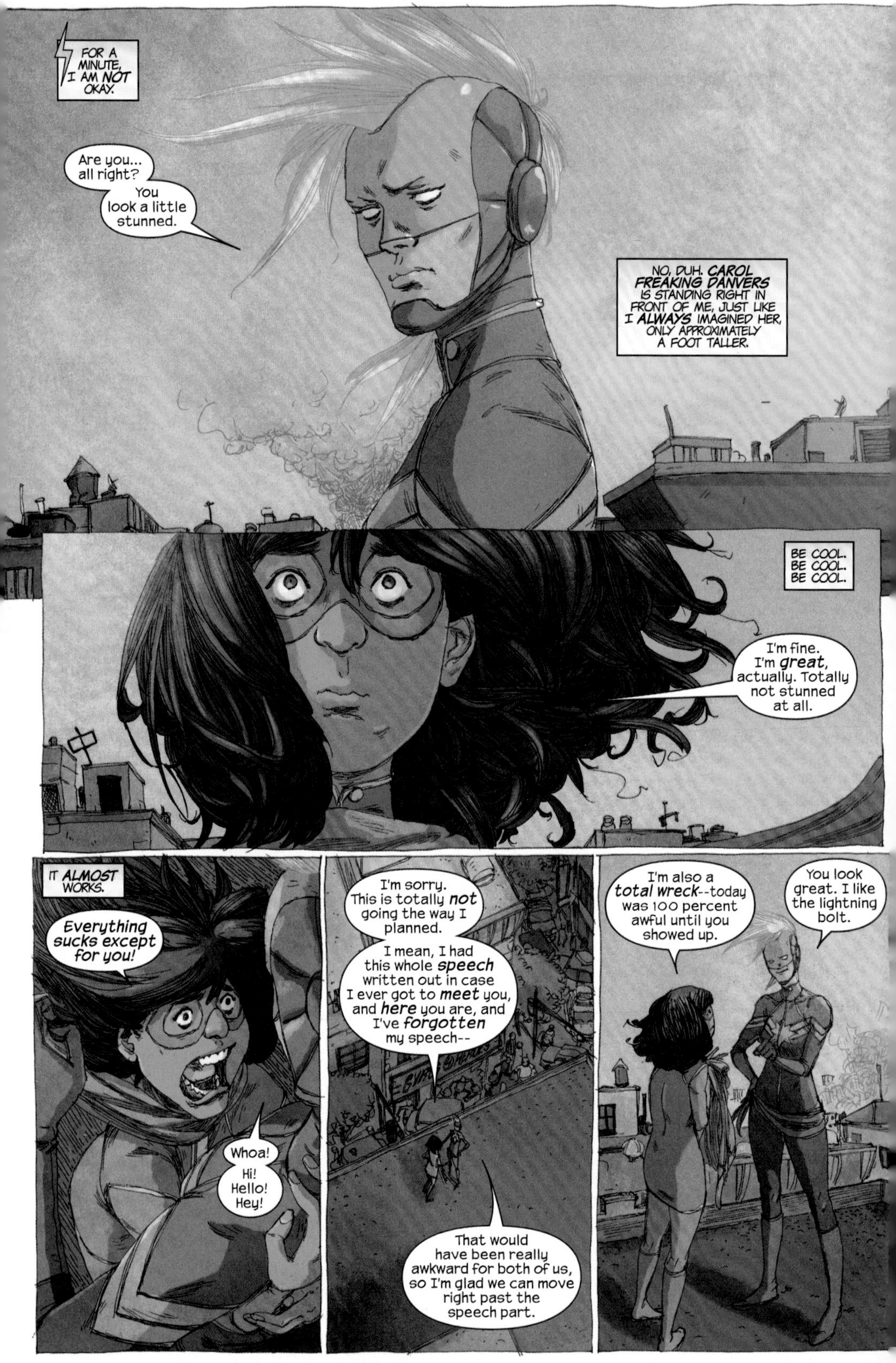
FOR A MINUTE, I AM NOT OKAY.
Are you... all right? You look a little stunned.
NO, DUH. CAROL FREAKING DANVERS IS STANDING RIGHT IN FRONT OF ME, JUST LIKE I ALWAYS IMAGINED HER, ONLY APPROXIMATELY A FOOT TALLER.
BE COOL. BE COOL. BE COOL.
I'm fine. I'm great, actually. Totally not stunned at all.
IT ALMOST WORKS.
Everything sucks except for you!
Whoa! Hi! Hello! Hey!
I'm sorry. This is totally not going the way I planned.
I mean, I had this whole speech written out in case I ever got to meet you, and here you are, and I've forgotten my speech--
That would have been really awkward for both of us, so I'm glad we can move right past the speech part.
I'm also a total wreck--today was 100 percent awful until you showed up.
You look great. I like the lightning bolt.

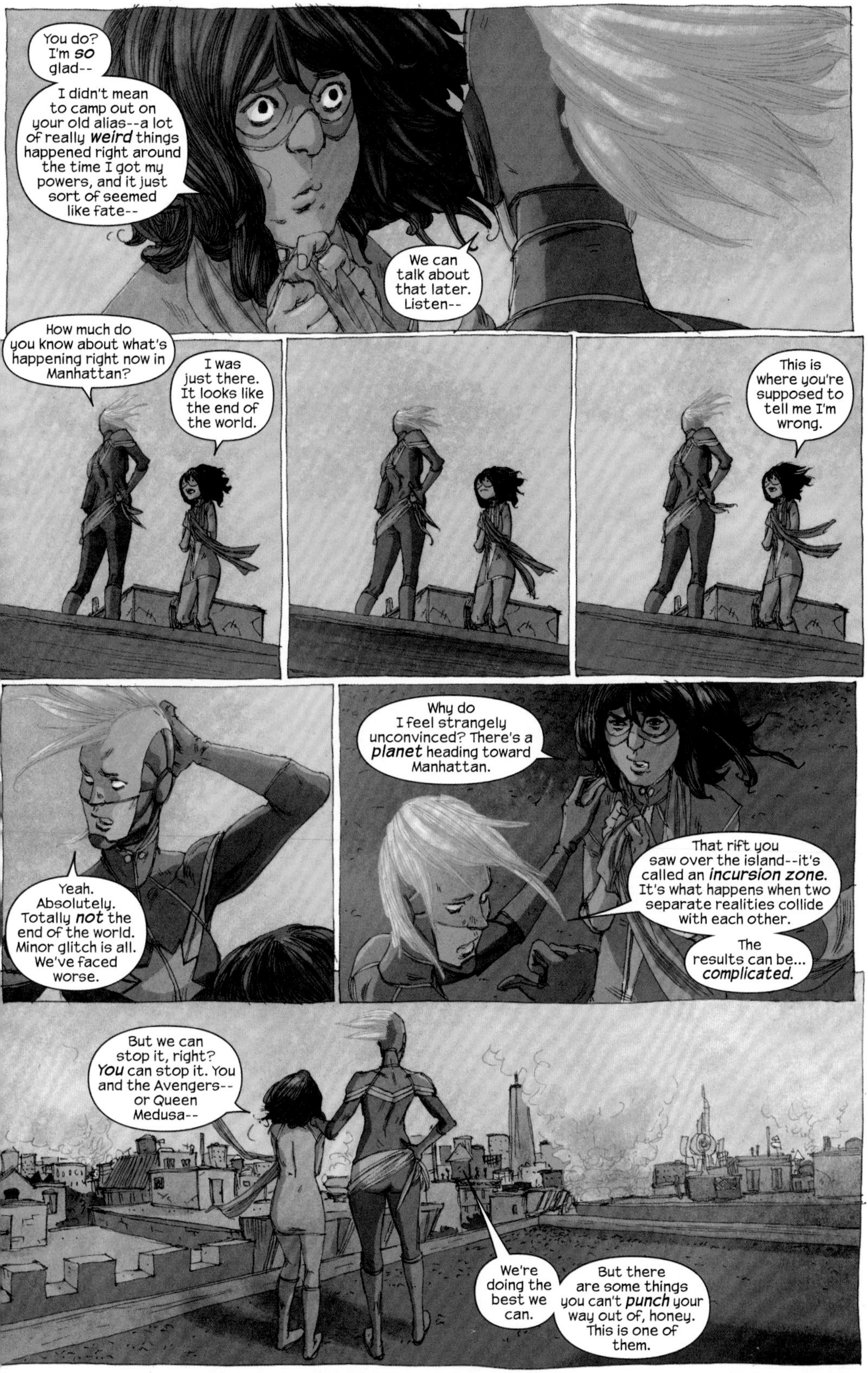
You do? I'm *so* glad--
I didn't mean to camp out on your old alias--a lot of really *weird* things happened right around the time I got my powers, and it just sort of seemed like fate--
We can talk about that later. Listen--
How much do you know about what's happening right now in Manhattan?
I was just there. It looks like the end of the world.
This is where you're supposed to tell me I'm wrong.
Yeah. Absolutely. Totally *not* the end of the world. Minor glitch is all. We've faced worse.
Why do I feel strangely unconvinced? There's a *planet* heading toward Manhattan.
That rift you saw over the island--it's called an *incursion zone*. It's what happens when two separate realities collide with each other.
The results can be... *complicated*.
But we can stop it, right? *You* can stop it. You and the Avengers--or Queen Medusa--
We're doing the best we can.
But there are some things you can't *punch* your way out of, honey. This is one of them.

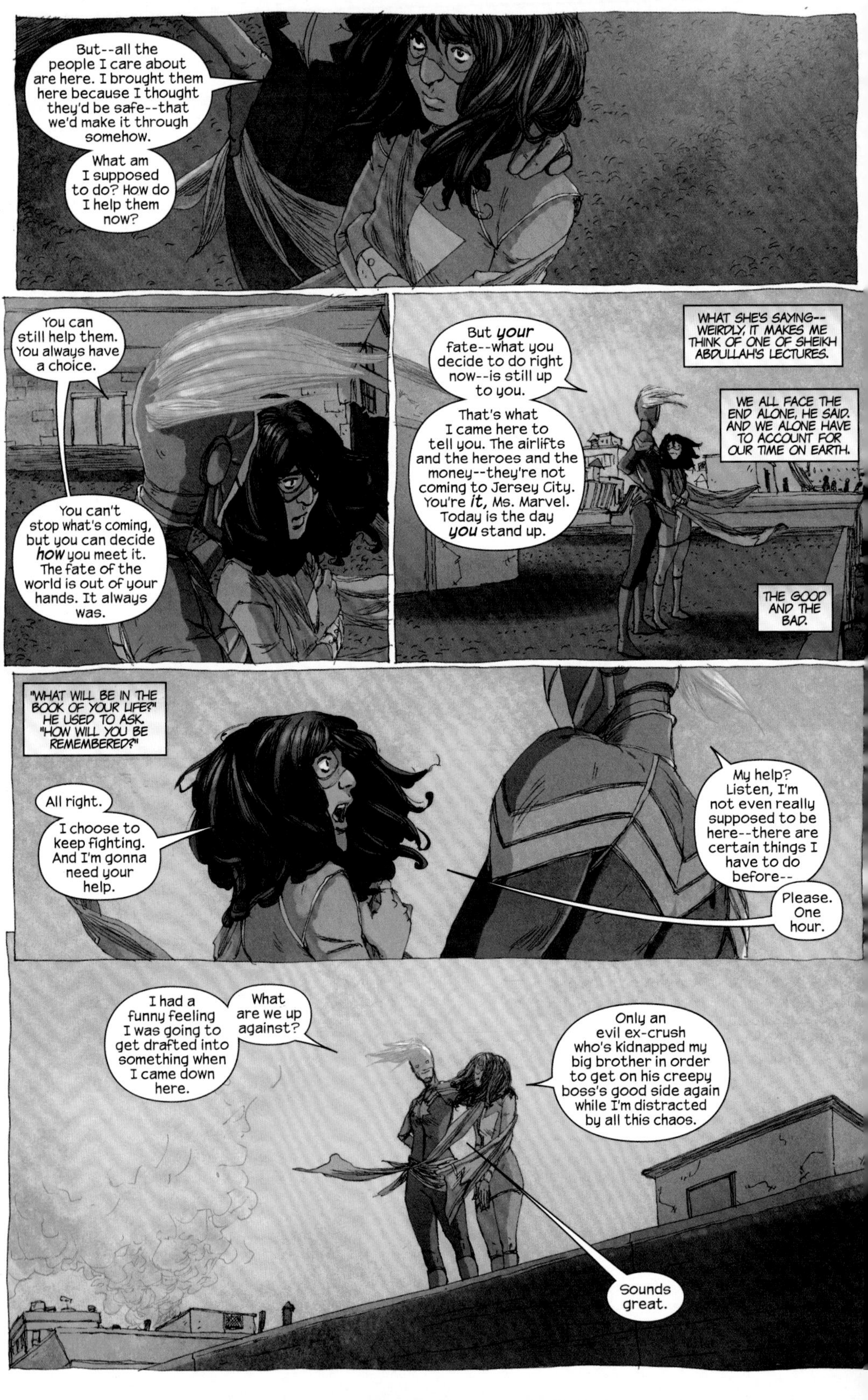
But--all the people I care about are here. I brought them here because I thought they'd be safe--that we'd make it through somehow.
What am I supposed to do? How do I help them now?
You can still help them. You always have a choice.
You can't stop what's coming, but you can decide how you meet it. The fate of the world is out of your hands. It always was.
But your fate--what you decide to do right now--is still up to you.
That's what I came here to tell you. The airlifts and the heroes and the money--they're not coming to Jersey City. You're it, Ms. Marvel. Today is the day you stand up.
WHAT SHE'S SAYING--WEIRDLY, IT MAKES ME THINK OF ONE OF SHEIKH ABDULLAH'S LECTURES.
WE ALL FACE THE END ALONE, HE SAID. AND WE ALONE HAVE TO ACCOUNT FOR OUR TIME ON EARTH.
THE GOOD AND THE BAD.
"WHAT WILL BE IN THE BOOK OF YOUR LIFE?" HE USED TO ASK. "HOW WILL YOU BE REMEMBERED?"
All right.
I choose to keep fighting. And I'm gonna need your help.
My help? Listen, I'm not even really supposed to be here--there are certain things I have to do before--
Please. One hour.
I had a funny feeling I was going to get drafted into something when I came down here.
What are we up against?
Only an evil ex-crush who's kidnapped my big brother in order to get on his creepy boss's good side again while I'm distracted by all this chaos.
Sounds great.

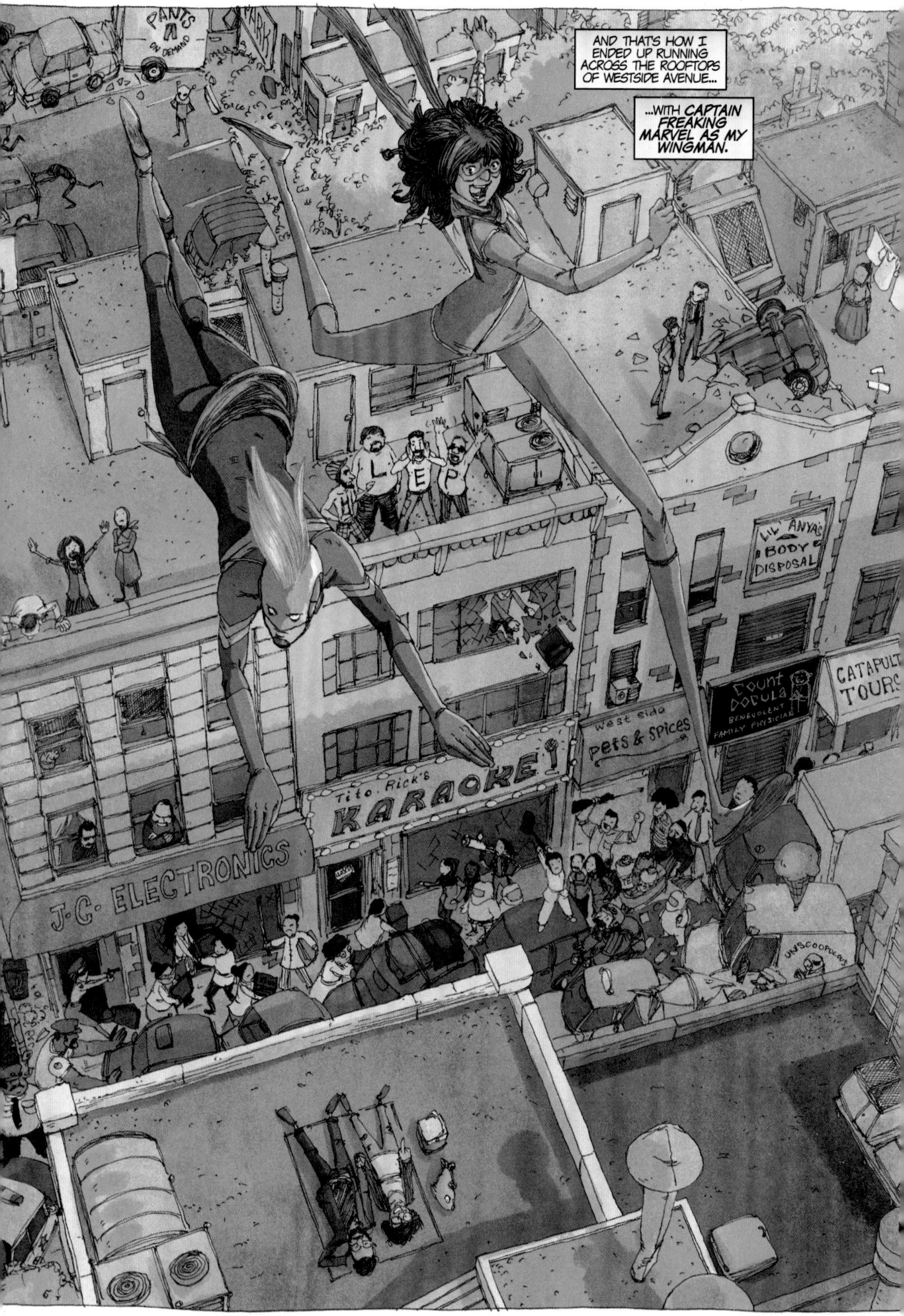
AND THAT'S HOW I ENDED UP RUNNING ACROSS THE ROOFTOPS OF WESTSIDE AVENUE...
...WITH CAPTAIN FREAKING MARVEL AS MY WINGMAN.
PANTS ON DEMAND
LIL' ANYA'S BODY DISPOSAL
Count Docula BENEVOLENT FAMILY PHYSICIAN
CATAPULT TOURS
West side pets & spices
Tito Rick's KARAOKE
J.C. ELECTRONICS

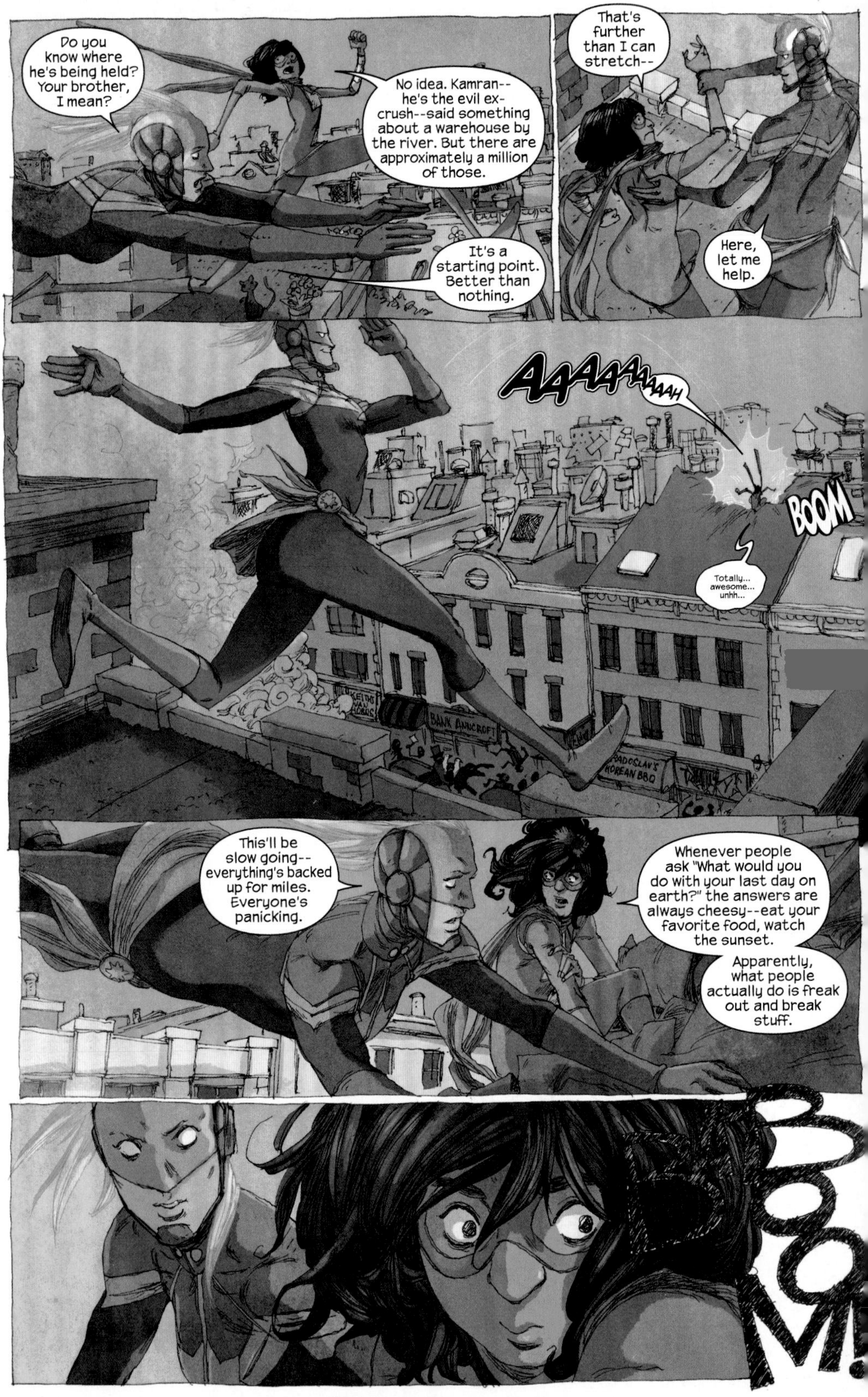

Do you know where he's being held? Your brother, I mean?
No idea. Kamran--he's the evil ex-crush--said something about a warehouse by the river. But there are approximately a million of those.
It's a starting point. Better than nothing.
That's further than I can stretch--
Here, let me help.
AAAAAAAAAH
BOOM
Totally... awesome... unhh...
BANK ANNCROFT
RADOSLAV'S KOREAN BBQ
This'll be slow going--everything's backed up for miles. Everyone's panicking.
Whenever people ask "What would you do with your last day on earth?" the answers are always cheesy--eat your favorite food, watch the sunset.
Apparently, what people actually do is freak out and break stuff.
BOOOOM!

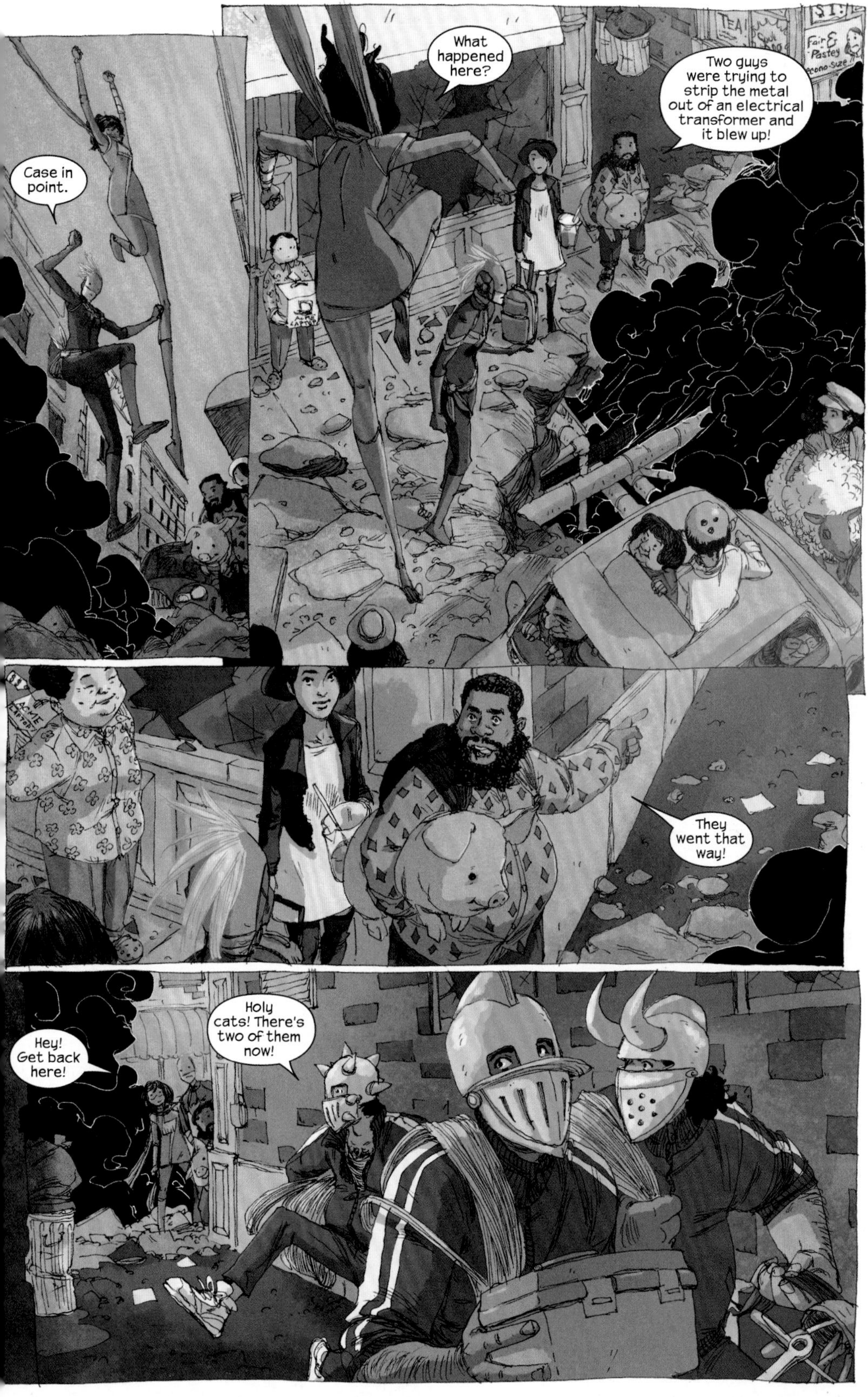
Case in point.
What happened here?
Two guys were trying to strip the metal out of an electrical transformer and it blew up!
They went that way!
Hey! Get back here!
Holy cats! There's two of them now!

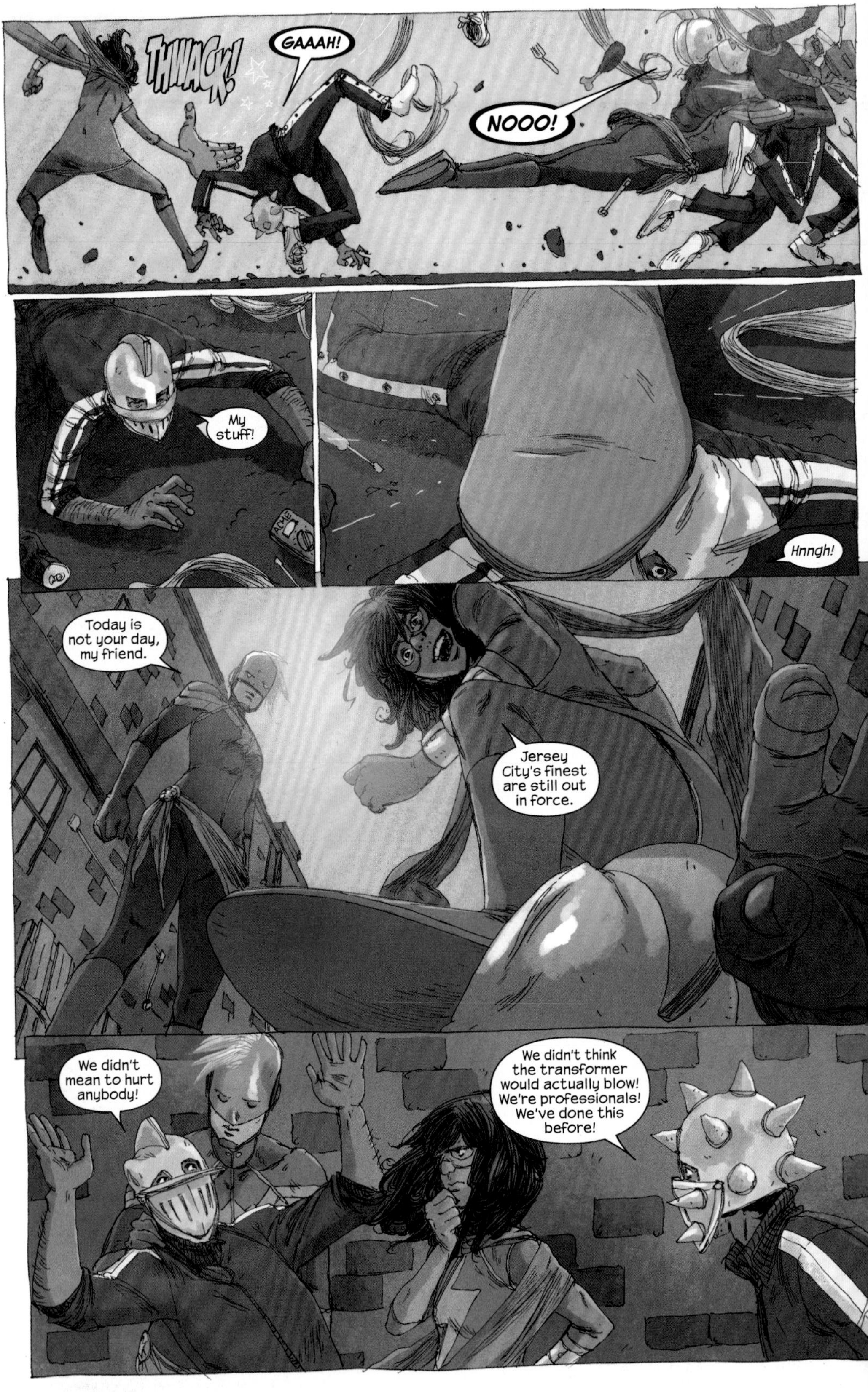
THWACK!
GAAAH!
NOOO!
My stuff!
Hnngh!
Today is not your day, my friend.
Jersey City's finest are still out in force.
We didn't mean to hurt anybody!
We didn't think the transformer would actually blow! We're professionals! We've done this before!

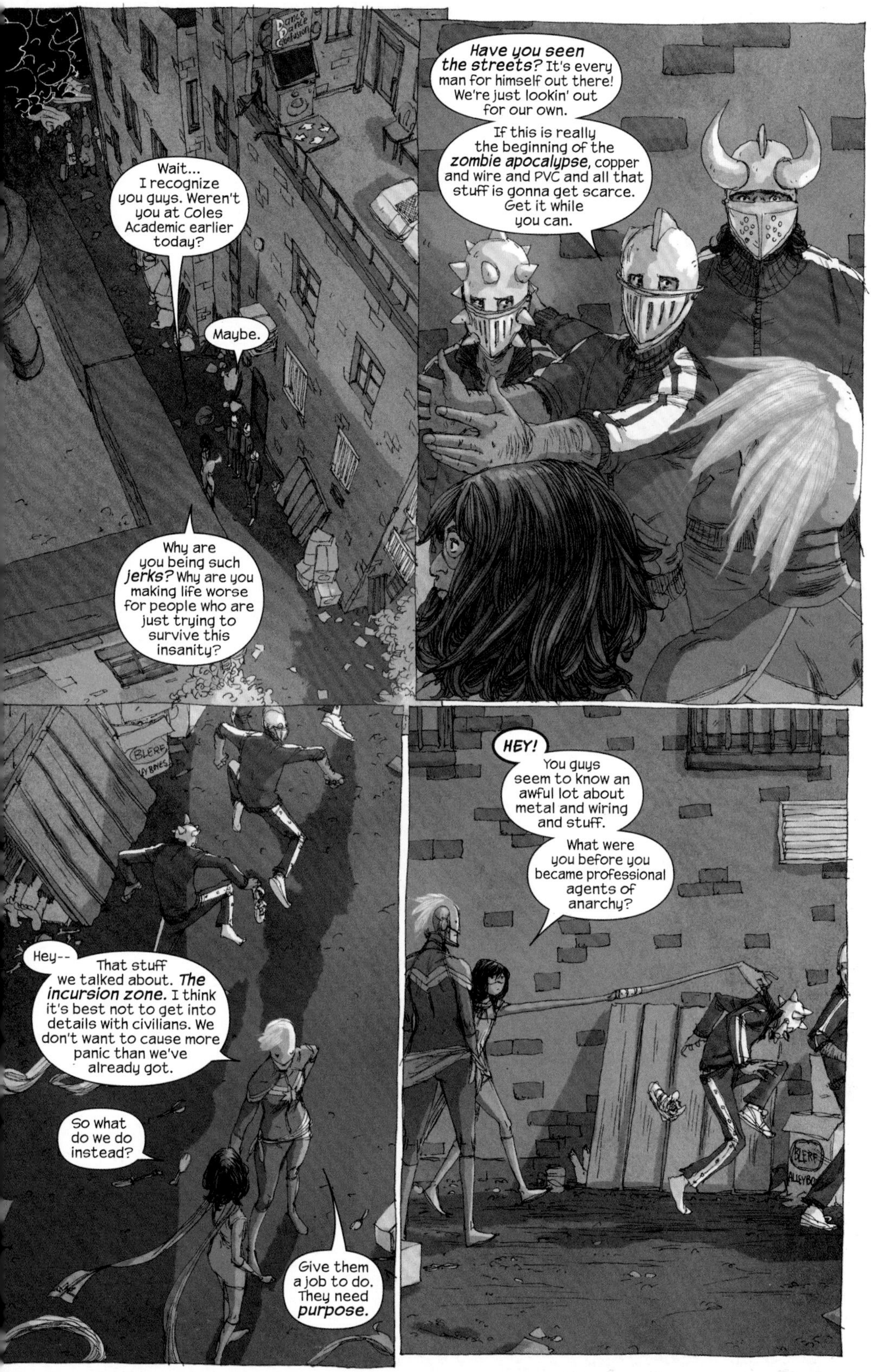
Wait... I recognize you guys. Weren't you at Coles Academic earlier today?
Maybe.
Why are you being such jerks? Why are you making life worse for people who are just trying to survive this insanity?
Have you seen the streets? It's every man for himself out there! We're just lookin' out for our own.
If this is really the beginning of the zombie apocalypse, copper and wire and PVC and all that stuff is gonna get scarce. Get it while you can.
Hey--
That stuff we talked about. The incursion zone. I think it's best not to get into details with civilians. We don't want to cause more panic than we've already got.
So what do we do instead?
Give them a job to do. They need purpose.
HEY!
You guys seem to know an awful lot about metal and wiring and stuff.
What were you before you became professional agents of anarchy?

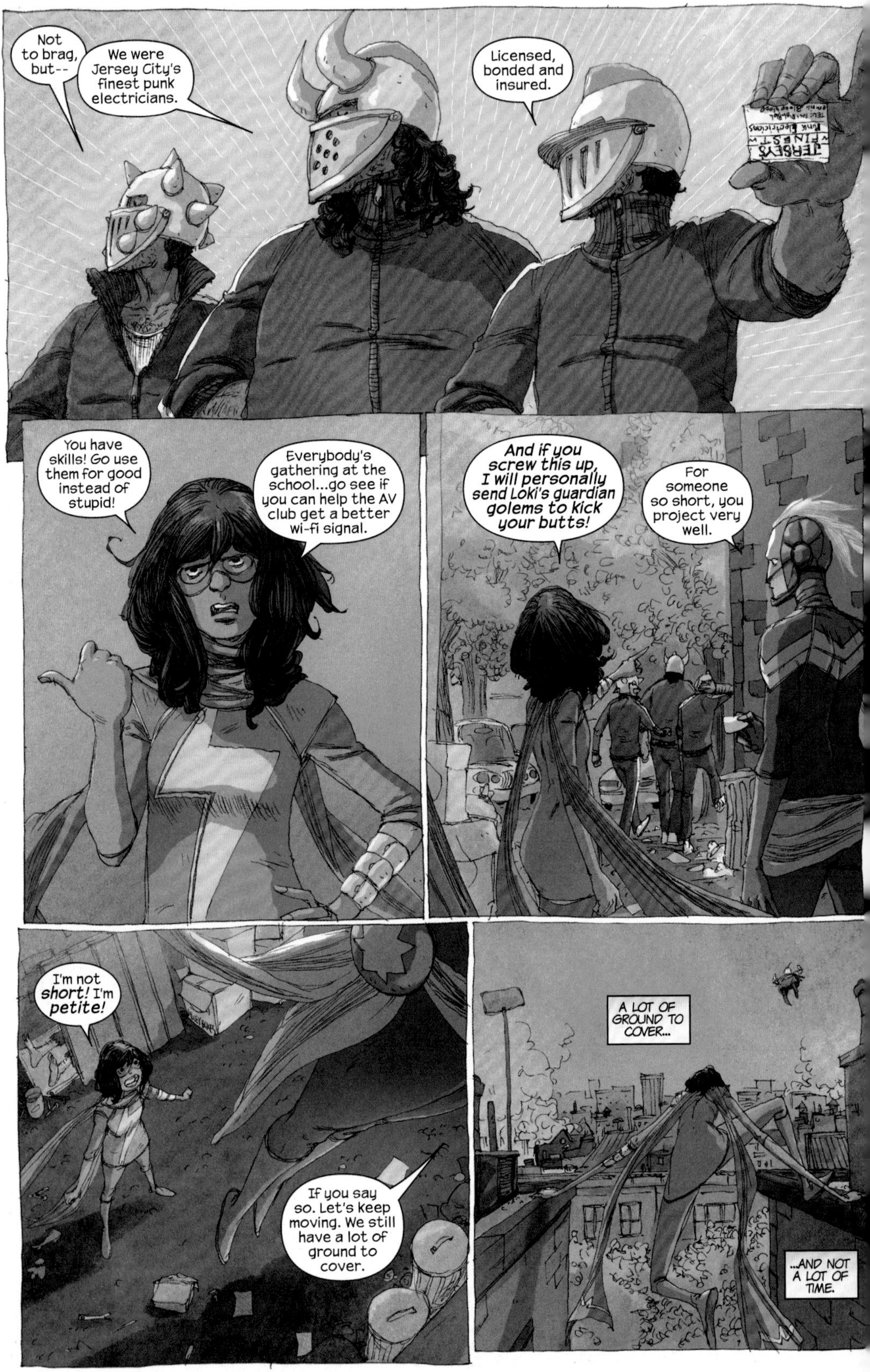
Not to brag, but--
We were Jersey City's finest punk electricians.
Licensed, bonded and insured.
You have skills! Go use them for good instead of stupid!
Everybody's gathering at the school...go see if you can help the AV club get a better wi-fi signal.
And if you screw this up, I will personally send Loki's guardian golems to kick your butts!
For someone so short, you project very well.
I'm not short! I'm petite!
If you say so. Let's keep moving. We still have a lot of ground to cover.
A LOT OF GROUND TO COVER...
...AND NOT A LOT OF TIME.

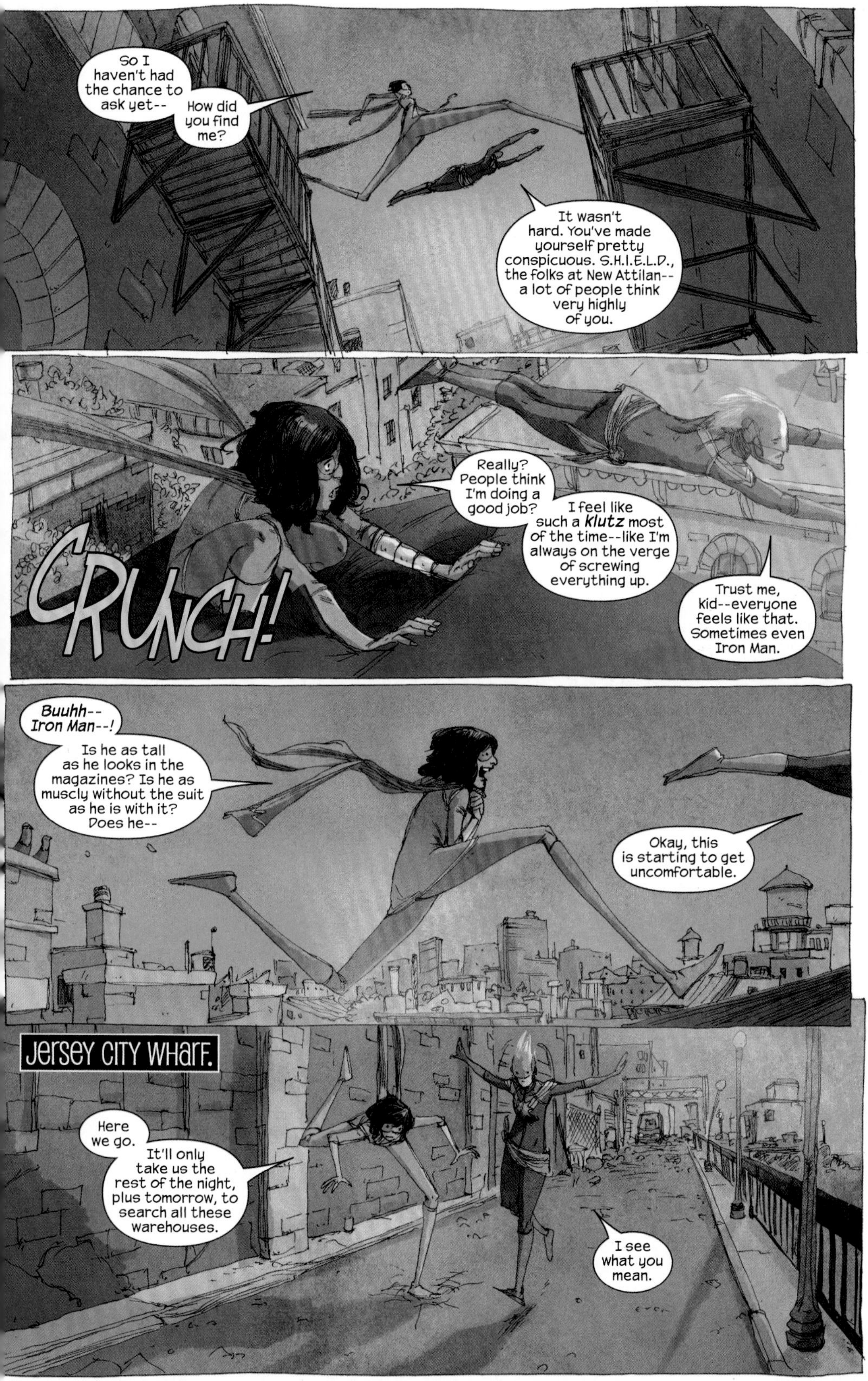
So I haven't had the chance to ask yet--
How did you find me?
It wasn't hard. You've made yourself pretty conspicuous. S.H.I.E.L.D., the folks at New Attilan--a lot of people think very highly of you.
Really? People think I'm doing a good job?
I feel like such a *klutz* most of the time--like I'm always on the verge of screwing everything up.
CRUNCH!
Trust me, kid--everyone feels like that. Sometimes even Iron Man.
Buuhh--Iron Man--!
Is he as tall as he looks in the magazines? Is he as muscly without the suit as he is with it? Does he--
Okay, this is starting to get uncomfortable.
Jersey City Wharf.
Here we go.
It'll only take us the rest of the night, plus tomorrow, to search all these warehouses.
I see what you mean.

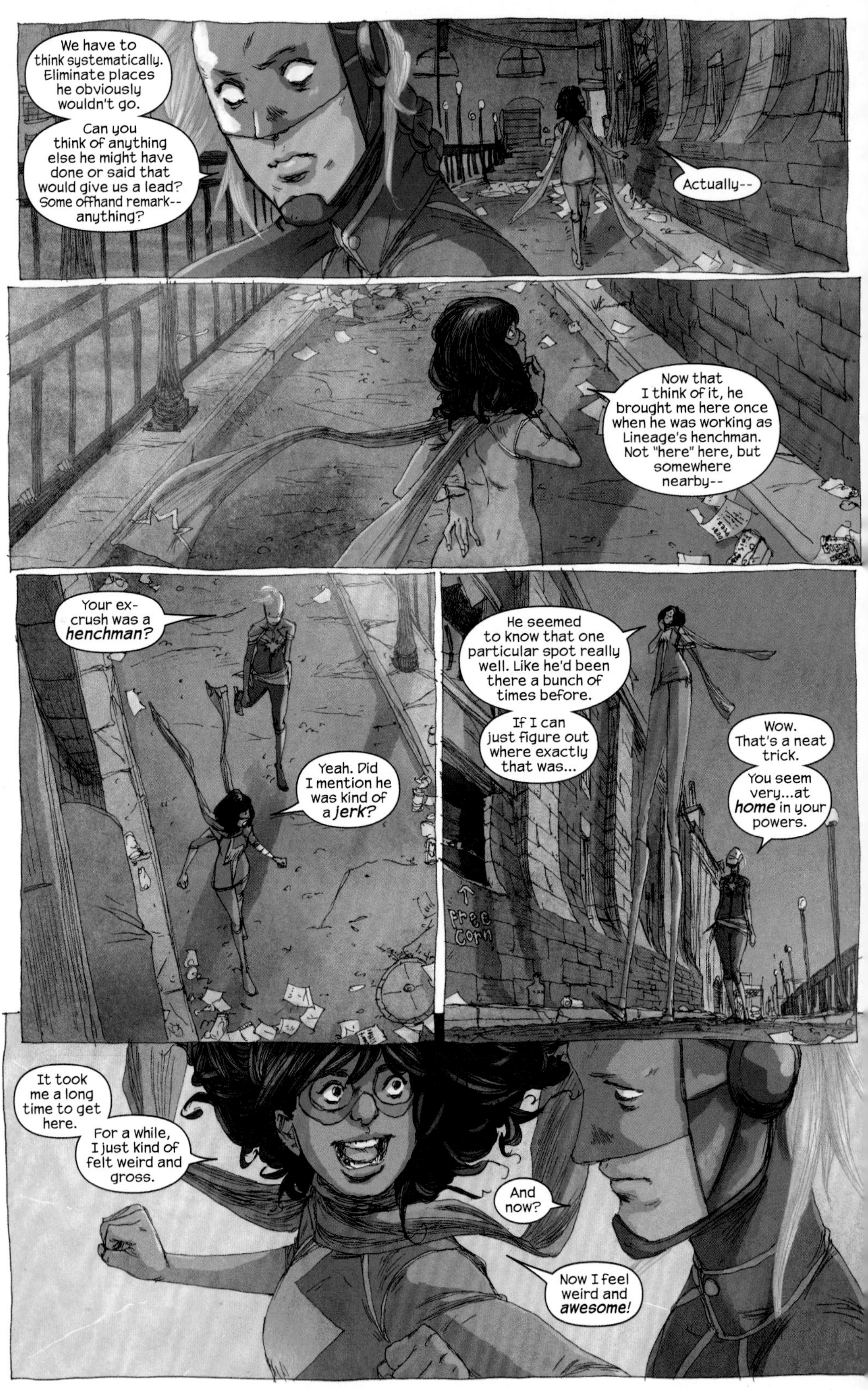
We have to think systematically. Eliminate places he obviously wouldn't go.
Can you think of anything else he might have done or said that would give us a lead? Some offhand remark--anything?
Actually--
Now that I think of it, he brought me here once when he was working as Lineage's henchman. Not "here" here, but somewhere nearby--
Your ex-crush was a *henchman*?
Yeah. Did I mention he was kind of a *jerk*?
He seemed to know that one particular spot really well. Like he'd been there a bunch of times before.
If I can just figure out where exactly that was...
Wow. That's a neat trick.
You seem very...at *home* in your powers.
Free Corn
It took me a long time to get here.
For a while, I just kind of felt weird and gross.
And now?
Now I feel weird and *awesome!*

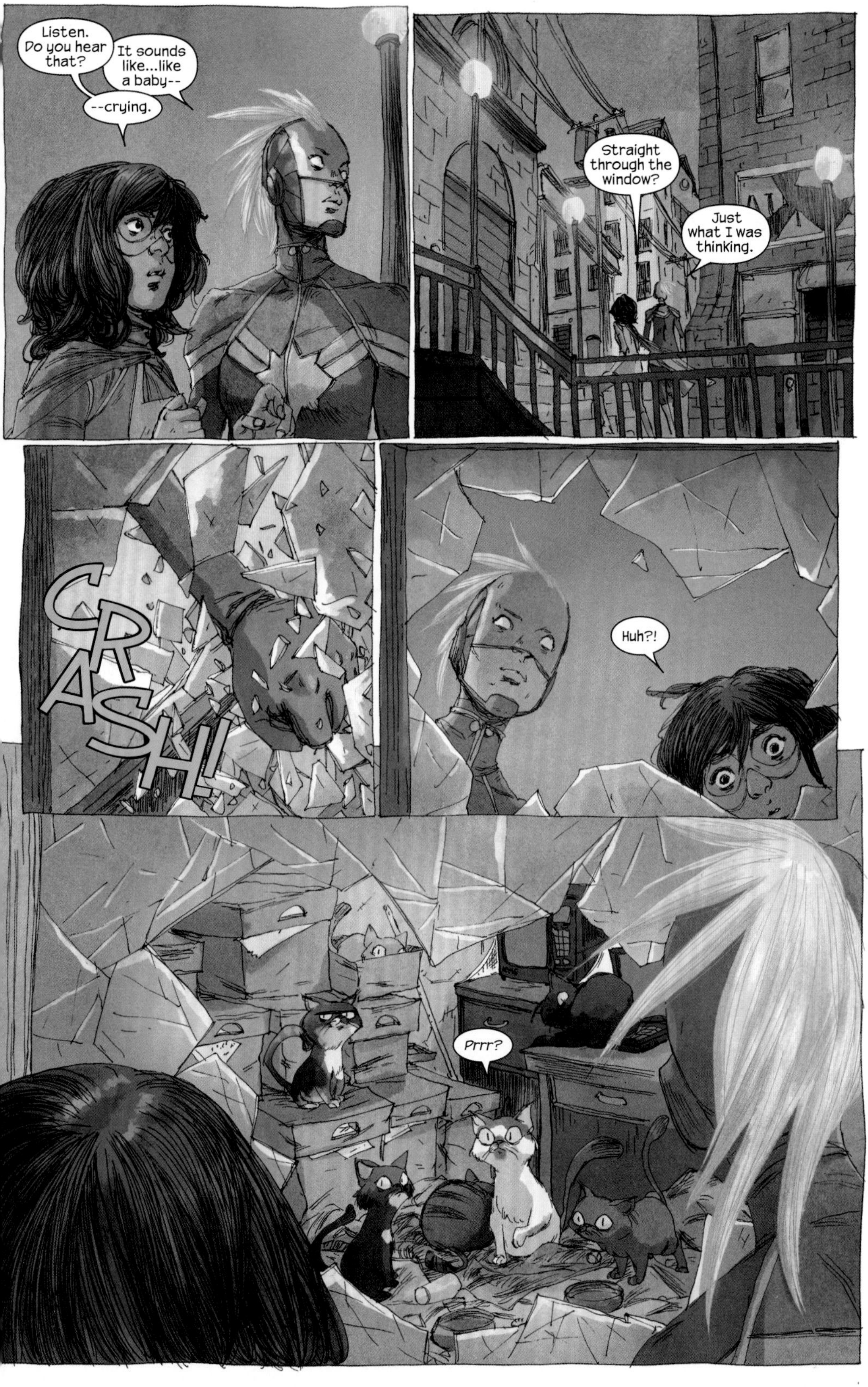
Listen. Do you hear that?
It sounds like...like a baby--
--crying.
Straight through the window?
Just what I was thinking.
CRASH!
Huh?!
Prrr?

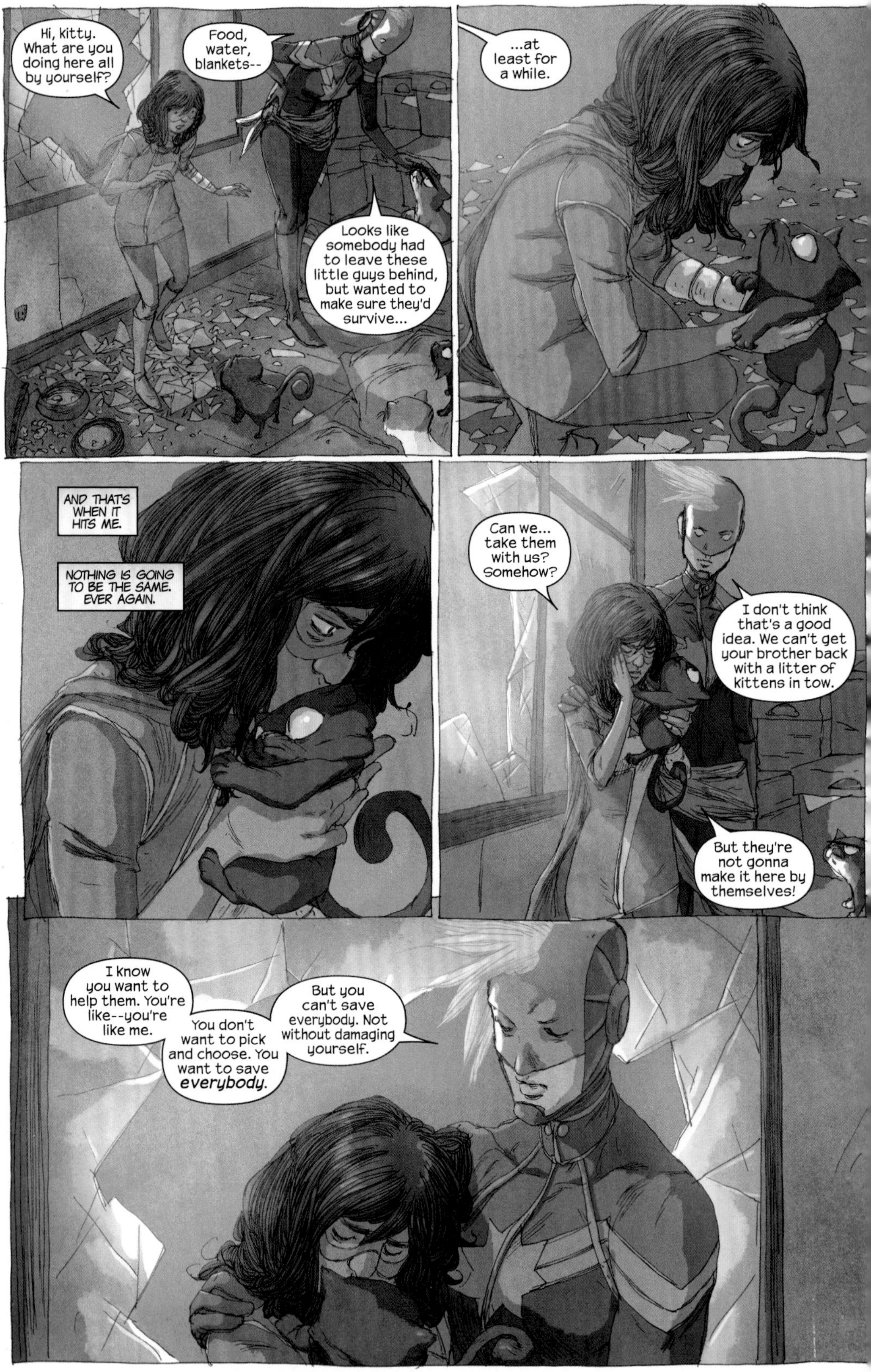
Hi, kitty. What are you doing here all by yourself?
Food, water, blankets--
Looks like somebody had to leave these little guys behind, but wanted to make sure they'd survive...
...at least for a while.
AND THAT'S WHEN IT HITS ME.
NOTHING IS GOING TO BE THE SAME. EVER AGAIN.
Can we... take them with us? Somehow?
I don't think that's a good idea. We can't get your brother back with a litter of kittens in tow.
But they're not gonna make it here by themselves!
I know you want to help them. You're like--you're like me.
You don't want to pick and choose. You want to save *everybody*.
But you can't save everybody. Not without damaging yourself.

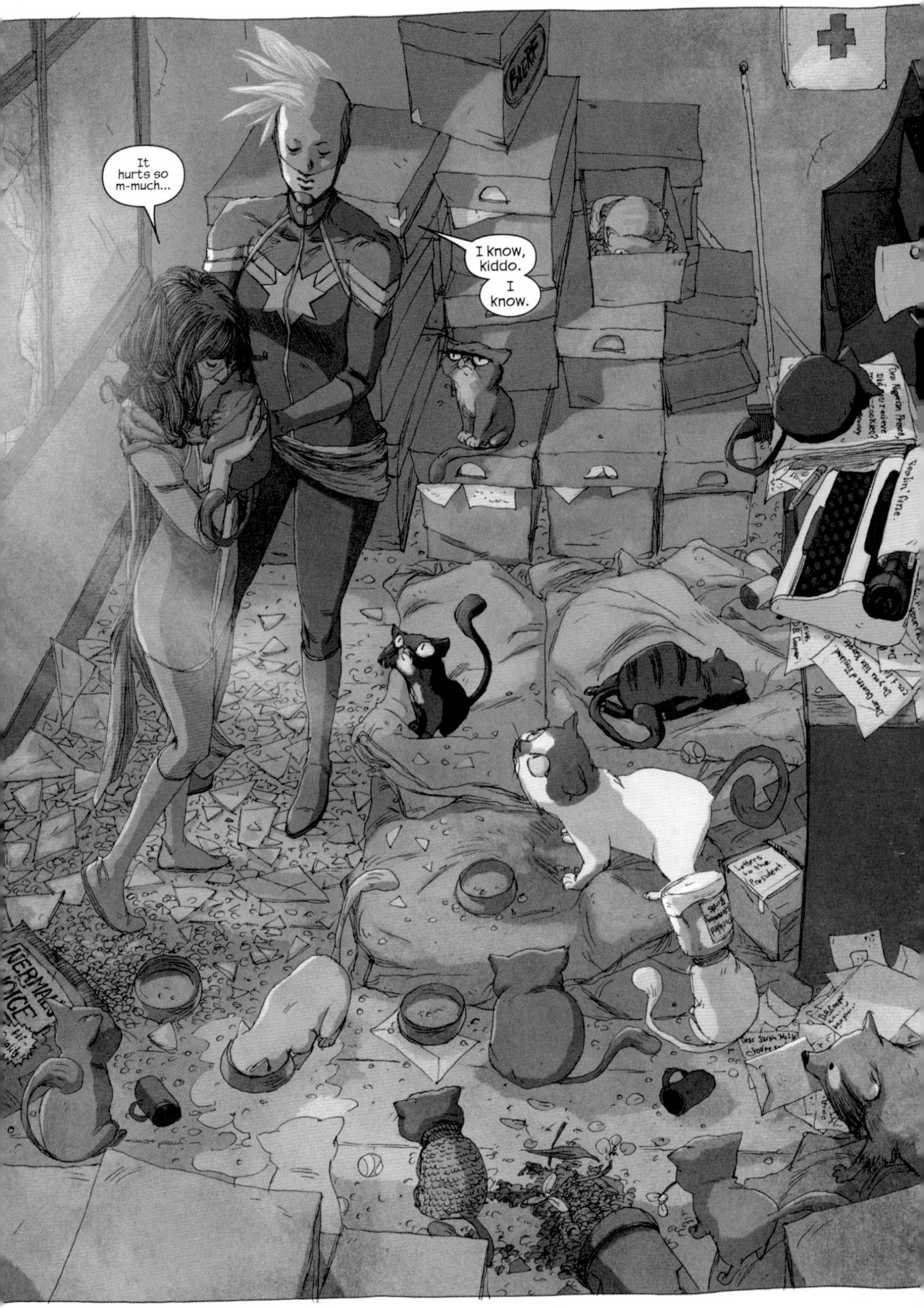

It hurts so m-much...
I know, kiddo.
I know.
Feelin' fine.
Love, D.B. Cooper
Letters to the President.

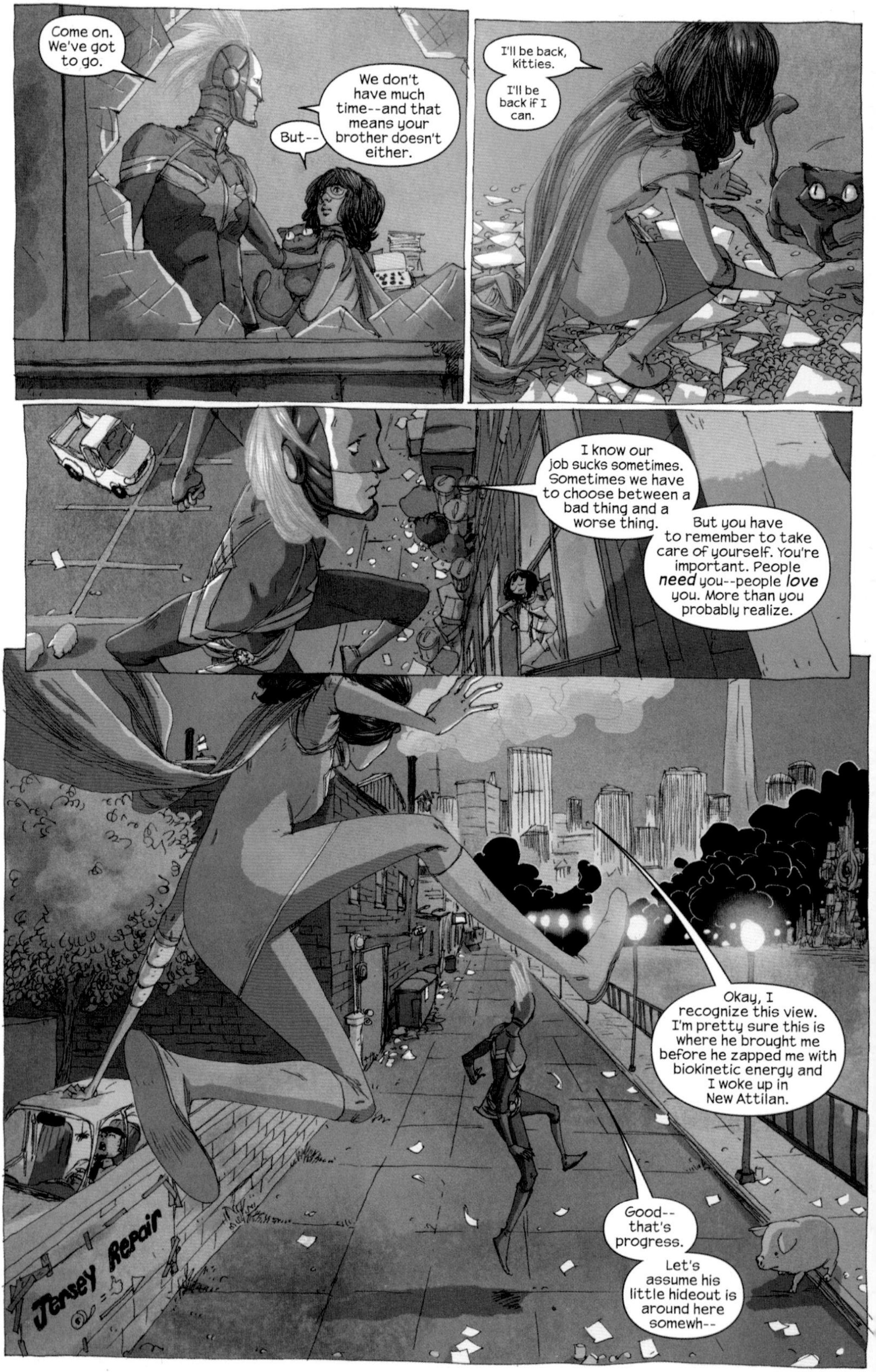
Come on. We've got to go.
But--
We don't have much time--and that means your brother doesn't either.
I'll be back, kitties.
I'll be back if I can.
I know our job sucks sometimes. Sometimes we have to choose between a bad thing and a worse thing.
But you have to remember to take care of yourself. You're important. People *need* you--people *love* you. More than you probably realize.
Jersey Repair
Okay, I recognize this view. I'm pretty sure this is where he brought me before he zapped me with biokinetic energy and I woke up in New Attilan.
Good--that's progress.
Let's assume his little hideout is around here somewh--

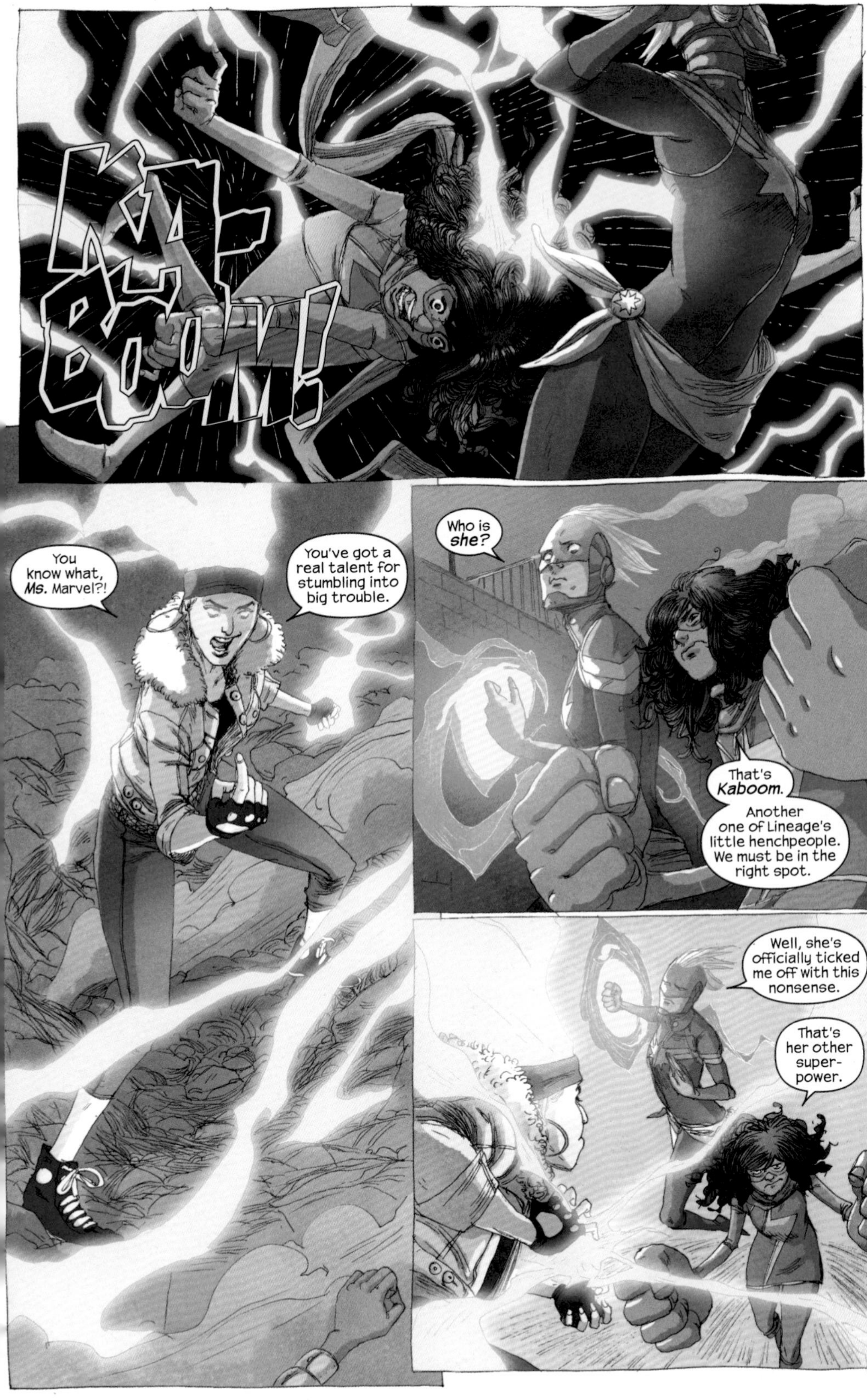
KA-BOOM!
You know what, Ms. Marvel?!
You've got a real talent for stumbling into big trouble.
Who is she?
That's Kaboom.
Another one of Lineage's little henchpeople. We must be in the right spot.
Well, she's officially ticked me off with this nonsense.
That's her other super-power.

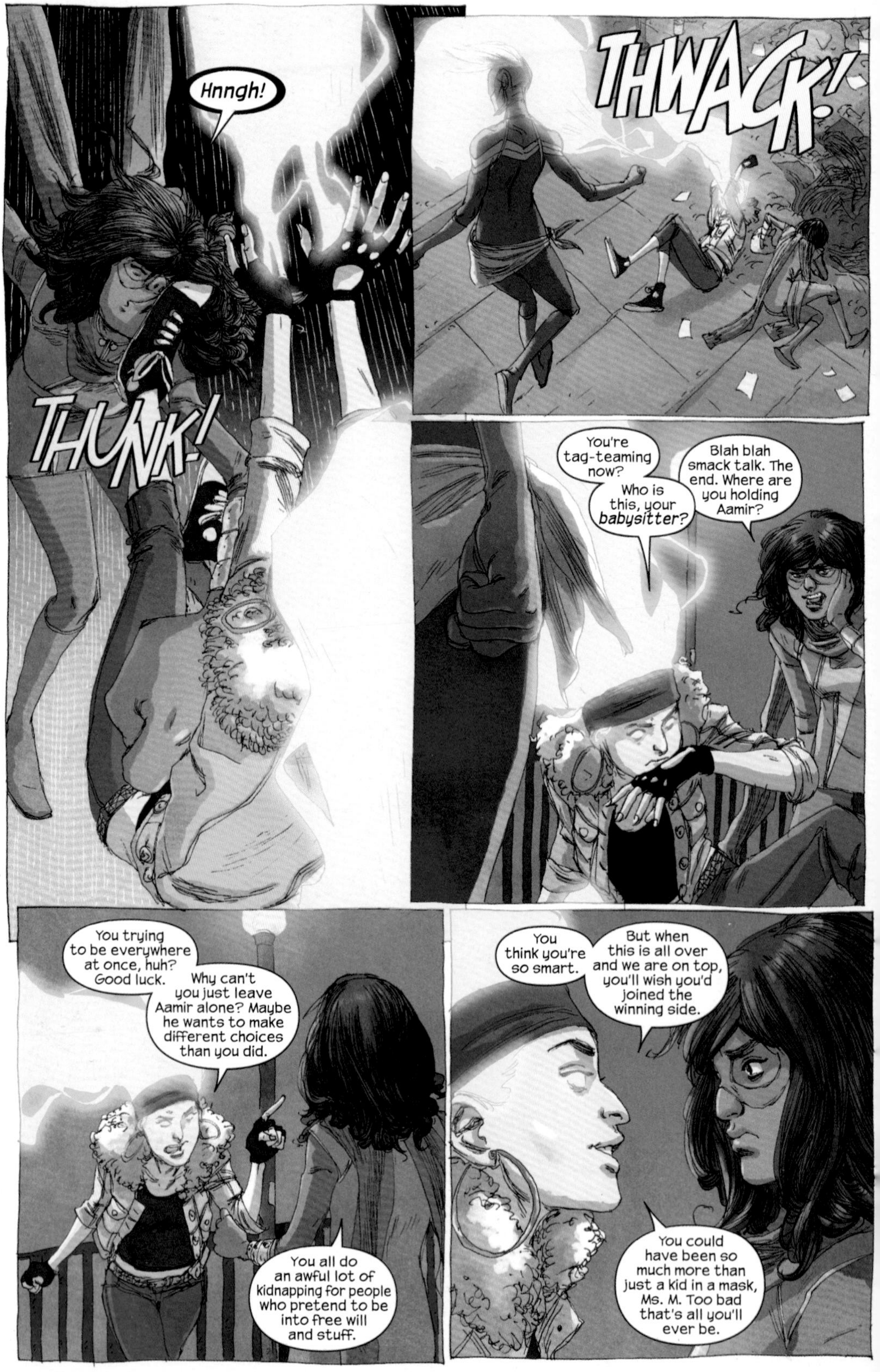
Hnngh!
THUNK!
THWACK!
You're tag-teaming now?
Who is this, your *babysitter?*
Blah blah smack talk. The end. Where are you holding Aamir?
You trying to be everywhere at once, huh? Good luck.
Why can't you just leave Aamir alone? Maybe he wants to make different choices than you did.
You all do an awful lot of kidnapping for people who pretend to be into free will and stuff.
You think you're so smart.
But when this is all over and we are on top, you'll wish you'd joined the winning side.
You could have been so much more than just a kid in a mask, Ms. M. Too bad that's all you'll ever be.

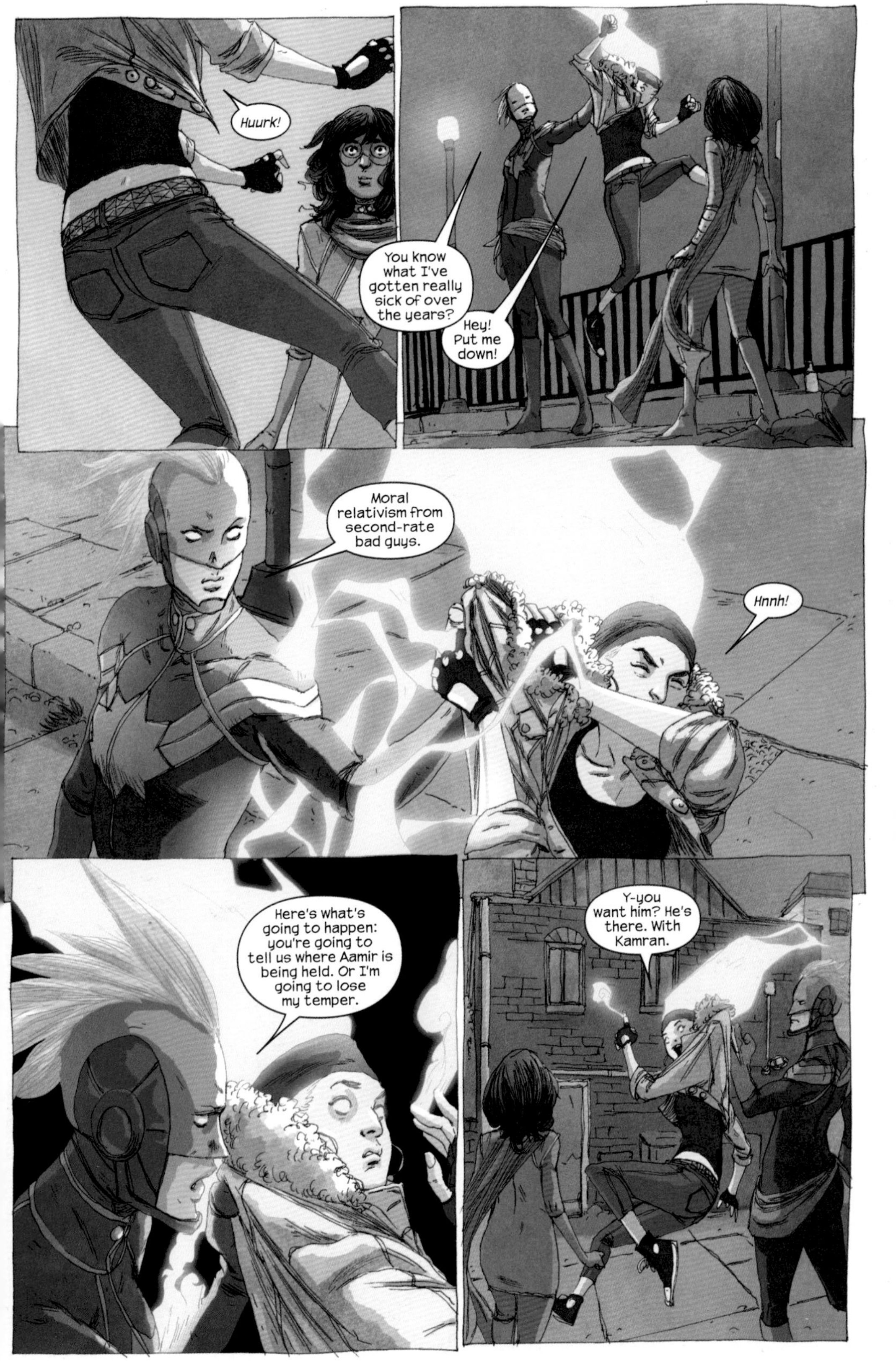
Huurk!
You know what I've gotten really sick of over the years?
Hey! Put me down!
Moral relativism from second-rate bad guys.
Hnnh!
Here's what's going to happen: you're going to tell us where Aamir is being held. Or I'm going to lose my temper.
Y-you want him? He's there. With Kamran.

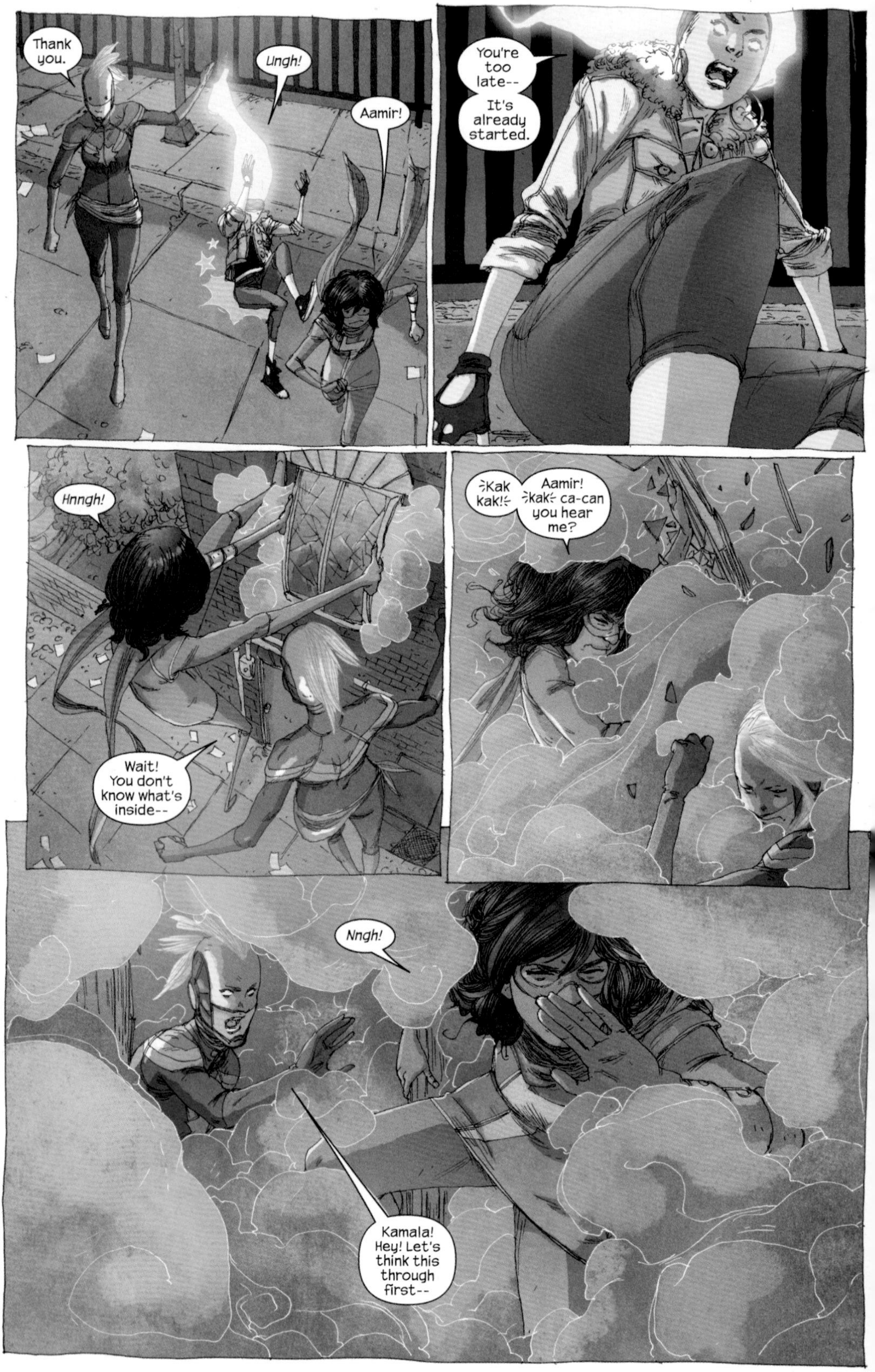
Thank you.
Ungh!
Aamir!
You're too late--
It's already started.
Hnngh!
Wait! You don't know what's inside--
Kak kak!
Aamir! kak ca-can you hear me?
Nngh!
Kamala! Hey! Let's think this through first--

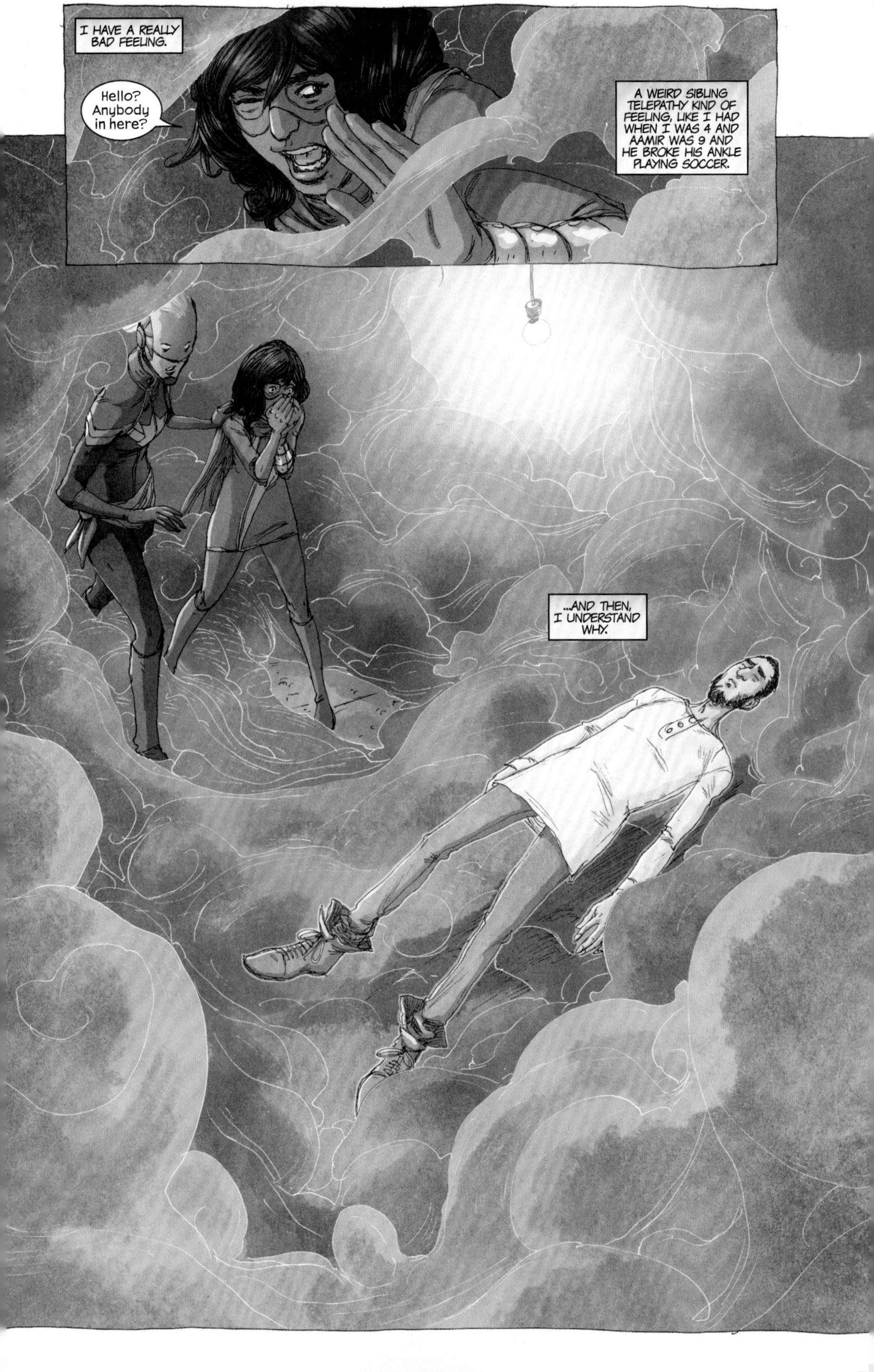
I HAVE A REALLY BAD FEELING.
Hello? Anybody in here?
A WEIRD SIBLING TELEPATHY KIND OF FEELING, LIKE I HAD WHEN I WAS 4 AND AAMIR WAS 9 AND HE BROKE HIS ANKLE PLAYING SOCCER.
...AND THEN, I UNDERSTAND WHY.

MS. MARVEL #18

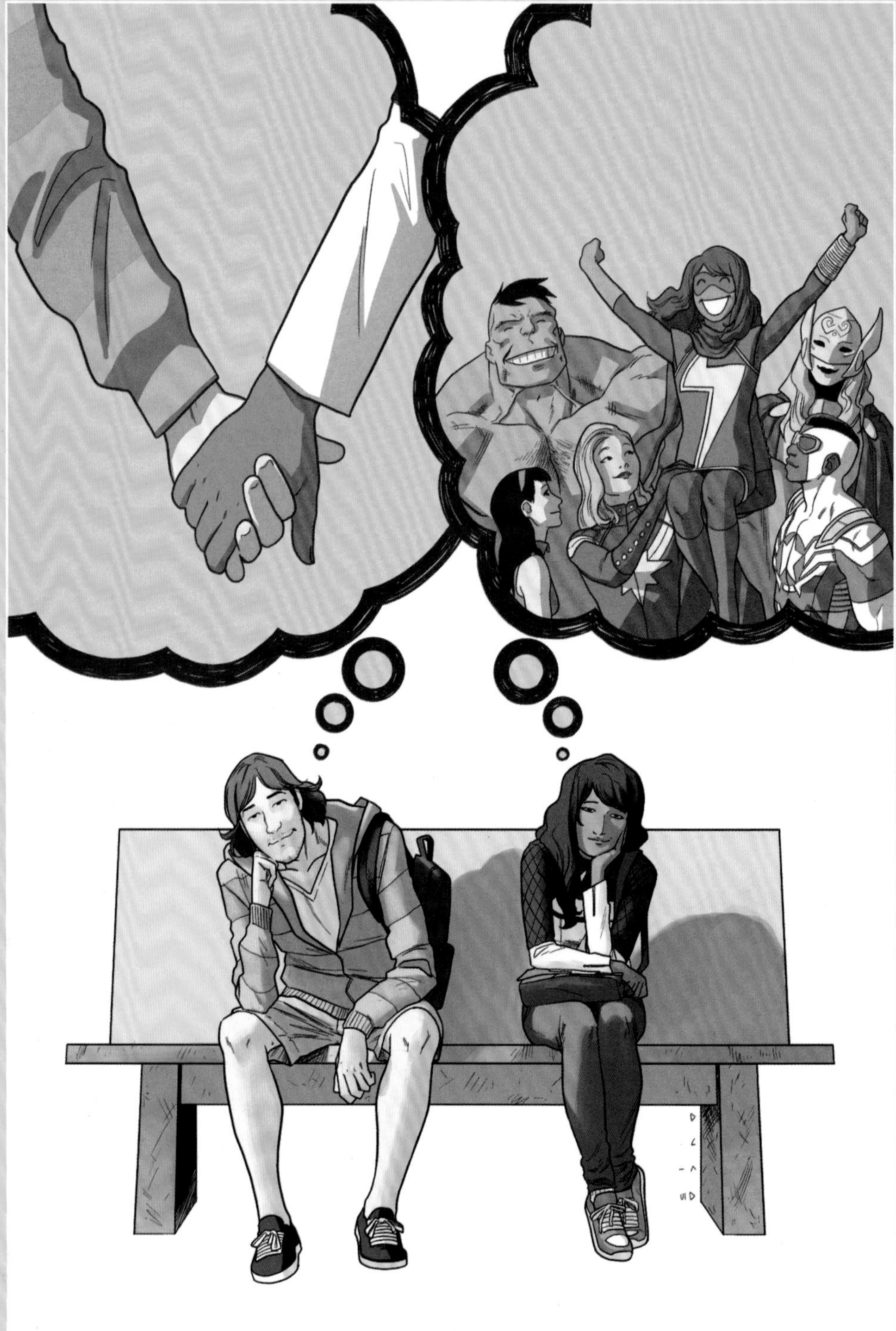

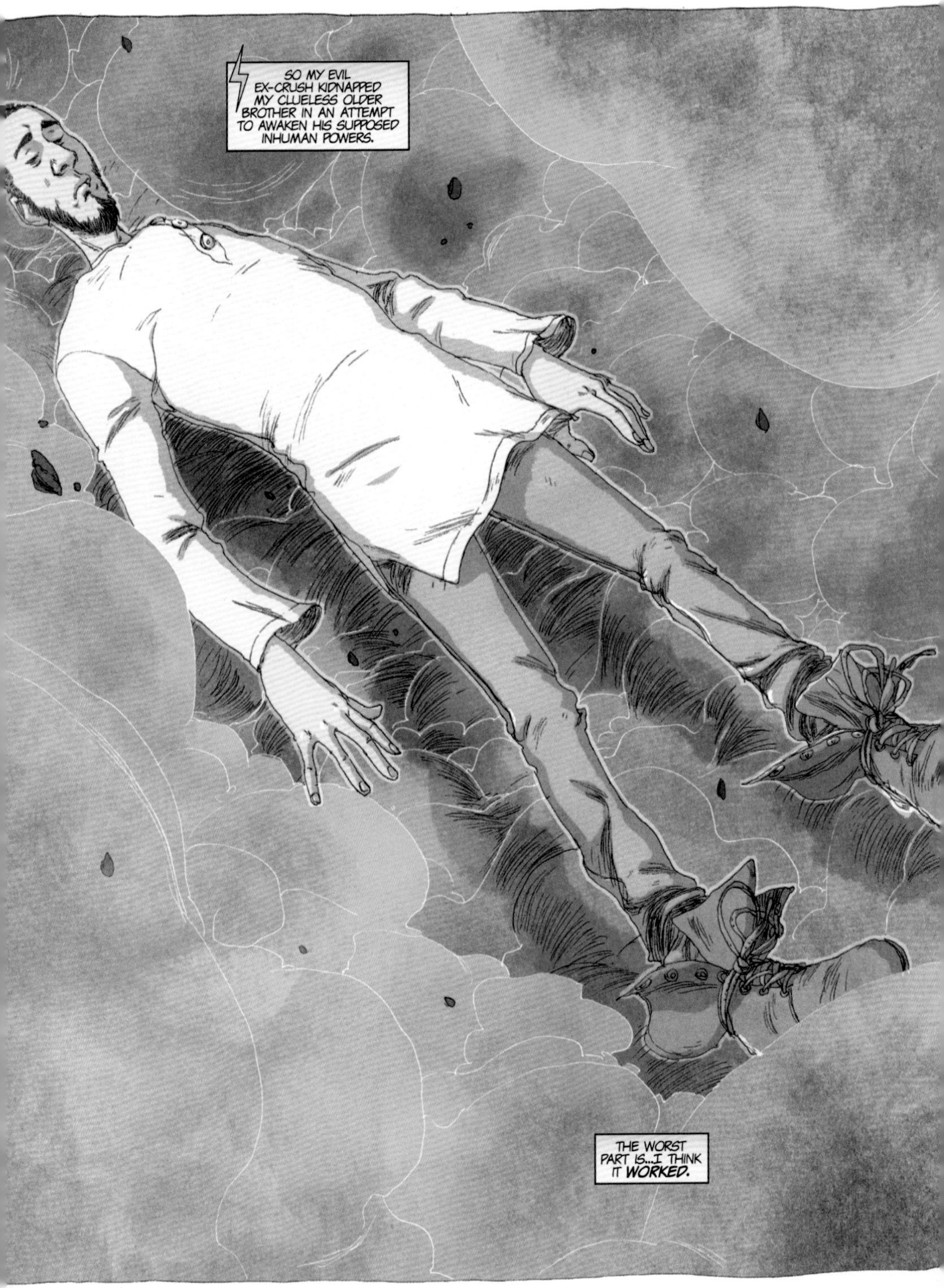
SO MY EVIL EX-CRUSH KIDNAPPED MY CLUELESS OLDER BROTHER IN AN ATTEMPT TO AWAKEN HIS SUPPOSED INHUMAN POWERS.
THE WORST PART IS...I THINK IT *WORKED.*

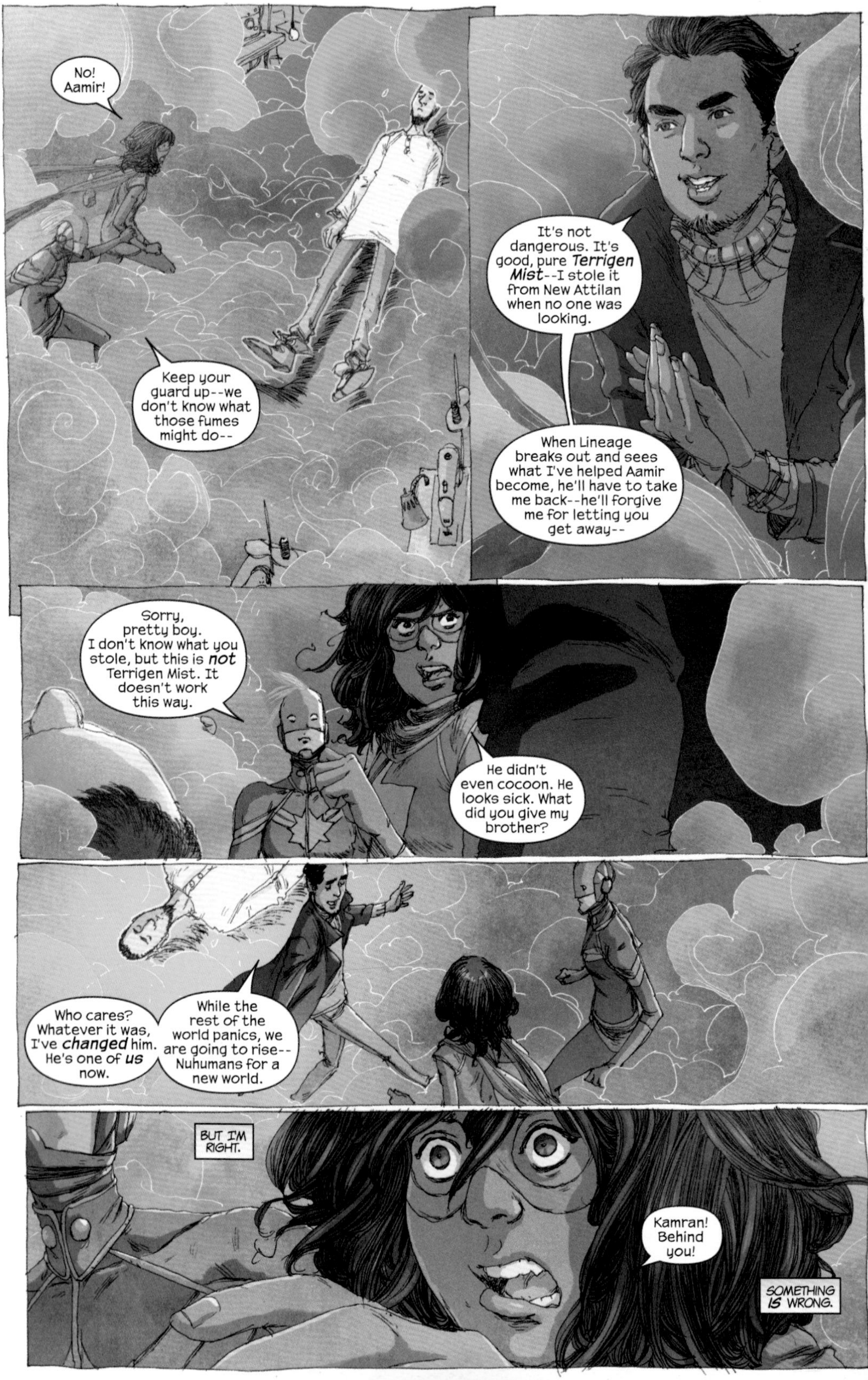
No! Aamir!
Keep your guard up--we don't know what those fumes might do--
It's not dangerous. It's good, pure *Terrigen Mist*--I stole it from New Attilan when no one was looking.
When Lineage breaks out and sees what I've helped Aamir become, he'll have to take me back--he'll forgive me for letting you get away--
Sorry, pretty boy. I don't know what you stole, but this is *not* Terrigen Mist. It doesn't work this way.
He didn't even cocoon. He looks sick. What did you give my brother?
Who cares? Whatever it was, I've *changed* him. He's one of *us* now.
While the rest of the world panics, we are going to rise--Nuhumans for a new world.
BUT I'M RIGHT.
Kamran! Behind you!
SOMETHING *IS* WRONG.

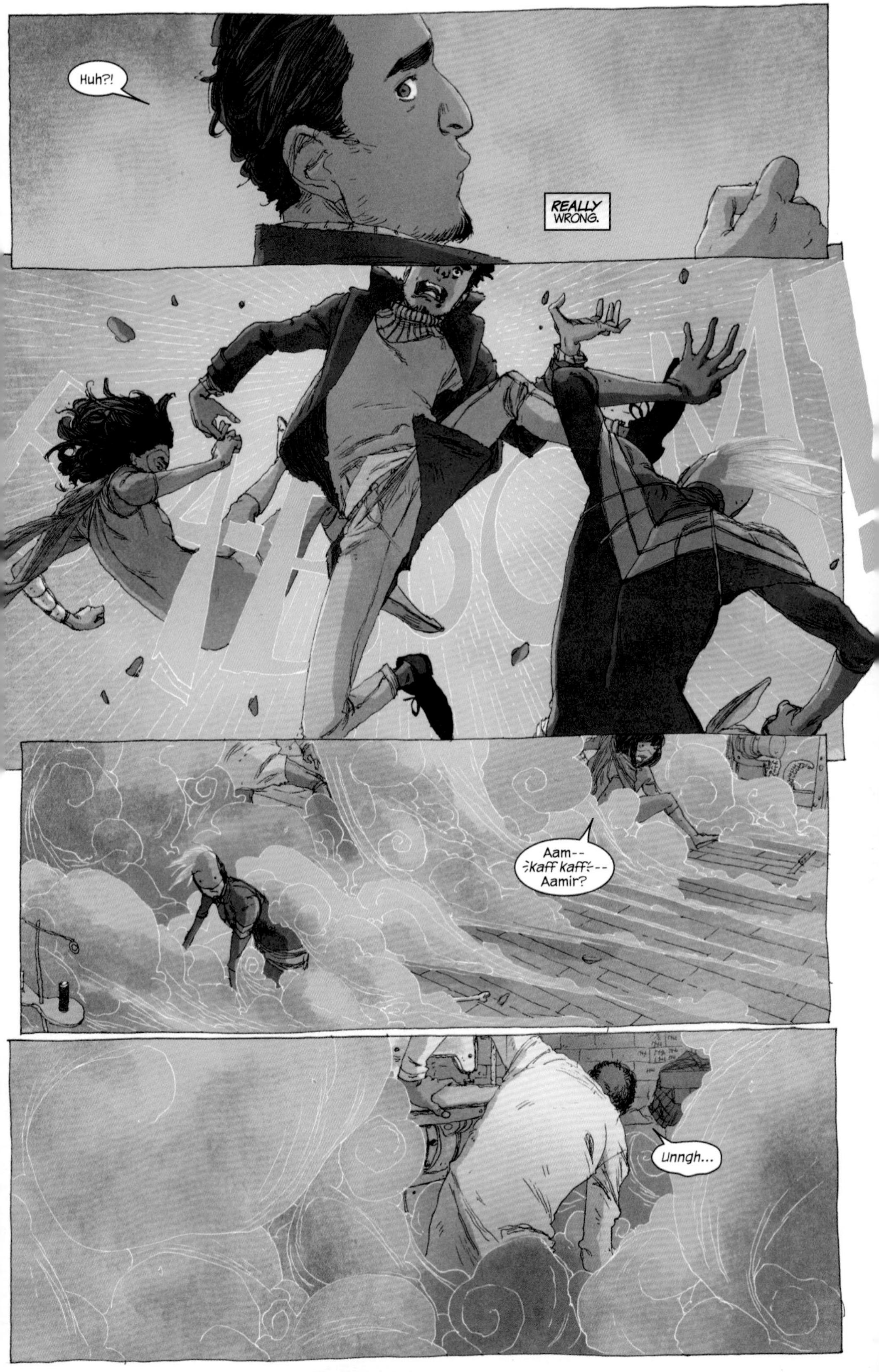
Huh?!
REALLY WRONG.
Aam--
kaff kaff--
Aamir?
Unngh...

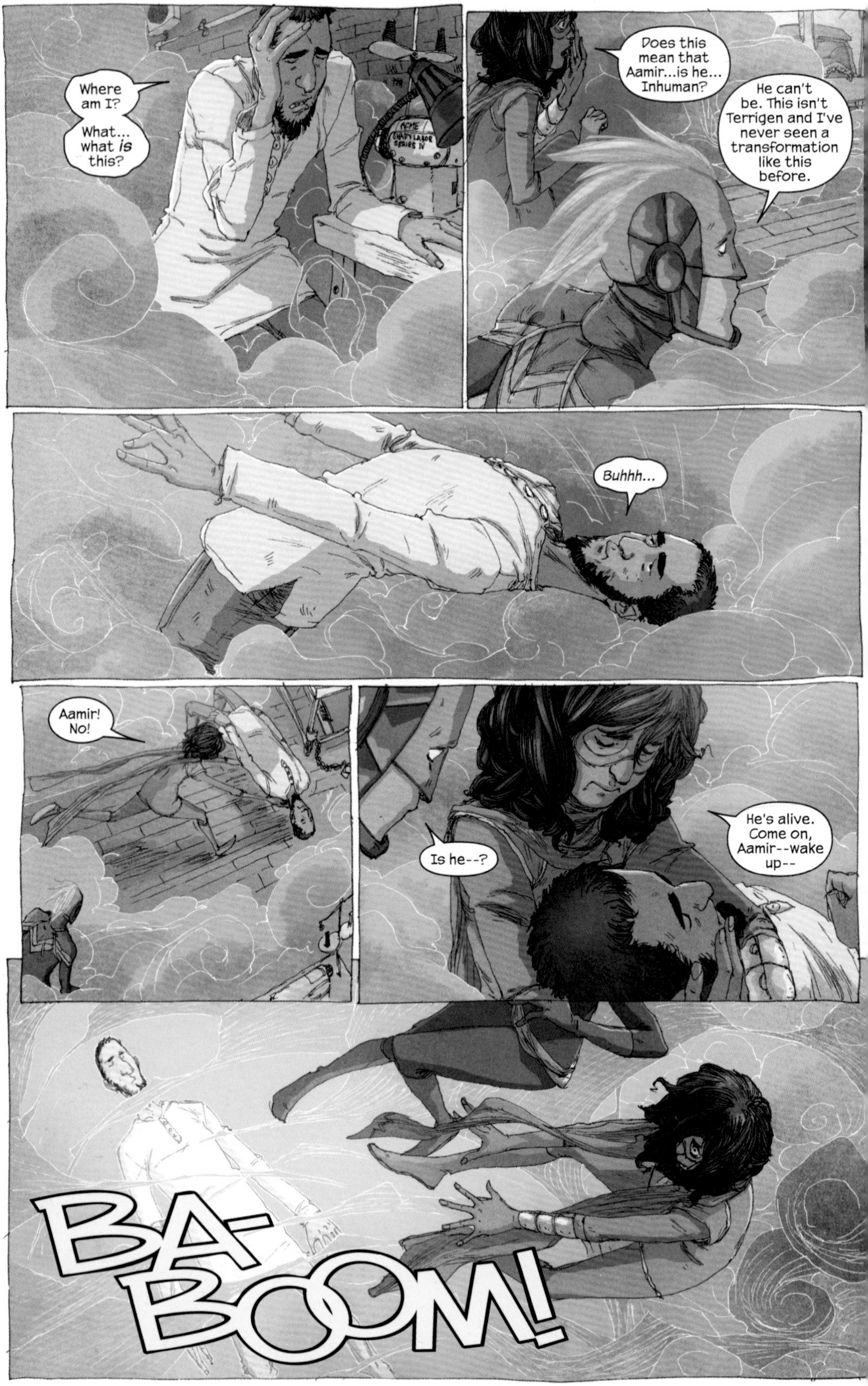
Where am I?
What... what *is* this?
ACME SHADY LABOR SERIES IV
Does this mean that Aamir...is he... Inhuman?
He can't be. This isn't Terrigen and I've never seen a transformation like this before.
Buhhh...
Aamir! No!
Is he--?
He's alive. Come on, Aamir--wake up--
BA-BOOM!

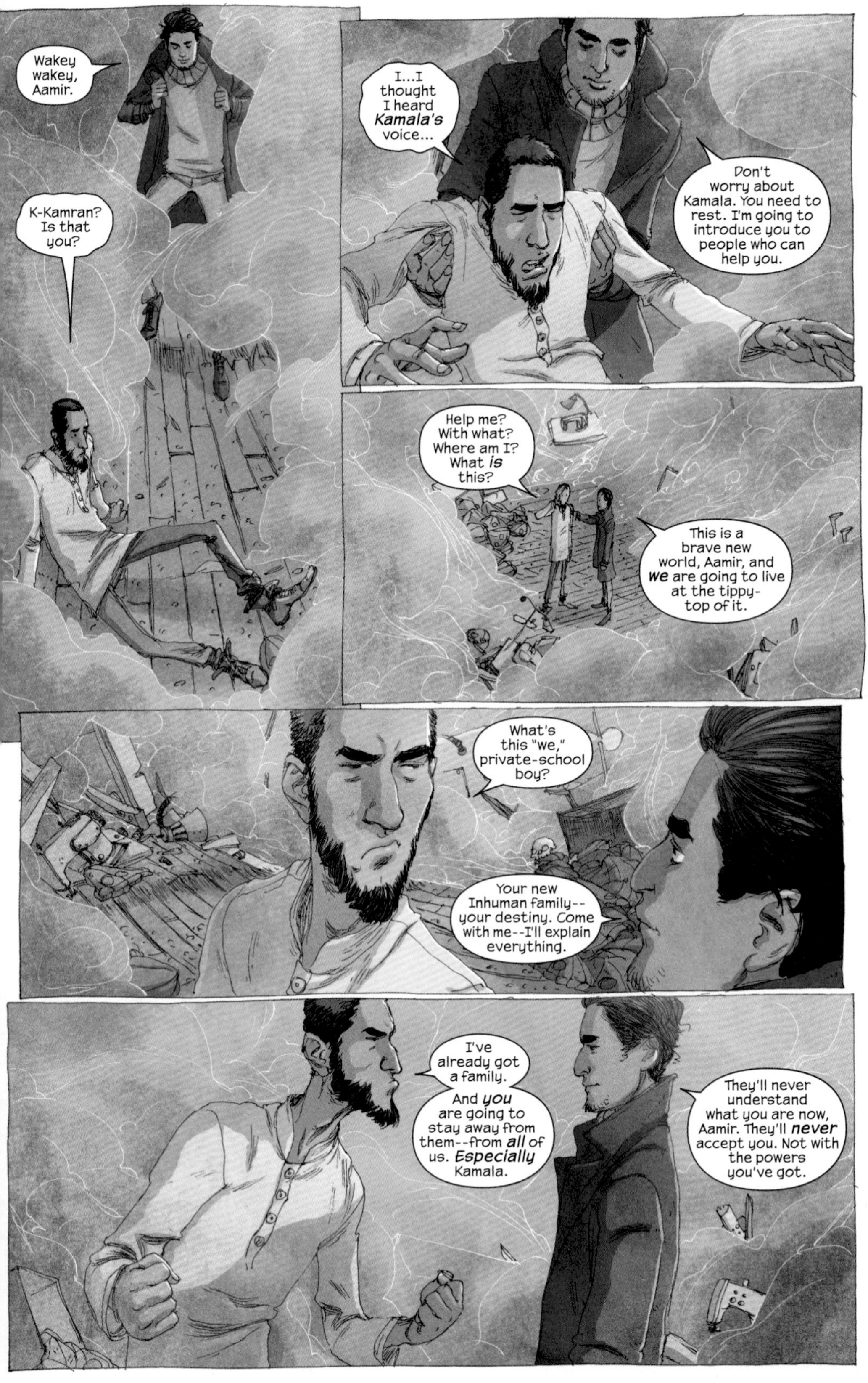
Wakey wakey, Aamir.
K-Kamran? Is that you?
I...I thought I heard *Kamala's* voice...
Don't worry about Kamala. You need to rest. I'm going to introduce you to people who can help you.
Help me? With what? Where am I? What *is* this?
This is a brave new world, Aamir, and *we* are going to live at the tippy-top of it.
What's this "we," private-school boy?
Your new Inhuman family--your destiny. Come with me--I'll explain everything.
I've already got a family.
And *you* are going to stay away from them--from *all* of us. *Especially* Kamala.
They'll never understand what you are now, Aamir. They'll *never* accept you. Not with the powers you've got.

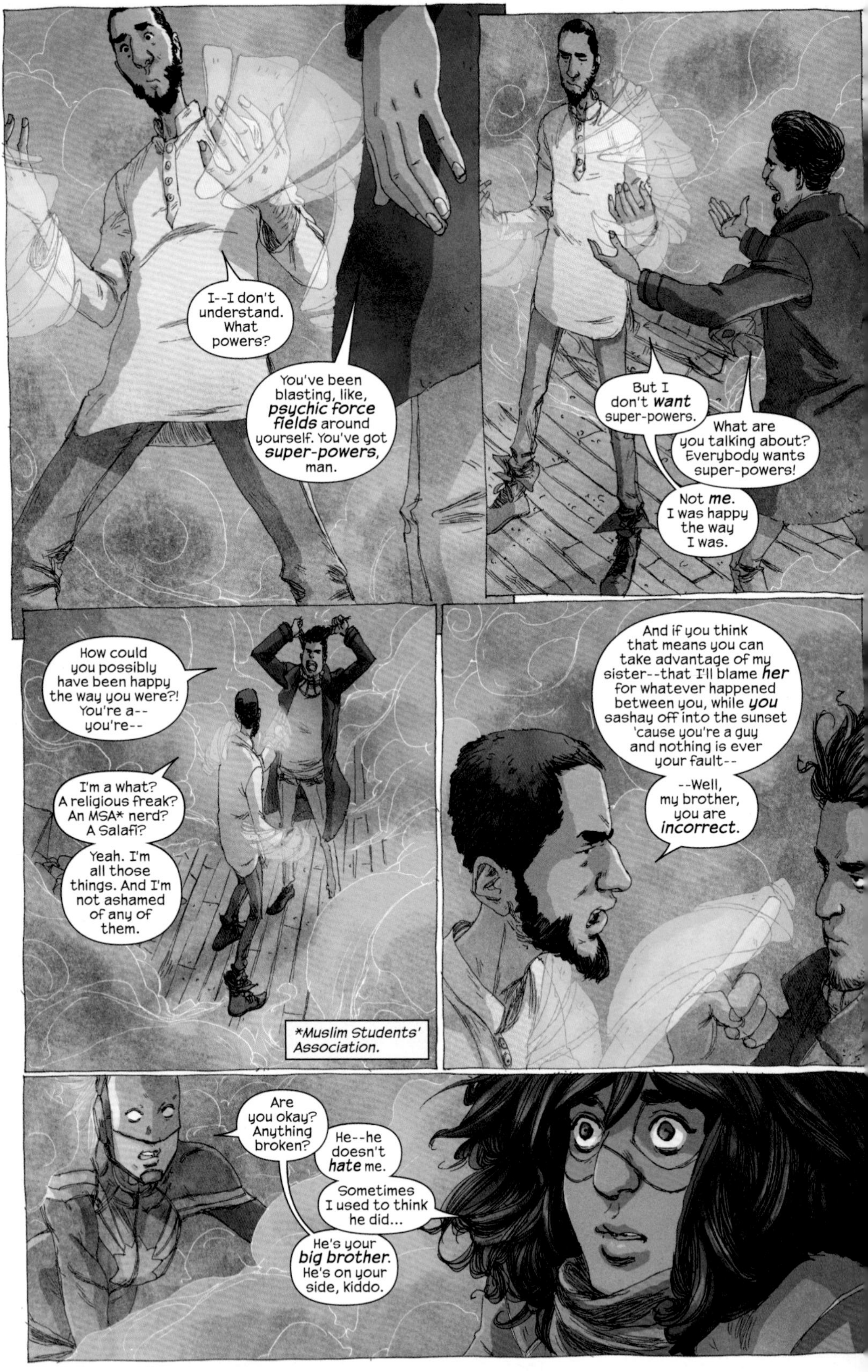

I--I don't understand. What powers?
You've been blasting, like, psychic force fields around yourself. You've got super-powers, man.
But I don't want super-powers.
What are you talking about? Everybody wants super-powers!
Not me. I was happy the way I was.
How could you possibly have been happy the way you were?! You're a-- you're--
I'm a what? A religious freak? An MSA* nerd? A Salafi?
Yeah. I'm all those things. And I'm not ashamed of any of them.
*Muslim Students' Association.
And if you think that means you can take advantage of my sister--that I'll blame her for whatever happened between you, while you sashay off into the sunset 'cause you're a guy and nothing is ever your fault--
--Well, my brother, you are incorrect.
Are you okay? Anything broken?
He--he doesn't hate me.
Sometimes I used to think he did...
He's your big brother. He's on your side, kiddo.

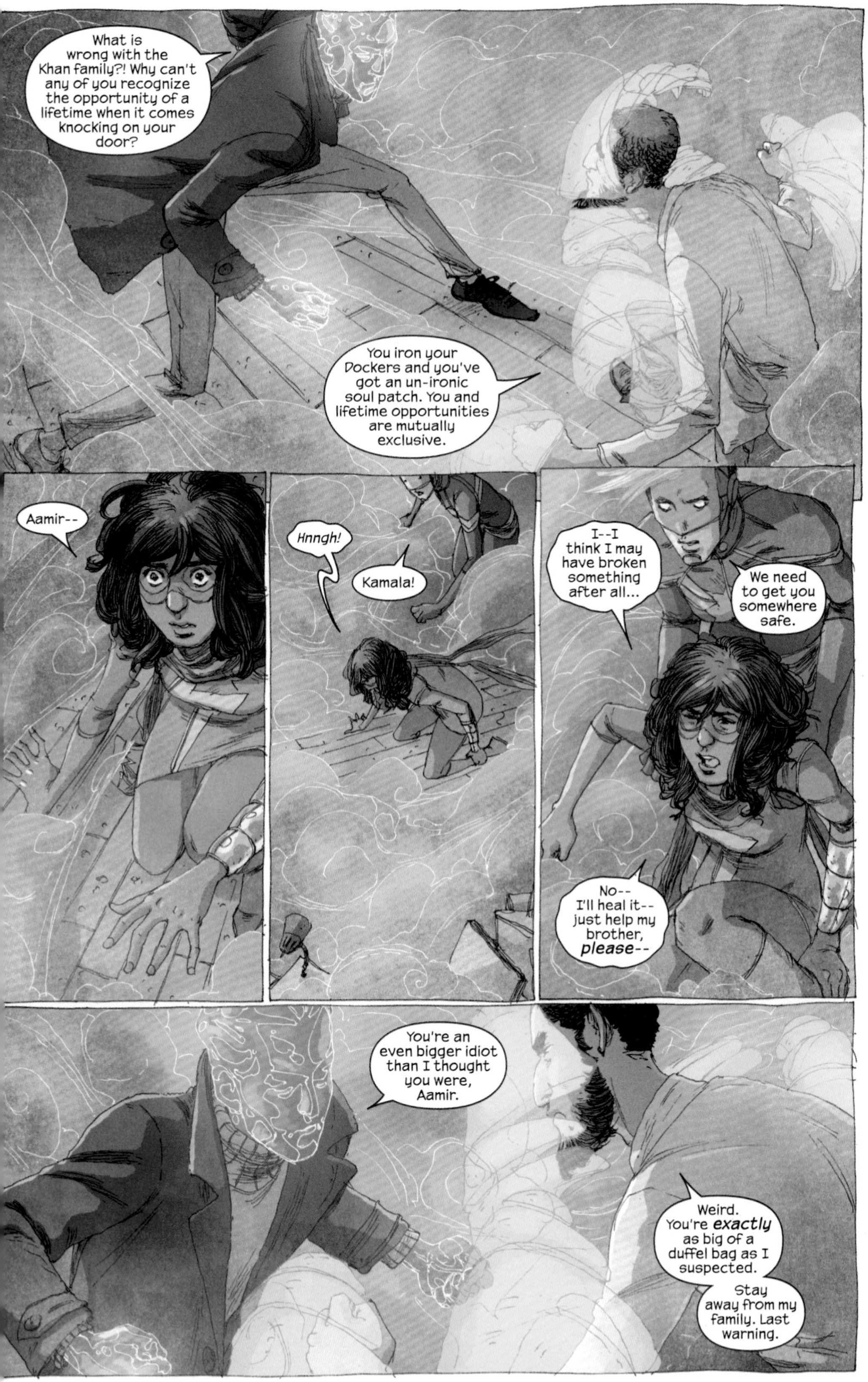

What is wrong with the Khan family?! Why can't any of you recognize the opportunity of a lifetime when it comes knocking on your door?
You iron your Dockers and you've got an un-ironic soul patch. You and lifetime opportunities are mutually exclusive.
Aamir--
Hnngh!
Kamala!
I--I think I may have broken something after all...
We need to get you somewhere safe.
No-- I'll heal it-- just help my brother, *please*--
You're an even bigger idiot than I thought you were, Aamir.
Weird. You're *exactly* as big of a duffel bag as I suspected.
Stay away from my family. Last warning.

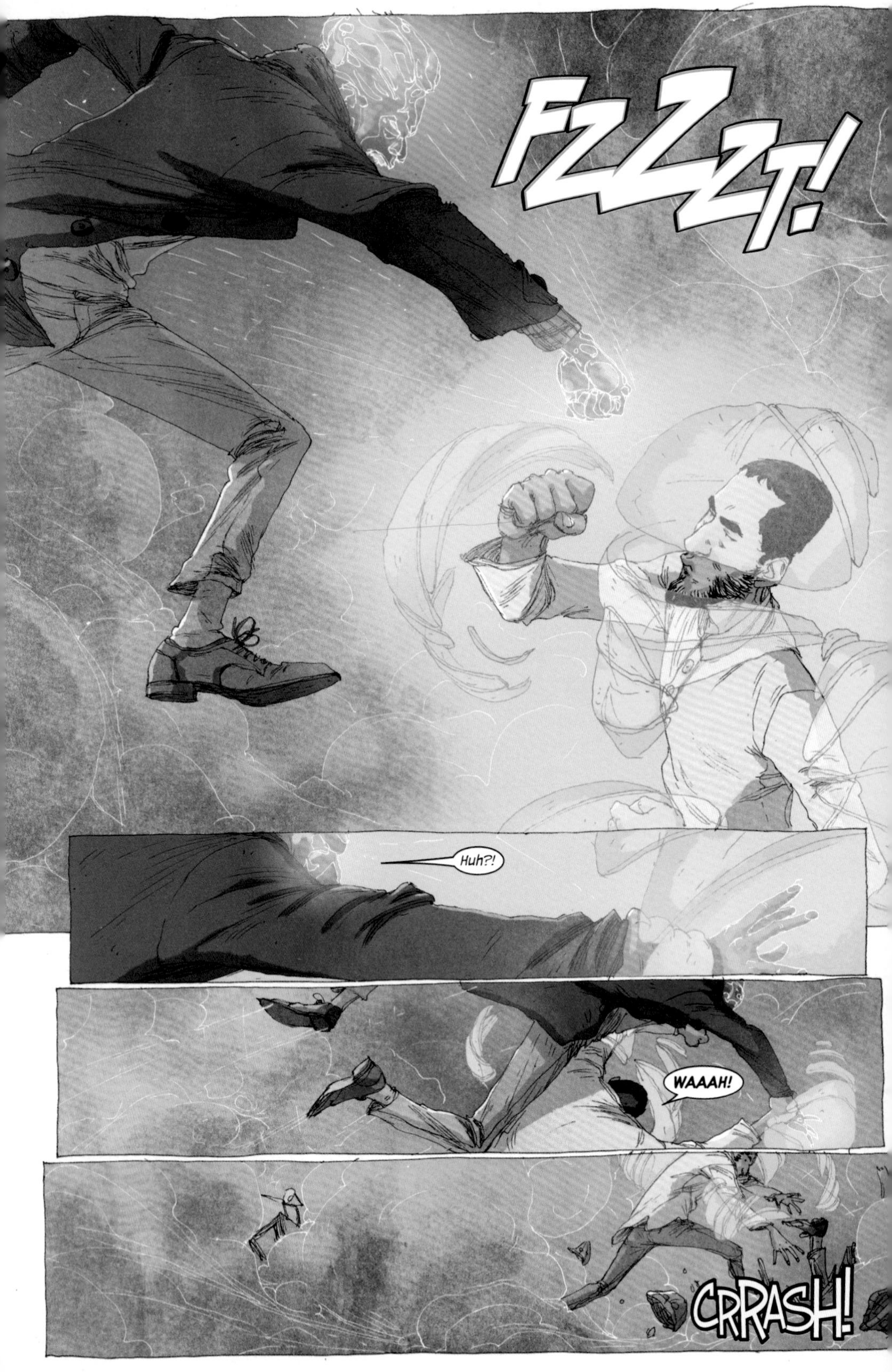
FZZZZT!
Huh?!
WAAAH!
CRRASH!

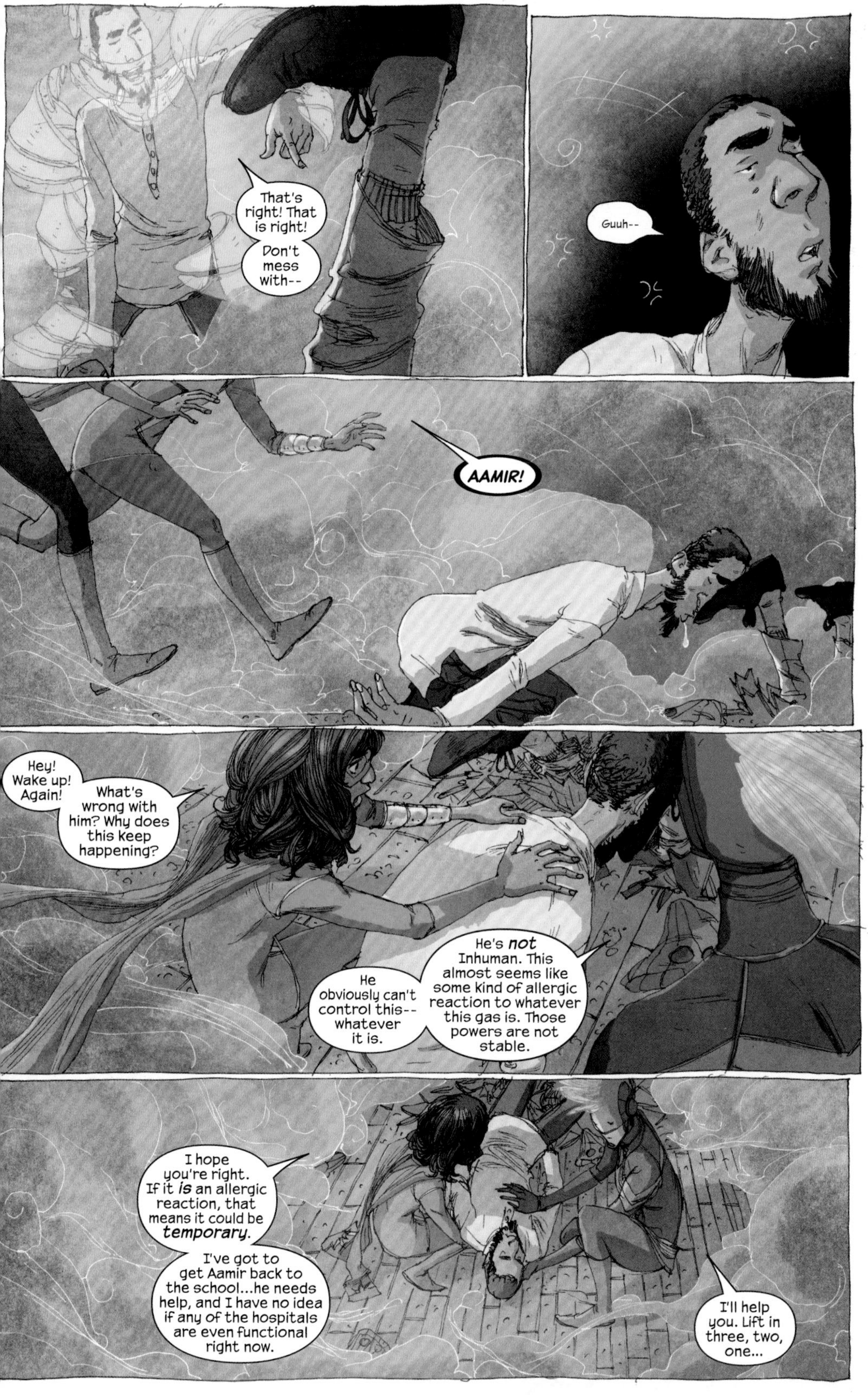
That's right! That is right!
Don't mess with--
Guuh--
AAMIR!
Hey! Wake up! Again!
What's wrong with him? Why does this keep happening?
He obviously can't control this--whatever it is.
He's *not* Inhuman. This almost seems like some kind of allergic reaction to whatever this gas is. Those powers are not stable.
I hope you're right. If it *is* an allergic reaction, that means it could be *temporary*.
I've got to get Aamir back to the school...he needs help, and I have no idea if any of the hospitals are even functional right now.
I'll help you. Lift in three, two, one...

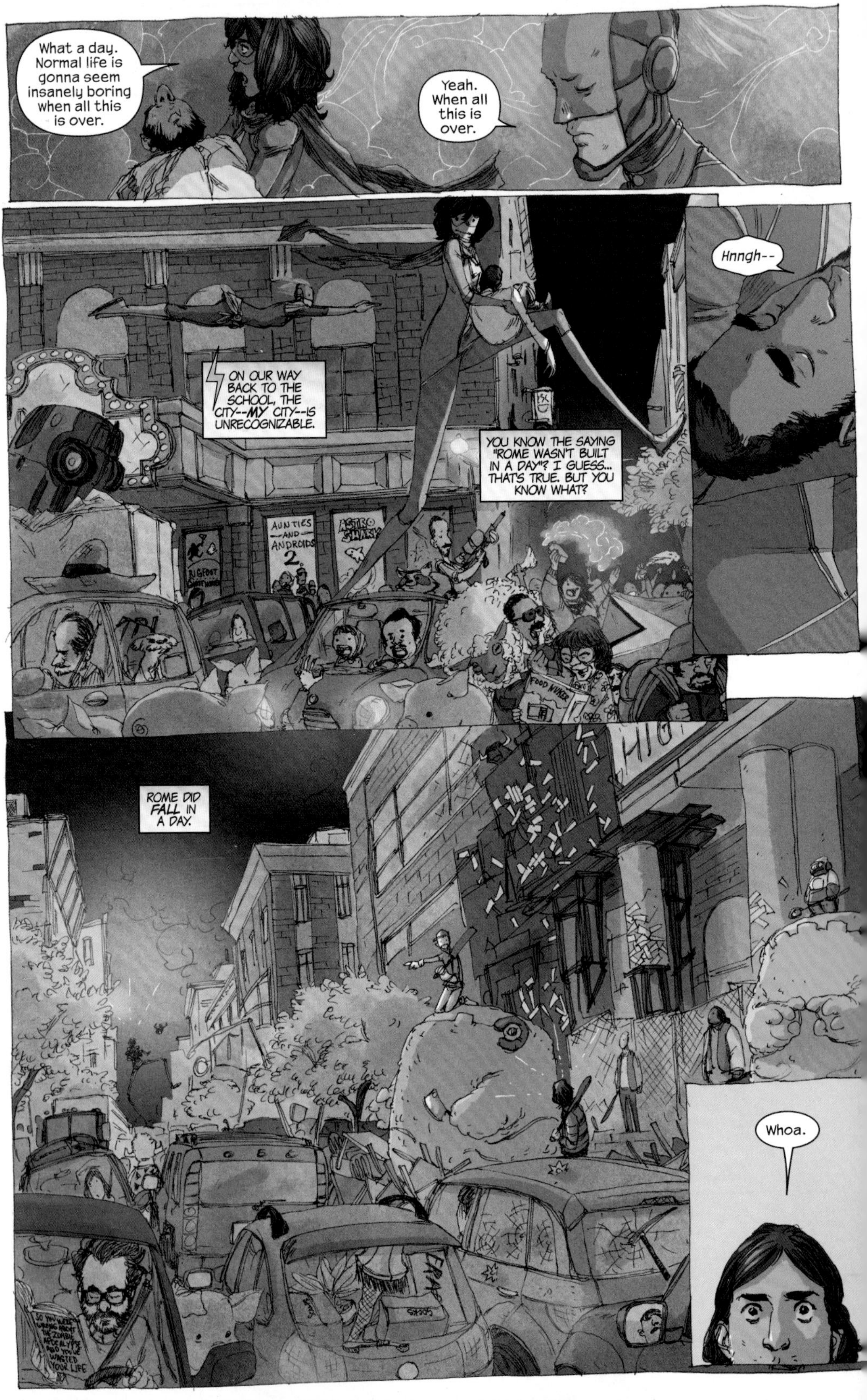
What a day. Normal life is gonna seem insanely boring when all this is over.
Yeah. When all this is over.
ON OUR WAY BACK TO THE SCHOOL, THE CITY--MY CITY--IS UNRECOGNIZABLE.
YOU KNOW THE SAYING "ROME WASN'T BUILT IN A DAY"? I GUESS... THAT'S TRUE. BUT YOU KNOW WHAT?
Hnngh--
AUNTIES AND ANDROIDS 2.
ASTRO SHARK
FOOD MAKER
ROME DID FALL IN A DAY.
Whoa.

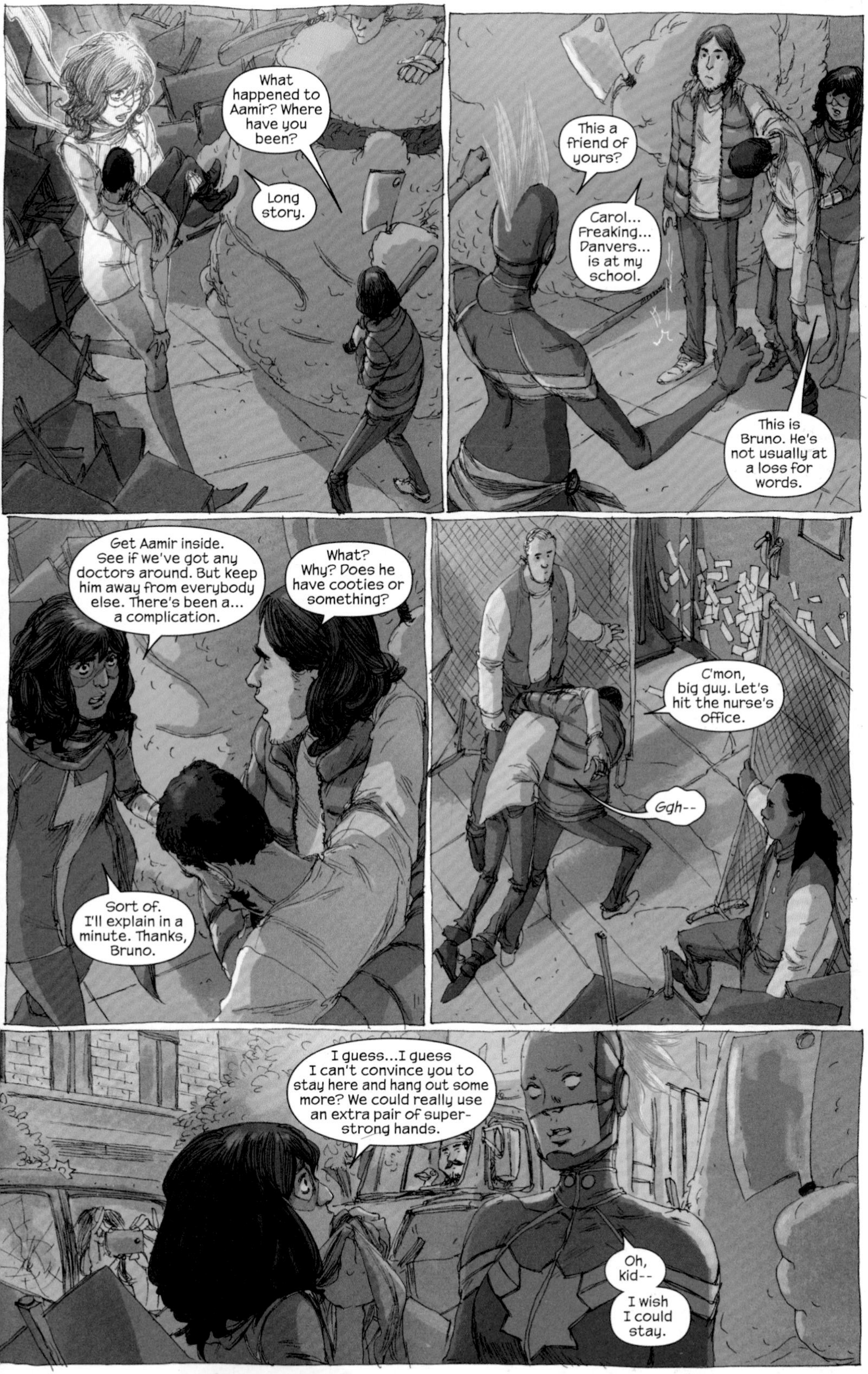
What happened to Aamir? Where have you been?
Long story.
This a friend of yours?
Carol... Freaking... Danvers... is at my school.
This is Bruno. He's not usually at a loss for words.
Get Aamir inside. See if we've got any doctors around. But keep him away from everybody else. There's been a... a complication.
What? Why? Does he have cooties or something?
Sort of. I'll explain in a minute. Thanks, Bruno.
C'mon, big guy. Let's hit the nurse's office.
Ggh--
I guess...I guess I can't convince you to stay here and hang out some more? We could really use an extra pair of super-strong hands.
Oh, kid--
I wish I could stay.

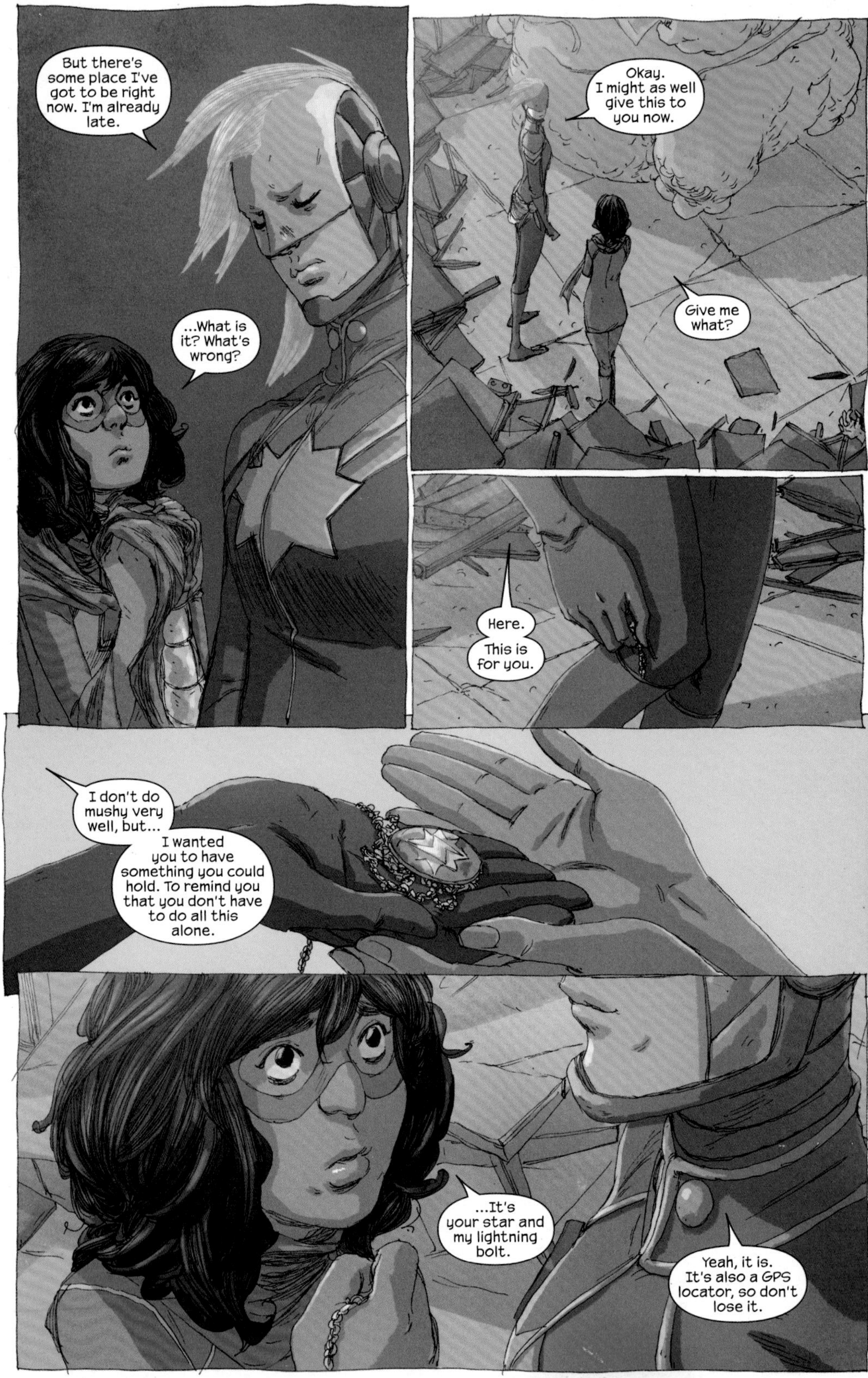
But there's some place I've got to be right now. I'm already late.
...What is it? What's wrong?
Okay. I might as well give this to you now.
Give me what?
Here. This is for you.
I don't do mushy very well, but...
I wanted you to have something you could hold. To remind you that you don't have to do all this alone.
...It's your star and my lightning bolt.
Yeah, it is. It's also a GPS locator, so don't lose it.

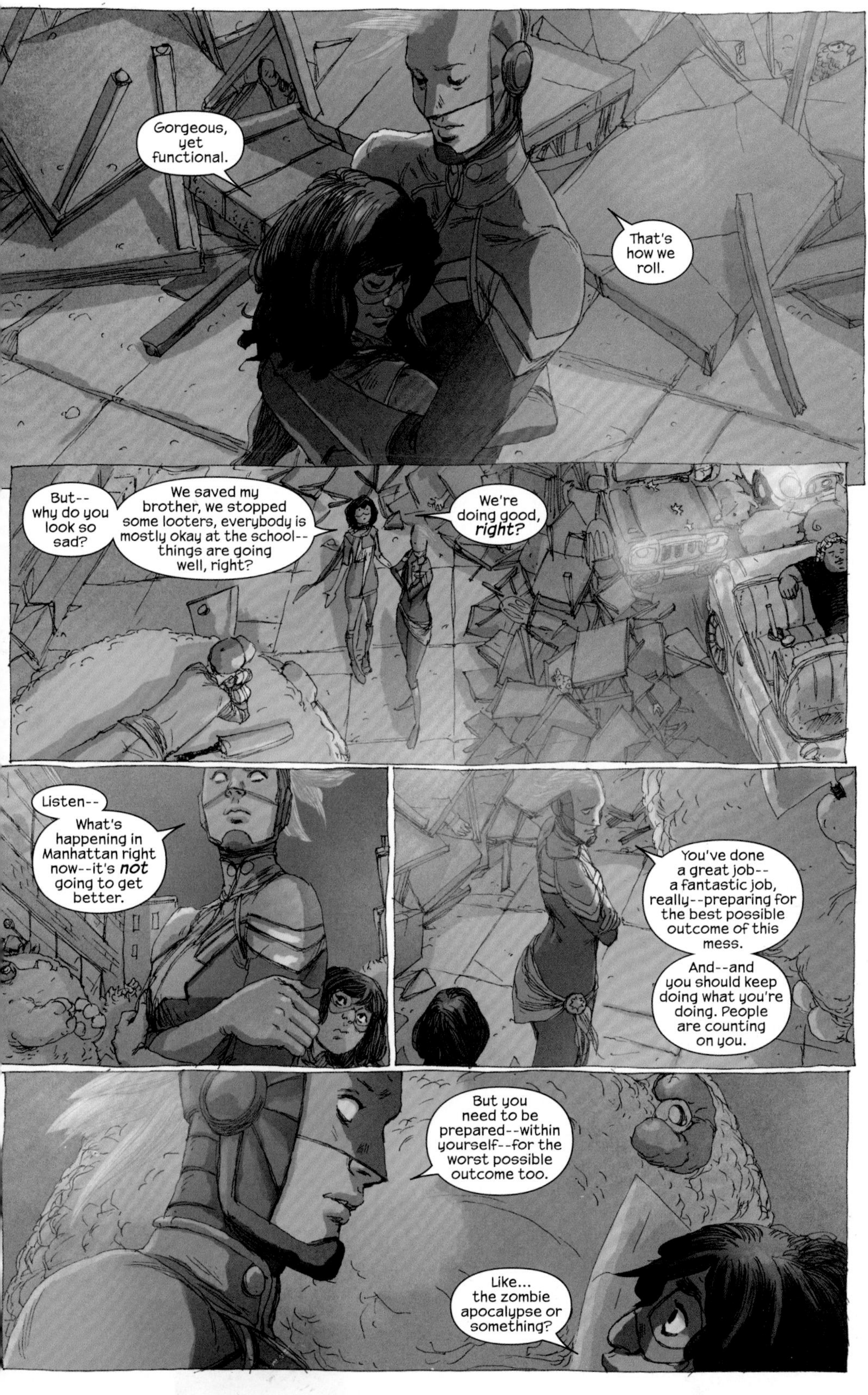
Gorgeous, yet functional.
That's how we roll.
But--why do you look so sad?
We saved my brother, we stopped some looters, everybody is mostly okay at the school--things are going well, right?
We're doing good, *right?*
Listen--
What's happening in Manhattan right now--it's *not* going to get better.
You've done a great job--a fantastic job, really--preparing for the best possible outcome of this mess.
And--and you should keep doing what you're doing. People are counting on you.
But you need to be prepared--within yourself--for the worst possible outcome too.
Like... the zombie apocalypse or something?

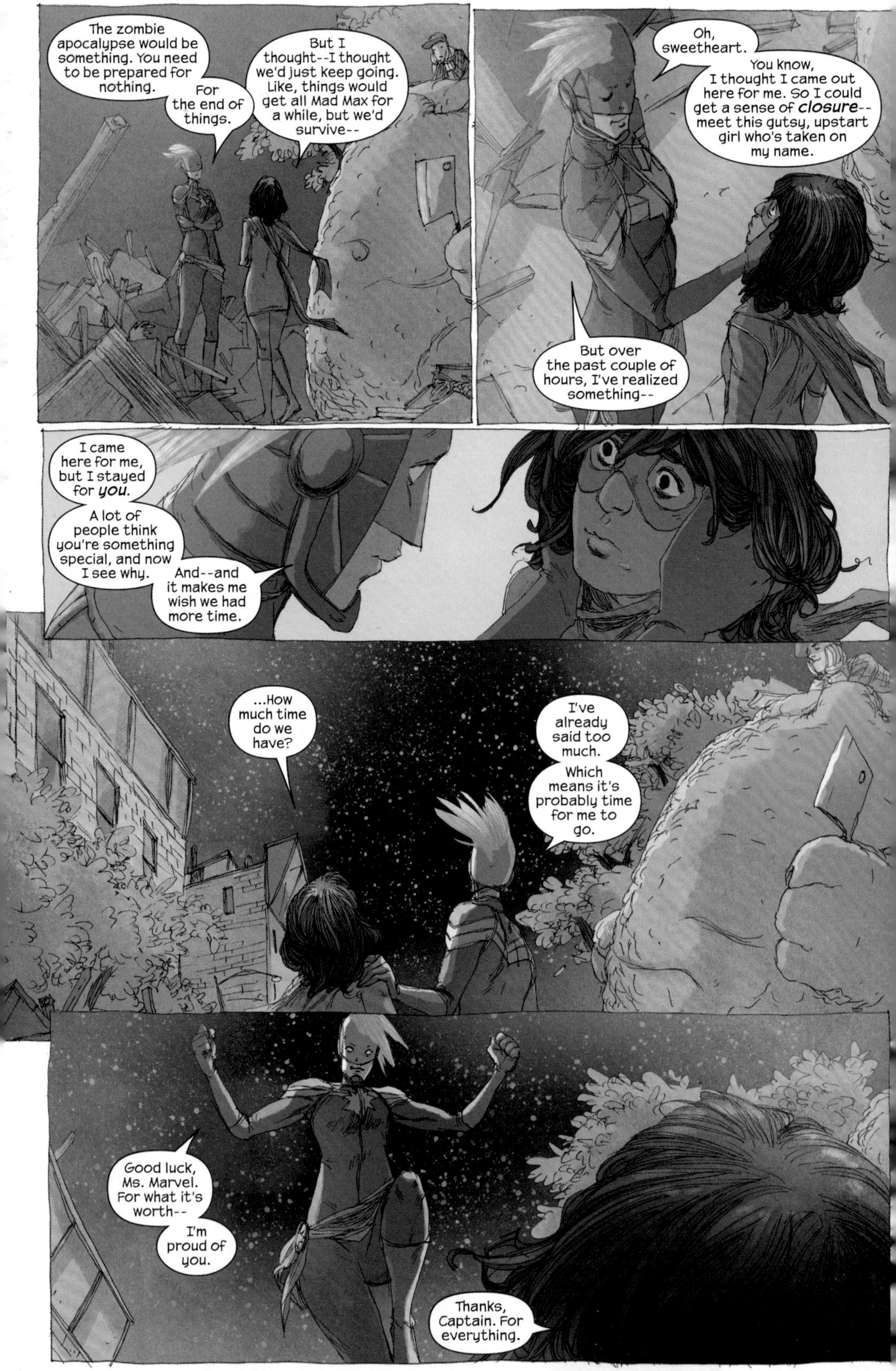

The zombie apocalypse would be something. You need to be prepared for nothing.
For the end of things.
But I thought--I thought we'd just keep going. Like, things would get all Mad Max for a while, but we'd survive--
Oh, sweetheart.
You know, I thought I came out here for me. So I could get a sense of *closure*--meet this gutsy, upstart girl who's taken on my name.
But over the past couple of hours, I've realized something--
I came here for me, but I stayed for *you*.
A lot of people think you're something special, and now I see why.
And--and it makes me wish we had more time.
...How much time do we have?
I've already said too much.
Which means it's probably time for me to go.
Good luck, Ms. Marvel. For what it's worth--
I'm proud of you.
Thanks, Captain. For everything.

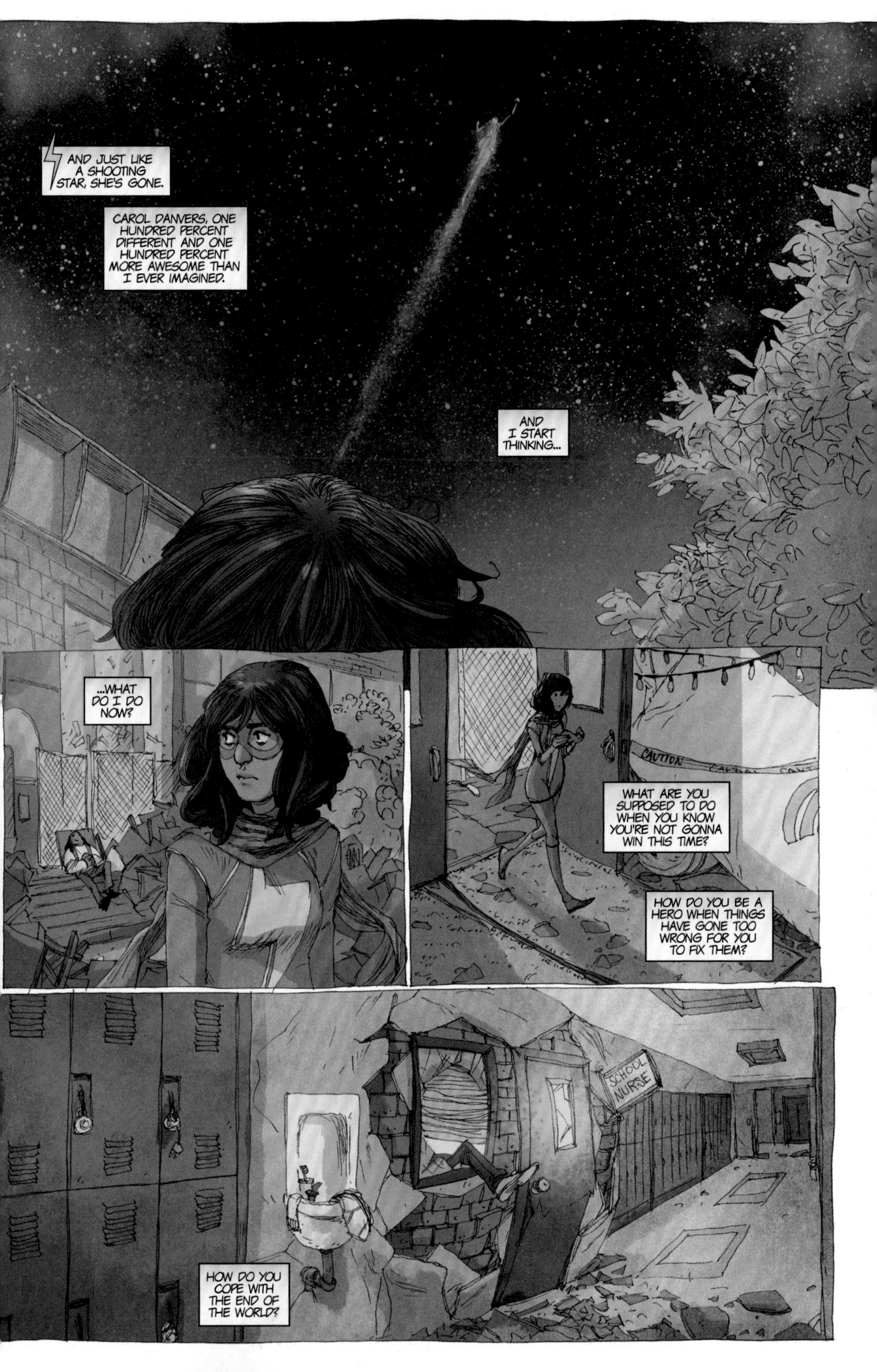
AND JUST LIKE A SHOOTING STAR, SHE'S GONE.
CAROL DANVERS, ONE HUNDRED PERCENT DIFFERENT AND ONE HUNDRED PERCENT MORE AWESOME THAN I EVER IMAGINED.
AND I START THINKING...
...WHAT DO I DO NOW?
CAUTION
WHAT ARE YOU SUPPOSED TO DO WHEN YOU KNOW YOU'RE NOT GONNA WIN THIS TIME?
HOW DO YOU BE A HERO WHEN THINGS HAVE GONE TOO WRONG FOR YOU TO FIX THEM?
SCHOOL NURSE
HOW DO YOU COPE WITH THE END OF THE WORLD?

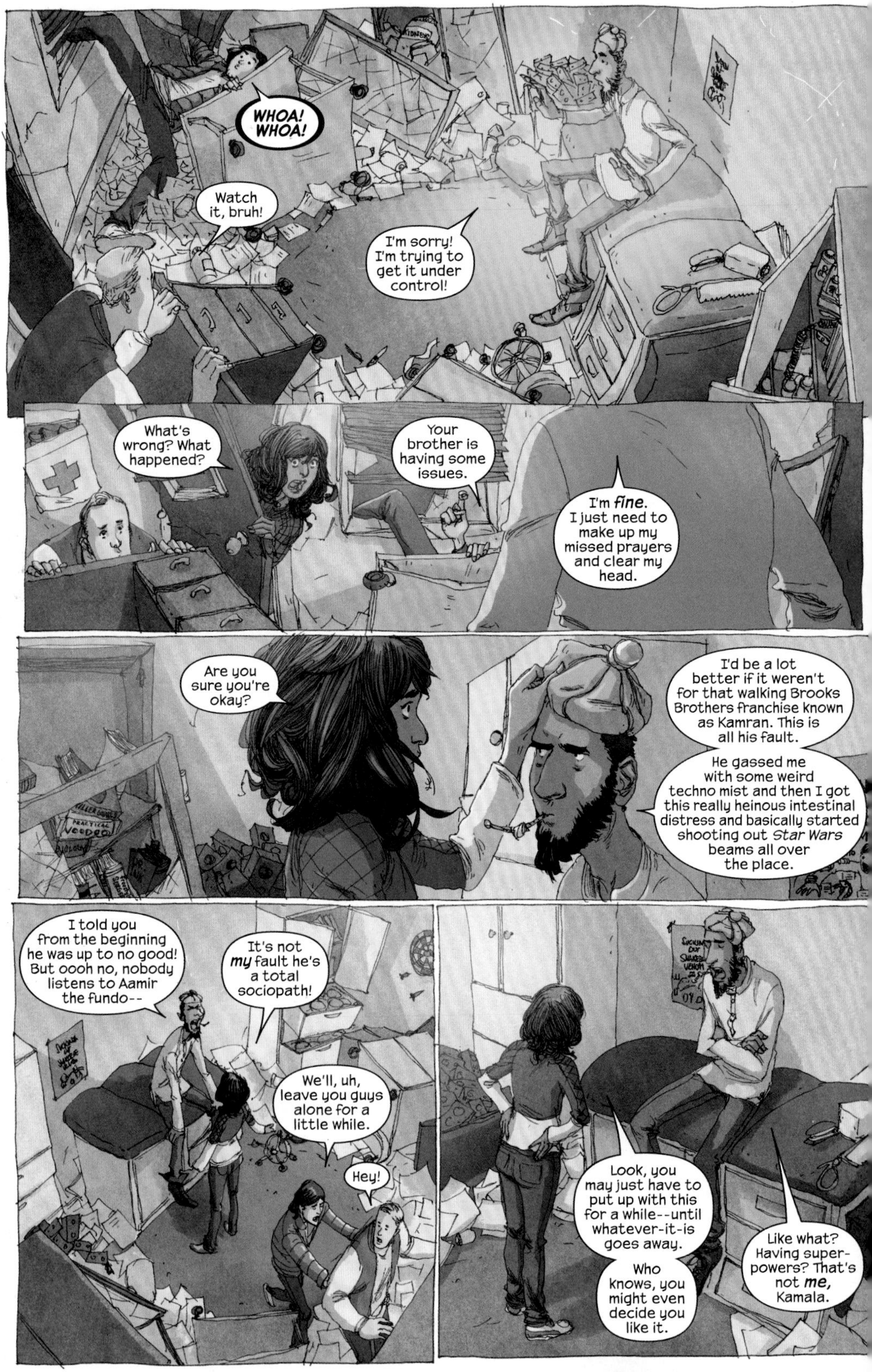
WHOA! WHOA!
Watch it, bruh!
I'm sorry! I'm trying to get it under control!
What's wrong? What happened?
Your brother is having some issues.
I'm *fine*. I just need to make up my missed prayers and clear my head.
Are you sure you're okay?
I'd be a lot better if it weren't for that walking Brooks Brothers franchise known as Kamran. This is all his fault.
He gassed me with some weird techno mist and then I got this really heinous intestinal distress and basically started shooting out *Star Wars* beams all over the place.
I told you from the beginning he was up to no good! But oooh no, nobody listens to Aamir the fundo--
It's not *my* fault he's a total sociopath!
We'll, uh, leave you guys alone for a little while.
Hey!
Look, you may just have to put up with this for a while--until whatever-it-is goes away.
Who knows, you might even decide you like it.
Like what? Having super-powers? That's not *me,* Kamala.

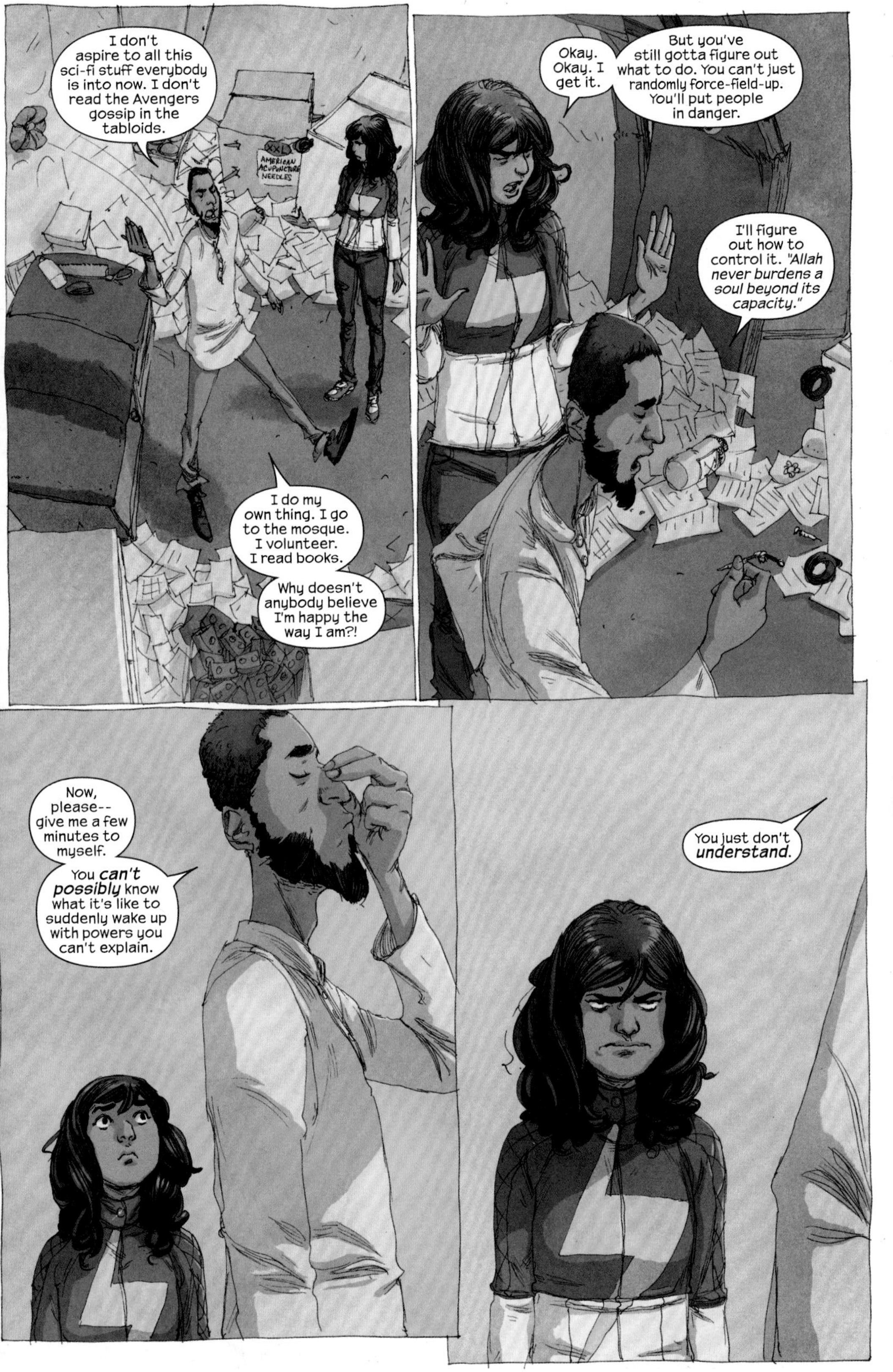
I don't aspire to all this sci-fi stuff everybody is into now. I don't read the Avengers gossip in the tabloids.
AMERICAN ACUPUNCTURE NEEDLES
I do my own thing. I go to the mosque. I volunteer. I read books.
Why doesn't anybody believe I'm happy the way I am?!
Okay. Okay. I get it.
But you've still gotta figure out what to do. You can't just randomly force-field-up. You'll put people in danger.
I'll figure out how to control it. *"Allah never burdens a soul beyond its capacity."*
Now, please-- give me a few minutes to myself.
You ***can't possibly*** know what it's like to suddenly wake up with powers you can't explain.
You just don't ***understand***.

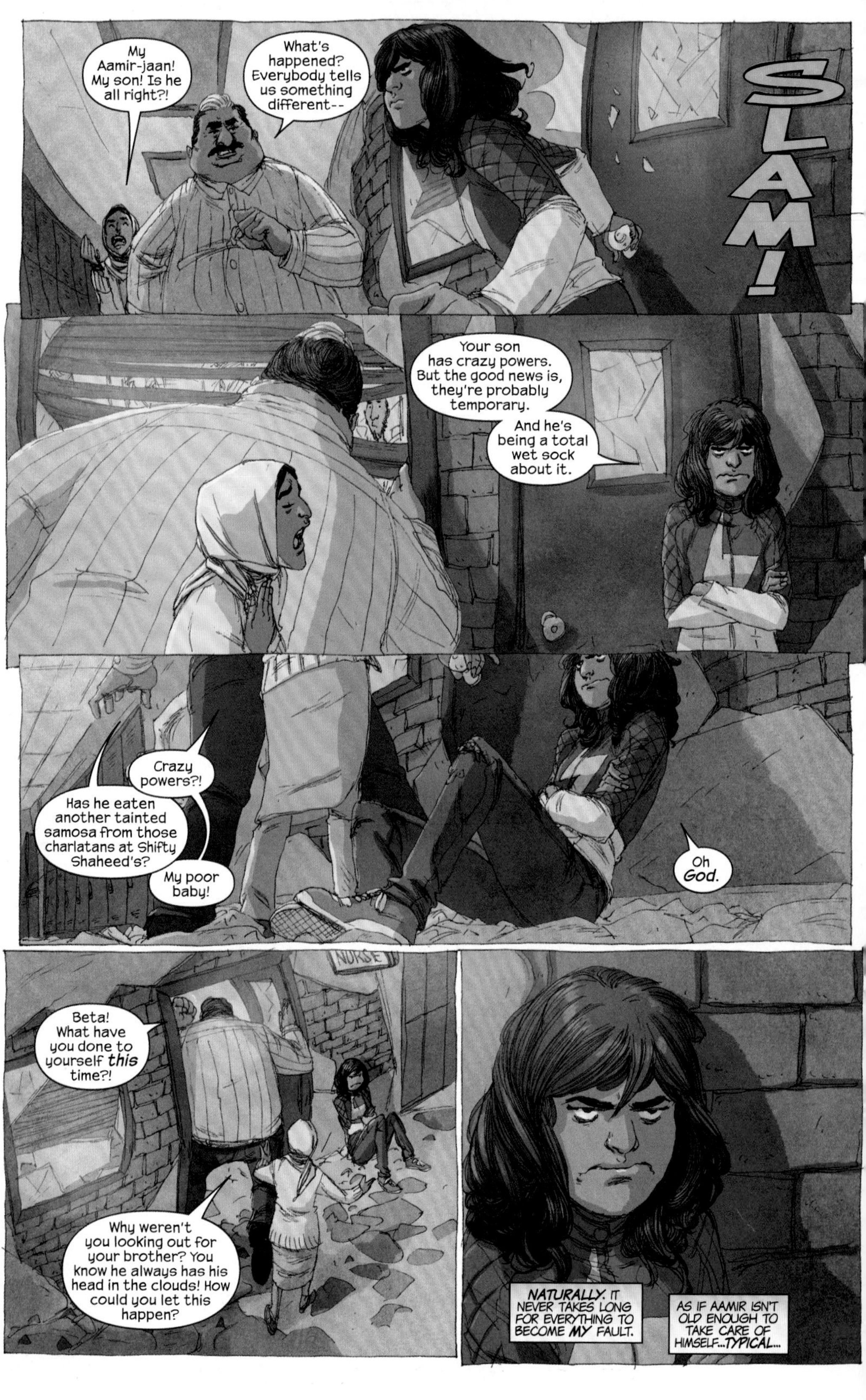
My Aamir-jaan! My son! Is he all right?!
What's happened? Everybody tells us something different--
SLAM!
Your son has crazy powers. But the good news is, they're probably temporary.
And he's being a total wet sock about it.
Crazy powers?!
Has he eaten another tainted samosa from those charlatans at Shifty Shaheed's?
My poor baby!
Oh God.
NURSE
Beta! What have you done to yourself this time?!
Why weren't you looking out for your brother? You know he always has his head in the clouds! How could you let this happen?
NATURALLY. IT NEVER TAKES LONG FOR EVERYTHING TO BECOME MY FAULT.
AS IF AAMIR ISN'T OLD ENOUGH TO TAKE CARE OF HIMSELF...TYPICAL...

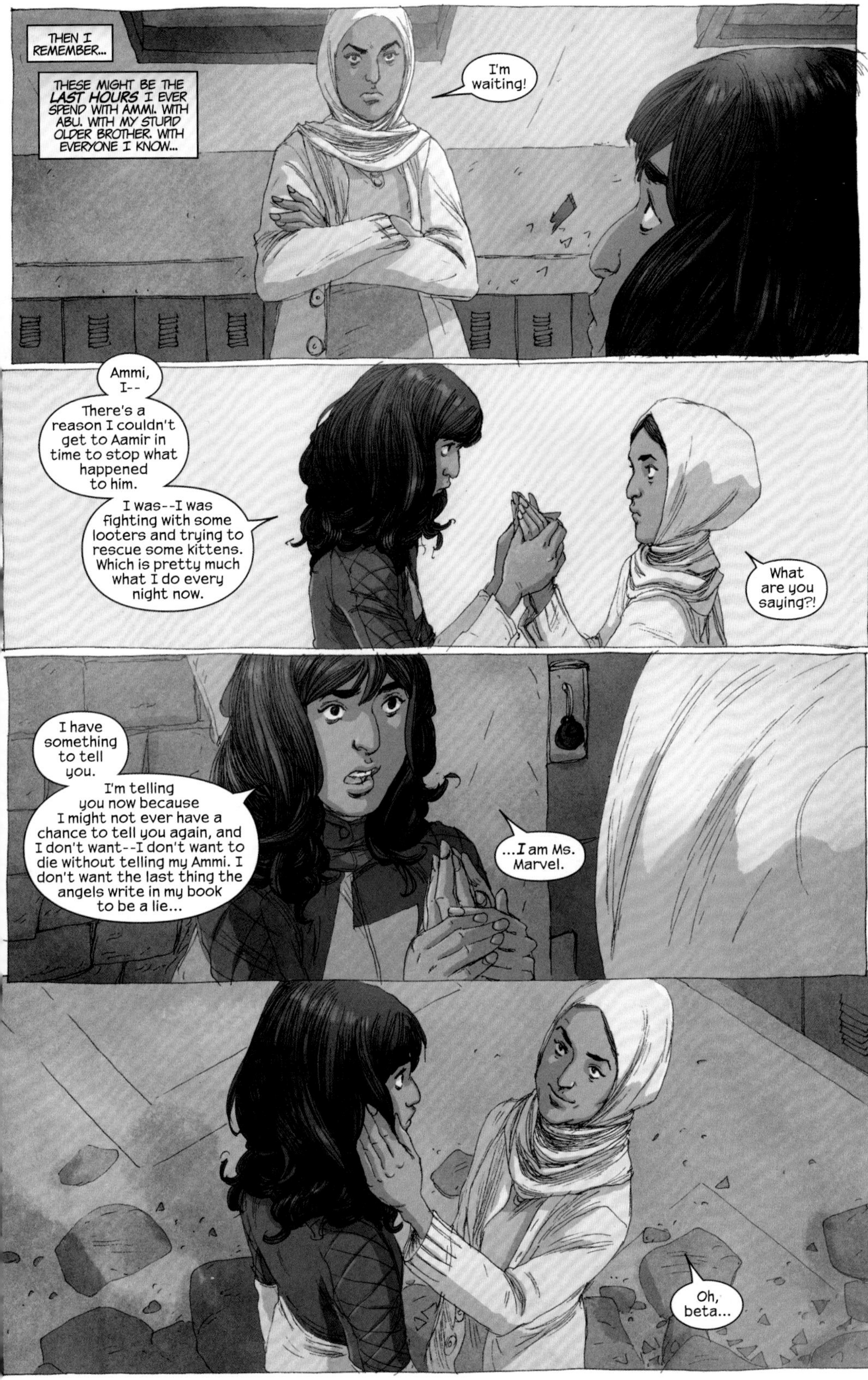
THEN I REMEMBER...
THESE MIGHT BE THE LAST HOURS I EVER SPEND WITH AMMI. WITH ABU. WITH MY STUPID OLDER BROTHER. WITH EVERYONE I KNOW...
I'm waiting!
Ammi, I--
There's a reason I couldn't get to Aamir in time to stop what happened to him.
I was--I was fighting with some looters and trying to rescue some kittens. Which is pretty much what I do every night now.
What are you saying?!
I have something to tell you.
I'm telling you now because I might not ever have a chance to tell you again, and I don't want--I don't want to die without telling my Ammi. I don't want the last thing the angels write in my book to be a lie...
...I am Ms. Marvel.
Oh, beta...

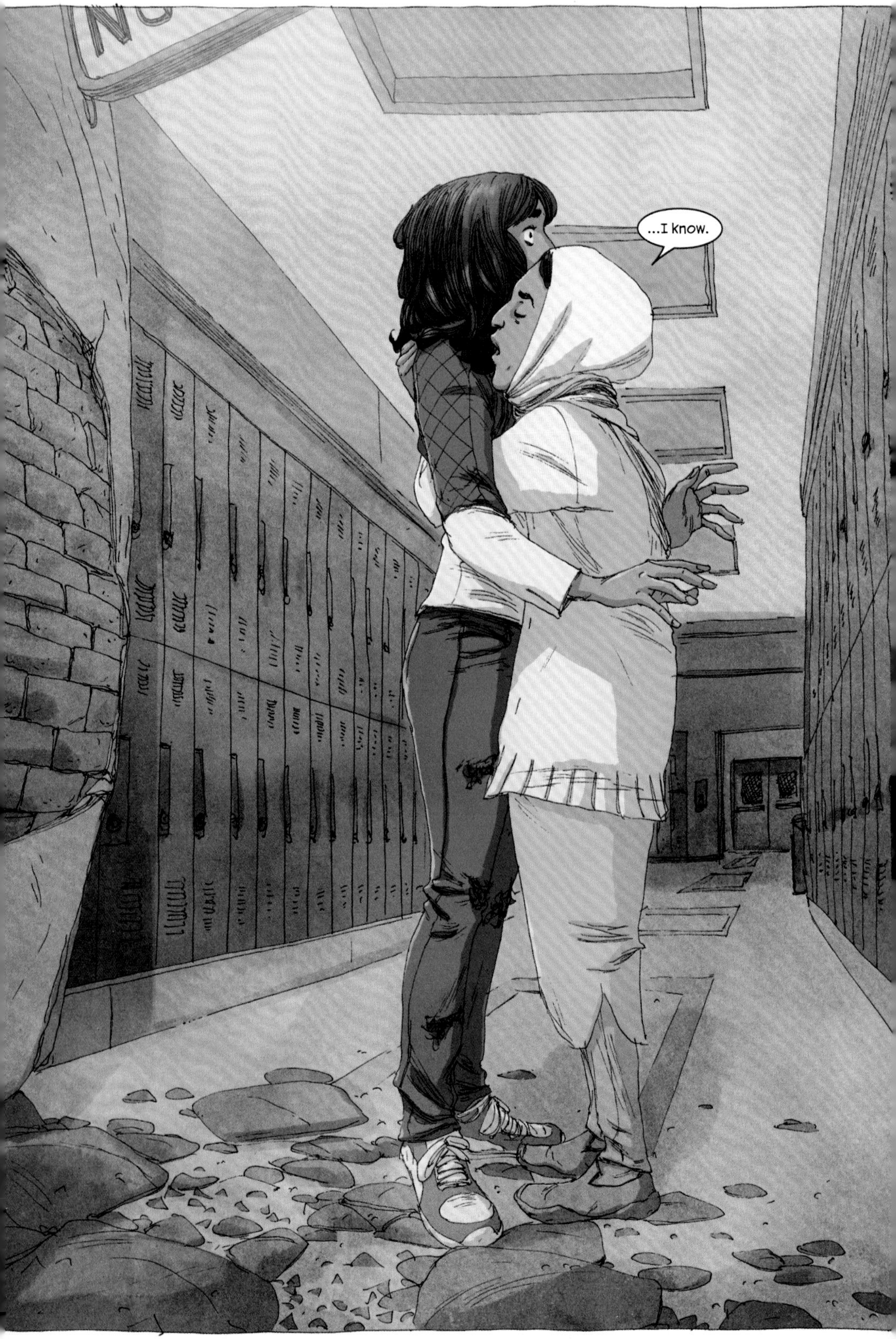
...I know.

FREE COMIC BOOK DAY 2015

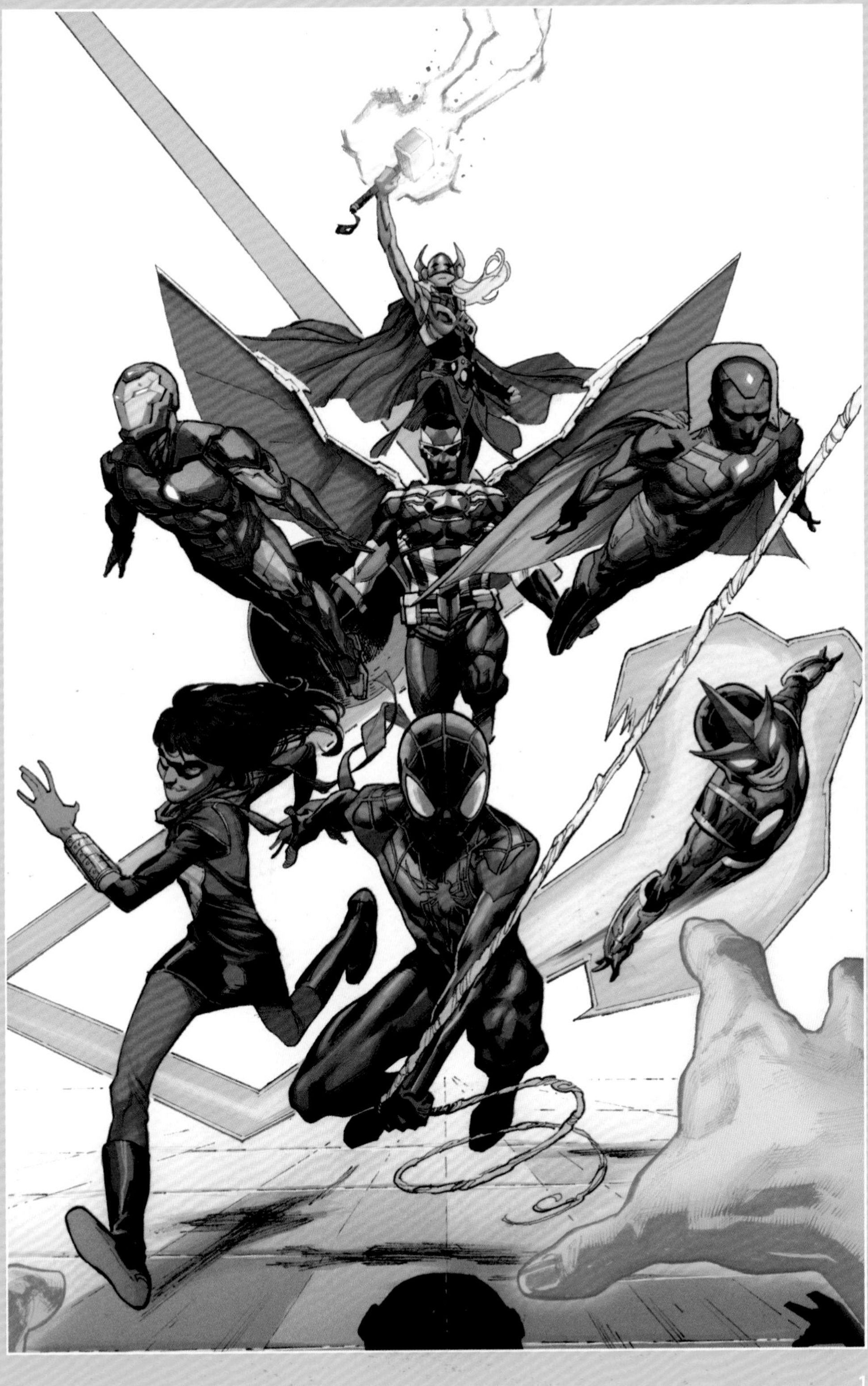

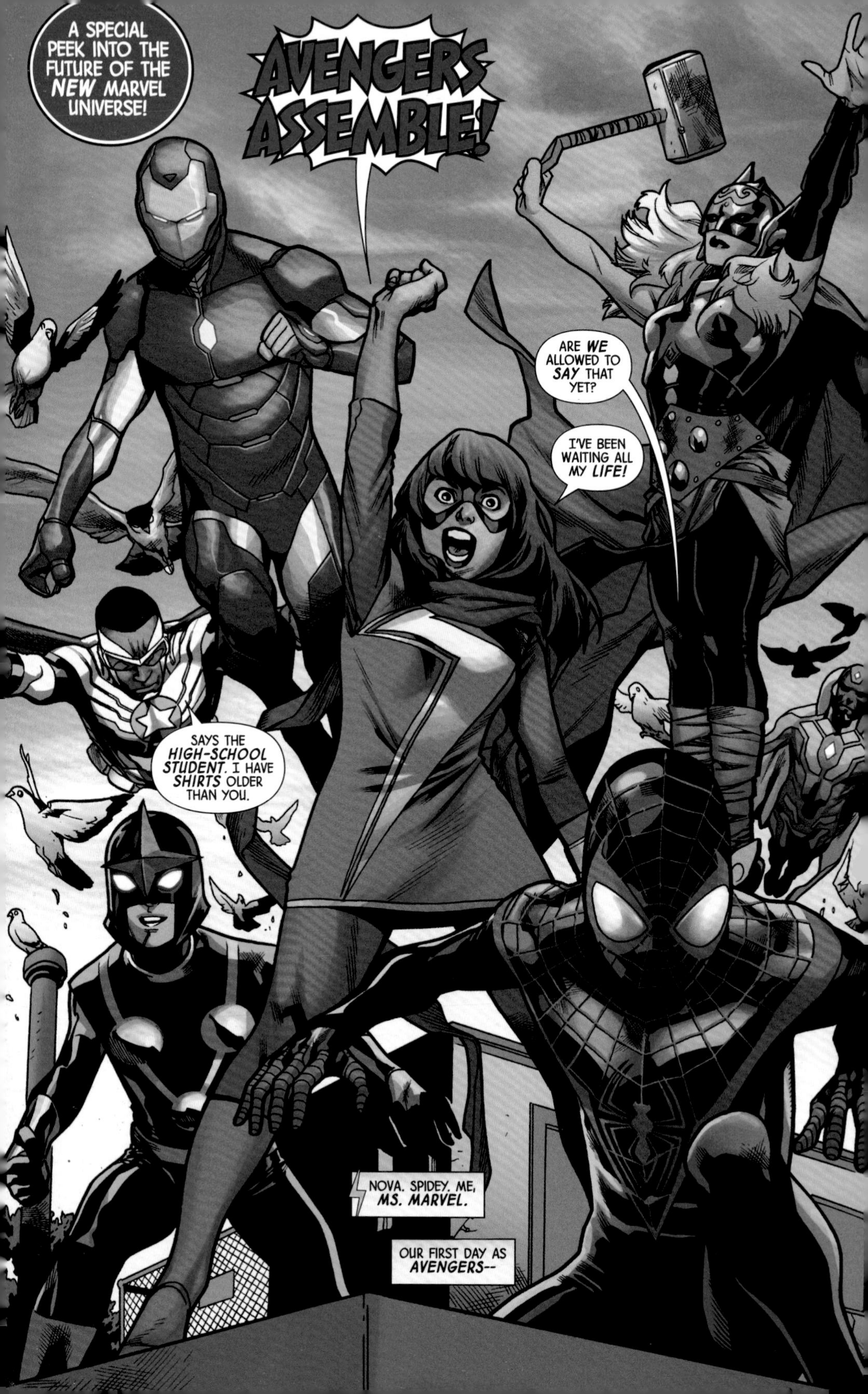
A SPECIAL PEEK INTO THE FUTURE OF THE NEW MARVEL UNIVERSE!
AVENGERS ASSEMBLE!
ARE WE ALLOWED TO SAY THAT YET?
I'VE BEEN WAITING ALL MY LIFE!
SAYS THE HIGH-SCHOOL STUDENT. I HAVE SHIRTS OLDER THAN YOU.
NOVA. SPIDEY. ME, MS. MARVEL.
OUR FIRST DAY AS AVENGERS--

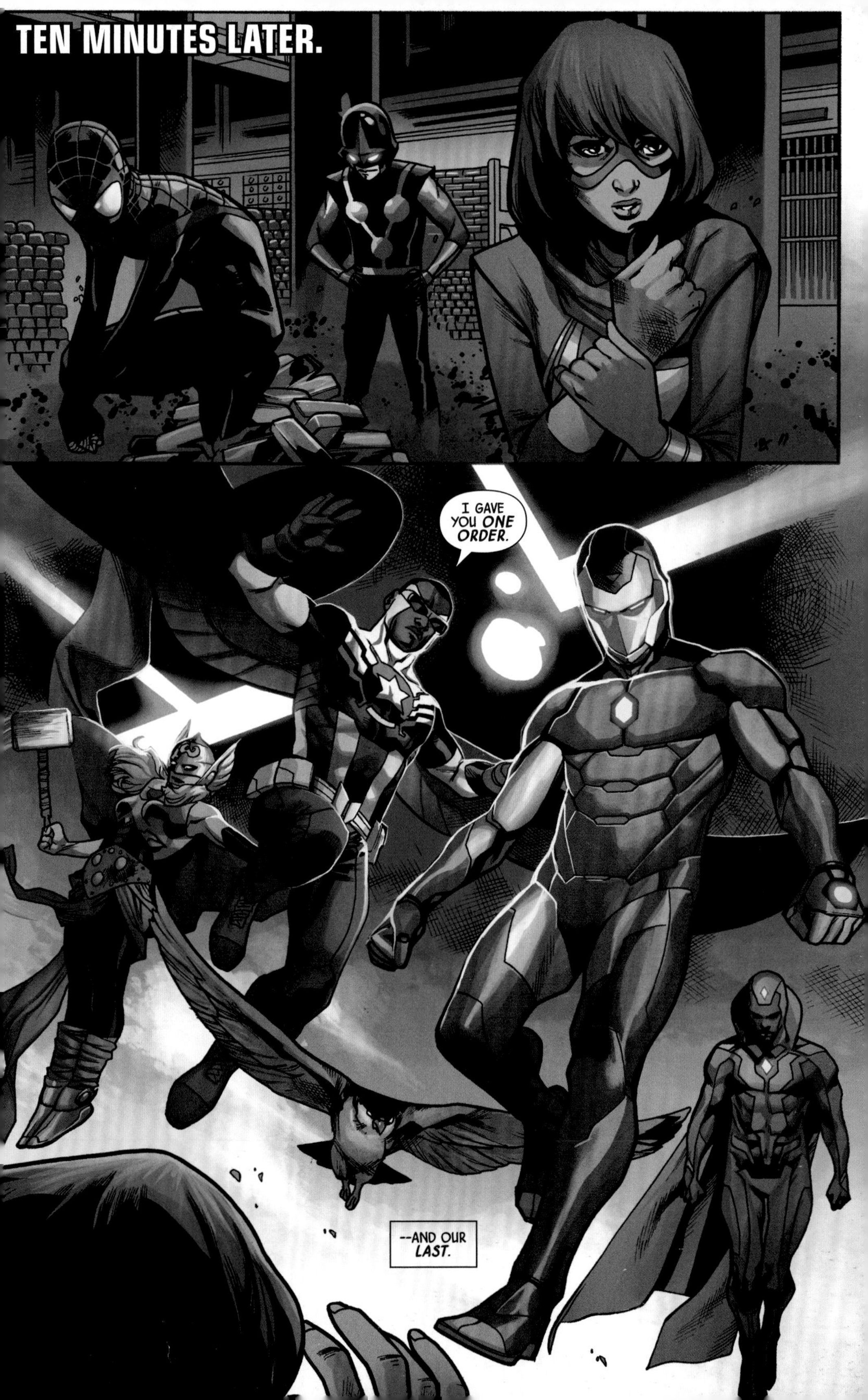

TEN MINUTES LATER.
I GAVE YOU ONE ORDER.
--AND OUR LAST.

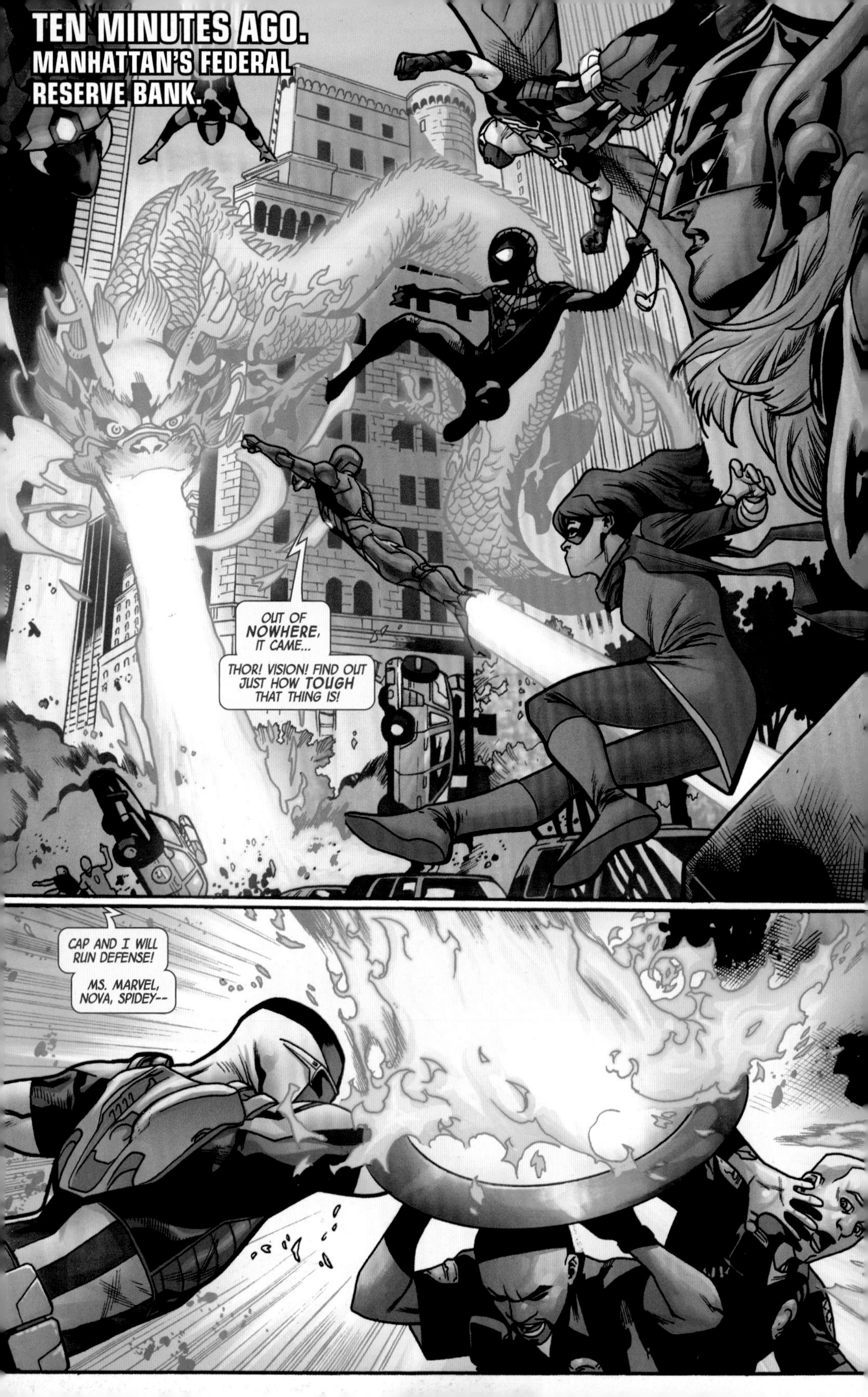
TEN MINUTES AGO. MANHATTAN'S FEDERAL RESERVE BANK.
OUT OF NOWHERE, IT CAME...
THOR! VISION! FIND OUT JUST HOW TOUGH THAT THING IS!
CAP AND I WILL RUN DEFENSE!
MS. MARVEL, NOVA, SPIDEY--

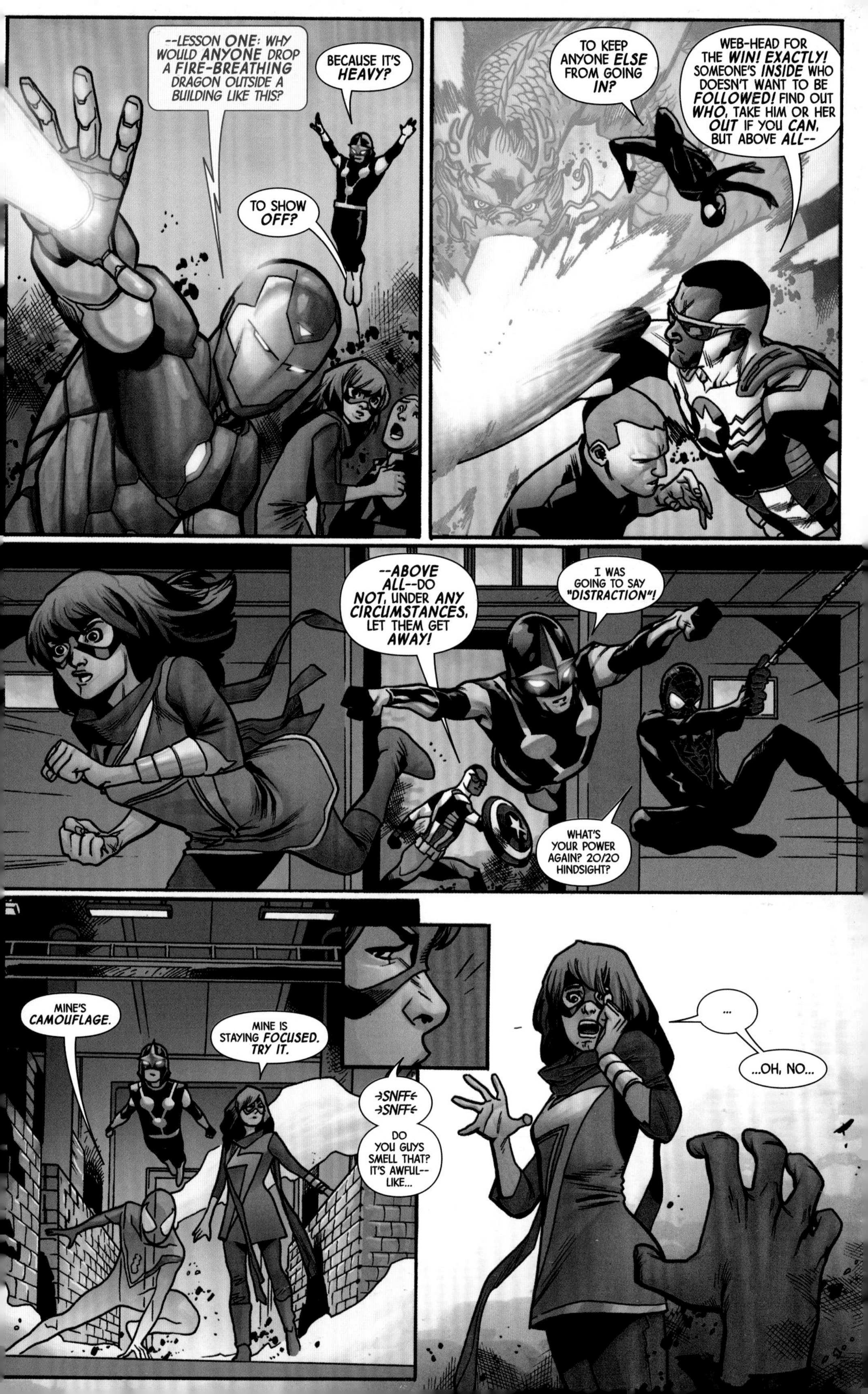
--LESSON ONE: WHY WOULD ANYONE DROP A FIRE-BREATHING DRAGON OUTSIDE A BUILDING LIKE THIS?
BECAUSE IT'S HEAVY?
TO SHOW OFF?
TO KEEP ANYONE ELSE FROM GOING IN?
WEB-HEAD FOR THE WIN! EXACTLY! SOMEONE'S INSIDE WHO DOESN'T WANT TO BE FOLLOWED! FIND OUT WHO, TAKE HIM OR HER OUT IF YOU CAN, BUT ABOVE ALL--
--ABOVE ALL--DO NOT, UNDER ANY CIRCUMSTANCES, LET THEM GET AWAY!
I WAS GOING TO SAY "DISTRACTION"!
WHAT'S YOUR POWER AGAIN? 20/20 HINDSIGHT?
MINE'S CAMOUFLAGE.
MINE IS STAYING FOCUSED. TRY IT.
SNFF SNFF
DO YOU GUYS SMELL THAT? IT'S AWFUL-- LIKE...
...
...OH, NO...

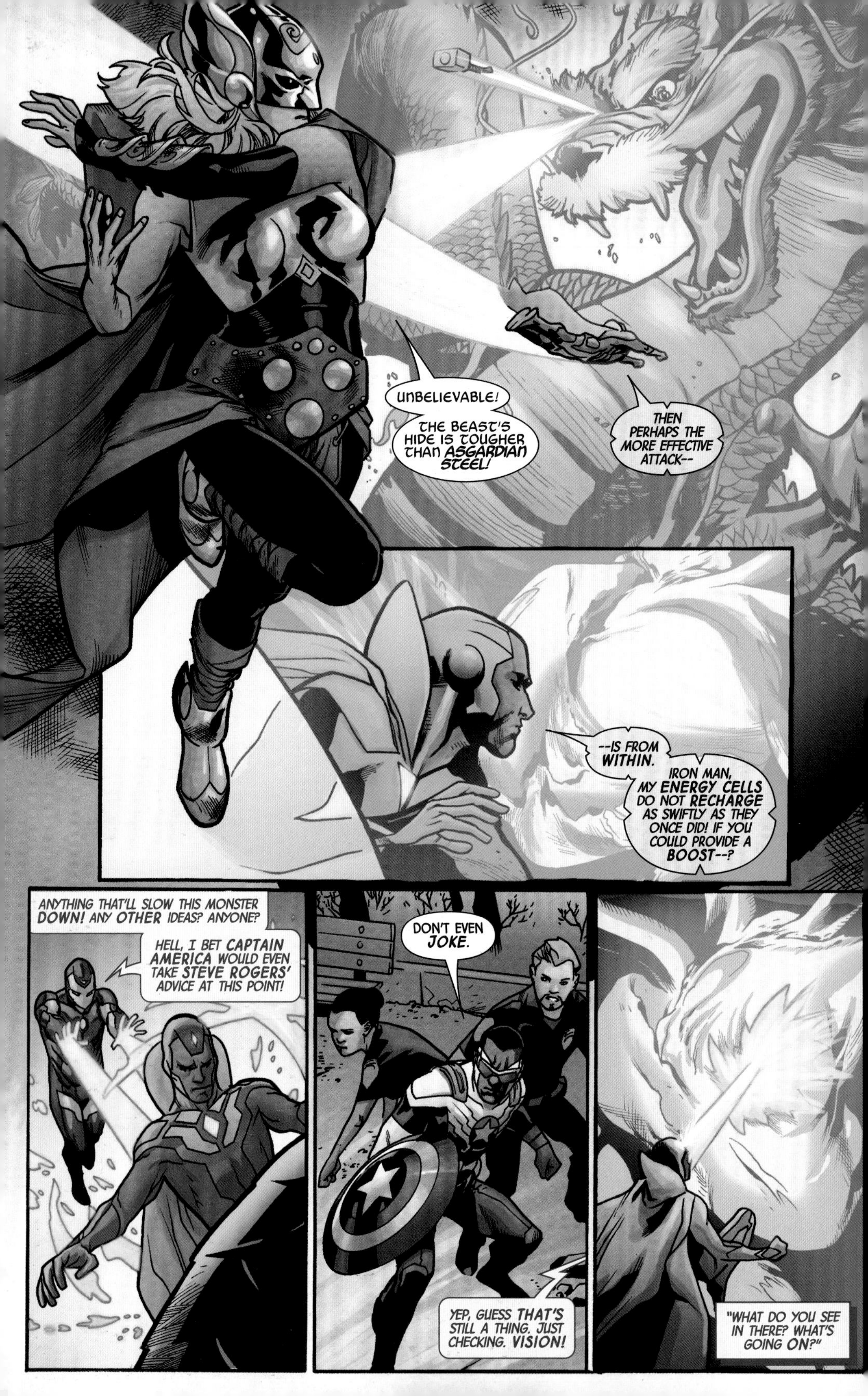
UNBELIEVABLE!
THE BEAST'S HIDE IS TOUGHER THAN ASGARDIAN STEEL!
THEN PERHAPS THE MORE EFFECTIVE ATTACK--
--IS FROM WITHIN.
IRON MAN, MY ENERGY CELLS DO NOT RECHARGE AS SWIFTLY AS THEY ONCE DID! IF YOU COULD PROVIDE A BOOST--?
ANYTHING THAT'LL SLOW THIS MONSTER DOWN! ANY OTHER IDEAS? ANYONE?
HELL, I BET CAPTAIN AMERICA WOULD EVEN TAKE STEVE ROGERS' ADVICE AT THIS POINT!
DON'T EVEN JOKE.
YEP, GUESS THAT'S STILL A THING. JUST CHECKING. VISION!
"WHAT DO YOU SEE IN THERE? WHAT'S GOING ON?"

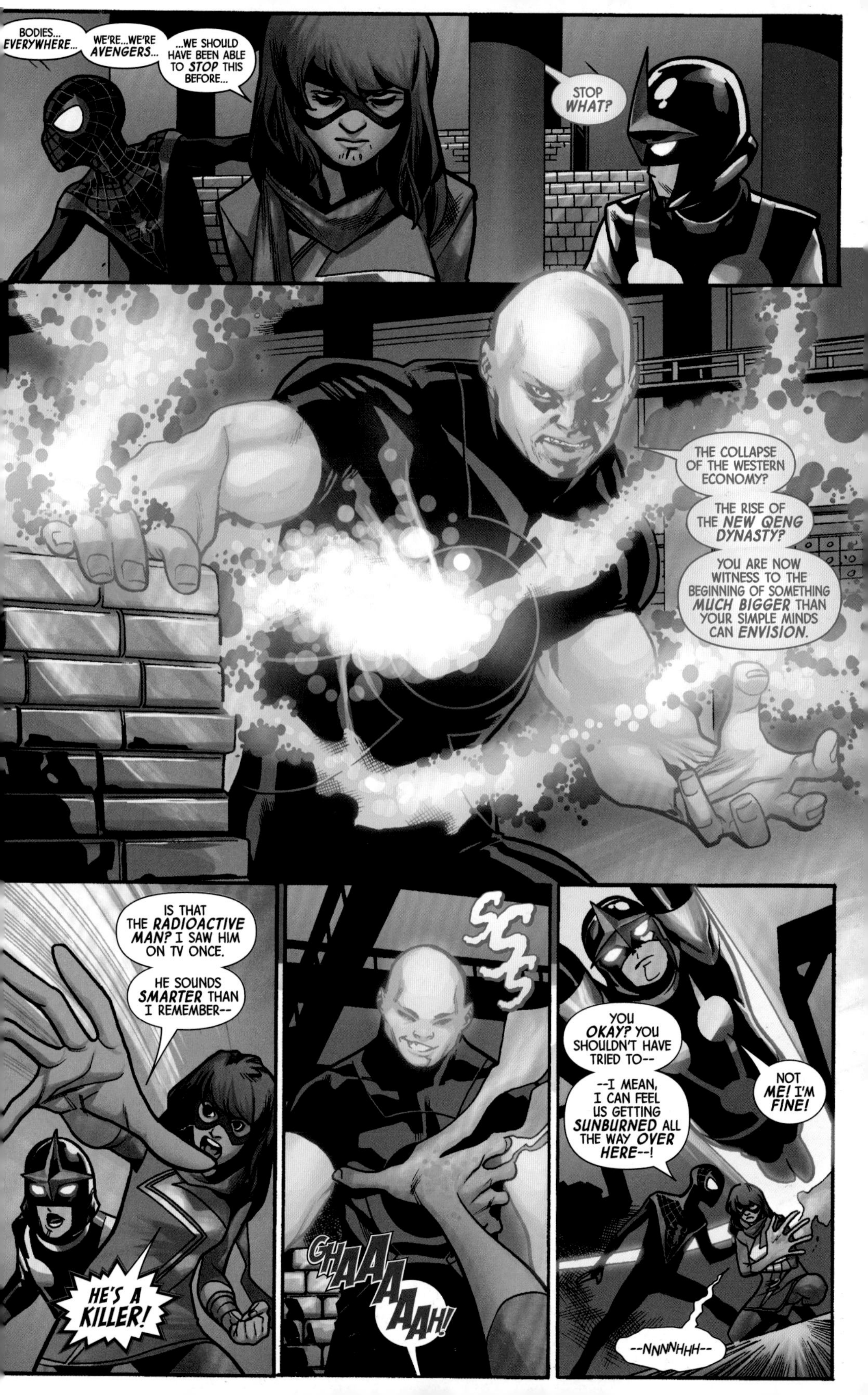
BODIES... EVERYWHERE...
WE'RE...WE'RE AVENGERS...
...WE SHOULD HAVE BEEN ABLE TO STOP THIS BEFORE...
STOP WHAT?
THE COLLAPSE OF THE WESTERN ECONOMY?
THE RISE OF THE NEW QENG DYNASTY?
YOU ARE NOW WITNESS TO THE BEGINNING OF SOMETHING MUCH BIGGER THAN YOUR SIMPLE MINDS CAN ENVISION.
IS THAT THE RADIOACTIVE MAN? I SAW HIM ON TV ONCE.
HE SOUNDS SMARTER THAN I REMEMBER--
HE'S A KILLER!
GHAAAAAAH!
YOU OKAY? YOU SHOULDN'T HAVE TRIED TO--
--I MEAN, I CAN FEEL US GETTING SUNBURNED ALL THE WAY OVER HERE--!
NOT ME! I'M FINE!
--NNNNHHH--

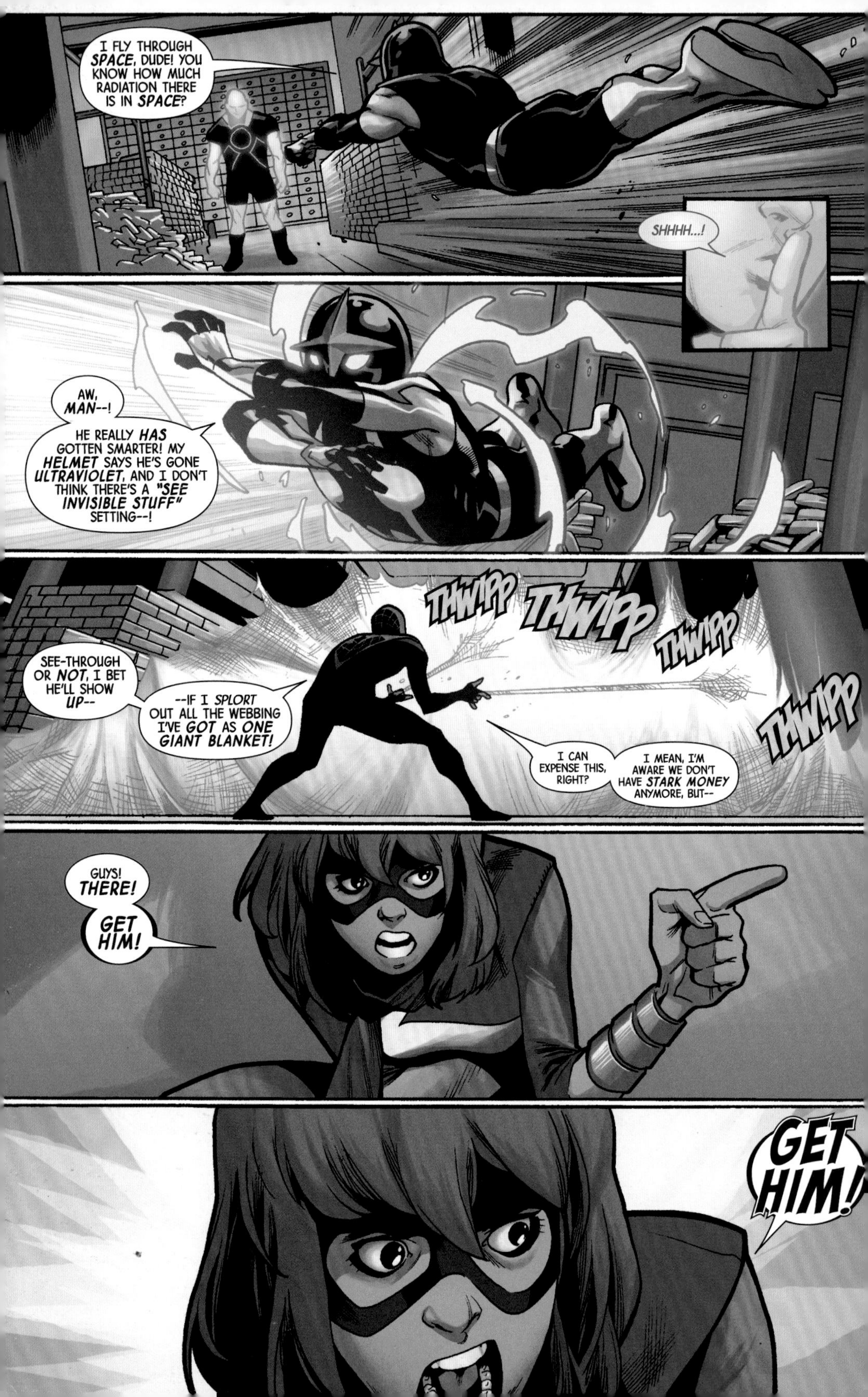
I FLY THROUGH SPACE, DUDE! YOU KNOW HOW MUCH RADIATION THERE IS IN SPACE?
SHHHH...!
AW, MAN--!
HE REALLY HAS GOTTEN SMARTER! MY HELMET SAYS HE'S GONE ULTRAVIOLET, AND I DON'T THINK THERE'S A "SEE INVISIBLE STUFF" SETTING--!
THWIPP THWIPP THWIPP THWIPP
SEE-THROUGH OR NOT, I BET HE'LL SHOW UP--
--IF I SPLORT OUT ALL THE WEBBING I'VE GOT AS ONE GIANT BLANKET!
I CAN EXPENSE THIS, RIGHT?
I MEAN, I'M AWARE WE DON'T HAVE STARK MONEY ANYMORE, BUT--
GUYS! THERE!
GET HIM!
GET HIM!

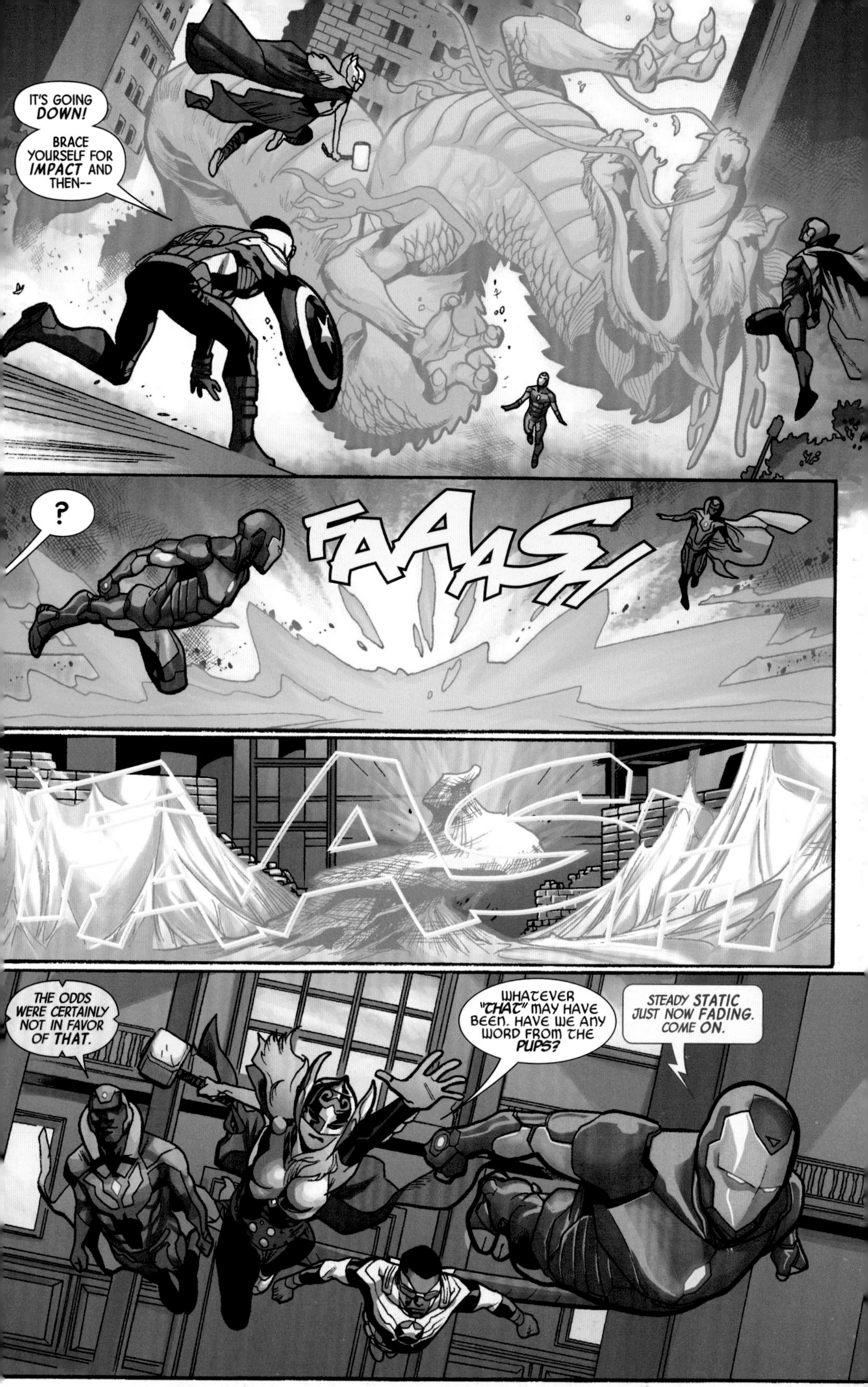
IT'S GOING DOWN!
BRACE YOURSELF FOR IMPACT AND THEN--
?
FAAASH
FAASH
THE ODDS WERE CERTAINLY NOT IN FAVOR OF THAT.
WHATEVER "THAT" MAY HAVE BEEN. HAVE WE ANY WORD FROM THE PUPS?
STEADY STATIC JUST NOW FADING. COME ON.

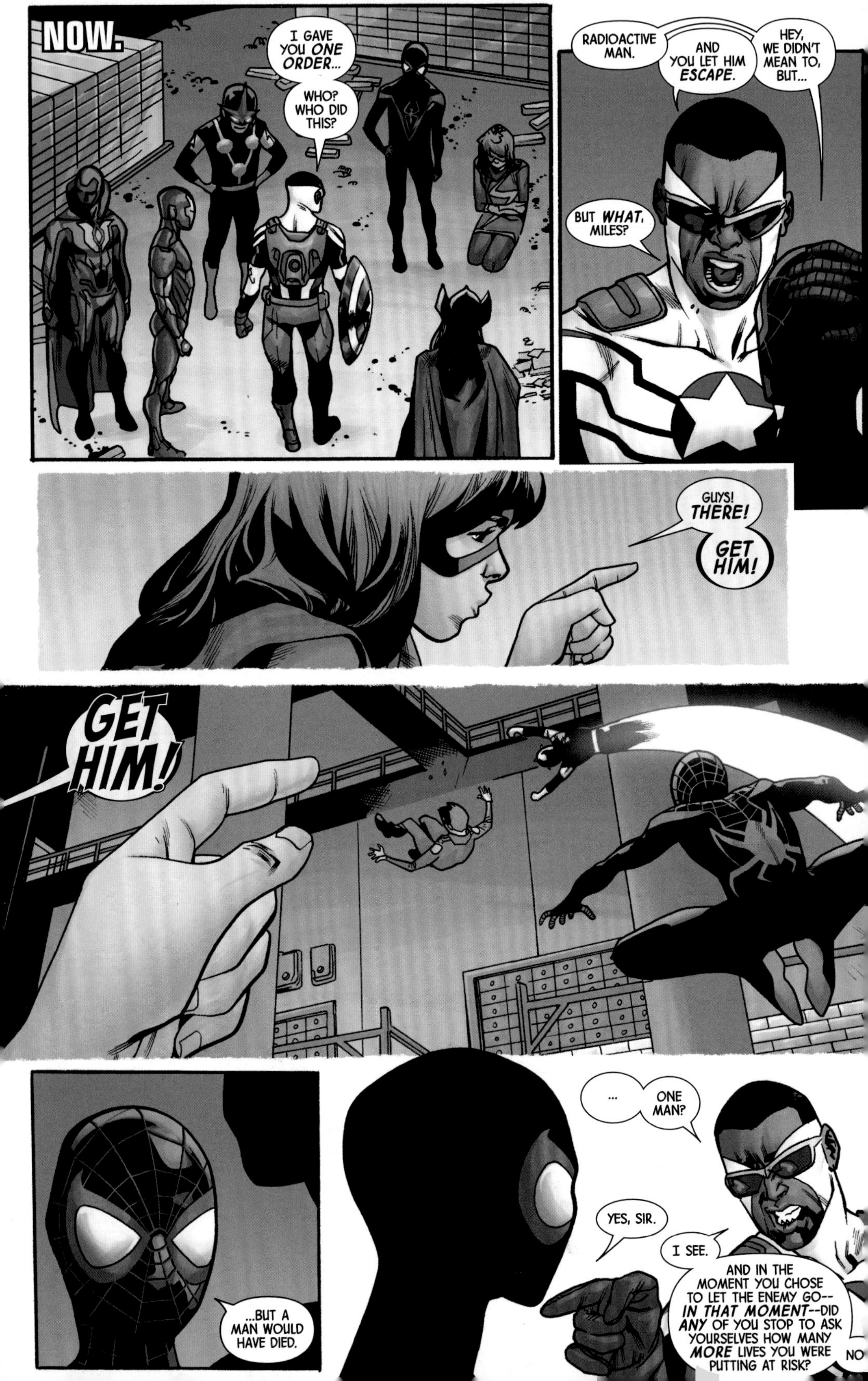
NOW.
I GAVE YOU ONE ORDER...
WHO? WHO DID THIS?
RADIOACTIVE MAN.
AND YOU LET HIM ESCAPE.
HEY, WE DIDN'T MEAN TO, BUT...
BUT WHAT, MILES?
GUYS! THERE!
GET HIM!
GET HIM!
...BUT A MAN WOULD HAVE DIED.
... ONE MAN?
YES, SIR.
I SEE.
AND IN THE MOMENT YOU CHOSE TO LET THE ENEMY GO-- IN THAT MOMENT--DID ANY OF YOU STOP TO ASK YOURSELVES HOW MANY MORE LIVES YOU WERE PUTTING AT RISK?
NO

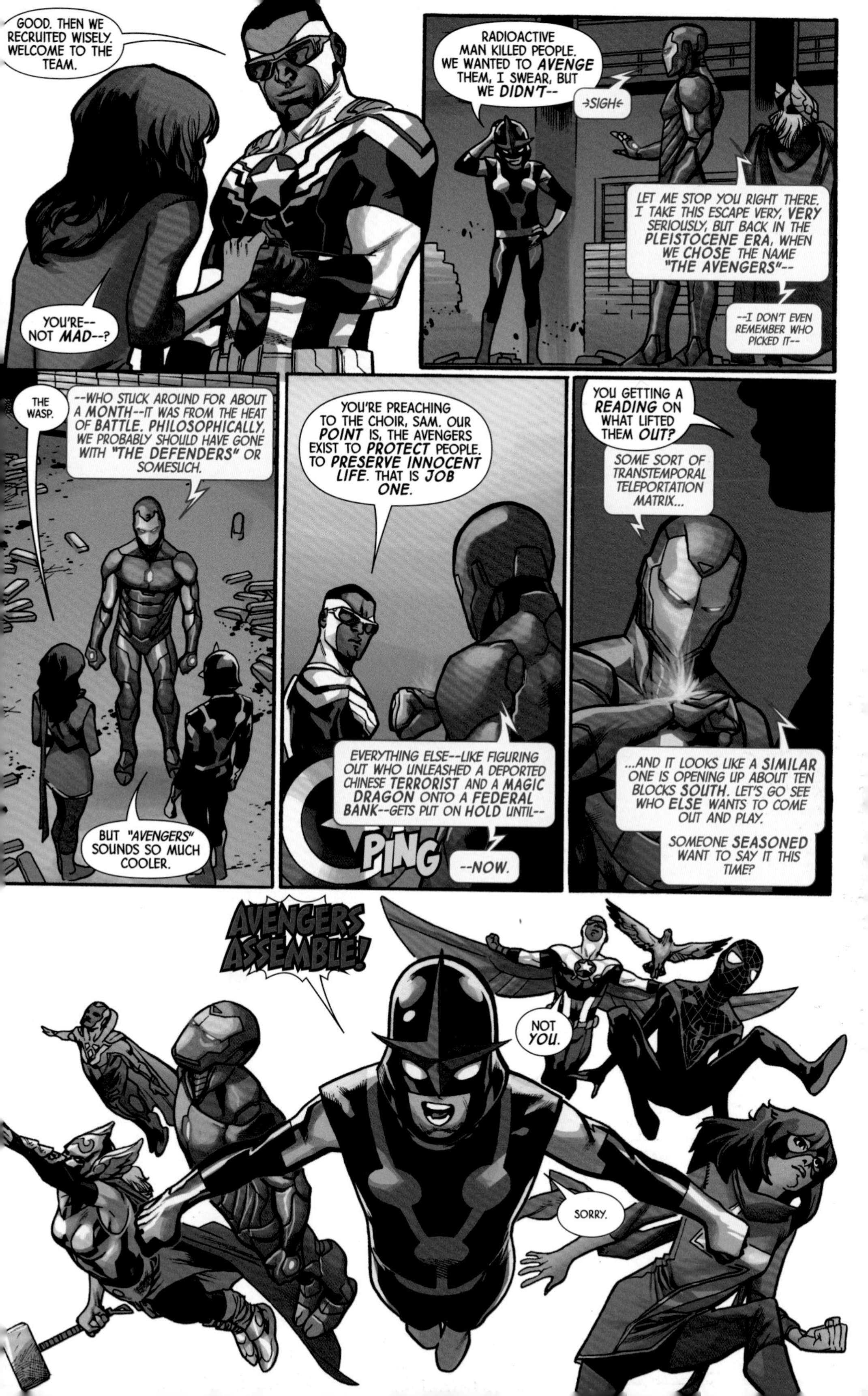
GOOD. THEN WE RECRUITED WISELY. WELCOME TO THE TEAM.
YOU'RE-- NOT MAD--?
RADIOACTIVE MAN KILLED PEOPLE. WE WANTED TO AVENGE THEM, I SWEAR, BUT WE DIDN'T--
›SIGH‹
LET ME STOP YOU RIGHT THERE. I TAKE THIS ESCAPE VERY, VERY SERIOUSLY, BUT BACK IN THE PLEISTOCENE ERA, WHEN WE CHOSE THE NAME "THE AVENGERS"--
--I DON'T EVEN REMEMBER WHO PICKED IT--
THE WASP.
--WHO STUCK AROUND FOR ABOUT A MONTH--IT WAS FROM THE HEAT OF BATTLE. PHILOSOPHICALLY, WE PROBABLY SHOULD HAVE GONE WITH "THE DEFENDERS" OR SOMESUCH.
BUT "AVENGERS" SOUNDS SO MUCH COOLER.
YOU'RE PREACHING TO THE CHOIR, SAM. OUR POINT IS, THE AVENGERS EXIST TO PROTECT PEOPLE. TO PRESERVE INNOCENT LIFE. THAT IS JOB ONE.
EVERYTHING ELSE--LIKE FIGURING OUT WHO UNLEASHED A DEPORTED CHINESE TERRORIST AND A MAGIC DRAGON ONTO A FEDERAL BANK--GETS PUT ON HOLD UNTIL--
PING
--NOW.
YOU GETTING A READING ON WHAT LIFTED THEM OUT?
SOME SORT OF TRANSTEMPORAL TELEPORTATION MATRIX...
...AND IT LOOKS LIKE A SIMILAR ONE IS OPENING UP ABOUT TEN BLOCKS SOUTH. LET'S GO SEE WHO ELSE WANTS TO COME OUT AND PLAY.
SOMEONE SEASONED WANT TO SAY IT THIS TIME?
AVENGERS ASSEMBLE!
NOT YOU.
SORRY.

MOON GIRL AND DEVIL DINOSAUR #10

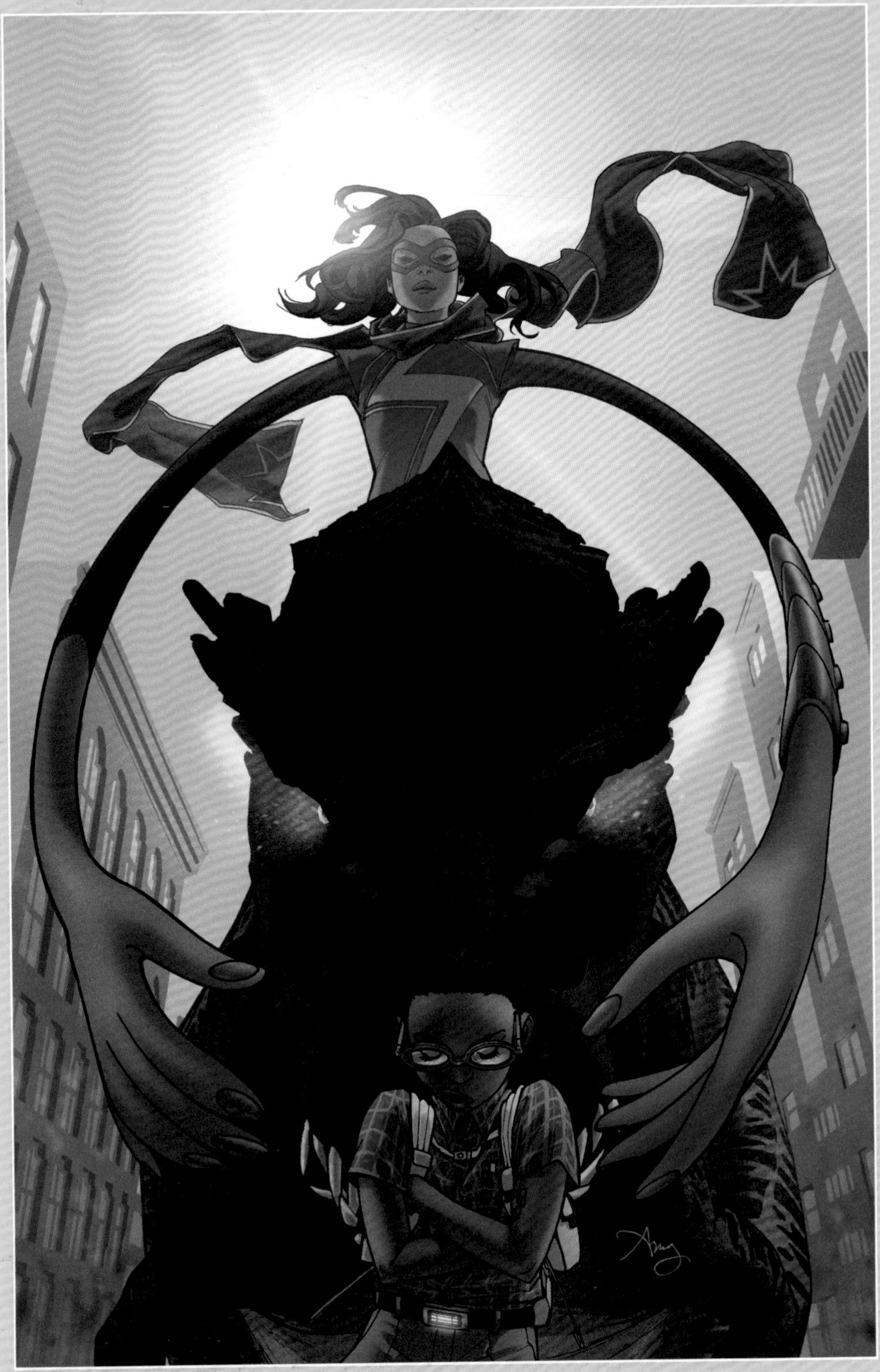
Amy

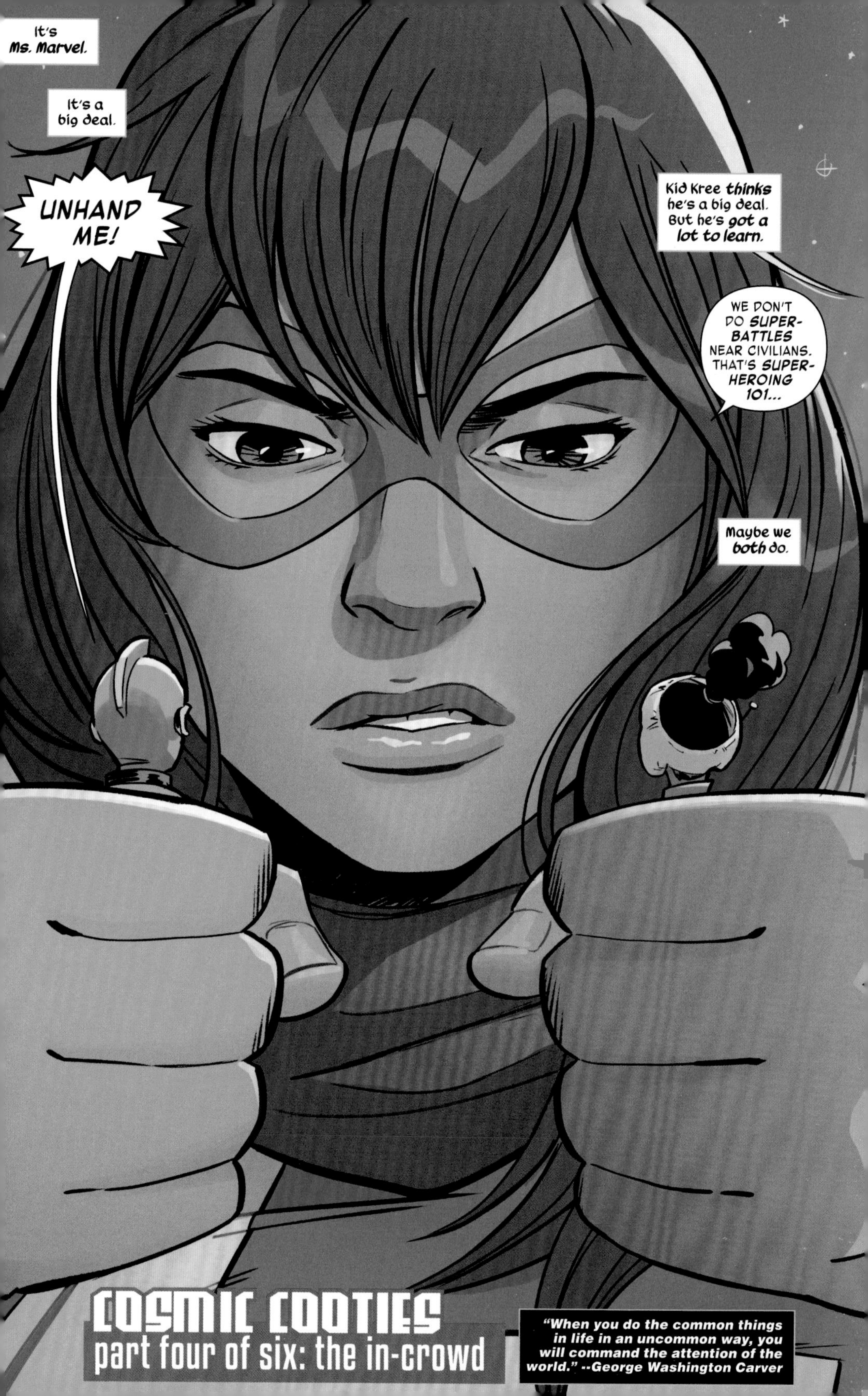
It's Ms. Marvel.
It's a big deal.
UNHAND ME!
Kid Kree thinks he's a big deal. But he's got a lot to learn.
WE DON'T DO SUPER-BATTLES NEAR CIVILIANS. THAT'S SUPER-HEROING 101...
Maybe we both do.
COSMIC COOTIES
part four of six: the in-crowd
"When you do the common things in life in an uncommon way, you will command the attention of the world." --George Washington Carver

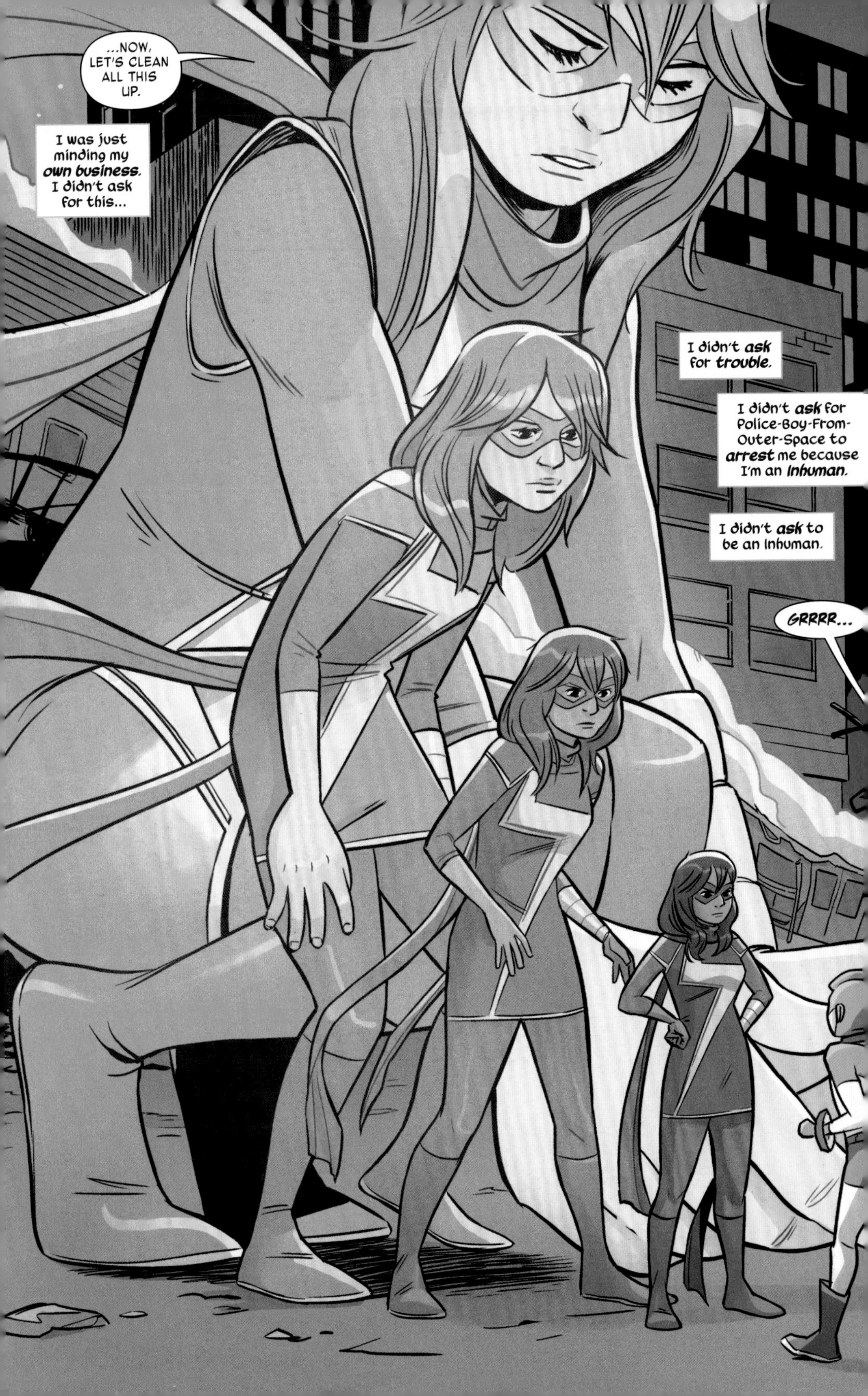
...NOW, LET'S CLEAN ALL THIS UP.
I was just minding my **own business**. I didn't ask for this...
I didn't **ask** for **trouble**.
I didn't **ask** for Police-Boy-From-Outer-Space to **arrest** me because I'm an **Inhuman**.
I didn't **ask** to be an Inhuman.
GRRRR...

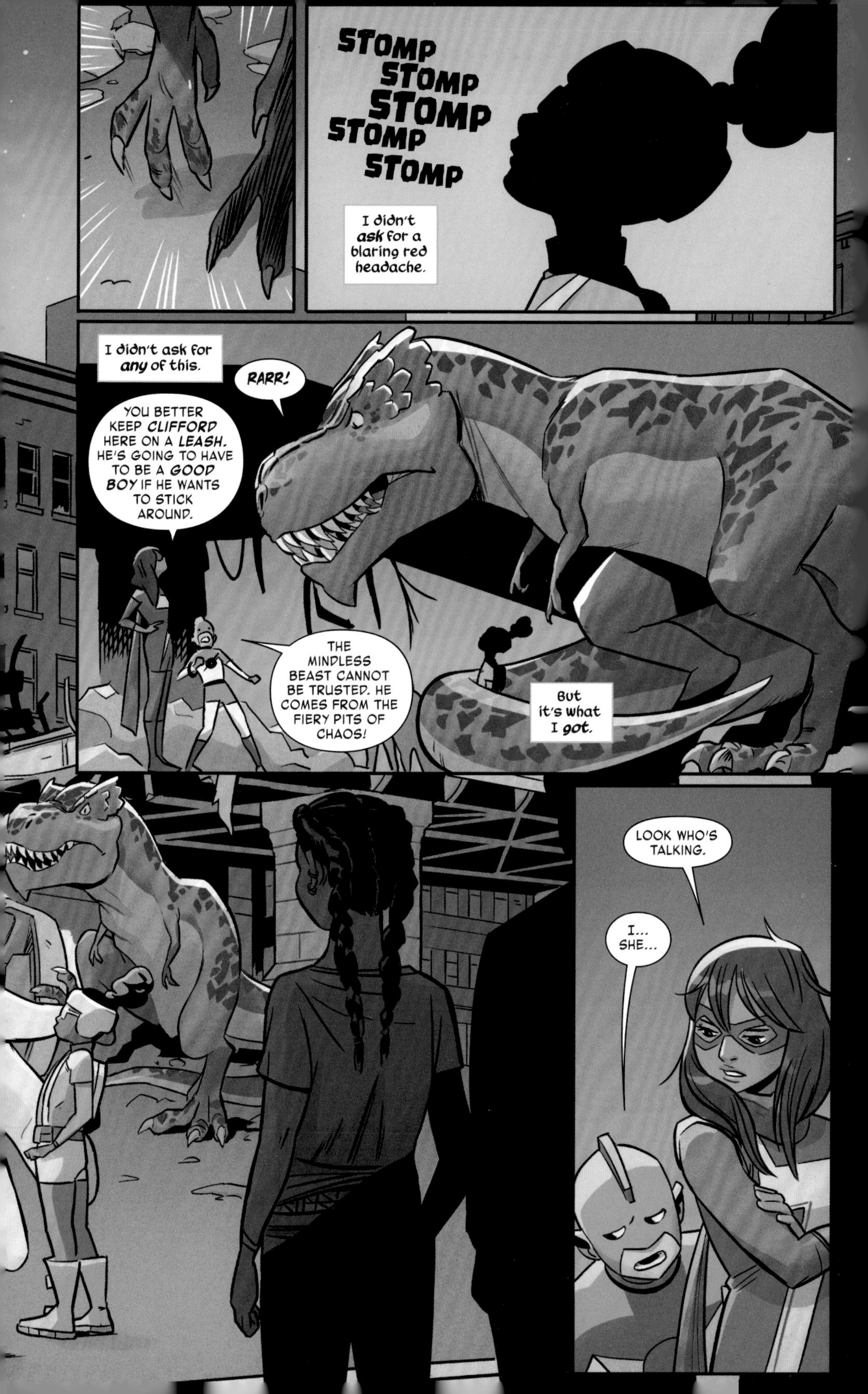
STOMP
STOMP
STOMP
STOMP
STOMP
I didn't ask for a blaring red headache.
I didn't ask for any of this.
RARR!
YOU BETTER KEEP CLIFFORD HERE ON A LEASH. HE'S GOING TO HAVE TO BE A GOOD BOY IF HE WANTS TO STICK AROUND.
THE MINDLESS BEAST CANNOT BE TRUSTED. HE COMES FROM THE FIERY PITS OF CHAOS!
But it's what I got.
LOOK WHO'S TALKING.
I... SHE...

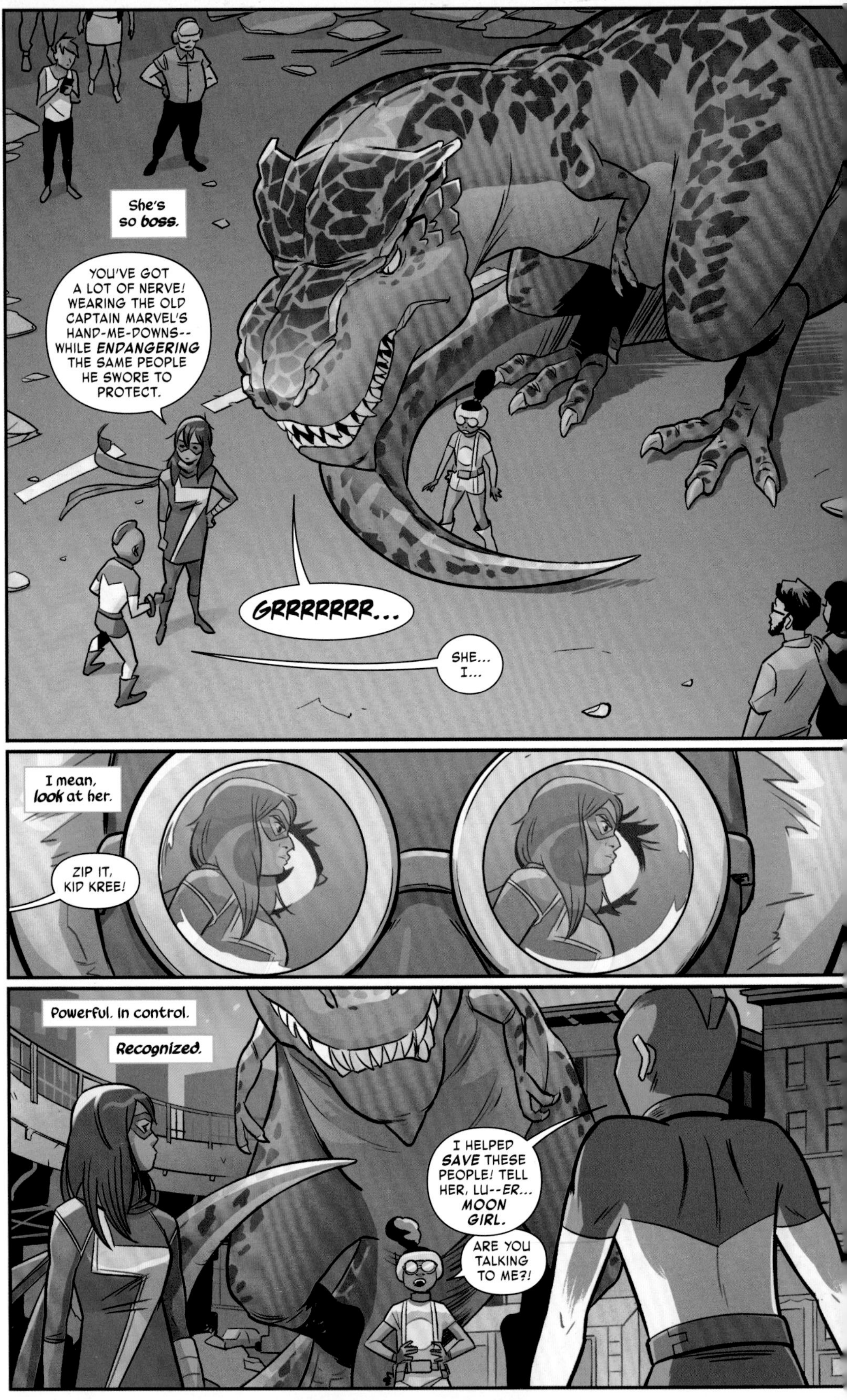
She's so boss.
YOU'VE GOT A LOT OF NERVE! WEARING THE OLD CAPTAIN MARVEL'S HAND-ME-DOWNS-- WHILE ENDANGERING THE SAME PEOPLE HE SWORE TO PROTECT.
GRRRRRRR...
SHE... I...
I mean, look at her.
ZIP IT, KID KREE!
Powerful. In control.
Recognized.
I HELPED SAVE THESE PEOPLE! TELL HER, LU--ER... MOON GIRL.
ARE YOU TALKING TO ME?!

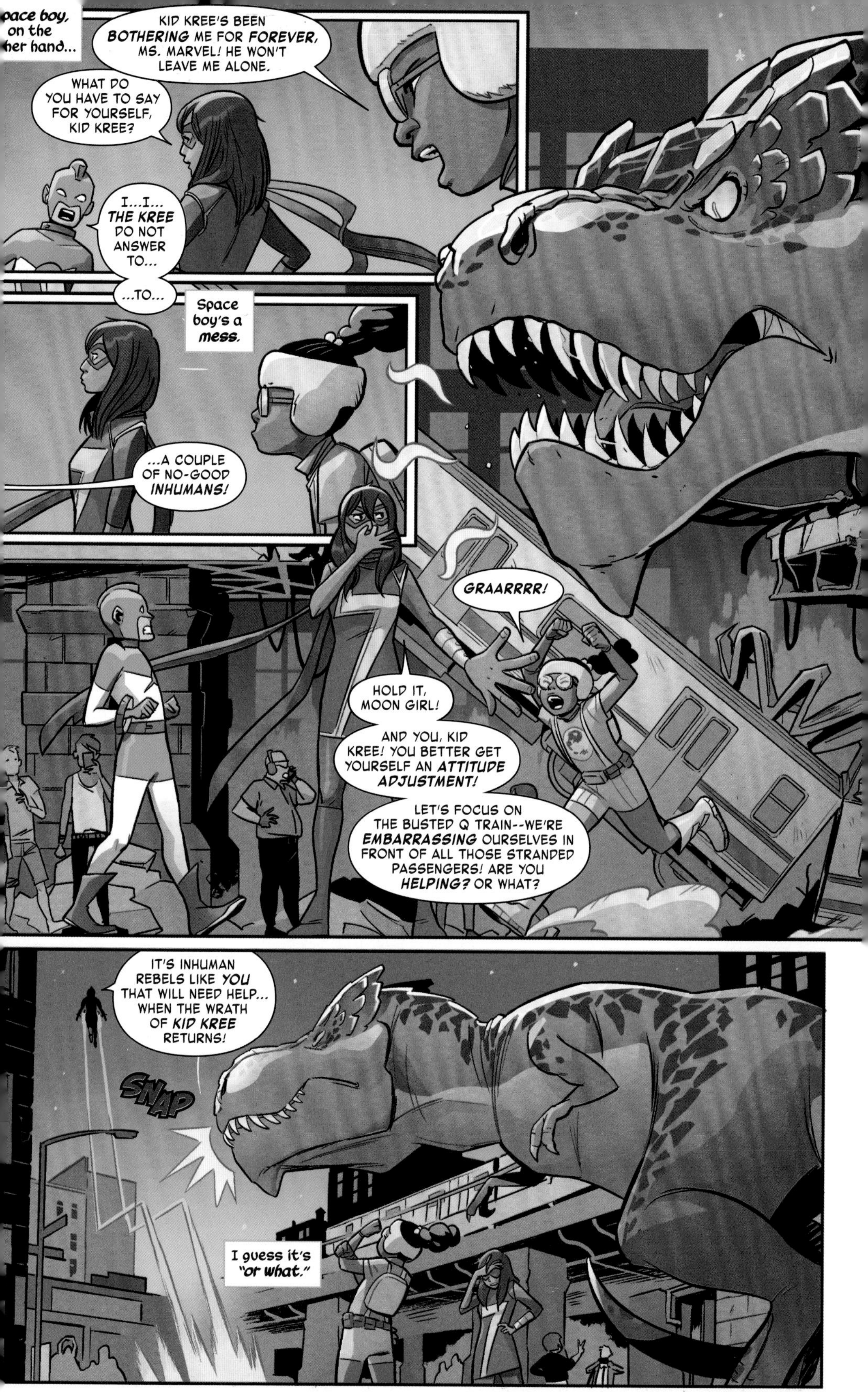
Space boy, on the other hand...
KID KREE'S BEEN BOTHERING ME FOR FOREVER, MS. MARVEL! HE WON'T LEAVE ME ALONE.
WHAT DO YOU HAVE TO SAY FOR YOURSELF, KID KREE?
I...I... THE KREE DO NOT ANSWER TO...
...TO...
Space boy's a mess.
...A COUPLE OF NO-GOOD INHUMANS!
GRAARRRR!
HOLD IT, MOON GIRL!
AND YOU, KID KREE! YOU BETTER GET YOURSELF AN ATTITUDE ADJUSTMENT!
LET'S FOCUS ON THE BUSTED Q TRAIN--WE'RE EMBARRASSING OURSELVES IN FRONT OF ALL THOSE STRANDED PASSENGERS! ARE YOU HELPING? OR WHAT?
IT'S INHUMAN REBELS LIKE YOU THAT WILL NEED HELP... WHEN THE WRATH OF KID KREE RETURNS!
SNAP
I guess it's "or what."

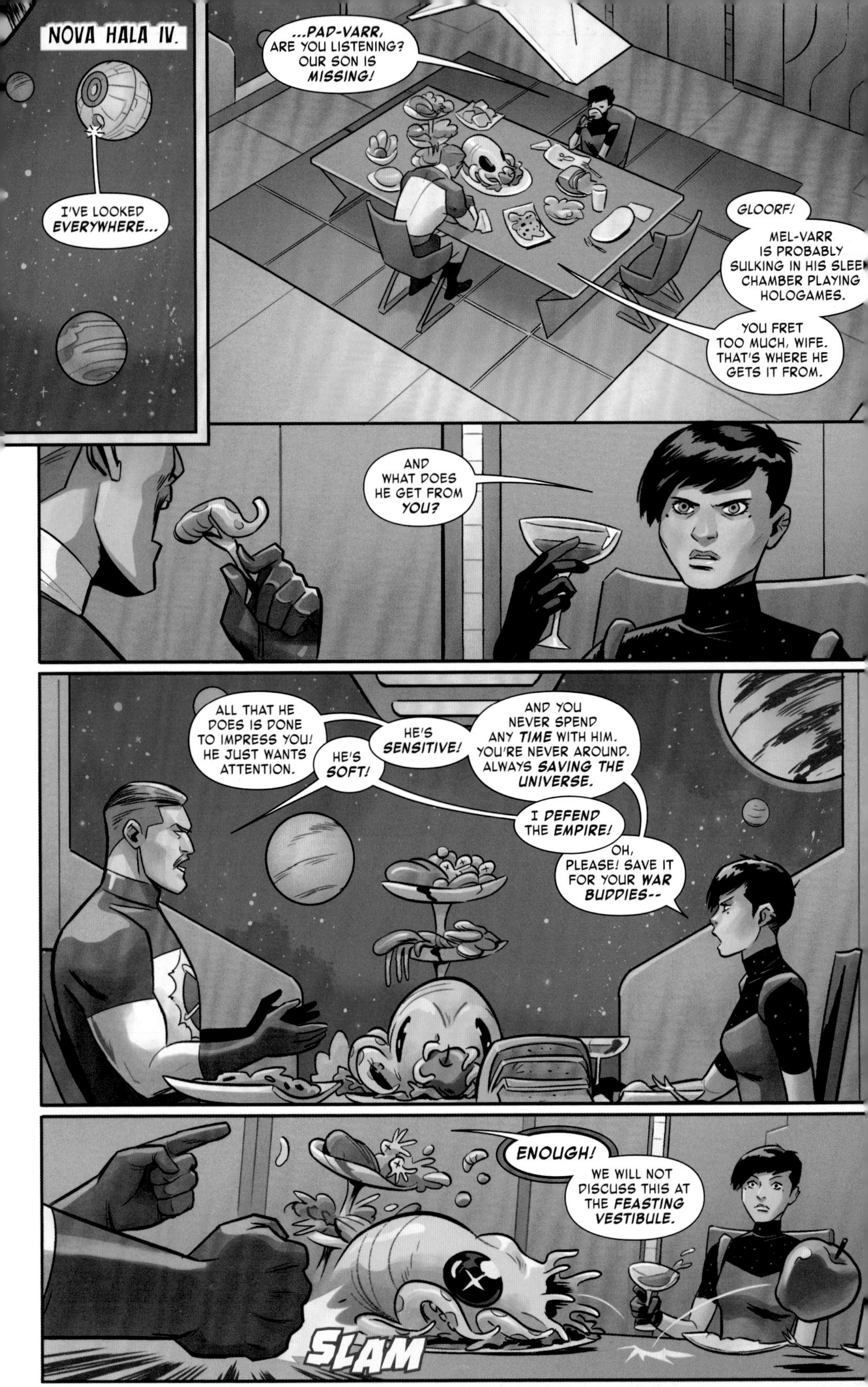
NOVA HALA IV.
I'VE LOOKED EVERYWHERE...
...PAD-VARR, ARE YOU LISTENING? OUR SON IS MISSING!
GLOORF!
MEL-VARR IS PROBABLY SULKING IN HIS SLEE CHAMBER PLAYING HOLOGAMES.
YOU FRET TOO MUCH, WIFE. THAT'S WHERE HE GETS IT FROM.
AND WHAT DOES HE GET FROM YOU?
ALL THAT HE DOES IS DONE TO IMPRESS YOU! HE JUST WANTS ATTENTION.
HE'S SENSITIVE!
HE'S SOFT!
AND YOU NEVER SPEND ANY TIME WITH HIM. YOU'RE NEVER AROUND. ALWAYS SAVING THE UNIVERSE.
I DEFEND THE EMPIRE!
OH, PLEASE! SAVE IT FOR YOUR WAR BUDDIES--
ENOUGH!
WE WILL NOT DISCUSS THIS AT THE FEASTING VESTIBULE.
SLAM

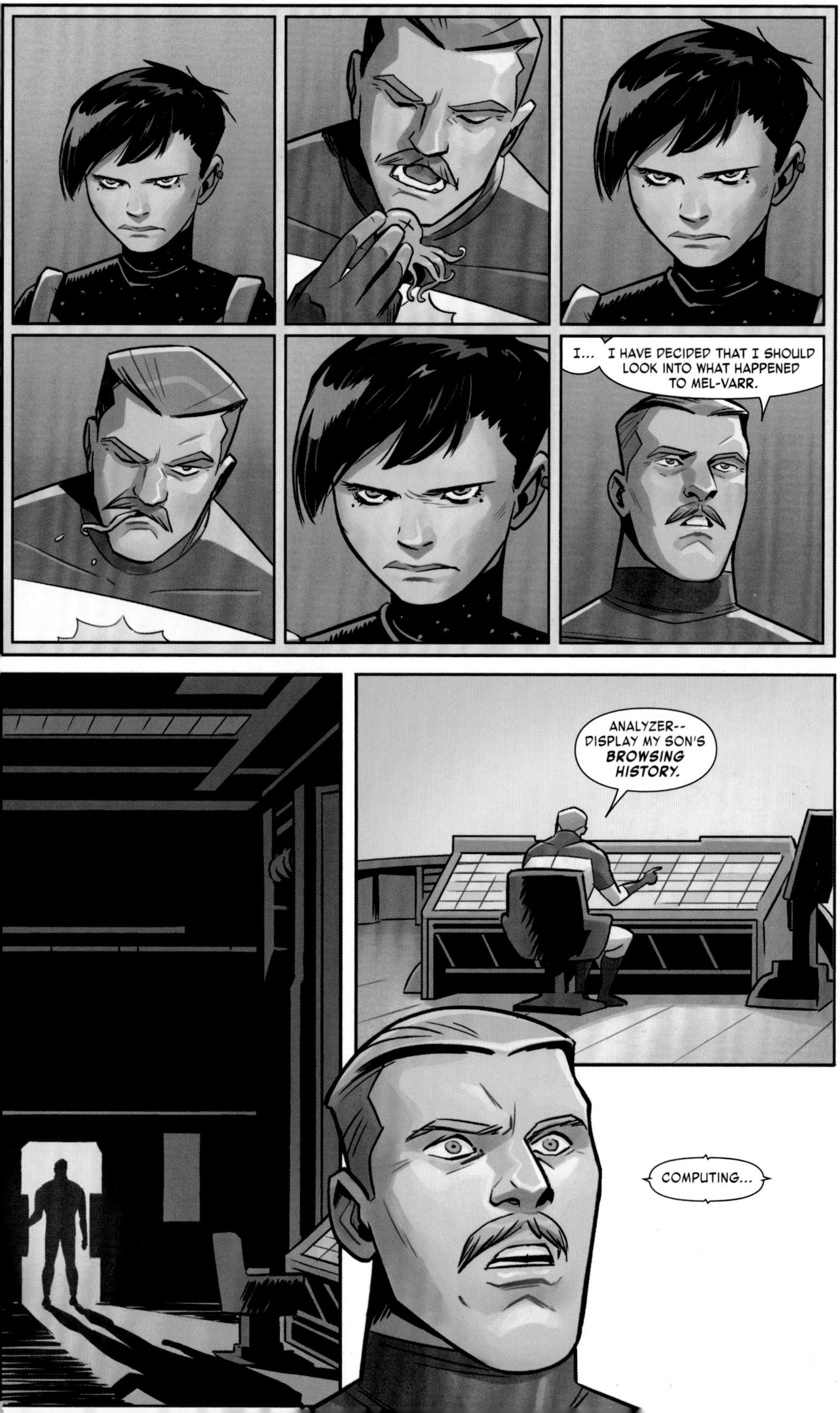
I... I HAVE DECIDED THAT I SHOULD LOOK INTO WHAT HAPPENED TO MEL-VARR.
ANALYZER--DISPLAY MY SON'S **BROWSING HISTORY.**
COMPUTING...

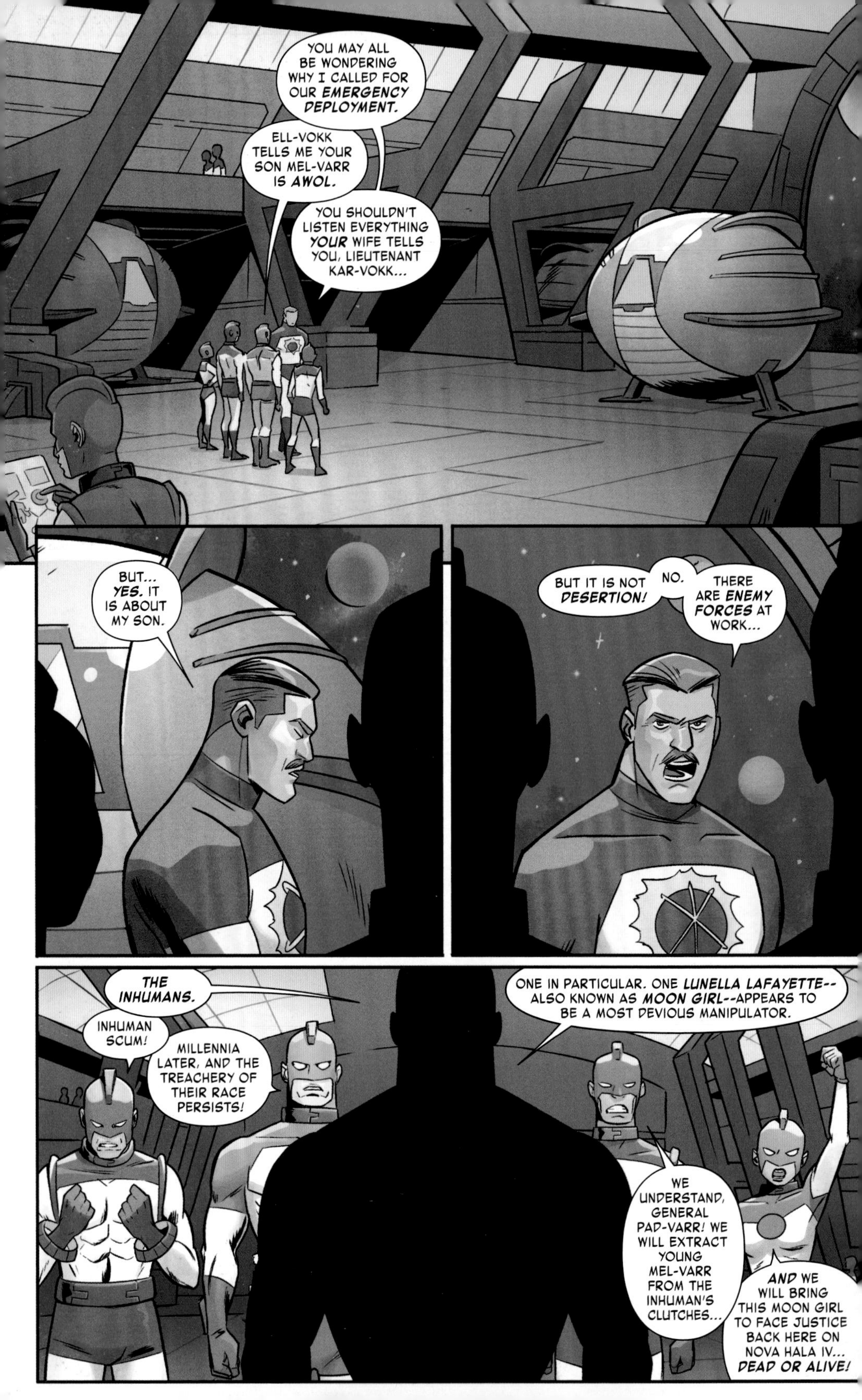
YOU MAY ALL BE WONDERING WHY I CALLED FOR OUR EMERGENCY DEPLOYMENT.
ELL-VOKK TELLS ME YOUR SON MEL-VARR IS AWOL.
YOU SHOULDN'T LISTEN EVERYTHING YOUR WIFE TELLS YOU, LIEUTENANT KAR-VOKK...
BUT... YES. IT IS ABOUT MY SON.
BUT IT IS NOT DESERTION!
NO.
THERE ARE ENEMY FORCES AT WORK...
THE INHUMANS.
ONE IN PARTICULAR. ONE LUNELLA LAFAYETTE--ALSO KNOWN AS MOON GIRL--APPEARS TO BE A MOST DEVIOUS MANIPULATOR.
INHUMAN SCUM!
MILLENNIA LATER, AND THE TREACHERY OF THEIR RACE PERSISTS!
WE UNDERSTAND, GENERAL PAD-VARR! WE WILL EXTRACT YOUNG MEL-VARR FROM THE INHUMAN'S CLUTCHES...
AND WE WILL BRING THIS MOON GIRL TO FACE JUSTICE BACK HERE ON NOVA HALA IV... DEAD OR ALIVE!

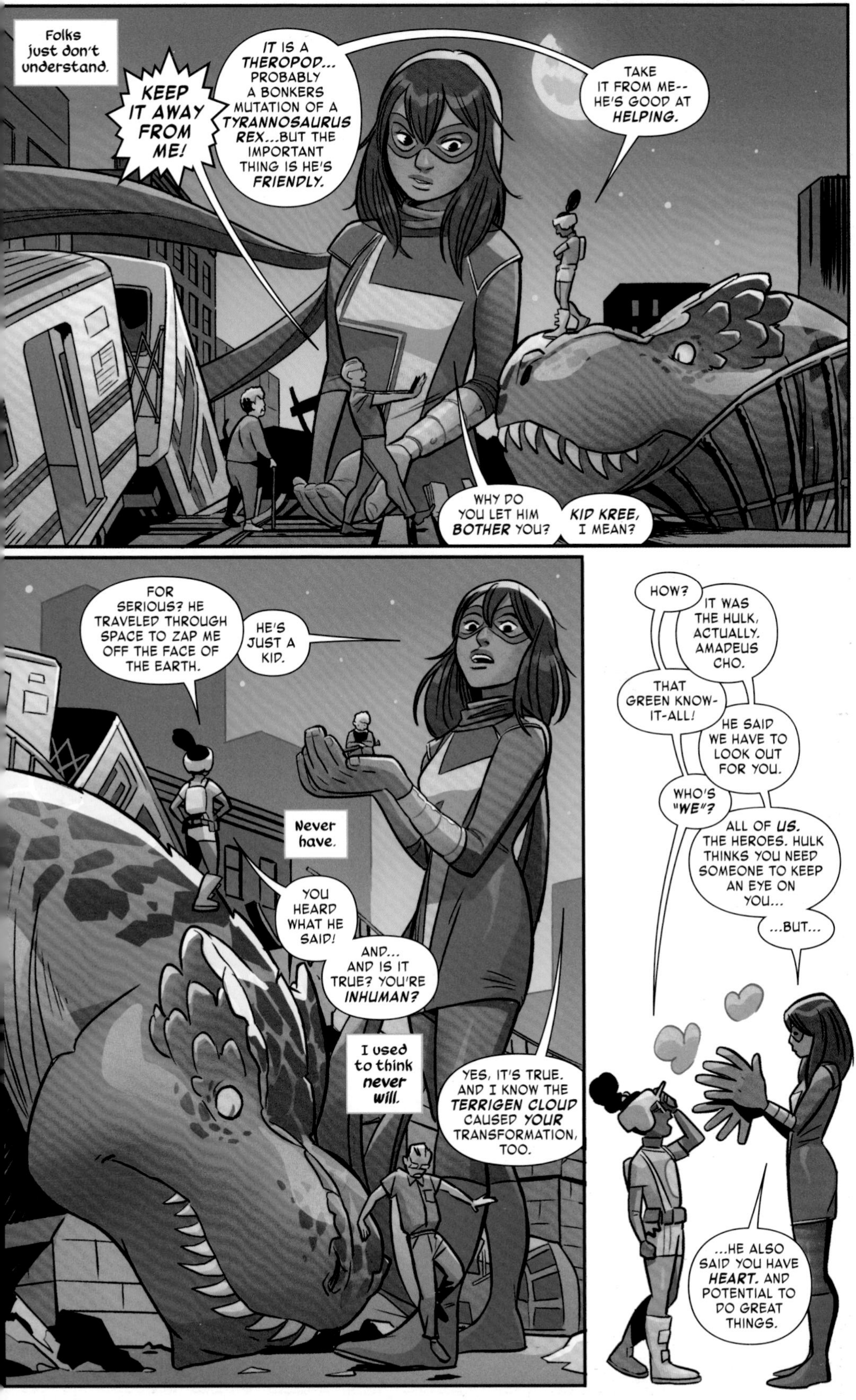

Folks just don't understand.
KEEP IT AWAY FROM ME!
IT IS A THEROPOD... PROBABLY A BONKERS MUTATION OF A TYRANNOSAURUS REX...BUT THE IMPORTANT THING IS HE'S FRIENDLY.
TAKE IT FROM ME-- HE'S GOOD AT HELPING.
WHY DO YOU LET HIM BOTHER YOU?
KID KREE, I MEAN?
FOR SERIOUS? HE TRAVELED THROUGH SPACE TO ZAP ME OFF THE FACE OF THE EARTH.
HE'S JUST A KID.
Never have.
YOU HEARD WHAT HE SAID!
AND... AND IS IT TRUE? YOU'RE INHUMAN?
I used to think never will.
YES, IT'S TRUE. AND I KNOW THE TERRIGEN CLOUD CAUSED YOUR TRANSFORMATION, TOO.
HOW?
IT WAS THE HULK, ACTUALLY. AMADEUS CHO.
THAT GREEN KNOW-IT-ALL!
HE SAID WE HAVE TO LOOK OUT FOR YOU.
WHO'S "WE"?
ALL OF US. THE HEROES. HULK THINKS YOU NEED SOMEONE TO KEEP AN EYE ON YOU...
...BUT...
...HE ALSO SAID YOU HAVE HEART. AND POTENTIAL TO DO GREAT THINGS.

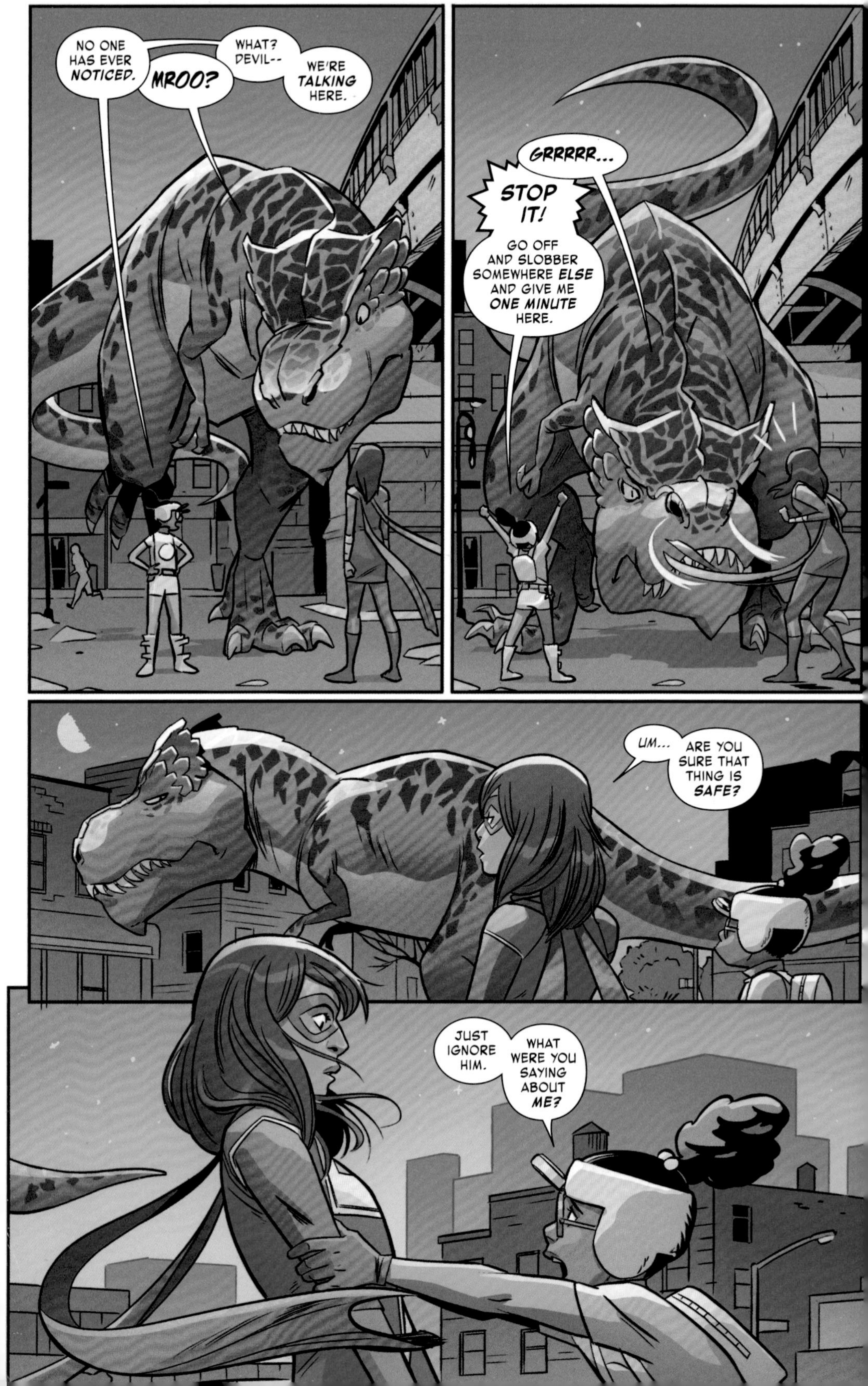

NO ONE HAS EVER NOTICED.
MROO?
WHAT? DEVIL--
WE'RE TALKING HERE.
GRRRRR...
STOP IT!
GO OFF AND SLOBBER SOMEWHERE ELSE AND GIVE ME ONE MINUTE HERE.
UM...
ARE YOU SURE THAT THING IS SAFE?
JUST IGNORE HIM.
WHAT WERE YOU SAYING ABOUT ME?

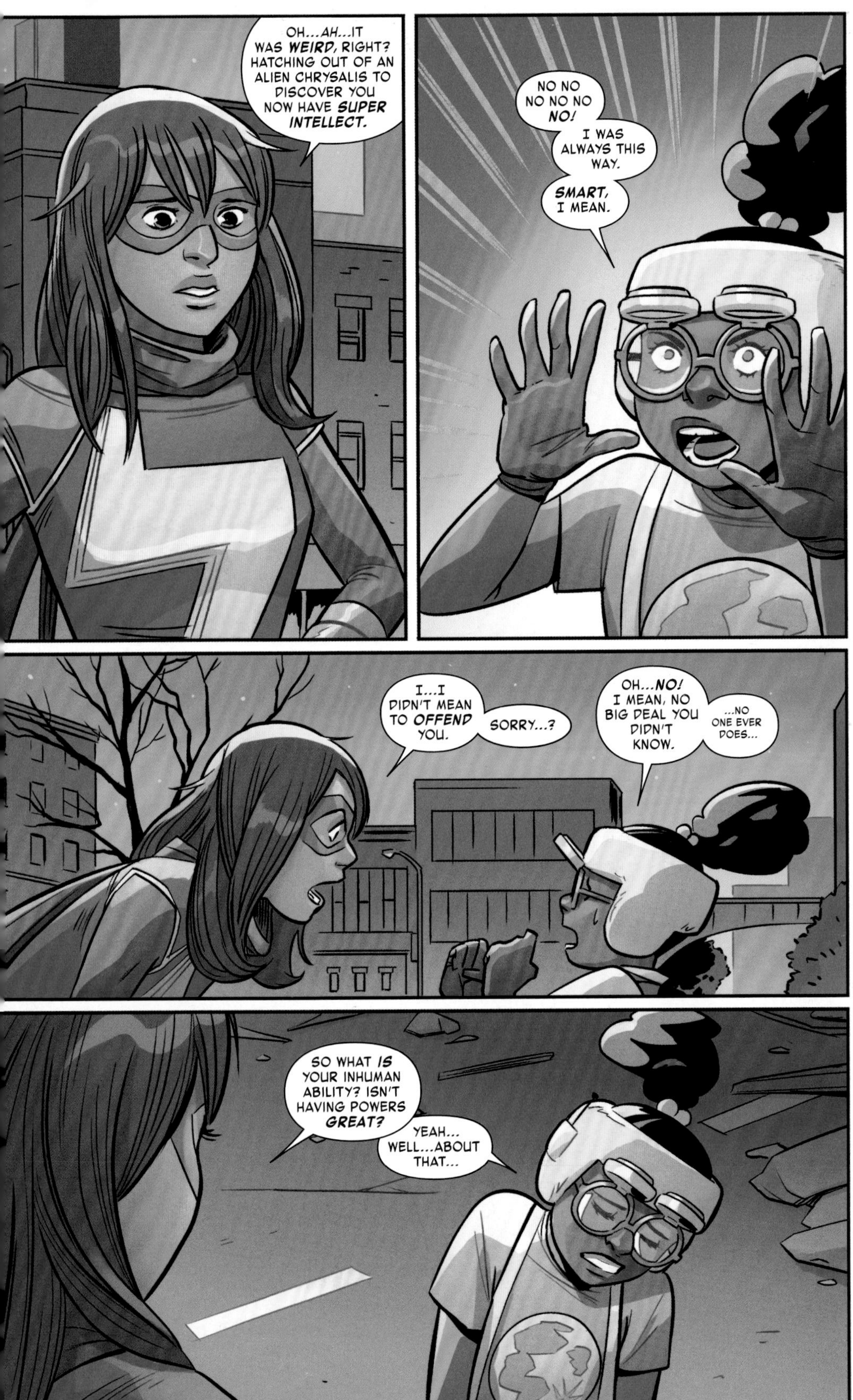
OH...AH...IT WAS WEIRD, RIGHT? HATCHING OUT OF AN ALIEN CHRYSALIS TO DISCOVER YOU NOW HAVE SUPER INTELLECT.
NO NO NO NO NO NO NO NO!
I WAS ALWAYS THIS WAY.
SMART, I MEAN.
I...I DIDN'T MEAN TO OFFEND YOU.
SORRY...?
OH...NO! I MEAN, NO BIG DEAL YOU DIDN'T KNOW.
...NO ONE EVER DOES...
SO WHAT IS YOUR INHUMAN ABILITY? ISN'T HAVING POWERS GREAT?
YEAH... WELL...ABOUT THAT...

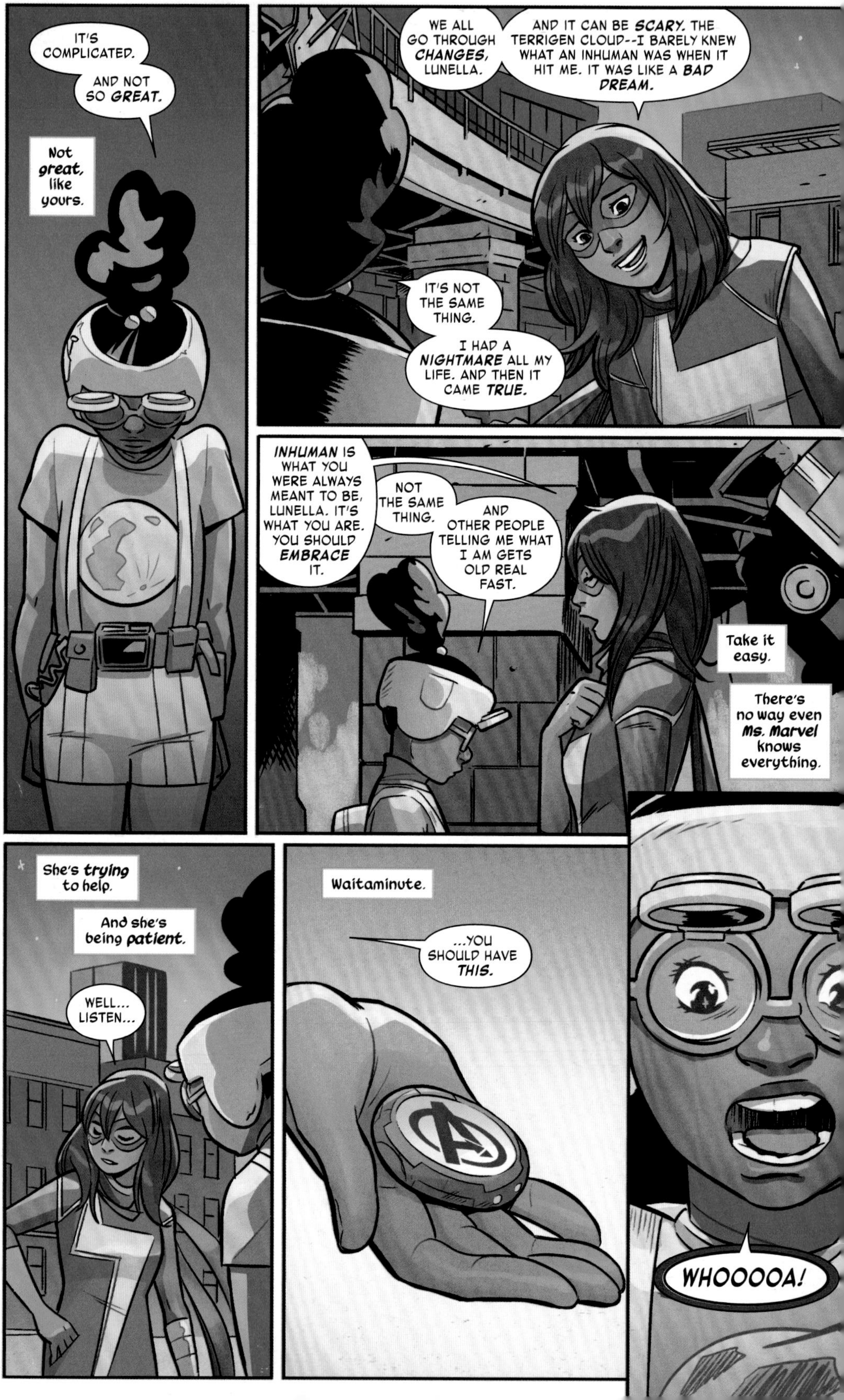
IT'S COMPLICATED.
AND NOT SO GREAT.
Not great, like yours.
WE ALL GO THROUGH CHANGES, LUNELLA.
AND IT CAN BE SCARY. THE TERRIGEN CLOUD--I BARELY KNEW WHAT AN INHUMAN WAS WHEN IT HIT ME. IT WAS LIKE A BAD DREAM.
IT'S NOT THE SAME THING.
I HAD A NIGHTMARE ALL MY LIFE. AND THEN IT CAME TRUE.
INHUMAN IS WHAT YOU WERE ALWAYS MEANT TO BE, LUNELLA. IT'S WHAT YOU ARE. YOU SHOULD EMBRACE IT.
NOT THE SAME THING.
AND OTHER PEOPLE TELLING ME WHAT I AM GETS OLD REAL FAST.
Take it easy.
There's no way even Ms. Marvel knows everything.
She's trying to help.
And she's being patient.
WELL... LISTEN...
Waitaminute.
...YOU SHOULD HAVE THIS.
WHOOOOA!

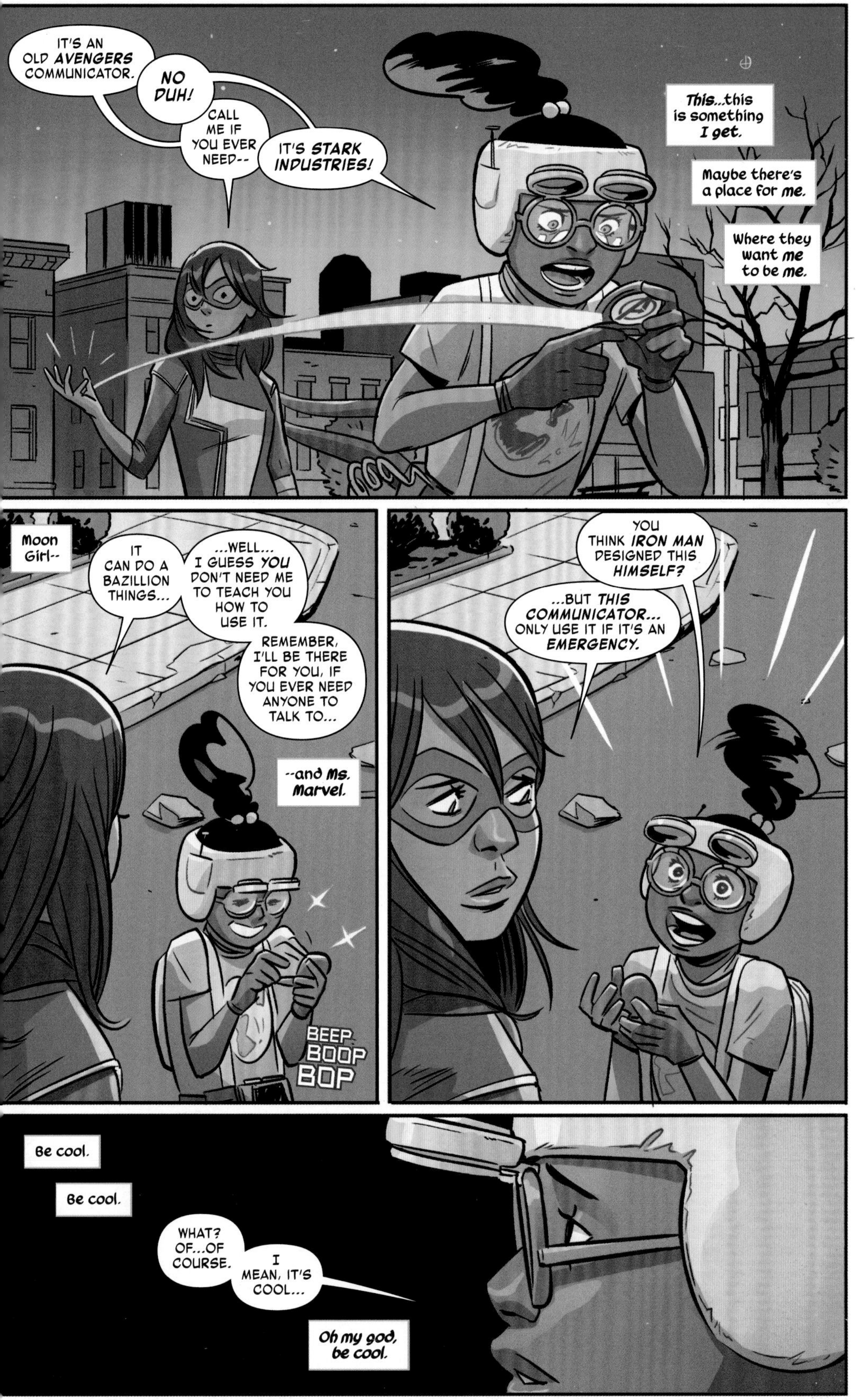

IT'S AN OLD AVENGERS COMMUNICATOR.
NO DUH!
CALL ME IF YOU EVER NEED--
IT'S STARK INDUSTRIES!
This...this is something I get.
Maybe there's a place for me.
Where they want me to be me.
Moon Girl--
IT CAN DO A BAZILLION THINGS...
...WELL... I GUESS YOU DON'T NEED ME TO TEACH YOU HOW TO USE IT.
REMEMBER, I'LL BE THERE FOR YOU, IF YOU EVER NEED ANYONE TO TALK TO...
--and Ms. Marvel.
BEEP BOOP BOP
YOU THINK IRON MAN DESIGNED THIS HIMSELF?
...BUT THIS COMMUNICATOR... ONLY USE IT IF IT'S AN EMERGENCY.
Be cool.
Be cool.
WHAT? OF...OF COURSE.
I MEAN, IT'S COOL...
Oh my god, be cool.

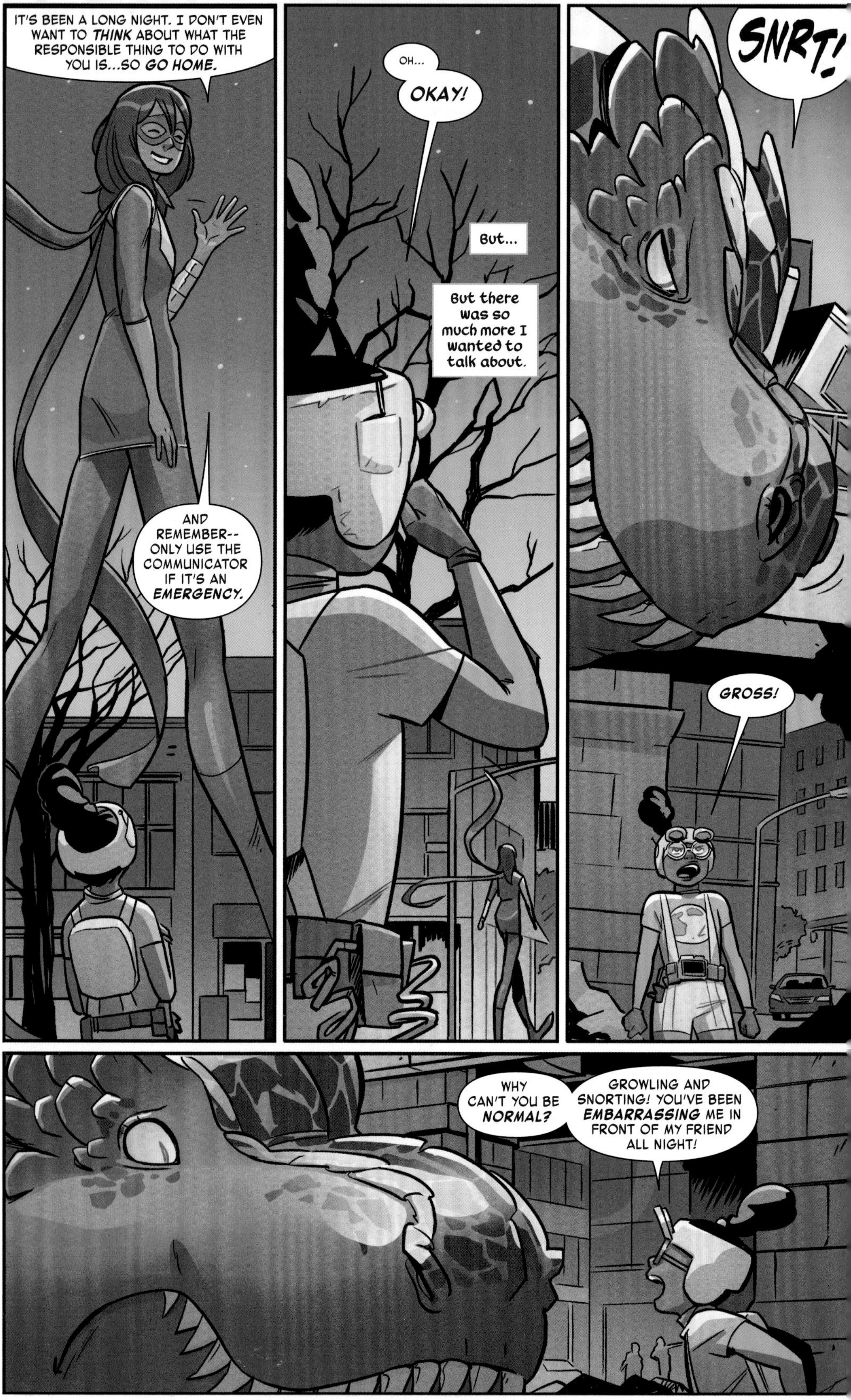

IT'S BEEN A LONG NIGHT. I DON'T EVEN WANT TO THINK ABOUT WHAT THE RESPONSIBLE THING TO DO WITH YOU IS...SO GO HOME.
AND REMEMBER--ONLY USE THE COMMUNICATOR IF IT'S AN EMERGENCY.
OH...
OKAY!
But...
But there was so much more I wanted to talk about.
SNRT!
GROSS!
WHY CAN'T YOU BE NORMAL?
GROWLING AND SNORTING! YOU'VE BEEN EMBARRASSING ME IN FRONT OF MY FRIEND ALL NIGHT!

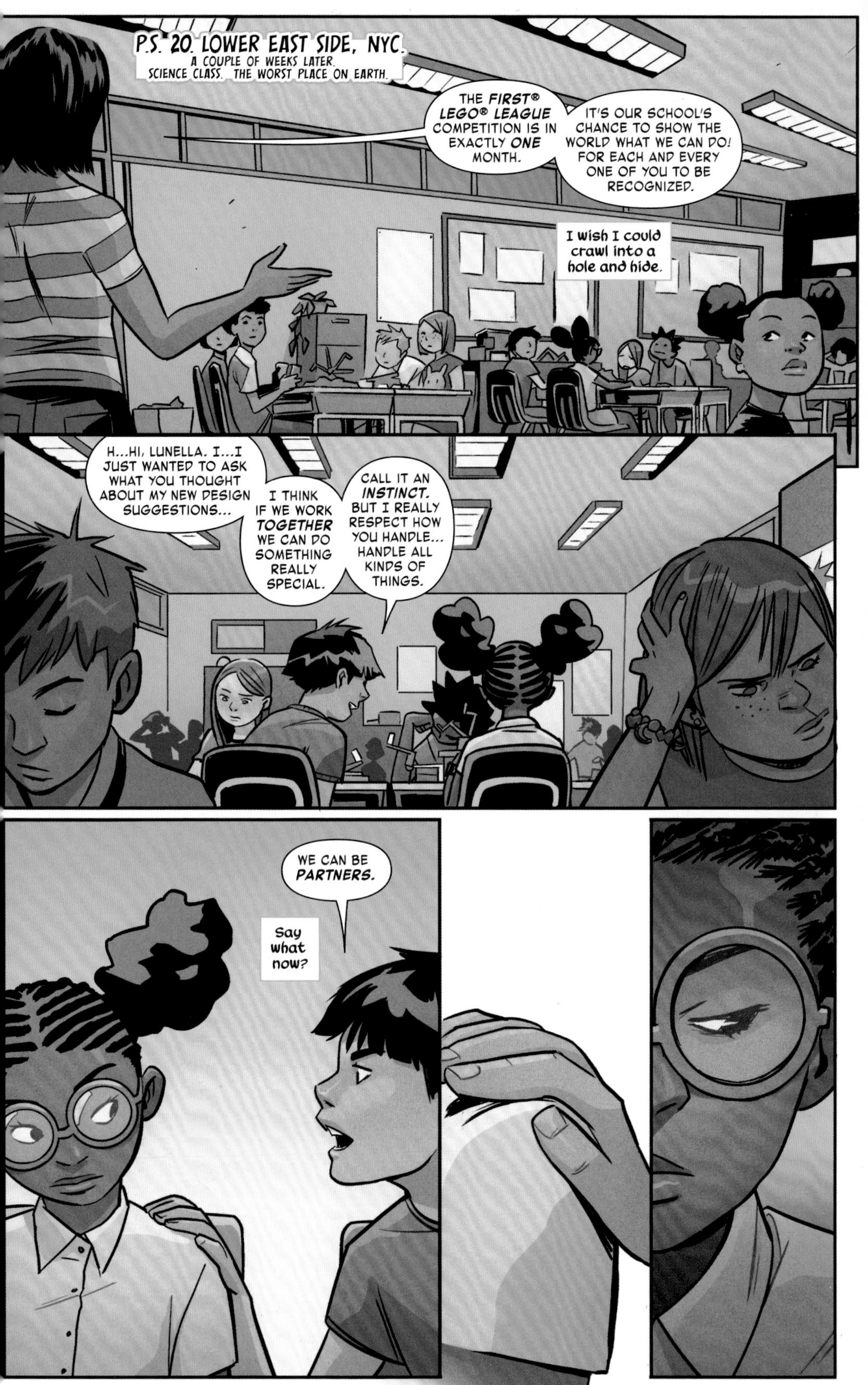
P.S. 20. LOWER EAST SIDE, NYC.
A COUPLE OF WEEKS LATER. SCIENCE CLASS. THE WORST PLACE ON EARTH.
THE FIRST® LEGO® LEAGUE COMPETITION IS IN EXACTLY ONE MONTH.
IT'S OUR SCHOOL'S CHANCE TO SHOW THE WORLD WHAT WE CAN DO! FOR EACH AND EVERY ONE OF YOU TO BE RECOGNIZED.
I wish I could crawl into a hole and hide.
H...HI, LUNELLA. I...I JUST WANTED TO ASK WHAT YOU THOUGHT ABOUT MY NEW DESIGN SUGGESTIONS...
I THINK IF WE WORK TOGETHER WE CAN DO SOMETHING REALLY SPECIAL.
CALL IT AN INSTINCT. BUT I REALLY RESPECT HOW YOU HANDLE... HANDLE ALL KINDS OF THINGS.
WE CAN BE PARTNERS.
Say what now?

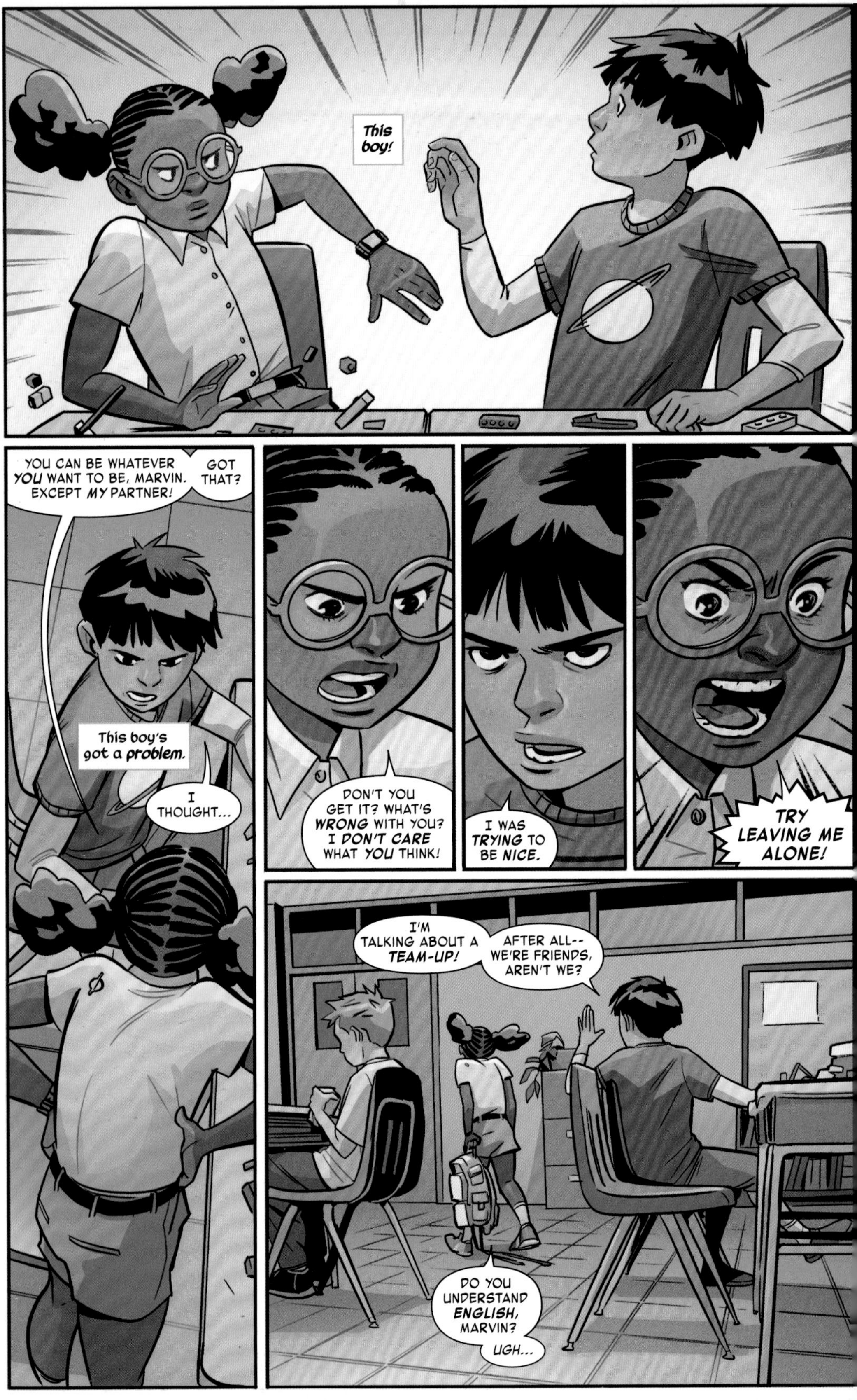
This boy!
YOU CAN BE WHATEVER YOU WANT TO BE, MARVIN. EXCEPT MY PARTNER!
GOT THAT?
This boy's got a problem.
I THOUGHT...
DON'T YOU GET IT? WHAT'S WRONG WITH YOU? I DON'T CARE WHAT YOU THINK!
I WAS TRYING TO BE NICE.
TRY LEAVING ME ALONE!
I'M TALKING ABOUT A TEAM-UP!
AFTER ALL-- WE'RE FRIENDS, AREN'T WE?
DO YOU UNDERSTAND ENGLISH, MARVIN?
UGH...

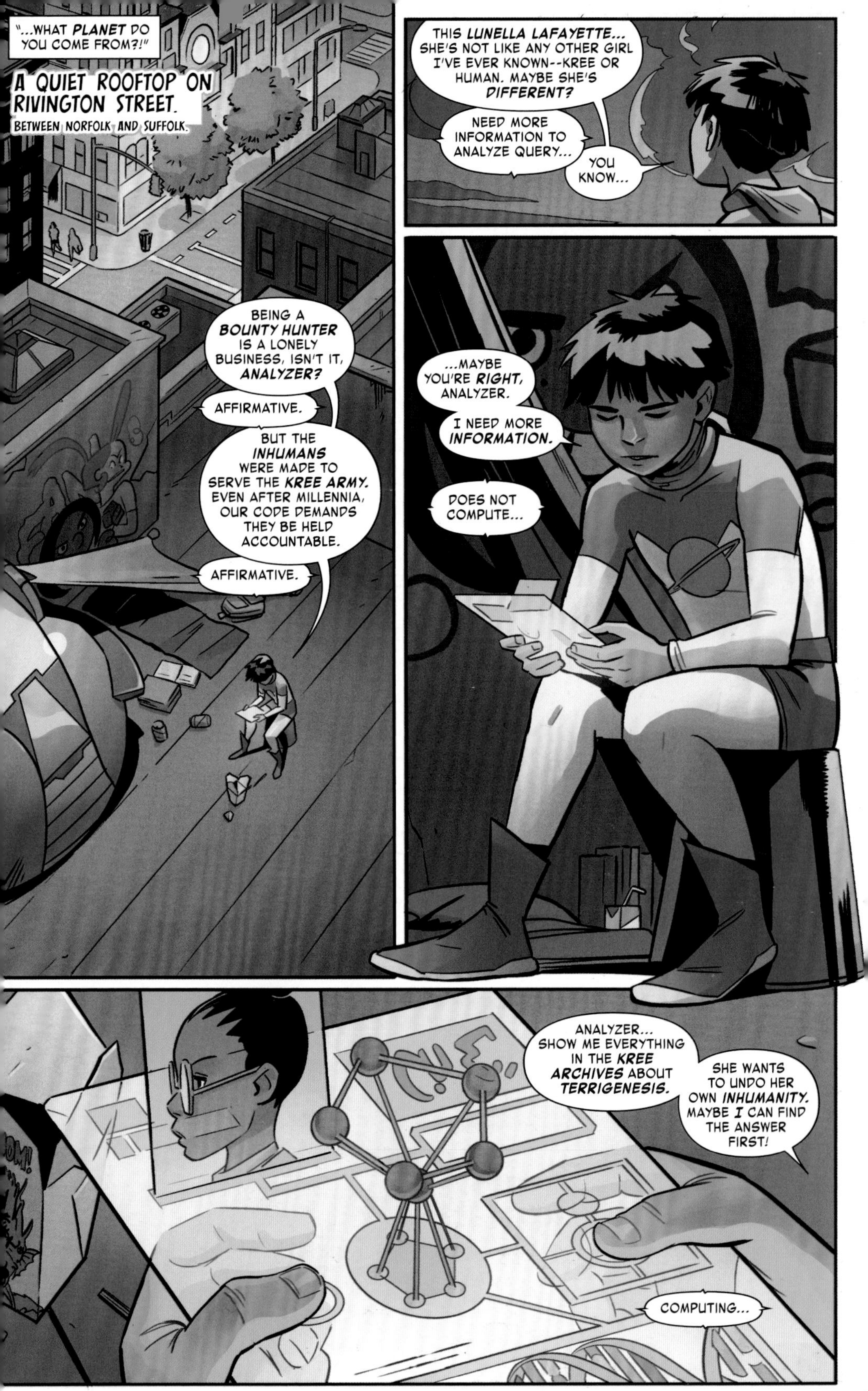
"...WHAT PLANET DO YOU COME FROM?!"
A QUIET ROOFTOP ON RIVINGTON STREET.
BETWEEN NORFOLK AND SUFFOLK.
BEING A BOUNTY HUNTER IS A LONELY BUSINESS, ISN'T IT, ANALYZER?
AFFIRMATIVE.
BUT THE INHUMANS WERE MADE TO SERVE THE KREE ARMY. EVEN AFTER MILLENNIA, OUR CODE DEMANDS THEY BE HELD ACCOUNTABLE.
AFFIRMATIVE.
THIS LUNELLA LAFAYETTE... SHE'S NOT LIKE ANY OTHER GIRL I'VE EVER KNOWN--KREE OR HUMAN. MAYBE SHE'S DIFFERENT?
NEED MORE INFORMATION TO ANALYZE QUERY...
YOU KNOW...
...MAYBE YOU'RE RIGHT, ANALYZER.
I NEED MORE INFORMATION.
DOES NOT COMPUTE...
ANALYZER... SHOW ME EVERYTHING IN THE KREE ARCHIVES ABOUT TERRIGENESIS.
SHE WANTS TO UNDO HER OWN INHUMANITY. MAYBE I CAN FIND THE ANSWER FIRST!
COMPUTING...

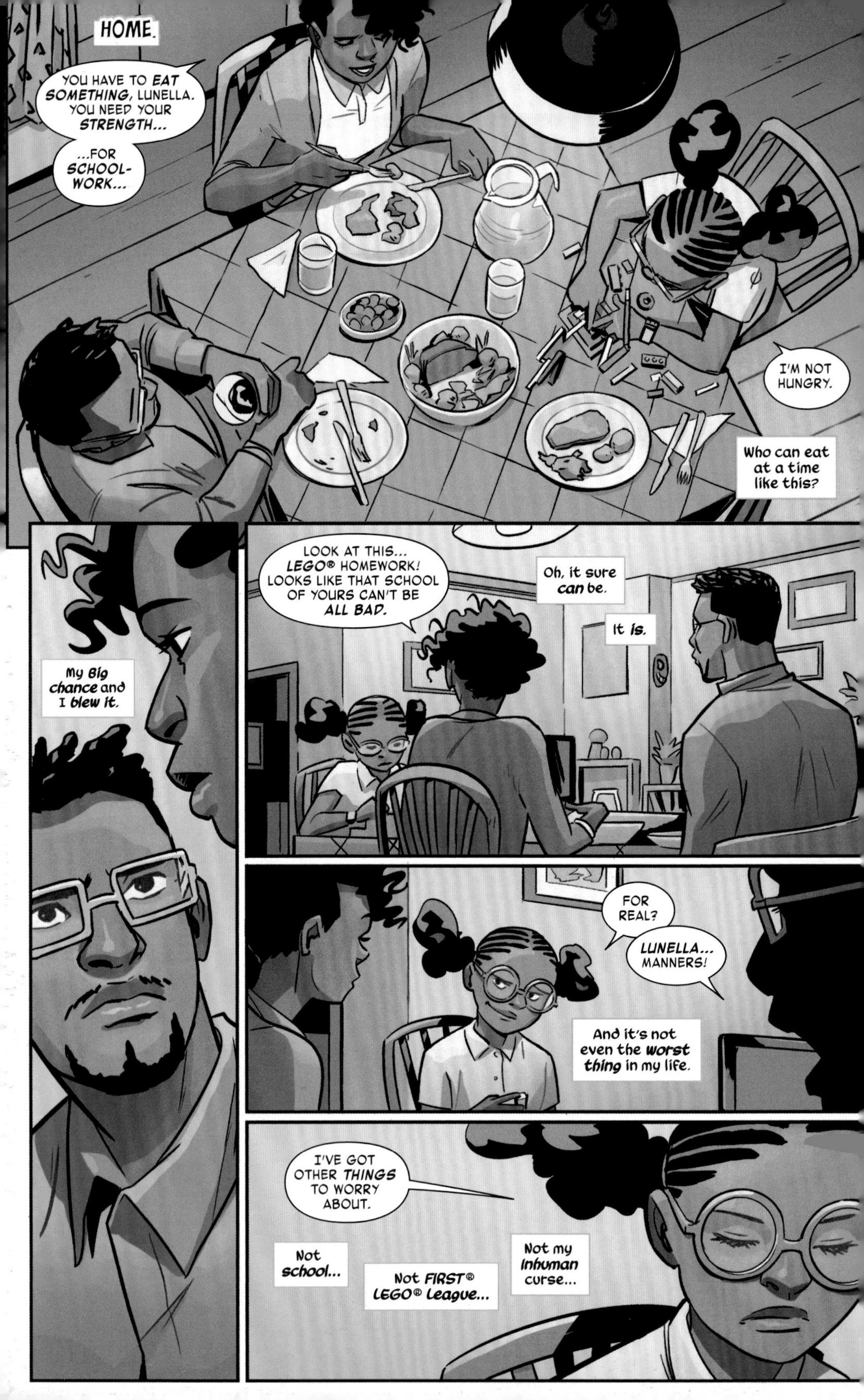
HOME.
YOU HAVE TO EAT SOMETHING, LUNELLA. YOU NEED YOUR STRENGTH...
...FOR SCHOOL-WORK...
I'M NOT HUNGRY.
Who can eat at a time like this?
My Big chance and I blew it.
LOOK AT THIS... LEGO® HOMEWORK! LOOKS LIKE THAT SCHOOL OF YOURS CAN'T BE ALL BAD.
Oh, it sure can be.
It is.
FOR REAL?
LUNELLA... MANNERS!
And it's not even the worst thing in my life.
I'VE GOT OTHER THINGS TO WORRY ABOUT.
Not school...
Not FIRST® LEGO® League...
Not my Inhuman curse...

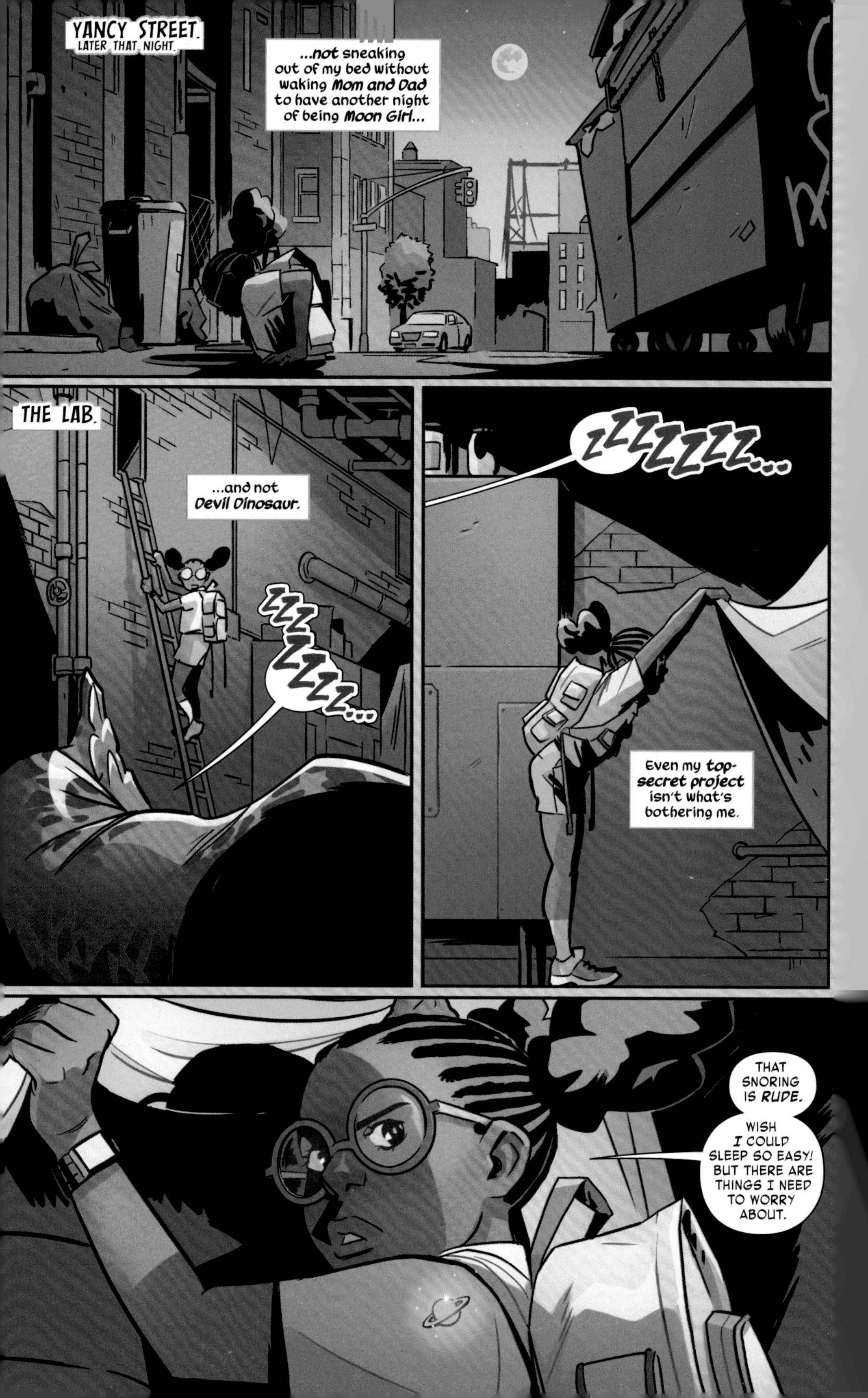

YANCY STREET. LATER THAT NIGHT.
...not sneaking out of my bed without waking Mom and Dad to have another night of being Moon Girl...
THE LAB.
...and not Devil Dinosaur.
ZZZZZZZ...
ZZZZZZZZ...
Even my top-secret project isn't what's bothering me.
THAT SNORING IS RUDE.
WISH I COULD SLEEP SO EASY! BUT THERE ARE THINGS I NEED TO WORRY ABOUT.

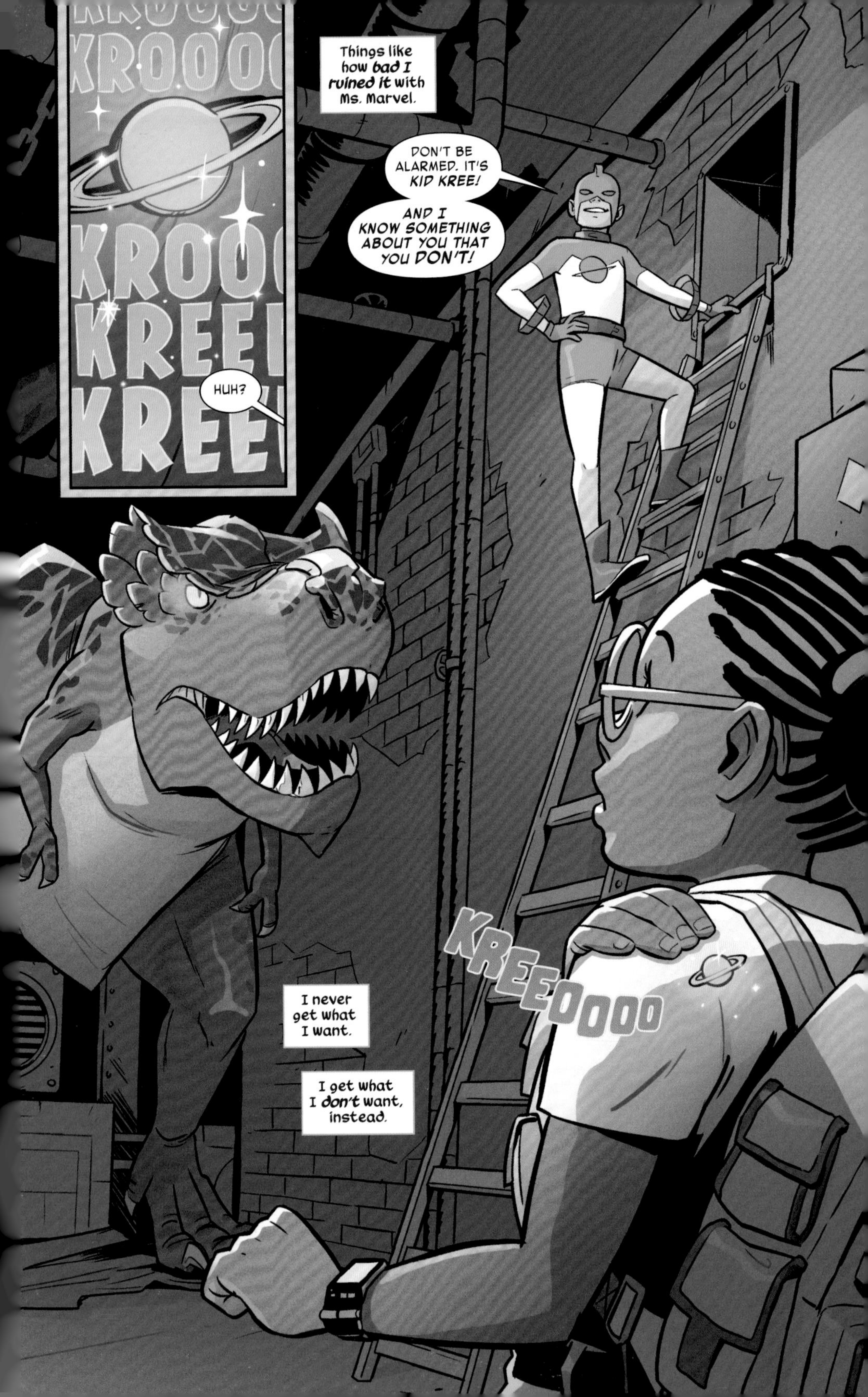
KROOOO
KROOOO
KROOO
KREE
KREE
Things like how bad I ruined it with Ms. Marvel.
DON'T BE ALARMED. IT'S KID KREE!
AND I KNOW SOMETHING ABOUT YOU THAT YOU DON'T!
HUH?
KREEOOOO
I never get what I want.
I get what I don't want, instead.

CHAMPIONS #1

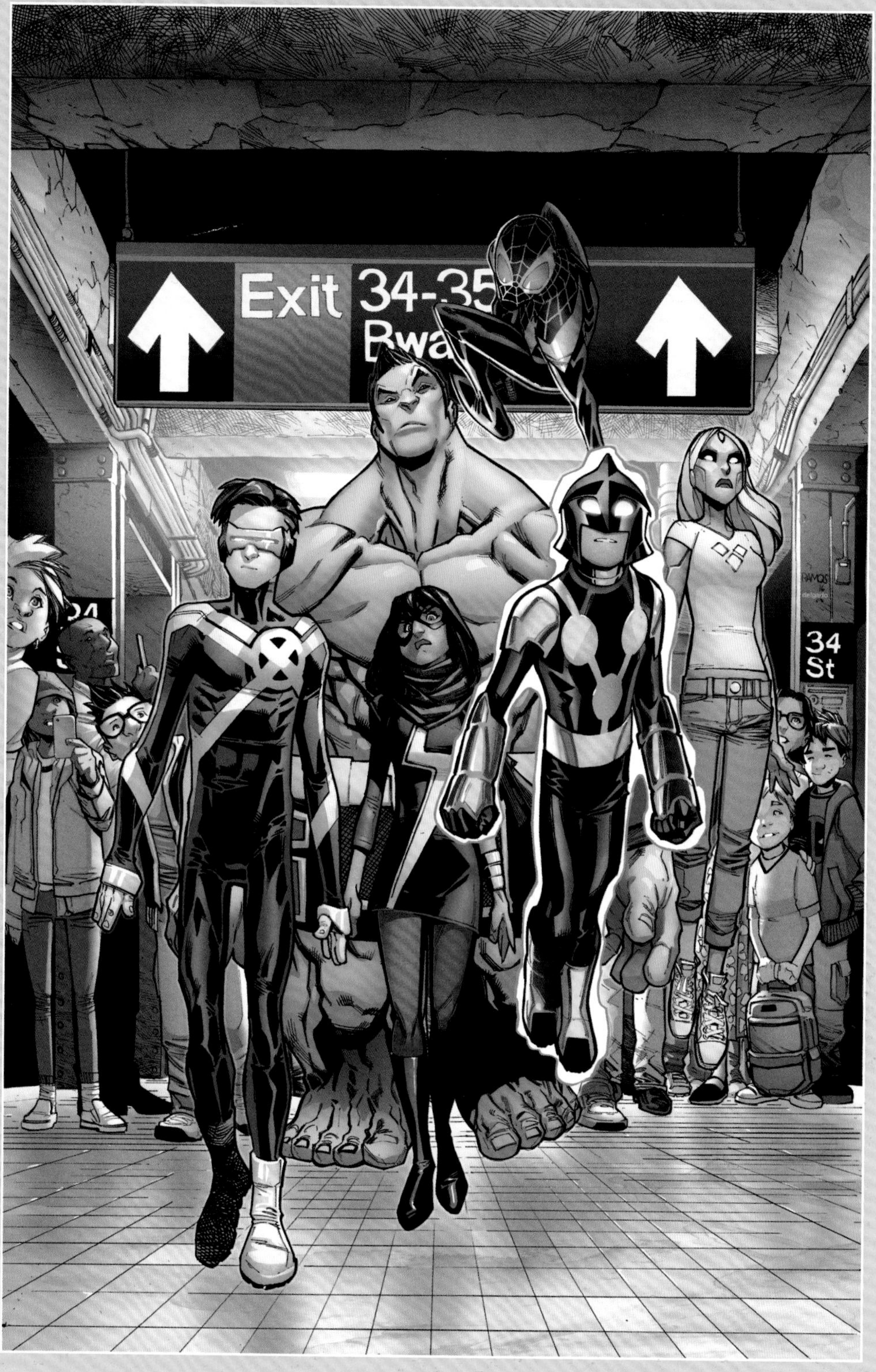
Exit 34-35
34 St

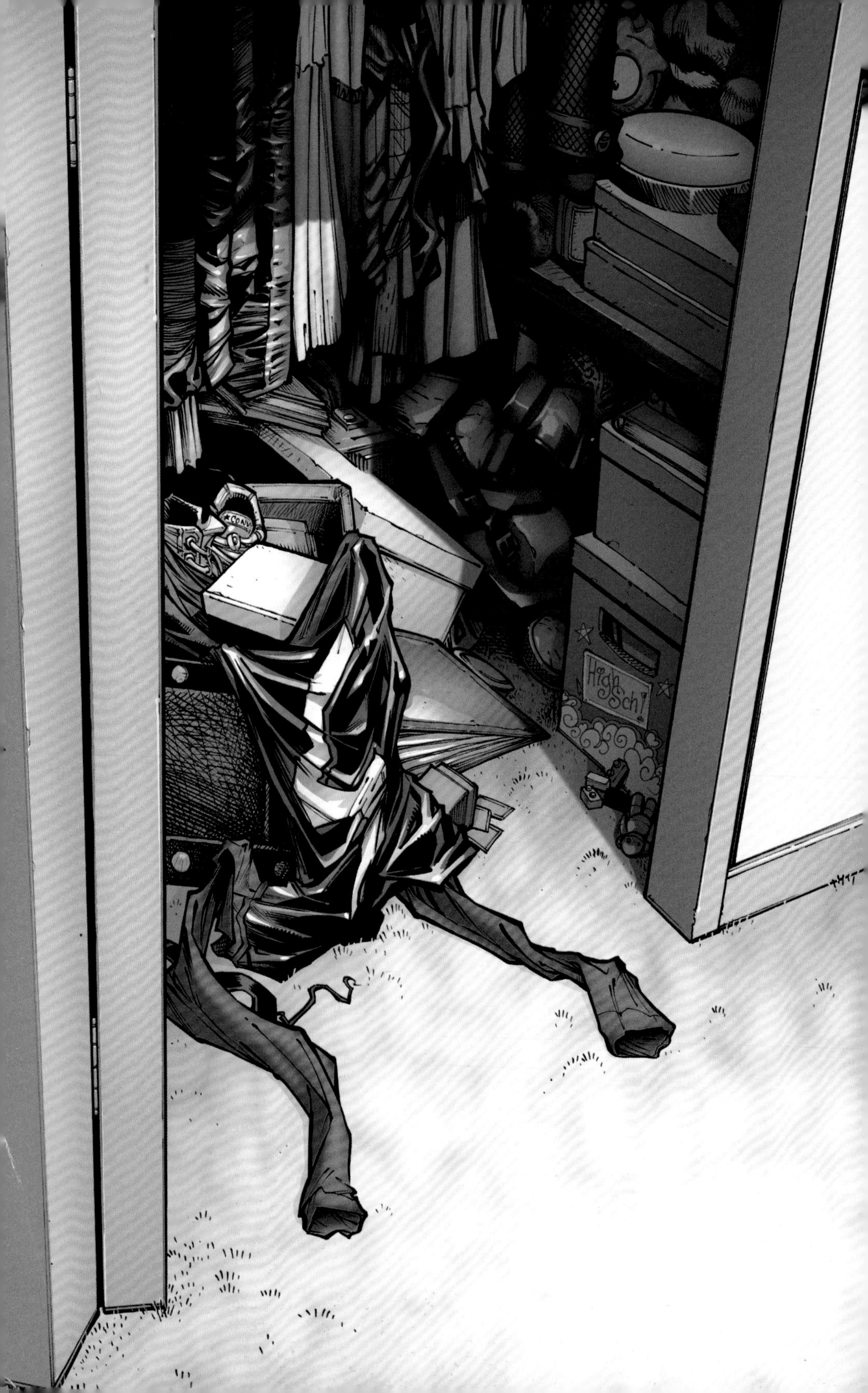
High Sch!

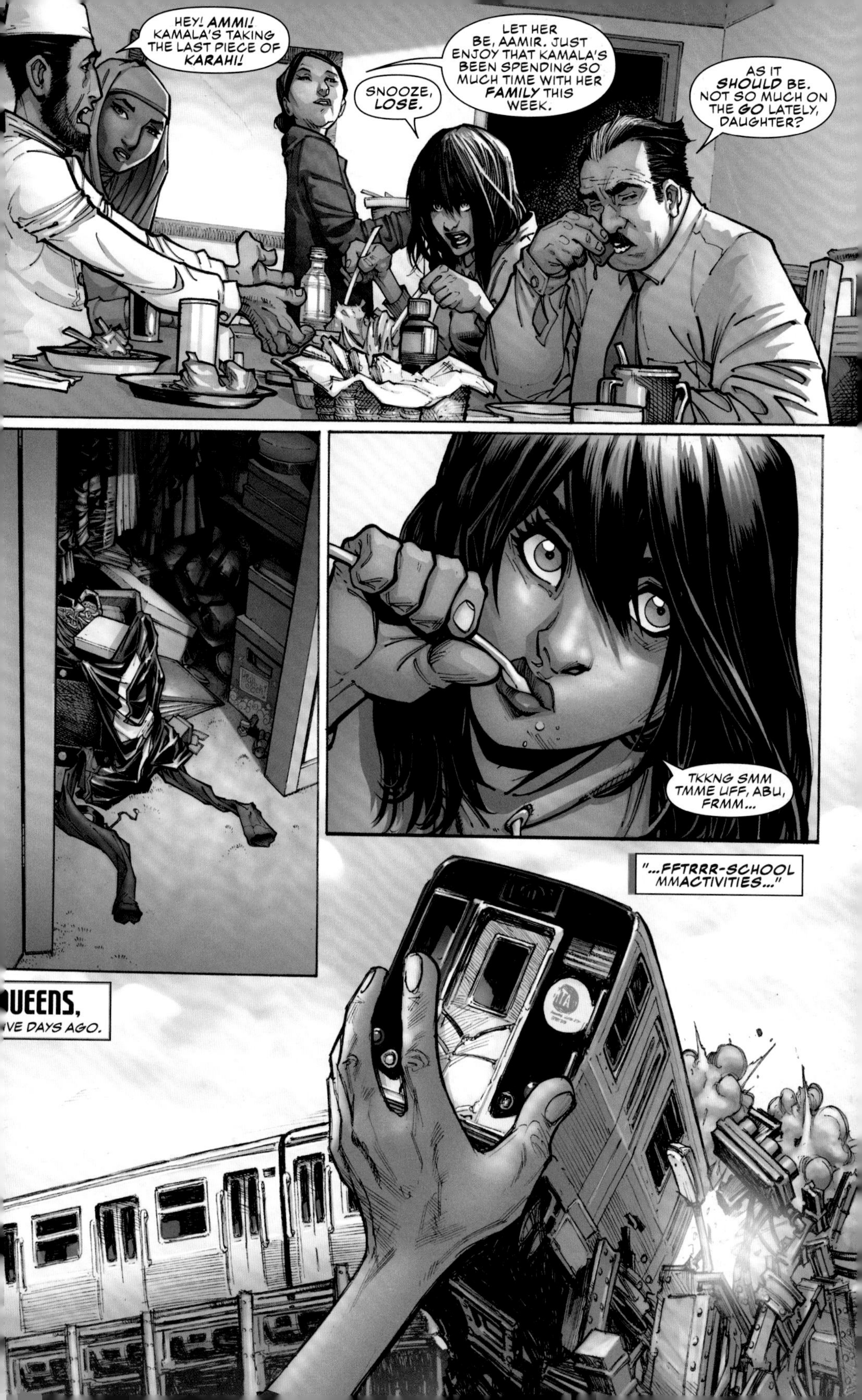
HEY! AMMI! KAMALA'S TAKING THE LAST PIECE OF KARAHI!
SNOOZE, LOSE.
LET HER BE, AAMIR. JUST ENJOY THAT KAMALA'S BEEN SPENDING SO MUCH TIME WITH HER FAMILY THIS WEEK.
AS IT SHOULD BE. NOT SO MUCH ON THE GO LATELY, DAUGHTER?
TKKNG SMM TMME UFF, ABU, FRMM...
"...FFTRRR-SCHOOL MMACTIVITIES..."
UEENS,
VE DAYS AGO.

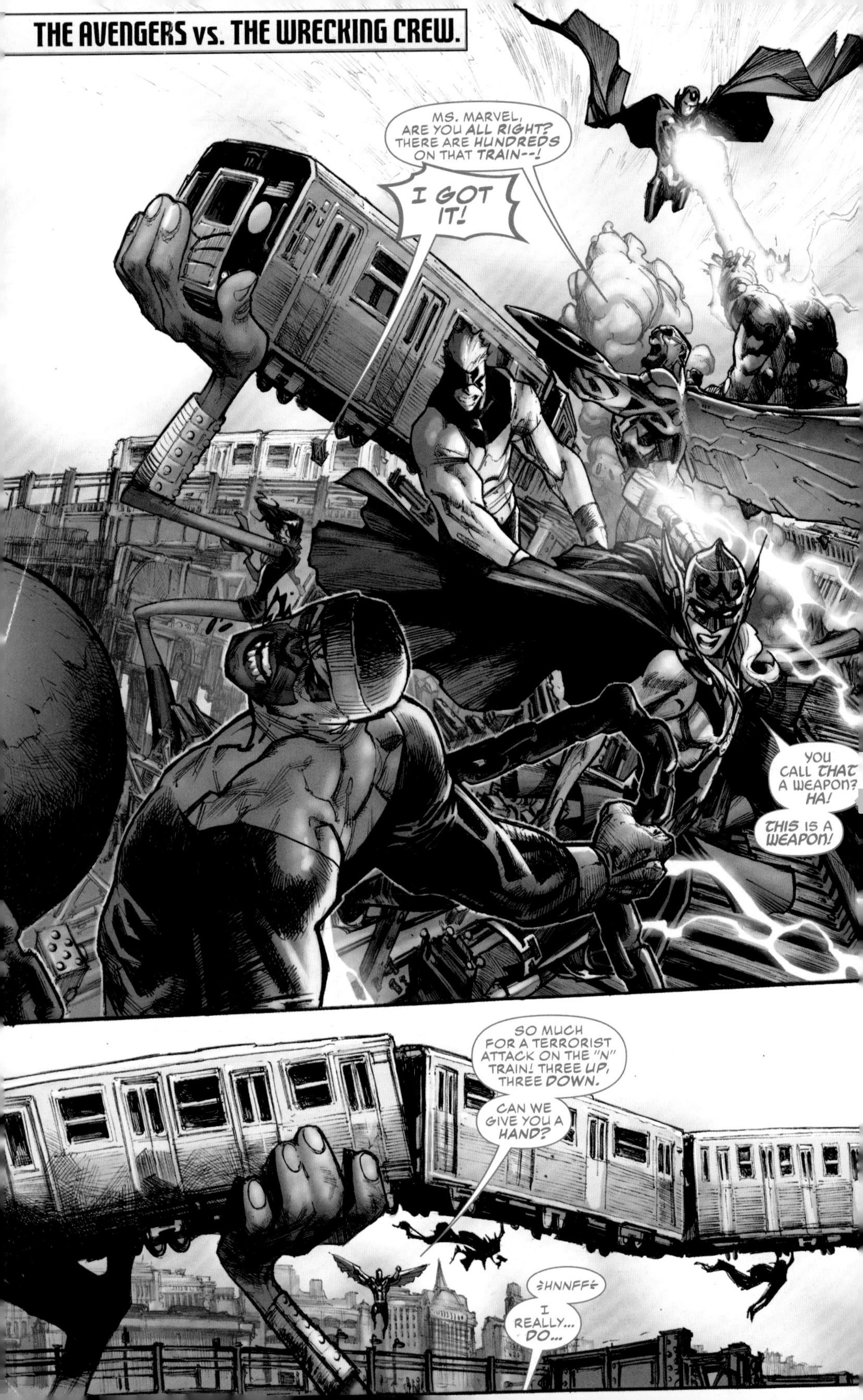
THE AVENGERS vs. THE WRECKING CREW.
MS. MARVEL, ARE YOU ALL RIGHT? THERE ARE HUNDREDS ON THAT TRAIN--!
I GOT IT!
YOU CALL THAT A WEAPON? HA!
THIS IS A WEAPON!
SO MUCH FOR A TERRORIST ATTACK ON THE "N" TRAIN! THREE UP, THREE DOWN.
CAN WE GIVE YOU A HAND?
HNNFF
I REALLY... DO...

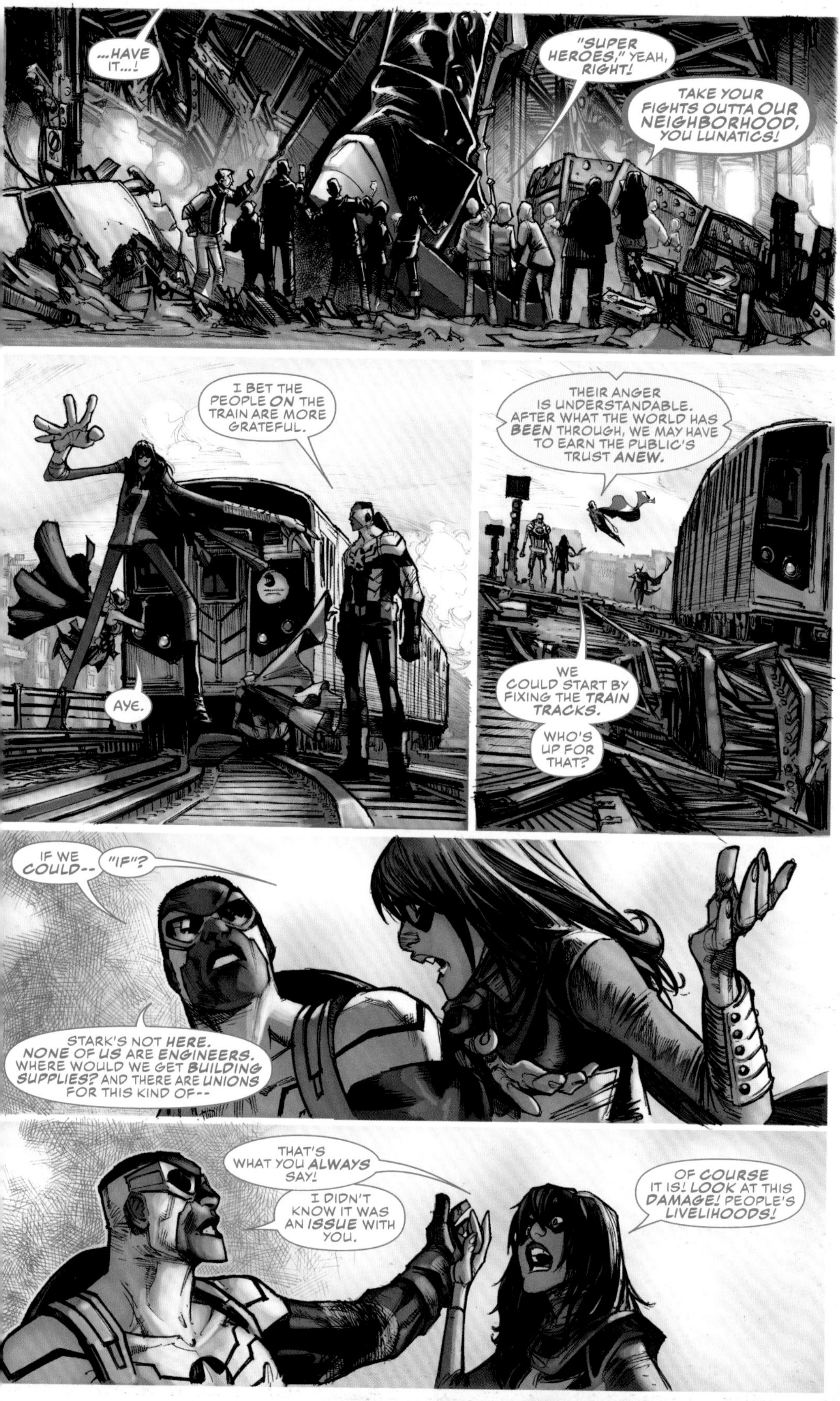
...HAVE IT...!
"SUPER HEROES," YEAH, RIGHT!
TAKE YOUR FIGHTS OUTTA OUR NEIGHBORHOOD, YOU LUNATICS!
I BET THE PEOPLE ON THE TRAIN ARE MORE GRATEFUL.
AYE.
THEIR ANGER IS UNDERSTANDABLE. AFTER WHAT THE WORLD HAS BEEN THROUGH, WE MAY HAVE TO EARN THE PUBLIC'S TRUST ANEW.
WE COULD START BY FIXING THE TRAIN TRACKS.
WHO'S UP FOR THAT?
IF WE COULD--
"IF"?
STARK'S NOT HERE. NONE OF US ARE ENGINEERS. WHERE WOULD WE GET BUILDING SUPPLIES? AND THERE ARE UNIONS FOR THIS KIND OF--
THAT'S WHAT YOU ALWAYS SAY!
I DIDN'T KNOW IT WAS AN ISSUE WITH YOU.
OF COURSE IT IS! LOOK AT THIS DAMAGE! PEOPLE'S LIVELIHOODS!

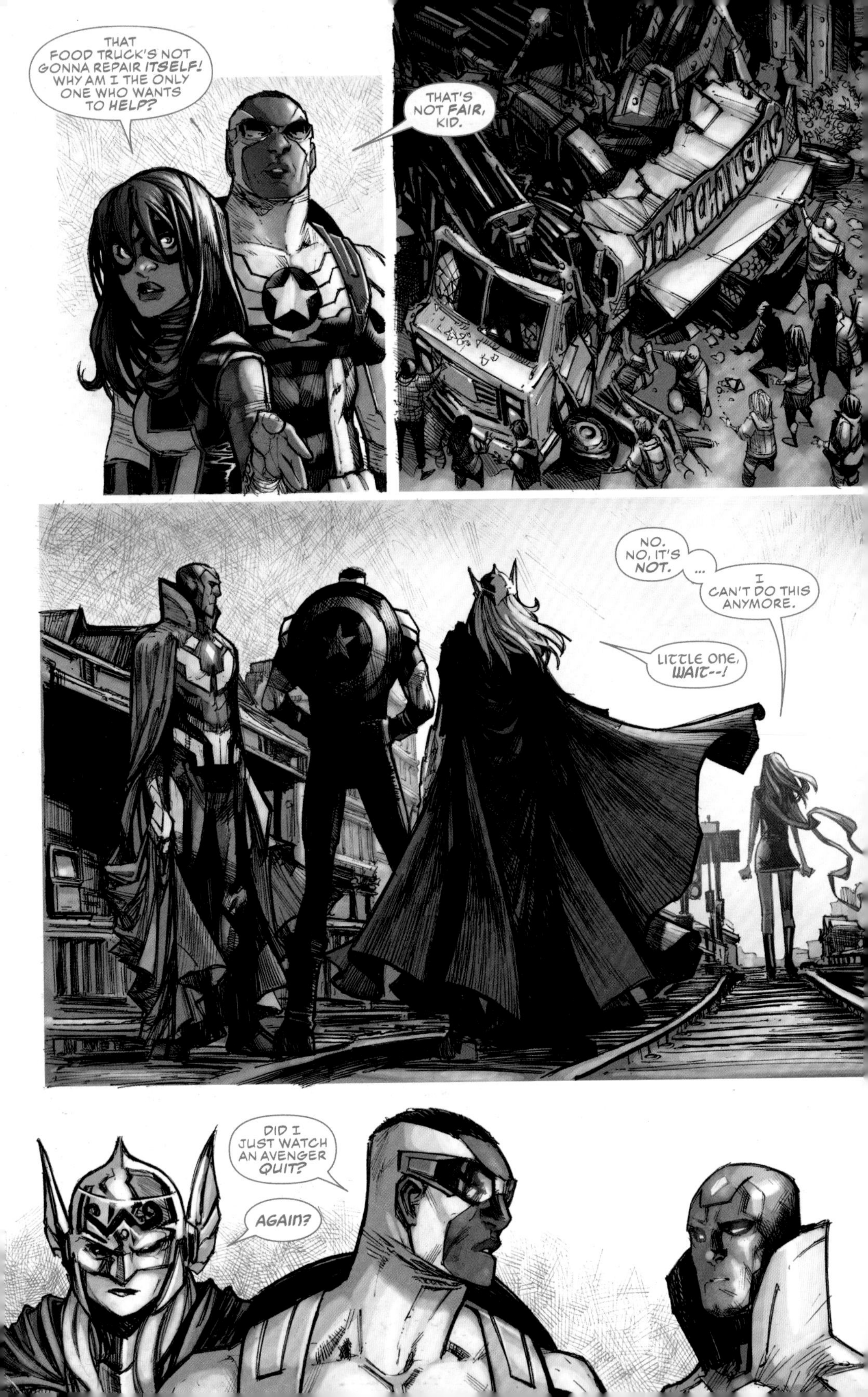
THAT FOOD TRUCK'S NOT GONNA REPAIR ITSELF! WHY AM I THE ONLY ONE WHO WANTS TO HELP?
THAT'S NOT FAIR, KID.
NO. NO, IT'S NOT.
...
I CAN'T DO THIS ANYMORE.
LITTLE ONE, WAIT--!
DID I JUST WATCH AN AVENGER QUIT?
AGAIN?

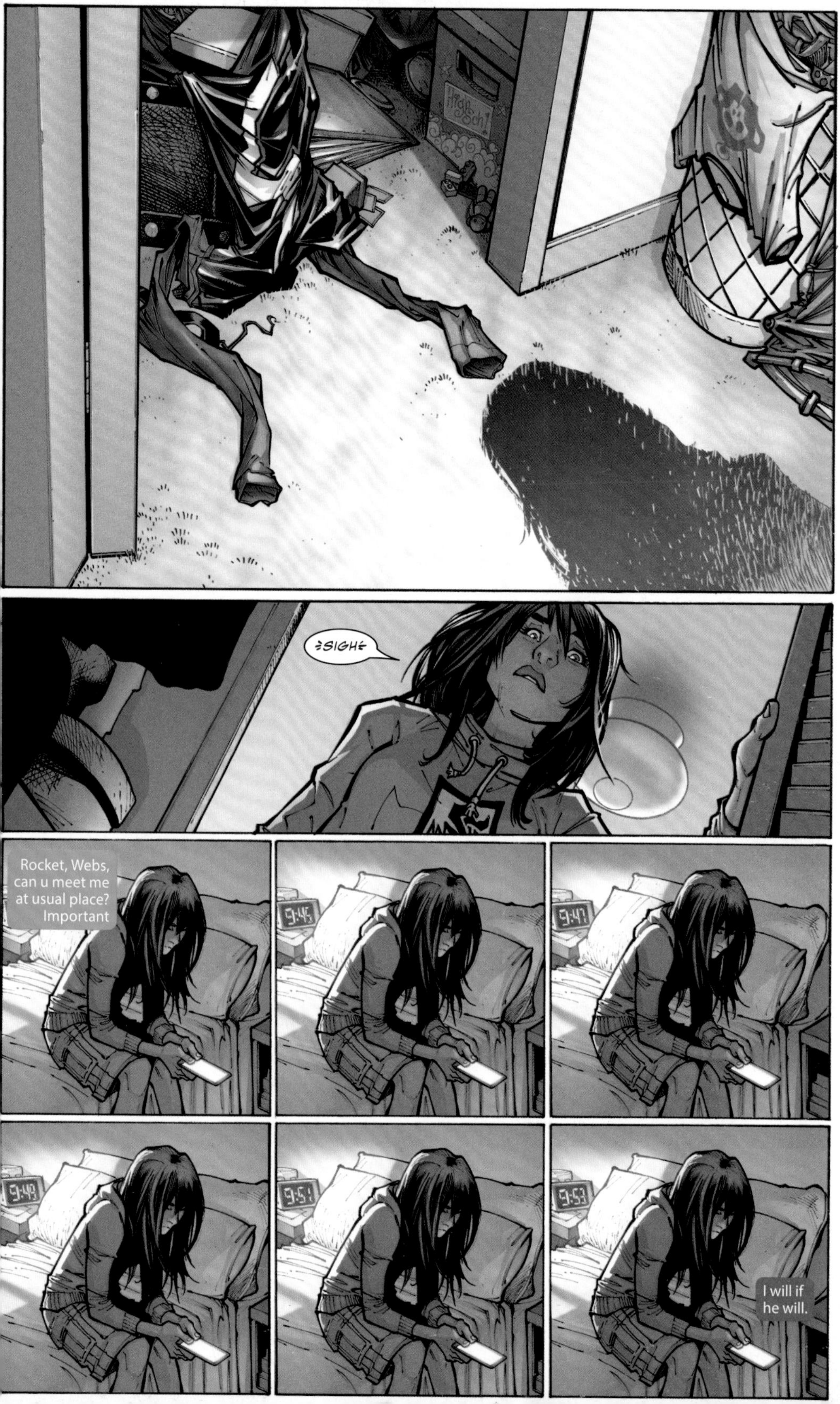
SIGH
Rocket, Webs, can u meet me at usual place? Important
I will if he will.

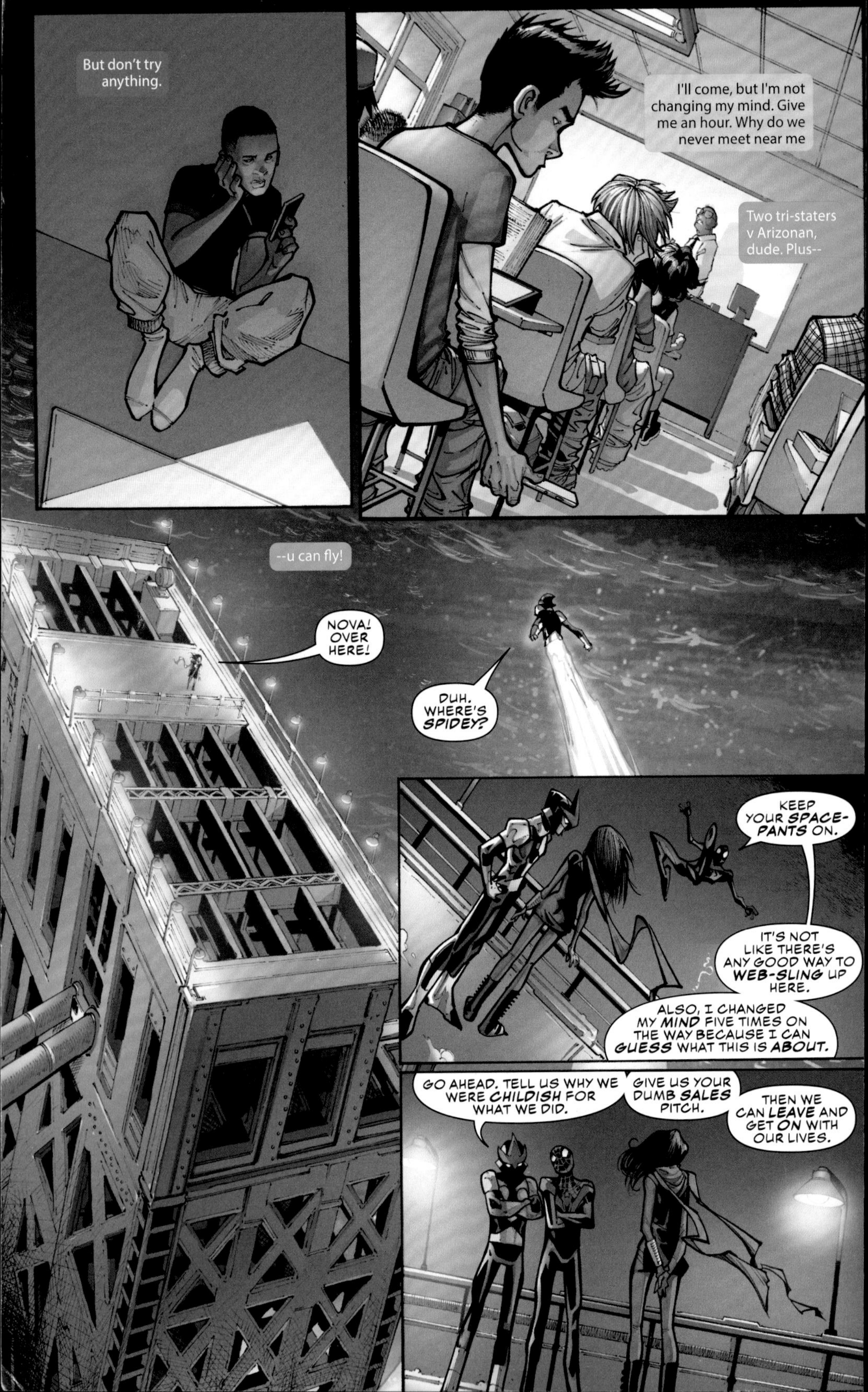

But don't try anything.
I'll come, but I'm not changing my mind. Give me an hour. Why do we never meet near me
Two tri-staters v Arizonan, dude. Plus--
--u can fly!
NOVA! OVER HERE!
DUH. WHERE'S SPIDEY?
KEEP YOUR SPACE-PANTS ON.
IT'S NOT LIKE THERE'S ANY GOOD WAY TO WEB-SLING UP HERE.
ALSO, I CHANGED MY MIND FIVE TIMES ON THE WAY BECAUSE I CAN GUESS WHAT THIS IS ABOUT.
GO AHEAD. TELL US WHY WE WERE CHILDISH FOR WHAT WE DID.
GIVE US YOUR DUMB SALES PITCH.
THEN WE CAN LEAVE AND GET ON WITH OUR LIVES.

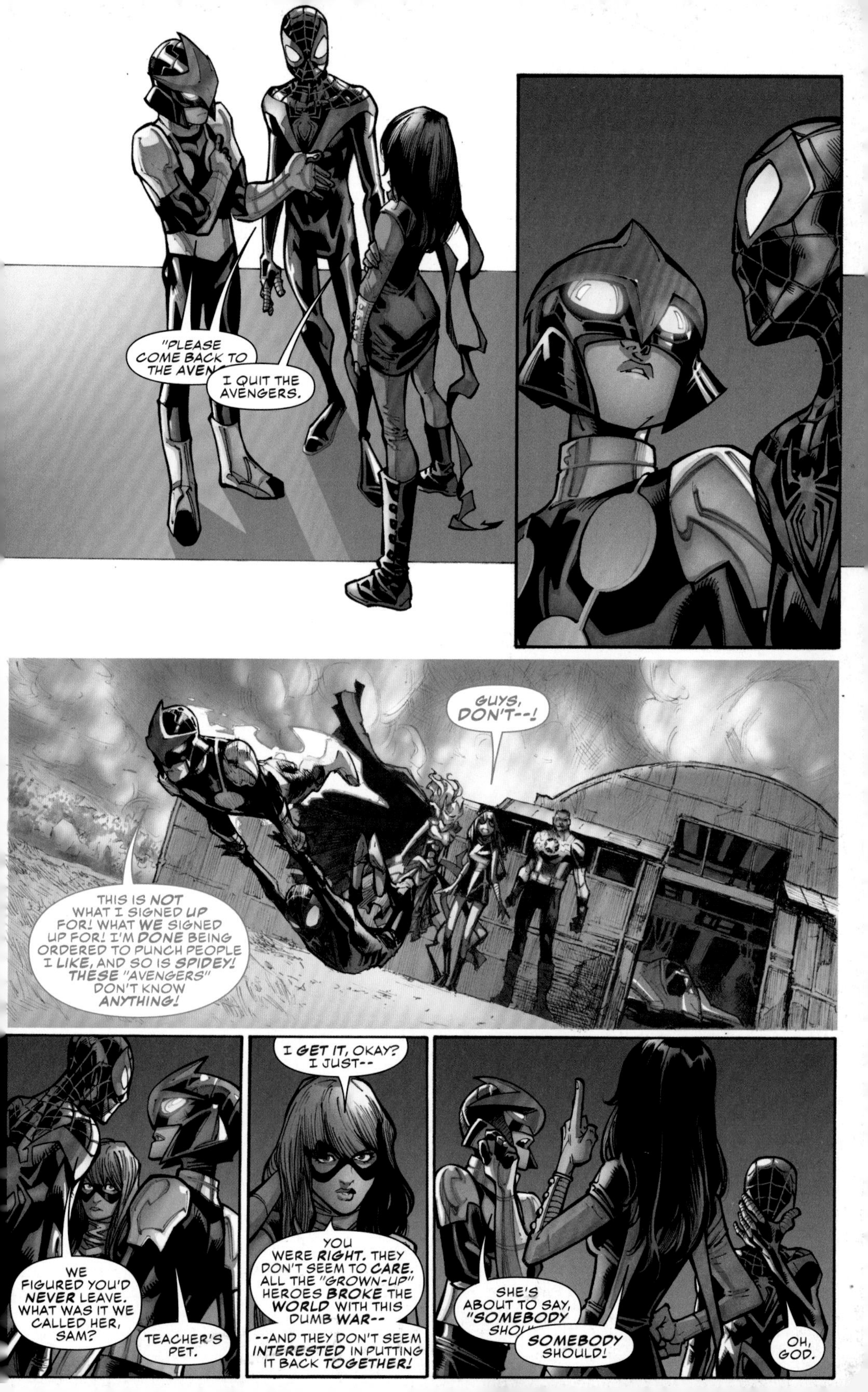
"PLEASE COME BACK TO THE AVEN-
I QUIT THE AVENGERS.
GUYS, DON'T--!
THIS IS NOT WHAT I SIGNED UP FOR! WHAT WE SIGNED UP FOR! I'M DONE BEING ORDERED TO PUNCH PEOPLE I LIKE, AND SO IS SPIDEY! THESE "AVENGERS" DON'T KNOW ANYTHING!
WE FIGURED YOU'D NEVER LEAVE. WHAT WAS IT WE CALLED HER, SAM?
TEACHER'S PET.
I GET IT, OKAY? I JUST--
YOU WERE RIGHT. THEY DON'T SEEM TO CARE. ALL THE "GROWN-UP" HEROES BROKE THE WORLD WITH THIS DUMB WAR--
--AND THEY DON'T SEEM INTERESTED IN PUTTING IT BACK TOGETHER!
SHE'S ABOUT TO SAY, "SOMEBODY SHOU-
SOMEBODY SHOULD!
OH, GOD.

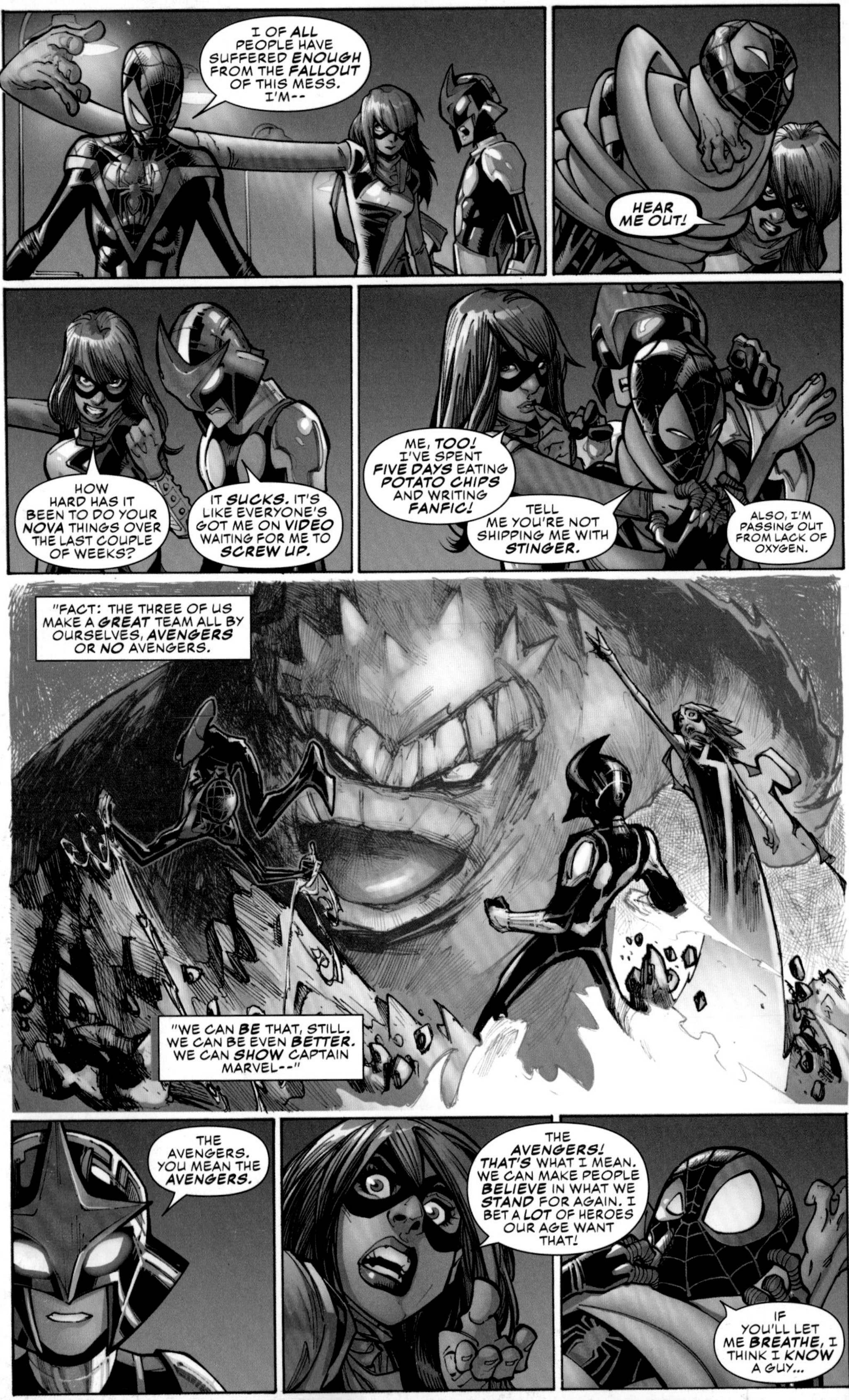
I OF ALL PEOPLE HAVE SUFFERED ENOUGH FROM THE FALLOUT OF THIS MESS. I'M--
HEAR ME OUT!
HOW HARD HAS IT BEEN TO DO YOUR NOVA THINGS OVER THE LAST COUPLE OF WEEKS?
IT SUCKS. IT'S LIKE EVERYONE'S GOT ME ON VIDEO WAITING FOR ME TO SCREW UP.
ME, TOO! I'VE SPENT FIVE DAYS EATING POTATO CHIPS AND WRITING FANFIC!
TELL ME YOU'RE NOT SHIPPING ME WITH STINGER.
ALSO, I'M PASSING OUT FROM LACK OF OXYGEN.
"FACT: THE THREE OF US MAKE A GREAT TEAM ALL BY OURSELVES, AVENGERS OR NO AVENGERS.
"WE CAN BE THAT, STILL. WE CAN BE EVEN BETTER. WE CAN SHOW CAPTAIN MARVEL--"
THE AVENGERS. YOU MEAN THE AVENGERS.
THE AVENGERS! THAT'S WHAT I MEAN. WE CAN MAKE PEOPLE BELIEVE IN WHAT WE STAND FOR AGAIN. I BET A LOT OF HEROES OUR AGE WANT THAT!
IF YOU'LL LET ME BREATHE, I THINK I KNOW A GUY...

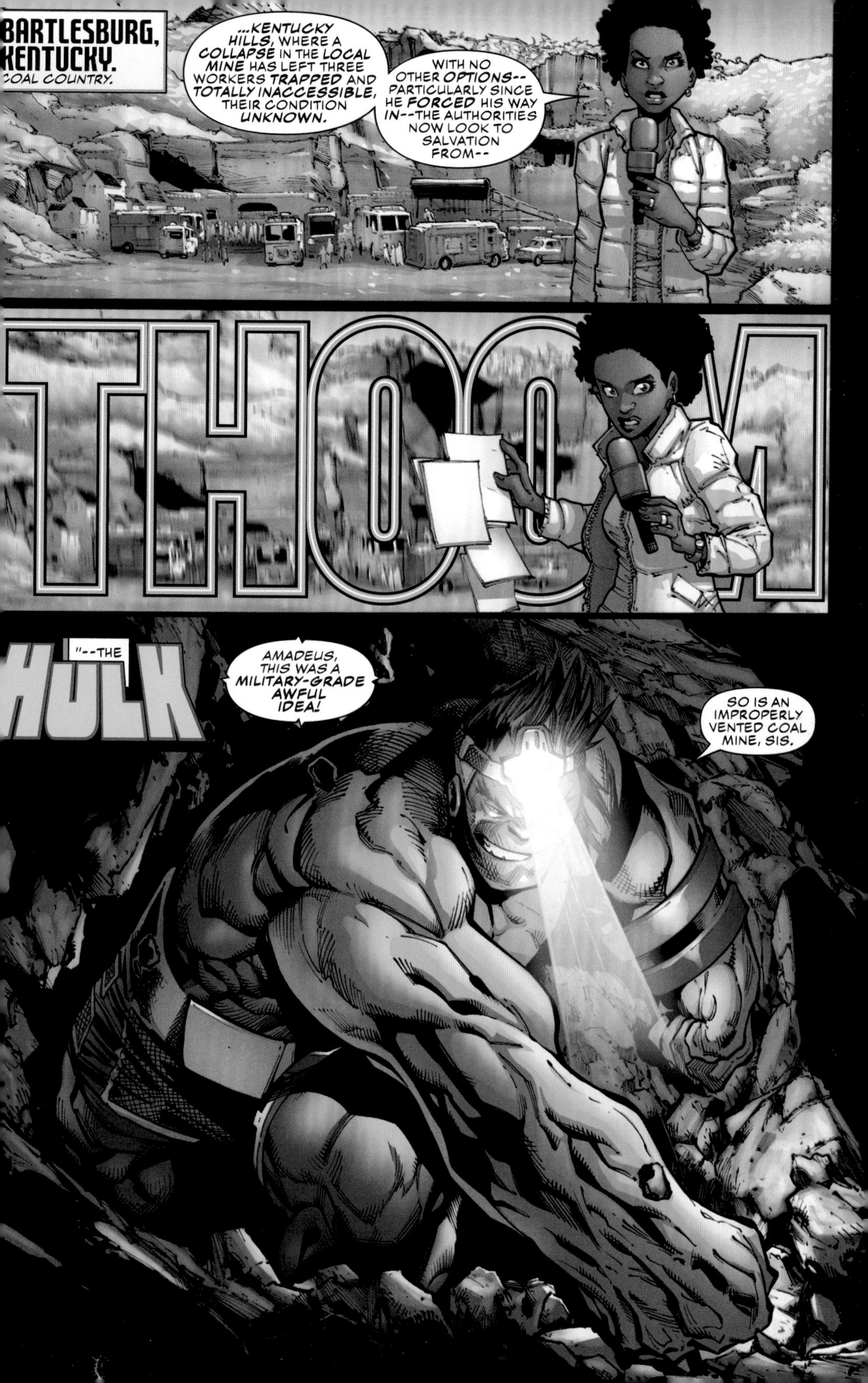
BARTLESBURG, KENTUCKY.
COAL COUNTRY.
...KENTUCKY HILLS, WHERE A COLLAPSE IN THE LOCAL MINE HAS LEFT THREE WORKERS TRAPPED AND TOTALLY INACCESSIBLE, THEIR CONDITION UNKNOWN.
WITH NO OTHER OPTIONS--PARTICULARLY SINCE HE FORCED HIS WAY IN--THE AUTHORITIES NOW LOOK TO SALVATION FROM--
THOOM
"--THE HULK
AMADEUS, THIS WAS A MILITARY-GRADE AWFUL IDEA!
SO IS AN IMPROPERLY VENTED COAL MINE, SIS.

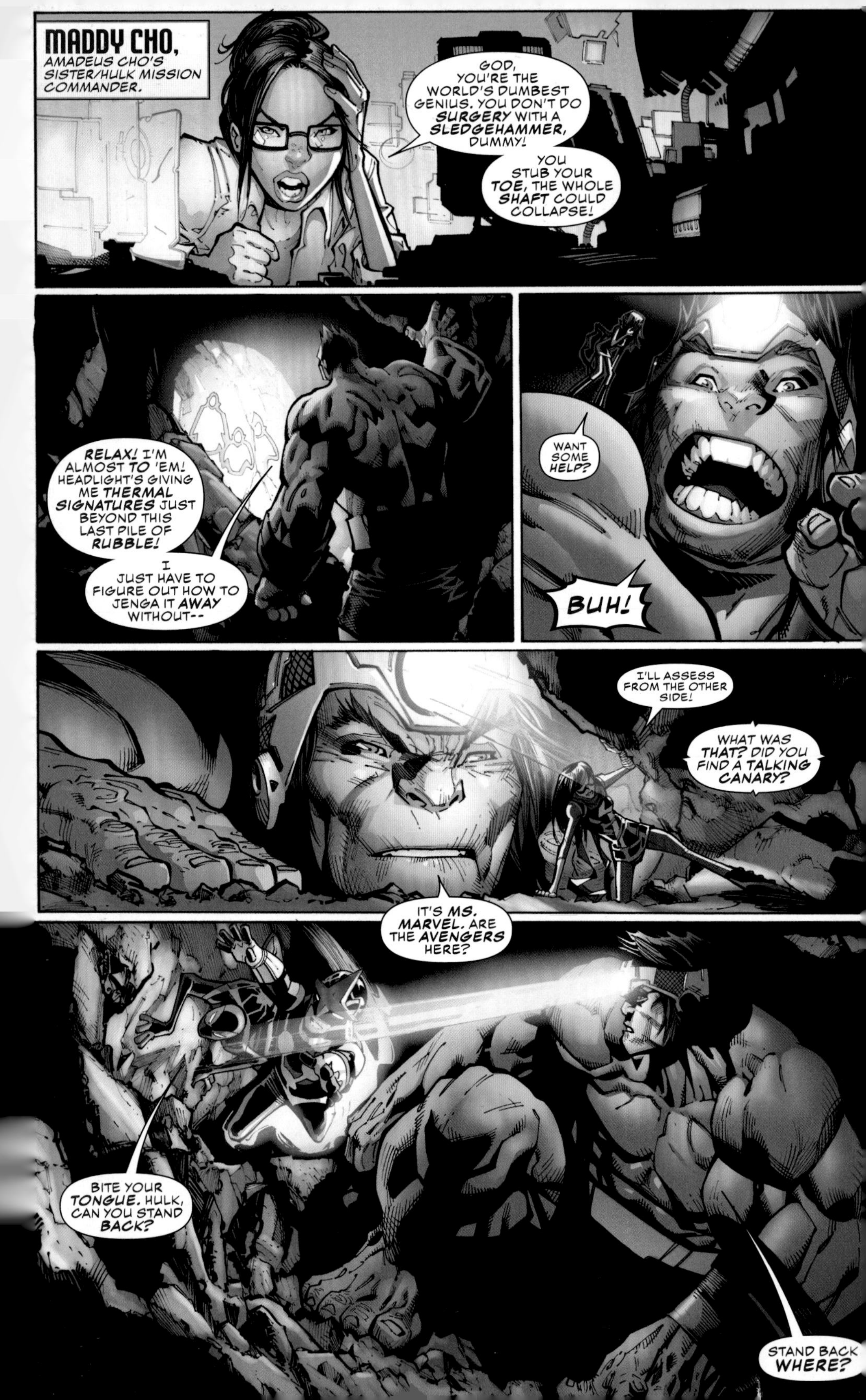
MADDY CHO, AMADEUS CHO'S SISTER/HULK MISSION COMMANDER.
GOD, YOU'RE THE WORLD'S DUMBEST GENIUS. YOU DON'T DO SURGERY WITH A SLEDGEHAMMER, DUMMY!
YOU STUB YOUR TOE, THE WHOLE SHAFT COULD COLLAPSE!
RELAX! I'M ALMOST TO 'EM! HEADLIGHT'S GIVING ME THERMAL SIGNATURES JUST BEYOND THIS LAST PILE OF RUBBLE!
I JUST HAVE TO FIGURE OUT HOW TO JENGA IT AWAY WITHOUT--
WANT SOME HELP?
BUH!
I'LL ASSESS FROM THE OTHER SIDE!
WHAT WAS THAT? DID YOU FIND A TALKING CANARY?
IT'S MS. MARVEL. ARE THE AVENGERS HERE?
BITE YOUR TONGUE. HULK, CAN YOU STAND BACK?
STAND BACK WHERE?

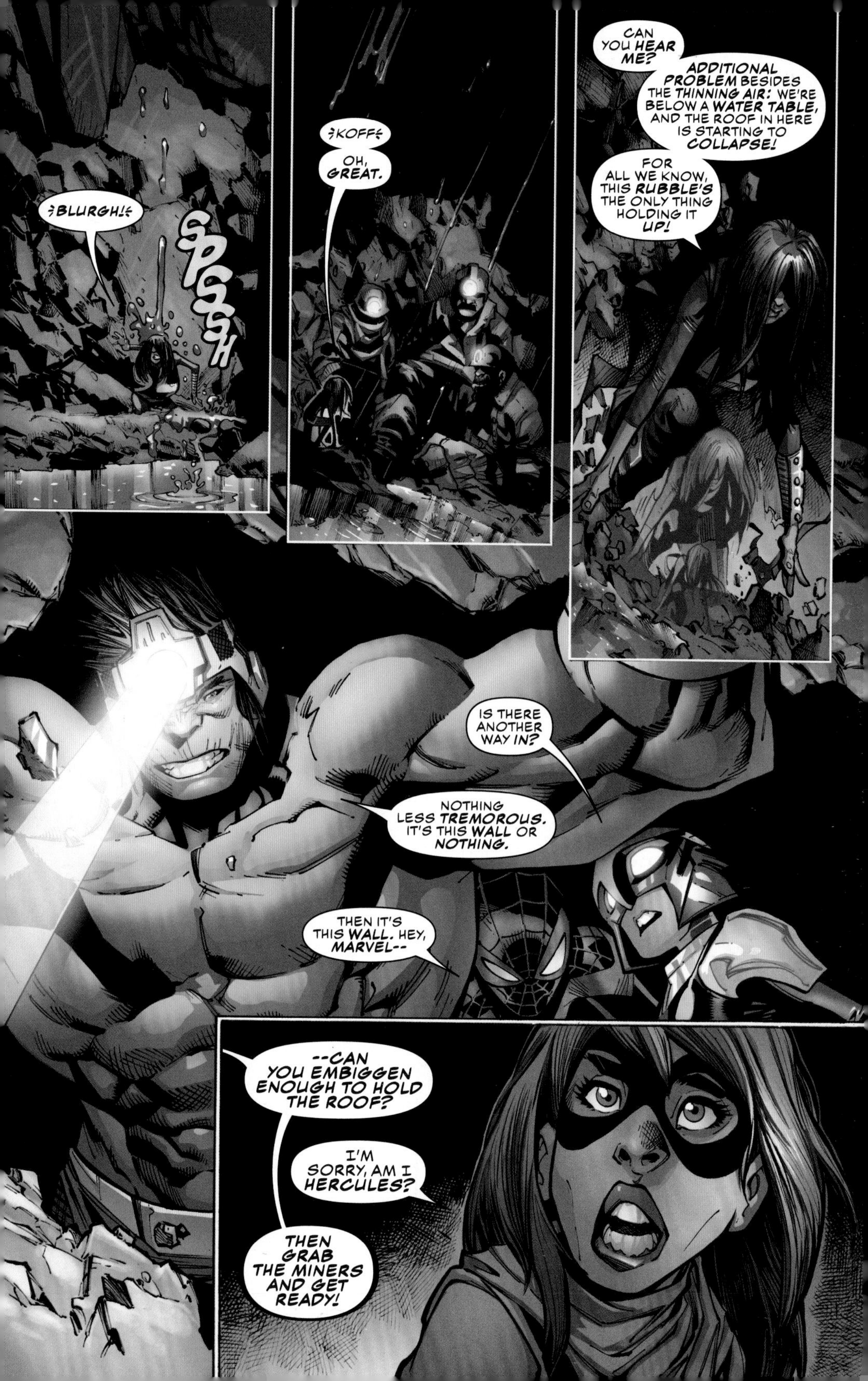

BLURGH!
SPSSH
KOFF
OH, GREAT.
CAN YOU HEAR ME?
ADDITIONAL PROBLEM BESIDES THE THINNING AIR: WE'RE BELOW A WATER TABLE, AND THE ROOF IN HERE IS STARTING TO COLLAPSE!
FOR ALL WE KNOW, THIS RUBBLE'S THE ONLY THING HOLDING IT UP!
IS THERE ANOTHER WAY IN?
NOTHING LESS TREMOROUS. IT'S THIS WALL OR NOTHING.
THEN IT'S THIS WALL. HEY, MARVEL--
--CAN YOU EMBIGGEN ENOUGH TO HOLD THE ROOF?
I'M SORRY, AM I HERCULES?
THEN GRAB THE MINERS AND GET READY!

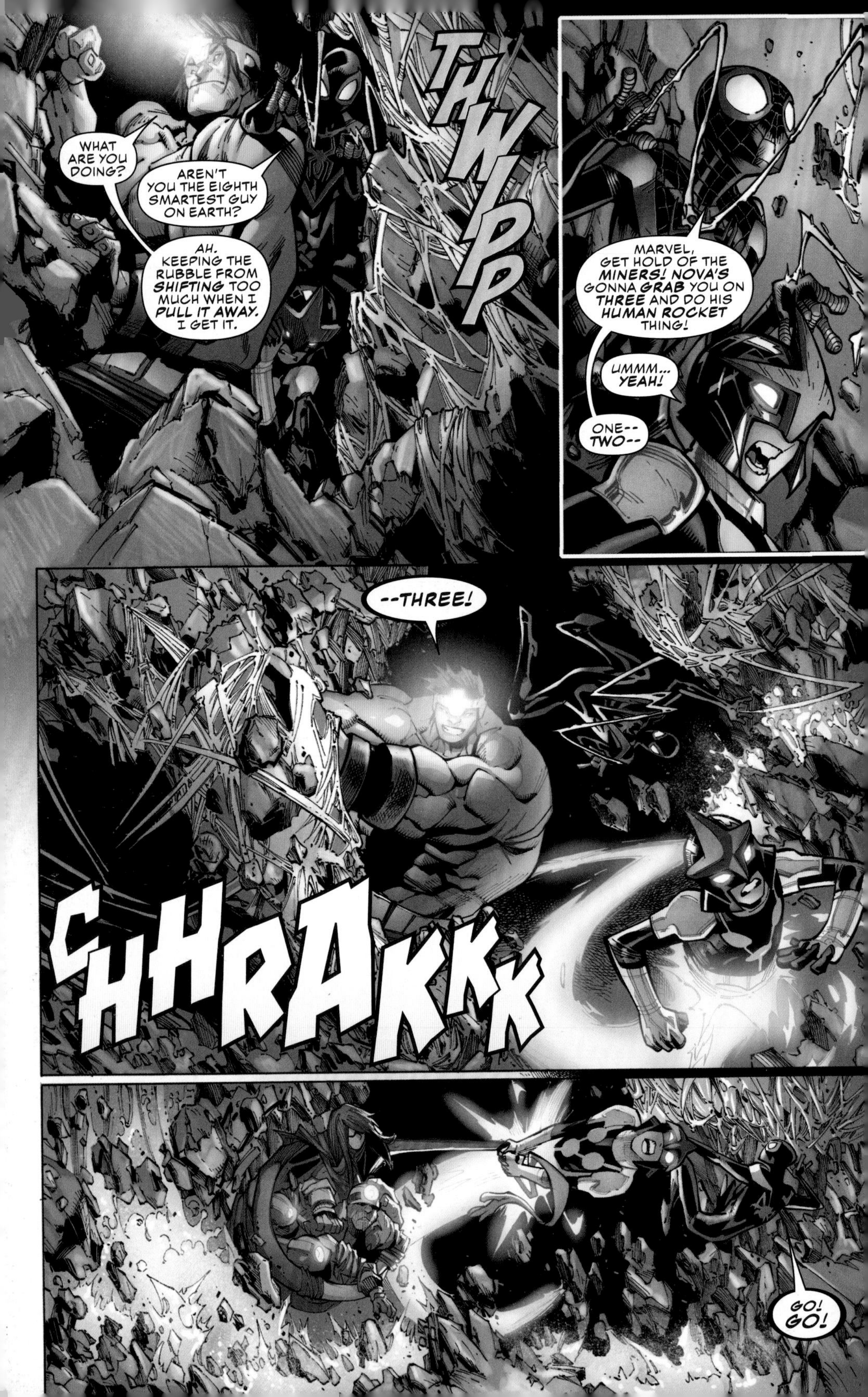
WHAT ARE YOU DOING?
AREN'T YOU THE EIGHTH SMARTEST GUY ON EARTH?
AH. KEEPING THE RUBBLE FROM SHIFTING TOO MUCH WHEN I PULL IT AWAY. I GET IT.
THWIPP
MARVEL, GET HOLD OF THE MINERS! NOVA'S GONNA GRAB YOU ON THREE AND DO HIS HUMAN ROCKET THING!
UMMM... YEAH!
ONE-- TWO--
--THREE!
CHHRAKKK
GO! GO!

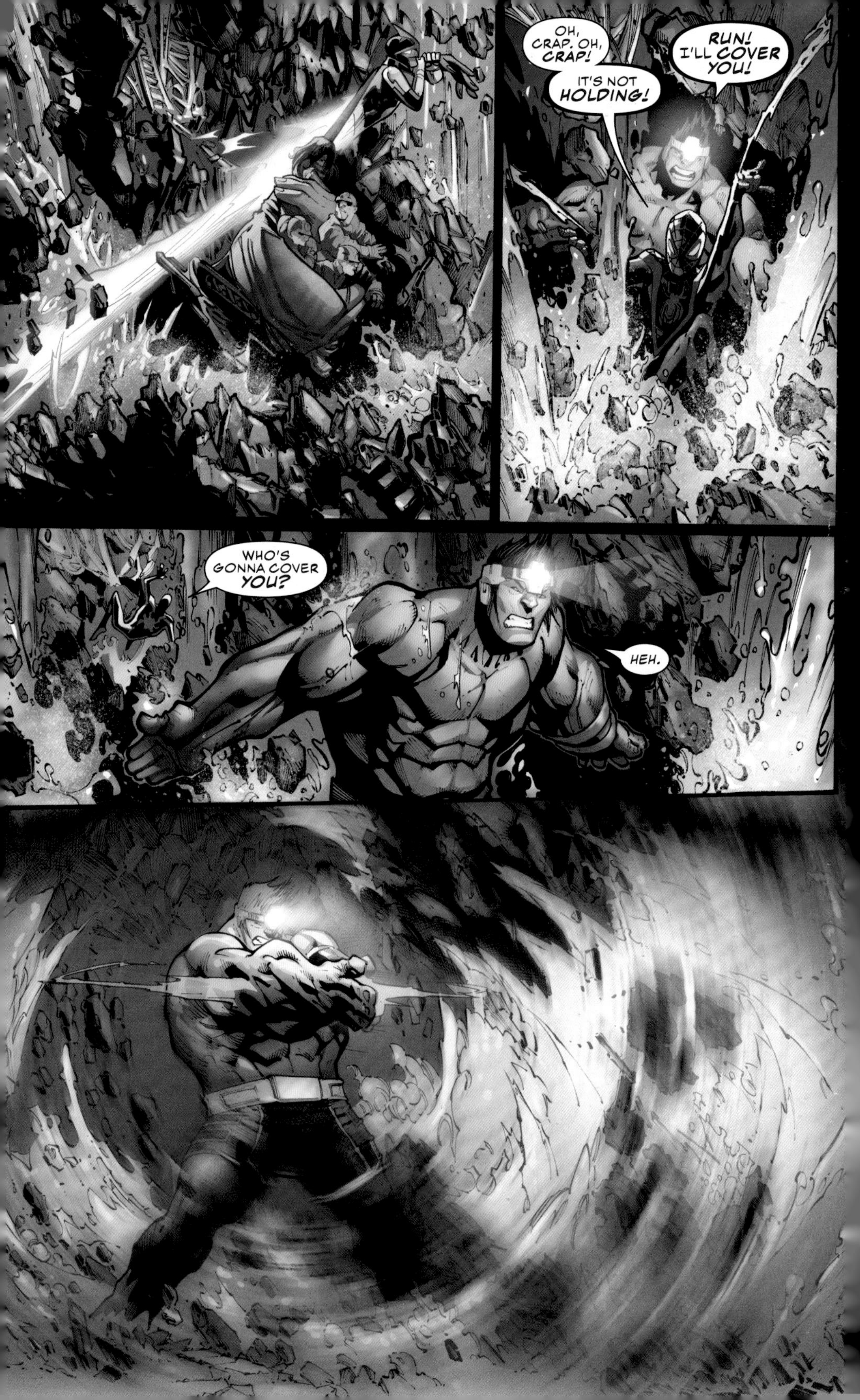
OH, CRAP. OH, CRAP!
IT'S NOT HOLDING!
RUN! I'LL COVER YOU!
WHO'S GONNA COVER YOU?
HEH.

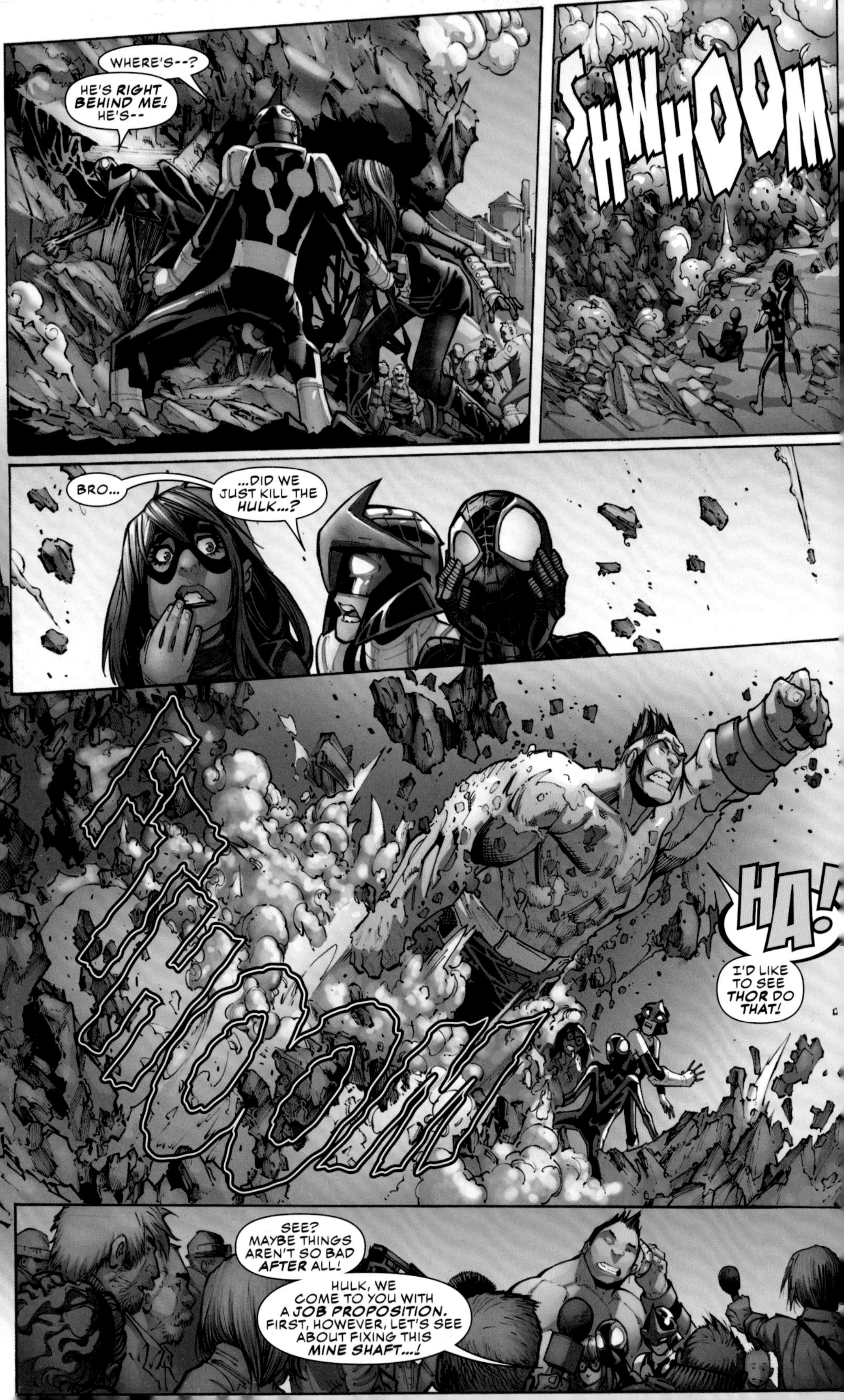
WHERE'S--?
HE'S RIGHT BEHIND ME! HE'S--
SHWHOOM
BRO...
...DID WE JUST KILL THE HULK...?
FWOOM
HA!
I'D LIKE TO SEE THOR DO THAT!
SEE? MAYBE THINGS AREN'T SO BAD AFTER ALL!
HULK, WE COME TO YOU WITH A JOB PROPOSITION. FIRST, HOWEVER, LET'S SEE ABOUT FIXING THIS MINE SHAFT...!

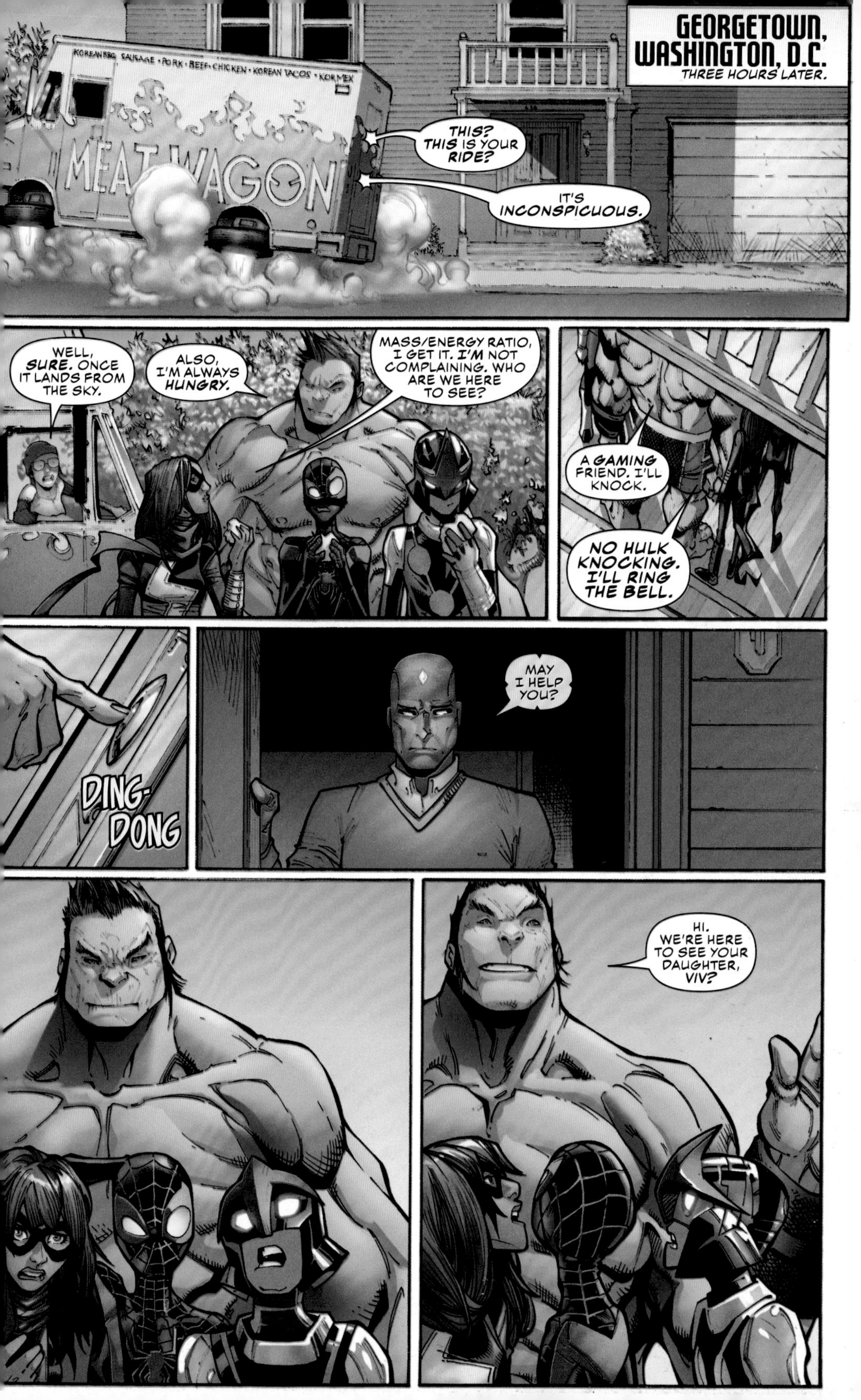
GEORGETOWN, WASHINGTON, D.C.
THREE HOURS LATER.
KOREAN BBQ SAUSAGE • PORK • BEEF • CHICKEN • KOREAN TACOS • KOR-MEX
MEAT WAGON
THIS? THIS IS YOUR RIDE?
IT'S INCONSPICUOUS.
WELL, SURE. ONCE IT LANDS FROM THE SKY.
ALSO, I'M ALWAYS HUNGRY.
MASS/ENERGY RATIO, I GET IT. I'M NOT COMPLAINING. WHO ARE WE HERE TO SEE?
A GAMING FRIEND. I'LL KNOCK.
NO HULK KNOCKING. I'LL RING THE BELL.
DING-DONG
MAY I HELP YOU?
HI. WE'RE HERE TO SEE YOUR DAUGHTER, VIV?

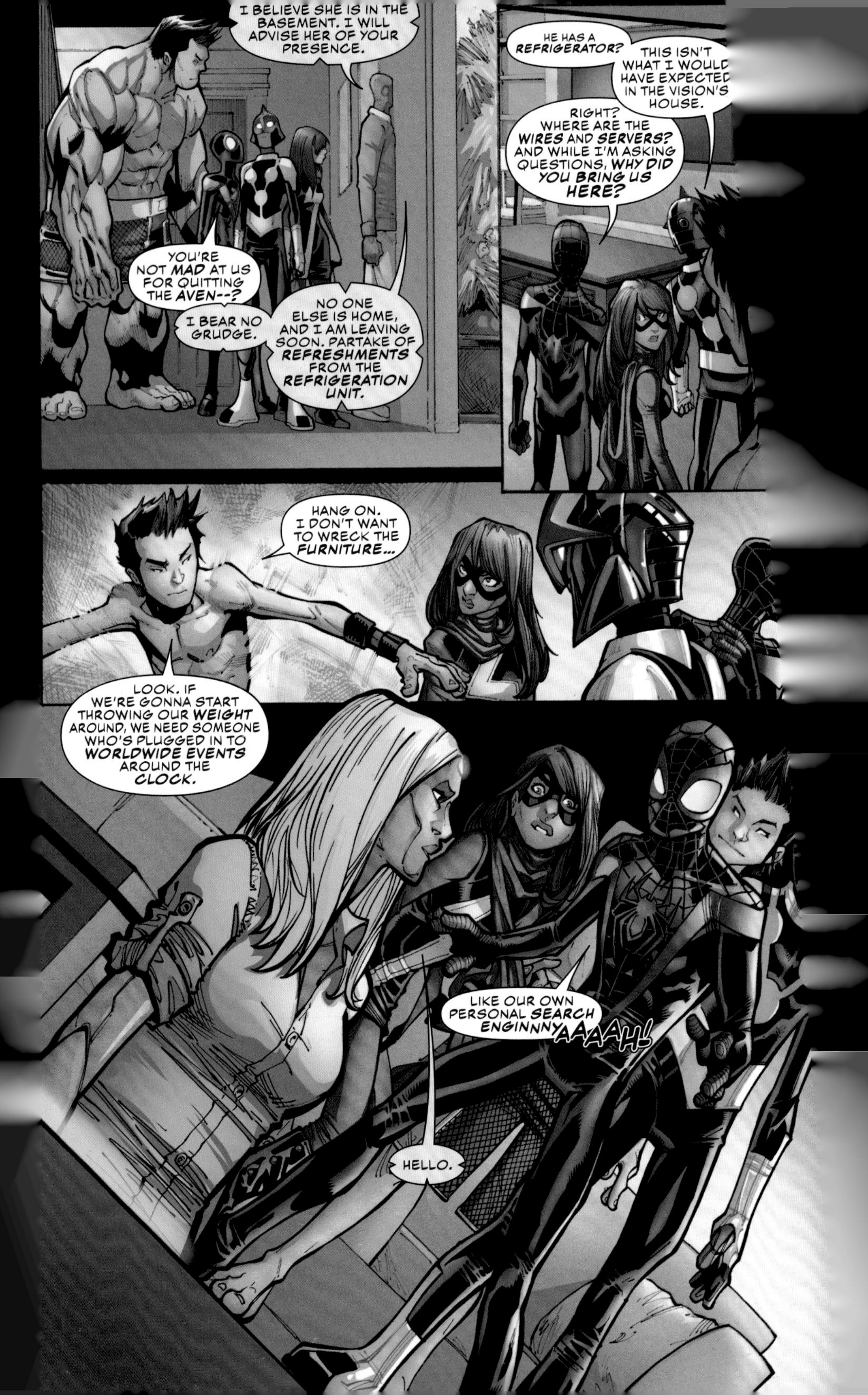
I BELIEVE SHE IS IN THE BASEMENT. I WILL ADVISE HER OF YOUR PRESENCE.
YOU'RE NOT MAD AT US FOR QUITTING THE AVEN--?
I BEAR NO GRUDGE.
NO ONE ELSE IS HOME, AND I AM LEAVING SOON. PARTAKE OF REFRESHMENTS FROM THE REFRIGERATION UNIT.
HE HAS A REFRIGERATOR?
THIS ISN'T WHAT I WOULD HAVE EXPECTED IN THE VISION'S HOUSE.
RIGHT? WHERE ARE THE WIRES AND SERVERS? AND WHILE I'M ASKING QUESTIONS, WHY DID YOU BRING US HERE?
HANG ON. I DON'T WANT TO WRECK THE FURNITURE...
LOOK. IF WE'RE GONNA START THROWING OUR WEIGHT AROUND, WE NEED SOMEONE WHO'S PLUGGED IN TO WORLDWIDE EVENTS AROUND THE CLOCK.
LIKE OUR OWN PERSONAL SEARCH ENGINNNYAAAAH!
HELLO.

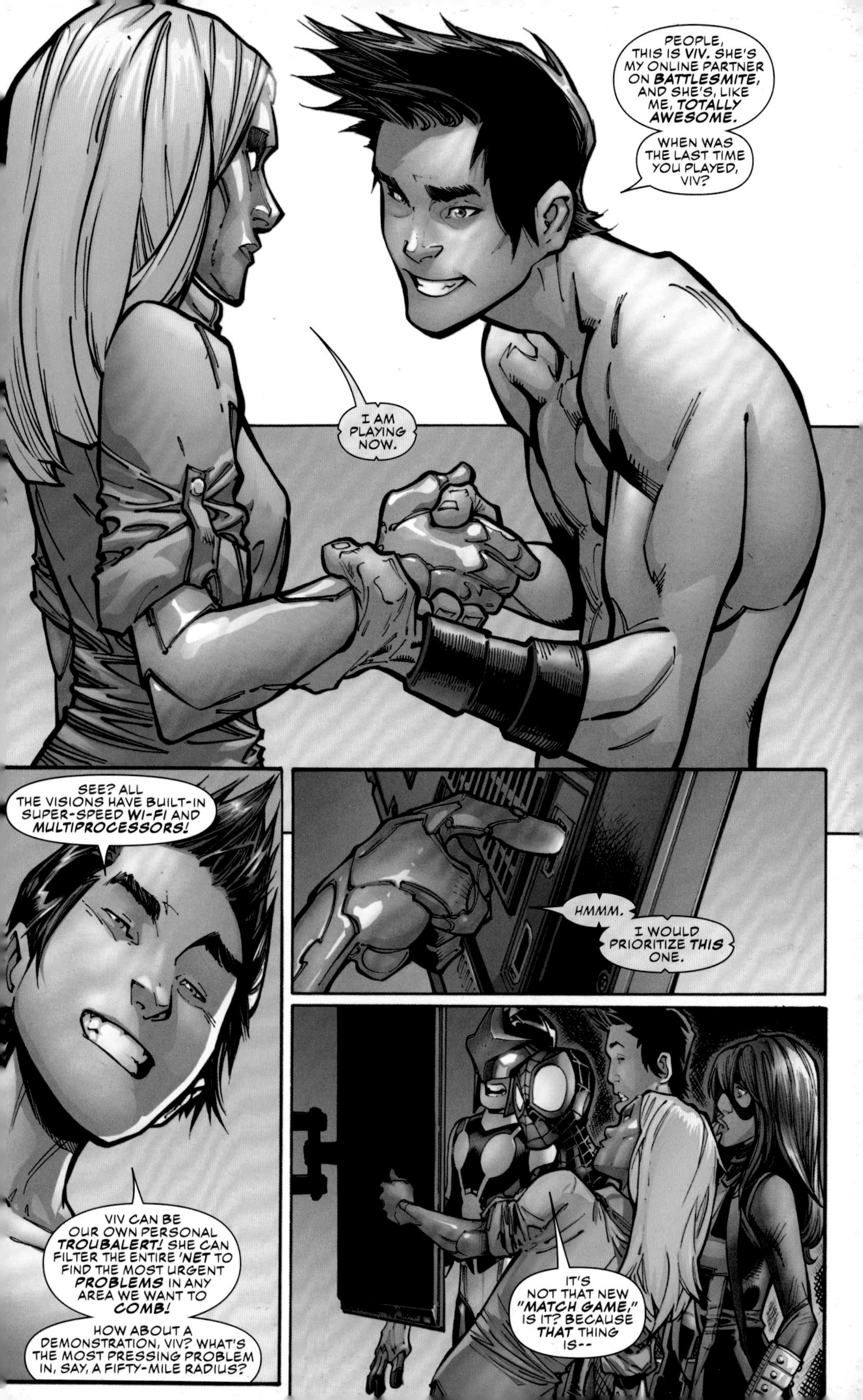
PEOPLE, THIS IS VIV. SHE'S MY ONLINE PARTNER ON BATTLESMITE, AND SHE'S, LIKE ME, TOTALLY AWESOME.
WHEN WAS THE LAST TIME YOU PLAYED, VIV?
I AM PLAYING NOW.
SEE? ALL THE VISIONS HAVE BUILT-IN SUPER-SPEED WI-FI AND MULTIPROCESSORS!
VIV CAN BE OUR OWN PERSONAL TROUBALERT! SHE CAN FILTER THE ENTIRE 'NET TO FIND THE MOST URGENT PROBLEMS IN ANY AREA WE WANT TO COMB!
HOW ABOUT A DEMONSTRATION, VIV? WHAT'S THE MOST PRESSING PROBLEM IN, SAY, A FIFTY-MILE RADIUS?
HMMM.
I WOULD PRIORITIZE THIS ONE.
IT'S NOT THAT NEW "MATCH GAME," IS IT? BECAUSE THAT THING IS--

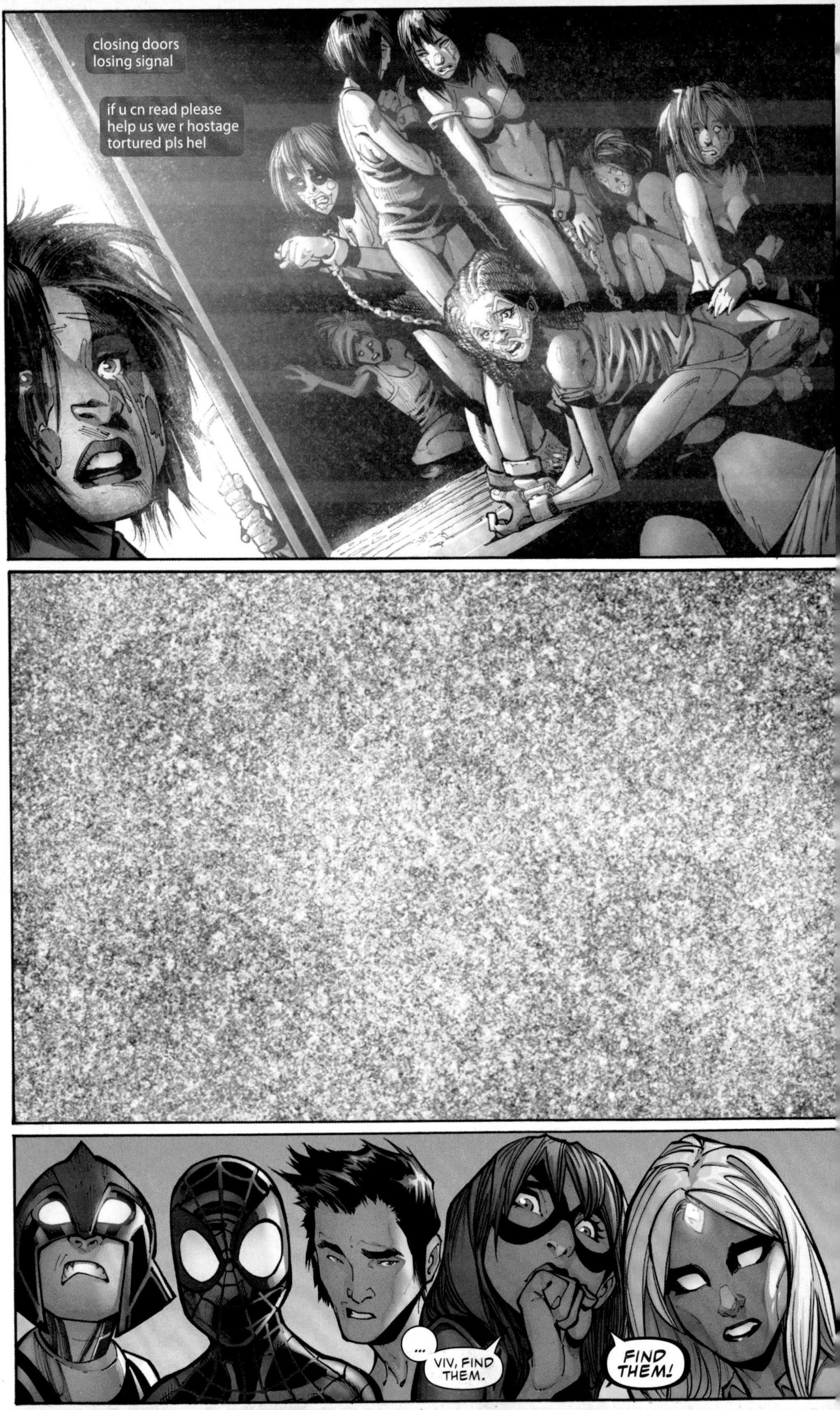
closing doors
losing signal
if u cn read please help us we r hostage tortured pls hel
...
VIV, FIND THEM.
FIND THEM!

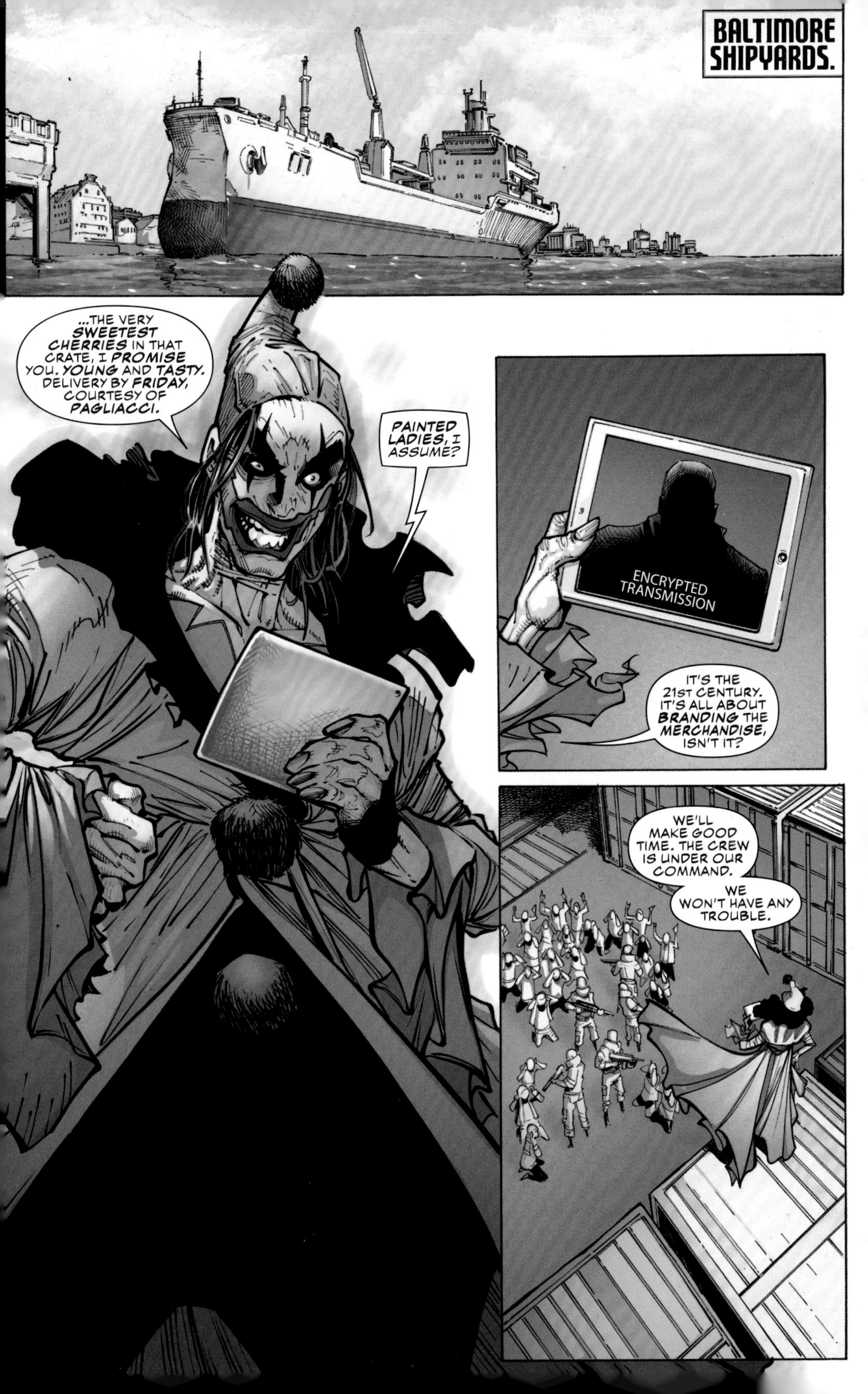
BALTIMORE SHIPYARDS.
...THE VERY SWEETEST CHERRIES IN THAT CRATE, I PROMISE YOU. YOUNG AND TASTY. DELIVERY BY FRIDAY, COURTESY OF PAGLIACCI.
PAINTED LADIES, I ASSUME?
ENCRYPTED TRANSMISSION
IT'S THE 21ST CENTURY. IT'S ALL ABOUT BRANDING THE MERCHANDISE, ISN'T IT?
WE'LL MAKE GOOD TIME. THE CREW IS UNDER OUR COMMAND.
WE WON'T HAVE ANY TROUBLE.

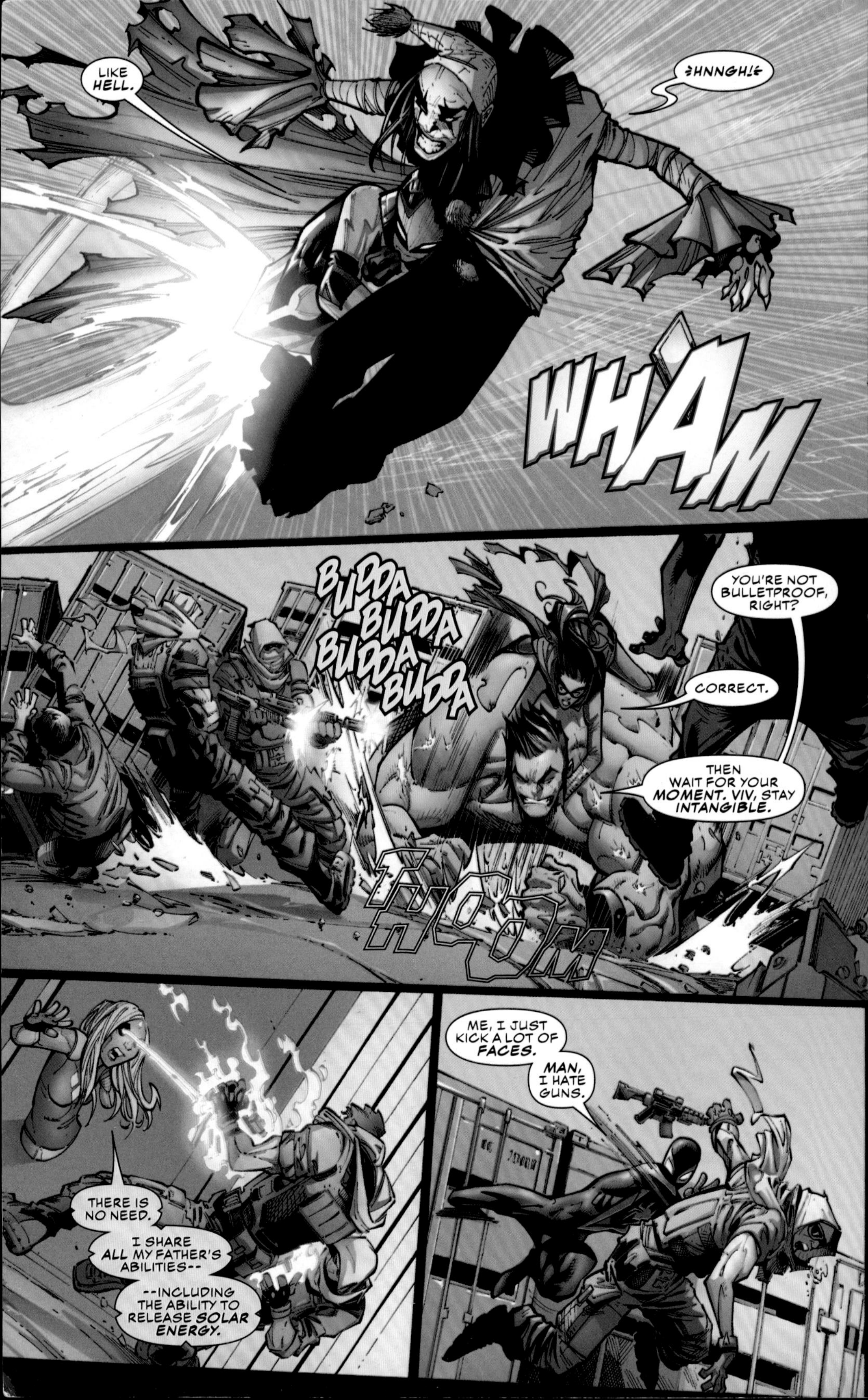
LIKE HELL.
HNNGH!
WHAM
BUDDA BUDDA BUDDA BUDDA
YOU'RE NOT BULLETPROOF, RIGHT?
CORRECT.
THEN WAIT FOR YOUR MOMENT. VIV, STAY INTANGIBLE.
THERE IS NO NEED.
I SHARE ALL MY FATHER'S ABILITIES--
--INCLUDING THE ABILITY TO RELEASE SOLAR ENERGY.
ME, I JUST KICK A LOT OF FACES.
MAN, I HATE GUNS.

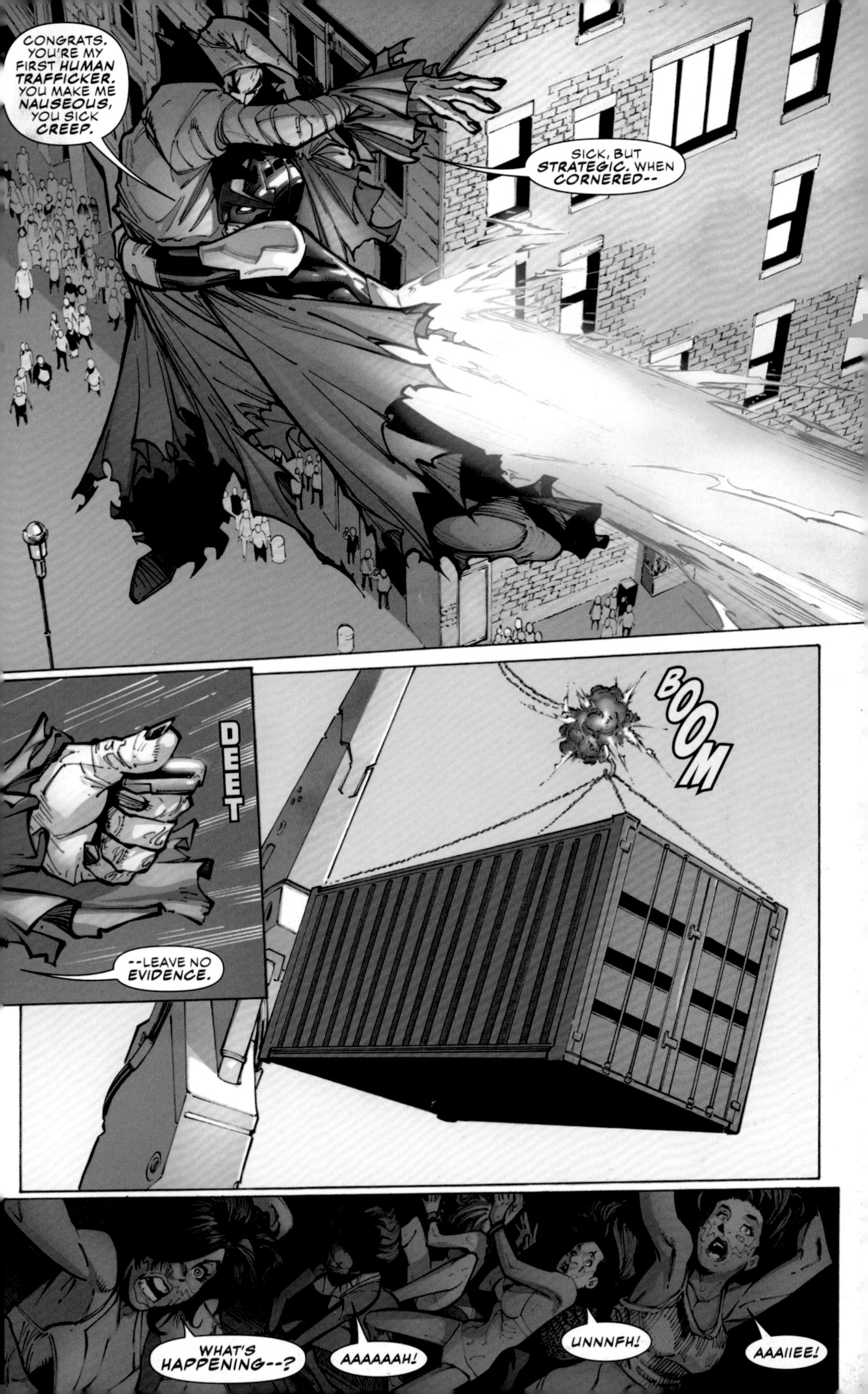
CONGRATS. YOU'RE MY FIRST HUMAN TRAFFICKER. YOU MAKE ME NAUSEOUS, YOU SICK CREEP.
SICK, BUT STRATEGIC. WHEN CORNERED--
DEET
--LEAVE NO EVIDENCE.
BOOM
WHAT'S HAPPENING--?
AAAAAAH!
UNNNFH!
AAAIIEE!

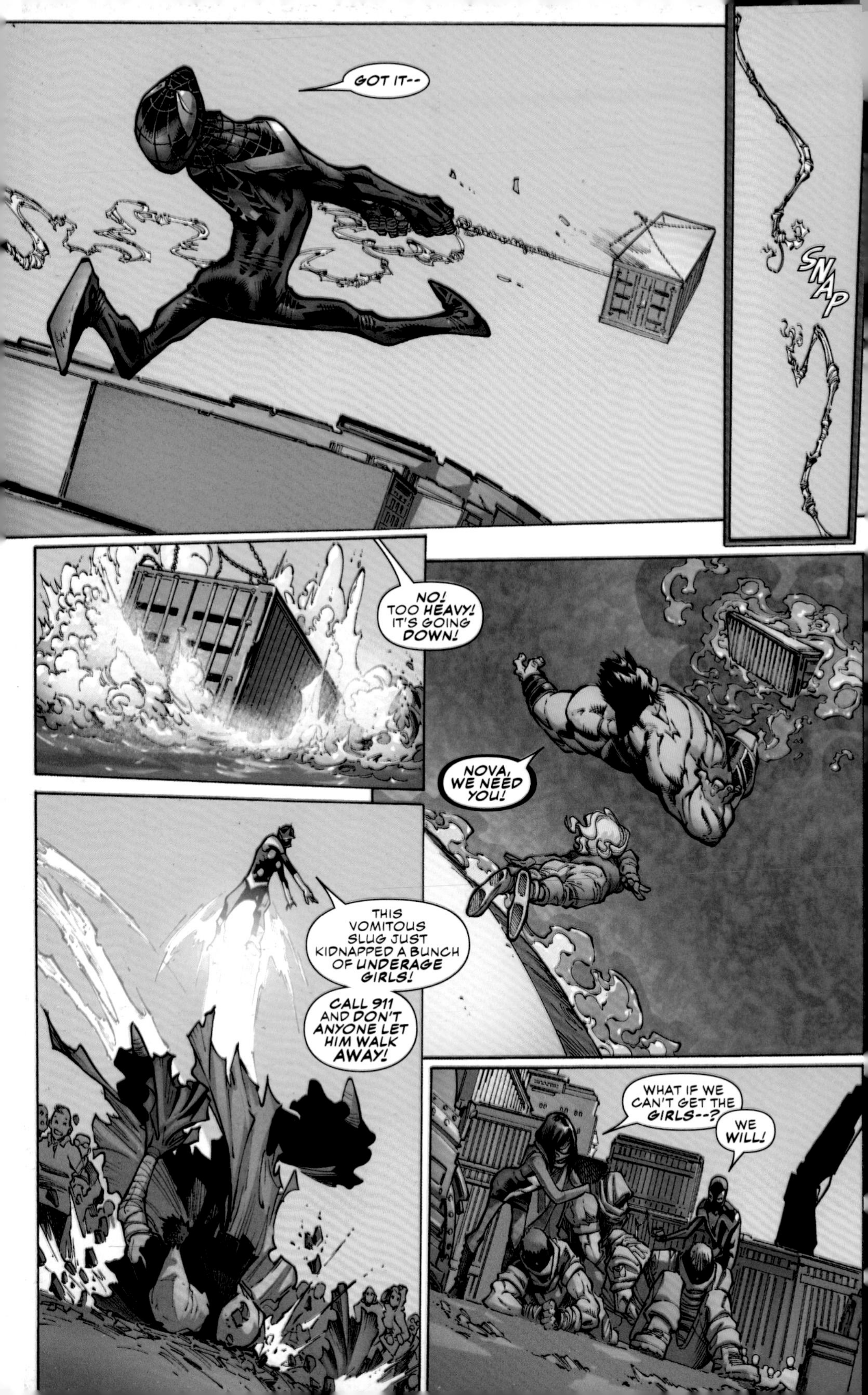
GOT IT--
SNAP
NO! TOO HEAVY! IT'S GOING DOWN!
NOVA, WE NEED YOU!
THIS VOMITOUS SLUG JUST KIDNAPPED A BUNCH OF UNDERAGE GIRLS!
CALL 911 AND DON'T ANYONE LET HIM WALK AWAY!
WHAT IF WE CAN'T GET THE GIRLS--?
WE WILL!

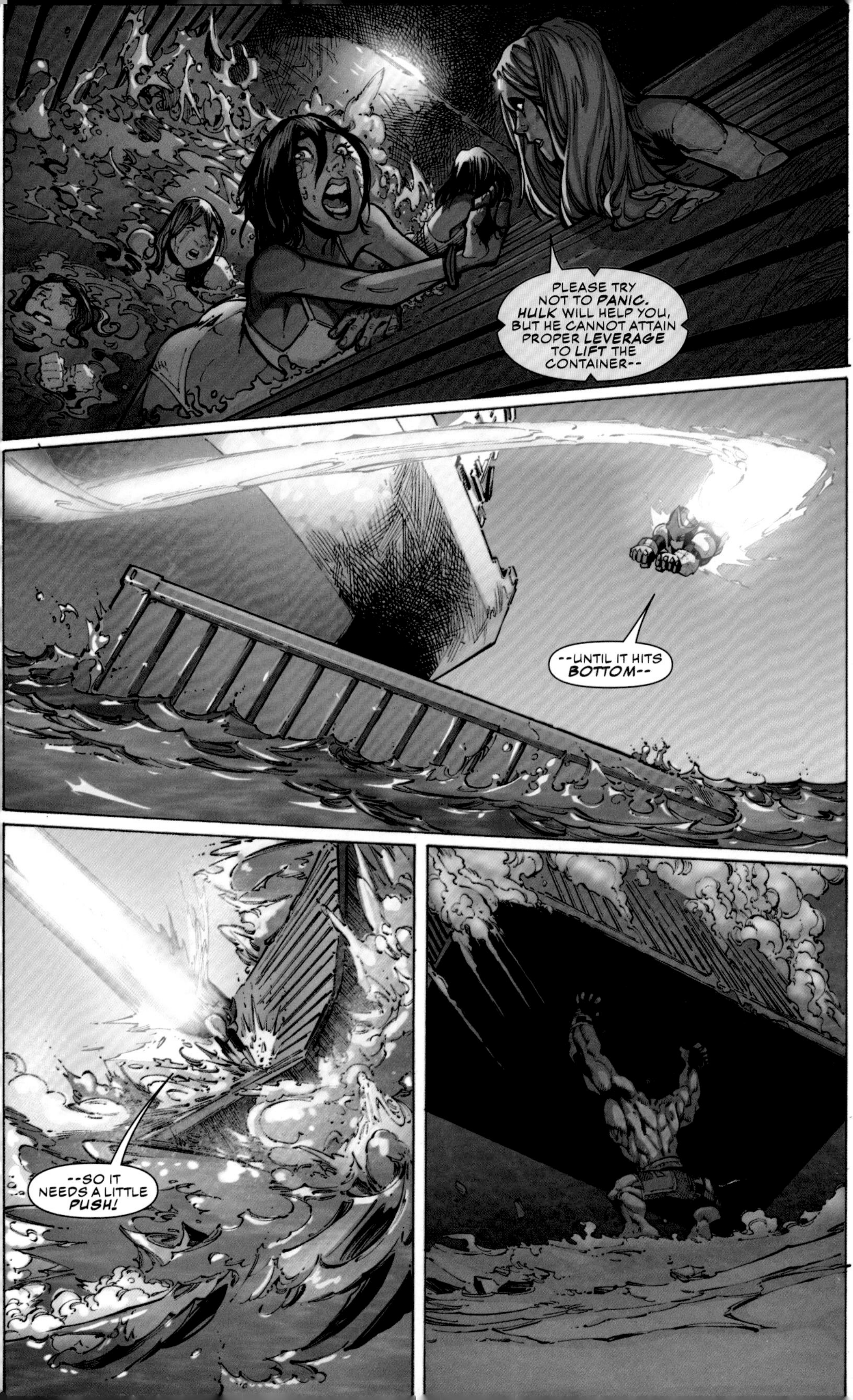
PLEASE TRY NOT TO PANIC. HULK WILL HELP YOU, BUT HE CANNOT ATTAIN PROPER LEVERAGE TO LIFT THE CONTAINER--
--UNTIL IT HITS BOTTOM--
--SO IT NEEDS A LITTLE PUSH!

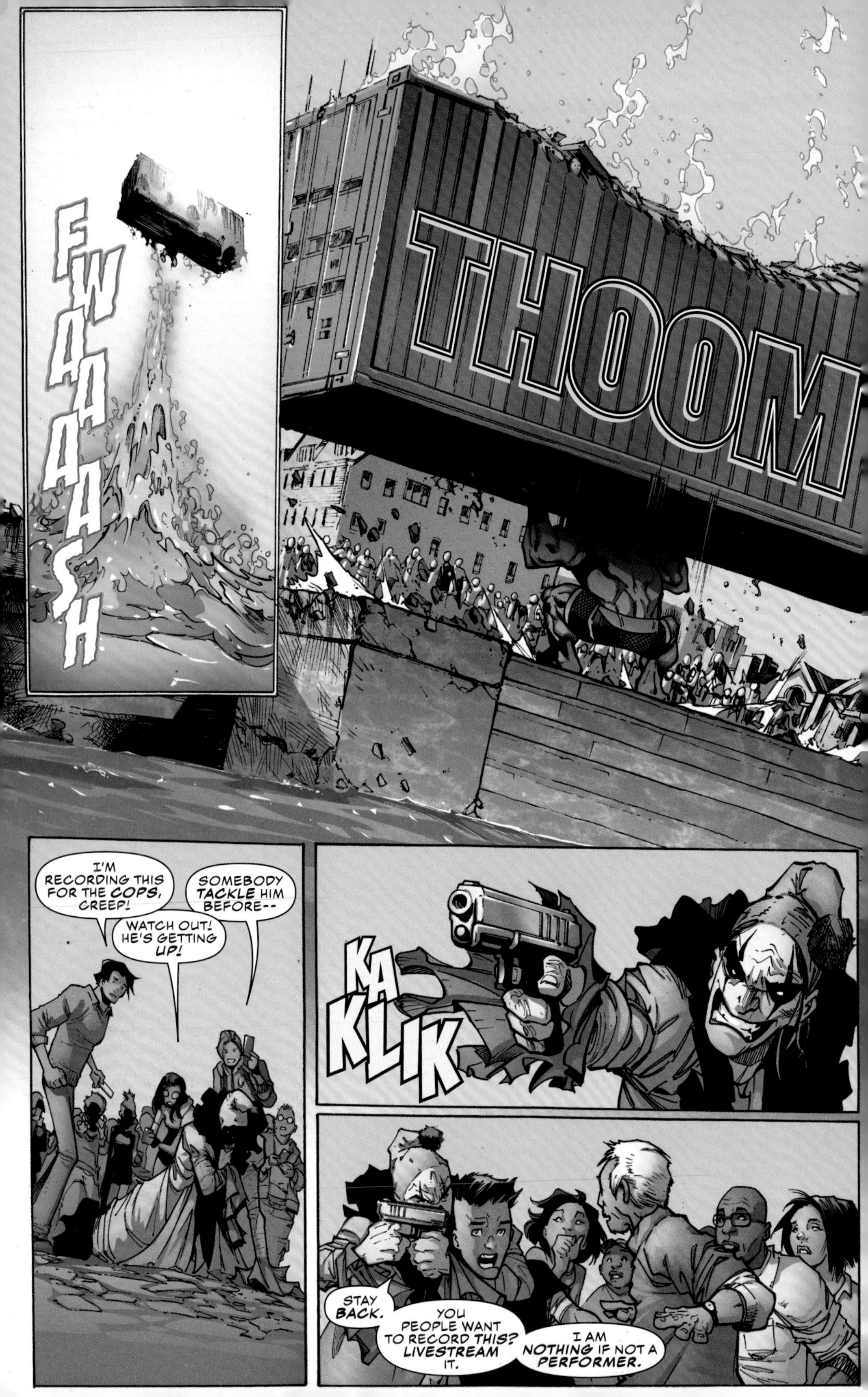
FWAAAASH
THOOM
I'M RECORDING THIS FOR THE COPS, CREEP!
SOMEBODY TACKLE HIM BEFORE--
WATCH OUT! HE'S GETTING UP!
KA KLIK
STAY BACK.
YOU PEOPLE WANT TO RECORD THIS? LIVESTREAM IT.
I AM NOTHING IF NOT A PERFORMER.

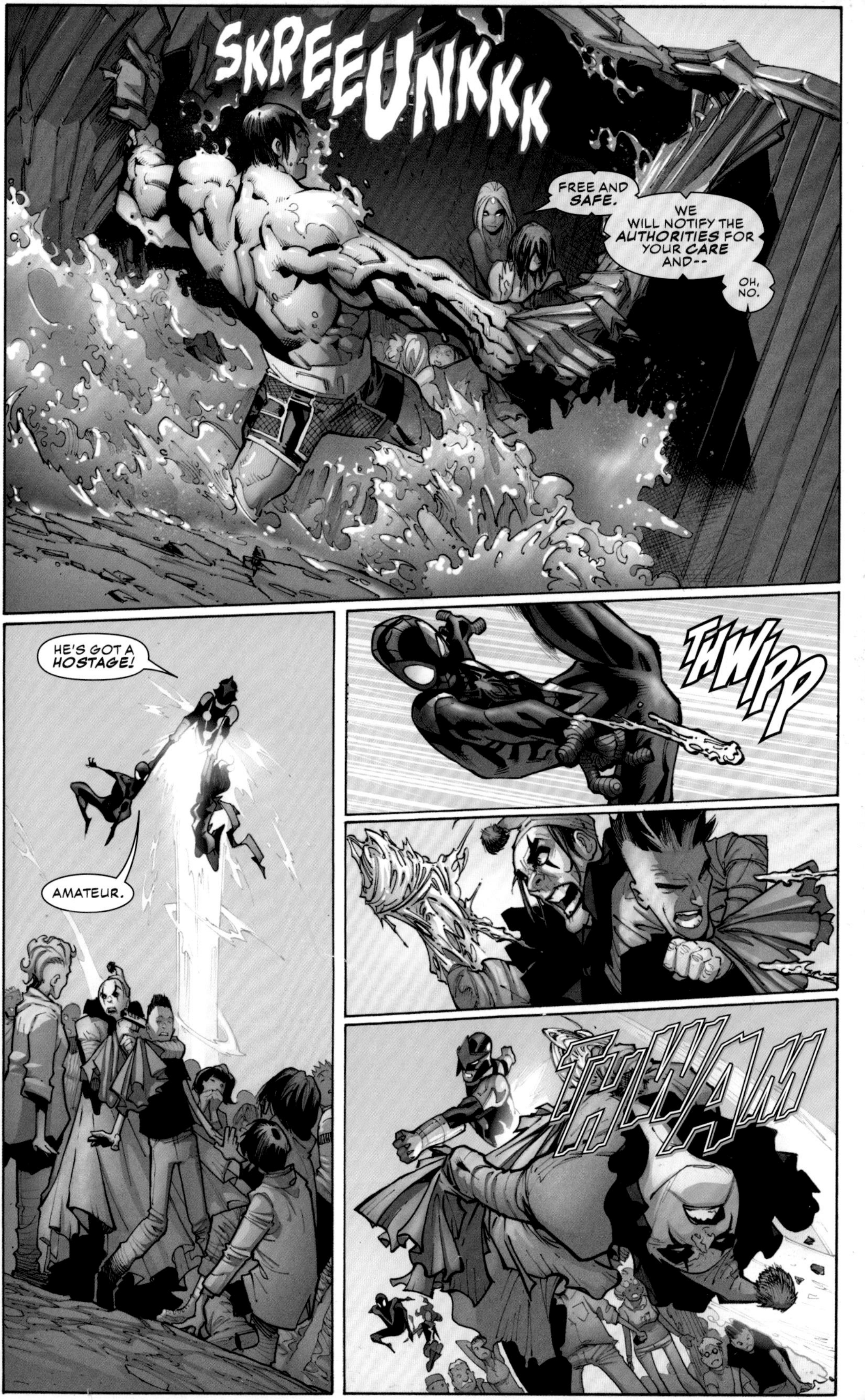
SKREEEUNKKKK
FREE AND SAFE.
WE WILL NOTIFY THE AUTHORITIES FOR YOUR CARE AND--
OH, NO.
HE'S GOT A HOSTAGE!
AMATEUR.
THWIPP
THWAM

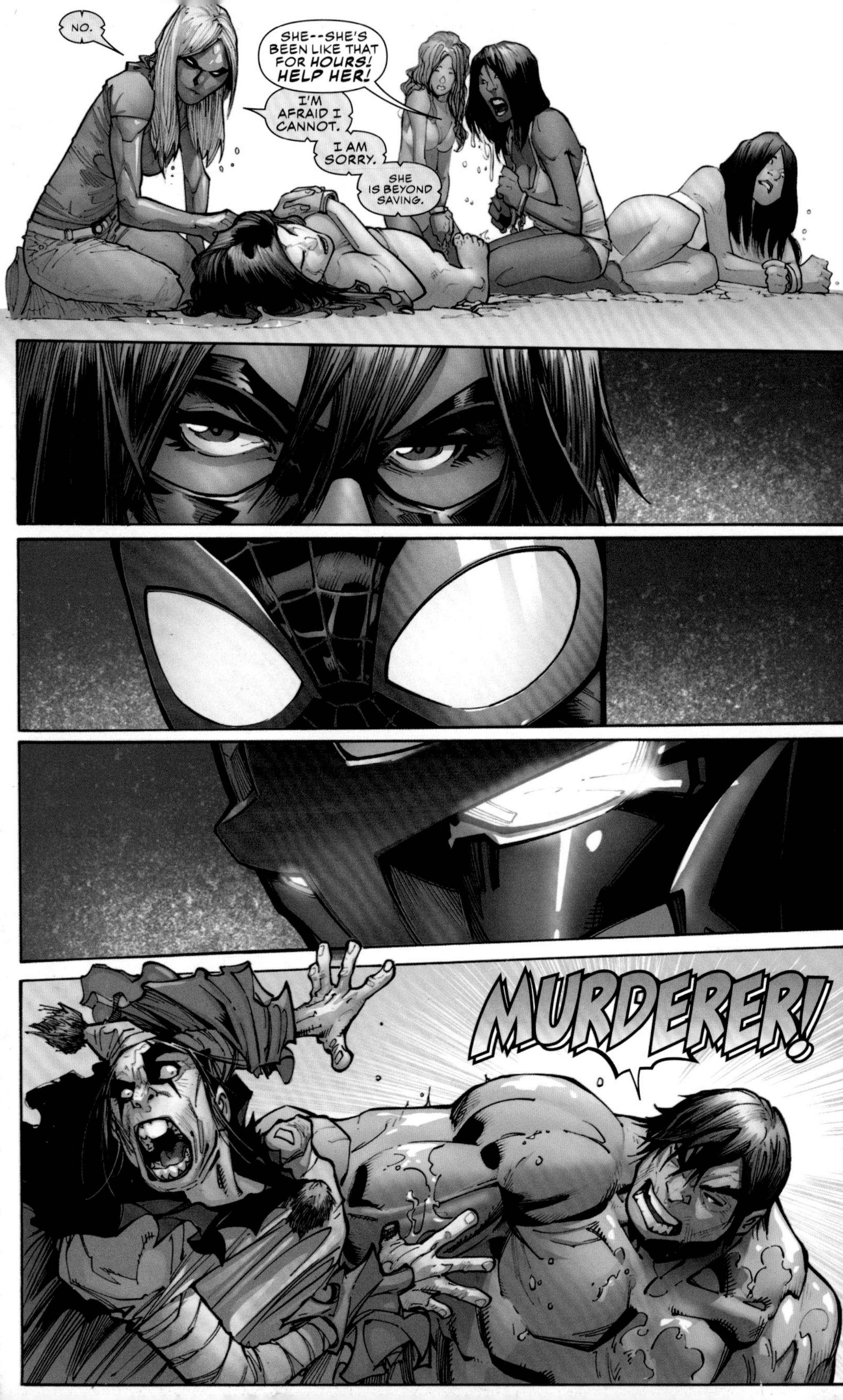
NO.
SHE--SHE'S BEEN LIKE THAT FOR HOURS! HELP HER!
I'M AFRAID I CANNOT.
I AM SORRY.
SHE IS BEYOND SAVING.
MURDERER!

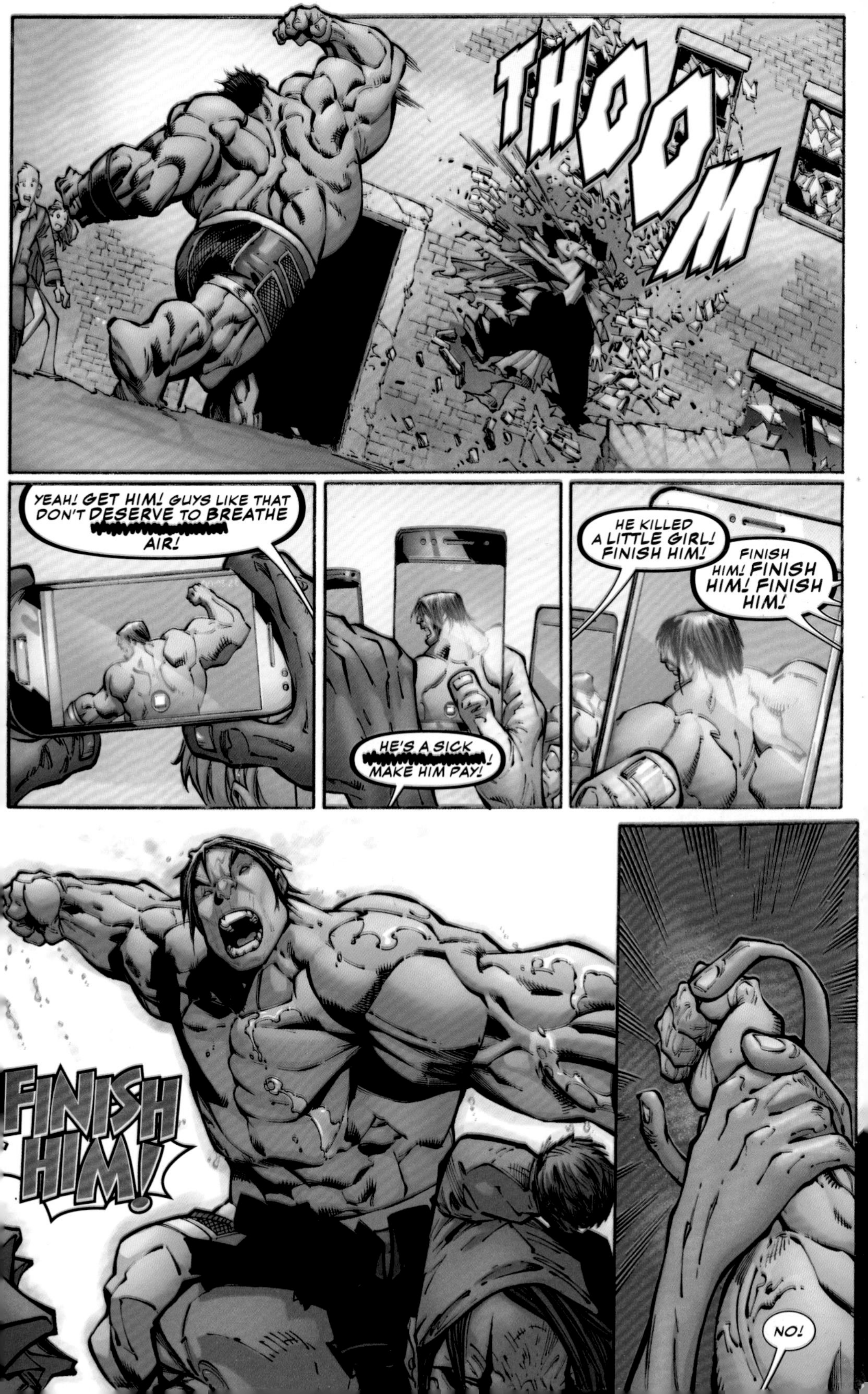
THOOM
YEAH! GET HIM! GUYS LIKE THAT DON'T DESERVE TO BREATHE [redacted] AIR!
HE'S A SICK [redacted]! MAKE HIM PAY!
HE KILLED A LITTLE GIRL! FINISH HIM!
FINISH HIM! FINISH HIM! FINISH HIM!
FINISH HIM!
NO!

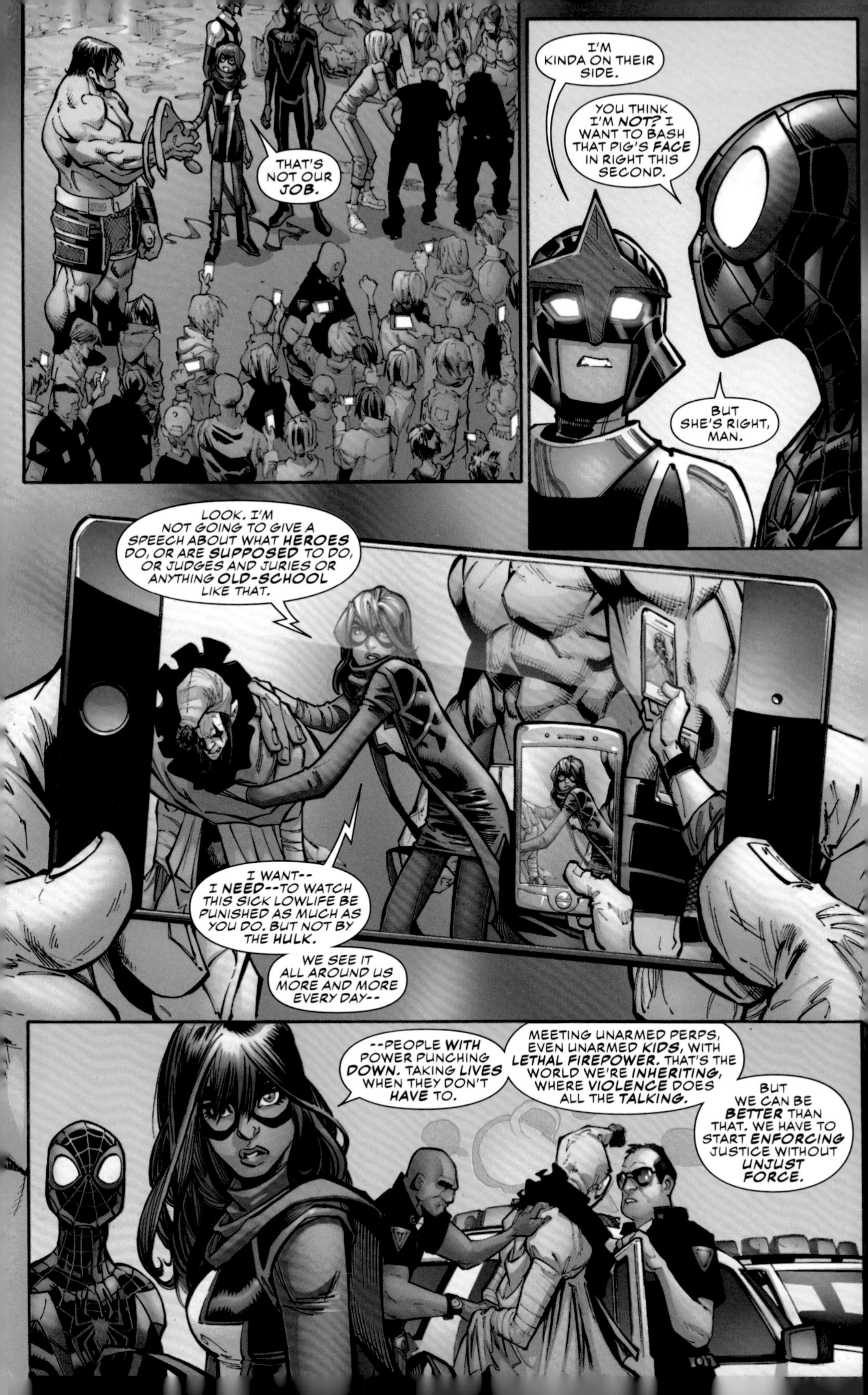
THAT'S NOT OUR JOB.
I'M KINDA ON THEIR SIDE.
YOU THINK I'M NOT? I WANT TO BASH THAT PIG'S FACE IN RIGHT THIS SECOND.
BUT SHE'S RIGHT, MAN.
LOOK. I'M NOT GOING TO GIVE A SPEECH ABOUT WHAT HEROES DO, OR ARE SUPPOSED TO DO, OR JUDGES AND JURIES OR ANYTHING OLD-SCHOOL LIKE THAT.
I WANT-- I NEED--TO WATCH THIS SICK LOWLIFE BE PUNISHED AS MUCH AS YOU DO. BUT NOT BY THE HULK.
WE SEE IT ALL AROUND US MORE AND MORE EVERY DAY--
--PEOPLE WITH POWER PUNCHING DOWN. TAKING LIVES WHEN THEY DON'T HAVE TO.
MEETING UNARMED PERPS, EVEN UNARMED KIDS, WITH LETHAL FIREPOWER. THAT'S THE WORLD WE'RE INHERITING, WHERE VIOLENCE DOES ALL THE TALKING.
BUT WE CAN BE BETTER THAN THAT. WE HAVE TO START ENFORCING JUSTICE WITHOUT UNJUST FORCE.

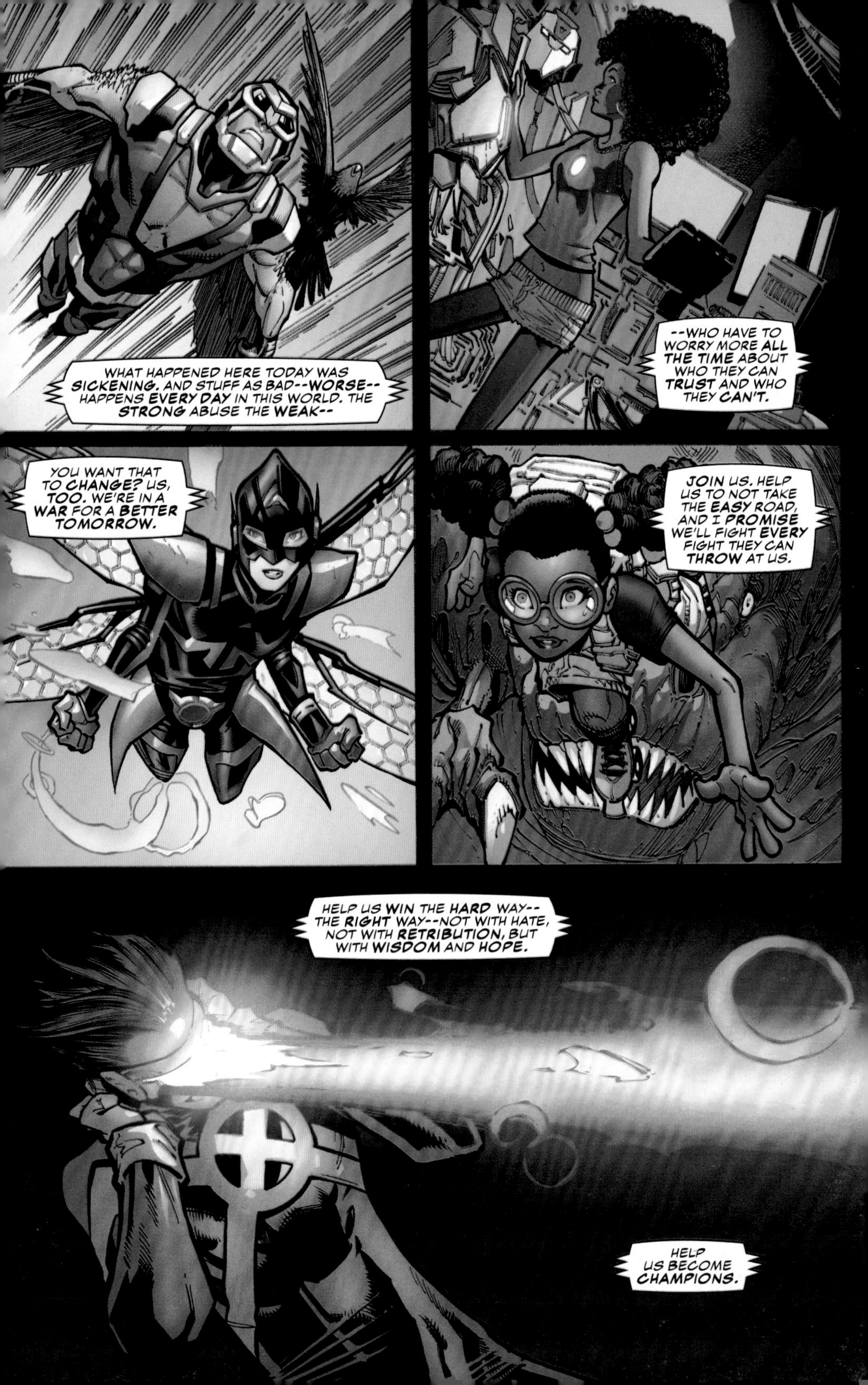
WHAT HAPPENED HERE TODAY WAS SICKENING. AND STUFF AS BAD--WORSE--HAPPENS EVERY DAY IN THIS WORLD. THE STRONG ABUSE THE WEAK--
--WHO HAVE TO WORRY MORE ALL THE TIME ABOUT WHO THEY CAN TRUST AND WHO THEY CAN'T.
YOU WANT THAT TO CHANGE? US, TOO. WE'RE IN A WAR FOR A BETTER TOMORROW.
JOIN US. HELP US TO NOT TAKE THE EASY ROAD, AND I PROMISE WE'LL FIGHT EVERY FIGHT THEY CAN THROW AT US.
HELP US WIN THE HARD WAY--THE RIGHT WAY--NOT WITH HATE, NOT WITH RETRIBUTION, BUT WITH WISDOM AND HOPE.
HELP US BECOME CHAMPIONS.

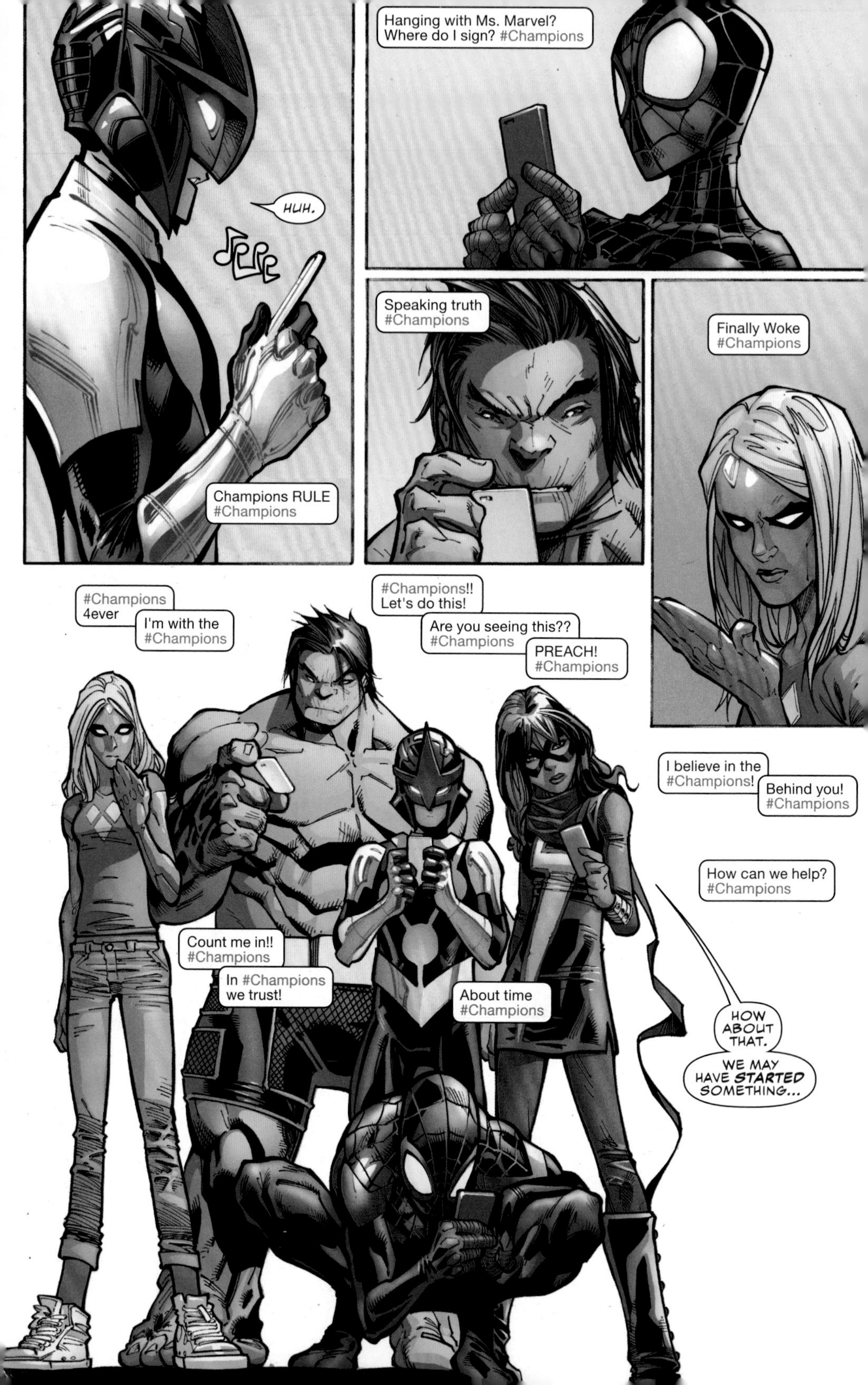
HUH.
Champions RULE #Champions
Hanging with Ms. Marvel? Where do I sign? #Champions
Speaking truth #Champions
Finally Woke #Champions
#Champions 4ever
I'm with the #Champions
#Champions!! Let's do this!
Are you seeing this?? #Champions
PREACH! #Champions
I believe in the #Champions!
Behind you! #Champions
How can we help? #Champions
Count me in!! #Champions
In #Champions we trust!
About time #Champions
HOW ABOUT THAT.
WE MAY HAVE STARTED SOMETHING...

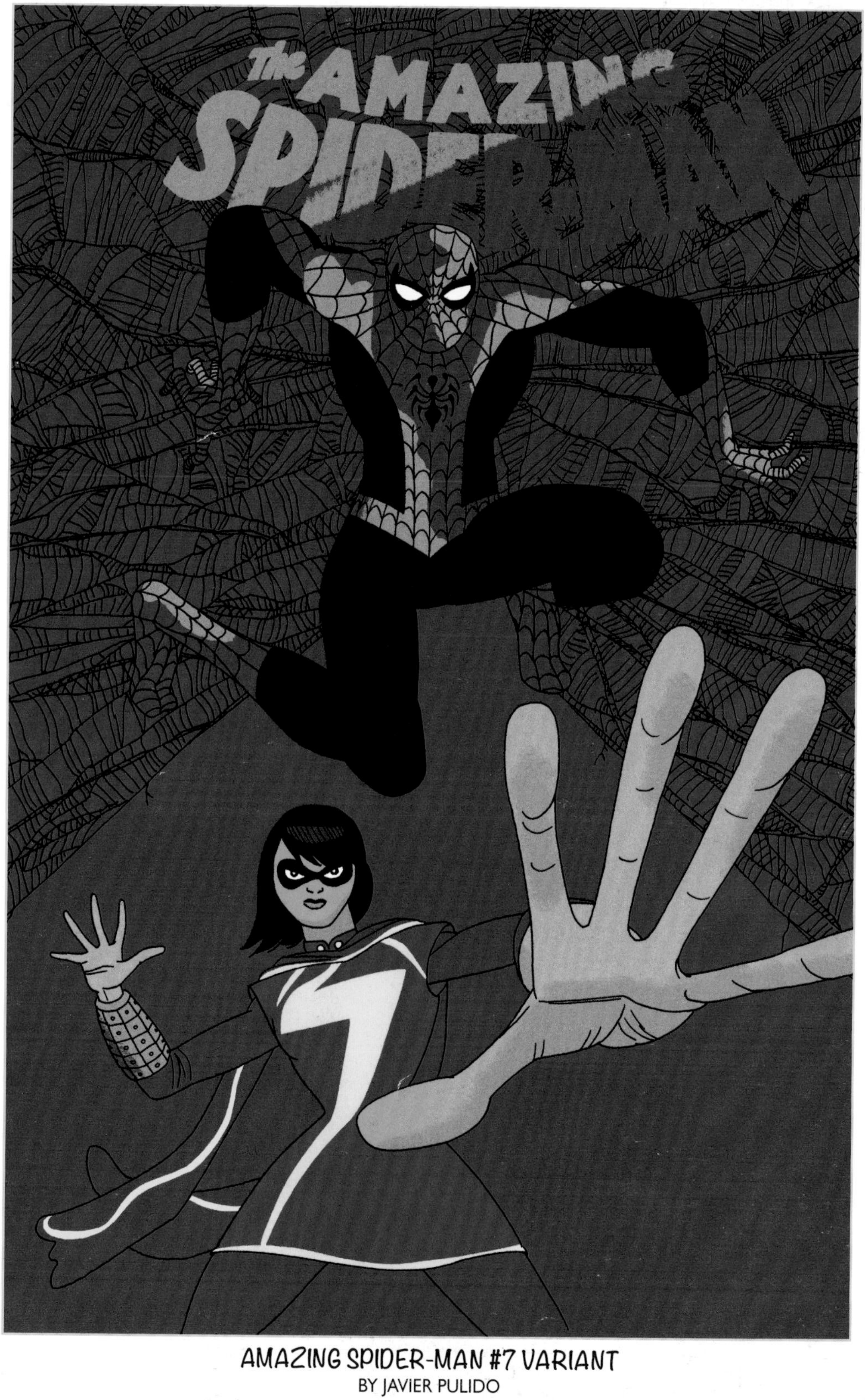
The AMAZING SPIDER-MAN

AMAZING SPIDER-MAN #7 VARIANT
BY JAVIER PULIDO

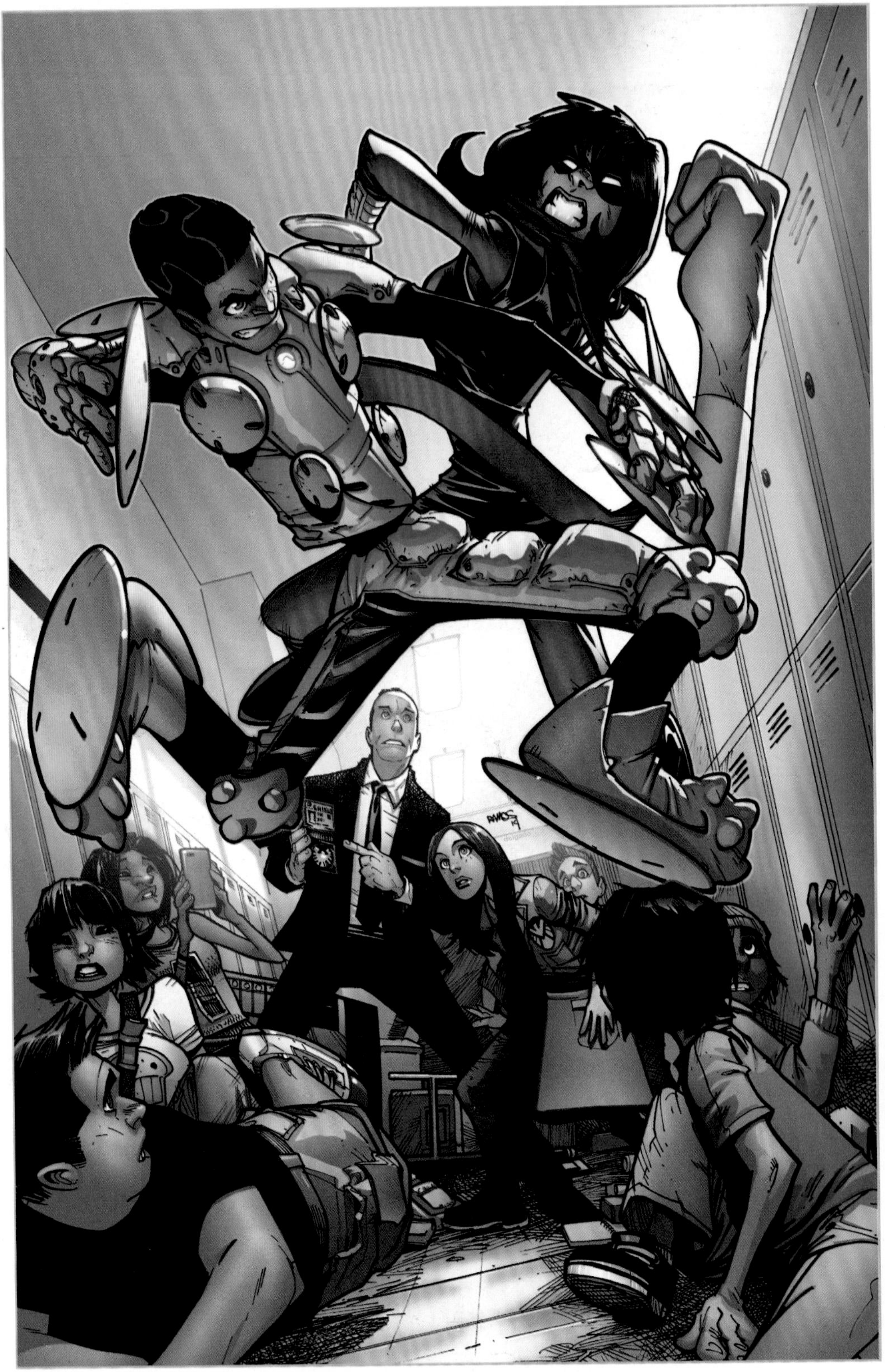

S.H.I.E.L.D. #2 VARIANT
BY HUMBERTO RAMOS & EDGAR DELGADO

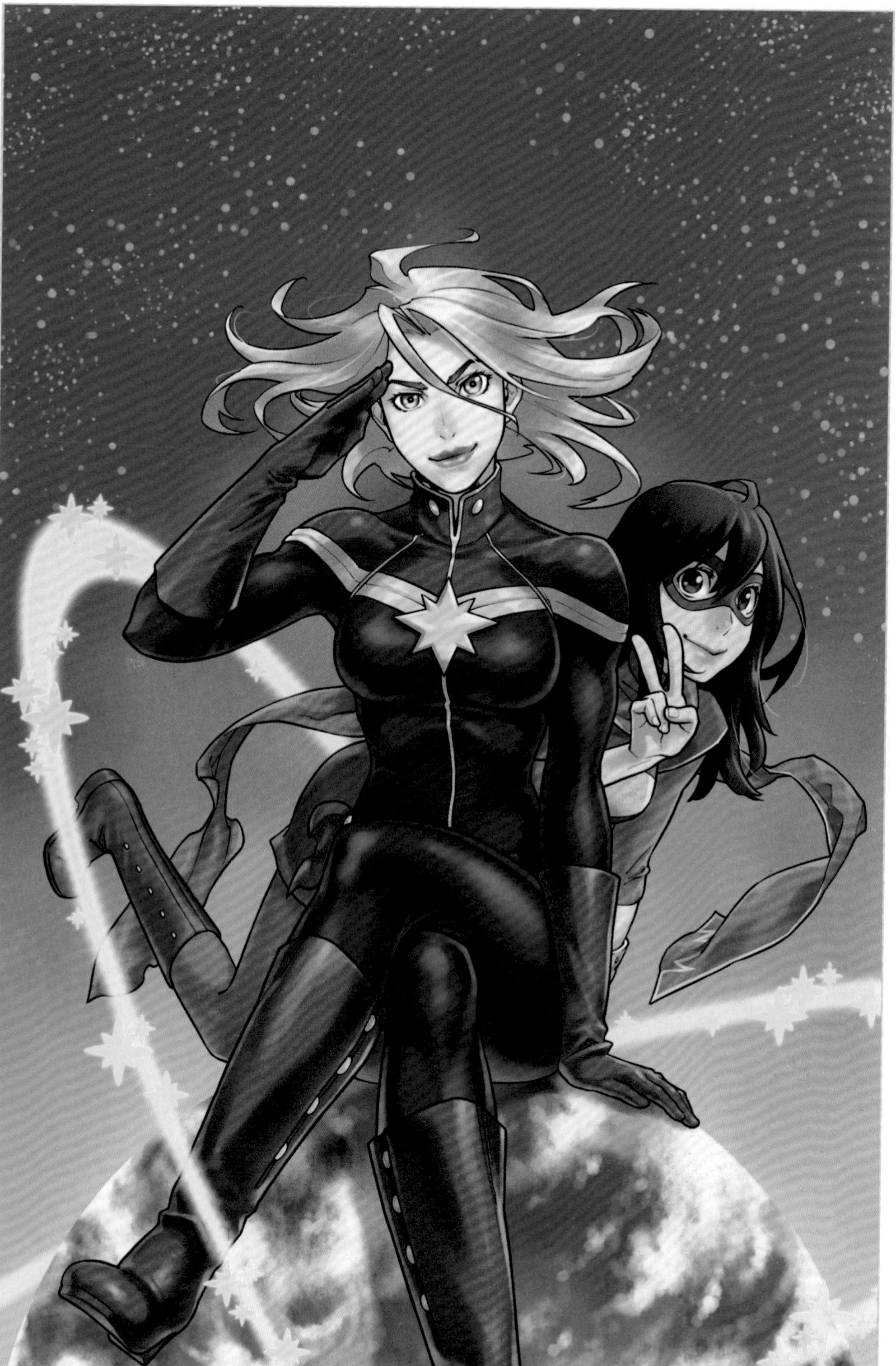

MS. MARVEL #18 MANGA VARIANT
BY RETSU TATEO

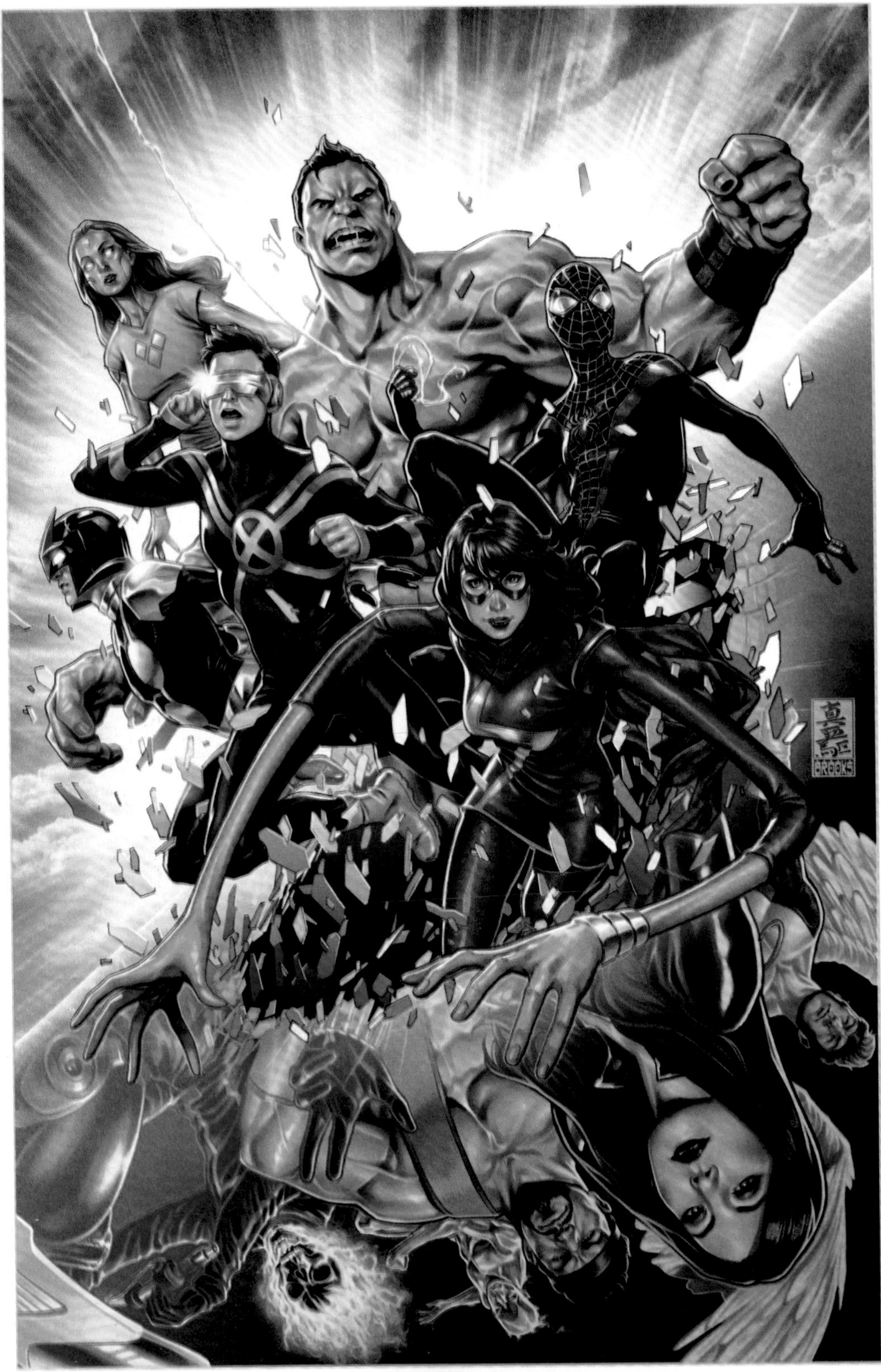
BROOKS

CHAMPIONS #1 VARIANT

BY MARK BROOKS

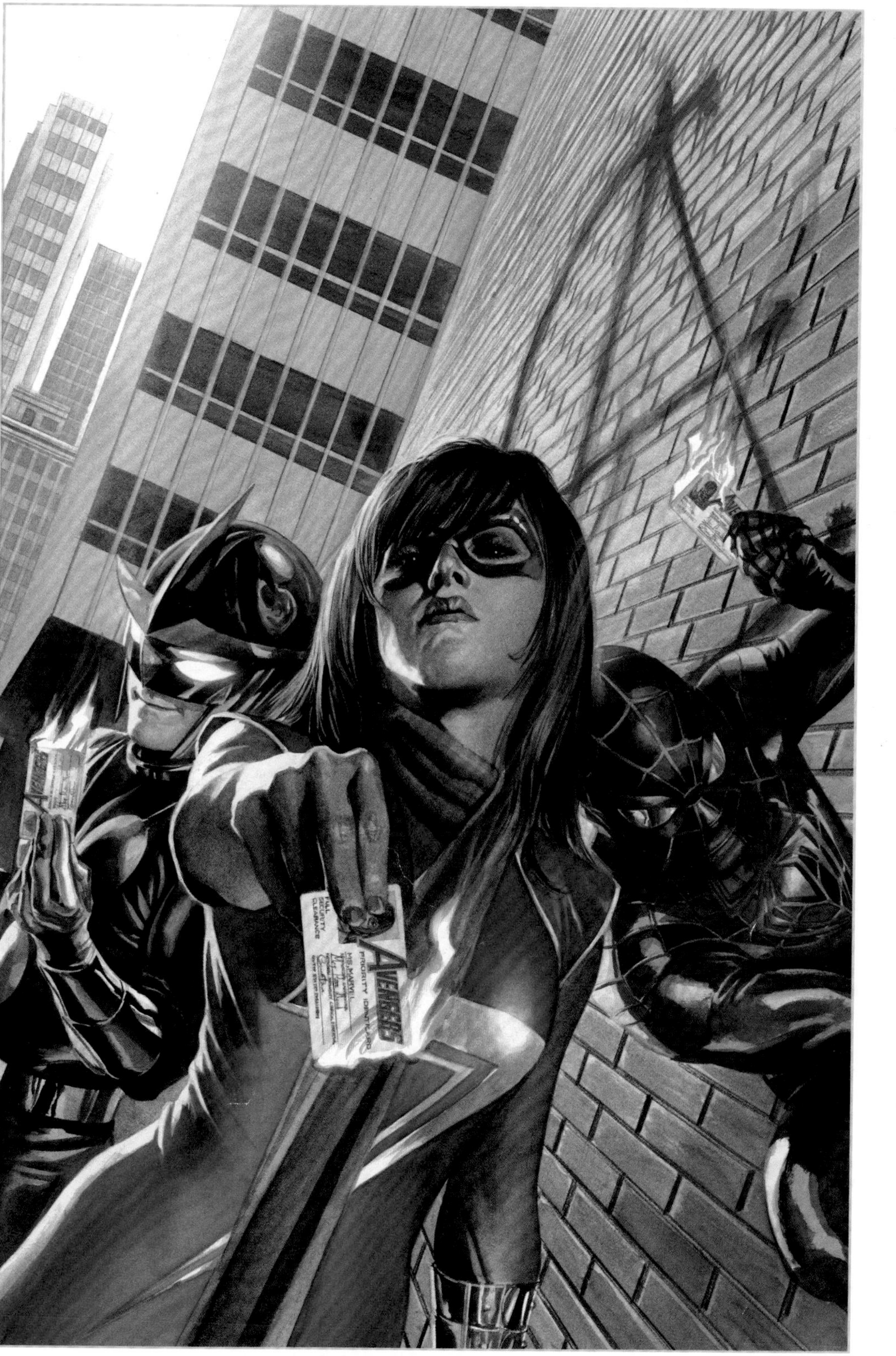
AVENGERS
PRIORITY IDENT CARD
MS. MARVEL
FULL SECURITY CLEARANCE

CHAMPIONS #1 VARIANT
BY ALEX ROSS

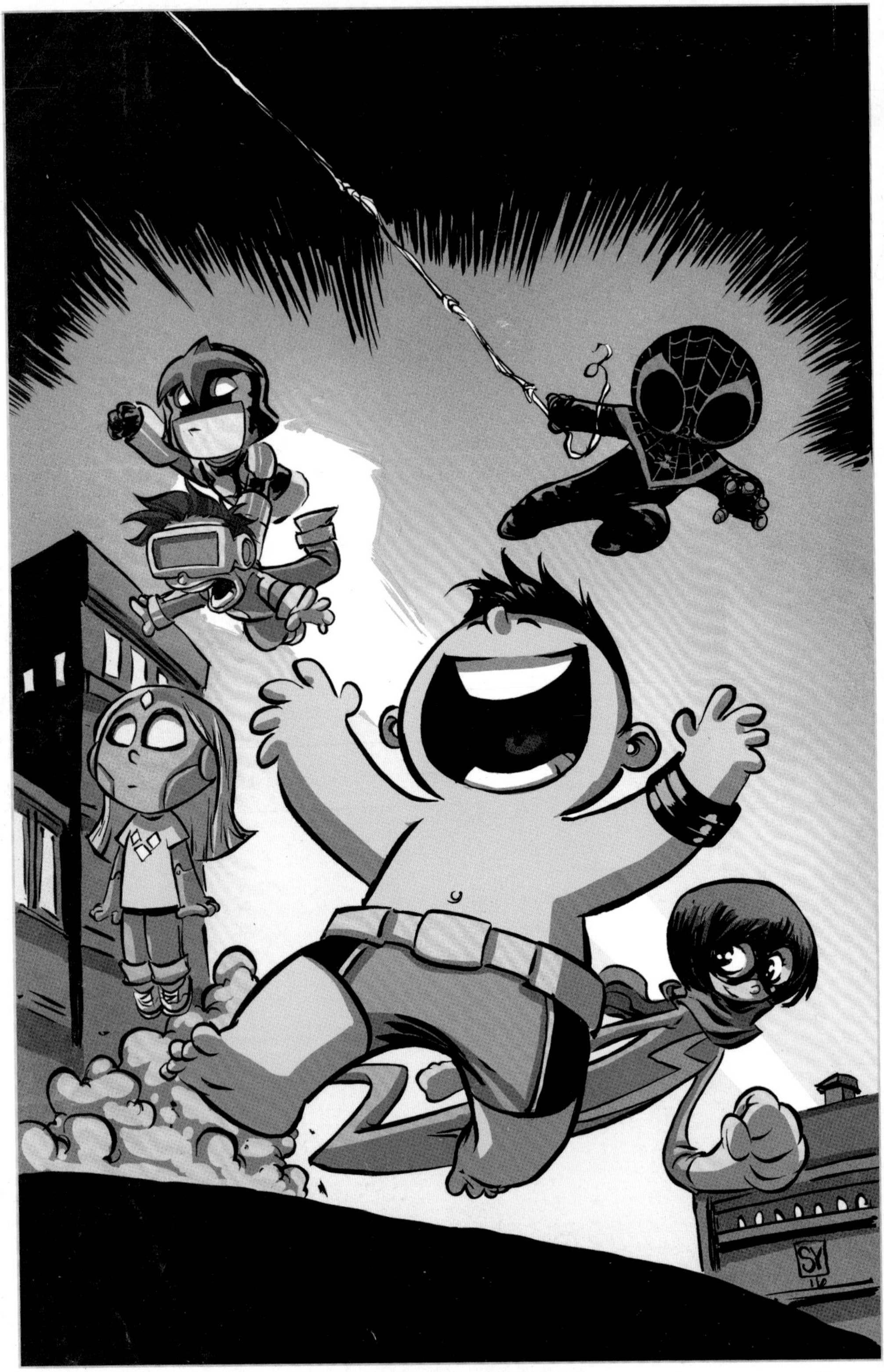
SY

CHAMPIONS #1 VARIANT
BY SKOTTIE YOUNG